The Upsilon Knot

Merle Darling

This is a work of fiction. Names, characters, places, incidents and cultures are either the product of the author's imagination or used in a fictitious manner; and any resemblance to actual persons, living or dead, business establishments, events, locales or cultures is entirely coincidental.

"There is no such thing as accident; it is fate, misnamed."

Napoleon Buonaparte

"A single ray of light from a distant star falling upon the eye of a tyrant in bygone times, may have altered the course of his life, may have changed the destiny of nations, may have transformed the surface of the globe, so intricate, so inconceivably complex are the processes of nature."

Nikola Tesla

CONTENTS

ADES GENII AUGUSTI

They woke the young lieutenant at midnight, and handed him a parchment scroll with a message from the Emperor himself. Dominic Soderini came alert immediately, as a legionary is trained to do. He dressed quickly, glad that for once he had polished his boots before lights out instead of waiting until morning. He brushed his hair, buckled on his sword and followed the corporal down to the barracks gate.

Two members of the Praetorian Guard stood waiting to escort him. Saluting smartly, he moved into place between them. As they crossed the Tevere, he noticed the moon shining like a pearl on the skin of the river. Nothing was more beautiful than Roma on a moonlit night.

The Guards moved more rapidly than he would have thought possible for such massive creatures; he was hard-pressed to match their pace. They marched past the Piazza Navona, oblivious to the glow of the moon-kissed fountains. They passed the ancient Pantheon, so quietly glorious that Baron Haussmann had bowed his head over his plans, rubbed out his pencil marks and let it be—as he had left little else in the nearly thirty years since Augustus had inherited the throne from his father, the Great Napoleon, the uniter of Italy.

To Dominic's surprise, the guards walked right past the Palazzo and turned in the direction of Santa Maria Maggiore.

"Where are we going?" His query was clearly the result of the case of nerves he was pretending not to suffer. He knew very well the *trecika* could not answer. Those forbidding lumps of clay that guarded the great Caesar Augustus II had no power of speech. It made them that much more intimidating. He wondered if they really did house demons, or if that was only a tale to frighten children. His grandfather had certainly used it as

1

such, but his grandfather, until he had grown too old and ill to do so, had served Caesar and knew many secrets.

They continued to march along in silence, save for the ring of his boots and mineral thud of their feet against the paving stones of one of Haussmann's grand avenues. After a few minutes as long as an hour, they turned onto an unfamiliar street that led to a narrow alley. Dominic could smell the age of the buildings as they brushed by. He knew he was near some of the many ruins of the First Empire, but none with which he was familiar. Another turn; the moon disappeared and the cobbles beneath his feet slanted downhill. They were going beneath the street. Had he not been a brave lieutenant in the Roman Imperial Army, he might have panicked.

His eyes adjusted to the darkness of the cryptoporticus. A faint glimmer seemed to pull him forward, making him eager to reach whatever destination lay in store. He drew ahead of his escorts, never noticing that they stopped within the archway, their bodies plugging the gap between the two-thousand-year-old stones.

The archway opened into an anteroom of sorts, lit by the wicks of a few brass bowls of oil that limned a path to another room. Dominic inhaled the damp, earthy air. He passed under the portico into a large, long room. The light was stronger there, but no less antique in source—pools of amber spreading from more of the rude lamps and a few branched candelabra. Dark doorways, or perhaps they were alcoves, loomed to either side; sometimes the lights threw menacing shadows from the shapes they contained. The near darkness smelled sweetly of beeswax and some unfamiliar resin, not the incense Dominic knew from Church but somehow like it.

The strongest light came from the far end of this hall, where a wheel-shaped chandelier dangled by a brass chain from the vaulted ceiling. Dominic moved toward it, as a weary swimmer makes for a ribbon of shore. On the other side of its glow, his eyes could just make out a shadow in the shape of an inverted pyramid. It reminded him of the seats the Baron's workers were restoring to the mighty Colosseum. When at last he could see the seated spectators, he nearly smiled at having reached such a fine conclusion; this was some sort of auditorium then, something familiar.

A white-robed man rose stiffly from the center of the stands, a very old man with an unmistakable brow.

"Hail Caesar!" Dominic trumpeted. He gave his smartest salute and hoped his boots had not become too scuffed on the long walk over.

Caesar Augustus II nodded briefly, then brought his staff down sharply on the stone. A blue-hooded figure scampered from the shadows with a round cup, which he offered to Dominic.

"Drink from the *situla*, boy!" commanded Caesar. Dominic drank. The liquid was thick and strangely sweet, like the must of rotting fruit. It tasted also of the metal of the vessel, which a spark from the chandelier revealed to be mellow gold. As the bearer removed the cup, Dominic saw a red burst on the side; it might have been a ruby, or perhaps it was merely the reflection of a flame.

There was a humming sound in the air, voices chanting something Dominic could not understand. There was some kind of zither and a reed or flute, the kind of music that made his teeth buzz. It was also making his head spin, which surprised him.

"Sit, boy!" commanded Caesar. Feeling a chair placed behind him, Dominic sank into it just before his knees would have given way.

A woman stepped into the open space between the stands and began to sing strange words in a high nasal drone. Her bare feet rubbing against the mosaic floor, she crossed to where Dominic sat and began to dance. Bangles chimed on her bare ankles and on the thin bloodless arms that writhed like snakes in the air above her veiled face. As she twisted and spun, her long yellow hair flew wildly, revealing the shocking whiteness of naked flesh. Old naked flesh: slack breasts and buttocks, a belly like a speckled mushroom and thighs that brought to mind a boy years ago at school, who had drowned and had been pulled from the river by a farmer's pitchfork. It should have been horrible, but somehow Dominic could not tear his eyes away from her gyrations.

The voice of Caesar, aged but still powerful, poured over him, invoking his gods. "*Henu* Nun and Naunet, of the Waters that flowed Before Time," Caesar called. "*Dua* All Infinite Heh and Hehet. *Suash*, the Invisible Power. *Suash* Amon and Amaunet. Kek and Keket of the darkness, *Ter*. *Djewi* Ogdoad!"

Dominic's eyelids fluttered. His body felt heavy and, as he noticed more of the trecika guards, the amphoraeka, in the shadows, he wondered if this was what it might feel like to be encased in a shell of clay. That was Dominic's last conscious thought.

Words were chanted that, even if he had heard, he would not have understood. A cymbal was struck and the blue-robed priest used a strange bronze knife to cut away the uniform of which he had been so proud. Two youths carried a large ceramic jar to the chair. They were naked except for thin linen squares held by a thong around the waist. They poured the herb-infused water over Dominic's body, washing him, then smashed the vessel. The naked priestess danced around the boy's chair. An acolyte brought her an alabaster bowl and she anointed the spot between his eyes with pungent oil. His mouth was prised open and a white feather tucked inside.

At a signal from Caesar Augustus, one of the Praetorian Guard lifted a very old man from the invalid's chair in which he had been sitting, just beyond the spill of candlelight. The clay giant grasped the old man under his arms and held him like a baby; it might have almost seemed tender, had there been any present with the eyes to note it. The priestess anointed the ancient as she had the boy. He opened his mouth to receive a scarab of lapis lazuli on his tongue. Augustus and the man, both old, locked eyes, the weary with the powerful. A beatific ferocity shone from the Emperor's face as he pronounced the final formula.

Dangling from the trecika's arms, the old man's body spasmed and shook. With a final mighty arch, something seemed to break free; the body crumpled like an empty stocking. At the same moment, the young man appeared to be thrown from the chair. He gasped, like an infant pulled from his mother's womb. His eyes, glazed opaque a moment before, sparkled with life. He stared, incredulous, at the empty husk held by the creature of clay. "Hail Caesar!" he whispered, falling to his knees at the Emperor's feet.

"Who is this?" Augustus looked deep into the boy's eyes.

"Soderini, Caesar," said the boy in an awed but oddly triumphant whisper. "Omberto Soderini!"

An equally triumphant smile spread across Augustus's face. "*Omberto Soderini, Giulia!*"

The priestess threw her arms around the Emperor. "Success, Patre! At last! After all those failures!"

"The Piscapetti translation," Augustus mused. "He was correct about the variant; an 'heir of the blood.' So it must be a direct descendant. Perhaps I shouldn't have been so quick to dispose of Piscapetti; he might have had further uses." Abruptly exhausted, but never taking his eyes off Soderini, Augustus resumed his seat. "Omberto!"

"Yes Caesar?" Soderini lifted his head cautiously. At the Emperor's signal, he too returned to his chair.

"What does it feel like?" Augustus asked in a friendly voice.

"Perfect," Soderini said, his astonishment clear in his voice. "I feel as young as my grandson. I am as young as he," he corrected.

"Is he there, Omberto?" The tone remained conversational.

Soderini's face furrowed in silent concentration. He seemed to be searching for something deep inside. His answer came on a sigh. "No, Caesar. He's gone. The body is only mine." Raising a finger to wipe his eye, he stared in surprise at the tear it found. "My grandson...I suppose the boy is dead."

"I'm sorry, Omberto," Augustus said sadly, flicking his hand in the air above his right ear. Another of the Guard, who had been primed for this gesture, moved from the shadows to just behind the chair. "I know you'd hoped to share his body, but we always knew it wasn't certain."

Soderini nodded sadly. "He was a good boy," he said. "Loyal to his Emperor and to his family. He would have been proud to know he gave his life for both."

The strong arms of the amphoraka reached around Soderini and crushed him, a cat's jaw crushing a hummingbird. "As would have you, Omberto," Caesar pronounced. "As would have you."

The clay giant stood unmoving, the broken body dangling from its arms. Ignoring it, Augustus reached a hand to where his daughter's hand rested on his shoulder. "I am spent, Giulia," he confided. "As much as if I'd led a legion into France."

"You've won a great victory, Patre. Napoleon himself never won anything so great." She moved around to face him. Her eyes glittered with excitement. "How soon do we prepare the boy?"

He stroked her fondly. "You are so impetuous, just like your mother. It will be soon enough. The moment is not yet ripe."

"But what we've seen here tonight…you must proceed!"

"We know what we have seen," he admonished, "but there is no telling what the process might disrupt in the body." The weakness in Caesar's left arm was becoming familiar. He disregarded it and found the leverage to push himself up from his seat. He allowed Giulia to take his weight on her shoulder and lead him down the stone steps. His bent foot throbbed, as it always had when he was fatigued. "Therefore," he grunted, "before we proceed, we must secure the bloodline to the next generation. Waiting is no longer acceptable. Gusto must be mated now."

"There would be no waiting if you would marry him to the young Duchess of Alba."

"Never!" His pinch would leave a red welt on her skin for days. "Everything I have ever dreamed of is finally within my grasp and you would have me settle for mere breeding stock? You disappoint me, Giulia."

"But Patre, we've made every effort—"

"There is always another way. We must find it. Rome will be complete again. First Britannia and then Gaul. We will have the English princess!"

Giulia bowed her head and kissed his hand. "As you say, Patre. May you live forever."

He smiled. "I may indeed," he said, and pulling his daughter close, he lifted her chin to kiss her firmly on the mouth.

1 ~ THE GOLEMS OF ROME

The workshop was in the Josefov, the old Jewish quarter, tucked safely out of sight at the end of a twisted alley. Not that there would be many passers-by to worry about; the street was just near enough to the Old Cemetery to keep casual traffic to a minimum. Nikola Tesla had done better than he had hoped. With all the Jews moving out to the recently opened suburbs, there were many buildings standing empty in Prague and the cost of renting them was correspondingly low. This one had been a warehouse of sorts. It was only a large shack, but it was watertight. Now that spring was creeping in, he could work without his fingers turning blue and chapped. The drafty space was heated with an old wood stove that he could also use for cooking, a blessing as he had to forgo the expense of a rooming house and was sleeping in a sailor's rope hammock that he had strung under the eaves of the loft. There was room enough for all of his tools and machines, and for trial after trial of his pet experiment. He had his brain and the determination necessary to succeed. What he was running short of was money—money, and time.

It had been a long day. Satisfied with the results of this last adjustment, he welded the panel in place with a tight, nearly invisible seam. His head ached and his goggles were steaming from the sweat beading up on his face. The comfort and safety of the light, unbreakable Vitriflex lenses far surpassed the old glass models, but it seemed to him that they fogged up twice as quickly. Cursing, he pulled them off and wiped them down again. It would take a few minutes for them to clear enough for him to resume work, minutes he could ill afford to lose. Haussmann's agents would be looking for him, soon if not already, and once they began it could only be so long before they'd find him. It was dangerous to make a name for yourself in the world.

ｇ●

Following his mother's death and the terrible episode in America, Tesla went home to Gospić to be with his sisters, the only people in the world left to him. He cleaned up his old workshop and gradually resumed the rhythms of his old life, hoping for nothing more than for his mind to be at peace. For a long time, he moved cautiously, limiting his mental stimulation to making minor improvements to existing inventions. When he was stable enough to feel restless, he allowed himself to begin work on an electrical clockwork man; it was a idea that had come to him in one of his visions, while he was still in the sanatorium. The work made him almost happy, until the day a man with Roman insignia on his sleeve appeared at the door.

Before his breakdown, Tesla had been privileged to work with Franklin Monteith, whose nimble mind and hobby of amateur detection had made him a popular celebrity in British America. Frank was possessed of a gift that dazzled even Tesla. Together, they had created a groundbreaking device for the mining industry, a remotely-operated digging apparatus. Brash young America delighted in the role of incubator of the future. Even lesser inventions were launched with acclaim. Something as significant as RODA (as Monteith's intractable hoyden had christened their machine) was major news. The ribbon-cutting ceremony had been a gala public affair. Photographs were published in the illustrated papers, one of which had eventually found its way to the Emperor of Italy's pet civil engineer.

The envoy at the family door explained that Baron Haussmann had identified Tesla as a coming man. Caesar had a special commission for him.

Any man of science would have shuddered. The Second Roman Empire was no friend to technology. Licking his wounds after the Gallic War, Augustus had lashed out at the modern world for failing him. Manufactories that produced new tools and machines were razed to the ground. Any owners too stubborn to flee were mowed down where they stood. Foundries and smithies were raided in the middle of the night, telegraph towers were burned to ash, inventors were hauled before tribunals that always ended in execution, universities were emptied by the reign of terror. Whatever Augustus chose to retain was controlled by him, by the State. To prevent dangerous ideas from infecting the Empire, travel to Italy and, to a lesser extent, its possessions in the Mediterranean, was restricted.

The Augustan Purge may have happened well before Tesla's birth, but elderly refugees kept the memory green. Instead of expressing deference and humble gratitude, Tesla flatly turned the envoy down. He said he was working on a project of his own and did not like to be interrupted. The Roman saluted sternly and left. That Sunday, while the family was at church, the barn that served as Tesla's workshop exploded. His sisters and the local fire brigade scolded him furiously for having been so careless with his materials. He held his tongue. He knew that nothing in the barn could have caused that particular type of explosion. It had been a warning—or a threat. The next day the envoy returned with two indisputable soldiers. Serbia was not officially part of the Second Roman Empire, but the nature of the alliance was such that it might as well have been. Tesla was powerless to resist; he packed a bag, embraced the girls and went quietly. It was a silent, uncomfortable journey.

In the wake of that introduction, Tesla was surprised by the warmth with which he was greeted by his debonair host. Georges-Eugène Haussmann had a humorous mouth and whimsical taste in cravats. He spoke any number of modern languages, including a bit of Serbian, with a slight Alsatian accent. The old Baron greeted Tesla as an honoured guest, as though he had come of his own accord. A brace of liveried footmen showed him up to a comfortable guest suite. Despite Tesla's protestations that he was accustomed to tending to himself, Haussmann was insistent that a servant be sent to draw his bath.

Rather than the extravagant stairway that might have been expected in such a villa, the footmen led him up a curved ramp. The walls were picked out with molding so simple that the quantity of gold leaf remained elegant. The ceiling, he thought, seemed unusually high. He passed one or two curiosities along the way—a marble gladiator, a small bronze Aquarius, a grouping of weathered glass bottles—all presented atop slim white plinths that emphasized their rarity. Looking down from the top, Tesla caught a tantalizing glimpse of what seemed to be a scale model of Rome laid out on a gilt octagonal table that was tucked into the curve.

The rooms assigned to him, in a small wing off the main corridor, were spacious and richly furnished in soothing tones of green and fawn. Despite the luxurious appointments, they were clearly a kind of prison. Tesla had never seen Rome, other than in paintings and photographs. The windows were fronted with iron grilles that let in the light but made it difficult to see any details beyond. He was trying to make out a bit of the view, when he heard the creaking of the large, iron-banded door.

Turning to greet the servant, he saw a mountain of clay moving toward him. His heart thrashed in his chest. It couldn't be; this was something out of legend! Tesla had spent some of his student years in Prague. His roommate, a young law student by the name of Sandtmann, had told him the old tales. Though he knew it was impossible, except for the strange helmet that looked like something off an antique Roman coin, he would swear that this was Rabbi Löwe's golem. It was formed of dry clay that didn't appear to have been glazed in any manner. Stepping into the marble bath, Tesla 'accidentally' flung out his hand so that his father's signet ring would hit against the creature's arm. Instead of the chink he would have heard from hitting a terra cotta pot, it made a muffled sound, as if falling onto damp earth. The creature seemed to have no constraints about standing within splashing distance; it loomed over him while he bathed. He wondered how it had been cured to resist water. Tesla couldn't say why this should fascinate him as much as its animation, but it did. It seemed ripely significant somehow. He watched it, covertly. A bluish light, like the core of a gas flame, flickered occasionally behind the empty sockets that were its eyes. After he had dressed, it led him down to a courtyard to dine with his official host.

Seated by a tinkling fountain, Tesla tried to enjoy what he understood, even with his limited knowledge of such niceties, to be an unusually exquisite feast. There was hot-house melon, served with ham sliced so thin that he could see through it to the pattern on his plate. There was an unfamiliar firm-fleshed white fish with a garnish of lemon, followed by tender veal that was bathed in a sauce savoury with garlic and green olives. All the wines, Haussmann noted, came from his own estate in Tuscany; '68 had been a particularly fine year.

There were only the two of them at table. Haussmann knew a flattering amount about his work and could talk about it most intelligently. This should have kept Tesla focused on the conversation, but he was distracted by the nagging feeling that someone was watching him. As the meat dishes were removed, Haussmann broke off to give some instruction to a servant. Tesla took advantage of the moment to stare frankly around him. It was a charming spot, designed for entertaining guests far more discerning than a Serbian tinker. The faint citrus perfume, he realized, came from the potted lemon trees set just outside the peristyle. Thinking he glimpsed a bluish light, he leaned forward for a better view. He spotted his golem and a number of its fellows stationed in the shadows between the columns. He couldn't say how he knew which was 'his,' but he did. He also knew that it recognized him.

The tap on his shoulder made him jump from his seat. Haussmann was openly amused at the reaction. "I see you are admiring our sentries," he said. "We are honoured. They include some of Caesar's own Praetorian Guard."

"They're golems!" Tesla blurted.

"Amphoraeka," the Baron correctly mildly. "What do you know of such creatures?"

"When I was at University in Prague, I heard the old Jewish stories. They were folk tales, I thought."

"Many folk tales turn out to have more than a grain of truth," Haussmann observed.

Tesla nodded. In his own life, he'd had occasion to see things that most eyes would doubt. "A grain indeed. Sandtmann claimed he was a descendant of sorts of the Maharal." Nikola could swear that 'his' golem had reacted to what he had said.

"Most interesting," Haussmann said blandly. "Our Roman amphoraeka have their beginnings in a more ancient time than the golem of which you speak. As you've observed, they're made of clay. But," he emphasized with a smug smile, "they were not quickened by any pleas to the God of Israel."

"So you've found some way to use electricity! How?" Tesla was excited by this notion. It would explain the bluish light. His vision of a self-propelled mannikin required a compact energy source, but none of his countless attempts to create a new type of Daniell cell had met with any success. It was staggering to think the Italians might have developed one. Perhaps Augustus had reversed his position on technology and wonderful things were happening here. If so, maybe this so-called commission would turn out to be to his benefit.

"Caesar does not favour electricity," Haussmann said, delicately evasive. "As a boy, Caesar's imagination was fired by his father's Egyptian campaigns. He dedicated himself to completing the Great Napoleon's reclamation of the heart of the first Empire; not merely the land, but the lost wisdom of antiquity. Men of talent and wisdom have congregated to help him." The Baron fingered a large curiously-carved jasper ring that he wore on his left hand. "I myself have been honoured to serve Caesar by using reclaimed ancient knowledge to engineer roads and aqueducts, and by restoring the majesty of his capital."

"I see," Tesla was carefully non-committal. He recognized the look on the Baron's face. He had seen it in the faces of other old men, drinking successive rounds of *rakia* in smoky rooms, exulting the names of comrades who had sacrificed their lives to the ideal of Nationalism.

"I doubt that you do, Mr. Tesla," the Baron replied. "But that is of no matter. I have brought you here because we need a scientist, not a magician. Caesar has achieved much with the amphoraeka, but is desirous of a few refinements before he expands the model beyond his personal guard. You have had success with the type of articulated mechanisms he requires. I look forward to your continued success on our behalf."

The next morning, Tesla was conveyed across the city to an isolated building that seemed half laboratory and half temple. It was guarded by a platoon of the amphoraeka, including the one he continued to identify as "his." The young soldier who was detailed to accompany him to and from the place referred to the creatures casually as 'trecika,' explaining this was slang for what they were: *creta che contiene*—three c's—*ka*; the clay vessel containing ka.

"What is 'ka' then?" Tesla asked. It was the one syllable shared by both the official and slang names, so it must be important. The young man, Dominic, shrugged. He had no idea; this was simply what they were called in the barracks.

A pair of rawboned, nut-skinned men took him from the soldier and brought him to their workroom. In their blue linen robes, they looked like monks or priests. As best he could tell, they were in charge of building the clay bodies. Tesla had limited fluency in Latin, the only language they seemed to share with him at all, so it took some while to find out what they expected him to do. He was surprised that the polyglot Baron had not come with him to translate, but apparently his impression of some religious component was correct and the Baron was not an initiate to these mysteries. Tesla fervently hoped that he was not about to be made privy to something so arcane that they would not permit him to live to tell.

The puzzle put before him was so absorbing that it soon buried this worry in the far depths of his mind. The arms of the amphoraeka were formed as a single tube from the shoulder and ended in fist-like lumps of clay. The priests conveyed that the Emperor wanted to improve the block-like structure with articulated arms. They showed him the detritus left from failed attempts at elbow joints. He intuitively saw that their problem was in trying to make clay, however animated, flex and recoil. In broken Latin and a few sketched lines, he tried to describe how a metal armature would resolve the issue in no time at all. Tesla's two new associates started babbling so frantically that he couldn't make out a word. They eventually made it clear that their religion demanded that the bodies be constructed of contiguous portions of earth. Metal might be used for bits that weren't integral to the structure, such as the headgear, but even then only a few specific metals were allowable. He shrugged helplessly; their constraints made this a dilemma that he couldn't solve.

He was marched, deliberately it seemed, through a city dump. Under the observation of armed centurions, emaciated men and women foraged through the rubbish for food and rags. Each of them, even the children with their swollen bellies, wore an armband with a badge, a green letter 'D'. "*Dissidente!*" Domenic's lip curled in distaste. "Enemies of Roma."

The air was still thick with sour milk and vegetable rot, when Tesla heard the sharp report of a rifle behind them. He jumped. Domenic shrugged philosophically. "They should be grateful that Caesar suffers them to live at all."

Back at the Villa Alsaziano, a shaken Tesla tried to explain that the task was unreasonable.

"I think not," Haussmann informed him, a fanatical look in his eyes. There was no reprise of the sociable evening in the charming courtyard. Dinner arrived at Tesla's room on a tray and an amphoraka was stationed outside the door.

Recalling the workshop explosion, Tesla realized he had no option but to try to attain the unattainable. The problem was inspiration. Tesla's best ideas always came to him full-blown, envisioned all at once and to a fine level of detail. With a vision beckoning at the end of a road, he would begin the expedition to reach it and could work twice as hard and many more times effectively than other engineers. Serving at the pleasure of Caesar Augustus, inspiration was a necessity he was having to do without. Each day for a fortnight, Tesla rose before dawn and spent his waking hours madly experimenting with bits of clay and even sketching, a method he ordinarily eschewed as frustratingly slow and lifeless, good only for communicating his completed designs to idiots. Each night, he tossed and turned in his silken prison, getting barely a wink of sleep. Food was sent up several times each day but turned to dust in his mouth. Desperate for rest and for ideas; he felt himself drifting away from life.

It didn't surprise him to feel one of his headaches coming on. He'd been subject to them for much of his life. The world around him would disappear in flashing lights, there would be whirring or humming in his ears, and he would slip into a kind of silent trance; he might forget to eat or drink for as long as three days. Mercifully, this wasn't one of his worst episodes. When the coloured lights started darting behind his eyes, he was already in his bed, too exhausted to do anything other than release himself into the pain. Across the blackness danced the image of a marionette that had belonged to his brother, Dane, who'd died when Nikola was five. The little ghost had haunted his childhood as the example of all that was ideal. His painted toy was kept on a shelf in the nursery as a constant reminder, to be touched at the penalty of a beating. Young Nikola had spent hours watching the wooden man, imagining it would come to life and play with him. Now in the headache fugue, watching the mannikin dance, Tesla perceived that his joints—elbows and knees, ankles and wrists—had been accomplished by balls and sockets carved to mimic a human skeleton. The following night, Tesla awoke and demanded that the sleepy orderly immediately fetch him his notebook and a pencil. He sketched until dawn when, drained, he dragged himself to the laboratory and explained it to the monks.

The design they accepted struck him as more fragile than he would have wanted but the monks were content. With a design to execute, they came into their own. Tesla was amazed at their speed and skill. Pieces were shaped and left to air dry to a certain point, then assembled and tested, in rapid succession. He was allowed to help construct prototypes of individual pieces of arm, and his molding of a mitten-like cleft hand was enthusiastically adopted, but when he asked to remove an arm from one of the amphoraeka and replace it with the newer model, he was made to understand this could not be. For some reason, he'd assumed that the arms could be broken off, as they could from a china shepherdess, and that the new arms would somehow be glued into place with damp clay; for expressly this reason, he had adjusted the design to include a type of curved epaulette. When he volunteered to begin disassembly, the monks' reaction was nothing short of horror. A religious reason was again implied but, as a scientist, Tesla wondered if it had more to do with the mysterious power source. He had kept a watchful eye all his weeks in Rome; but he had never seen anything remotely like a battery, nor any other portable source of energy. What was the secret? If he broke off an arm, would whatever element that made these creatures move leak out of the hole? When he tried to probe further, one of the monks shook his head vehemently and gestured for a soldier to escort him 'home.' They must have gotten word to the Baron; at dinner that evening by the lemon trees, Haussmann suavely explained that assembling an amphoraka was a sacred task that lay persons such as Tesla and himself were prohibited from performing. The monks were embarrassed at the awkwardness their overreaction might have caused. They were most grateful for his help and looked forward to showing him the results of their shared labor. In the meanwhile, Caesar Augustus had suggested he enjoy a few days on Capri to recover his strength.

Young Dominic came to fetch him the next morning. They went by boat to an island of great beauty, for what turned out to be a bacchanal beyond Tesla's imaginings. When they returned to Rome, his head was so muzzy that he barely glanced at the trecika guarding the villa until the creature greeted him with the ancient Roman salute, a fist to the chest followed by the straightening of the now-articulated arm. Tesla was gratified by the success of his design. The clay giant then dipped its cleft hand in a small mud puddle and dragged it along the wall, leaving marks on the marble. Tesla hardly had time to register this odd behaviour, no less to understand it. The Baron met him with a celebratory glass of prosecco and a few hours later, a bag of gold coins in his handbag, Tesla was on his way back to Serbia.

It was not until days later, back in his own workshop, that he recalled the moment and recognized that it had been 'his' trecika, and that the marks on the wall had looked like awkward writing. The more he thought about it, the more it haunted him and the more certain he became that the creatures weren't simply animate, that they were somehow alive. Caesar was a madman with an army of slaves that he, Nikola Tesla, had helped to make even more functional, which meant more dangerous.

How had he been allowed to leave Rome with his life? He wouldn't wager that Haussmann or the Emperor or even the nervous monks might not still change their minds. Tesla knew more than was safe for any man to know. The response to this situation was clear and two-fold: he needed to hide; and he needed to build something strong enough to destroy the amphoraeka before Caesar Augustus turned them on the world.

Setting aside the welding torch, Tesla carefully pushed himself upright. His knees ached from hours of kneeling on the brick floor. A piece of carpet, or even linoleum, would be nice, but the workshop didn't run to homely frills. Not only was money better spent on brass or saved for Prometheum but, between the stove, the torches and the acid, there was already too much danger of fire.

As he stood, a blinding lightning began to rage behind his eyes. He let his canvas coat fall where it might and staggered up the ladder to the loft, hoping only to reach his bed before he lost consciousness. He needed to be somewhere safe. He somehow managed to fumble off his boots and fall into the hammock. He pulled off his collar, sending the studs dancing across the floor; chances were they would disappear forever between the planks, but he didn't care. It was essential that he rid himself of anything that might cause him harm. His late mother used to slip him into his nightshirt, tuck the sheets around him, and fold a damp towel over his eyes. He still couldn't believe she was gone. The lights were exploding like fireworks now. He pulled the old knit coverlet up to his chin and closed his eyes. It was going to be a bad one. Sometimes, as in Rome, the headaches would bring him a solution to a seemingly hopeless problem. Tesla devoutly hoped that would be the case this time.

2 - THE FRANKLIN LEGACY

Nan Hudson led the strangers down the rear stairs to the basement gymnasium. They couldn't see her frown, but her narrow back radiated clear disapproval. She remembered their type all too well: their impeccably neutral suits of black Burberry gabardine; their good leather boots, carefully polished to a discreet dull shine. Her late husband Ian, God rest his soul, had been one of them. The one who called himself 'Baxter' even wore the same fiendishly costly spectacles as Ian had, the rimless kind that disappear against the skin, making it unlikely that the face would be remembered as wearing such an appliance. One of Frankie's patents of course and, considering that their own great-grandfather had designed the bifocal lens, it was most seemly for him to have devised it. She presumed the duo also had some of Frankie's less seemly contrivances concealed about their persons. 'Baxter' and 'Chandler' indeed. Baker and candlestick maker; did they think she was a fool? She sniffed audibly. Where was their 'butcher' then? Sending another poor soul like her Ian to his patriotic rest, she didn't wonder.

"Gentlemen," she quietly, her Scots burr exaggerated by dripping scorn. "Ah advise you remain verra still and keep to this side of the lines. Ma brither does nae take well t'interruption." They nodded, predictably vacant of expression.

The hinges were well-oiled; the door opened silently at her touch. Stepping through, the two strangers were promptly appreciative of their guide's caution. Within the confines of the painted lines, the scuffed softwood floor was the scene of a mighty skirmish. There were only two combatants, but each was double-armed with saber and knife, and they moved with such swift ferocity that they appeared to be triplets. The two

16

were more or less of a height. The slightly smaller one was slimmer and moved with the freedom of youth. The older and more muscular man moved with no less speed, and with more control of his limbs and greater precision in his parries and thrusts. The match seemed to favour him, until a flick of the other's wrist sent the saber flying from his grip. It was a move to make a spectator's wrist twinge in sympathy but, to the admiration of Chandler and Baxter, the older warrior seemed to grow in resolve. A dazzling feint distracted the younger combatant, who was quickly likewise without saber and, all too soon, without any weapon at all.

By any reasonable rules, the duel ought to have ended there, but the pair kept at it. "Use what you have!" the older man grunted at his opponent. The younger body twisted and collided with the older, feet first, in such a way that the final blade spun away to the farthest corner of the room. The older, knocked breathless, and the younger, fallen to the ground, merged into a ball of flailing limbs. The only sounds were grunts and thuds as they rolled, first one on top and then the other. The younger appeared to feel a surge of energy and leapt up, only to be felled by a quick jerk of the ankle. Then it was the elder who rose and, with a clever jump like a circus acrobat's, pulled back beyond arm's reach. The younger struggled upright. The two began to revolve in a close circle, first one and then the other, attempting moves that were instantly preempted. It seemed this circuit would never be broken.

Nan Hudson blew an impatient puff of air between her teeth. Though neither combatant registered awareness of the sound, the older of the pair broke out an impromptu series of kicks and slashes, his legs and arms poised from a lateral rotation that appeared to support unusual power. More wonderful still, the younger parried these with a series of defensive moves that seemed perfectly wedded to these thrusts. This went on for more than a minute, until the older delivered a three point kick-kick-slash that the younger was unable to counter. Instead, the youth jumped and twisted into a backwards flip. It would have been breathtaking to watch, had not the older jumped as well with a move that landed the younger face down on the ground, himself sitting upright on the youth's bottom.

"Enough?" the older man said with admirably steady breath. The younger pulled off a glove in supplication and tossed it aside.

"If ye be done then, Frankie," Nan said with some asperity, "there be some gentlemen here to see ye." She said the word 'gentlemen' as if it were an insult. The older man helped the younger upright, then came towards the uninvited audience. Nan flicked her fingers in their direction: "Messieurs Baxter and, ahem, Chandler."

Franklin Monteith pulled off his gloves and mask. He was older than anyone might have expected from his recent performance, his sandy hair thickly speckled with silver, a fine net of lines around the clever grey eyes that swept his visitors from boot to crown. "Pinkertons, aye," he stated rather than asked.

"Sir," Baxter replied, as if in affirmative, clicking his heels in salute.

"And what brings two Pinkertons all the way from London to the Wild West?" He raised his hand to forestall any possible reply and turned to his sister. "We'll be in my office, Nan, if you can see your way to a wee pot of tea." She nodded briskly; she had anticipated as much.

They left the room, the door closing silently behind them. The younger combatant pulled of her mask and shook out her long chestnut hair. "What's all this about, I wonder?" Her large eyes, also grey, sparkled with curiosity.

"Well might we both wonder," her aunt replied, "until your father decides what's fit to tell." She looked at the tall, disheveled Amazon in fond despair. This was what came of a man raising a lass. Even that women's college back in the civilized East seemed to have left no gentle traces, except when she was willing to play act in the service of one of Frankie's so-called 'cases.' Mrs. Hudson started up the stairs. Casually, as if it made no never mind, she called back, "see about making yourself decent. I expect we'll be having visitors to dine."

❧

"Is Pinkerton dead? Because there is no other excuse for this intrusion." His voice was low and cold and, if granite could blaze, Frank's eyes would have been doing a worthy impersonation. "I'd made it quite clear that there was not to be any presence in my home. Not ever. This was primary among the terms of continuing to enjoy my services. Pinkerton has managed to adhere to this for twenty years. Now in you stride, bold as brass and obvious as a pair of bears in a perfume shop, announce yourselves as visitors, spy on a private lesson…"

"To be fair, Sir Alastair," began the Chandler…or was it the one calling himself Baxter?

"I am called Franklin Monteith!" he snapped.

The Baxter smoothly picked up his junior's thread of thought. "We assure you, sir, we would never have breached your privacy if it hadn't been absolutely necessary. It wasn't feasible to employ the usual methods and have your regular contact arrange to rendezvous in Pittsburgh."

"He can't," Chandler said bluntly. "Kellogg is dead."

18

Before Frank could react, there was a knock at the door. He opened it; his visitors noticed that the outside of the door had no knob, only a blind keyhole.

A tall, lean man entered, his reddish brown skin at odds with his finely tailored black coat. His nose was chiseled like an arrowhead. Above the high, flat cheekbones, his almond-shaped eyes were entirely black. He wore his long hair, equally black, neatly bound with a leather thong. From the ease with which he maneuvered the massive tray of tea things and set it down on the table, it was obvious that his strength was formidable. "Mrs. Hudson thought you would prefer that I bring this," he told his employer.

Frank nodded approval. "Thank you, Firewalker."

Chandler and Baxter couldn't tear their eyes from the man. In the course of their business, they had travelled to many corners of the world, but never before had they found themselves in the presence of a genuine American native. It was thrilling, yet somehow to be expected, that Sir Alastair Franklin Menzies would have such a man in his household. Despite, or perhaps because of, having chosen to be sidelined to the Territories, Menzies was a legendary figure to the men of the Special Service, particularly those too young to have ever served with him. He'd spent time in India and China, learning peculiar disciplines of fighting and controlling the body. The stories of his daring and narrow escapes could keep a dormitory of boys enthralled every night for a year. Yet physical prowess and a knack for cryptography were the least of his accomplishments. His favourite puzzles were the secrets of nature. Like the famous ancestor whose name he bore, he wielded curiosity like a scalpel. He was a born scientist and an inventor of brilliant practicality; half the equipment in the current Service arsenal bore his name.

"What do you mean, Kellogg is dead?" Frank handed a cup of tea to Chandler, who was so startled he nearly dropped it.

"Exactly that," Baxter answered for him. He looked significantly at the tribesman, who went on pouring.

Frank nodded. "You may talk freely in front of Firewalker. I trust him as much as I trust myself. More perhaps—he's never so daft."

Baxter couldn't tell if that was meant as a joke. No matter; his Pinkerton training was in charge. "I'm sorry, sir, but regulations…"

"Damn the regulations!" Frank exclaimed, smashing his hand against the desk in such a way that Baxter expected the elegant nacre stars and planets to vault from the border and orbit the room.

The tribesman coughed and Frank caught himself. "My apologies, sir," he said, with the merest sketch of a bow. "Allow me to introduce

Wakhangli Mani. In the language of his people, the Lakhota Sioux, the name means 'He Walks With Lightning.' The tall man bowed gravely. Chandler felt compelled to bow in return. "You may call him 'Firewalker.' I once had occasion to save his life and, by the customs of his people, he owes it to me. I don't relish the position, but I've done my best to make things right. Now do you understand why you're free to speak in front of him?"

Baxter nodded and resumed. "Only a week ago, following procedure, we wired a coded message to Kellogg through the usual channel." Kellogg posed as the owner of a titanium sheeting factory, a personae that facilitated innocuous contact with Menzies. "In return, we received a message to contact the Boston police. We did and were told that Kellogg's body had been found in the harbor, his arms bound behind his back and a bullet between the eyes."

"Execution, not murder," Firewalker opined, to the Pinkertons' surprise.

"Yes!" Chandler put down his cup and struggled to lean forward out of the deep leather bucket of his chair. "Evidently his identity had become compromised. The hand of our enemy is reaching even across the Atlantic. The information we had for Kellogg was meant to be passed to you, sir."

"One of you ought to have become the Kellogg and contacted me according to the standing protocol." Frank tapped his disapproval on his armrest.

The Baxter, who was the senior remaining agent and therefore the likely candidate, shook his head decisively. "No time to establish a transfer of cover. There wasn't even time to take ship to Boston. The Chief had us booked on the next aership to New York, and a second aership straight from there to here."

Only from the direst need for speed would Allan Pinkerton reach into his purse for the outlandish cost of a trans-Atlantic dirigible. This was indeed a sign of the Apocalypse. "What was the message?" Frank asked. "The message so important that you had to come to my home?"

Baxter produced an oiled canvas envelope from his breast pocket. Frank unwound the string from the fastener and slid out a piece of heavy linen paper, folded and fastened with a seal he knew well. He took the paperknife from Firewalker without looking up, lifted the seal and unfolded the page to read what was written there in a cramped, angular and very familiar hand. It was, in effect, a Royal command, from Charlotte Antonia Sophia, Queen of Greater Britain, to her loyal servant Alastair Franklin Menzies, that he return to London at once to lend his unique talents "to prevent the destruction of Our House." Uncharacteristically for a Royal command, it ended "please, I beg you."

Frank set the paper on his knee, his hand cupped protectively over it. With the thumb and forefinger of his other hand, he rubbed the sides of his nose. "Brief me," he said.

"Lord Pinkerton wants to brief you himself in London," Baxter apologized. "I am only to say that it's the Italian Emperor…"

"He's mad, you know," Chandler seemed eager to register as a presence with the tall silent American. "Barking mad."

"We have our newspapers on this side of the Atlantic," Firewalker observed.

"Rome may have isolated itself, but information continues to leak out. And I do receive communiqués," Frank said with touch of impatience.

Baxter stifled the urge to shake his junior. He reminded himself that they had traveled rapidly across time as well as land and sea; some men do not adjust quickly to a change of sun. "Sir, I've been instructed to tell you that the Emperor's exploits go well beyond the buffoonery of Caligula with his horse. As disturbing as it is to contemplate what that might imply, our primary concern is the more immediate threat to Britain. Lord P didn't dare commit anything to paper, but he's had a young protégé working undercover in Italy for almost three years now. Horner's made great strides. Horner is his code name, no one knows who the man is…he's uncovered information…" Baxter cleared his throat. He stopped speaking like a dispatch and fixed a reluctant eye on Frank. "Sir, we now know that the Emperor was behind the so-called 'accident' that killed the Princes of Wales and York."

Frank was duly shaken. It was hardly more than a year since the terrible accident that had taken the lives of both the Queen's heir and his only brother. Prince Richard of Wales, a man who had shown every promise of being one of Britain's great kings, had been on his way to the ceremonial opening of Paxton-Brunel Station, traveling the private spur from Windsor to London. Since the assassination of Prince Albert more than twenty years before, the Queen wouldn't allow the princes to appear together at the same public function, and so Prince Frederic of York was leading his regiment through a demonstration of maneuvers for the edification of the boys of Eton. Somehow, the Royal train had jumped the rail, just as York and his men were passing through the field. It had been a bloodbath. Eight horses had to be put down and twelve men died, among them the two Princes and the train's engineer.

"The engineer and Prince Frederic's groom Avery were both in the pay of the Roman Emperor. Poor Avery was being blackmailed," Baxter shook his head sadly. "The engineer was an agent. You'll recall, sir, that this tragedy occurred soon after the Queen refused yet again to affiance the Princess Maud to the Emperor's grandson."

"And as a result of these deaths, the Princess has since become the heiress-presumptive to the British throne." Frank now understood the message "prevent the destruction of Our House."

"Yes, sir. Horner says there's reason to believe that the Emperor will stop at nothing to bring this marriage about as soon as possible. We believe the Princess to be in extreme danger. That's why Lord P wants you working with him in London. As does the Queen herself."

❧

They had been waiting in the library for the better part of an hour, on display as if in the tea room of the Palmer House. Aunt Nan wouldn't let up on her efforts to turn Claude into her idea of a young lady. To dine with two men of whom Aunt clearly disapproved, she had been told—make that ordered—to change into a tea gown and put up her hair with the garnet combs. She came down prepared to talk ridiculously about the weather or even, upon request, play the piano after dinner. Aunt Nan had also dressed up, in her good olive bombazine with the French frills that set off her surprisingly elegant hands.

Father stuck his head in the door. His eyebrows jumped in comic surprise. "Why are the two of you dressed like the Christmas goose?" He claimed that the men, having urgent business to attend to, had regretfully declined their kind invitation. Claude knew him better than to believe that; he'd sent the two men packing. So much for Aunt's efforts.

They sat down to an elaborate floral arrangement and a roast beef dinner clearly fit for English visitors. When Father began his story, she thought it was part of the same joke. Those two bland men couldn't be spies; spies were supposed to be dashing and handsome! She laughed aloud.

Father ignored her. He calmly admitted that he too was a spy; not just any special agent, but right hand man to Allan Lord Pinkerton, the Queen's own spymaster. He went on, as calmly as discussing the weather, to tell them a terrible secret about the tyrant in Rome and the poor dead Princes. The Queen, he announced, needed him in London.

She felt like such a little fool. Aunt Nan went on chewing roast beef as if it were an ordinary dinner. Why not? Whether or not she'd guessed he was still actively spying, she had known her brother's history. Firewalker probably had too. Only Claude had been left in the dark. She pushed away her plate. Ordinarily she had a hearty appetite, particularly on gymnasium days, but it was too difficult to digest both shock and dinner.

Aunt finally swallowed and asked what he was going to do.

Father shrugged. "It's a Royal command. If nothing else, I have to go to London and hear Pinkerton out. Perhaps he has it wrong."

Claude's discomfort was offset by pleased anticipation. She had gotten a taste for playacting and being in on the chase, but there had been no new cases in almost year. There was always plenty to do in the workshop, but it lacked that thrill. Life felt dull. London would be an exciting diversion. It was one of her few points of contention with her father, that he had never permitted her to travel abroad. She wondered aloud about the clothes she might need to pack.

Father cut her off, without a second's pause. "You're not going anywhere. You'll be staying here with your Aunt Nan."

"You might be there for months! What if it takes years? Don't you want to have me with you there?"

Even Mrs. Hudson seemed surprised. "It would be a treat to be away from the Wild West and meet with civilized society."

Father calmly speared a potato. "I made a choice to leave London and raise my daughter here. I had my reasons, just as I have good reason to return alone."

"But I can help you! I'm your assistant!"

"This won't be like one of my cases," Father replied. "Spying is warfare, not a game."

That "my" stung her like a slap. "Games?" she protested. "I could have died helping you trap that murdering landlord!"

"Aye!" Aunt Nan exclaimed, triumphantly. She might have been feeling her own disappointment, but she couldn't resist the opportunity to make one of her points. "I always say these investigations are no proper occupation for a lass." Her mouth pursed in a satisfied smirk.

Nan always did say that. As if there were some other occupation suitable for someone of Claude's gifts and training. What better use of her education than to help her father with his investigations? Anyone might work at a settlement house or teach infants until they got married. Claude wanted to do something more with her life, something important. She turned a beseeching eye on her father.

Frank shook his head. "Your Aunt has the right of it. I should never have involved you in my work. Living with danger is one thing; putting my own child in the thick of it…" When she was small, he had worried about her every waking minute of the day. He had finally outgrown that; then the landlord case brought it all back. "Never to know from minute to minute whether or not you were safe, imagining you laid out cold…" His voice thickened with emotion and he clenched his hand into a white-knuckled fist. "I never," he said fiercely, "never want to live through that again!"

So that was why she'd been twiddling her thumbs; not because there weren't any cases, but because he wouldn't allow her to share them. "What about what I want?!" She jumped from her seat, gripping the dining table to keep from flying across it. All of the frustration she hadn't even known she'd pent up came bursting out. "You want to lock me in the house, and she won't let me speak. I might as well still be in the nursery! When will you start treating me like an adult? I have college classmates who are married and have two children already."

"As you might, if you put half a mind to it," Mrs. Hudson remarked smartly.

"I ask to be excused!" Claude threw her napkin down on the table and stalked out of the room.

Claude Monteith was angry: she was frustrated; she was perturbed; she was discomfited, aggrieved and a little titillated. She paced furiously, glad for the education that had provided her with so many words to describe what she was feeling, because what she really wanted to do was thrash someone and that option wasn't available.

Whirling to yet again reverse her course down the hallway, she caught her skirts on the carved teak idol and stumbled. Father had found the idol in Sumatra, when he had travelled there once for business. What business was that, she wondered now? He'd said the idol had been used to smuggle opium and silly Claude had been amazed that he could possibly know such a thing. Well, marvel no more. Father was a spy, an agent of Her Majesty's Special Service; moreover, he had been a spy all her life and she had never caught the faintest whiff of it. She supposed that made him a superb spy, which should have made her proud but only made her angrier.

Father built fabulous machines and solved baffling puzzles; he feuded with Edison and dined with Carnegie; he was equally at ease in a ballroom and a tipi. He had shared all of this with her. She had been so proud to be treated as a partner, the way that he might a son. Claude would have sworn that she knew everything about him. Now she wondered what other secrets she didn't know.

She gave her skirt a disgusted tug to free it from the idol and heard the rip; a bit of the brass channeling that held the ivory inlay had come loose, snagging the fabric. Not a simple seam rip, oh no, but the worst—a three-cornered tear. There would be another lecture from Aunt Nan on the importance of learning to "act like a lady." Oh, the throwing-up of hands and rolling of eyes that would ensue! Angry tears stung her eyes. There would be no point in protesting that even the most ladylike of the girls she'd known at Vassar tore their skirts on a regular basis. What else should you expect, when fashion had women dragging the parlour draperies on the ground behind them wherever they walked? There were any number of practical reasons to prefer to wear trousers, not merely because your father had "raised you like a lad."

It was time for Aunt Nan to stop harping on that subject. Claude liked the way Father had raised her. It didn't stop her from being able to be feminine beyond Aunt Nan's wildest dreams. When Uncle Andrew had asked Father's help in investigating a notorious adventuress who was leading naive, newly-wealthy men to their destruction, it was Claude, in a dark wig and a few slightly questionable gowns, who had played the seductive decoy. She had been so successful that, as well as helping to net Gwendolyn Fortescue, she'd garnered a few marriage proposals. You would think that would have stopped Aunt Nan's sighing about "a lass your age and not a beau in sight," but no.

She knew Aunt Nan meant well. She only wanted to see Claude happy and, to Aunt, that meant married and settled into an establishment of her own. It wasn't that Claude didn't want that as well; it was that Claude wanted more. She had a good mind and a strong body, both of them well trained. Why was it so wrong in wanting to use them? She admitted it was challenging to find a way to balance who she was with what society expected her to be, but college, where she'd met other educated young women, had helped. So had helping Father. She was no longer that rough girl, mooning awkwardly over Nikola Tesla one day and short-sheeting his bed the next.

She drew herself up proudly in front of her mirror. Let Father play his spy games and Aunt Nan dream of picking wallpaper. She was confident that somewhere, if only she could find it, were a man and a world that would appreciate the woman she was.

She did look exceptionally well in this gown. It was a glossy sherry-coloured silk, cut like one of the Liberty gowns she'd seen in the fashion plates. Aunt Nan was wrong to think she didn't like fashionable clothes. If only they weren't so inconvenient to wear! Sitting on the edge of her bed, she smoothed the fabric across the coverlet and examined the damage with regret. If she could catch-stitch the tear and shift the ruffle to hide it, maybe she could avoid another harangue. If she and her aunt were to be left on their own together for months on end, it was worth the effort of avoiding conflict when she could.

Claude sought out a matching silk in her thread box. With a wry smile, she opened the slim needle case on the belt chatelaine that hung from her waist. This was one ladylike art she was glad her aunt had insisted she master. It was only sensible that everyone should be able to wield a needle. That and bake a loaf and disarm an opponent who was holding a knife to your throat. She didn't see why there should be 'manly' and 'womanly' skills. Knowledge belonged to everyone; her father had had always said this. She'd thought he really believed it, but now she wasn't so sure. She bet a son would be going to London.

3 - THE WHITE QUEEN'S KNIGHT

It was not without qualms that Frank picked up his leather handbag and said his farewells. In the two days since Baxter and Chandler's visit, the atmosphere at home had been chilly. Claude stalked through the house, slamming doors and saying not a word to him nor, apparently, to anyone other than Firewalker, who passed her grievances along. Firewalker had always indulged Claude in his way. As a small child, she had enchanted him with her affectionate nature and audacity. He held the young woman she'd become in the highest esteem and often subverted Nan's attempts to press her into a more ladylike mould. Typically, Firewalker expressed no opinion of his own about the current situation, but Frank could sense his disapproval.

In retrospect, Frank thought he might have handled the revelations more gracefully; but speed was of the essence. Even with all the time in the world, his decision would have been exactly the same. He had devoted a score of years to protecting his child. He was not about to drop his vigilance now. He owed nobody any explanation. It was not the Lakhota's place to judge him, any more than it was Nan's or Claude's.

He bid goodbye to his sullen daughter and thin-lipped sister at the door, and to his taciturn man at the end of the Chicago Aerodrome road. It was a relief to hand his ticket to an indifferent gatekeeper and mount the gangway. Frank felt grim amusement at the nervous chatter of the first-time flyers; no disaster in the air would disturb his peace more than what he was leaving behind on the ground.

In New York, he transferred to one of the colossal new titanium dirigibles that sailed across the Atlantic. Even Frank was impressed by their elegance and luxury. Compared to these metal-skinned behemoths, the aership that had brought him from Chicago was as quaint as something a child might pull along on a string. Standing on the observation deck, he accepted a flute of champagne from the circulating waiter. From the other end of the lounge, he caught the pleasant tinkling of a clockwork piano playing some modern piece of musical frippery. The inventor of Vitriflex raised a private toast to the extravagant windows that he had made possible, then allowed himself to relax and watch America drift slowly away.

❧

As a modern man of science, Frank considered that aerships mingled comfortably with the mechanized bustle and ever-taller buildings of the New World. Though it was always glorious to see their gleaming ranks, he felt only a careless satisfaction at their presence above the sheds of American cities. Disembarking at Shooters Hill, a very different perspective brought a catch to his throat. Why would he have pictured London unchanged? It might feel like yesterday, but nearly twenty years had passed since he had removed his daughter across the Atlantic. Back in 1868, who would have conceived of an aerodrome? Aerships then had been nothing more than dangerous toys. Frank looked up from the platform and paused to marvel. Tethered to the red brick tower, casting dancing shadows down the hill to London below, the silvery balloons seemed more magic than science. Except, as he was fond of saying, Frank didn't believe there was any such thing as magic; there was only science that we don't yet understand. Nonetheless, it was an other-worldly vision. It was with regret that he tore his eyes away and boarded a train that was as prosaically modern and dusty as any back in Chicago, Boston or New York.

He had expected to get off at Charing Cross and get a little taste of the city beneath his feet. When he noticed that the new route stopped at Paxton-Brunel Station, Frank decided a longer walk would do his legs good. A stop earlier than planned, he pulled his bag from the brass rack. What he had in mind wasn't a scene of the crime examination; he would need to request the Service files for that information and, in any case, the long-buried Princes hadn't been killed at the station itself but on the Windsor spur. No, this was purely a pleasure excursion.

The original Lambeth Station had still been in use when he'd last set foot in London, although Paxton's plans had indicated it would ultimately be replaced by a larger and more efficient structure. As a member of the original committee, Frank knew those plans well. Leaving that project had been one of his few regrets in deciding to relocate.

During the trans-Atlantic flight, Frank had resolved that whatever this business required of him, he would carve out the time to walk the entire finished circuit of the Great Way. The Prince Albert Great Way, he corrected himself. He remembered the Queen renaming the stalled project when she had insisted it be completed as a memorial to her beloved husband, its greatest champion. Other than opening Parliament, that speech, at the opening of the phase connecting Queen's Station to Lambeth, had been her first public appearance after the death of the Prince Consort. She'd been thin with grieving, and her widow's black had made her appear even taller than her already impressive height. "No matter how long it takes to complete!" she'd vowed, her eyes blazing in her white face. She had been electrifying. There was not a man alive who could have refused her. Still, the vast project had taken nearly a quarter of a century more. What bitter irony, that celebrating the final piece of the memorial to her husband had cost the Queen her sons and heirs.

Frank emerged from the platform and made his way to the center of the main concourse. He knew it was the center because of the compass of rare marbles laid into the floor, just the sort of useful decorative note the Prince Consort had favoured. Starting with one foot East and the other West, he shuffled slowly from point to point, craning his neck to take it all in. Inspired by two men whose vision had led the empire into the future, Paxton-Brunel Station was everything it should be. The epitome of British engineering, a magical confection of glass and iron, the building hummed with energy. Throngs of people went about their business, gliding along fantastical moving sidewalks to and from the platforms and surging everywhere in-between. Busy shops and food stalls packed the mezzanine with exciting colours and aromas. Overhead, message capsules flashed through a network of pneumatic tubes. Frank felt his face stretching into a broad, contented smile.

Taking up his bag, he followed the signs to the egress that lead towards what he saw had ultimately, not surprisingly, been named the Albert Bridge. As Paxton had envisioned, it was an occupied bridge in the manner of the Ponte Vecchio or the old London Bridge. Frank strolled past the shops, his eyes occasionally pulled upward by the flutter of awning from the balcony of one of the flats above. It was cheerful and bustling and, from the casual attitude of the crowd, it already seemed to have been there forever. At the midway point, an archway sheltered a pair of ledges that overlooked the river. Frank sat on the oak bench on the south-facing side. A gust of Thames-borne wind fought him for his hat and he had to clamp a hand down on the crown. It was all so familiar and all so strange. Ahead of him was Westminster and the august implications of Barry's Gothic palace; yet if he leaned forward and looked to his left, he could make out the sunlight glinting off the vaulted roofs of the ultra-modern railway station. He had forgotten how much London could thrill. His pulse quickened to match the pulse of the capital around him and he allowed himself a moment of lightness he hadn't felt in years. His excitement was underscored with a pang of regret; it struck him forcibly that there was no one left who might share his joy. The Prince and Paxton had both died before more than the first steps of the Way had been accomplished. Poor Kingdom Brunel had seen only the vision. He wondered what they would have made of all this.

Frank would have sat there for an hour if he could have, but the sun was fading and so, he was chagrined to admit, were his energies. He ambled across the bridge and onto the moving walkway of the new Median Arcade to Piccadilly; there taking leave of the glorious and scarcely explored Way in favour of streets that, even after all these years, seemed comparatively dull with familiarity.

Arriving at last at the Diogenes Club, he was greeted by a steward who seemed only slightly more decrepit than he had when last met. By fortunate contrast, the room had improved with time. Frank noted with satisfaction that his small trunk had preceded him, together with his wish to have it left undisturbed. It wasn't that he had brought anything of particular sensitivity, but security was the habit of a lifetime and, unless Firewalker were traveling with him, he preferred to unpack himself. One of the advantages of the Diogenes, the reason that of the several clubs to which he belonged this was the only one in which he would stay over night, was the sinecure against prying eyes that was part of its very charter. Another was their very decent cellar. He was looking forward to a good claret with his dinner. A good claret and a good night's sleep. He would need to be at his best tomorrow.

₰

Pinkerton's note, delivered with the Stilton, said that Frank would be fetched from the club at three. That was a surprise but, all things considered, a pleasant one. Considering the tenor of Queen's message, he had assumed he'd be kissing hands directly after breakfast or spending his first day locked in a room at Whitehall. Instead, he'd had a long morning free to reacquaint himself with familiar sites and absorb some of the inevitable changes.

To Frank's mind, there was no substitute for proper London tailoring. Despite the minor drawbacks, no matter how mercilessly his daughter might chide him for snobbishness, he persisted in ordering his furnishings by mail. After endless fruitless correspondence, it was a relief to be able to demonstrate to his shirtmaker exactly why his new patented-design cuff fasteners required a differently shaped eyelet; and it was a pure pleasure to select suiting fabric off the bolt instead of from a six-inch swatch. He was, however, left almost literally wrong-footed by his final stop on Jermyn Street. Old Duckworth, who had always made his boots, had passed two years ago. Though the bespoke work was, reassuringly, continued by his apprentices, Duckworth the Younger was more interested in picking Frank's brains regarding the plans for his new steam-powered manufactory. Frank allowed that the plans were impressive but he believed some things, his feet included, should be left to individual craftsmanship. Even he, the most forward-looking of modern men, was always sad to see generations of excellence discarded in favour of a gamble for a quick fortune. Frank hoped the ambitious cobbler wouldn't throw out the baby with the bathwater. He had always intended to have a Duckworth last carved for his daughter. It would be a shame if, when he finally got her here to be measured, there was no Duckworth's worthy of the name.

Feeling measurably less Colonial, and fortified by the first honest Dover sole he had tasted in years, Frank gave his best coat to the club porter to be brushed and pressed. He used the pleasantly modern facilities and exchanged his lemon cravat for the silvery-blue foulard that Claude said flattered his eyes. An hour later, just as he fastened the star of the Most Ancient Order of the Thistle to his breast, two anonymous looking men arrived in a black automobile.

They drove him to Windsor, where the Royal Standard was flying. Entering through one of the lesser doorways, the trio made their way, through a series of corridors of ever-increasing grandeur, to a guarded door. They stopped and were saluted. The door was opened. "Sir Alastair only," the guard said.

Cool as marble, Sir Alastair Franklin Menzies nodded once and entered alone. The doors closed heavily behind him, on a room that was larger than it needed to be. The lone occupant rose from the high-backed chair to meet him. Tall for a woman, taller than he, she wore her malachite silk gown with careless elegance. As she drew near, he could see that her hair, once a rich chestnut full of slumbering fire, was liberally threaded with silver. She looked at him with eyes that were as large, liquid and golden as any of the great cats. She held out her hand in greeting. "Frank," she said simply. "Thank you. It was good of you to come."

"Majesty," he said, with a courtier's bow. He took the proffered hand gently and kissed it. As he raised his head, he saw her mouth quirking in a private smile. All so familiar and all so strange. "Charlotte," he murmured, smiling in kind. He took a small step back. A glimmer of disappointment crossed her face. Both standing, they gazed at one another for just a moment until the ceremonial thud of the guard's baton against oak announced a visitor and broke what had the aspects of a spell.

The Queen had resumed her seat before Lord Pinkerton stumped emphatically into the Private Audience Chamber. Frank felt a twinge of sadness in his chest. For a man whose habits were known to be abstemious, Allan Pinkerton had developed a surprising paunch. As he walked, the unconscious way in which he shifted his body told of some persistent ache in his bones.

"Menzies!" Pinkerton exclaimed, once he had made his bow. Despite the depredation of the score of years on his person, he greeted Frank with a thump on the back that was as stout as ever. "You haven't changed, not a wee bit!"

"Pinkerton!" Frank was glad to embrace his old friend. "Not true. Silver threads among the gold. For all of us, I fear. Begging Her Majesty's pardon."

"There's no call to apologize for the truth, Sir Alastair." The Queen smiled graciously. "Gentlemen, please do be seated. I expect it will take some time for Lord Pinkerton to share what we've learned."

"Not unduly long, I hope, Your Majesty. I take it, Menzies, that you know what we've discovered?"

Frank nodded. "I've been told some of it."

"Time enough for details tomorrow. I'm dedicating my entire day to you. Mind, Joan insists you join us for breakfast. She remembers how you enjoy her marmalade." Behind the thick spectacles, Pinkerton's weak eyes sparkled.

"My pleasure. Quite like old times."

"Quite. Now then, my men informed you…?"

"That you say the Emperor Augustus is responsible for the deaths of the Princes. Aye." Frank spoke quickly and tried not to look at the Queen. It seemed cruel to be discussing this in her presence.

"Aye," Pinkerton agreed. "But that's not all." He sighed deeply. "Menzies, I couldn't have trusted this to any channel of communication. An agent died simply to protect Her Majesty's letter." He paused a moment, as if to honour the departed Kellogg, then lifted his chin and took a steadying breath. "We now have reason to suspect a prior attack from Rome; the assassination of His much-beloved Royal Highness the Prince Consort."

Frank felt a shocking chill. It had been a quarter of a century since he'd done his mourning, but with these words, Pinkerton exhumed the Prince's corpse. Albert had been Frank's patron and friend as well as his Prince. They had spent hours together discussing engineering problems; no one was a better sounding board for designs for new machines. When Albert was killed, the personal loss to Frank had been immense. "The Prince Consort was attacked by a random lunatic in Toronto!" he protested.

"A lunatic, yes," the Queen agreed. "But perhaps not so random. Remember how we laughed when Augustus proposed marriage?"

How could he ever forget? It had been the first time she'd laughed in months, the first sign to the Court that she was returning to life.

Pinkerton frowned. "We thought we had the Emperor neutralized after the Gallic War. We were wrong." Even schoolchildren knew the roots of that war. The young Augustus Napoleon, consumed with the desire to hold all that his Julian namesake had held, had believed he could claim France in the name of his wife, daughter of the deposed last Capet king. His noble father was still alive but sidelined by apoplexy, when Augustus attempted to annex the shaky French Republic. Her allies, led by Britain, had beaten him soundly back.

"Albert called that war 'the tragic cost of one man's delusion,' " the Queen reminded them. "How relieved we were when Augustus isolated himself in Rome. All the allies: Ourselves, Austria, Spain, Prussia. It was over and we didn't have to set a dangerous precedent by disposing of him."

"Except that it wasn't over, Ma'am," Pinkerton corrected. "Merely hidden. And his focus shifted to Britain in revenge."

"And perhaps," Frank speculated, "some twisted logic that if Britain were in his power, the rest of our allies would simply fall to him."

"Augustus's mind is as twisted as his bad foot," Pinkerton agreed. "The evidence my team has amassed is irrefutable, Menzies. You'll see for yourself tomorrow. It was no coincidence that the Prince Consort's death came so soon after the death of the Empress Philippine. We have documentation, including support for the rumours that the Lady Giulia had some hand in the Empress's final decline in health. Augustus was careful to make himself available before making his move. However, when Her Majesty proved to be too…uh, 'recalcitrant'," Pinkerton carefully adjusted the more vivid phrase Agent Horner had employed in his reports, "Augustus shifted his focus to the next generation."

"As I refused to bestow this crown on him as my dowry," the Queen explained with a note of bitter humor, "he determined that Rome would absorb Britain through our joint descendants. You do know that he set his sights on a marriage between Maud and his grandson when the two were quite small."

"I know you refused the match on multiple occasions, Ma'am. I sense that Lord Pinkerton and yourself are now thinking this connected, in some manner, to the death of the Princes."

"From what we've learned, Menzies, Augustus assumed he would weaken Her Majesty's resistance by removing what he saw as the obstacles to his success. He thought the Queen would be defenseless without male heirs, certain to jump at an alliance with Rome."

At that last observation, Frank let out a series of coughs to cover his desire to laugh. If there was any incontrovertible sign of Augustus's madness, it was the persistent notion that Charlotte of Greater Britain was a flower who would crumple without the protection and advice of a man.

Pinkerton ignored him and continued. "He finally seems to have accepted that he won't obtain Her Majesty's agreement. However, there are implications that he nurtures some fantasy of kidnapping the Princess, marrying her to Prince Augusto by force or perhaps even marrying her himself."

This time Frank didn't bother to conceal his laugh. "Ach, this is absurd, Pinkerton! This is the nineteenth century! He can't expect the world would condone that type of behaviour."

"That's the thinking of a *rational* mind, Menzies. Caesar Augustus, as he insists on calling himself, doesn't much seem to care what the world might condone."

"Regardless," Frank waved the issue away. "No doubt it's a moot point. I'm certain you have the Princess more than adequately protected."

The spymaster nodded. "She's unaware of it, but aye."

"Unaware of it?" As the father of a young woman, Frank thought that sounded extremely unlikely. "She would have to be what, seventeen, eighteen? A lass that age…what about public events, dances and so forth?"

"She's been in mourning, of course," the Queen said, evenly.

"And now that she's out, only secure venues are allowed. The Press has been cooperative. Her engagements are entered into the Court Circular retrospectively. Even her image hasn't been printed for some years, to avoid fueling the Emperor's passion for the match. Young Walter's idea. Able man, Walter."

"Extremely loyal," the Queen agreed. "We are grateful."

"Naturally, an armed detail accompanies her wherever she goes. Undercover. Currently led by my man Piper. Young, but one of our best. Decorated for heroism in the Mexican War, and merely a cadet at the time. And on the dashing side. If she's noticed him hanging around Bucharest, she's delighted."

"Bucharest?!" Frank was openly amazed.

"Relax, Menzies," Pinkerton chuckled. "Sleepiest capital in Europe."

"Then why...?"

"My son's widow remains in a fragile state. It was thought that Queen Elisabeth might provide her sister with the consolation that I cannot." A wry smile twitched at the Queen's mouth. "Maud asked to accompany her mother and Catarina would have thought me heartless to refuse."

"The Princess shows a proper sensibility and respect," Frank observed cautiously.

There was no humor in the Queen's laugh. "I'm certain her true motive was to have a holiday from me. My granddaughter does not enjoy her responsibilities. So different from myself at that age. Still, I don't have much choice of heir and I need to draw up an instrument of succession soon. Would that I had never allowed Emilie to marry Belgium but, at the time, how would I have guessed? The York children are too young to even consider; should something happen to me while Augustus lives, a Regency would leave the kingdom vulnerable." She said it coolly, as if it were not her own death that she was contemplating. Not for the first time, Frank marveled at her ability to divorce the Queen from the woman. She tipped her head in an almost invisible nod, as if she knew what he was thinking. "I worry greatly," she continued, "that Maud won't be ready to ascend the throne, but she's my best hope. She does have a brain, when she chooses to use it. And people are fond of her; she can inspire loyalty. The child can be moulded. I also know that if she's driven too hard her mind turns into a butterfly and flits away, so it's to my advantage to sometimes allow her to think she is breaking free. What could be safer than Bucharest?"

"Indeed," Pinkerton agreed. "Though we take no chances."

"It seems you have everything well in hand, Pinkerton. The young woman seems safe as houses. I confess I'm at a loss..."

"Against some of what we've recently learned, Menzies, abduction would seem to be the most reasonable of the Emperor's plans. The man's declared himself a god."

"Very Roman of him," Frank said drily. "But surely of no matter to us."

"He's decided if he can't recreate the Roman Empire in a lifetime, he's he'll find a way to live forever."

"Insanity!" Frank dismissed the idea.

"Of course," Pinkerton agreed, "but he believes eternal life to be an achievable goal."

Frank had to laugh again.

"Deranged the Emperor may be, but he's not a joke," Pinkerton admonished. "For decades he's applied himself to the scrolls and tablets his father brought back from Egypt. Whatever secrets they hold might now be his. The man's as dangerous as a wounded animal."

"Not half so dangerous as I," the Queen said in voice all the more terrible for being soft. "I would be happy to find myself locked in a room with Augustus Napoleon and a dull blade." She flicked her lashes at the startled Pinkerton. "Pain counts."

"An assassination, is that what you've brought me here to plan?" Frank considered the possibility. This was not how the British dealt with their enemies however, if done properly, it would be preferable to a declaration of war. From what he knew, he'd be glad to kill the man himself.

The Queen sighed so deeply that Frank could feel his own chair vibrate in sympathy. "You are here to help me, Sir Alastair. We have not yet determined how. Lord Pinkerton, please continue…"

"You'll think we're all daft, Menzies, but here it is!" Pinkerton pulled a square of cardboard from his coat and threw it down on the little French table as if he were calling a trump.

Frank picked it up and squinted. It was a blurred photograph of a large white villa, a pair of ungainly statues standing to either side of the entrance. "Pity. There was a time Rome was renown for her statuary."

"Perhaps you need a pair of Franklin Magnifiers," the Queen suggested. He thought she was teasing him until she unlatched the chain from her neck and handed him a pair.

He held the lenses over the picture and peered at it closely. They still looked like statues, lumpen but roughly human in shape. A man stood between them, bald and neat, his waistcoat strained over his rounded belly.

"He seems familiar," Frank mused.

"Baron Haussmann, or so it's written on the back of the card."

"Haussmann? There was a Georges-Eugène Haussmann. A civil engineer. Worked for Napoleon. The Prince Consort and I met him at a conference in Amsterdam to discuss drains." Haussmann had been both knowledgeable and charming. The Prince, Frank recalled, had been most favourably impressed. Frank look at the photograph again, this time focusing on the man. Haussmann hadn't much hair left to lose even then, and he'd been very fond of his dinner. "But it couldn't be the same man. He'd be…"

"Nearly eighty," Pinkerton confirmed, stroking his own silvered chin whiskers. "And exceptionally vigorous, by all report. It would be wonderful if he hadn't turned his talents to serving Augustus."

"But the man was an engineer! Augustus is against everything he stands for."

"Augustus might reject modern technological advances, but he wants a new imperial city. We're told entire neighborhoods have been ploughed under to make way for boulevards and civil palaces."

"We have had to do some of the same ourselves, in order to complete the Way," the Queen admitted.

"We build for the future, Ma'am. Haussmann has been given free rein and nearly unlimited funds to keep that city planted firmly in the past. Some of their most ancient buildings have been restored to their original glory. Something for our troops to marvel at when we march into Rome," Pinkerton noted with a bleak smile.

"Invasion? Has it come to that?" Dating from the gilded, if not actually golden, Ricardian era, most Britons found the concept of invasion repellant. Even the quixotic Mexican War had been fought only after a direct act of military aggression.

"Look again at the picture," the Queen advised. "Carefully. They're not statues."

Frank looked again. Haussmann, if that's who the man was, stood at a slight angle to one of the figures and seemed to be looking up at its face. One of the figure's arms was blurred, as if the camera had caught it in motion. Slowly, Frank put down the picture and met Pinkerton's eyes.

Pinkerton nodded. "Even before this picture was smuggled out, we'd had word of this; clay giants who serve as the Emperor's personal guard. There is some evidence that they're not mechanical constructs but animate." He pressed on, before Frank might object. "We can't begin to speculate how Augustus has done this, but Horner believes there is magic involved. And if Horner believes it, then I believe it."

Frank didn't believe it. He knew there were energies in the atmosphere that no one as yet understood, but energy was science and could be measured and quantified. His own aether spectrometer, for example, was a beginning. Calling something "magic" was assigning it power from belief rather than fact, the opposite of science. He turned from his old friend to look at the Queen. Her face showed complete acceptance of this impossibility.

"This Horner has convinced you as well, Your Majesty? He must be an unco persuasive lad. I look forward to meeting with him."

"He is a very brave young man," she said crisply. "I have read his communiqués, as will you. That is sufficient."

Frank understood. "Deep cover. Little Jack Horner, sat in a corner."

"Pulling out many a plum, Sir Alastair. We do not wish to compromise his safety. Only Lord Pinkerton is aware of his identity, and the agent who serves as his courier."

"Little Boy Blue? Really, Pinkerton…"

"Tucker." If she hadn't been the Queen, it might have been called the ghost of a grin. "Tommy, naturally."

"With all due respect, Pinkerton, these daft code names predispose me to doubt. Even my sister Nan…"

Pinkerton showed as much anger as he dared to reveal in the Royal presence. "Agent Horner is not a fanciful young man, Menzies. Quite the contrary. I've known him for most of his life and would swear he has a mind as logical and dispassionate as…well, not to put too fine a point on it, as your own. The evidence is compelling. Moreover, I share his conviction that the Emperor doesn't mean to stop at building an honour guard. Horner reports that the ranks of these creatures have swollen visibly in this past year. They're a growing presence in Rome and in other Italian cities as well."

"So you would have me believe that Augustus is planning to march on Britain with an army of magical monsters?" Frank folded his hands across his chest and shook his head.

"It's possible," Pinkerton said crisply. "We're trying to learn as much as we can."

"We would expect you to apply an unbiased mind to the evidence, Sir Alastair." Despite the smile, the Queen was not pleased with the skepticism she heard in Frank's voice.

"I assure you that I shall, Your Majesty." Frank kept his voice and eyes steady. "I am a scientist. I look forward to making a start tomorrow."

From the mantel, Queen Marie-Antoine's ormolu clock seemed to countenance this assumption by prettily striking the hour with its distinctive chime.

"Ah…" After so many years, Pinkerton was still never certain what to do when his hour had ended.

"Thank you, Lord Pinkerton. You've been most generous with your time."

It was a clear dismissal. "Ma'am" he replied, bowing. "Menzies? My driver…"

"I require Sir Alastair's attention to another matter," the Queen interrupted. "He shall have the use of an automobile to return to London. And a driver, if he prefers not to drive himself."

"You are most gracious, Ma'am." Frank bowed.

"Well then, Menzies. See you at breakfast. Your Majesty." Pinkerton bowed once more before backing out of the room.

⁊₰

They were alone once more. The Queen pointed to the gilded French cabinet and sank into the cushions of one of the low velvet chairs. It might have been twenty minutes instead of twenty years. Without hesitation, Frank produced the crystal decanter concealed within, poured a pair of whiskies and, handing one to the Queen, sat opposite her. They raised their glasses in silent salute and took a deep, appreciative sip. The ghillies on the Balmoral estate continued to brew an excellent draught. Frank wondered if Prince Albert had ever known about it. With the examples of his father and brother before him, the late Prince Consort had tended to veer to the other extreme when it came to drink. No one had liked to see him distressed. One of Frank's earliest assignments in the Service had been to supervise the transportation of potables to the various Royal residences. Discretion had been a priority.

"It's good to have you here, Frank. You look well. America seems to agree with you."

"It suits me there. I can't complain. "

"You must find me much changed." She leaned forward, turning the full power of her attention on him as she had all those years ago, a quarter of a century that simmered between them now.

He felt unexpectedly shy. "Not in the least wee bit."

"Don't be ridiculous. You're no courtier, Frank. You never were. Of course I've changed."

He had been sure she hadn't kept him there to speak of the Roman Emperor, much as it might have been easier if she had. "Not to me," he insisted. His sincerity must have been obvious. She relaxed against her chair with a sigh.

"Did you come alone?" she asked casually. "To London, I mean."

"Aye. It seemed best, not knowing what might be required of me."

"Your daughter must be quite grown up then, to leave her alone in America."

"She's not alone," he said shortly.

"Oh yes. I'd heard your sister joined you after Hudson's death. Another sad loss."

39

"Nan has been a boon to both of us. It's not easy for a man to raise a child alone, especially a lass."

"No, I didn't expect it would be."

Frank refused to react. He took a deep, calming breath, followed by a deeper mouthful of whiskey. He slowly adjusted his top three vertebrae, the better to keep his eyes safely on the ceiling. Like all the ceilings in the various Royal Residences, it was heavily illustrated. The Queen's illustrious ancestress Queen Anne was depicted as Juno, blessing the marriage of her daughter Princess Sophia to George of Hanover. Frank was surprised by a pang of sympathy for poor George. A Queen for a mother-in-law and a future Queen for a bride. No wonder Hanover had thrown himself so avidly into the Battle of Oudenarde.

Finally, she spoke again. She had to; he had always been the better one at silence. "What does she look like?" the Queen said abruptly.

"Not like me, thank goodness. Though she's said to have my eyes."

The Queen looked into those splendid grey eyes and her own grew more liquid. She was unprepared for this. She lifted her glass toward the chandelier of incandescent bulbs, pretending to admire the glow of the whiskey against the light.

"Tell me all about her," she said; "does she have many beaux?" It was an inane question but the first that came to mind and she had to say something. She was fearful of another lull.

"I think it's your granddaughter we should be talking about," he said carefully.

"Yes, of course. You're quite right. You must ask me anything you need to know. But not now. Questions can wait. Why shouldn't we enjoy a moment's peace? Such moments come rarely enough these days." She smiled at him again and indicated her empty glass.

Frank stood slowly and returned to the cabinet. When he turned back with the decanter, he saw that she'd risen to meet him. The air between them was so charged they might as well have been touching. She held out both their glasses and, his eyes never leaving hers, he refilled them. She handed one to him. Was it his, or was it the one that had kissed her lips? He took it from her and the tips of his fingers brushed against the back of her hand.

"Stay," she said. "For dinner." It was as much like a request as she could manage.

He nodded. What else could he do? She smiled. Few people ever saw her natural smile and those that did could never forget it. She was just as beautiful to him as she had ever been, and she would always be the most fascinating woman he would ever know. What else could he want to do?

Hours later and Frank still couldn't sleep. Sandford Fleming's Mean Solar Day was sound in theory but, in practice, it meant that his body still thought it was ten o'clock at night while his watch said three o'clock the next morning. He hoped he would have settled by now. Or maybe it was Pinkerton's briefing that was keeping him wide awake.

Frank had once known the pulse of Europe like his own heartbeat, but for two decades now his attentions had been trained westward. The young Mexican jaguar skulked hungrily along the left flank of Her Majesty's American possessions, and the Russian bear loomed over Her shoulder. What he had heard that afternoon was preposterous, but whatever the precise facts turned out to be, there was a powder keg in Rome. It was time for him to recalibrate his focus.

A little before five o'clock, Frank gave up trying to sleep. He splashed some water on his face and resigned himself to a day of black coffee and catnaps. She stirred, just as he was slipping on his coat. "Don't leave," she murmured, reaching for him.

He turned her outstretched hand and ran a gentle finger along her forearm before softly kissing her palm. She shivered and tried to pull him closer.

"I have work to do," he admonished. "I'm here on the Queen's business."

"Then I mustn't keep you." She pinched his nose tenderly before turning away.

"And the Pinkertons are expecting me for breakfast."

"See that they don't expect you for dinner," she said, closing her eyes.

He watched her for a moment. He felt an unexpected tenderness at the sight of the dent his head had left in the pillow beside hers. Quickly, before he might think twice and refrain, he removed a photograph from the soft leather wallet he kept in his coat and laid it down.

4 - A LETTER & A REPLY

"Tesla." Claude regarded the letter with some trepidation and a bit of a thrill. She'd recognized the handwriting at once. She'd had to transcribe enough pages of that crabbed scrawl; now here was an envelope with her name in that hand, and in green ink. "Why green?" she'd asked, the first time he'd handed her a letter to post to his family. He'd explained he always used coloured ink for his correspondence, so that he wouldn't confuse a letter with the sheaves of jottings on his desk and inadvertently send his mother his ideas about rotating magnetic fields or a record of his latest dream. He put great stock in dreams, she recalled.

She recalled so much more than that. She'd been half-past fifteen when Father had brought him home, and she'd never dreamed of a man like Nikola Tesla. He was handsome, like someone's idea of a poet, with a white face, tumbled waves and those dark haunted eyes. But he wasn't a poet or a painter.; nor was he on any of the boring paths followed by the young men of whom her aunt approved. He was a scientist and, after Father, the most intelligent man she'd ever met. He was someone who should have appreciated her. Even though she'd been younger than her age in certain ways, he should have been able to see her potential; but, for a man of science, Mr. Tesla had been oddly conservative about women and frustratingly blind.

She took the envelope from the tray and felt its presence in her hand. It was puzzling. Green ink meant 'personal.' Nikola Tesla had nothing personal to say to her, yet here was a letter indisputably addressed to her in green ink.

"He said that I was a terrible hoyden and that Father had ruined me for polite society." The observation had rankled then and had nagged at her ever since. "Not that he would know polite society if it stepped on his foot. He hated me."

"Perhaps not so much," Nan Hudson observed. You could hear that she was dubious. She'd seen Mr. Tesla's lack of regard for her niece and had been most insulted. Not disappointed, as he was a Serbian with no compensating fortune or title; but while she wouldn't have relished the match, she'd expected, with some complacency, that a young genius would be the category of man to appreciate her niece's finer qualities. Moreover, she'd seen that Claude had wanted him to. Even now, years later, the bairn's cheeks were flushed with emotion. Whatever did that exasperating man want from her? "Stop toying with the letter lass, and open it."

Claude neatly slit the envelope open. If it turned out to be that kind of letter, she wanted to preserve it as a souvenir. She'd never had one before; that is, she thought, recalling the Fortescue case, not one addressed to her in her proper person and certainly not one from Nikola Tesla.

My dear Miss Claude, it began. *I regret how long it has been since last I wrote. I have been traveling, and know you will understand how the beautiful villages of France can cause one to lose all sense of time...*

"And why hadn't you said that Mr. Tesla had been writing to you?" Her aunt was hurt. "Why did you pretend..?"

"He hasn't," Claude snapped. She rang for Firewalker.

"How can you say that? He says as much" Mrs. Hudson objected. With a grudging sniff she added, "the letter does begin well. Who would have thought the genius had such sensibilities?"

Claude frowned impatiently and counted off the points on her fingers. "He has never written to me before, not in all these years, not since Mr. Carnegie's doctor took him from this house. And he never used to call me 'Miss;' as I recall, that used to upset you more than it did me. Also...the 'beautiful villages of France?' He knows very well I've never left this blessed continent! He taunted me mercilessly for being so provincial. Something is very wrong here."

Firewalker appeared in the doorway. "*Leski*," she began. Leski was Lakhota for "Uncle," a respectful endearment that was permitted her. She often employed it when she meant to wheedle, an unconscious action on her part that was familiar to Lem.

"Leski, please bring a bowl of water to Father's office." There was a queer excitement in her voice. A lifetime of being the daughter of Frank Monteith, detective or spy or whatever he was, had honed senses in her that most people didn't even know they had. She'd been moping around the house for the last two days, longing for something real to do, and she sensed this letter might have delivered it. From Nikola Tesla of all people. Deus ex machinist, she quipped to herself. "I believe, Mr. Firewalker, that we may have a case!"

She unlocked the office door with her own key. Going straight to the fireplace, she removed the dome from the little brass clock and wound it with a second key off her silver chatelaine. A bit of the mantel shifted to reveal a hidden lever. She pulled, springing open the bookcase. She knew the contents of the hidden cabinet well enough to find what she needed without a light. By the time Firewalker had returned with the water and a linen rag, she was seated at Frank's big desk with a lacquer box, a soft sable brush and a pair of ruby lenses. She opened the box and tapped some of the lavender crystals into the bowl. They dissolved almost instantly; Firewalker had known precisely what temperature of water to bring.

Taking a deep breath, Claude lay the sheet of paper face up on the leather desktop. She dipped the brush in the water and stroked it across the first line of writing. Forming the edge of the linen into a point, she dabbed carefully where she had brushed. The green ink bled from the page into the cloth.

"What are you doing?!" Mrs. Hudson couldn't contain herself. "You haven't even read that letter!" Why was her niece deliberately destroying her chances? Even a mad Serbian genius was better than no suitor at all. She tried to pull the letter away but Firewalker, gently but very firmly, kept her back.

"Hush, Aunt," Claude murmured, "I know what I'm doing. This isn't a letter, it's a message." She continued to brush and dab, gradually wiping the page clear of writing.

"How can it be a message if nothing's there?!" Mrs. Hudson fretted.

"The message is in code. It's one of Father's, a kind of double code. This one's triple in a way, seeing that it was those ridiculous opening sentences that made me twig to what it was." Firewalker nodded his approval. "There's an ink that Father developed…It's invisible when it dries, and permanent." It was one of many of what she'd always thought were over-elaborate toys that he'd invented to entertain himself, just as he'd seemed to detect for amusement. Ha! Since the day of the Pinkertons, her eyes were shedding scales and constantly re-interpreting what they'd always seen. "I suppose he really developed it for spying, didn't he? You write your message, let it dry, then write another message over it in water-soluble ink. The recipient uses water, mixed with certain chemicals, to remove the top layer of writing," she held up the now-blank page in illustration, "and the message is available to be read and de-coded. As long as you have the proper spectacles, that is!"

Pushing the goggles onto her nose, she stared intently through the red glass at the sheet in her hand. Mrs. Hudson and Firewalker waited so silently that they could hear Claude's breath brushing the paper as she read. She reached for the pad of foolscap always kept at hand, even when Frank's desktop was as painfully clear as it was now, and made a few rapid calculations. At one point she whistled through her teeth, one of Mrs. Hudson's least favourites of her niece's habits. Finally, with a sigh of satisfaction, she put the paper down. "So much for Mr. Tesla's low estimation of young women!" she remarked, with a lop-sided grin. "It's clear that he addressed this to me as additional subterfuge. His expectation was that Father would read all of my letters and discover the message meant for him."

"It's common enough," Nan Hudson sniffed, "your father's peculiar ideas of female education not withstanding."

"What is the mission, *mit'anksi*?" Firewalker asked calmly. His own impression had been that the young genius was far too independent, what the *wasicu* called a 'loose cannon,' and would be unlikely to ask for help unless he had gotten himself very deeply into trouble.

"It's a most peculiar message, Leski." The eyes Claude turned on him were bright with speculation. "He seems afraid to say very much, even in an unbreakable code. Only that he's working on a project of tremendous importance, something that requires Father's assistance. He urgently needs money for supplies, but dares not risk a banking wire. He begs Father to come with all haste to meet him in Prague—why Prague, I wonder?—and to bring the gold with him. Also an ounce of Prometheum, in 18-grain nuggets."

"Prometheum! Does he ken what he's asking?" Mrs. Hudson was stunned by the audacity.

"I assure you, Aunt, that he does." She waved the paper, blank to all excepting herself. Firewalker took it from her. She handed him the goggles and waited.

After a few minutes, he placed them on the desk. To someone who knew him as well as Claude did, he looked grave. "If only this had arrived yesterday Wohitika Capa is over the Atlantic now. The wire will have to meet him in London."

"Why?"

"The message was meant for him."

Mrs. Hudson nodded her firm agreement.

"We can't wire this to Father," Claude protested. "We would have to send him a coded letter, like this one. We'd lose days. And then we'd lose still more time because, in the end, the Prometheum would have to come from here." This was simple fact. It wasn't as if you could waltz into a store and buy Prometheum. It was rare and not entirely stable. Refinement required large quantities of a silicate found in a black sand common to the area around the Lakes, so the elaborate manufactories had needfully been built near to the source. Generally, Prometheum nuggets were processed to exact specifications and were transported in specially designed lead-glazed vessels that ensured they didn't accidentally collide and combust outside their destined housing. Not many people had the ability to tell a Prometheum manufactory that he needed an ounce of nuggets in any configuration and expect to have it handed over at once and without question. Franklin Monteith, as part owner of such a facility and a world-renown expert on the properties of the element, was one of them. In his employer's absence, and legally empowered to act as his steward, the man known as Lemuel Firewalker was another. "This says 'urgent', six ways to Sunday."

"I will make my arrangements for Prague and leave tomorrow," Firewalker nodded.

"Oh, no, Wakhangli Mani," Claude used the Lakhota name with quiet emphasis. "Don't you see? You would stand out in Europe as much as I would in the Athletic Club. People would take notice, maybe gossip or ask questions. Discretion is critical. I must be the courier." She laughed, forestalling his objections. "No one would ever suspect that a young woman was carrying such valuable cargo in her bag. And if I learn that Mr. Tesla requires further materials, you are much better equipped to provide them from Chicago than I would be."

"If you think I'm going to allow you to travel to Europe unchaperoned and meet with a young man..." Mrs. Hudson broke in, alarmed at Firewalker's tacit agreement with this bold proposal.

Claude turned to her and smiled. "But you're going with me of course, Aunt Nan. Together we're the perfect pair of spies! Who would suspect a silly young lady being taken on an improving trip to Prague by her long-suffering aunt? We'll need a suite, Leski. For a week, don't you think? At the hotel he stipulates."

Firewalker gave one of his rare smiles and nodded. "I will arrange for the Prometheum as Tesla requires. How much gold does he say he needs?"

She handed him the page. "Whatever he says, add ten percent more. I don't know what he means to purchase with it, but men are never very good at shopping. Oh, and I'll need spending money as well. What is there to buy in Prague, do you think?"

"Crystal," her aunt said wistfully. "And **garnets**. They have the bonniest garnets. Your father bought you those combs in **Prague**."

"Maybe I'll buy earrings to match," Claude grinned mischievously. "Or perhaps a bracelet. I'll want a souvenir of my first trip abroad!"

&

For the first leg of the journey, Claude had prudently foregone her own preference for a dirigible in favour of the railroad. Traveling by air wouldn't have saved much time. It was relief enough that her aunt hadn't insisted on taking a hackney coach all the way to New York. Nan Hudson did not travel well, and the more modern the conveyance the worse her suffering. To Mrs. Hudson, the Iron Horse was exactly that, a disquieting modification of the brougham she'd insisted Firewalker use to drive them to the station (she refused categorically to set so much as a toe on the running board of that devilish machine the automobile). The railroad was a modern disruption, rendered barely acceptable only by the most extraordinary situations. She always kept her lips pressed so tightly together that Claude assumed she feared that the rattling of the carriage would shake her teeth loose. She was certainly afraid to open her mouth for a cup of tea, or perhaps she didn't want Claude to leave her side long enough to find a porter and request one.

Aunt Nan acceded to the train with martyred grace. Crossing the Atlantic, however, was another thing entirely. In view of her aunt's fears, Claude had tried hard to conceal her glee when Firewalker, unasked, produced tickets for the transoceanic aership. Aunt protested, but it was a lost battle. Tesla was waiting, possibly even in some kind of danger, and there was no comparison between three days in an aership and twelve at sea.

The aership was every bit as gorgeous as Claude had imagined. Yes, the cabin she and Aunt Nan had to share was smaller than her bath at home, but what did that matter when there were dining rooms and parlours and observation decks to wander? The gondola was so beautifully fitted out in titanium and bamboo—the lightest weight of everything, as she instinctively understood—and everywhere she looked, there were the most breathtaking views of the water. Leaving New York, they had just accepted a glass of champagne from the waiter when Aunt Nan took one look past the rail and dropped her glass, her face a perfect eau de nil. Clutching at the corridor walls, she staggered back to the cabin. She fell into her bunk, where she curled up in a ball and refused to stir for the remainder of the journey. The dipping and swaying was worse than seasickness, she claimed. Claude thought it unlikely. The floor of the aership was perfectly steady and calm beneath her feet; she felt none of the lurching of which her aunt complained. It must have been vertigo, the result of Aunt Nan finding herself looking *down* at the tower of the New York Tribune building. Claude couldn't understand this weakness; both she and her father had a fine head for heights. Poor old Aunt! With nothing she could do beyond ensuring that the steward provide a steady supply of wet towels and clear broth, Claude spent most of the voyage wandering around the ship, thoroughly enjoying the experience and having the most fascinating conversations with unlikely people.

As much as the sheer joy of heading for someplace new, Claude adored the freedom of traveling. Daily routine was set aside; one felt free as a bird to do whatever one pleased. As nearly every person was unknown, one couldn't *not* talk to strangers. After she had exhausted the possibilities of the other passengers, Claude went on to happily question the porters and stewards and, thanks to a fortuitous dinner seating the second night, the First Officer, from whom she wangled a tour of the engine room.

Claude hadn't always seen the point of flirting. To be fair, some girls truly needed the security and position of any kind of marriage at all, but Claude was in a fortunate position. She wanted a man who she could respect. She could afford to forgo all that flutter and vacuous laughter and wait for someone who would appreciate her for her differences and not try, like Millie Spafford's handsome but otherwise horrible cousin Archie, to turn her into who she wasn't. So no, she hadn't seen much benefit in flirting until she'd realized it could get her something that she genuinely prized—information. Then, as with any skill she thought it behooved her to master, Claude became quite good at flirting indeed. She was more than adept enough to compel First Officer Smith to not only escort her to the engine room, which was forbidden to passengers, but allow her to examine the very valves and dials that regulated the steam pressure. She was so charming to the men that one of the wipers agreed to smuggle her into the crow's nest the last morning, to have the best first view of the coast of England.

Unlike its sailing ship ancestor, the dirigible had a crow's nest slung at its lowest part, below the belly of the passenger gondola. Protected by an oiled canvas duster borrowed from the wiper, and the work gloves and goggles she'd providently thought to pack, Claude knelt on the platform. She held onto the ropes for dear life. Her ears rang with wind. Tendrils of hair escaped their pins and battered against her face; it was like being whipped by spider webs, but she didn't care. It was worth any discomfort for the thrill of sailing majestically across the threshold of what was, after all, the land of her birth. The farms and forests didn't look much different from home, but she could spot a ruin or two. A train steamed across a bridge that might have been an ancient aqueduct, and surely that long, broken wall must be something important.

Just as she was wondering what below might be a scene from her history lessons, one incontestable sight met her eyes. Pressing herself as flat as she could, she stuck her face over the platform to peer down at the enigma that was Stonehenge. The shadow of the dirigible slipped through the stones as if modern science had no place here and they were trespassing. It gave her a queer feeling along her spine.

The wiper, returning soon after to bring her back to the gondola, found her sitting on the platform with her eyes closed. "Stonehenge?" he asked.

She blinked in surprise.

He nodded sympathetically. "It takes a lot of us that way. Seeing what they did all that time ago, and who knows why or how. Makes you feel small. It's like this ship, all our science and all, like it don't much matter, not in the scheme of things."

"It has to matter," she insisted. "Science and learning things. My father invented Vitriflex, you know." She didn't know why she'd said that.

"Well there you go now," he said comfortably, helping her up. "That's a wonderful thing, that is."

"I mean that we can't stay the same as we were thousands of years ago. Mankind has to grow and get smarter and better."

"Yes, Miss, we do. But we've still got that thousands of years ago inside of us. No matter how smart we get."

Claude flashed him her best smile. There are more philosophers on earth than we dream. This wasn't the first time she'd found one with grease under his fingernails.

As yet, overseas flight was a novelty; the only regular service ran between New York and London. Disembarking at Shooters Hill, the logical course would have been for Claude and her aunt to change to a Bohemia-bound continental aership. Instead, they took a sedate train down to Dover. It was the wrong call. Crossing the Channel by steam ferry, Mrs. Hudson became greener by the minute and even Claude found her digestion somewhat disturbed.

They boarded another train in Calais. In the wake of the Channel, Mrs. Hudson found jouncing over the rails to be comparatively placid. She was able to take some toast with her broth, but she was still wan and shaky on her feet when they finally arrived at Prague. Though longing to explore the strange new city at once, Claude heroically restrained herself. She ordered some poached fish to be brought up to their rooms on a tray and they shared a quiet evening in.

The next day, after breaking her fast, Mrs. Hudson was well enough to deign to venture out to see the famous astronomical clock. Clutching Claude's elbow, she moved so tentatively that the brief walk from the hotel seemed to take an hour.

It was Claude's first walk ever in Europe. The least little thing fascinated her. Even the air, she thought, smelt somehow more cultivated than the air she breathed back home. Aunt Nan, on the other hand, had some disparaging comment to make about everything they saw. The Church of Our Lady, with its four fairy-castle towers, was "too Catholic" for her Presbyterian sensibilities. The medieval buildings, pink or buff or covered with sgrafitto, seemed amazingly old and wonderful to Claude but were dismissed as nothing compared to the wonders of Edinburgh. Even the sweetly jingling bells on the harnesses of carriage horses were judged as not being in the best of taste. Aunt Nan positively turned up her nose at the "quaintness" of Old Town Square until the clock began to strike, and she was compelled to stop speaking and look up. Claude, enchanted, stared with all her might. Even the very newest bit of the clock was older than anything at home. Imagine someone being so clever hundreds of years ago! Wheels, representing the sun and the moon and every sign of the zodiac, circled within wheels. To either side of the face, little figures jerked into life, including a dance of Death that marked the hour; all twelve apostles appeared at the pair of blue windows at the top. Eleven strikes were not nearly sufficient to appreciate the glory of that clock. Mrs. Hudson allowed that it was "unco skeilie." She unbent enough to agree to stroll for a while and see what might be on offer at the nearby shops. After spending two hours deliberating between two nearly identical crystal rose bowls and deciding against both, she was exhausted. She insisted they return to the hotel for tea, toast and a rest.

Claude was already contemplating ways to slip out to explore the city on her own, when she espied Mr. Tesla lurking in the shadows across from the hotel. Giving him a signal that she thought he seemed to catch, she hustled her aunt up to the room and ordered a pot of tea. It was the matter of a moment to add a few drops of chloral hydrate from the vial in her vanity case. Once Aunt Nan's eyes had closed, Claude planted a hasty note and slipped from the room.

Tesla had indeed caught her signal. He was waiting in the hotel receiving room. "It is Miss Monteith, isn't it?" he seemed bewildered.

So, for a second, was she. Not only had he never called her "Miss" before, but he'd hardly used any piece of her name, preferring to say "you" when he needed something handed to him, and otherwise to speak as if she weren't even present. And though, towards the end of his time in Chicago, there had been times when she'd wished he would, he'd never looked at her like this. It made her feel a little odd inside to be seen by those mournful eyes. "Hello!" she said brightly, not using his name in case anyone was taking notice. "I didn't know you were in Prague! What a lovely surprise!"

"Y-yes," he stammered. "Surprise." He bowed over her gloved hand as if he had never seen one before.

"My aunt and I arrived only yesterday. We are so enjoying this beautiful city. I was about to take luncheon. Won't you join me?"

He was hesitant at first, but she managed to coax him into the dining room. She was glad. He looked more like a poet than ever—one of the consumptive ones. She would bet that the man hadn't eaten in days. He had two servings of pork and sauerkraut and so many of the *knedliky*, the little bread dumplings, that she felt quite full watching him. He finished by devouring a large slab of poppy seed cake with a generous mound of whipped cream. As they (or mostly he) ate, Claude murmured an explanation as to why it was she, rather than Frank, who had come. He complimented her for decoding the message and also for grasping the urgency of his situation. His gratitude was delightful.

"I have much to tell you, for you to tell your father. But not here. There might be ears anywhere." He looked honestly frightened. She recalled what it had been like in those weeks before Uncle Andrew's doctor had come to take him away.

"Where then?" she asked softly.

"My workshop. We could go at once. That is, if it would not trouble you to visit such a place." He eyed her modish dun-coloured traveling suit and the extravagant eruption of silk hyacinths that was her hat; she hadn't wanted to seem provincial on her maiden trip abroad.

Claude rolled her eyes. "You forget," she chided. "Our most civil conversations were held in such a place."

He nodded thoughtfully. "It's not far to walk, but we'll take an indirect route."

"Naturally," she agreed. It was pleasant, being treated so sensibly. As they left the hotel, she took his arm. Walking like any young couple, they would draw no attention. She looked up at him. Even with her wearing French-heeled boots, he was taller than she. That was nice. He seemed to think so, too.

❧

Nowhere between Chicago and Prague had there been any sign of spies, nor even ordinary thieves who one might imagine on the trail of a valuable consignment. Claude was nonetheless glad that she had replaced the sinkers in the hem of her walking skirt with the encased grains of Prometheum. Aunt had thought it silly, but Mr. Tesla was impressed. He was so jubilant to learn she had brought them with her that, for a moment, she fancied he was about to kiss her. She had been prepared to let him, too, a thought that made her blush to recall. She was grateful for a task, even a tedious one, that kept her face turned down so that he wouldn't see.

It was taking forever to pick the capsules out with the tiny scissors on her chatelaine, pop in a washer and stitch back the hem, but this was of no matter. She had learned long ago that even Father's most apparently random advice had its good reason. He cautioned that one must always anticipate the worst outcome and prepare for it, hence she had hidden the Prometheum. "An ounce of prevention is worth a pound of cure," as great-great-grandfather Franklin had said. She grimaced. At least that part of her family's history was true; Father had confirmed as much and, whatever truths he might conceal from her, he would never directly lie. She stopped to shift her weight and pull the last few yards of skirt over her lap. As she did, she looked around her. It was an impressive sight, the makings of Mr. Tesla's of clockwork mannikins. To one side, she saw a shelf with a row of metal arms that reminded her of RODA. All were bent or dented to some degree.

"What happened to those?" she asked.

"Clay. I had to test to see which metal would bear up best." He began to explain. "I moulded a tube from eight kilos of clay. When it was dry enough, I swung it at the arm. Not the same, I assure you, as the trecika, but as near as I could conjure and still lift it." As they'd walked through the cemetery, he'd told her about the Emperor's golems. In addition to being more courteous, the Tesla of this afternoon had been far more forthcoming than the one she recalled from Chicago.

"So titanium?"

"In a carbon fiber alloy. Still light enough to have mobility without requiring much thrust, but more rigidity than titanium alone."

"Where do these go?" she gestured to the little pyramid of capsules growing beside her. The only sensible way to remove them was by sitting on the floor. Mr. Tesla insisted on pulling the blanket from his bed for her to sit on, but it was a rough wooly thing, really not so much cleaner than the bricks. She must be careful and give herself a thorough brushing before returning to their rooms. What Aunt Nan wouldn't know couldn't hurt her.

"Here, in the chest." He pointed to the open cavity of the nearest of the assembled figures. "Eighteen grains each to power the boiler. I originally thought to use the Prometheum as an electrical power source," he explained, "but I was wasting months trying to find ways to stabilize the engine in such a way that the balance of the gears wouldn't be disturbed. For the short term, steam was a better option." He seemed wistful at having drawn this conclusion, like a little boy wanting a 'real' train for Christmas and having to make do with a tin locomotive with a wind-up key. Men could be like that.

"It's a prototype. Later you'll do it the other way," Claude said lightly. "It's only a question of the time. So, with the engine you've designed, do you still control them with radio waves, like RODA?"

"Clockwork and radio were more than sufficient for RODA because it was designed to perform a single repetitive task. These machines require instructions for dozens. I wish brain waves could travel like radio waves!" he said wryly. "You know, for years, even when I was working with your father, I've experimented with the idea of a thinking engine."

"Is that even possible?" Claude was both intrigued and horrified. Imagine a machine that could think!

"Not truly thinking, like a brain," he explained, "but more like a jacquard loom. You might plan any number of complex sequences and use…well, some theorize a system of punch cards, but while that might be fine for a stationary machine it would never work for something mobile, certainly not with this form." He was surprised to feel how much he missed having someone to talk to, someone who understood what he was talking about. His work had always absorbed him to the extent that he never thought of himself as lonely, but perhaps he was. "Now I'm working with celluloid ribbon…"

"Celluloid's no good," she countered promptly. "It'd burn up from the friction and then your entire Rodaman would explode. A copper ribbon maybe or, better still, titanium…"

"What did you call it?"

"Titanium. You thought of it first."

"I mean the machine. You called it something." He screwed up his mouth in that shape that, in the old days, meant he was about to tell her to quit bothering grown men who were busy with serious work.

"Rodaman?" she repeated, with a little laugh that she'd appropriated since those same old days. "You know, like RODA but a mannikin. Why? What have you been calling it?"

"My Automaton," he proclaimed grandly.

"Uninspiring," she said, giving the machine a friendly smile. "He deserves better."

The figure did appear to be a 'he.' In his earliest sketches Tesla had made the head a blank cylinder, but staring at the drawings gave him nightmares worse than the memories of the trecika. There was something about a faceless colossus that was too horrible to even contemplate. He might have wanted to put fear into the hearts of his enemies, but he didn't want to drive innocent bystanders mad and so, while his device had no need of it, he decided to make some gesture at welding eyes, nose and mouth to the faceplate. He wasn't much of an artist; it had a slightly foolish expression.

Claude placed the final capsule on the pile and rose to her feet. She stretched her fingers to the ceiling and felt her vertebrae release. It felt wonderful, like doing one of Father's qigong exercises. She bent from the waist to stretch the other way and touch her toes. Her eyes went again to the pile. "One capsule each? How many of these are you expecting to make?"

"Several dozen. The rest of the Prometheum will power the weapons."

"Weapons," she repeated dully. She had gotten so caught up in the excitement of a new project that she'd forgotten he was building an army.

Tesla abruptly put down his tools. "How much chloral did you say?" he asked, a look of concern on his face. "We must get you back to the hotel."

Aunt Nan was no longer supine on her bed, enjoying a restorative sleep. She was awake and furious, but luckily also still muzzy-headed enough that she could be handled.

"Oh, no, Aunt Nan," Claude insisted firmly, "it can't have been much more than an hour. You must still be confused from your recent indisposition. All that pitching and rolling and swaying way up in the air, and then that choppy English Channel." Mrs. Hudson swallowed visibly. "I went down to luncheon so that the smell of rich food wouldn't disturb you, remember? And when I returned, you'd fallen quite asleep. No wonder. You must be so exhausted." Claude made her voice as contrite as she could manage. "I sat by the window for a while, reading," here she feigned a yawn, "but it was such a beautiful day, it seemed a pity to be cooped up indoors. I thought you'd want me to get a bit of fresh air and exercise." She sounded gently reproachful. Aunt opened her mouth to speak, but Claude sailed on, certain she'd hit her mark. "The hotel steward told me of a shop in Wenceslaus Square that might have exactly the rose bowl you want..." Indeed, she'd made sure he had. "Wenceslaus Square is very fashionable, you know. I thought I would go and see. I hadn't taken more than two steps when there was Mr. Tesla, approaching the hotel to see if Father had yet arrived. He was most amazed. I knew you wouldn't be happy about my speaking with him alone, but I really couldn't send him away. It is a mission of sorts, after all, not a holiday outing. He was anxious that we should keep moving, so as not to be overheard, so we took a walk. I explained our presence and he explained some of his situation." That part, at least, was bare truth. "All very proper and seemly. We are to meet him tomorrow, you and I, at a charming pâtissierie he says every visitor to Prague must experience."

"I cannot credit that Nikola Tesla would frequent a 'charming pâtissierie'," Mrs. Hudson commented drily.

"It does seem strange," Claude laughed in relief. The pastry shop had actually been recommended by a girl in one of the glass houses, while Aunt Nan's attention had been elsewhere. "You would scarcely recognize him, Aunt. He's quite altered. So courteous and thoughtful. Most respectful of me."

Mrs. Hudson turned a considering eye on her niece. This was a change indeed, but she couldn't be certain it was not in her niece rather than the Serbian.

"Not his appearance though," Claude continued. "He looks as melancholy and disheveled as ever. Somewhat more gaunt. It's the weight of what he's trying to accomplish," she added soberly. "And the constant worrying about the Emperor. Oh, Aunt! The things Mr. Tesla has seen!"

"Which Emperor?" Mrs. Hudson, ever practical, asked. There were, after all, several scattered around the globe.

"The Roman Emperor, of course," Claude said with distaste; "that Augustus."

ֶֹ֞

"We need to contact Frankie," Mrs. Hudson insisted for the thousandth time. She touched a finger to the face—face!—of one of what the Serbian called an 'automaton' and shuddered. To think he expected to make these things move! They were horrible. More horrible still was what Mr. Tesla had described seeing in Rome. The dark creatures he had encountered were unimaginable, but she had looked the young man in the eye and would swear that, this one time, he was as sane as she.

Tesla stared at her intently. "Yes, we do," he agreed. "That was why I *did* contact him. Not only for the money."

"And the Prometheum," Claude reminded him.

"Of course the Prometheum. But I also need him here. It's not that I'm not grateful for what you've done by coming here, but I need to tell him what I've told you. I need to show him all of this. I need his ideas and his advice. I need…" He ran his hands despairingly through his hair. "This is beyond me. Frank is the man for this, not I."

Claude disagreed. "You've done wonderfully. Father would say the same. He will when he gets here. And he will get here, won't he Aunt?"

"I'll wire him from the hotel."

"NO!" the young people shouted.

"We can't wire this Aunt Nan," Claude said crisply. "If the Emperor's men are looking for Mr. Tesla, even a coded letter might fall into the wrong hands."

"They must be searching for me," he groaned miserably. "I know they must." The thought overwhelmed him. Putting his elbows on his workbench, he cradled his head in his hands. If only his message had reached Monteith. The pressure was too great.

"Exactly. There's too much to say. A letter would have to be pages and pages to tell Father what he needs to know. The best thing would be to send a messenger." She smiled brightly. "I know! I could go to London and fetch him here."

"He's on the Queen's business," Aunt Nan reminded her. She said 'the Queen' with as much respect as though she were standing before the monarch in question.

"*This* is the Queen's business, Aunt!" Claude exclaimed. "Didn't she beg for him to come because of the Emperor?"

"You wouldn't be able to find him. You dinnae ken the least thing about London."

"*You* know London, Aunt," Claude spoke carefully, picking her way through her thoughts. "Maybe not for years, but you know more than I. And you know Lord Pinkerton. Didn't you say Uncle Ian worked for him, too? If Father is somewhere secret, Lord Pinkerton would speak with you and help you find him. You're the perfect messenger! If you leave in the morning, you'll be there in two days. Father can fly back no time at all.

And I," she concluded with satisfaction, "will make certain not a moment is wasted. I will stay and help Mr. Tesla."

"Stay here? Alone?!" Mrs. Hudson was aghast.

"Oh for goodness sake, Aunt Nan, what could be safer than the hotel? You'll have more eyes on me than in our own house." Mrs. Hudson swiveled her neck so that her nose pointed significantly in Tesla's direction. Claude rolled her eyes and gave a snort of exasperation. "Don't be ridiculous, Aunt! He's the same Nikola Tesla who lived in our home for nearly two years. He thinks I'm his bratty little brother; you know that!" She took Mrs. Hudson's hands between hers and held them tight. "He needs help, Aunt Nan," she pleaded. "Look at him. He's been carrying this all alone. He was so certain Father was on the way. He needs another pair of hands. Until Father can come, who can better assist him than I? I did help to build RODA."

Her last comment registered with Tesla. He raised his head to look at her. It was almost as if he were seeing someone else. "You did," he remembered. "You're not bad. You have good hands with the gears and wires. Small hands. Steady."

"Plus, I know a fair bit about how to set a grain of Prometheum," she added, beaming.

"What do you ken about Prometheum?" Mrs. Hudson was thunderstruck.

"More than most people," Claude said, a little smugly. "I met all kinds of men when we were working on RODA. For a lot of them, Prometheum was their entire life. You'd been surprised what cranks and boors are willing to tell a girl if she acts interested."

Nan Hudson gave a troubled sigh. She didn't know what to do. She had spent the last dozen years of her life trying to protect her brother's child. To leave her alone in a strange city, in these surroundings, went against everything she held dear. Nevertheless, she was a Menzies and this was War. She shook her head as if to clear it, and clenched her fists. "We need haste," she said grimly. "I'll fly if I have to."

"Oh, Aunt Nan, you're wonderful!" Claude threw her arms around her aunt as she hadn't done in years. Aunt Nan hugged her back.

The brother of three sisters, Tesla marveled yet again at the excitability of women.

5 - AUD IN B_EST

Sitting in her conservatory, Helena Blavatsky communed with the Masters of the Great White Brotherhood, her face tilted gratefully upward to be kissed by a beam of sunlight.

Modern 'mediums,' as they tend to style themselves, prefer to sit in a darkened room. Night's blackness is most efficacious in concealing the threads and bladders that support mysterious music, apparitions and the flying open of doors. By contrast, there is something about the drowsy blue-grey afternoon shadows of a velvet-draped room that saps the spectators' abilities to doubt their senses; for that very reason, late afternoon is favoured by those who produce ectoplasm from their mouths. Madame Blavatsky, however, preferred the sun.

Madame Blavatsky did not regurgitate yards of cheesecloth, nor did she require cymbals or black-garbed servants with painted-pale faces. In point of fact, despite what some of her clients thought, she wasn't a medium at all. She was a Spiritualist, whose travails in Tibet had confirmed her as a true messenger and servant of Theosophy. Her allegiance was to her Spirit Masters, her teachers and to those she taught in turn.

Helena knew that patterns of this life had been determined by actions in previous lives and would weave themselves. Someone like herself served merely to observe and, when commanded, guide the threads. She had no personal ambitions; she did as the Brotherhood required.

In dealing with persons of temporal power, it was her karma to be the instrument of theirs. In her Cairo days, when Baron Haussmann sought her out, Madame Blavatsky had not been difficult to find. Her servant heard whispers in the souk, even before her spirit guides had volunteered the information, and made certain that the Roman Emperor's man was led to her door.

The Baron had been one of those clever ones who thought to challenge her authenticity. She satisfied him by delivering, upon request, a message from the Great Napoleon. It was child's play to impress such clever ones and win their trust. They didn't understand how easy it was to contact the recently departed. It took many decades to adapt to existence on the Other Side. Souls that had recently crossed over missed their earthly lives; they were pleased at the opportunity to chat with the living, even with those who had been their enemies in life; they came eagerly when called.

For someone of Helena's natural gifts, contact was a trivial matter. However messages, whether from new arrivals or essences long-translated, had to be interpreted. This was a delicate task, one that Helena would be loathe to attempt had she not elevated her talent through the Discipline. One had to know exactly how much information to disclose, how much of the pattern of the universe it was prudent to unveil. What did the seeker truly seek?—for it was certain that no one ever sought a plain response to a plainly spoken question. What was wise and good for them to know? Such intercession required delicacy of touch and the ability to read the human heart. Helena could not read minds, though she had no doubt there were others walking this earth possessed of that talent. What she had was a native ability to see how a phrase here or there, or a certain gesture, could paint a picture that spoke more eloquently of need or intent than an entire speech.

Twenty years ago, she had told the Baron exactly as much as he had needed to hear, and thus secured the patronage of one of the most powerful men in the world. It had been, as she had known it would be, a mixed blessing and a grave responsibility. Today's message from the aether gave her pause. She wished she knew where it might lead, but the Seven Rays did not choose to elaborate.

She turned her gaze on one of the Children who sat meditating at her feet. Her pale stare bored through his aura. He automatically rose to serve her. "A message for Baron Haussmann," she said tersely. The young man nodded and prepared to listen. His memory had been trained to instantly preserve prolonged exchanges. This one was only a few words. "Tell him the moment he has awaited is now. Tell him that I have seen 'aud' and she is far from home. She is in…" Madame paused and appeared to again consult the Rays. The little bow of her mouth spread into a wide smile. "Say that I cannot see clearly where she is. I can hear that it begins in 'B' and ends in 'est', that is all that I know." He bowed and ran from the room. Madame sighed deeply. Letting one hand fall heavily to each knee, she slipped into a trance as deep as sleep.

❧

Bucharest was a pokey little city, or so thought Charlotte Maud Albertine of Wales, half-orphan and heiress presumptive to the throne of Greater Britain. How such a drowsy place could be the capital of anywhere was beyond her. Worse yet, she was hardly even permitted to be in Bucharest; Court was at Uncle Carol's castle in the Peles valley, more than two hours away by automobile. It was worse than staying with Grandmama at Windsor.

Uncle Carol was very proud of the brand new castle, which everyone said was one of the most beautiful in Europe. Maud agreed that the outside was unusually pretty but, other than the glass ceiling above the entrance hall, which could be made to slide open to the night sky, it seemed disappointingly similar to every other castle she knew. One might think that if one were going about designing a frightfully modern building, one might choose to avoid such a quantity of heavy carving and perhaps use a bit less gold. Maud did appreciate the electricity and the central heating, although the warmth made it difficult to stay awake during yet another so-called entertainment by one of Aunt Elisabeth's friends. This one was some kind of poet, but either he was reciting in Roumanian or his accent made a more familiar language impenetrable. Maud's ear could make out nothing beyond a perilously soporific drone. Shifting again in her odd little chair, she tried to stay away by following a pattern through one of the Moroccan carpets. She frowned just enough to appear to be thinking deep thoughts.

Maud had thought it was brilliant to bring Mama to Roumania. Something had to be done; she couldn't bear all the wailing and keening. It wasn't that she didn't miss her Papa terribly. There was an achey hole inside her that she didn't expect would ever be filled. Even now she would find herself caught by tears at the sight of a coat that looked like Papa's or the sound of that song that Uncle Fred used to whistle when Grandmama couldn't hear him. It was natural to feel such grief but, with the wisdom of her seventeen years, Maud knew that your life didn't stop because someone else was gone. Mama was unable to accept this. She was like one of those storied Indian widows who throw themselves on the funeral pyre. It was exhausting to be with her. Maud thought it would be a relief to let Aunt Elisabeth cope with her mother. Grandmama had no patience; she was a widow herself, as she noted more than a little sharply on multiple occasions, and she had lost both her sons in one day.

Grandmama didn't understand women like Mama. Neither did Maud, but she also wasn't sure she understood Grandmama. She had no doubts that her grandmother cared for her, but it wasn't a comforting kind of love. People who meant to encourage Maud would allow that Grandmama was formidable. Maud disagreed: the Prime Minister was formidable; Grandmama was more like something on a mountaintop, with lightning bolts in both her hands. Maud could remember bursting into tears whenever they'd put her in the prickly dresses that meant Grandmama had called for her to be brought. The Queen would kneel down so that her eyes and Maud's, so much alike, would meet. Maud always felt as if her grandmother's eyes drilled a hole into her head to lay bare all her thoughts. There would be a perfunctory embrace and she would be given back to her nurse. Even as a tiny child, Maud remembered feeling that she had been weighed and found wanting. Often after those meetings she would do something extremely naughty.

Once it had become clear she was unlikely to have a younger brother, Maud's education became far more stringent than other girls'. Since Papa and Uncle Fred had died, Grandmama had become increasingly demanding. There were even more and drier things to learn. She was perpetually having to visit manufactures, scientific societies and other dreary places, where she was expected to ask well-informed questions of their inhabitants. She had to stand at the Queen's side for audiences with visiting dignitaries, all so stupid and pompous, and afterward be quizzed by Sir Henry as to what had been said. For two hours every day, with no possible demur, she must sit at her own small desk in the Queen's office, reviewing dispatches and reading aloud from the Parliamentary Record. Youth did not excuse her from these responsibilities. As no one ever tired of repeating, Grandmama had ascended the throne when she was barely older than Maud was now. It was too disquieting to contemplate. The Second Act of Succession enabled a reigning monarch to select any of his or her legitimate issue as successor. With Papa and Uncle Fred gone, and her cousins so very tiny, Grandmama's immediate choice came down to Maud. She prayed that Grandmama would live a long life.

The reprieve from learning to be Queen was the only thing about Roumania that was turning out to Maud's satisfaction.

Aunt Elisabeth was an especial disappointment. All Mama's relatives were eccentric but, from afar, the world of Carmen Sylva (as Aunt Elisabeth preferred to be called) had also seemed glamourous. Either writers and actors and artists weren't as witty or romantic a breed as Maud had always fancied, or Carmen Sylva's circle were a uniquely sober bunch. When her aunt wasn't talking politics or philosophy with her friends, she and her lady-in-waiting Madame Kremnitz, were constantly visiting hospitals or establishing orphanages. As worthy and admirable as they were, good works were crashingly dull.

Moreover, Aunt Elisabeth seemed determined to make up a match with Uncle Carol's dull nephew. Ferdinand wasn't bad looking, but he was so earnest that it made him seem plain. Not that Maud's opinion of

Ferdinand mattered worth a tick; now that Uncle Carol had adopted him as his heir, Grandmama would never approve him. One would think Aunt Elisabeth should know better and stop throwing them together. To make his way onto Maud's list of suitors, a young man had to be a Protestant prince who was willing to live his life as consort to a reigning queen, not one who had his own kingdom, however insignificant, to worry over. It was difficult to find a man who met these criteria and also had looks; it would be a certain miracle to find one who had a personality. Grandmama had been impossibly lucky. Maud had seen the pictures; in addition to all his other apparently sterling qualities, when Grandpapa had come calling, he'd been beautiful. The old ladies at Court said he'd also danced like an angel. Axel of Sweden had danced well, Maud recalled. He was nice looking too, or at least she remembered thinking he was. He had been one of the suitors invited to her ball, at what was to have been her first Season. A few short weeks later, Papa had died and a thick veil dropped over the memories of that time.

Mourning was lifted now. Maud expected that once she returned to London, Grandmama and her advisors would spare no efforts in matching her with someone suitable. This visit to Roumania might be her last chance to have some fun. She'd looked forward to being nothing more significant than 'Caterina's girl' here: choosing gowns, gossiping with other girls over the attractions of various potential beaux, and enjoying a little flirtation. Only there were no other girls, the shopping was two hours away and whenever she saw the cadets she was in the company of one of Aunt Elisabeth's tedious retainers.

A decorous smattering of applause roused Maud from her private sulk. The poet, or whatever he was, had finished and was kissing Aunt Elisabeth's hand. After the other guests had paid similar homage, they would go to the white and gold reception room for a protracted tea.

Maud mechanically smiled and nodded as people she would never recognize at second sight were briefly introduced and moved on. It was only the sound of "Your Majesty" in a well-bred British voice that made her suddenly pay attention. It belonged to the wife of the British ambassador. Lady Lascelles had been absent from Peles for several days, presumably engaged with duties at the Embassy in Bucharest. Her presence reminded Maud that, even so far from home, she must keep up the standards Grandmama would expect. She straightened her posture and made an effort to appear alert as well as gracious.

The effortlessly elegant Lady Lascelles gestured to the young woman beside her, who dipped her auburn curls and curtseyed low to Aunt

Elisabeth. "Your Majesty, may I present my niece, Miss Bell, who has recently arrived from England."

A smile of wonder spread across Maud's face. Gertrude Bell! Maud hadn't seen her for ages, but they were friends of a sort. Her grandfather was an influential man in England, a wealthy businessman and a member of Parliament. Grandmama got on well with Sir Lowthian. Having got wind that his granddaughter was a brain, she had invited her to join Maud's lessons. Gertrude was a few years older than Maud, but Maud's studies were rather advanced and Grandmama thought having another girl to share them would be stimulating. The arrangement hadn't lasted long. Gertrude was like a sponge, if a sponge could be a predator. She had a thirst for knowledge and the instincts to hunt it down wherever it might hide. After a few months of shared lessons, Maud felt limp in more parts of her body than she could put a name to (though she didn't doubt Gertrude could). It wasn't that she didn't like Gertrude. On the contrary; Gertrude could be quite jolly when she wasn't mapping the source of the Ganges or ferreting out the names and lineage of the chieftains of the Iroquois Confederation. She also loved beautiful things and, being something of an heiress, cultivated a substantially modish appearance and knew all the best shops. But these feminine diversions did nothing to blunt the quality of her scholarship. It was hard work to keep up with her at lessons, and frankly embarrassing for a presumptive ruler to be so thoroughly challenged. Maud had had to make it crystal clear that she refused to thrive on classroom competition. Ultimately, Grandmama had seen the wisdom of calling an end to the experiment. Gertrude moved on to a crammer's in Sussex, to prepare for the University entrance exams, and Maud resumed her solitary studies. It was far less stimulating, but she could breathe easy again.

Being far from the schoolroom now, Maud was delighted to see Gertrude. It was so droll when her friend approached and murmured "Your Royal Highness" with such gravity, giving as deep a curtsey as she would to be presented before Grandmama.

"Miss Bell!" Maud exclaimed with unreserved enthusiasm. "How lovely to see you here!"

At tea, Gertrude explained that her parents had insisted she go abroad for some between-terms frivolity. They had chosen Bucharest because, as Maud should have remembered, Lady Lascelles was Gertrude's aunt.

"Frivolity?!" Maud didn't try to disguise her skepticism. "In *Bucharest*?"

"It isn't quite the Elizabeth Gardens at Christmastime," Gertrude said with just the slightest touch of asperity; "but it seems pleasant enough to me."

Maud laughed. It was nice to have someone who would talk to her as if she were an ordinary girl. Nicer still was that she now had a companion of whom even Grandmama approved. Perhaps she would no longer have to waste day after day with Mama and Aunt Elisabeth, or else be constantly begging for an escort. With Gertrude, if there were places to go, they might go there alone or, when a male escort was necessary and a stuffy one provided, it would be much easier to ignore his presence.

"Then you must take me around," Maud insisted. "Starting tomorrow."

ॐ

There were known to be exactly two telegraph wires in all of Italy, one at di Bari's headquarters in Venezia, the other at the Villa Alsaziano. Both were used only to communicate with operatives outside the country, a function crucial enough that Caesar was willing to close his eyes to their existence.

The young page copied the message off the chattering wire and ran to find Signor Gallante, the Baron's major domo. As was appropriate for such precious communications, Gallante placed the transcription on a silver tray and delivered it to his master immediately, even though, in this instance, immediately meant interrupting the weekly therapeutic visit of the estimable Signorina Rosalba.

Baron Haussmann found his spectacles on the bedside table and read the message twice, to be certain it was not a trick of the eye. For years, even when the pair were in their cradles, the Emperor had been trying to secure the English princess as his grandson's bride. In recent years, it had become his primary ambition; he had done and would do anything to make it come about.

It would be secure enough to entrust the message to one of the amphoraeka, but Caesar would want a human face to witness his joy. Haussmann could not delegate this task to any messenger other than himself. He bade a reluctant adieu to Rosalba and set off for the Imperial Palazzo with far more speed than even a spry octogenarian could comfortably sustain.

Caesar lay dozing in Giulia's arms in his garden, serenaded by his cherubic eunuch. He'd had a sleepless night. He had them increasingly often of late. Haussmann felt the same restlessness himself; he assumed that, with ever fewer days to witness, the body was loath to lose any hour to sleep. Augustus had surmised that it was a sign of a battle being waged between the sun (who he alternately called **Ra** or **Apollo**), with whom he now dwelt, and the gods of the underworld who were fighting for him to join them. There was not too much difference between the men's views; they were both descriptions of old age.

"*Divina*," Haussmann puffed, his lungs cramping further as he fell painfully to his knees. One of the tame historians had found this form of address in a volume of Suetonius and, inasmuch as like the first Augustus he had founded a temple to his own genius, Caesar felt that it was only his due and commanded it be adopted. "A message from the Pythia, Divina."

Augustus signaled for the castrato to stop his tune and waved the Baron to his feet.

Staggering breathlessly, Haussmann hauled himself upright with his gold-knobbed ebony stick. "Her message," he said carefully, "is that her spirit guides have shown her that 'aud' is far from home. I have read this multiple times, Caesar and it is 'aud' that she mentions, just in that way. This 'aud,' she tells us, can be found somewhere that begins in the letter 'B' and ends as 'est.' This is the entire message."

Augustus savoured the words. "So," he gloated, "The Principessa Maud has left Britain. We will have her at last!"

"So it would seem, Divina. So it would seem."

"But where is she? What place begins in 'B' and ends in 'ess'?"

"*Est*, Patre mio," Giulia corrected him impatiently. "Est, not ess. She is obviously in Budapest."

"I was going to suggest Bucharest, Daughter of Light," the Baron said, with a resumption of his usual poise. He could remember back to when Giulia had been a young and almost beautiful woman, though never as lovely as her mother had been. Now she was a raddled hag who fooled only herself by tinting her hair with saffron.

"Tut! Why would anyone go to Bucharest? They are practically Republican."

"There is a family connection, Madame."

"Be that as it may, Budapest is the obvious choice. There is much more there to lure a young woman." Giulia had a reminiscent look in her eye.

"What does it matter? We send to both. No effort is too great for such a prize." Augustus gave a peremptory wave and a page appeared with paper and ink. He scrawled a quick note and gave it to the boy. "This must reach the Conte di Bari. Your hand to his. You will wait for a message in return. At once!" The boy ran off before Caesar could ask him to do something less possible than hop a train to Venezia.

Augustus yawned. "I think I will sleep now," he said, falling back on his couch. "Rafello?" The angel-faced eunuch picked up his lute and resumed his song. The Baron felt himself began to sway under the influence of the lullaby.

"Go, old man," Giulia told the Baron, not unkindly for her. "You have a wedding to prepare."

A sleepy childlike smile crept over Caesar's face. "We will triumph, my jewel," he murmured. "Your mother will be so pleased."

The Baron made a courtly bow and backed out of the Imperial presence to hobble home at a comfortable pace. Rosalba had no doubt left his sheets, but he could treat himself to a bottle of the '68 with perhaps a dish of shrimp and hothouse peas.

In the corner of Caesar's most private cabinet, in an alcove that was always garlanded with fresh flowers, stood a golden statue.

Giulia entered the room and the statue moved towards her. It was an amphoraka, smaller and finer than the others and with its clay skin entirely sheathed in gold leaf. The dome of its head, unprotected by the usual bronze helmet, had been shaped so that it appeared to wear a cluster of curls, bound with a gilded circlet. Giulia nestled close and rested her head against the clay breast.

"Such news, Mama," she said, stroking the oval that did for a face.

The creature lifted a jointed arm and, with more gentleness than might have seemed possible, placed it around her. From behind two holes, a bluish glimmer danced.

❧

Benvolio Rappaccini was a keen centurion. He turned the exhausted page over to the barracks *tessarius*, who would provide the boy with food and a bed, then delivered the message to Conte di Bari's *praefectus* by his own hand.

The Praefectus waited while his commander read the note. Ermanno di Bari was a brisk, effective man. It was the work of the moment for him to select two of the several teams of agents who had trained for the eventuality of this mission. Send one to Budapest and one to Bucharest, and their quarry would surely be found. He handed the Praefectus a reply for the page and instructions to code for the agents, then returned to the recent dispatches from Ethiopia.

A few minutes later, there was another knock. "*Entrare!*" he barked.

Rappaccini strode through the door and gave a smart salute. *"Eminenza,"* he began.

"Si, si, Rappaccini, what is it?"

"It is ungrateful I know, and I apologize for asking such a favour, but my brother…"

Di Bari nodded. He had heard the story when Rappaccini first transferred to his cohort. The brother, born a month before his time and unfinished, had suffered his entire life and required constant tending. To ensure his care, Rappaccini had bestowed the family fortune on a Benedictine community somewhere in Piacenza.

"I've received word that he has taken a bad turn," Rappaccini continued. "I would not ask for myself, Eminenza…"

"Of course." As a family man himself, and a devout Catholic (though naturally one did not speak much of this in the current imperial climate), di Bari thought highly of his centurion for such devotion and was inclined to be generous. As a commander, he hoped the brother would either, God keep him, recover quickly or move on from this world. "You have my permission to go at once. I hope it will not be long…" di Bari reddened, realizing that such a sentiment might be misconstrued. He crossed himself piously. "That is, I hope it may be God's will that your brother recover quickly."

"Grazie, Eminenza." Rappaccini kissed the Conte's hand in gratitude. "Truly you may have saved a life today."

❧

Frank had walked from Whitehall all the way to the park at Kensington. He didn't much care for pleasure gardens, but he needed a thinking walk and it helped to have a destination; London in April was not a place for aimless strolling.

Chilly and damp as it was, it felt good to be out. He had already started to feel trapped in his office. It wasn't *his* office, of course; Pinkerton's quartermaster had long ago laid claim to his old room overlooking the Thames, with the special gadgets he had imported a Swiss watchmaker to help fit out. This room was a reasonable enough size. If you stood at a particular angle at a time of day when the light allowed, you could negotiate a sliver of a view. He supposed some disgruntled rising junior was mourning the lack of it every day. To Frank, after only a week, it felt like a cage. There were just so many hours a man could sit behind a desk and read. Plus, he was exhausted. Life would be slightly easier if the Queen hadn't taken against Kensington Palace after the death of the Prince

Consort. As it was, he'd been spending every night at Windsor, slipping out in the early morning to make it to Pinkerton's jolly daily breakfast briefing. The automobile made the trip more quickly than his old hunter had used to, but he'd been younger back then and sleep hadn't seemed to matter.

He yawned continually, not caring who might see him. Manners would have to take a back seat to oxygen if he were to get a second wind and get any work done this afternoon.

The mountain of papers he'd been set was a testament to the efficacy of Her Majesty's Special Service in gathering and transferring intelligence. There were copies of what were alleged to be actual memoranda from key members of the Emperor's court and government, including Augustus's own spy service. Transcripts of interviews included the painful examination of Mrs. Avery, widow of the late Prince's compromised groom, which had led to the unraveling of her husband's betrayal. Unsavoury gossip could be mined for fact, and was sometimes equally valuable for what it said about the emotional climate of court and country. There was a particularly ugly rumour that Augustus's beloved niece, the Lady Giulia, was actually a daughter he had sired on his own sister, Paulette. That Paulette, despite being a famous beauty, had never wed and had ultimately committed suicide gave credence if not substance to the rumour.

Pinned to the walls of the office were a dizzying array of photographs. They showed an Italy little changed over the many years since Frank had last been there himself in his student days, a sliver of time between the Gallic war and the orgy of killings and expulsions that came to be known as the Augustan Purge, when one might still travel through Italy more or less freely. Even then there had been a joke that Augustus only permitted indoor plumbing was because it was thought that the early Romans had invented it. In Frank's recollection, the country had been short on nearly any other modern convenience. There had been few bicycles in the street and at night the lamps had still been lit by oil. These pictures showed that he would see the same today, but with streets that were wider and much better paved. The railroads had been accepted, it seemed, if not welcomed, and many of the ancient buildings appeared to have been reborn. All, according to Pinkerton's files, thanks to Baron Haussmann.

That had been a particularly upsetting disclosure. The Haussmann Frank recalled had been one of the most innovational civil engineers of a generation. As much as he hated to think of talent gone to waste, it troubled him more to consider how Haussmann had managed to stay in the Emperor's confidence when hundreds of men of science had been murdered and exiled. A thick file contained the testimonies of those who had survived the Augustan purge. It was the one set of documents Frank had no need to read; he'd done much of the debriefing himself, as one of his earliest assignments for the Service. It would always haunt him. So many had been broken; men of profound intellect, reduced to shaking huddles. Only a few dozen had been strong enough to build some new life in the universities of Europe or the scientific haven of Visby.

Every time Frank thought he had read everything at least once, something new seemed to surface. One box had yielded a flutter of Italian newspaper clippings, sent over the years by a Spanish informant. Frank presumed the Spaniard was the Emperor's cat's paw and was fed information Augustus wanted to leak out of Rome to the rest of the world. Understood through the prism of the Emperor's manipulation, both the clippings and the Spaniard's reports provided fascinating insights.

For a closed kingdom, the Second Roman Empire had been exceedingly well documented and analyzed by Pinkerton's organization. What Frank had been brought out of his self-imposed exile to provide was what the rest of the team, talented though they were, could not. Frank was a scientist. Thus far, the one thing he couldn't find in all this paperwork was what he needed most: any clues to the science that might animate figures of clay. What perturbed him was Agent Horner's assertion that it might not be science at all.

Augustus does not believe the future depends on science, at least not in the way we think of science. Frank had copied this from the transcript of an early debriefing of Horner's courier, Tucker. He read that statement several times a day, a reminder to look beyond the obvious in trying to understand what was behind these amphoraeka or trecika or whatever they were called.

Turning reluctantly back towards Whitehall, Frank heard a peal of girlish laughter. Turning at the welcome sound, he was nearly knocked over by a young man, who was following his hat. The wind had knocked it off his head and was bowling it along the ground. The young man manage to retrieve the hat before it was lifted over the Serpentine. He bowed apologetically to Frank. The giggling young woman made a small curtsey, ducking her yellow head in Frank's direction. She took her beau's arm and pulled him towards the gardens.

They were a courting couple, their humble means betrayed as much by their willingness to promenade in this weather as by their clothes. Frank smiled; their happiness had momentarily lifted his spirits. The sight of those curls dampened them again.

Back in Chicago, Baker and Chandler had mentioned a maid in the Lady Giulia's household, smuggled out to England by Horner. The poor girl was in a sanatorium in Aberystwyth now. She'd told them of a young

Florentine who had shared her room: fair, golden-haired, blue-eyed, and virginal; so elated to be called to serve at Augustus's temple, that despite a vow of silence, she confided in her roommate. She had been ordered to bathe that evening, an odd request, and had been sent a kind of white chemise and sandals to wear. The excited girl left the servants' quarters close to midnight and never returned. When the maid asked after her, she was told that the girl had been homesick and sent back to Florence. This was a lie. On several occasions, the girl had spoken to her of the hopeless poverty of her family's farm and had always said she would rather throw herself in the Tiber than return.

She was not the first blonde girl known to have disappeared in the middle of the night. Horner had implied that these rites might in some way be connected with the soldiers of clay. If Horner were correct, and Pinkerton clearly believed the young man walked on water, then who knew what atrocities Augustus might have performed to quicken the creatures. It seemed to Frank as if some of the lost knowledge of Egypt would much better be left buried.

᠊ஓ᠊

Princess Maud put down the poetry she wasn't reading and looked around the pretty room with disgust. Even a room decorated in the height of modern style was still, once one had sufficiently admired it, four walls. She sighed as deeply as she could, loud enough for Gertrude to look up from her Roumanian dictionary or whatever it was that she was writing. Surely Gertrude didn't keep a diary?

"Would you like to come back to town with me this evening?" Gertrude suggested, blowing on a page to dry the ink. To excuse herself from writing anything longer than an invitation, Maud refused to have the sand shaker filled. "We could go shopping tomorrow."

"We've seen all there is to buy." Maud sighed again, this time more naturally. "How is it that you're never bored?"

"An intelligent person should never be bored," Gertrude said in that governessy voice that sometimes adopted her, and which Maud cattily thought matched her uncompromising features. "There's always something to do. The sun's come out. What about a ride?" If she hadn't had to amuse the Princess, she would be taking advantage of King Carol's plentiful library.

"The cadets have their drills in the afternoon and won't be there to meet us." Maud shot what she thought was a coy look at Gertrude, through her eyelashes. "Perhaps if I come with you, your cousin Billy will escort us to the park tomorrow." The Ambassador's older son, who was about to take commission with the Guards, was very handsome.

"He went climbing with your cousin Ferdinand and his household, remember? They're not back yet."

"Poor Billy! I suppose he had to go, once he'd been asked."

"I think it might be interesting," Gertrude considered. "What sort of boots would one need, do you think? Of course, one couldn't climb a mountain in a bustle…"

Maud was following her own train of thought. "It might be rather fun to have him assigned to my personal detail. Once I'm properly invested as Princess of Wales, that is."

Gertrude stopped thinking about mountains. Her tongue made an exasperated click. "Honestly, the things you think of!"

"Why not? Thinking is the one thing I don't need to ask permission to do."

It always fascinated Gertrude that a girl so beautiful could pull such horrible faces. Like a petulant infant, Maud threw the morocco-bound volume against the desk.

Gertrude's patience snapped. "It's not my fault that we seem to have done all there is to do in Roumania. And it's certainly not the fault of William Ashbless!" She scooped up the abused little book and slipped it into her pocket. "It's not as if we can simply go somewhere else!"

"Why not?!" Maud jumped out of the depths of the slipper chair, ran to the window and stretched her arms wide. There was a wild look in her eye that Gertrude didn't like. "Mama doesn't need me; she's got Aunt Elisabeth. And you're on holiday. Why shouldn't we see something more of the world?"

"Because." Gertrude could think of several good reasons, all of which would only make the contrary Maud more determined. "Because we'd first need to get permission from your grandmother, and once you asked her, your mother would hear and forbid you to go."

"We won't go far," Maud urged. "Somewhere nearby. Uncle Carol keeps a few pteries in a barn by the little airstrip. Two-seaters. One of the cadets gave me a grand tour." She fluttered her eyes suggestively. "He was very charming, and so was I. Of course he had to be, seeing as I'm most likely the future Queen of England."

"Can you fly a ptery?" Gertrude asked with some asperity.

Maud had never even been up in one. Grandmama thought it was too dangerous, not for a girl, but for the Succession. This was something of a sore point with Maud, who had, as a child, coined the name for the small light-weight helio-porters. "Just like Mr. Marsh's Pteranodon!" she'd told her governess, and a reporter had been within hearing. The name had stuck; soon it was all that anyone called the contraptions, that or 'ptery' for short. There had been a flutter of public affection for the well-educated little princess. Grandmama had been pleased, as she certainly would not be if she could read the mischief Maud had in mind now.

"Nooo," Maud admitted, melting into her most charming smile. "I was assuming you could. I know you can do just about everything."

In fact, Gertrude did know how to pilot one of the little machines. After Billy learned last year, she had insisted that he show her. It seemed the sort of thing that might be useful to know. But she had only made a few short hops from Father's land to the Lascelles' estate and back again, hardly enough to qualify her for ferrying others. She certainly didn't want the responsibility of taking the heir to the throne...

Her hesitation cost her. Maud, always more astute than others realized, saw her thinking and exclaimed "Aha! I knew you could!"

Gertrude blushed and, angry with herself, flushed redder still.

Maud pretended not to notice. "I know where we can go!" she said brightly, as if they'd been wondering for hours. "It's close enough that we can be gone for a day or two and no one will even miss us." Her eyes glowed like Baltic amber. "We are going to have such fun!"

The Abbot had not expected the Centurion's visit, but the respectful young man was always a welcome visitor. It was admirable how devoted he was to poor Signor Guido. Such devotion should be encouraged.

The dispensary brothers of the Abbazia di San Colombano, however, sometimes wished that Rappaccini were not so attentive to his brother. It took days to recover from one of these visits. Signor Guido, ordinarily content to sit for hours with his wood carving (he had a particular affinity for spoons, for which the brethren were most grateful), had a tendency to become over stimulated in the Centurion's presence. And there would inevitably be some confrontation with Tómas that would send the hapless manservant off on one of his sprees. Signor Guido's man had a sunny disposition and a kind nature, and no one was better at communicating with Signor Guido and caring for his frequent night terrors, but the fellow had an unfortunate weakness for drink.

The Centurion's visit began pleasantly enough. He arrived in good humor, with a gift of fine beeswax candles, and a piece of colourful

Murano glass that the Abbot would not use himself but would barter for needful things. Rappaccini's strong back was put to good use, helping raise the roof on the new shed. Tómas stayed indoors with Signor Guido all that day. There had been strict adherence to the Rule at the evening meal but, some time between Vespers and Matins, there must have been an opportunity for an exchange of some kind because the two young men were seen to be glaring at one another over their morning bowls of bread and milk.

They were working side by side at the far end of the garden, when the altercation broke out. None of the monks saw it begin, but they heard the slap ring out and turned toward the intrusive sound. The Centurion loomed over a cowering Tómas, who was nursing his cheek. Shamefaced at his show of temper, Rappaccini reached out an arm, palm up in peace. Tómas took the hand, twisted it and pulled the Centurion down into the grass. The two tussled briefly. Then, just as some of the brethren drew close enough to break up the fight, Tómas pushed himself up and ran towards the thicket of trees that led to the road.

The monks helped Rappaccini to his feet and would have taken him to the dispensary. He insisted that only his soul required tending and asked to be allowed to repair to the chapel to confess and repent this shameful transgression of the peace.

The brethren knew from experience that Tómas was headed off to a local inn, where the barmaid would no doubt pity him with grappa enough to set off one of his sprees. They didn't expect to see him for a few days; it was whispered he'd broken the hearts of girls as far away as Tremona, across the border in Switzerland. Tómas was incorrigible, but Signor Guido was fond of him, as were the brothers who rather charmingly kept hoping they would be able to reform their pet sinner. And the Centurion would no doubt make a gracious contrition that would more than offset a few days inconvenience.

❧

It was that time of evening when Frank stopped work and headed toward dinner. The garage was oddly situated near the Horse Guards parade grounds. He was walking briskly in that direction when Pinkerton hailed him from the kerb, waving for him to wait.

He had no choice. He couldn't pretend to have not spotted his old friend. Pinkerton walked in a painful hurry, red-faced and dragging his black document box. His free hand clutched a stitch in his side. "I'm coming with you," he wheezed, when he was close enough to be heard.

Trying to think of an excuse to leave his friend behind, Frank grabbed his forearm to brace him.

Pinkerton latched onto his shoulder. "Don't...be so daft." He struggled to catch his breath. "Of course I know...Always have. I'm...her bloody...spymaster!"

Frank stared at him in astonishment. He had never known Pinkerton to use foul language. And in all these years, he was embarrassed to admit, it had never occurred to him that Pinkerton knew anything about this most secret relationship. Thanks to his brilliance in establishing and administering a network, Pinkerton was an excellent spymaster, but he had only ever been an average to middling spy.

Seeing this now in Frank's face, Pinkerton grinned. "Ha! Been wanting to catch you out for years! Think..." The laugh made him sputter. He crouched for a moment to ease his breathing. "Otherwise, do you think...I would have wasted your talents out West all these years? But if she wanted you there...I admit it never crossed my mind you might start back up after all this time."

"Does she know that you...?"

Pinkerton shook his head in firm negative. "Even now, she'll assume that I thought that *I* was bringing *you*. Sorry, Menzies, but there's no choice. I've got an urgent message you both need to hear."

"What?"

"You'll hear it when she does." Pinkerton's natural colour seemed to have returned and he took a deep breath with a rueful smile. "I'm all peched out. I'm getting too old to go running through Whitehall. Drive carefully so I can catch forty winks along the way."

It was a token of her innate noblesse that Queen Charlotte managed to appear not in the least discomfited when her lover arrived accompanied by his commander. She welcomed them both into the private drawing room and acted as if she were not wearing a décolleté copper evening dress and there were no such thing as a whiskey decanter and two glasses on the table nearest her chair.

Pinkerton bowed unusually low. "I beg Your Majesty's humble pardon. You know that Sir Alastair and I would never presume to arrive without invitation except in a moment of crisis."

She inclined her head, inviting him to continue. If she'd looked at Frank from the corner of her eye, she would have noticed his minute shrug.

"I've had an urgent communication from Agent Horner. Something I felt necessary to deliver in person." Pinkerton cleared his throat, twice.

"We've intercepted an extraordinary message from Madame Blavatsky to the Emperor. The Princess must return from Bucharest at once. We believe her to be in danger there."

Frank ran his fingers through his hair, as if sifting through the mass of information. "Blavatsky. That's the mysterious Russian seeress, aye? She, what? She 'predicted' that the Princess is in danger?"

Pinkerton drew a sharp breath. "She is widely rumoured to have some genuine dealings with the other world. Augustus sets great store by her." Two pair of skeptical eyes turned on him. He opened his palms in appeal. "It's natural to doubt, but doubt this if you will."

He lifted the black box and looked around for a convenient place. Frank scooped the glasses from the table. Setting down the box, Pinkerton used the key chained to his wrist to unlock the bottom. Reaching inside, he pulled out what appeared to be a dead pigeon. The red eyes were glassy and the sooty grey plumage showed nary a tremble. He flipped the creature over and plunged his fingers into its belly.

The Queen gave a startled gasp.

Frank chucked, a pleased expression shining across his face. "So you've found a use for the wee thing!"

Pinkerton seemed surprised. "Oh, aye! We made some for Tucker." He pulled a tiny roll of paper from the cavity and handed to the Queen. "I thought you would want to read it with your own eyes, Ma'am."

The Queen took the clean, dry bit of paper. Before she unrolled it, she raised her eyebrows at Frank. "It's a machine," she said, distinctly unamused. "One of yours."

"My carrier pigeon," he confirmed. He was incapable of concealing a boyish pride at seeing his invention employed. "I thought it was a skeilie notion, but I didn't think it we could put it to work as yet. The transmitter can follow a signal for no more than twenty miles."

"Aye," Pinkerton agreed. "It can be made to work if there's a regular route, like this one. We put a series of relays on towers along the way. Still, it's not foolproof. Tucker will have crossed to Switzerland after launching it. I expect we'll see a wire from him by tomorrow."

The Queen had fished a pair of magnifiers from the table drawer and was reading. "Message intercepted. Endora suggests..." The Queen looked at Pinkerton. "Endora?"

"Code name for the Blavatsky," he explained. "Book of Samuel."

"Run out of nursery rhymes, Pinkerton? Really, these names..."

"Never mind the names. Gentlemen, would you please explain why I can read this message? Why hasn't it been encrypted."

"If you would continue reading, Ma'am, you'll see that it wouldn't have been possible."

The Queen continued. "Endora suggests Bootsie seek 'aud' in 'B_est.'" The colour drained from her cheeks. "Bucharest," she whispered.

Pinkerton rushed to reassure her. "I've wired my man, Piper. He'll have the Princess home in a trice. If you would excuse my impertinence, Ma'am, I ask leave to return to London at once. Augustus will doubtless be sending his best men to any place that matches that description. I'll need to be monitoring the situation. I can leave Menzies here to await whatever personal message you might have to transmit to the Princess and the Dowager Princess of Wales."

"Thank you, Lord Pinkerton. Of course." The Queen seemed almost about to take his hand before she gestured that he might take his leave.

"You can see, Menzies, why we needed you here. The villain refuses to give up!"

As soon as the door had closed behind his old friend, Frank poured a glass of whiskey and pressed it into the Queen's hand.

"She'll be fine," he said gruffly.

"Of course." She looked up at him with a tremulous smile. "But it's good not to have to worry alone."

6 - MOVING PIECES

Upon arriving in Bucharest, and following Conte di Bari's explicit instructions, the two men who were Squadra Rosso went openly to the Roman Embassy to present their diplomatic credentials. Following the failed Gallic war, guarded relations had gradually resumed throughout Europe, but the other nations were wary of official Italian presence and kept a weather eye on visitors. It was important to prove that one had nothing to hide.

The Ambassador, a foolish man who held his post by virtue of his obvious harmlessness, was delighted to have the distraction of guests from home. Along with an excellent bottle of wine, he shared all the local news, capped by the fact that the Queen's sister, the Dowager Princess of Wales, was visiting Court with her daughter.

"The Queen would like to marry the young principessa to Prince Ferdinand, but the match is said to be unlikely." The history of Caesar's negotiations was not public knowledge. "Such a beautiful young lady," he reflected wistfully. The ambassador, a small man, had an especially fondness for tall women.

The squadra leader, who was traveling as the Conte da Rossi, hid his thrill of excitement by extravagantly praising the Ambassador's chef.

Later, as he coded his wire to di Bari, visions of an elegant villa in Palermo danced in his head. "Aud in B_est" indeed! Their team would bring home Caesar's prize.

Da Rossi was well-experienced as a courtier. Conspicuous—large and heavily bearded—he was the logical one of the pair to perform their reconnaissance. The next day, he pinned the decorations to which he was entitled (but rarely wore) to his substantial chest, to attend a levee at Peles as part of the Ambassador's train. Upon being presented to the Queen and her visiting sister, he kissed hands elegantly. He made no mention at all of the Princess Maud, whose absence he nonetheless noted.

The following afternoon, he and his secondus, Arancione, took the air in one of the capital's lovely public gardens, where it had been arranged that they would accidentally encounter a certain music teacher. It was interesting that no one in any of the capitals of Europe seemed concerned by the many resident Italian instructors of music and painting. Those who might have fleetingly questioned their presence assumed the artistic nature to be incompatible with war or espionage, thereby discounting the power of information gleaned from casual gossip. Possessed of a gentle manner and a romantically shabby appearance that appealed to young ladies and their mamas alike, this particular musical young man had established a roster of students from the best-connected families in the city. The squadra's presence flustered him. He reported, apologetically, that he had no idea where the Princess Maud might be found. He was surprised to learn that this was of any consequence. Several of his young ladies had dropped hints to the effect that it had been days since anyone had seen her. Rumour had it that she had tired of Bucharest and was sulking at Peles; rumour also had it that she was prone to sulks.

Da Rossi hadn't seen her at the castle. The Embassy was certain there had been no announcement in Court Calendar of any conclusion to her visit. Where was the girl? None of their plans for seizing her could work if they didn't know where she was!

Dottore Arancione, the type of man who could yell "fire" in a crowded theatre and still remain unnoticed, started lingering around the types of saloons and brothels where the better class of soldier took his leisure. The musician's scuttlebutt was quickly confirmed. The titled young captains, lieutenants and Embassy factotums had neither ridden with nor been required to dance attendance on the Princess for several days. At the bar where he found himself at last call, Arancione targeted a few susceptible ears and planted the idea that this should be cause for great concern.

That hint remained with at least one of these young roués after the haze of alcohol had lifted. He was troubled. As third Secretary to Lascelles, he'd seen the beautiful princess regularly since she'd arrived. It was odd, wasn't it, that she'd suddenly vanished from sight? If she were ill, wouldn't someone have said? He decided to seek out the Ambassador's son and see if he knew anything about it. They were friends of a sort; Lascelles had fagged for him at Eton.

Billy Lascelles laughed. "Oh, she's with Gertrude! They're old friends. My cousin has her own ideas of fun," he explained. "I'm sure they're poking around in some museum or something of an equally improving nature." The soldier went away reassured, but Billy began to wonder. It was peculiar that he hadn't seen his cousin once since he'd returned with Prince Ferdinand. He raised the issue at the luncheon table.

Billy's parents hadn't seen Gertrude either, nor had the Embassy servants. Everyone had assumed she was with Maud at Peles, though it was generally agreed it was queer that she hadn't been home at all. The maid sent to check her room found her walking suit and several minor garments missing, together with her toiletry case. It seemed odd to wear a walking suit to Court. Ambassador Lascelles' concern began to rise. When he'd been told of plans for the royal visit, he'd been warned of the need for additional security. One of Pinkerton's men was hidden in the Princess's train, and her actions were to be closely monitored. Although Gertrude didn't know it, this had been the primary reason for inviting her to spend her holidays with the family.

Hurrying to Peles, Lascelles quickly established that the girls were not there. Neither, as Catarina's now frantic equerry discovered, was Pinkerton's agent. It was impossible to guess how no one had noticed this. Lascelles blamed the comparatively casual nature of Carol and Elisabeth's court, but as a diplomat he couldn't say a word. Then Billy blurted out that his cousin knew how to pilot a ptery. Catarina fainted. The Ambassador ran to wire Pinkerton.

In all that time, no one had paid any attention to young Florence, Billy's little sister. Her singing lesson went on as it did on any Tuesday afternoon. While she did her scales, her governess flirted, as she always did, with the handsome instructor.

"Oh, and such a to-do about Miss Gertrude going away. We are all quite frantic about her!" Miss Trigere fluttered her eyelids dramatically. Gertrude had once commented that Miss Trigere seemed more suited to the stage than to the classroom. Florence's mama had laughed; she was quite a good governess, and not every girl wanted to be an Oxford bluestocking.

"I know where they've gone," Florence piped up.

Both adults looked at her skeptically. Children who wanted attention might say anything.

"Well then," Miss Trigere snipped, "you should have said."

"You said children are not to speak at meals unless spoken to," Florence replied calmly; "and no one ever thought to ask me. No one ever asks me anything."

Miss Trigere turned to the singing teacher with her hands raised in supplication as if to say 'deliver me from other people's children.' "Where then?" she demanded of the girl. "If you know so much, where is she?"

"They went to Budapest. They were bored here and thought it would be more fun." Florence sighed sympathetically. She was often bored here. There were so few lessons that were at all amusing and there weren't many English-speaking girls for her to play with. She wished Papa's job didn't have to take them so far from home.

Miss Trigere yanked the child unceremoniously by the arm and dragged her downstairs to her mother. No one noticed when the music instructor left the house.

Da Rossi was aware that Squadra Verde was already in Budapest. He wired di Bari for further instructions.

☺

The Conte di Bari read the decrypted message that his Praefectus set in front of him. He smiled. By sending top teams to both places, he had nothing to worry about. The question now was whether there was anything Squadra Rosso might accomplish on the Emperor's behalf in Bucharest, or if he should bring them back home.

He encoded a message for the Emperor and rang the pool for someone to bring it to Roma. It was an exhausted Benvolio Rappaccini who entered.

"Excellent!" di Bari said. "Just the man for the job! And your blessed brother?"

"Grazie, Eminenza. It is God's will that he should live." Rappaccini crossed himself.

"Amen," the Conte replied. "Now I must send you to Roma, as fast as you can manage."

"Si, Eminenza," Rappaccini said, stifling a yawn and taking the message. He saluted and prepared to exit.

The Conte stopped him. "Rappaccini? Do I recall correctly that you speak some English?"

"Si, Eminenza," Rappaccini said diffidently. "Not for many years. We had a tutor…"

Before Rappaccini could begin another elegy to his wealthy past, di Bari stopped him. "Some words will be fine," he said brusquely. "I expect to have a new assignment for you very soon. Now take your leave."

"Si, Eminenza," Rappaccini said. "Grazie." He shut the door silently as he left.

For all his talk, Rappaccini was good at silence. And he had many uses, di Bari thought with satisfaction.

❧

Maud had been correct, as she usually was when it was in her self-interest to be so. It was shockingly easy to appropriate a ptery; they'd had only to coordinate their arrival in the shed with the afternoon drill period. They slipped past the dozing steward with their handbags and the driving dusters Gertrude had the foresight to acquire from the Embassy garage. While most cadets had their own kit, there was a locker in the shed with leather caps and goggles that were used for training. They quickly selected some of the smaller ones and crept into the vehicle at the farthest end of the canopy. Though the instrument panel was similar, the machine differed slightly from the leisure model Billy had taught her to use. Gertrude hoped this meant that it was built for longer runs.

Inwardly cursing herself for allowing Maud to have pushed her into this corner, she put her hand on the throttle and pulled. Her mood instantly changed to one of elation. It was thrilling to feel the frame tremble as the Prometheum boiler kicked in. To control such power; then to rise over the trees in that fragile openwork cab! It was truly like a dream of flying. Even over the roar of the engine, Gertrude could hear the Princess crowing behind her.

While Maud was enjoying her first flight, Gertrude found herself happily absorbed in the intellectual challenge of flying to an unknown location. She'd made herself a rough plan from the maps in the library, but features that had seemed so distinctive on paper were less obvious from the air. She kept glancing from map to ground to instrument panel. If she were going to make a habit of flying, she would need to learn more about navigational devices. A new course of study was always an agreeable prospect. Gertrude pushed the thought to the back of her mind to be reconsidered once she'd gotten them safely home from this adventure.

Gertrude accomplished the flight with minor error and only one stop to tend the boiler. She didn't ordinarily seek accolades but, in this case, it would have been pleasant if Maud might have recognized her achievement. The Princess, exhilarated by her own accomplishment, took Gertrude's lightly.

"See how easy?" she said, debarking in the tiny aerodrome. "I knew you could do it! Do you think they have cabs here? How do we get to the city?"

The driver recommended a hotel suitable for visiting young ladies, where they checked in under the assumed identities of Miss Stuart and Miss Lowthian. They took a pleasant stroll through the streets of Castle Hill and, at Gertrude's insistence, poked their noses into a few of the more flamboyant churches. Maud discovered it was fun to be an ordinary tourist; even the most officiously lauded 'sights' were enjoyable when you weren't coerced into visiting them and no one quizzed you after.

That evening, they headed down to the hotel's dining room in good spirits and excellent appetite, neither of which was more than momentarily disturbed by the discovery that one of Maud's most devoted followers had trailed them from Bucharest. It would have been difficult not to notice such a dashing man, particularly in the tight, blazing white pants and scarlet coat of his regimental uniform. Captain Piper had the good grace to blush when Maud waved him over. He had seen them take the ptery from the barracks, he explained, and a good British officer could not allow two lovely ladies to be unprotected in a strange city. He had requisitioned his own machine and followed them.

Maud graciously invited him to join them for dinner. He was amusing as well as handsome. She also realized that a tame male escort might provide them with even more freedom. She suggested he meet them the next morning for a drive. The prospect from Gellért Hill was said to be exceptional; or perhaps an excursion out to Margareth Island and a picnic luncheon.

The captain appeared overjoyed at the invitation. In point of fact, he was enormously relieved. After dinner, he returned to the British Residence and used the diplomatic telegraph key. He sent a terse message before going to his allotted room to enjoy a well-earned untroubled sleep.

§▲

Where in Budapest does one look to find a princess? Squadra Verde had arrived in the double city with no idea where to begin.

Assuming the guise of a specialist in women's nervous disorders, the Primo, Signor Verdi, made the rounds of all the spas. As there were at least as many of these in Budapest as in Montecatini, this took him the better part of three days.

His more attractive junior, calling himself the Barone d'Azzuro, had spent most of his working life in the region and kept a series of discreet and delightful mistresses stationed along the Danube. The ladies had surprising resources that could be very useful to a spy. On this mission, however, his Hungarian could provide nothing beyond his personal comfort and the discouraging observation, a tickling whisper in his ear between kisses, that there were no members of the Royal family in residence. So the charming D'Azzuro accompanied the ambassador's elderly sister on her morning drive and eavesdropped on the conversation of many a fashionable lady. None of them so much as mentioned the word "principessa." Rigid with pastries and numb with pointless gossip, he dashed over to the zoological gardens for a breath of unperfumed air and to leave a substantial bribe with the head gatekeeper.

They were beginning to doubt they were in the right place when a wire came from di Bari, confirming that Princess Maud had come to Budapest. They looked at one another in chagrin. How could they have missed her? They sat down to make a list of all the places they would have to check...again.

*

Joan Lady Pinkerton heard the electric buzzer, turned over on her other side and quickly fell back asleep. No matter what the fashionable folk might do, she had never held with the idea of separate bedrooms and was therefore long inured to having her sleep disrupted for the sake of the Empire. One thing you could say for modern technology: the sound of a buzzer, however irritating, was far preferable to the days when a scout had used to knock on the door in the wee hours, sending her burrowing modestly under the bedclothes.

Lord Pinkerton stuck his feet into his slippers and pulled on his dressing gown. His bifocals were on the bedside table. He stuck them in his pocket. If he didn't actually have to slip them on, perhaps he might get back to sleep tonight.

One of the Ministry pages was standing shyly at the door to Lord Pinkerton's study. He looked as if he, too, had been roused from his bed. Pinkerton took the folded piece of foolscap and, with a sigh of regret, donned his spectacles. It was a wire from Piper. Smart lad, Piper; he led off with the most important thing. The Princess was safe and sound. But she was in Budapest. Fortunately, so was he. Pinkerton sank heavily into his chair and gestured for the boy to do the same. He had a feeling he might need a messenger. And a pot of strong tea. Budapest. With a tiny twinge of guilt, Pinkerton rang for his man. Like Pinkerton's, Thompson's sleep belonged to Greater Britain.

A few hours later, all the arrangements were in place to bring the Queen's private dirigible back from Cowes, where the Duchess of York had taken her two little girls for sea air, and prepare it to retrieve the Princess and her party. Pinkerton did not want to risk more adventures in any city that might be 'B_est.' He wired Piper to find the most discreet way to get the girls to Prague, where an aership would meet them in two days time. By not specifying how this might be accomplished, he reasoned that he was adding a layer of security should the message be intercepted and deciphered.

Before dismissing the boy, Pinkerton scrawled a message for the Queen. It could wait for morning. Menzies could take it up. He managed a good three hours of sleep before the housemaid came with their eye-openers and drew the curtains.

❧

The reply to Piper's telegram came via the maid who brought his morning tray. He gulped his tea so quickly that he scalded his mouth. Dressing at campaign speed, he ran down the stairs. After consulting with the Resident, he took a cab to the hotel where the young ladies were breakfasting in their rooms, at leisure and in dishabille, discussing what they preferred to explore later with the assistance of their unexpected swain.

They thought it presumptuous of the Captain, to materialize so early in the day; being dashing did not excuse that kind of behaviour. They sent the hotel maid back down to him without a reply. When a second message appeared, with the ominous words "at your honoured Grandmother's behest," Maud turned her most contrary. Gertrude, however, thought perhaps the Captain should be answered. She sent down asking him to attend her in the parlour and quickly changed into day clothes.

Piper was relieved to see her. Miss Bell was an Oxford scholar. He could tell her the simple truth and trust her not to call attention to herself by fainting or screaming.

"Miss Bell," he gave one of his most elegant and respectful bows. "I apologize for my unceremonious arrival, but I've come on an urgent errand. I must speak with you and you must speak to the Prin...your companion."

Gertrude looked at him as if she were much older and taller than she was. "Be seated," she said, taking a seat herself.

He scanned the room from the corners of his eyes and found it satisfactorily empty. "Miss Bell, asking for your strictest discretion, I reveal to you now that I am an agent of Her Majesty's Special Service."

"A Pinkerton!" Gertrude was thrilled. Her family connections were such that she'd heard of Pinkerton's elite team of spies. The idea fascinated her. What minds such men must possess! She wondered if women could be spies as well. Her clever eyes regarded the handsome captain with a new degree of respect.

"Quietly Miss, if you please. You must remain calm, as I explain." She nodded, brushing a finger quickly against her lips. He continued. "I am here on a mission of the greatest urgency. As long as she remains in this city, your companion is in danger. Extreme danger. We have reason to believe that agents of a foreign power are aware that she is here and mean to do her harm."

It sounded like the type of fabulous adventure tale one might find in the trashier type of novel, not that Gertrude wasted her time reading that sort of thing. However, her logical mind saw an obvious flaw. "But no one knows we're in Budapest. I don't even know how you…"

"I explained yesterday that I followed you here. What I didn't say was that I am specifically assigned to follow the…your companion. I have been following her every move since she left London. We must all be grateful that Lord Pinkerton takes such extreme precautions. As for the foreign agents, I am told they have some supernatural assistance."

"Oh really!" Gertrude made the impolite clicking sound that her family, Maud and the girls at Lady Margaret Hall equally would have recognized. "That is simply too much! You can't expect me to believe…"

"Miss Bell, it is of no matter to me what you believe. My only concern is to extract you and your companion from this city without delay. I will not permit the Emperor's agents to succeed on my watch!"

"The Emperor!" she exclaimed.

"Hush! I have arranged for a carriage, a good British carriage, to arrive at this building in thirty minutes."

She was cowed by his sudden martial sternness. It was not unpleasant. The Captain was a most attractive man.

"You will go upstairs now and tell your companion to be prepared to leave at that time. If she is not, I'll carry her downstairs myself."

"It's their job to believe there's an assassin under every bed," Maud grumbled, cramming garments into her hand bag. She was peeved. All that trouble to get here and not even two days of fun to show for it.

"That's ridiculous and you know it." Gertrude had caught the Captain's concern and was in no mood to humor a spoilt princess.

"You don't understand," Maud pouted. No one did. She gave a sad look around the room. At least she'd been in a hotel, she comforted herself. And she had finally flown in a ptery; that was a happy thought.

Sir Alastair Franklin Menzies was elegantly boning kippers and trying to keep his eyes open. Joan hadn't joined them this morning. Perhaps she'd finally tired of the novelty and Pinkerton could move their daily meeting to luncheon. Now that he knew Pinkerton was in on the secret, there was certainly no reason not to discreetly hint that he would appreciate an extra hour's sleep. He cleared his throat.

Pinkerton ignored him and took another swallow of tea. He wasn't to be pressed. At his age, he was careful of his digestion. And there was no need to rush; everything was under control.

"I've heard from my man Piper," he said at last, spooning marmalade on his toast. "Seems our princess flew the coop before he could bring her home. More trouble than a circus, that lass. Good news is, he was right behind her."

"That implies there's bad news as well," Frank observed.

"Mmm, aye," Pinkerton said. "How was it that the Blavatsky woman put it?"

"You mean starts in B, ends in est?"

"Exactly. Piper found the lass in Budapest."

Frank's hand slipped. The Blavatsky woman and her voices went against his every belief. "Damn it!" It was only a fish knife, but it still hurt. He pushed away the kippers and walked over to the sideboard to check for something less dicey. Perhaps some buttered eggs. "He's getting her out of there immediately, of course." Frank said testily. "Presumably not back to Bucharest, but straight home. Through some other city, I would hope; some city that neither starts with B nor ends in est. Though I hear Brest is bonny this time of year." He couldn't resist the quip. If one didn't have to worry about the fate of a Nation, and could ignore the ghosts and ghoulies, the entire caper would almost be amusing.

"Via Prague," Pinkerton confirmed. "The Queen's yacht is prepared to retrieve them."

"Them?" Frank asked.

"She went off with a friend. A Miss Gertrude Bell. Surprising, that is. The Queen considers Miss Bell to be extremely level-headed."

The men smiled at one another, not bothering to disguise their relief. An irresponsible female companion was still a female companion. It was also good that this one was known to the Queen.

"I'm only waiting to hear how Piper is planning to get them to Prague. Obviously the train is out of the question."

Frank nodded vehemently. "Any public transport. The Emperor will surely have his men watching."

There was a discreet rap at the door.

"Come!" Pinkerton called. His manservant entered with a salver. Pinkerton took the message, straight from the crytographic pool, and read it. His forehead wrinkled, then smoothed in quick succession. Going to the small corner table, he scrawled a quick note, rolled the square of paper tightly and tucked it into a capsule that he popped, with the heel of his hand, into the pneumatic tube that dangled overhead. "He's going by carriage," he told Frank. "One of ours." He realized his man was still standing there with the tray. "What is it, Thompson?"

"A visitor, Lord Pinkerton. A lady."

"I assume you explained Lady Pinkerton's hours for receiving."

"She was most insistent that it was yourself she wished to see and not Madam." It was hardly the most peculiar demand a guest had ever made. Thompson proffered the salver and Pinkerton lifted the card.

Pinkerton smiled broadly. "Well, well! Please bring the lady in, Thompson. And have a fresh pot of tea sent up."

A few minutes later, there was another knock at the door. It opened, admitting a wan, travel-stained woman.

"Lord Pinkerton, I cannae begin to apologize, but I dinnae ken..." Her eyes flew to the other man and she blinked back tears of relief. "Oh Frankie! You're here!" Nan Hudson collapsed gratefully into the chair her brother pulled out to meet her.

"That I am," Frank replied. "But why are you? And where's my lass?"

Mrs. Hudson had just arrived on the milk train from Dover having, to her great relief, been unable to book a ticket on a timely dirigible. She'd crossed the Channel the night before. The combination of sleeplessness and the lingering effects of the sea and rail made it difficult for her to temper her message. "Prague," she said baldly. "With Nikola Tesla."

"Prague?!" Frank barked. "What in the blazes is Claude doing in Prague!"

"Tesla," Pinkerton mused. "Why do I know that name?"

"The Serbian," Mrs. Hudson said, reaching for the cup of tea that the maid had poured for her before making a well-trained exit (lady visitor or not, this was a Service breakfast and Thompson ran a tight ship).

"The inventor," Frank said simultaneously.

Pinkerton's face cleared. "Of course. Rather brilliant young man. Electricity, aye? And radio waves?"

Frank nodded. "Amongst other things. An extraordinarily versatile mind."

"Like your own."

Frank brushed away the compliment. "I had him with me in Chicago a few years back. Sound thinking, but not the most stable soul. And what he's doing in Prague and with my daughter..." his voice rose dangerously and he fixed his eye sternly on his sister.

Nan Hudson straightened her spine. "It's the Emperor's monsters, those Tracys!" she exclaimed.

"You know about the trecika?" Pinkerton asked intently.

"Mr. Tesla told us..." She turned to him, astonished. "You mean to say, Lord Pinkerton, that you already knew?"

Pinkerton answered her solemnly. "The Service has that information."

She sank back in her chair with a sigh of relief. "Thank the Heavens!" She hadn't been at all confident of her ability to explain, no less convince anyone of what still sounded to her like a nasty fairy story.

"How does Tesla figure into this?" Pinkerton pressed her to continue.

Nan seemed about to collapse from fatigue. Frank spooned some eggs onto a plate; if they wanted any sense out of his sister, he'd better try and get her to eat.

"They brought him there, to Rome, to do some work on the evil craiturs."

"And let him leave?" Frank was dumfounded.

"He knows too well that he saw too much," she nodded. "He's building a machine to fight those Tracys before they find him." She pushed away the eggs with a shudder, but took a tentative nibble off a piece of dry toast.

"What kind of machine?" Frank asked

"Some kind of clockwork soldier. That's why he wrote to you!" Her voice rose accusingly. "But you weren't there, so that lass of yours and your man Firewalker," she spit the name and toast crumbs like a curse, "had the brrrrilliant idea that she would bring him the Prometheum herself."

"Prometheum!" Frank didn't know what was more dangerous to his only child, the unstable genius or the unstable element. He jumped to his feet and turned to Pinkerton. "When does that aership leave?!"

Pinkerton addressed him with brisk authority. "Calm yourself, Menzies. We'll hold it for you. But first we must allow Mrs. Hudson to tell us everything she knows."

Nan turned sheet white. "I cannot go on another aership!" she protested.

"Dinnae fash, dear Madam. You'll stay here with us," Pinkerton patted her hand comfortingly. "Joan will be glad of the company. But your brother needs the benefit of your knowledge before he leaves. Mrs. Hudson," he said, adjusting his spectacles and fixing her with his eyes, "your Queen is depending on you."

§.

Claude perched on a high stool at the workbench, meticulously punching a series of tiny holes into a ribbon of titanium. Her back was cramped after so many hours hunched over the narrow strips of foil, and her face was hot from the magnifying goggles that she needed to wear, but it was all in the best of causes. She was proud of her growing proficiency in the task. This was the fourth one she'd punched since Nikola had completed graphing out the sequence, and she was nearly finished; at this rate, she'd be able to complete another whole tape today.

"How many did you say?" she asked, wiping her forehead with the back of her hand. "Altogether?"

"Thirty-six."

Their voices sounded furry from lack of use. They both felt the need to hurry, as if they could feel Augustus's shadow looming over the workshop. The peculiar courtesy of their first day together in Prague had quickly been supplanted by the shared professionalism of equals. They worked intently, speaking only when necessary, except when taking a short break to eat. For Claude, the companionable silence was a better compliment than a bouquet of hothouse flowers or a sonnet. It meant that Nikola really saw *her*, not her eyelashes (unusually long and lustrous though they were).

Tesla looked across the workshop at the girl, bent intently over her work. Her face shone, brighter that the light that he'd angled there to help. Dust motes danced across her hair like fireflies. He felt oddly elevated, the way he did when stray thoughts unexpectedly fell into place and the pattern of an idea began to emerge. He wanted, he understood with a shock, to kiss her. He was afraid of such buoyancy. He couldn't afford to be vulnerable and he couldn't risk distraction, not right now. There was too much work to be done.

Today, with the algorithms calculated, he was spending every minute trying to perfect the engine. The Prometheum steam engine had a copper boiler to drive the pistons. A system of tubes would circulate, catch and condense the steam, processing the droplets back to be used again for a prolonged number of cycles. All would be encased in nickel housing, protecting the remainder of the machine from moisture. Tesla calculated that this ought to provide propulsion for up to six hours without requiring additional water. He'd gotten the idea from pteranodon engines. Radio control would be needed to remotely activate the coded sequence, as it had for RODA. Clockwork would accomplish the finer motions, and to that end, the jacquard patterns Claude was now punching.

"I wish I could build a machine that calculated autonomously," he sighed; "a true thinking machine."

"Do you?" Claude looked up from her work and stared at him intently. "I should be terrified to do that."

"You follow where the science wants to go."

"Surely not always," she objected.

He shrugged, looking so melancholy that she immediately wished she could take it back. He was, she thought, like some hero standing on a drawbridge, being told he was fated to open the gates but never cross through. It made her want to hug and shake him, both at the same time.

They worked in silence for another half hour or so. Finishing her tape, she started to massage the back of her neck and found herself looking up at the silly metal face of the mannikin Tesla was working on. "Do Augustus's creatures think, do you think? Are they truly alive?"

"It's difficult to explain. They move by themselves..." Sitting beside her, he scattered his handful of rivets carefully on bench and started forming them into ranks. He spoke slowly, wading through his endless thoughts on the subject. "That is, there's no obvious sign of clockwork or any other machinery. How would you fit that into lumps of clay? I told you, it's not baked. You would think unbaked clay would seize around the armature; it couldn't sustain motion." His sigh, when it came, was as uneasy as it was perplexed. "I do think they're alive in some way," he finally admitted. "That they're aware. I felt one looking at me, more than once. I knew it could somehow distinguish me from other people." He lowered his voice and mumbled something else.

"I didn't hear..." She leaned in closer.

He lifted his head. She saw an expression of abject misery that went straight to her heart. Instinctively, she reached to stroke his curls.

"It was worse than that," he said. "It recognized me, Claude, that I'm me, Nikola Tesla. I had the most horrible feeling that monster was someone I knew!" His face creased with the pain of the memory.

It wasn't the return of the old delusions. He meant it and she believed him. Whatever he had seen in Rome had been real. It seemed strangely credible that those creatures were alive in some way, and if that were so there could be only one option.

She looked trustingly into his eyes. "Then we must free them," she said calmly. "The way you free any wounded creature, by helping it to die."

Her hand had slipped down to the curve of his chin. He covered it with his own. Their faces were so close. A look of awe stole across his and he pressed his lips to hers. His other arm wrapped around her waist and crushed her to his chest.

She couldn't tell if what she was feeling was pure joy or a queer sort of triumph, but she didn't want it to end. It ached to feel him come back to himself and pull away in embarrassment. He jumped up and started tidying the workbench.

"Look at the time!" she said brightly, as if they'd been lost in their work. "I think we've earned a plate of *palačinky*, don't you?" He needed to be made to laugh. What might amuse him? "I can tell you all about my debut as a femme fatale. 'The Case of the Society Snare,' Father and I called it. It started when Governor Adams contacted Father a few weeks before Christmas. Not this past Christmas, the year before. It was one of the last things the old governor did before he died. Governor Adams' grandfather completely disapproved of my great-grandfather Franklin, you know. But the governor always showed Father great respect…"

৯

Leaving the dirigible in its berth at Petřín Hill, Frank took the funicular railway down to Mala Strana and the Vltava. Looking back uphill, he was satisfied that, with the hull panel in place and displaying the false registry, the royal yacht did not appear out of place among the handful of similar conveyances dotting the sky. Piper couldn't be expected for another day, so there was plenty of time for a leisurely stroll across the river. Walking would help him to compose himself before confronting his wayward daughter.

He had argued with himself the entire trip over from London and accomplished nothing beyond keeping a better head of steam than the dirigible. Nan was right, he had treated Claude too much like a son and this was his reward: at the first opportunity, she'd run off on her own and right into the jaws of danger. But wasn't this what he had trained her to do? According to Nan, she'd decrypted the note as handily as he would have himself, and had wasted no time in forming a plan of action. And she'd convinced Firewalker to support her; save for himself, there wasn't another person on Earth who could have done that. It was difficult not to feel a burst of pride. She had been successful in making contact with Tesla and effecting the delivery. What's more, Nan said the genius seemed truly pleased to have her assistance in his efforts. Frank was proud of that as well, or he would be if he weren't so furious.

Stopping at a drinking establishment, he had a Becherbitter—to settle his stomach, he told himself, but really because, for the brief time he was in Prague, he might as well enjoy something of the city. Once Piper arrived, he would be loading his lass and the other two delinquent young women onto the yacht and bringing them all back to London. And if his unreasonable bairn thought he'd let her stay with him in the capital, she was heading for a rude awakening. He was not about to reward her recklessness! Frank brought his glass down on the bar so resolutely that the saloon keeper assumed he was ordering a refill. No, indeed; he would be putting her and Nan on the first steamship home! After everything the lass had put her through, his sister deserved a first class transatlantic cruise. If Tesla needed a lab assistant, he would wire Firewalker to come. Frank picked up his bag, downed his second shot and left before he inadvertently ordered a third.

He explained to the hotel clerk that he was Miss Monteith's father and would be using Mrs. Hudson's room for the next few days. Miss Monteith, he was advised, was out. Frank had no idea where to find her. With no point wandering aimlessly around the city looking for her, he might as well have a lie down. He closed the curtains and let his head fall back on the pillow. It was a comfortable bed. It had been a long day.

A burst of light across his face awakened him abruptly. He bolted upright, only to be smothered by his daughter's delighted embrace. "Oh, Father! The clerk at the desk told me you'd come!" She hugged him hard, her hat mashing against his face. The last time she'd hugged him like this, he had let her solo with a ptery. "What time is it?" he said groggily, pushing a feather out of his nose.

"Not even seven," she said. "That's very early for Prague. We were working so hard that we forgot to stop for our bread and cheese, so we decided to go to the coffee house for palačinky. That's pancakes. They make the best one's here, with lovely jam and almond tucked inside..."

Maybe it was the preposterously stylish hat that made him look at his child and finally grasp she was a young woman. A young woman who had been on her own for nearly a week in a strange city with a young man. "Where is Mr. Tesla?"

"Back at the workshop. He sleeps there, you see, so we're very careful that I should leave at a respectable time. Not that anyone would see me. No one even knows where the workshop is but us and Nan, and soon you will…Oh, Father! I'm so very glad you're here!"

It was difficult to scold her after that. She wanted to drag him off to the workshop at once, but he convinced her that first thing in the morning, when everyone was fresh, would be a much better time. In the meanwhile, she was to tell him everything she could and, if the pancakes had left any room in her stomach, they would have a civilized dinner together.

Ⅎ

Frank shouldn't have been surprised that Claude insisted they breakfast downstairs rather than in their rooms. Sure enough, there was Nikola Tesla, looking much as Frank remembered he had before his illness. The hotel staff seemed familiar with his preferences.

"It's the only way to be certain he's had a real meal," Claude whispered. She was not generally a maternal young woman, but Frank saw she was rather protective of Tesla. The young man did seem in need of care. He was thin and too pale, but admirably composed and, if fervent hand-wringing could attest, unambiguously delighted to see Frank. They ate quickly, eager to leave the exposure of the public dining room and get to a place where they could speak freely. As they left the hotel, Tesla tipped his hat to Claude and strode off, checking his timepiece as if late for an appointment.

Claude linked her arm around her father's and, leaning against him, nudged him in a different direction. "We always separate," she confided, "in case we're being watched, and we're careful to vary how we go." She patted his hand affectionately. "This way, even if one of us were taken, the other might get through. I could never do what he does, but I know where his notes are. I could help." Frank was alarmed at the danger she was so casually accepting, but felt his chest swell. This was his lass alright. Now if only he could get her home before she found herself so deep in international espionage that she'd ruin her life forever!

Frank had no clue that they had reached their destination, until Claude selected a key from her chatelaine and, pushing aside a clump of vines, unlocked what looked like an abandoned door. He surveilled the area with satisfaction. Tesla had chosen his hiding place well.

Inside, it seemed like a temple dedicated to a god of war. Piles of limbs and a pyramid of heads, all in a dull bluish metal, took up a large part of the floor. Around them were neat stacks of what looked to be torsos, each parti-coloured metal barrel having a good-sized window cut out of the front. Four fully-assembled metal men stood sentry in the area with the best light. They were nearly seven feet high, from boot-shaped foot to domed head. Frank had to tilt his neck back to see them in their entirety. There was something majestic about them, their vacant faces sweetly calm, like the most innocent young soldiers who had not yet seen battle. Tesla, his coat already put aside in favour of a battered leather apron, stood beside them, flushed with nervous pride.

"Aren't they wonderful?" Claude breathed. "Nikola, show him everything!" Frank tucked away his daughter's fond use of the young man's first name for later consideration and watched intently as Tesla did so, leaving not so much as a rivet unaccounted for. He pulled down schematics, and showed the shelf of dented arms and his notes about testing. They spent considerable time looking at the latest version of the engine. Frank was impressed.

"May I?" he asked, pointing at the chest cavity of one of the automatons (Tesla had been firm about the name). Tesla nodded. Frank slipped on the thin chamois gloves he always carried in his coat pocket. Ever so slowly, he lifted the mechanism and, turning it to the proper angle, slid it into position. "You've got a gyroscopic mounting!" he said, delighted. "The hours we spent going over this!"

"It works here," Tesla said, a little shyly. "It wouldn't have for RODA."

"And with the Prometheum here..." Frank poked his finger into the cavity. "Yes, I can see. Neatly done."

"Claude set that, sir." Tesla hastened to give credit.

Frank looked at his daughter, who winked. "Faerie fingers," she said. It was an old family joke.

Finally, Tesla showed Frank the work they'd been doing on the 'brain.' As he spoke, he handed Frank his magnifying goggles so that the older man would be able to examine the titanium ribbons, and the delicate shuttle pins he'd built to 'read' them.

"Magnificent!" Frank all but whispered. "How many motions can you map out?"

"We think maybe as many as two dozen!" Claude said proudly.

Frank handed the goggles back to Tesla, regarding him thoughtfully. "Why so many?" he asked. "It will be a tremendous achievement, of course, but why?"

"You haven't seen the trecika, Sir," Tesla said, a blossom of fear shimmering in his eyes. Now that he could share the burden, it seemed to have become too heavy. He looked about to dissolve like rice paper in the rain. Claude slipped a warm hand over his cold one and gave a comforting squeeze. "They're all but alive," he said, his voice almost to low to hear.

"Perhaps they are alive. We need our automatons to be as near to thinking machines as we can make them."

Frank sat down heavily and began to rub his eyes as if he'd been staring into a lamp for too long. "There are things I am not at liberty to discuss," he said. "Not even with my dear lass, nor with you, Mr. Tesla, despite all that you already know. Combined with what you've told, I am left with no doubt that this Emperor is the most dangerous man on earth. We know his ambition is boundless. We know that he wants...no, that he *thinks* that he *can* live forever. If he has control over the life force itself...As one scientist to another, Tesla, do you think this can be possible?"

"I don't know if it's possible. But I would come close to swearing he'd done it."

"And you think he's building an army of these deathless creatures." Frank massaged the sides of his nose with his thumb and forefinger. Pinkerton might trust his Horner, but Frank wanted confirmation from someone whose habits of observation he knew to be as rigorous as his own.

"I think he already has, sir. We need to build an army of our own to fight him. No human soldier would be able to stand against that host. I've done as much as I could alone. That's why I called on you."

Frank looked around the room and took a deep breath. "Show me what type of weaponry you had in mind."

7 - PAWNS IN CZECH

Arancione checked the message twice, then handed it to Rossi. "That's it then."

Rossi shrugged. "A thank you would have been nice. The Blavatsky woman didn't actually find the Principessa. We did."

"She was correct about B_est," Arancione reminded. "We happened to draw the wrong city. Maybe we'll be luckier next time."

"Start packing. Once the photograph arrives in the diplomatic pouch, we leave for Prague and start looking for some scientist of the Baron's." Rossi sighed. In his mind, the soap bubble villa in Palermo popped. It had been a nice dream.

After coffee and *kolach*, Squadra Verde said goodbye to d'Azzurro's cheerful mistress and left the flat to begin another sweep of Budapest. As it was evident that their quarry was not here on an invited stay, they decided to focus on the better type of hotels and on cafes patronized by well-bred young ladies and their chaperones. Two young women traveling alone (as, thanks to Squadra Rossi, they now knew to be their quarry), would certainly be noticed in such places.

D'Azzurro, dashing in a Habsburg uniform, threaded his way through the room with Verdi just behind him. "I am looking for my sister," he would begin by way of introduction, holding out a photograph of the Princess. He spoke in the nocturnally-acquired Hungarian that had qualified him for this mission, but with an intriguing Italian lilt and accompanied by exquisite gestures. "She is angry with my father for forbidding her match with the young man she prefers and betrothing her instead to this gentleman." He would indicate Verdi, a weasel-faced man whose expensive coats never looked to be his own. "He has land in three counties, but you can see her point." Verdi, who spoke no Hungarian beyond *igen*, *nem* and *köszönöm*, would give the ladies what he believed to be a hopeful smile. The girls would titter and a look would cross their faces: determination to help the unlucky girl at all cost if ever they saw her. Spotting this, their mothers and governesses would be just as determined to aid d'Azzurro.

Hotel clerks were eager to avoid a scandal, particularly when one gentleman was a Hussar and the other wore a very expensive ring on the ungloved hand that held the silver knob of his cane.

Despite all of this eager assistance, the squadra had no more luck than they'd had on previous days. After drawing the most recent blank, they decided to pause for refreshment. Turning the corner, to search for a suitably manly establishment that they'd noted earlier, they heard a sound of running feet coming up close behind them. Verdi whirled around, whipping a blade from his cane.

The urchin in front of him cowered. "Please master," he whimpered. "Please don't harm me. I only came to say I heard you at the hotel," he jabbed a thumb over his shoulder, indicating the direction from which they'd come, "and I think I know something that can be of service to two fine gentlemen."

Signaling to Verdi to put down his weapon, d'Azzurro fixed the lad with a commanding stare. "You do? You?"

"Yes, your lordship," the boy babbled, his eyes darting furiously in every direction but d'Azzurro's. "I saw them, I think. Your sister and the other young lady."

With the concern a good brother might be expected to show, d'Azzurro pulled the photo from his sash and showed it to the boy. "My sister. You saw her...and her friend?"

"Yes, lordship." He licked his lips nervously and looked at the picture. "Yes, I'm sure it was her. They arrived yesterday, the two of them."

"The clerk didn't say," d'Azzurro frowned sternly.

"He wasn't here. Biro don't come on until noon. Ranody's the morning clerk. You didn't see him. He was here when they came. Also when they left."

"They left! They were here and we missed them?!"

Not understanding the conversation, but seeing his partner's agitation, Verdi started to move on the lad.

D'Azzurro caught his arm and frowned again at the boy. "You've upset her betrothed," he said grimly.

"That's not anything to how he'll be upset when he hears the rest," the boy grumbled. Was he going to get a reward or not?

"What 'rest'? Where did she...where did my sister go?" d'Azzurro grabbed the boy by his skinny arm, half-dragging him forward.

"Prague!" the boy screamed, kicking and struggling. "They got in a carriage and were going to Prague!"

"Prague," d'Azzurro repeated, dropping the boy's arm.

"I heard the man say so." He leered at Verdi, exposing a mouth full of unpleasant teeth. "The man who was with them. I bet he was the lover. He was that handsome. And the gold braid..."

Understanding nothing but the impudence, Verdi reached out and smacked his face. Before the boy could react, d'Azzurro pulled a coin from his purse and tossed it into the road. The boy ran after it with a guttural cry.

"We need a taxi to the station," d'Azzurro muttered to his commander. "We take the first train to Prague!" There was no time to waste. Verdi could wire the Conte when they arrived. If d'Azzurro were lucky, he'd be able to find a boy at the station to take a message to his mistress. If he disappeared without a word, she might throw a fit of pique and toss his good coat and boots to the rag and bone man. Not that it wouldn't be fun to punish her for it later, but he really loved those boots.

❦

Rossi pretended to read what appeared to be an engraved invitation of the highest quality. Tucking it back into the envelope, he turned regretfully to the Ambassador.

"*Mi dispiace*," he said, with a deep sigh. "Duty calls. Our presence," he gestured across the table to include Arancione, "is required elsewhere."

"Signore?" Impersonating a good secretary, Arancione pulled out a small silver pencil and memorandum and awaited instructions.

His eyes dancing with curiosity, the Ambassador craned to try and read the return address.

Rossi was too quick for him, dipping the envelope in coquettish waves as he gave his instructions. "Have the trunks packed. We will be leaving this afternoon."

"Must you? So quickly?" the Ambassador was crestfallen. He'd enjoyed having a fellow Roman diplomat to gossip with.

"I'm afraid so. You know how it is." The envelope skimmed temptingly past the Ambassador's nose on its way into Rossi's pocket. "It's the Principe Giroleme," he explained. "He was to have represented Caesar, but he's not as hale as he once was. He's fallen ill. I've been asked to go to the Court of Vienna in his stead."

"Ah!" the Ambassador breathed. He was envious. Even after the depredations the Great Napoleon had wrought on the Habsburg Empire, Vienna was a prime posting. This Conte da Rossi must be even more important than he had inferred. "There's a sleeper train," he remembered, brightening. "I would be honoured if you'd stay to dinner." Perhaps he might be able to hear a thing or two more.

Rossi smiled. The Ambassador set a fine table and there was no real hurry to get to Prague. It wasn't even certain that the Baron's scientist was there.

ex.

Claude had forgotten how exhilarating it could be listening to Nikola and Frank bounce ideas off one another. She was proud to think she'd managed to hold her own in that room, but now she was exhausted. Nikola's fire was burning low, too; he was getting that strained look in his eyes. If anything, the good dinner Frank had insisted they have was making them sleepier. She expected they would go straight to bed and sleep like babies. That is, she and Nikola would. Frank would likely be up all night. The agent he was supposed to be meeting in Prague was expected within the next few hours and Frank wanted to speak with him as soon as he arrived. She could see her father was restless now. She didn't know where he got the energy.

"Why don't you go?" Claude asked. "Wait for him at the Embassy. Nikola will see me back to the hotel."

"You're sure you don't mind if I leave you?" Frank wondered if *he* minded. He looked from his tired but radiant daughter to the young man who, it appeared, might soon have to be considered in the light of a suitor. It seemed only yesterday that Tesla was begging him to lock 'the brat' out of the workshop. And now, well, she was as beautiful as her mother and Nikola Tesla was not a fool. Not the most stable young man, but by no means a fool; and there was no doubting his integrity. Frank's hesitation was as ridiculous as it was inconvenient.

Claude reached up to kiss him on the cheek. "Go on, you! And, no, I won't wait up," she said before he could. It was another favourite tease. "I'll see you at breakfast."

Frank paid the bill, leaving the waiter a generous gratuity. He left the young people sitting with their heads close together, deciding between chocolate and chestnut gateaux.

$\clubsuit$

Arriving in Prague, Verdi and Azzurro sought out the home of an Italian expatriate known locally as a painter of elegant murals. Following the plan they had worked through on the train, they informed him of their need to requisition his carriage and his trusted driver. They provided their new servant with a coded message to telegraph to di Bari. Next, availing themselves of the shed the painter used as a studio, they made their preparations. The Principessa and her party might arrive in the city at any time and they wanted to be poised to act instantly.

Verdi produced the slim leather case he had insisted on keeping with him in Budapest. Azzurro had teased him for spoiling the lines of his coat; now he couldn't say too much in praise of his primo's foresight. Because they'd had it with them, they'd lost not a minute of their pursuit.

Months ago, when the Emperor had resolved to have this bride at any cost, each elite team of agents had been outfitted with such a case and trained by the Lady Giulia herself in how to use the contents. The case held a colourful row of glass tubes, syringes, a box of needles as fine as eyelash and a set of silver tools. The tubes were filled with rare drugs. The Lady Giulia had explained that some of these had been given her by the Emperor's Sybil, who belonged to a secret society that channelled their knowledge across the veil. Others were ancient potions, lost for more than two thousand years. The contents of this case was beyond value.

Having washed the zinc table with methylated spirits, Azzurro unrolled a bit of clean linen. They scrubbed their hands and opened the case flat on the cloth. Ever so carefully, Azzurro eased the top off one particular vial. Verdi removed his large ring. There was a small button concealed in the bezel. When pressed, it opened the onyx intaglio like a door. A tiny needle sprung up from the recess. Verdi fixed a jeweler's loupe in his eye and held the ring steady in one hand. With his other hand, he slid a silver pick into the tube and very slowly withdrew a single drop of viscous yellowish stuff, which he let fall on the tip of the needle. Neither man moved for three minutes, which they timed by chanting a charm in a language neither of them knew. When they had finished, the needle showed not a trace of fluid. Verdi used the silver pick to press the needle gently back into its nest. Hearing a tiny click, he returned the onyx to its original position.

They both exhaled in relief. This was their most subtle appliance and the most difficult to prepare. Should that fail, or should they find themselves needing to take the Principessa's companion as well, they prepared a few syringes, capping them with the silver tips designed for the mission. They secreted the syringes in their pockets, to have them ready at a moment's notice. They also pocketed the violet-coloured tubes, wrapping them in clean cotton handkerchiefs; the sedative within them, though tricky to apply to the subject, was said to be powerful.

They felt certain of success. They would start their search tomorrow, and when they found their quarry, they would be ready to act.

After clearing the shed of any hint of their presence, Verdi and Azzurro followed the recommendations of their temporary landlord, and found their way to a cafe that did a reasonable local-style chicken with dumplings. It had been a long day; they were glad to see an end to it. Azzurro wanted to stretch his legs, so they chose a return route that led them by the river. It was a pleasant walk.

Passing a well-lit restaurant, they nearly collided with a young couple who were exiting, hand in hand, laughing and a little unsteady on their feet. Azzurro politely doffed his hat. The young woman gave him a brilliant smile before the pair moved on.

Beside him, Verdi drew in his breath in a loud hiss. It was she, the English principessa! She was with a man, just as that rascal in Budapest had said! There was no sign of the other young lady Squadra Rossi had reported. Azzurro felt his feet rooted to the ground.

Keeping to the shadows, Verdi took off behind the couple. She was unchaperoned: easier for the mission, but shocking to see what those English would allow. One would never, upon pain of death, question the Emperor; but one had to wonder what he was thinking, to want a brazen English hussy as a bride for his grandson. Principe Gusto was a fine young man, if a little retiring. He should have a principessa worthy of him, an immaculate jewel. This one was beautiful, and she would bring Britannia back to the Empire, but someone would need to train her to be a good Roman wife.

"What do we do?" Azzurro had caught up with him.

"What do you think? We take the Principessa."

"What about the man? Kill him?"

"We don't know who he is. It seems a very bad idea to kill someone who is with a principessa."

"What then? Knock him out? Stage a robbery?"

Verdi couldn't waste too much time thinking. They were on a dark street with the Principessa in their sights, and no bystanders other than her escort. He did not want to lose this opportunity. "We take him, too," he said impetuously. As soon as he said it, he could see the wisdom. "The instructions were to take the Principessa to the Sybil. She knows the secrets of the mind. We'll take him to her and she can decide what to do."

They were rounding a corner. Azzurro could see that they were nearing a busier street. "When?" he asked.

"Now. Distract the man," Verdi said. "I'll get the Principessa. Then you get him."

Azzurro nodded and started running toward the couple. "Sir!" he called out, using the English he had learned from a lonely widow in a resort in the Swiss mountains. "Sir, you drop this!" He held his handkerchief in his outstretched hand.

The couple stopped and looked at him, perplexed.

"I didn't lose anything," the young man began.

"Check your coat," the girl advised. "Maybe you did without…Oh!" As he started to check his pockets, Verdi walked briskly by and bumped into her.

"'Scusi, Miss," Verdi said, making a great show of bowing. "So very sorry."

"Oh that's quite alright," she said vaguely, her attention on Azzurro and her escort.

"No, no," Verdi insisted. "Make apologies!" He took her hand as if to kiss it and stuck her with the needle in his ring.

"Ow!" she cried. "What was…?"

Verdi sped off, leaving her staring around in confusion.

Her young man spun round to face her. "Claude! Are you alright? What happened?"

"I don't know. This man ran into me. He was so apologetic, but something stuck me and…I don't know," she started to waver a bit. "I think perhaps that was too much wine." She stumbled forward, and he caught her.

"Help me!" the young man said to Azzurro.

Instead, Azzurro reached around and covered his face with a handkerchief drenched in ether. The young man kicked out and struggled. The young woman was starting to crumple. Verdi reappeared in time to catch her and support her tenderly to the shadow side of a large statue nearby. Azzurro dragged the limp body of the young man to the same spot and placed him close against the base of the plinth. Azzurro sat himself on the steps, his back against the plinth, the girl leaning against him. To the casual passerby, they would appear to be a couple sleeping off the night's indulgence. The young man was completely concealed by her skirts and the shadows.

Verdi ran back to the painter's house to get the carriage and driver. Fortune had favoured them tonight.

❧

After Piper had them well on the road, he had been able to relax his vigilance long enough to provide a brief history of Augustus's plot against the royal family. Maud, who had been protected from this information up until now, was not surprised to learn that her grandmother had made multiple refusals of the suit for her hand.

"It's pointless to ask Grandmama twice," she observed. "Once she's made a decision, she only gets more determined if you ask again." She seemed oblivious to her own identical proclivity.

When he reached the part about 'aud in B_est,' Maud rocked with laughter until her breath came in gulps.

Gertrude was impressed with Madame Blavatsky's prophecy. "Don't mock," she scolded Maud. "There are mysteries beyond our comprehension."

"Is that what they teach you at Oxford?" Maud scoffed.

"I've learned enough to know my limitations."

Maud thought it was hilarious bunk. The woman had made a lucky guess. She admired the fortuneteller's nerve, though. She hoped that any agents sent to Bucharest would gather proof that she'd been there and earn the woman a fat reward.

Piper's horse-drawn carriage might have been the most secure option, but close quarters and bumpy roads made for a relentless two days.

Gertrude would have been content to read for most of her waking hours. She had indeed produced an onionskin travel copy of Burton for that purpose, but Maud required conversation. An attempt to amuse her by reading the story of "The Sweep and the Noble Lady" failed, to the gratitude of the embarrassed Piper (Burton was rather more racy than any of them had anticipated). In the end, they exchanged senseless gossip about people they scarcely knew and didn't much care about. Gertrude told some amusing second-hand stories of undergraduate scrapes at Oxford. Piper chimed in with his own carefully edited youthful escapades.

They were all a little hoarse, as well as bone sore, when they finally pulled up at the Embassy door. No one was in the best of tempers.

Despite the odd hour, Ambassador Hutchinson and his wife were there to greet them, along with a man who was introduced to Maud as "Sir Alastair Menzies, a trusted friend of your grandmother." He was a neat but unimpressive figure, Maud thought; not much taller than she, although she acknowledged herself to be tall for a woman. He had a bent nose and a somewhat whimsical expression, but his eyes were like steel and she found herself shrinking under his steady gaze.

Dinner had been held for their arrival. Frequently throughout the meal, Maud noticed Sir Alastair, who did not dine but merely sipped companionably at his claret, looking at her in quite a considering manner. It became most annoying. Putting down her fork, she turned to challenge him. "I find your attention most impudent, sir," she said in her haughtiest manner.

Sir Alastair only looked at her more frankly still. "My sincerest apologies, Your Royal Highness," he said, with what might have been either a nod or a bow. "I mean no offense. It was only that you bring to mind…"

"My grandmother," she sighed, exasperated. She was tired of hearing how much she resembled the Queen. It made her have to imagine that someday she would be as old as the Queen was now. This was something not at all pleasant to contemplate.

Gertrude had been longing to go up to bed for some time, but couldn't leave the table until Maud did. She politely muffled another yawn. This time, Maud noticed. Rising, she graciously thanked her hosts for their generous welcome and bid the table good evening. Adding her own thanks, Gertrude quickly followed.

The gentlemen had just resumed their seats when the Princess reappeared in the doorway. "Captain Piper," she instructed; "I should like to do some shopping tomorrow, and show Miss Bell some of the sights of the city."

Piper looked at Frank. "I believe it best for Princess Maud to return to London at once," he said, "but the decision is in Sir Alastair's hands."

Maud was not pleased. "I wish it," she said.

"Then I hope we will be able to make it so," Sir Alastair said mildly. "Your Royal Highness shall have your answer in the morning. Captain Piper and I have much to discuss tonight."

There wasn't anything to be said to that, so Maud swept off without another word.

"Was the Queen really so much like the Princess?" Piper asked, watching after her.

"Oh yes!" Mrs. Hutchinson was a near contemporary of Her Majesty's. "As alike as two peas. But then her father, the late Prince of Wales, God rest his soul, greatly favoured his mother. Not a bit of blessed Prince Albert about him. In looks, that is to say. He had many of his father's other fine qualities."

Piper had been a mere boy when the Prince Consort died, but the two older men nodded in solemn agreement. The reverent silence put an end to dinner. After putting a small parlour at the disposal of their guests, the Ambassadorial couple went up to their own beds.

Frank turned to the liveried ancient who had remained behind. "I apologize in advance for the inconvenience, but the Captain and I have much to catch up on. I expect we may be here deep into the night. Is the kitchen up to a wee pot of coffee?"

The answer was affirmative and came with a smart salute. Ambassador Hutchinson, he said, had anticipated the need and assigned him to be available throughout the night to wait on them. He, Lummis, had been the Ambassador's batman during the war, he explained, and was a true English soldier proud to serve the honoured gentlemen who were no doubt on the Queen's own business. The door closed behind the old soldier.

Frank took off his coat, turned up his sleeves and poked up the fire. "Might as well make yourself comfortable, Piper," he advised. "It's going to be a long night."

§ॐ

Minutes after the Conte di Bari arrived at his office, his Praefectus brought the tray with his small pot of coffee, morning pastry, and the first messages of the day.

There was a wire that had arrived an hour or two before, in the code restricted to the Emperor's business. The Conte got out the code pad to work it out. It was from Squadra Verde, announcing that they had found the Princess in Prague and were already on their way to Dubrovnik.

It was wonderful news, but a little puzzling; he could have sworn that he'd sent Verde to Budapest. Wasn't it Rosso, the Bucharest team, that he had just dispatched to Prague?

Confused but jubilant, he scrawled a quick note for the Emperor and sent his Praefectus to get Rappaccini. The Emperor would always remember this messenger. It should be someone worthy of the honour.

"A most felicitous moment!" de Bari told the bowing centurion. "I need you to leave at once. For Roma. Deliver this into the hands of the Emperor himself."

"Si, Eminenza."

"From there, you will leave for Ragusa to meet Squadra Verde at Madame Blavatsky's and escort the Principessa to Roma."

"The Principessa?" Rappaccini came instantly alert.

"Yes," the Conte said proudly. "*Vittoria!*"

Maud flounced into Gertrude's bedroom. Having slept well and breakfasted to her taste, she was ready to meet the day. She was extremely disgruntled that no one seemed to want to meet it with her.

"There has been no word from Captain Piper," she sniffed.

Gertrude, also up and dressed, was happily reading a two-day old copy of the *The London Times* with her morning tea. She put down the paper and offered the Princess a pastry. "They're delicious," she said.

"I've had some," Maud replied. "And now I'm ready to go to the shops."

"I assume he's still sleeping," Gertrude said.

"At this hour?" Maud reached for the bell-pull.

"He may have kept late hours. I formed the impression that he and Sir Alastair had business to transact. You do understand that Captain Piper is a spy?"

Maud hadn't thought about it. "I'm not an idiot," she retorted automatically.

Gertrude sighed at this reminder of their briefly shared tutorials. "I didn't say you were. I was merely confirming…"

"Do you think Sir Alastair is as well?"

"I should be very surprised if he were not."

"Trusted friend of my grandmother's indeed! He examined me as though I were some kind of specimen in a jar. It was extremely presumptuous."

A maid knocked and entered. "Madame?" she said, curtseying.

"Is Captain Piper awake?" Maud demanded loftily.

"No, Madame," the girl replied, looking down at her apron. "We've been instructed not to disturb him."

Gertrude was curious now. "Did Sir Alastair stay the night?"

The maid looked uncomfortable. "Mr. Lummis was to wait on him. He wasn't at breakfast." The two young ladies stared at her, waiting for more. She squirmed miserably, trying to think of something else to tell them. "We cleaned the hearth this morning and it was cold." She brightened. "So they were long gone by seven!" she concluded triumphantly. Maud waved for her to go and with a wash of gratitude across her face, she scampered off.

"What if he doesn't waken until noon?" Maud said, thinking of her own post-ball lie-ins.

"Then we'll have to wait until after noon," Gertrude said calmly. "Why don't we go downstairs and pay a call on Mrs. Hutchinson?"

"If we wanted to sit around talking with dowagers, we might as well have stayed in Bucharest," Maud pouted. "I want to go to Karlova and look in the shops! And I so wanted to take you to see the astronomical clock," she added cunningly. "It isn't far from here at all."

"It isn't?" Gertrude couldn't keep herself from asking. She did want to see that clock.

"Well, we did arrive at night so I don't know exactly where we are, but it can't be too far," she said airily. "I'm certain I can find it easily. I have been to this city before, you know. Many times." Only two or three, and never without at least one parent and a retinue, but why confuse the issue with details. "We'll pop out for an hour or so and be back in time for luncheon. By then Captain Piper will surely be awake and we'll learn what else we'll have time to see."

"We shouldn't go out on our own," Gertrude said. "It might be dangerous. We should wait for the Captain." She could see the mulish set of Maud's mouth. "Oh, just this once, can't we please do things my way?"

"What if he says we have to leave immediately and we don't get to do anything at all?" Maud asked. "It's not as if anyone knows we're in Prague," she added, exasperated. "I'm supposed to be in B_est, remember?"

It was a waste of breath to argue with someone who never gave way. Gertrude threw up her hands in resignation. Maud flashed her an exuberant smile and flew back to her room to grab a shawl and her purse before she could raise another objection.

"We should at least leave a note for him, in case he wakens before we return," Gertrude muttered, opening the lap desk on the bedside table.

Still tired when he woke, just before ten, Piper obliged himself to shave and dress before he rang for a pot of tea. It was the best way to be sure of not putting his head down on the pillow and falling back asleep.

The maid arrived with a full breakfast tray, including a folded note. Piper's head was clouded from trying to keep up with the legendary Sir Alastair Menzies all night. He moved slowly, adding his cream and sugar, taking little tastes of the different preserves to see which would make more of a treat on his toast, and finally nibbled at a bit of bacon. Unfolding the note, he prepared to tangle with a morning missive from Sir Alastair.

"Gone shopping. Be back soon."

Dropping the bacon, he leapt to his feet and rang the bell. His pulse racing, he pulled on his boots and started to load his arsenal into the proper pockets.

The maid returned as he was slipping his loaded pistol into his belt. She gave a little scream.

"Is this true?" he asked, waving the note in his other hand.

"I'm sorry sir, I don't know what you're asking!" Someone had left the note in the kitchens, to be taken up whenever the Captain rang for breakfast. "I'll have to ask Mr…" She started to leave. To her horror, the Captain came after her. Despite her protests he followed her all the way down to the kitchens, where he proceeded to question everyone he met until he found the maid who had taken the note from the Princess.

He and Sir Alastair had decided to allow the young ladies a well-escorted propitiatory outing to a jeweler recommended by Mrs. Hutchinson, then remove them to the aership directly after luncheon. They hadn't anticipated being outflanked. Piper didn't know what would be best to do, but he sensed that inaction would be worst of all.

The girls had left only half an hour before, and on foot. He thought about their long heavy skirts, the tiny waists that didn't allow for deep breaths and the dainty boots of soft leather. How quickly could they walk? They couldn't be far, but he had no idea which way they might have gone. If he went one way and perhaps sent Lummis another…He was about to dash off a message for Menzies to come right away, when he realized he had no idea where the senior spy was billeted; when they'd parted at dawn, he'd said only that he was going to catch some shut eye and would be back by eleven.

There was nothing for it. While waiting for the old soldier to report, Piper put together a reasonable memo and left it with the butler to be given to Menzies the moment he arrived. There was not a moment to lose.

Having slept past his usual hour, Frank wasn't surprised to find Claude's room was empty. Her bed was already neatly made up and everything was tidy.

It was going to be a busy day. First he would see Piper off with the Princess and Miss Bell, then he could decide what to do about his daughter. The minute he'd seen Maud, he had realized his initial plan wasn't feasible. When she'd paraded into the Embassy last night, only a lifetime of discipline had enabled him to contain his shock. For a moment, he would have sworn he was staring at his own child, the resemblance was that strong. The longer he'd looked, the more distinctions he'd noted, the colour of their eyes being the most obvious. The other differences were more subtle ones of expression and bearing. The tall, slim frame, the abundant chestnut hair, the shape of the face and features were astoundingly alike.

He couldn't put them on the yacht together. He could not risk Claude catching even a glimpse of Maud, nor the other way around. Nor did he dare have his lass meet up with anyone who knew the Princess. No, he would have to see Princess Maud and her friend safely off to London with Piper, and then he would get his daughter to France. Nan could meet them there. He'd already wired Pinkerton to say he'd be remaining in Prague for a few days.

No doubt the Princess would have to have her shopping before she left. Before he left for the Embassy, he would leave a note for Claude at the desk, in case he missed her at the workshop. He'd ask her to avoid tourist sites and the shops until they had a chance to speak.

"Such a civilized mode of travel," Rossi remarked as he and Arancione left the rosewood-paneled dining car and returned to their compartment to put away the last of their possessions. They had been able to book a first class sleeper car and pass the night in comfort. Breakfast was fine enough to meet even Rossi's high standards. The train was due to pull into Prague in twenty minutes.

They exited the terminal as Professor Ross, a Doctor of Natural Science, and his assistant, Monsieur d'Arancione and proceeded to a small hotel near the University that catered to visiting academics. Leaving their bags, they decided to stretch their legs and refresh their recollections of the city.

Arancione had been stationed here in his first years of active duty. It looked much the same, he was pleased to note. He wondered if he would be able to find the coffeehouse he remembered so fondly. They turned a familiar-looking corner. He thought the place might be nearby, perhaps another block or two. "Look for a green door," he told Rossi. "And the name in gold on the windows."

Rossi forbore to point out that all the windows had names in gold. It was a pleasant day for a walk. When his lieutenant tired of his search, they could stop at the first agreeable cafe for their coffee. He noticed Arancione had stopped a little behind him and was staring fixedly at a building across the street. Perhaps he had found his coffeehouse after all.

Rossi walked back and tapped him on the shoulder.

"The jewelry shop across the way," he said in a strangled whisper, not moving his eyes.

Rossi followed his stare. Two young women in mouse-coloured walking suits were standing in front of a shop window, admiring the goods on display. Rossi gave a grunt of triumph. They had spent enough time memorizing her features to be certain beyond any doubt. They had her, the English princess herself!

"She was supposed to be in Budapest," Arancione said in wonder. "Andretta told us the little girl said…"

"The little girl was wrong," Rossi hissed. "And the old biddy in Dubrovnik made a mistake. What does that matter? She's ours!"

They could hardly believe their eyes. Squadra Rosso had been sidelined, sent to hunt up some scientist for Haussmann, but the grand prize was so close they were breathing the same air. They ambled a little closer, remaining on their own side of the street and staying a little behind the girls. Their quarry was in site, but how were they to capture her?

The shop door opened with a gay little tinkle and the girls were welcomed by a smiling old man. Rossi and Arancione hoped he was one of those shopkeepers who liked to charm ladies out of their purses. If so, the girls might be in there an hour or more. Every minute they were behind that door meant more time for Squadra Rosso to come up with a plan.

❧

Frank waited in the Embassy sitting room, reading the Captain's memorandum over and over. The girl is told that her life is in danger and she waltzes out on a shopping expedition? The Queen's reservations were well founded; the irresponsibility of this young woman was staggering.

The Ambassador poked his head in again. "Any word from Piper or Lummis?"

Frank shook his head.

"Piper wasn't half an hour behind them. How quickly could they walk?" Hutchinson thought he was being comforting, but Frank was starting to have a bad feeling.

"Why are you so certain they were walking?"

"They didn't ask for a carriage, and all the horses are accounted for."

"They might have walked for a wee bit and then hired a cab."

The Ambassador shook his head. "I expect the Princess wouldn't know a cab from a milk cart."

Frank raised his eyebrows. "Perhaps. But Miss Bell is presumably familiar with both. We need to send out search teams. I'd rather make a sooch over nothing than rue that we hadn't. Call in your most discreet men—embassy staff, any military men we have available."

While the Ambassador was assembling his men, Lummis dragged in, distraught at having let down the Queen. Despite Frank's urging, he refused to sit but gave his report leaning on the back of a chair, blinking his rheumy eyes to hold back tears. Frank listened closely, making notes, and began a rough map that centered on the embassy.

The searchers, sent out in pairs, were assigned their routes, given detailed descriptions of the missing girls and ordered to report in at one hour intervals. With Piper still unaccounted for, Frank himself took the most promising lead, an area of streets that Mrs. Hutchinson considered would be most attractive to young ladies. Despite his protests that he only needed a cup of tea to be as good as new, Lummis was appointed to help the Ambassador monitor messages and update the map.

The girls left the shop, the Princess giggling and touching her hand to her neck; presumably they'd made a purchase. From his post across the street, Arancione waited until they had been welcomed into another shop.

He ran back to the jewelry store. It was a risk, exposing himself this way, but it was necessary to their plan.

"My betrothed!" he cried, apparently frantic. "Have you seen her? There's been...oh!" The proprietor tried to calm him and offered a drink of water. He shook his head. "A beautiful young woman, tall like a goddess, hair like an autumn leaf. I know that she and her cousin were coming this way after we left the coffeehouse. She wanted to buy a necklace to wear at our wedding." A spark of interest flared in the old man's eyes but he said nothing. He was a careful one, this jeweler. Arancione resumed, glad he had concocted a story more elaborate than Rossi had urged. "Her father...it was all so sudden! Reading the newspaper. It dropped from his hands, he held his chest and then...I must find her before it's too late for her to say goodbye!" It was histrionic, but he knew he didn't make a romantic figure of a bridegroom; an abundance of passion might lend him sufficient verisimilitude.

Perhaps the old jeweler was an opera lover. The drama touched something in him and he responded. "She was here, yes. You only just missed her."

"A blessing on you!" Arancione cried, and fled the shop without waiting for further details.

Rossi had followed the girls, occasionally turning his head to look back. When he could see Arancione running towards him, it was time to approach them.

What Rossi did not see was the soldier rounding the corner. And in the slice of street visible to him, the soldier saw no one apart from a familiar pair of young women, a pair he could cheerfully have throttled but who would be gratefully taken into his safe custody whether they liked it or not!

"Princess!" Rossi said in English, politely tipping his hat and bowing. As expected, she turned to him, startled.

"Do I know you?"

Her companion turned as well, giving Arancione the opportunity to arrive beside her unseen and stick her with the pin that had held the boutonnière in his lapel. There had been no time for them to return to their rooms and get their full kit, but they had the contents of Rossi's snuffbox: a folded paper of sleeping powder, and a bit of silk that had been soaked in a hypnotic drug and stored in a tightly-stoppered silver tube. They had wiped two pins with the silk, one for each girl. Rossi had decided they should also take Miss Bell. Having her there might calm the Principessa and make things easier for them once she was awake. Besides, they would have to drug her in order to take the Principessa. Rossi had become sentimental since the birth of his own small daughter; he wouldn't like to leave a drugged girl wandering the streets of Prague alone.

"Ow!" Gertrude exclaimed, slapping the back of her neck and whirling angrily to face him. "What was that?!"

"*Una vespa*," Arancione said, turning out his hands apologetically. The pin dropped between his fingers to the ground, unnoticed.

"You're Italian!" she said accusingly, in that language. "Who in the world are you?! Leave us alone!

The Princess turned as well, providing Rossi with his own target. She shrieked at the pinch, but he quickly covered her mouth with his hand and pulled her towards him, into a nearby alley. His lieutenant did likewise.

Captain Piper burst into the dark alley like an avenging angel, his pistol extended and ready. He had a clear view of Rossi then, and would have shot at once; but the Italian was holding up the Princess, on whom the drug had taken effect almost instantaneously. The girl was like a shield. Gertrude saw that Piper dared not shoot for fear of hitting her.

Arancione's hand was still pressed against Gertrude's mouth. She bit down hard and tried to move towards Maud, to push her out of the way. But the drug was affecting her too. She stumbled clumsily and fell. Her fall was enough of a distraction to enable Arancione to slip behind Piper and, with an elegant but brutal gesture, slash his throat with a stiletto.

Piper crumpled silently to the cobbles, his blood pooling around him, his hand reaching out as if he might still save them. The girls watched him fall, the horror burned into their minds as their own bodies grew too distant to feel.

Within minutes, the girls, now limp and easily managed, were guided by Arancione back to the shop, where the sympathetic jeweler was more than willing to have the presumably bereaved maidens wait while his shop assistant found them a cab.

Lavishly tipping the assistant, and thanking the jeweler again, Arancione helped the girls into the cab. He loudly gave the driver the name of a fashionable hotel but once they were sufficiently far from the store, he ordered the cab to drive them instead to a small square by the Manes Bridge. He tipped the driver enough to please him but not so much that his curiosity was raised.

Frank and his footman went from door to door, questioning storekeepers and waitresses. It was unfortunate that there had been no maids familiar with their wardrobes, who might have been able to extrapolate what the Maud and Miss Bell might be wearing; the waitresses were more prone to notice a bonnet or gown than another girl's face and it seemed there had been numerous pairs of young ladies exploring the offerings of this neighborhood.

At the sixth or seventh shop, a milliner thought she might have seen the gentleman's niece...but perhaps not. "If only," she said apologetically, "you had her likeness." Frank thanked her and was about to leave when inspiration struck. He reached into his breast pocket and pulled out his leather wallet. Charlotte might have Claude's studio portrait, but he had the photograph that Firewalker had taken of the two of them at her college commencement. To someone who had met only one of them, it would be the same face.

The milliner's face brightened. "Oh yes!" she said. "She was here. With her friend. They were very interested in this bonnet," she pointed to a gooseberry velvet confection with a mauve veil. "They were going to Old Town Square to see the clock. She said they might return on their way back."

Partly by way of thanks and partly from superstition, Frank bought the bonnet. He gave it to the footman and told him to return to the embassy with a message that the search should concentrate on Old Town. He himself continued along the current street in that direction. If they had stopped at one shop, they were likely to have stopped at others. He had no Czech, but his German was up to the task. Entering each establishment, he showed his daughter's picture. Two other shopkeepers recognized Claude's face. Frank was headed in the right direction. With growing confidence, he pushed open the door of an elegant jewelry shop. The bell tinkled gaily.

"Oh yes!" the jewelry said, with alacrity. "She was here with her cousin and her young man. Such a tragedy, her poor father!"

It was clear that the worst had happened. The Princess and Miss Bell had been kidnapped. By "such an unassuming gentleman," average height and weight, dark-haired and clean-shaven, who spoke good Czech, albeit "with a foreign accent." The story of the stricken father, and the jeweler's description of the girls' dazed state, indicated they had been drugged and the abduction well planned, likely with a confederate. The jeweler's assistant confirmed that he had found the cab two streets away and that the driver was known to him. The assistant was tipped again by Frank and given promise of a more significant reward if he would find the driver and see him to the British Embassy.

Having gleaned all that he could from this source, Frank set off for the square to rendezvous with the footman and intercept the other teams that would eventually congregate there. On the way, he stopped to down a sausage roll and short stein of pilsner. He hadn't eaten since the breakfast that now seemed a day away. He was glad he'd left a message for Claude.

He would never make it to Tesla's workshop today. It would be a miracle if he made it to dinner.

Sitting on a bench with two catatonic young ladies, Arancione felt the minutes stretch to hours. At one point, Miss Bell's eyes began to focus. Fortunately, Rossi had left him the snuffbox. He had no more pins but, after first cleaning his stiletto on the grass, wiped the tip with the silk and, with apologies to the young lady, stuck her finger. He hadn't been certain there was enough of the drug left on the silk, but her eyes glazed over again. The Princess never even blinked; either Rossi's pin had had a stronger coating or else she had a more susceptible constitution.

Finally, or what felt like a half a day later to Arancione, Rossi arrived in a hired carriage. He settled the young women as comfortably as he could. "The powder," Rossi reminded, passing him a flask of lukewarm tea and a tin cup.

Arancione poured the contents of the folded paper into the bottle and shook it to dissolve the powder. He poured some of the tea into the cup and brought it to the Princess's lips. "Drink, Principessa," he said compassionately. "It will make you feel better." She swallowed obediently, and he tilted the cup until it was drained. He repeated the process with Miss Bell, who required a bit more coaxing but eventually relented. Both the young women gradually slipped into a deep sleep. Only then did Arancione allow himself to relax.

Every few hours, Rossi would check the girls' colour and lift their eyelids. When he judged it necessary, he would inject the girls with an opiate to keep them asleep. When they stopped to change horses in Moravia, he sent Arancione to find a telegraph office and send a message to their chief.

The Conte di Bari studied the message his Praefectus had just handed him and rubbed his head in confusion. Sent from Olmütz and signed "Rosso", it claimed to have acquired the English princess. But Verde had already procured the Princess. And both were claiming to have found her in Prague.

He was glad he already had Rappaccini on his way to Ragusa. Such a clever young man. Rappaccini would sort things out. Really he was due a promotion.

At first, the cab driver was reluctant to speak. He was intimidated by the Embassy, both the grandeur and the knowledge that it had something to do with kings and possibly the army. The word 'kidnapping' frightened him beyond silence into garrulousness and made him spill every detail he could muster. He kept reiterating his own innocence. How was he to have known? The young man was so well mannered, and the ladies more sad (at least that was how he'd interpreted their lassitude) than distressed. He'd known something was up, but had thought it was a simple elopement, the young ladies a touch melancholy at leaving home. He'd seen others…

Frank cut him off again and sent him on his way. They had learned all that they could from this avenue of questioning. They could rough in a timeline. Frank had been driven to the park, but found nothing but a scrap of yellow silk. With a description cobbled together from the jeweler's and driver's testimonies, search teams had been sent to make the rounds of hotels and stables to learn if anyone had seen the man, or rented him a carriage or a room.

Piper still hadn't surfaced. Frank was hopeful that the resourceful young captain had spotted the abductors and was even now tailing them somewhere. Lummis dozed in a chair by the embassy's telegraphy key, waiting for a message.

Now it was time to draft and encode a lengthy message to Pinkerton. Not for the first time, Frank wished there was a way that a telephone might be used to convey such messages. If only there were a way to secure the lines against eavesdroppers. Perhaps, once those automatons were armed, Tesla and he might turn their attentions to that development.

It was past nine by the time Frank had decided there was nothing more to be done that day and ordered everyone to get some rest.

"Any messages?" he asked the night clerk who handed him his room key.

"Only for Miss Monteith," the man replied.

"From Miss Monteith?" Frank repeated, confused.

"No, sir," the man corrected him. "For Miss Monteith." He handed Frank two messages—the two messages Frank had left for Claude—and stared as Frank ran from the hotel.

By the time he reached the workshop, Frank's chest was heaving. He pounded on the locked door loud enough to wake a sleeping Tesla. There was no response. All the windows faced on the rear courtyard, which could not be reached from the street. He knelt on the ground, peering through the crack beneath the door to see if there were any light coming from inside. There was nothing, not a sign of life.

With a sinking feeling, he went to the restaurant where they had eaten the night before. They weren't there, nor were they in the coffee house Claude had singled out for their admirable pancakes. He could see his daughter's face in front of him, exuberant at having discovered something special in a strange city. He felt a crease of pain in his chest and stumbled back to the hotel.

The night clerk confirmed the worst. Claude had not returned to the hotel. She had not, it turned out, returned to the hotel the night before. What he'd mistaken for a neatly made bed was a bed that hadn't been slept in. All day long, when he'd imagined her working happily and safely with Tesla, she'd been...where?

Had Tesla had been found, as he'd feared? Had she been with him and Augustus's men taken her as well? Or had she been injured during the incident—he refused to contemplate the more extreme possibility—and left in some dark corner of the city? He would have to begin at the hospitals. He needed someone who knew the city. Perhaps that cab driver.

Spinning around to head back out into the streets, trying to ignore the pain in his chest, Frank nearly collided with one of the Embassy pages. The boy had been running hard and he seemed about to cry.

"Please, Sir Alastair," he panted, "you have to come at once. It's horrible. They've found Captain Piper."

A lesser man would have bellowed and raged. Frank nodded once and followed the boy.

8 - THE WALLED CITY

With her first slight tickle of awareness, Claude felt a gentle rocking. At first, her befuddled mind supposed she was in a cradle. If she opened her eyes, she would see her father smiling down at her; or maybe the face of the mother who had died when she was born. The sheer impossibility of this last thought jolted her fully awake.

She sat up carefully, her body heavy and slow. There seemed to be daylight coming from somewhere, but she couldn't see a window; something overhead was blocking her view. Swinging her legs over the mattress, she leaned forward and craned to see the rest of the room. The soles of her boots pressed against the floor. She didn't need to be able to see the water to confirm its presence beneath her; she felt it. She was on a ship. The daylight was slipping through the slats of a shutter that was nailed over a porthole. What was she doing on a ship? And where was Nikola?

She tried to clear her head. They had left the restaurant. They were walking to the hotel when something...some man...Something about a coach, too. Or had that been another dream? Darkness and the clatter of horses on a hard road. It had seemed so real. She remembered having thought how cruel it was, to force horses to gallop over stone. Yes, and she'd cried out. Then there had been a struggle of some kind. Nikola yelling; she remembered Nikola yelling. She had been thrown across something and hit her elbow against a sharp corner. It had hurt. And then this odd smell, sweet as decay, followed by...nothing. A dark blank.

Claude hugged herself for comfort and nearly yelped at the pain. Rolling up her sleeve, she saw the small purple bruise. Not a dream then. She had been rendered unconscious. For how long, she had no way of knowing. Now she was awake and on a ship, and she didn't know why or how she'd gotten here.

She was extraordinarily thirsty. There was a pitcher of water on the table. She poured a glass and was about to drain it when she realized that it might be drugged. Something had kept her asleep long enough to get her here. In dismay, she dropped the glass. It shattered. The noise brought people running.

She snatched up a large vicious-looking shard and thrust it into her chignon, then went for a woman's best defense: she sat on the bunk, shrank back against the wall, and willed herself to look meek and terrified. The door flew open. Two men burst in, sabers drawn, yelling in some language that wasn't English but sounded familiar. It was Italian, though not quite as Signora Murphy had taught it. With a thrill she understood: these must be the Emperor's men; they had found Nikola, just as he'd feared; she'd been with him, so they'd taken her as well. She raised a shaking arm to point at the broken glass and started to cry piteously, a tactic filched from La Fortescue's arsenal. The burly man grunted with disgust and left the room. The other waited in the doorway with what might have been some sympathy. He stayed to watch over the servant who arrived to clear the mess. When a new glass was brought, he poured some water and handed it to her. She mimed her fear well enough that he understood and took a sip to show her that it was safe.

So they weren't planning to drug her again, at least not now. She took the glass with gratitude. He nodded respectfully and left. She heard the door lock behind him.

Her mind raced in every direction at once. If Nikola was a danger to the Emperor, then so was she. They were...Oh! She felt her face grown hot. This was not the time to wonder about that! Nikola and she were *friends*, she told herself firmly; they were friends and she had been working as his assistant. The Emperor's men might have assumed the former but certainly not the latter. Unless they knew she was the daughter of Franklin Monteith. If they didn't know who she was, they would never guess that a young woman might be an engineer. Did they know her name? She would need to listen carefully, and be very certain not to volunteer it. She was not going to volunteer a thing, not even that she understood Italian. She would have to find a way to make certain that Nikola kept her name to himself. Unless Nikola were dead.

No! That was the thinking of a frightened girl, not a trained consulting detective. Fear caused panic. Panic only got in the way of facts and logic. Of course Nikola was alive. They said the Emperor Augustus was crazy, not that he was stupid. He had needed Nikola's genius once before, and now he wanted to be sure he would always have it at his command. His men would have been ordered to keep Nikola alive. That was only logical.

So she would not be foolish. She must look at this as a puzzle to solve. What would be wise to do next?

It was tempting to consider how she might break through the shutter and open the porthole but, with or without Nikola, there was no sense in trying to escape off a boat. She was a strong swimmer, but even if she knew where they were holding Nikola and could miraculously free him, the chances were that, like most Europeans, he couldn't swim. And without knowing where they were or where they were headed, even if she could escape alone she would have no way of sending help. That was another thing she'd been taught: when caught in a moving vehicle, wait; eventually you'll come to a stop.

Sipping her water, she calmly began to inventory her assets, the way Father and Leski had trained her to do. She was glad they had gone to dinner straight from the workshop. She was wearing her walking suit and boots; if the opportunity arose, she would be able to run. Her chatelaine, which had any number of useful items, was still hooked to her belt. Clearly her captors hadn't seen it or (so insulting!) had thought a woman's bits and bobs posed no risk of either fight or flight. And now she had a lovely jagged piece of glass. She slid it out of her hair and examined it with grim satisfaction; it was, in essence, a dagger. Tearing a scrap from the flounce of her petticoat, she wrapped the glass carefully before tucking it away in a pocket that she'd sewn into her stays for just such a purpose. There was one thing to be said about women's clothing: lots of hiding places, especially if one had some imagination and planned for every contingency.

She checked the cabin for anything that might be of use. Someone had diligently emptied all the drawers, leaving nothing so much as stray pencil. A fruitless rummage through the bed clothes only further proved the efficiency of the housekeeping. Apart from the water, there was nothing but a basket of grapes. Useless. Unlike nuts or even crab apples, you couldn't even hoard grapes for later. She pocketed the linen napkin, more as a matter of principal than for any purpose it might serve.

With the boarded porthole obscuring the view and not even the presumed courtesy of a Bible to divert her, Claude felt her eyes begin to close. She resisted only briefly. Whatever she had been given was probably still working its way through her system. There was nothing else she could do; at least she could let her body try to recover and prepare for whatever might happen next.

❧

The two men were brisk but courteous as they handed her up onto the quay. She still didn't know where Nikola was and she couldn't understand why they kept calling her "Principessa," but she kept silent. Watch, listen and learn, that's what Father always said.

There was plenty to see. Though she'd read about walled cities, a real one was different from what she had envisioned. She had fancied they must be dark and gloomy, but this place was full of light and life.

It must have been late afternoon. As they passed through the gates, she noticed a lovely square and a broad, straight avenue, all paved in gleaming white stone that she took at first for solid marble. The city was bustling. People were clustered around the large fountain and in front of the old church. More people strolled along the avenue as, to the casual eye, she and her escorts would appear to be doing. It was reassuring to see so many people. Everyone seemed prosperous and beautifully dressed. Wherever they were, it was clearly a city of culture with a large number of shops and pâtissieries. There was music playing somewhere nearby, the kind of music she associated with bandshells and ice cream. At least it didn't seem that she'd been smuggled off to meet some ignominious death. This made her feel quite cheerful.

It was all so fascinating that she didn't know where to look first. She was grateful that her escorts didn't seem to mind. It would have been horrid to have been blindfolded and miss all of this. The buildings here were close together and very old, possibly even older than in Prague, but as clean and well-kempt as if brand new. They passed the façade of a building that seemed particularly ancient, even for here. She craned her neck to look around the corner at its side and saw that the streets ran up the side of a hill.

"Principessa, per favour," the handsome one said, taking her elbow and steering her off the avenue. They led her through a warren of narrow streets, much of it uphill. Ultimately, she was pushed through a stone archway into a small courtyard that was sweet with orange blossom. A bell was rung, almost as if they were paying a call. A tall, tea-skinned man came to greet them.

This man also addressed her as "Principessa," bowing low and setting the sleeves of his spice-coloured kaftan to fluttering. He gestured for her to follow him inside. "Please to sit," he said, pointing to a dark, carved chair that reminded her of the idol on the landing back home.

She sat obediently, folding her hands demurely in her lap, and took stock of what she had learned along the way. The people in the street had reminded her of the people in Prague, not at all exotic, just subtly different from the people back home. She had heard a strange language, as well as some more of what she was now certain was Italian, though it was odd to hear it spoken so glibly. This confirmed her hunch that this abduction had to do with the Emperor. No one seemed to want to harm her—yet. Other than having been drugged and kidnapped, she had been treated with care. Right now, she was sitting in what seemed to be someone's home, albeit an eccentric one. The large circular entry hall was hung with queer coloured flags, and there were chimes that tinkled whenever the air around them was stirred. Her nose caught a faint whiff of something like sandalwood.

She was kept waiting for a long time. She wondered if the waiting was meant to discomfit her. If so, she thought stoutly, it wasn't going to work. Anyone who had been babysat by Wakhangli Mani knew how to sit motionless in a damp field for the better part of a day, waiting to glimpse an eagle flying overhead. Sitting in this chair was no hardship at all.

Eventually, the same brown man came and bowed once again. She rose with as little visible concern as she could muster and fairly glided behind him to wherever he might lead. He pushed open a pair of doors. "Ama," he murmured, bowing low to whoever was within.

Holding her head high, Claude swept into the room.

The first thing she saw was Nikola, seated in a chair. He looked miserable, all shrunken and dazed, as if his mind hadn't caught up to his body. Whatever he had been dosed with had affected him badly. Perhaps he hadn't been given water. His hands were bound; he must have caused some trouble. He was rather beautiful in his misery, his eyes so great and dark against his pallor. She would have liked to reach out to him, to reassure him, but she sensed that the guards or whatever they were would not take this kindly. It was important not to give them reason to want her restrained.

"Your Royal Highness is concerned about the welfare of this man?" It was a woman's voice, low and compelling. She spoke English, but her accent, which Claude could not describe, seemed to hint at many languages. Claude followed the sound to its source: a squat middle-aged woman who sat on a heap of embroidered cushions at one end of the tiled floor. Her iron grey curls were piled haphazardly on the crown of her head. A loose red garment, half coat, half shawl, covered her unfashionable black gown. She plucked a date from the brass bowl in her lap and nibbled it thoughtfully with her small, white teeth. "This is good," she observed. "You will cooperate with us and he will be safe." Her eyes, a paler grey than Claude's own and even more fierce than Father's, fixed on Claude's face. "What is he to you?" she asked.

"He's a friend," Claude snapped, "not that it's any of your business!" She regretted it as soon as it was said. She had meant to remain detached and enigmatic, but the sight of poor Nikola and then this biddy's insinuation…What was it about old women!?

The woman raised her eyebrows. "You do not sound like a princess," she remarked. "Does she, Signore?" She gestured to a slim, elegant man who stood behind her in the shadows, half-obscured by his well-fitting black uniform tunic.

The Italian looked down his long thin nose at Claude, raking her from top to toe with a gaze as jeweled and fathomless as a snake's. She felt her first real thrill of fear since awakening on the boat. "The English, Madame" he said with a supercilious sneer, "suffer their daughters to learn mathematics and ride bicycles. It is unlikely that their princesses would be maidenly."

The older woman laughed humorlessly. "Perhaps she is fatigued from her journey. Gephel," she gestured with one finger and the man who had brought Claude arose with a single motion of his crossed legs. "See that our guests," she indicated Nikola as well as Claude, "are made comfortable."

"Yes, Ama," he said, with a bow.

The woman looked at Claude curiously. "Dinner and a good night's rest," she said. "We will meet again tomorrow."

Claude nodded with as much dignity as she could muster, then followed Gephel from the room. She heard Nikola being helped to his feet, but she dared not look back and add fuel to whatever fire was slumbering in the old biddy's mind.

As she left, she heard the old woman say "Ramasee, what news of the other ship?"

Other ship? Claude wondered. And, because once she left that room her brain seemed to function more efficiently, why had the old woman addressed her and not Nikola? It was almost as though she had been the one they wanted, as if Nikola had been taken because he'd been with her, when surely it was the other way around. And she still wanted to know why everyone seemed to assume she was a princess.

*

They were left to wait in the entry hall for what felt like hours. Claude and Nikola could see each other. Or at least she could see him. His eyes didn't seem to be focused on anything in this world. There was a strange look about him that worried her, but she dared not speak. The armed men at the door looked like men whose patience a sensible person would not want to test. She wondered what had happened to her gentlemanly escort from the boat.

Finally Gephel reappeared and signaled the men to lead Nikola away.

"No!" She couldn't help it; she jumped up. One of the armed men pressed her shoulders down to keep her in her seat. The movement was enough to spark some awareness in Nikola. For just a second, he saw her clearly. Even if the day that she died were very very far away, Claude would never forget the depth of sorrow she saw in his eyes at that moment. She tried a reassuring smile, but didn't have much confidence that she'd succeeded.

Gephel, accompanied by a bear of a man, led her in the opposite direction. When she saw they wanted her to start down the stairs, she tried to resist. It was inconceivable that there could be anything good at the bottom of a steep, stone staircase. Gephel was insistent. It was communicated that, if she didn't move of her own accord, the big man would sling her over his shoulder and carry her. They nudged her firmly down the stairs, then along a wide, dark hallway. Even with minimal light, she could make out the iron bindings on the door; it was a prison. She turned to Gephel, who was mildly but implacably moving her forward. "Your Ama or whoever she is said there was to be dinner," she said, as loftily as she could manage.

He smiled placidly. "You will dine," he said, "and rest. As Ama has said." He thrust a small bundle into her hands and gave her a little push. The door slammed behind her. She pounded it fruitlessly with her fist. "Is this how you treat princesses?!" she yelled. "My people will hear about this!" She knew it was ridiculous, but it made her feel better to register some protest.

The footsteps faded away, leaving her alone in the dark. Gephel's bundle was presumably her "dinner." She wasn't about to put it down on a floor that might be littered with straw or crawling with insects or some other unappetizing things. Awkward as it was to manage, she kept it tucked it under her arm while she fumbled at her waist for her match safe. The Emperor's spies or whoever they were certainly seemed confident of their ability to contain their prisoners; once again, her chatelaine had been ignored. Anxious to prevent sparks in such a place, Claude struck carefully and shielded the resultant tiny flame. She needed to see as much as possible before it burned so low as to scorch her fingers. This was no dungeon; it was merely a close room, bare of everything save an iron bed and, poking out from under, a chamber pot. It was almost disappointing. The bed had sheets; what's more they seemed clean. These people had assumed that, alone in the dark, she'd imagine the worst. They weren't torturing her.

They were only trying to frighten her, to soften her up for whatever questions they'd planned for her for tomorrow.

Claude had better uses for her mind than conjuring up spurious horrors. She blew out the flame and placed the spent match in the chamber pot. No point in risking a fire to test whether they would come to save her.

On the wall across from the door, up high near the ceiling, she thought she could make out a patch of a lighter shade of black. She sniffed carefully. The air was fresh. The air couldn't be fresh if the only ventilation was the small grille in the door. This patch must be some kind of window. But it was letting in no light. Night must have fallen while she and Nikola had waited in that hall. Was there no moon tonight, or did the wall face into an alley? It might not signify, but she wished she knew. "Knowledge is power," as Bacon had said. At least she thought it had been Bacon. She bet great-great-grandfather Ben had wished he'd said it.

Standing close to the door, Claude felt above her head for the grille. Not a mote of light was coming through. The corridor, like the room, was dark and silent as a cave. "Nikola?" she called, keeping her voice calm and steady as she pushed it up and through the little square, "are you there?"

To her surprise, a woman's voice responded. "We are prisoners here!" the other woman called stoutly. "Are you also being held again your will?"

Before Claude could reply, a rough male voice shouted out "Silencio!" Wherever they might be stationed, in the dark, or just beyond, the guards obviously could hear her.

The woman, Claude realized, had spoken with a British accent. Whoever she was, she had nothing to do with Nikola. How many prisoners were being kept in this house, and why were they there?

There was no purpose in thinking about it, nor anything else to be done right now. Claude's top priority must be to ensure she would be alert and refreshed for whatever might happen tomorrow. She sat on the edge of the bed and untied the napkin. Bread and cheese, and a small flask of what her nose told her was wine. Her mouth began to water. How long had it been since the dinner that had been her last real meal? She thought wistfully of the chestnut gateau. She was so hungry! Would the food be drugged? Did it matter? She needed to eat. If she were going to be drugged, she thought philosophically, at least she was already on a bed. Once she took the first bite, it took no time at all for her to devour everything to the last crumb. She swallowed the last of the wine and found herself yawning. Not that she was any kind of expert in these matters, but it felt like a normal sleepiness, not the effect of drugs. It was, after all, probably quite late and it had been a turbulent day.

Claude removed her boots and stretched out. It was a perfectly reasonable bed, no worse than her college dormitory's. The sheets were not even coarse. She allowed herself a congratulatory smile. Someone who allowed fear to cloud her perception, as the old woman must have planned, would find it impossible to get a decent night's rest, but not Claude Monteith. She hoped the English woman, whoever she was, had also learned enough to not be afraid.

Drowsy now, she curled up on her side (as she always did for serious sleeping), sinking into the modest mattress. She flinched; something hard was pushing into her leg. It was a trick! She'd been lulled into complacency and caught off guard. Gritting her teeth against whatever revolting thing she might find there, she thrust her hand between her leg and the blanket... Foolish, she chided her sleepy self. There was no blanket on the bed; it was her own skirt. She groped gingerly and found nothing but crumpled wool. How Princess and the Pea of her, to be startled by a wrinkle! Aunt would have been thrilled. Wryly amused by this unprecedented symptom of feminine delicacy, she smoothed the fabric. Her hand caught a raised lump in the hem. It was one of the Prometheum capsules! She would have sworn she'd removed them all on that first day at the workshop, yet all these days she'd been walking around with it still in her skirt. Such carelessness! She'd be berating herself now, except that it meant she had a significant asset that only she would know of. This was even better than the glass dagger. She had no idea how it might be useful, but she was awfully glad to know that it was there. She patted the lump fondly before shifting the bit of hem away from her legs.

This new bit of knowledge acted like a pot of strong coffee. As much as she knew she ought to sleep, as much as she wanted to, she was suddenly wide awake. Rolling over on her back, she folded up her arms to make a pillow for her head, as if she were gazing up at the stars. As long as she was awake, she might as well think and this was an excellent posture for thinking. Father always said that to solve a problem you began by...Ouch! She hadn't taken her hair down tonight and one of the pins was poking into her skull. She wriggled some of them to make a comfortable spot.

Hairpin! Claude sat bolt upright. What type of lock was it, she wondered, in the door? She jumped up and, sticking her feet back into her boots, hobbled over. She ran her fingers over the plate. It would be a shame to waste another match for nothing. Anyway, if it were one of the kinds of locks Father had trained her to open, she wouldn't need any light. She unbent a hairpin and began to probe the keyhole. Excellent! It was a pin-tumbler lock and not the latest model. If she held it right here and moved the other prong very very slowly...Yes! She felt the click and gave a little push. The door swung open. Claude knelt to quickly tie her bootlaces;

no sense in escaping prison only to trip on an unlaced boot. She stepped into the deep silence. At her waist, her little silver mechanical pencil clicked against the match safe. It was a slight sound, but even that might give her away. Removing her chatelaine, she turned it around and hooked it inside her waistband so that the chains dropped, muffled, between her skirt and petticoat.

Stepping further into the corridor, she turned left, the direction from which she had been led to her cell. Her goal was to find a way out of the building and make her way back to the town square. She assumed Nikola was somewhere on the premises, but she couldn't begin to guess where to look for him; even if she managed to find him, he hadn't seemed in much condition to escape. It would be more sensible to go for help. She wasn't adrift at sea now. There was a church in the square, she'd seen it. A person could get sanctuary in a church. Perhaps the priest or minister would help her wire Father.

Hugging the wall, Claude moved stealthily, as she had been trained to do on countless walks in the woods. It was simpler without twigs and rocks underfoot. It seemed the matter of only a moment before her hand could feel the large empty space that was the stairwell. Taking a deep, steadying breath, she started up the stairs. Partway up, there was a kink where the steps veered a bit and were temporarily more closely spaced. She tripped up, one foot slipping out from under her. The loss of balance sent her slipping down several steps. It was only by grabbing at the rail with every bit of her strength that she prevented herself from tumbling all the way down. Her heart jumped so high she thought it might pop out her mouth. She'd managed not to cry out, but had anyone heard that thumping? Hardly able to breathe, she froze where she was, clinging to the rail. Hours passed in that minute. There wasn't a sound. She was safe. There would likely be an enormous bruise on her shin by morning, but she wouldn't mind as long as she were alive somewhere with light to see it.

Bracing herself, she continued up the stairs. At the top, she paused to take her bearings. She was in a dark foyer, but not so dark as the corridor from which she'd surfaced; a bit of ambient light was coming from somewhere. She knew she needed to make her way to that rotunda where she had first waited. It was at the front of the house…House? It was larger than the Carnegie mansion! The foyer was thick with doorways, all alike. Which was she to choose to get there? She hadn't remembered there being so many. There had been a wall-hanging where she'd passed through, a silk panel painted with a story of some kind. She made her way from wall to wall. There seemed to be panels hanging on every one of them. How was she to tell the difference?

There was no other choice: she would have to explore each route in turn. She decided to be very scientific about it. She would begin with the door to her immediate right. If it turned out to be a wrong choice, she'd make her way to this spot to try the next one to the right, and so on.

The first door led past a row of closely spaced plain wooden doors to a narrow stairway that only went up. The second door also led to a dead end. Halfway along the third corridor, she ran into trouble. There were voices coming from one of the rooms ahead, two men talking. She instinctively started to move backwards, one step at a time, and walked right into the arms of a third man.

Pushing her roughly, he pinned her arms behind her and said something loud in a language she didn't understand. Somehow she was certain it meant "what have we here?"

The others came running from the room. One carried a lamp. Her captor held her tightly by the arm. He would have shaken her but the man with the lamp, apparently his superior, stopped him.

It was the sinister Italian. "No damage to Her Royal Highness," he said, "by the Emperor's orders." He said it in English, she noticed, as if he specifically meant for her to understand. He then said something in the strange language; it must have been the same thing, as her arm was released. She stood there, afraid to move. He made a mocking little bow. "Signorina," he said, holding out his arm. "Please allow me to escort you back to your chamber. For tonight, you will be safer there."

She had no choice but to take his arm and let him lead her back to the foyer, back down the stairs, back to the iron-bound door. He held the lamp to better see the door and noticed the hairpin on the floor. He looked at her with what might have been admiration. "I would have had someone whipped for leaving it unlocked," he said.

She acted as if he hadn't spoken. Refusing to give him the satisfaction of forcing her to do so, she entered the room of her own volition. He followed her, the lamp held high and making a pool of amber light around her head. As he had that afternoon in the audience chamber, he seemed to be looking into her, beyond her face. Emboldened by her rebellion, she stared back. His eyes, she couldn't help but notice, were a startling dark blue with a thick fringe of the blackest lashes. She felt herself blushing and fought to control her breath. He reached out a hand and touched her hair. She shrank back.

"Mi dispiace," he apologized. "You will pardon the liberty, Your Royal Highness, but I do not suppose you would yield them all and we cannot risk another attempt at escape. Had I not been in the mess just now..." he nodded significantly at the guards looming behind him and raised his eyebrows, telegraphing a disastrous consequence. He pulled the pins from her hair slowly, one at a time, and tucked them into his pocket. Her chignon tumbled down, lock by lock, falling over her shoulders. He reached out one last time. She thought he was about to touch her face. Her heart thumped. She raised her hand to block him and stared back at him as fiercely as she knew how, preparing to meet any advance with a quick stomp on his instep. Instead, he took her hand and kissed it suavely. "You must trust that I serve your best interests," he said. His voice, a mellifluous baritone, vibrated from his lips through her bones, making her shiver. "Sleep well."

She burned at his presumption. Serve her best interests! She supposed he meant that he might have easily punished her in some hideous way, or allowed those guards to do so. Though not too hideously, she suspected. She was being treated with particular respect, if abduction and incarceration could be called respectful.

With her ear to the heavy door, she could hear the men's boots fade away from her locked cell. She was glad she'd hidden her chatelaine and vowed it would remain tucked inside her skirt until she was free. She still had that and she still had the Prometheum. And she had tried. She had done her best. Father would have been proud.

Alone in the darkness, she would not cry.

ॐ

Benvolio Rappaccini made his way across the compound with the casual yet martial stroll he had perfected, exchanging salutes, acknowledging the bows of Madame's scurrying household and all the time mentally racing ahead to the room where he could lock the door and devote himself to the maze in his mind. His grandmother had been an opera singer. He had often found himself of late wondering if this had been what she'd felt on stage, this sense of sitting on his own shoulder, watching himself perform. If Grandmother Violet had passed him this gift of duality, he was grateful to her. As agitated as his thoughts were now, he knew no one would read them in his face.

It was the Princess who was making such a singular assault on his thoughts. His pulse had raced to see her held by that coarse brute of a guard. It was the rush of combat of course; a soldier's duty, rising to protect a vulnerable girl. Or perhaps it was the same thrill he'd felt witnessing the bravery and regal confidence in her confrontation with the Blavatsky. Whoever it was that Squadra Rosso had found in Prague, Squadra Verde had captured the prize. There was no mistaking the heir of Charlotte of Britain. Beyond her looks and bearing, there was her bold purpose.

Imagine a princess who could pick a lock and nearly engineer a successful escape! He would be proud to swear fealty to a sovereign like that.

But when he'd removed the hairpins, what he had felt then had nothing to do with respect. The sight of the curls tumbling down around her shoulders had set him to imagining the whiteness of those shoulders beneath her clothes. His blood had stirred. He had felt a response in her flush and shortness of breath. She might not be long out of the schoolroom, but this princess was a woman. A beautiful woman. A desirable woman.

He needed to wipe these thoughts from his mind. Remember the poor fellow Verde had taken along with her. He must have fought like a lion for her sake. Who could blame him? But look at the toll it had taken; the man was on the brink of madness, and all for naught. It was interesting that the Blavatsky had been so angry about the man's condition—and Rappaccini could tell she was, although she liked to pretend she was above such things as anger. Whatever drugs Madame might have supplied to the Lady Giulia, it was evident she hadn't planned these results. The man was a ruin, and Squadra Rosso's unknown girl had still been unconscious when their boat arrived. Word was that they'd had to wait for the cover of darkness to carry her to the house on a litter. Poor thing, whoever she was. Madame had sent a healer to watch over her, just as she had with the man.

Another surprising woman, Rappaccini conceded; the Blavatsky was not what he had expected. Whatever else she might do, her curious religion espoused respect for life. He had noticed the lack of meat at her table; the Italians and Ragusans who complained most loudly were requested to take their meals at a tavern in town. Since arriving at the compound, Rappaccini had observed her household enough to see that she was served from a loving devotion, not from fear. Yet for all that, the woman would apparently condone, even facilitate kidnapping. She guided Augustus's villainy—he had read her message to the Baron with his own eyes—but she seemed to have her own agenda. Some referred to her as Caesar's Sybil, but he thought she was more of a Sphinx. There was no penetrating the thoughts beyond that pale stare. Who was this woman and what did she want?

※

Claude was awakened by a shaft of light from the high window. She still didn't know where it faced. It wasn't important any more; they would be watching her closely now. She combed her hair with her fingers as best she could. Twisting it into a knot, she was about to skewer it with the mechanical pencil from her chatelaine, when she stopped. He knew he had taken her hairpins, that Rapacious or whatever his name was. He already knew she could pick locks. She didn't need him wondering what other tools she might have and how she might put them to use. Regretfully, she let her hair fall. It was so heavy, and such a mess. She often wondered why girls couldn't crop their hair as boys did. Hers would look very well, she thought. It would curl and she could wear a filet, like that Greek statue Uncle Andrew had in his garden. It would certainly be less fuss. But Father insisted that having long hair, like other women, was a useful disguise. With a sigh, she braided it back and hoped it wouldn't unravel too quickly.

She hadn't heard the footsteps (there was someone in this household who walked as silently as she) but she heard the key in the lock and jumped up to face whoever entered. It was only a young man, a boy really, very pretty in his long white tunic. His legs were wrapped in soft, narrow tubes of the same stuff and his feet were bare. He carried a large tray of food. She was hungry, but the opportunity seemed too good to waste; he was defenseless. She was calculating how best to place her strike to avoid being scalded by flying tea, when she spotted the other man, large and well armed, lurking beyond the door. Of course. With both hands occupied with the tray, the boy wouldn't have been able to use a key. Claude was disappointed in herself, as if she had failed some test; she was starting to be ruled by her emotions.

The boy set down the tray on the foot of the bed and, putting his hands together, bowed. "Namaste," he murmured, and backed out of the room. "Thank you!" she called as the door closed once more. Something about his courtesy made it seem the proper thing to do even if, rationally speaking, she was a prisoner thanking a jailer.

She looked at the tray. Tea, fruit, a laden toast rack and a covered dish that smelled extremely savoury. The napkin this morning was fine linen, daintily bordered with cross-stitch in blue and yellow silks. Everything was as nice as could be, not like a prison breakfast at all. Last night they had tried to make her feel afraid; today she was an honoured guest. If they were trying to throw her off balance to make her more vulnerable, it was very clever—or it would have been if she hadn't caught on. No doubt it would be an interesting day.

❧

For the longest time, it wasn't interesting at all. They picked up the tray and left her sitting in her cell for the entire morning. She wasn't bored; she had plenty to think about. She calculated that it had been three, perhaps four days since she and Nikola had been abducted. What was Father doing now to find her? If only she had been aware that she was being abducted, she thought crossly, she would have tried to leave some clues. Locks of hair or symbols written with a bloody finger. Well, no use crying over spilt milk. She would have to be more careful now. Think before acting. Be observant and remember everything she saw and heard. Assume that anything she did or said could become a weapon in her enemies' hands. It helped to think of herself as two people: Claude, who had been kidnapped; and the intrepid Miss Monteith, consulting detective and, now it seemed, spy.

Eventually they came to fetch her back to what she thought of as the audience chamber. The portly woman, Madame, was again sitting on her cushions with an adoring circle at her feet. They were an exotic group: men and women, but mostly men; old and very young, but nothing in between; they seemed to come from around the globe, but were all dressed in the same style of loose-fitting tunic.

As Claude entered, a substantial, bearded man and his younger companion rose from a pair of gilt ballroom chairs and bowed. It seemed only polite to bow her own head in acknowledgement. On the other side of the room, as if to balance them, were another pair who also stood and bowed. She remembered one of these as her gentlemanly escort from the boat. As she inclined her head in their direction, the sight of him with his partner pushed at a sore place in her memory. Where had she seen these men together before?

While she tried to marshal her thoughts, both pair of men began to nudge and whisper. Something was happening behind her. She turned to look. Another girl had entered the room, a girl who looked as confused as she felt.

"You see, Signor Rappaccini?" Madame said, with a sparkle in her eye. "We have twins. I find this quite intriguing, don't you?"

Claude's midnight jailer stepped forward from where he had been standing to one side, a shadow in stern black, keeping an eye on the proceedings. He moved slowly in a kind of figure eight around and between the girls, looking from one to the other and back again.

Rappaccini seemed amused. "I see now why the Signori," he indicated the two pair of men, "would have each believed that they had the prize."

"Ah, but which truly did?"

Claude found it hard to believe their captors could be so easily confused. There was a similarity of height and hair colour, and they were coincidentally wearing walking suits of the same, fashionable dun broadcloth, but she knew the resemblance was superficial. For one thing, while recent hardship might have blurred this distinction, Claude could tell that the other girl was younger by a few years, just out of the schoolroom. More significantly, even in her distressed state, the younger girl had the grace of someone in a painting. Claude had occasionally wished that she could look like that.

Madame trained her odd stare on each of the girls, considering them carefully. "Which one is the princess?"

Neither young woman so much as coughed. Claude didn't know about the lovely girl, but it was pure mulishness for her own part. She had been kidnapped and brought here against her will. She was a prisoner. Prisoners don't answer questions. Actually, she had a lot of questions herself. Since everyone seemed certain there was a princess here and she knew she wasn't one, then the other girl must be. Was she the English princess, the one the Queen had sent for Father to protect? How peculiar that was. The Princess was, in a manner of speaking, Father's case. If this girl were she, Claude had an obligation, to Father and to the Queen, to do whatever she could to protect her. Why hadn't Father told her there was some resemblance between them? He must have thought as little of it as she did. And yet, to people who knew neither of them, it was pronounced enough that she'd been abducted. That *she* had been abducted. It wasn't about Nikola after all. They'd been taken because of her, and it was only horrible luck for him that he had been with her! It dawned on her that she now had a more compelling reason to keep silent. She mustn't risk accidentally revealing Nikola's identity to the Emperor's people.

"Are they proud, Rappaccini, do you think? Or do you think perhaps they are shy?" Madame raised two fingers. One of her attendants rose and went to the door. "We'll see what the others have to say."

Another young woman was brought in, a frank-faced person with a great puff of curly auburn hair. She had the brisk stride of someone who would take no nonsense from anybody. She turned her blue-green stare on the tableau in front of her, shifting her head like a spectator at a tennis match.

"Which is the Princess Maud?" Madame Blavatsky asked.

"Don't say a word!" this young woman exclaimed stoutly, reaching out her hands as if to stop the mouths of both girls. "She won't know unless someone tells her." She turned on Madame and stuck out her chin. "And who might *you* be? I demand to be taken to the British Embassy!"

It was the same clipped voice Claude had heard in the darkness, the other prisoner. What she was doing now was ridiculous, but one had to admire her spirit. Claude instinctively liked her and hoped she wasn't putting herself in danger.

"I am Madame Blavatsky," the older woman said.

A peculiar expression dawned on the young woman's face. "Well then, you don't see everything, do you?" she said, sounding queerly triumphant.

"Show respect to Madame!" Rappaccini snapped.

The Blavatsky only laughed. "No, no. We have another heroine! Brava, Miss…?"

"Bell," she said proudly. "Miss Gertrude Lowthian Bell."

"Miss Bell." Madame had a sweet smile, an odd contrast to those moonstone eyes. "I do not claim to see anything," she explained. "I only know what my Masters tell me, the Seven Rays, the White Brotherhood." She brought her hands to her heart, and swept them through the air in a gesture that reached first out, then up. Everyone's eyes followed them. When they had returned to their beginning, the palms pressed tightly together beneath her chin, she bowed her head. The circle of acolytes repeated the gesture.

There was a lingering hush, underlined by the broken notes of the wind chimes overhead. It was disturbed by a pair of boots scuffling along the tiles.

Nikola looked as bad as he had the afternoon before. Even worse. His eyes were rimmed with red and his hands, though unbound, were shaking. Claude longed to reassure him, but knew she must remain still.

"Which is the princess, sir?" Madame asked him.

He didn't seem to hear her. He gazed at them, rubbing his eyes ferociously. "Claude?" he moaned. "My eyes! Everything is doubled!" He began to cry, great choking sobs.

Gephel bowed to Madame. "Ama," he said, "I fear there is no sense to be gotten from this one."

"Be calm, sir," Madame said in a low, soothing voice. "There is nothing to fear. What is your name?"

"K-k-kola," he stammered.

For a second, Claude allowed herself to think it might be a clever performance. If he were astute enough to give a false name…Then she remembered: this was the name his family had used for him when he was small; it was how he had referred to himself when he'd become ill in Chicago. Things were worse than she'd suspected.

He moaned again, and it tore her heart. "My eyes, my eyes! There is a bird's nest in my head!" He started grabbing at clumps of his hair.

Madame signaled to one of her servants, who hugged Nikola's shoulders and rocked him tenderly until he was calm. She turned a merciless face to the seated spies. "Which of you took the man?" she demanded. They flinched; her voice was like the whip of a rapier. "Which dose did you give him? How much?"

"The sleeping sponge, she did not work," the weasel-faced spy huffed disparagingly, in broken English. "So then the special syringe. Only one."

Madame was a large woman. In fury, she grew to the size of a mountain. "An entire syringe? Surely no! That was sufficient for two men!" To emphasize this, she repeated it in Italian. The handsome spy turned ashen. His companion gave a harsh laugh and continued to defend himself, fluently, in his own language.

Italian sounded much different rattled off at top speed by people who spoke it naturally. As best she could make out, whatever they had given Nikola to keep him unconscious had worn off too quickly. Then there was something about the boat... Before reaching the boat? She wasn't sure. And then something had happened. There was a lot of gesturing that indicated Nikola had been forced to swallow something. This caused Madame to purse her lips and narrow her eyes in an extremely ugly way.

Claude glanced over at the other girls. Miss Bell's eyes were alive with comprehension. The Princess wasn't listening at all, but was looking around like a doe surrounded by a hunting circle. Like that deer, she made a fleeting break for what appeared to be an opening and headed toward the door. The enormous armed man was standing just outside the archway and pushed her back.

Still arguing in Italian, Madame Blavatsky called out "Stupid girl! There is no place to run!"

"'*Scusi*," the Princess mumbled.

A curious expression crossed Rappaccini's face. "You speak Italian, signorina?" She nodded. He looked at the other girls. "And you?" Both nodded. He smiled his satisfaction and waved patronizingly in the direction of the spies. "Then Madame, I suggest we continue all discourse in that language, for the edification of these gentlemen."

"Not today, Rappaccini," Madame said. "There is too much turbulence in the ether. I prefer everyone to have time to restore themselves before we continue." She addressed the girls impartially. "Tashi will see that the gentleman receives proper attention. Do not concern yourselves. All will be well."

Tashi, the comforting servant, led Nikola from the room. He stared back over his shoulder with sad, moist eyes. Claude wanted to smash something, just for the relief of it.

Madame Blavatsky clapped her hands sharply, twice. "The rest of us shall share a cup of tea before we part. Then I think the young ladies will enjoy the gardens. Sit please."

She gestured for everyone to join her on the heap of cushions. As they settled themselves, some more gracefully than others, they could hear a faint creaking. A servant hastened to a painted panel, sliding it open to display a large brass samovar. Within moments, a tea table had been assembled from the contents of the dumbwaiter.

The water was boiling. Madam Blavatsky held the teapot under the spigot, releasing a delicious, spicy aroma.

"How do we know it's not drugged?" Gertrude asked bravely.

"I serve myself from the same pot," Madame explained. She was visibly amused when Claude snatched up two of the silver-jacketed glasses at random and checked to see that they were empty of any residue.

Smiling, Madame filled the glasses and passed them, gesturing for everyone to help themselves from the dishes of cream and sugar and honey and lemon. As many of the teas at home were herbs that Firewalker brewed as remedies, Claude had acquired the habit of taking hers plain. This tea had a pleasing flavour, a bit of cinnamon and nutmeg, some faint hint of black current, and something else with a sweet yet pungent note that she couldn't identify. There were sweet biscuits, little cakes really, to nibble alongside, once Madame took a bite and emboldened them to take their own from the plate.

After their tea, Gephel brought the girls to the garden, which was actually a conservatory filled with potted trees and a small, pleasant fountain. Even the dark presence of Rappaccini couldn't dispel the air of joy in that place. It smelled of citrus and bay and honeyed flowers. Bright little birds darted around, trilling happily. The girls became giddy, no doubt from relief from all the tension they'd been holding.

Claude longed to find out who Miss Bell was and how she knew the Princess, but that was exactly the conversation they could not have. They didn't dare say much of anything while under the surveillance of the Italian. They mostly just laughed and pointed to pretty things. Claude found herself spinning around in a circle, her arms spread wide and her face lifted up to the sunlight pouring through the glass. Gertrude started a game of tag. They must have exercised themselves more than they realized because, despite all the little cakes they'd so recently had, one by one they became hungry. Ravenously hungry; Claude would have eaten Aunt Nan's haggis and she hated haggis.

The Princess asked Rappaccini if they could have some food—told him, more than asked. For someone who had seemed so cowed earlier, she was extremely imperious now. Claude took note. She was thinking of herself as her father's deputy, which meant she now had some responsibility for this girl. People thought they looked a lot alike. It might be useful, in this place, to act alike, too.

9 - MIXED MESSAGES

Rappaccini slipped his hands into his pockets, a habit of his when deep in thought. The condition of his coats had been the despair of his mother, he remembered fondly. She'd threatened to try and break him of it by slipping a mousetrap inside, but she'd been too softhearted to ever follow through. What he touched now also made his fingers recoil. It was a small bundle of hairpins. Yesterday, he would have sworn the girl he'd taken them from was the English princess. This morning, seen side by side, the young women were as alike as two peas.

Was she a spy then, his intrepid lock-picker? It struck him in retrospect that, when she'd spoken yesterday, he'd heard something like a Colonial drawl. It was a subtlety most likely beyond the ears of di Bari's men, but he had engineered the switch to concealing Italian, just in case. They spoke equally abominable Italian, but with no tell-tale distinctions. And now, since Miss Bell's intercession, both young women were affecting similar gestures and bearing even when they thought they were unobserved. How clever of Miss Bell to muddy the waters. Clever, or professional? So two spies then? Three. He'd forgotten about the man called Kola, who perhaps was no mere smitten courtier after all.

What was the lock-picker's mission? If she had been meant as a decoy, the ruse hadn't worked. With two teams of agents in Prague, both young women had been taken. Why would she have tried to escape last night, leaving the Princess behind? Perhaps she had broken out of her cell with the purpose of tracking down the Princess, setting her free before anyone had seen the two of them together, and taking her place. With her escape foiled, what plans might she be making now?

With Madame's staff hovering everywhere, this would require more than usual subtlety to untangle. He hoped there would be enough time. As if young women needed any assistance in loosening their tongues, Madame had confided that she was lacing their food with cannabis. Before long, they would babble enough to betray the identity of the Princess. As much as he needed to know this, he also needed to know the other young woman's purpose, to see if he could use it to forward his own cause.

The girls were facing one another across a plate of tea sandwiches. They seemed to be looking in a mirror. It was their eyes that were so different. He must fix that detail in his mind and use it while looking for other clues. He tried to remember which pair had turned away from his last night. What was he to do if he couldn't tell which girl was which?

He was starting to feel the burden was too great for one man after all.

❧

Yet again, Madame Blavatsky didn't dine with the men. Apologies were sent via Gephel, who provided his own annotation to the effect that Ama led a contemplative life and was used to a simple bowl of porridge on a tray in her rooms.

"She knows how heated barracks talk can be," Rappaccini said slyly. "All the ins and outs of our business." The others laughed. There had been a sufficiency of wine.

"Speaking of which," Azzurro said, "I could use some rough and tumble. I've been away from Magda for…this will make five nights. No, worse! Six!"

Rappaccini had guessed Azzurro would be the one most likely to bite the bait. He waited until a few more randy thoughts were voiced, then cast his line. "When we were pushing off from Pescara, there was a seaman who said he used to work the docks here. He recalled the merchants talking about a certain house outside the Ploče Gate. Most discreet. I, ahem, encouraged him to recall the name."

The men looked eager but uncertain. They were spies, not guards, but it still seemed a dereliction of duty to leave the scene for nocturnal adventures. Rappaccini dropped an eyelid suggestively. "I was told the proprietress is French and hires a number of her compatriots."

As anticipated, Azzurro spoke up. "The things they can do with their tongues," he reminisced, his eyes lighting.

"I haven't had a French whore in years," said Rossi, wistfully. He had been based in Vienna of late. Such delicacies were available there but, now that he had a family to support, far too dear for him to taste.

Rappaccini called for more brandy. The men grew increasingly boisterous, trying to outdo one another in the bawdiness of their recollections.

Azzurro leapt impulsively to his feet. "Well I don't care about the rest of you. I'm going!" he cried. "Rappaccini, give me the name!"

"I wouldn't want you to wander the city alone," Rappaccini said coolly.

A rap of the dragon's head knocker brought a liveried strong-man to the door. Rappaccini spoke the password. He hadn't been given it by a random seaman; he had the names of many such places by rote; the map of Europe was carefully peppered with them.

It was an unassuming place from the outside but, having gained admittance, they saw enough gilt-veined mirrors, cupids and red velvet to satisfy Azzurro's now inflated expectations. The men were greeted delightfully, with champagne and rosy, disheveled girls who were pleased to sit on their knees and feed them strawberries. They made it known that they had a preference for entertainment of the French variety. Rappaccini allowed Azzurro to choose first, a dimpled girl with jetty curls who led him up the stairs with peals of good-humored laughter.

Once he was well out of sight, Rappaccini approached the Madam. "I am a man of peculiar tastes," he said quietly. "I have been told that you have a young lady here who might satisfy them. Mademoiselle Alouette?"

The Madam tilted her head. "Alas, Monsieur, Alouette is indisposed tonight."

"*C'est dommage*," he replied with a bow of the head. "Then I would be pleased to have you make the selection for me."

She nodded once and summoned a liveried manservant. "The dungeon," she said, raising her voice just enough for some of the revelers to hear. "I hope that you enjoy the entertainment."

Rappaccini mounted the stairs behind the servant. Several of those in the parlour watched with open curiosity. He swaggered past with a spectacular show of contempt.

He strode through the door with an air of inspection. The room was hung with black satin and smoked mirrors. There were manacles affixed to one wall, and a rack of whips and scourges. In the middle of the floor he saw a leather-upholstered device whose purposes he wouldn't begin to wonder about. "Very satisfactory," he said, casually tossed the servant a generous tip. The servant bowed and left the room. When his footsteps had faded, Rappaccini shot the bolt. No one else was expected and he had no intention of being disturbed by an accidental trespasser. Starting at the door, he moved slowly about the perimeter of the room. A screen concealed nothing more than a comfortable chair. Sitting in it, he saw a hole cut through the screen at eye level; not intended for his kind of spying. A wardrobe, painted to disappear into the wall, held nothing but ecclesiastical robes and other odd garments. He wasn't keen to open the trunk that stood opposite; he was less keen after having done so.

He had discovered every place it might be possible to conceal the appliance. Where was it? He was losing precious time. Azzurro wasn't the type to take overly long about his pleasure. With a sigh, he began again. This time, when he opened the wardrobe, he pushed all the clothes to one side. Still nothing, but now it was obvious that the floor was raised unusually high. He gave an experimental tap and smiled, relieved. False. Feeling carefully with his fingertips, he found a latch set flush into the wood in the front of the wardrobe. A firm press of the panel rewarded him with a soft click The shelf popped up and slid forward. He knelt by the telegraph key to tap out his message, then put everything back exactly as he had found it.

He sat gingerly on the 'visitor's chair' for five minutes more before carefully dis-arranging his appearance. He removed his coat, in order that he might make a big show of putting it on again once he'd exited the room. He moved slowly and stiffly along the corridor. As he reached the stairs, Azzurro rolled out from a nearby room, followed by peals of feminine laughter. Azzurro was grinning from ear to ear. He clapped Rappaccini's shoulder in good fellowship. Rappaccini made sure to wince.

"Oh, ho! And what have you been up to, *ragazzo*?!" Azzurro asked.

Rappaccini glared. "Mind your business and I'll mind mine!" he snapped. Azzurro laughed heartily.

There was no question what tomorrow's gossip would be about Benvolio Rappaccini and that was fine with him.

Madame Blavatsky had received a cable. Augustus having decided he could not trust a mere centurion to bring his prize to Rome, Baron Haussmann was on his way to Dubrovnik with the Royal yacht. This gave her three days to choose which girl to give him.

It wasn't a choice she relished. She had petitioned the Masters long and hard for guidance. It was Their doing that there was a decision to be made, but They were keeping silent now. That meant that her own karma was in play. She must remain conscious of this and not allow the pressures of time and an Emperor's wrath to influence her.

She would continue to consult the Masters and hope they would relent and supply an answer. Meanwhile, she must find a way to make the young women reveal the truth. Many would advise torture, but Helena could not condone such violence. There were subtler tactics that must eventually bear fruit. A fearful night isolated in the 'dungeon' should have shaken the gently-reared young ladies, yet it hadn't made a dent. Neither had the contrast of the following day disoriented them as she had planned; nor, despite the herbal assistance, had they relaxed their guard and confided in one another in the garden.

The companions that had been taken with the girls were turning into a liability. Where a shrinking violet would have helped Madame's cause, Miss Bell had alas turned out to be a virago. The plight of the man called Kola had, if anything, caused them to be more intent on resistance.

Fated or not, it was a pity that the poor young man was so damaged that few intelligible words could be gotten from him. The challenge was to free the girls' minds from discipline without causing similar results.

During the years of her apprenticeship, her more esoteric studies had introduced Helena Blavatsky to the herbologies and pharmaecopias of several ancient cultures. She had formulae she had created, as well as those she had been taught. She knew much about venoms and other animal-based substances, but she preferred to avoid them. Nature had intended these to serve as weapons; even when employed for non-lethal ends, they endangered the lives of those to whom they were applied. The fluid provided to the Emperor's men, for example, was milked from a rare African spider. In small enough doses, it slowed the limbs of the victim, and paralyzed the will. Too much and the victim suffocated in a matter of minutes. If Squadra Verde had misused that, Kola would have been dead. Instead, they'd overdosed him on the moonflower extract and coddled his brains.

When not administered by idiots, Madame much preferred essences of plants. They could be equally poisonous, of course; but someone well versed in herbalism would learn of ways to achieve more subtle influences. Her goal now was information, not destruction. There were compounds that would help, but they would need to be administered gradually, in order to properly control the dosage.

The cannabis-laced tea biscuits had been her first such gambit. Rappaccini's observation told her that it had been too small a start. The young women had lost some of their inhibitions in the garden, but not enough to loosen their tongues. Her preference would have been to try again, raising the quantity of herb, but with Haussmann on his way, time was strictly limited and she could not chance another failed experiment.

She would have to escalate the process. A browse through her cabinet of potions and powders brought the answer to hand. There was a form of ergot, used in rituals by a sect of lamas in Mirik. This could be introduced into their food to nudge them, as quickly as possible, into a delusional state.

She considered this approach and deemed it possible. While the cannabis had made less impact on their tongues than she had expected, their appetites had performed according to custom. She could keep the girls hungry enough to eat with un-ladylike abandon. This would enable her to feed them enough of the potent fungus to produce the desired condition, but balanced with enough of certain foods that would protect them from the worse side effects.

She offered her plan to the White Brotherhood. There were no objections. So be it.

She was about to rise from her meditation, when an apparition broke through the Veil. The old woman was well known to Helena; when still in this world, she had been the nurse of her sister Vera. Beneath the babushka, her familiar face was as sweetly wrinkled as a withered apple. She held up one finger in warning, as she used to when the girls had been about to do mischief and she wished to stop them. When she was sure Helena was watching her, she moved that same finger to her lips, the gesture of silence, and disappeared. It had been a warning, that much was clear. A warning about what? To be careful? To keep her deeper purpose a secret from anyone else? Helena would do both.

❦

After their enormous meal, the three young women had been given facilities to wash before being returned to their rooms for the night. Having now been seen in daylight, the cells weren't at all discomfiting and the odd day had been extremely tiring. Maud undressed down to her chemise and petticoats and slept soundly. She awoke to the morning feeling much restored.

After breakfast, which had been enhanced by the addition of a pair of tiny sweet muffins with a pleasantly familiar aroma that she couldn't place, one of the oddly-garbed servants returned to fetch her. She assumed they were going back to the room with all the cushions, to be stared at by the woman with the weird eyes and those horrible Italian men. It was a happy surprise to find herself in a large, sunny room with three beds and a familiar face.

"Hello," she said.

"Hello," her twin replied. "It appears they think they'll learn more if they keep us together."

143

They stared at each other, burst into giggles and collapsed onto the nearest bed.

The door opened again and they both jumped up.

"Gertrude!" Maud cried.

"Gertrude!" Claude echoed quickly, adapting her voice to sound as much like the Princess as possible. It seemed such a funny thing to do, they both laughed again. Claude didn't understand why she was giggling all the time.

Gertrude rolled her eyes. "Ladies," she scolded playfully, "one of you is the Princess Charlotte Maud Albertine of Greater Britain. I don't care to know which."

Quick thinking! Once again, Claude thought how much she could like this girl.

Maud's face lit up. It was like that story of Mr. Twain's that everyone had found so enthralling—everyone but Grandmama, who thought it was ridiculous. When all this was over and they were safely home, as Maud had no doubt they soon would be, she would have to see that her grandmother was introduced to this young woman. She wouldn't find Mr. Twain's tale so ridiculous after that! "It appears to be a lovely morning," she said carefully. "Do you think we'll be permitted the conservatory again?" She sounded just like her mama did when obliged to speak English. It was difficult not to laugh.

Claude smiled broadly. Now that there were three of them acting in concert, it felt more like a real case. As the only one with experience in these matters (at least she assumed that must be so), she would have to take the lead. First she needed to find out what the others knew. If only there were a way for them to communicate without being heard. She had her little silver pencil, but written notes could be found and read by unfriendly eyes. There was a type of finger language Father had taught her; he'd learned it from that Mr. Gallaudet, who ran a college for the deaf. Father had thought it might make a useful code, but most of the time it was easier for them to fall back on Lakhota. Claude didn't remember much of the finger language, but she did recall the alphabet. The others seemed to be an intelligent pair; she should be able to make them understand. She cleared her throat to get their attention. "I do hope so," she said, making the sign for the letter 'i'; "don't you?" She made the sign for 'u.'

Both girls looked at her as if she were one of those clown dogs that were trained to dance on their hind legs. She stared at them fiercely. She pointed to herself with her left hand, while making the 'i' sign with her right, then pointed to Gertrude and signed the 'u.' She did this several times.

Comprehension dawned on Gertrude's face. She turned to Maud and said firmly "yes I do," mimicking the 'i.' Maud looked confused. Gertrude had another idea and pointed to her eye while signing 'i.'

"Aha!" Maud crowed; she'd always been fond of charades.

Claude sat tailor-fashion on one of the beds, leaving room for the others to sit on the edge. When they had angled themselves to face her, they formed a close circle. Anyone who entered the room or spied through a hole would be looking at someone's inscrutable spine. Very slowly, Claude made the signs of the alphabet, starting with the thumbs up closed hand that was 'a.' After she'd limned the zig-zag of 'z,' she began again, this time making them mimic each letter in turn.

It wasn't easy going through the alphabet over and over. Oh yes, everyone had the idea, but for some reason they were all finding it difficult to concentrate and retain anything. Sometimes one of them would find one of the signs absolutely hilarious, like when Maud thought the 'n' looked like little legs and started to march her hand along the bedcover. It made them all dissolve into giggles, until one would manage to compose herself and get the others back on track.

Claude realized she was famished. She signed 'i m hungry.' Gertrude nodded to concur.

Maud rose and stretched. "Is there a bell anywhere?" she said, loudly and clearly. "I should like some luncheon." The three looked at one another and burst into helpless peals of hilarity.

Allan Pinkerton hadn't left his office in days. After the first 36 hours, Joan had finally sent Thompson to make him up a bed on the Chesterfield. He was definitely feeling his age; there was a time when he would have been able to sleep like a baby on that sofa.

First had come the long, detailed message from Menzies, announcing the terrible news of Princess Maud's abduction, together with all the information they had been able to gather about how she and Miss Bell had been taken. This was followed closely by a second wire, telling of the death of young Piper.

Pinkerton had to bring the news to the Queen. It was one of the most unpleasant hours of his life. So many of his worst hours had been spent giving bad news to Queen Charlotte.

She demanded that Menzies return to London at once. Menzies, shockingly, ignored the message and the one that followed. He had finally been conveyed back by the Royal aer-yacht, only to tersely insist that he would be more effective working from Prague. When pressed, he explained that Tesla had also been abducted.

How many Roman kidnappers had been running around Prague without their knowledge? Pinkerton felt like an old deluded fool. He had prided himself on what he had accomplished in the thirty years since becoming the Queen's spymaster. One could never boast about the excellence of an organization that was clandestine, but he was guilty of having silently patted himself on the back. Now he could scarcely face himself in his shaving mirror.

Tesla had made great progress developing a weapon against the Emperor's amphoraeka. Menzies was the only man who might be able to continue the work. He had already sent to Chicago for supplies. With Firewalker to assist him, he could pursue this as well as his share in the search for the Princess. Menzies requisitioned a ptery and returned to Prague the same day. Every wire since spoke of dead ends. Despite an elite team of men spread across Europe, the situation had only gotten worse.

It was no wonder Pinkerton couldn't sleep. He punched the pillow into what he hoped would be a more accommodating shape and tried again to stifle the thoughts swirling around in his head. At least he wasn't keeping Joan awake. It was almost a relief when he heard the boy's knock. If he couldn't sleep, he might as well have something to do, even if it was only to read more bad news.

It wasn't good news, but in its way it was the best news he'd had all week: a brief message from his protégé, young Fairservis. The Princess and Miss Bell were being held in Dubrovnik. They were none the worse for wear and being well cared for. He would do everything he could, but he reminded Pinkerton that he would need to be extremely cautious. He also asked why Pinkerton had neglected to tell him about the female agent, the Princess's double.

The last bit made no sense. They had no female agents in the Service, although Mrs. Besant had raised the issue at a recent dinner party and was unlikely to let it go. No matter. There was no way to get a message back to Fairservis until he was back in Venice. Well, he was a clever lad; he would sort it out. Meanwhile, they needed to mobilize their forces to be ready to support whatever opportunity presented itself to him.

The messenger yawned. Pinkerton quickly penciled instructions for the same message to be recoded and sent to Menzies in Prague. Perhaps he and the boy would now both get some sleep.

A terse reply arrived with breakfast. "Will continue to coordinate efforts from here," Pinkerton read. "Do not tell Q about other girl."

§.

There was no reason for Rappaccini to take either of the girls aside. He wouldn't in any case have known which to approach. It had gotten progressively more difficult for him to distinguish between the 'twins' when they were together. He still wasn't certain who had which colour eyes, and between himself and Miss Bell, the only other easily distinguishable feature, the accent, had been erased.

He continued to assume that the spy meant to effect a substitution. He could appreciate the elegance of such a plan. With a decoy in his grasp, the real princess could be smuggled home without the Emperor being any the wiser. He would like to assist this spy, but only if it were possible to do this without damaging his own position. It had taken him years to get this far in the fight against Augustus. He was not about to risk losing all that he'd gained.

That fight meant everything to the man who called himself Rappaccini. His grandfather had lost his life and his land to the self-proclaimed Caesar Augustus. Then his father had died fighting the Emperor. His widowed mother had dedicated her life to avenging them both, working from Napoli, sending information to the British Special Service until it became far too dangerous. Lord Pinkerton had managed to extract her and her child just in time. In London, she raised her son on tales of honour and valour. She taught him the proud history of his family, and the wrongs done to them by Augustus. She died when he was twelve. With his suit of mourning, he put on his first long pants. He stood by her grave and vowed to her ghost, "*io mi prenderò la rivincita!*" The Pinkertons took him in. They had seen him well-educated and turned Michaelo Leopoldo Benvolio Rianero into Micah Fairservis, a British gentleman. When he finished university, he naturally joined the Service. Since then, he had made his way through the shadows of the world, serving his adopted country superbly and devotedly, but always holding his inheritance close to his heart.

He would take his revenge slowly and carefully. He had been satisfied with his progress, but now his attention was torn between two fronts. It was a dilemma that Augustus's father would have appreciated. The Great Napoleon had famously pulled back from the Austrian front so as not to jeopardize his fight against the Turk for the Mediterranean. For similar reasons, Micah might have to leave this princess to her fate. As dastardly as the abduction plan was, it was but a portion of the Emperor's scheme to satisfy his greater ambition. The plight of a girl who might be married against her will must be far outweighed by the good of the many who lived under Augustus's thumb. She would be safe enough. Augustus wanted this marriage far too much to harm her.

§.

After another large meal, the girls spent the afternoon in the conservatory where, under watchful eyes both seen and unseen, they continued to sit closely together in apparent silence. The giggles wore off after they'd eaten, and as their focus improved, they made progress with their communication. By the time Gephel announced afternoon tea, they had managed to exchange some valuable information. They were pleased to see more of the little cakes on the tray; they felt they had earned a reward.

Claude felt restless after tea. She was accustomed to exercising her body. With so many eyes watching ceaselessly for any un-princess-like behaviour, she couldn't exactly run through any of Father's training disciplines. She sensed that the other girls felt equal need to move. Maud was trying to start another game of tag. That was fine but the room, pulsing with colour, was so beautiful that Claude wanted to do something beautiful in it. Funny, but she hadn't noticed yesterday that the fountain played music. She found herself swaying to it. Maud, she saw, was doing the same. On rainy days at Vassar, they used to practice their dancing in the wide corridors. Claude gave her best imitation of a gallant's bow and swept her into a waltz.

Gertrude watched the spinning figures melt into a single girl. She wanted to sing, like the fountain. She climbed on the rim of the basin to try. Her foot lost its purchase and she landed with a splash that set her laughing. Claude and Maud, laughing too, tried to pull her out. Before they would all end up in the fountain, two of Madame's servants ran to help them.

The girls were led back to their dormitory. Maud and Claude collapsed giggling on their beds while Gertrude exchanged her sopping wool for drier garments. Popping her head through the borrowed robe, she looked at the servant who'd brought them.

"I'm utterly famished!" she said, clearly surprised.

"So am I," the other two said, in perfect unison which only caused them to giggle more.

They had spoken in English, and the servant looked puzzled. Maud mimed eating. Smiling in comprehension, the servant bowed and went quickly to tell Ama.

❦

Madame Blavatsky, who had already been told of the behaviour in the conservatory, was delighted to hear of the order for dinner. Things were proceeding according to plan.

After her own modest evening meal, she made a brief appearance before di Bari's men in the dining room. The men rose respectfully and Rappaccini made to yield his seat. She refused him with a smile.

"I am not here to interrupt your evening," she smiled. "I only wish to reassure you that I will have the answer for the Baron when he arrives."

After she left, the men could not stop debating among themselves. Did she already have the answer? Or did she mean to say she knew that she would have it? More importantly, who had won the prize? This was not an ordinary mission. Whichever squadra had brought in the genuine princess was bound to be rewarded by Caesar. Would there be honours, money perhaps? Rossi was still hoping for his estate.

Rappaccini listened in apparent envy that he had no horse in this race. In reality, he was piecing together every shred of detail, trying to decide for himself which girl was which. What could he do to make one of the girls give herself away to him? He'd need to do it discreetly, but he needed to do it before the Baron arrived or not at all.

❦

Claude awoke at dawn. She'd had such strange dreams, but they had been wonderful. When she turned thirteen, Firewalker had taken her and Father on a camping trip to the lake. He explained that, if she had been born to his people, a holy man would have performed the coming of age ceremony. In token of this, he had thought it right to take them to a place of power, as his people did. That week, the three of them lived only on what they could catch or forage. At night, they looked up at the stars and Firewalker, Wakhangli Mani, told his stories. He had always told her stories, but this was the one and only time he spoke of his vision quest. Not long after saving his life, Frank had returned to London and the young man, feeling abandoned, had gone to claim a vision. He'd wandered many days, fasting and rarely sleeping, until at last his spirit animal, the snake, had visited him. Snake told Wakhangli Mani that he must make his way across the ocean to find his family. "And so I did," Firewalker finished the tale. He'd smiled then, a true smile from deep inside. It was the only kind of smile he ever gave and he did not give it often. It had been Claude's best birthday.

Perhaps now she was on her own vision quest. Her mind lived in a cave. There were stars outside, exploding like beautiful flowers. They beckoned and she ran like quicksilver to the door and trickled down a winding path. Here in the cave, the sun was coming up. Somewhere, she knew, her spirit animal was watching, breathing quietly in the shadows. It would flee from the light. But the day, so beautiful, was very strong. Claude started to fight, as Father had taught her, but the day fought harder. She wondered if Jacob had struggled so with the Angel. She pulled out a shining diamond sword and stabbed the day. She felt herself rip, like a petticoat caught on a nail. One half floated off, listening, to the stars. One half was pulled into the morning.

She heard Leski's voice. "Mit'anksi," he said, "Little Sister. Always remember to protect the weak. The Princess doesn't have a sword."

A few hours later, just before breakfast, the clouds in Claude's mind parted briefly and she remembered her dream. She thought about how defenseless Maud was. Claude knew how to fight, she had several weapons to hand and could turn other items to her advantage. As long as they were together, she could protect the other girl, but how much longer would that be? And how much longer would she be able to focus on this thought? She could feel herself starting to drift again. She fluttered her hand at Maud. Maud didn't notice; she too was in a world of her own.

Claude pushed herself to lean forward. She pulled back her hand; it took every ounce of focus she could summon to stop it from flopping down. She bit her own tongue. The pain, and the taste of blood, gave her a brief moment of alertness. She slapped the other girl across the face.

Maud's eyes welled with tears and she looked at Claude in reproach, in aware reproach.

"Change corsets," Claude signed quickly.

The three girls spent the day in the conservatory but, unlike the previous day, there were no giddy romps. They rarely moved; what actions there were, were languid and solitary. Gertrude spent a full half hour trailing her fingers in the fountain and staring at the droplets that clung to her nails.

Rappaccini observed them off and on, sometimes standing only inches away, marveling at the quiet.

"What is it that you've given them?" he went to Madame to ask.

"A form of ergot," she explained. "A fungus that grows on damp rye. Ergot expands the mind beyond the boundaries of this world. Ingested as it grows, it is dangerous, even deadly. Properly distilled, and taken in

150

carefully measured doses, it may be the gateway to a higher form of human consciousness."

"Higher human consciousness," he repeated. He tried to grasp what that might mean. To see more? To sense more? Perhaps to touch the hem of true divinity, not the parody of godhead Augustus thought he had achieved.

Madame Blavatsky saw the glint in the young man's eyes and shook her head firmly. "Not you. You have walls within you. I would fear the repercussions if they were to be breached."

If you sliced the top off your egg, you would find the sun tucked inside like a coin in a bit of cotton wool. Bend closer and stare and the sun would grow bigger and bigger and swallow the egg and the room and you would roll around the sun, a laughing planet with fingers that stretched like taffy into rainbows.

And the black-eyed snake winds around your brow and slips nimbly in through your ear to read your thoughts, and they were all wrong but the strawberries. The strawberries were like nothing except what music must taste like, Mozart perhaps. Look in the water and there you are looking back, except with someone else's eyes. A face looks down out of the sky, so close you feel the breath on your nose and smell cardamom. Yes, that was the name of that spice, it was cardamom, like the cakes from the Swedish bakery. How funny! But the face isn't funny, it stares like the moon, closer and closer, and it speaks.

"Which one is the Princess?" it says, zooming in and disappearing, zooming in and disappearing, over and over. So insistent. So much wanting you to say. A tiny sprout in your brain says if you say, you can help, you can help the weak. You open your mouth to speak, but the sound doesn't come. But you've been talking for hours and hours and days and days about things that mean nothing at all. Why not now?

And you hear another sound. The face again, talking upward, not talking down to you. Saying "Yes, my Masters. Now I see." And it doesn't ask you again.

Still, you struggle, because you are stubborn as a mule your Aunt always tells you. "I am," you manage to say weakly. Your chest opens and in pours all the breath in the universe. "I am!" you shout.

The face looks down, queerly kind, and someone pulls you to your feet.

"I am," you whisper.

The hooded eyes are pale and burning. They can see where other eyes cannot. The voice is low and sweet. "You are not the princess we seek."

৶

For her final interview, Madame Blavatsky had been alone behind closed doors with the two girls and the spirits of the White Brotherhood. She emerged exhausted but triumphant. The girls had not told her what she needed to hear, but the walls had dissolved and the Masters allowed her to see past them. She had her answer now.

She gave instructions for the girls to be brought to the bedroom, where Miss Bell was already resting safely. She ordered baths drawn with a fistful of rosemary, and a broth of beetroot and herbs for their supper.

Helena was confident that she'd managed the doses well enough that, given some respite and clean fluids, their healthy young bodies would begin to correct themselves. Even Kola's had begun at last to respond to the herbs Tashi had been administering. It was a pity that they would only have the one day before they must be dosed again, but it was better than leaving their fate to the Emperor's men. In the karmic balance, that day would weigh favourably for her.

৶

The breakfast gossip among Conte di Bari's men was that Bell and one of the 'twins' had risen early and asked for breakfast in the conservatory so as not to disturb the other girl. Everyone wondered what that meant. Was the sleeping beauty the Princess? Or was this proof that the double was a girl of lesser breed whose constitution compared unfavourably when put to the test?

Rappaccini made a quick meal and excused himself on the pretext of having much to do to prepare for the Baron. This might be his best opportunity. He slipped up the stairs to the wing where the girls had their room. The corridor was empty. He tested the knob. Fortune was with him; whoever had escorted the others downstairs had neglected to lock the door.

The girl certainly looked like a sleeping princess, with her bright chestnut curls spread across the pillow. She was so pale. He could see the blue veins in her eyelids, and her lashes spread like fans across her cheekbones. He was not usually a sentimental man, but he was moved to think of the trials this fragile young woman had recently endured, trials that were not over yet. If she was the agent, she had a hard mission still to come. If she was the Queen's heir, it would not be easy to get her home.

While he thought these solicitous thoughts, the eyelids began to flutter. He found himself staring directly into a pair of terrified amber eyes. "Don't scream!" he said quickly in English.

She didn't seem about to cooperate, so he put his hand over her mouth.

"I can help," he whispered. "We need to speak."

Struggling like a wildcat, she tried to bite him. With one hand over her mouth, he only had one left free to hold her down. He was astonished at her strength. Somehow she managed to twist away and plunge her own hand down her bodice. She pulled out a dagger-shaped wedge of glass and held the point under his chin. Her eyes rolled madly and her lips curled to display a wall of barred teeth. What had the Blavatsky given these girls?

He made himself stay very still. As calmly as he could, he said, "I am a friend. I will leave now, if you allow me. I will take my hand away from your mouth, if you promise not to scream. There are things we need to discuss, about your mission." He had no doubts as to which girl he addressed. Drugged, even a princess might fight like a madwoman, but she wouldn't carry a concealed weapon as his lock-picker surely would. He removed his hand. She didn't move hers but held it steady and continued to glare at him fiercely.

"Leave," she hissed; "now."

"As you wish," he said. He paused at the door. "Until later," he said, with a bow. They still needed to speak, but at least he could identify her now. And, he noted gratefully, whatever undercurrents he had sensed during their first encounter were no longer troubling him. Whatever came, he could handle it with complete professional detachment.

10 - TRANSPORTED

The three young women spent a quiet day together, much of it in the conservatory which Madame seemed to have consigned for their exclusive use. They felt such lassitude that they were glad to lounge on the cushioned rattan chairs and let the pulse of colours and sounds ebb and flow in their heads. Occasionally, two would find the same moment of clarity and they would sign brief conversations until one was once again lured away.

In later days, Gertrude would have some hazy memory of sitting in a music room, dazzled by the spectacle of two identical figures seated side by side on the bench playing Herr Brahms' waltzes for four hands. Or trying to play. The hands drifted onto other keys, and then one girl said something about the colour of the music hurting her eyes and stopped. The other played the same five notes over and over, a beatific smile on her face. Gertrude would never be able to confirm if the memory were a true one.

There were no meetings with Madame Blavatsky on this day. With clear heads, the girls might have realized that something had changed, but their minds were untrustworthy and they finished their dinner unaware. Not all of them even finished dinner. The meal had been laced with opium. They began to nod out before the raspberry sponge. They fell into a deep sleep, right at table.

§

Baron Haussmann had arrived some hours earlier and would begin his return trip that same night. The two squadre had gone together to the French whorehouse, Verdi and Azzurro to drown their sorrows at the expense of the magnanimous victors. Tomorrow, they would be returning to their various homes to await their next posting. Rossi, his villa nearly

154

within his grasp, thought perhaps he might request some leave to explore Palermo.

It was left to Rappaccini, who would be returning to Rome with the Baron, to be stationed at the dock and accept the precious parcel from Madame's strongman. The large man walked carefully up the ramp, which shook under his every step. Rappaccini stopped him on deck, under the lamp. He cautiously lifted the eyelid of the sleeping girl. The iris rolled up and he saw it was the colour of honey. It was the spy. Blavatsky's servants had confided that she planned to release the other girls; that meant the Emperor would not be involved their fates and the Princess would go free. Rappaccini signaled the man to continue down the ladder with his bundle and saw that the girl was placed in a comfortable position on a bunk that had been fitted with a purple silk coverlet. He escorted the servant topside and watched him disappear through the gate.

An amphoraeka had been installed below and was guarding the ladder. Rappaccini descended, making a show of brandishing the key to the cabin. He didn't know if the creatures registered anything other than direct orders. If they did, it was best to appear confident in one's actions.

The girl's breathing was heavy, but within reasonable bounds. It seemed only gallant to remove her boots. Her posture seemed comfortable enough. She appeared as frail and defenseless as she had that morning. That morning, the frail, defenseless girl had tried to kill him with a piece of glass. His eyes narrowed and he gritted his teeth. What he was about to do was definitely not gallant, but he saw no other option. He lifted her gently and tilted her forward. Her head flopped, like a rag doll's, onto his shoulder. He unfastened the tiny buttons behind her neck and eased the fine cotton from her shoulders. Shifting her carefully, he was able to slide two fingers into her chemise and find the bit of glass in the corset's cunning pocket. He managed to safely rearrange her garments and fasten the buttons. Throughout the entire operation, she hadn't so much as stirred. Neither, he noted with relief, had he.

He left the cabin and took up his post outside. When the lock-picker awoke, he would finally learn her mission and they would continue it together. Then he would return her weapon. Or perhaps he had better throw the glass into the sea. If she saw he had it and she understood how he had gotten hold of it, she might try to kill him again, even if they were both on the same side.

ॐ

The Baron was dining alone with Madame Blavatsky who, in deference to him, was apparently willing to forgo her simple tray. The Princess, she was explaining, had been heavily dosed with hallucinogens. "*Mení shkóda,* but it was necessary."

"Caesar would have been most displeased if the body had been damaged," the Baron agreed.

The Blavatsky shot him a look of extreme distaste. "Torture is barbaric," she spat. "And ineffective. People will lie to avoid pain. We must instead dissolve the barricades that hold back the truth."

Baron Haussmann gave a magnificently cavalier shrug. "However you accomplished it, Caesar will be most pleased. It will wear off, will it not?"

"In time. She should respond well to fresh food and clean water. She will want to sleep a great deal. Let her do so. Sleep is best healer of all. There might be occasional recurrences of the illusions, an unavoidable side effect of the ergot. If anything, her fear of these will make her more tractable."

Haussmann nodded. He could appreciate the wisdom of this.

Blavatsky hadn't finished. She set a black leather bag between them on the table. She unbuckled it and he could see it was fitted with rows of small blue bottles. "Should you require assistance while she adjusts to her circumstances, this is my particular compound, a distillation of poppy combined with a few roots and herbs. In measured doses, it will maintain a languid state." Helena didn't relish this treatment, but her Masters had advised it was necessary. Were the girl to have all her wits about her when she found herself in the Caesar's power, her nature would react in such a way that she would set off a disastrous chain of events.

She unrolled a silk-lined purse to display a pair of delicate syringes and a set of needles. She fitted a needle into a syringe and, plucking an orange from the pyramid of fruit, proceeded to show him how to use it. "Between the toes," she suggested, "will leave no trace to mar the affections of the Prince for his bride."

He practiced filling the syringe with water from his otherwise untouched glass and shooting streams of it into the fruit. When she was satisfied with his technique, she put everything back and buckled the case.

"I expect the others have been disposed of?" Haussmann remarked, gesturing for the white-robed servant to refill his wine. The Blavatsky did not herself partake, but she had selected an impeccable vintage and her table was excellent.

She bestowed one of her sphinx-like smiles. "In my own fashion," she said.

"But they are dead?" He did not enjoy being blunt, but this was not a matter to be cryptic about.

She shook her head. "It is against my Teachings to take a life," she noted, most serenely.

"If you require some assistance then…" It was an effort to remain calm. He did not advocate killing as a routine, but there were three witnesses to an act that, when it became known, would cause an international outcry. If they lived to tell, the Emperor would send a centurion to skewer the Baron with a sword or, even worse, enjoin him to do it himself. Damn those ancient Romans and their tradition of honour suicide! He was an old man with few years left, but planned to die uneventfully in his own bed and only when his natural time came. "If you and your people are unable to act, use my men. There is even one of the Caesar's amphoraeka guarding the yacht. Pfffttt! You can feel no compunctions about using one of them!"

"The Masters believe compassion is the Law of Laws," she said, staring at him with her hypnotic eyes. Haussmann tried to look away; he had a fear of looking into those eyes and losing himself to her power. "Your prisoners," she emphasized his ownership, "have been well cared for. Preparations have been made to convey them far enough from here to deflect suspicion when they should be found."

He pushed back. "And you expect them to be found alive?"

"The decision of life or death is not a decision for one man to make for another. It will out as it is meant to be." Never blinking, she explained: "They will be driven from Ragusa, through Herzegovina, to the woods at the Hungarian border. They will not know this; like your princess, they are in a secure sleep. They will be released at night, each with a satchel containing food and drink enough for at least two days. All the contents are dosed. Should it be their karma to be found alive, their story will be so garbled no one will believe it. If they are not meant to survive…" she shrugged. "Either way, their condition when they are found will be out of human hands."

The Baron nodded his head and gestured to have his glass refilled again. Dead or insane. Augustus would be satisfied. It seemed to him that a swift death would more merciful. This woman terrified him. Each time he had to face her, he rued that day in Cairo. Whatever compassion she might claim, she was as cold as ice; he was trapped between her and Caesar's wild burning. He took a deep draught of wine and, as he did in such moments, forced himself to think on the magnificence he had caused to rise from the rubble of ancient Rome. It had been worth dealing with devils to bring that about; of that he was certain. The beauty and harmony of the city would outlive him, would outlive them all.

❧

The carriage had been fitted for the journey through Herzegovina, the curtains rolled down and nailed in place. Tashi, who was to accompany them to the release point and keep them unconscious all that time, stood by to arrange all the prisoners comfortably inside. Gephel had the two largest of his men lift the young women from the remains of their dinner and carry them.

Poor Kola, for whom Tashi was much concerned, was too heavy for the men to handle. The only member of the household strong enough to lift him had been tasked to carry the Princess to the yacht. Gephel recalled the Baron's armed escort waiting in the kitchens and asked for their assistance.

Kola lay unconscious on the bed on which he had spent most of the last three days. The legionaries hoisted him upright and, draping one arm around each of their necks, they would drag a comrade from a bar. He was more of a dead weight than any drunk. They put him down to try again. This time, one took the head and one the feet, and they moved him like a corpse. When they reached a well-lit foyer, the legionary at the head happened to look down. There was something so familiar about this man.

"What did you say his name was?" he asked Gephel.

"Kola," Gephel replied.

"And he came from where?"

Gephel shrugged. "Where they all came from. Prague."

"I could swear I've seen him in Roma." Every time they passed by a good light, the soldier had his partner stop so that he might take a better look. The memory teased him, but wouldn't come.

With Gephel in the lead, they crunched across the gravel to the carriage. The soldiers wanted to slide him in and lay him across the seat, but Tashi had planned to sit beside her patient. She demanded they drag him into a sitting position while she bolstered him with cushions. His head lolled to one side. The angle or the light of the carriage lamp or something clicked.

The soldier turned to his comrade. "Get the Baron," he said, with dawning excitement. "I think we may have something he wants."

Haussmann was annoyed at having to quit the table before he had finished his brandy, but the soldier was atypically insistent. Curious herself, Madame Blavatsky came with them.

Kola had been pulled from the carriage and propped up on the box, Tashi fussing protectively around him. As the Baron's party approached, the legionary holding Kola saluted with his free hand. "Eminenza!"

Haussmann bent to look at the unconscious Kola. An incredulous smile spread across his face. He beamed at the clever soldier. "Well done! You will be rewarded for this, you have my word. Now see him loaded on the yacht and then we will be off."

The two soldiers lifted him as they had before. Tashi tried to stop them.

"Don't worry, my dear," the Baron said with a twinkle. "I will take good care of this young man. Very good care. He, uh, works for me. He was lost and I have been searching for him for some time."

Uncomforted, Tashi reached out again but a single look from her mistress stopped her in her tracks.

"The Baron must care for his own," Blavatsky said softly. "I need you to care for the young ladies." Tashi bowed and climbed miserably into the carriage.

"You have restored my treasure. Thank you, Madame," Haussmann said, with his most respectful bow. "May I offer my most sincere apologies to you and your Masters for any previous doubts? Compassion is indeed the Law of Laws!"

❧

"What do you have there?" Rappaccini called to the men. They were lugging something heavy between them.

"Property of the Baron," one said smartly. They stood by the ladder, wondering how to proceed.

"We could just roll him down," the other said. "He's out so deep he's as good as dead."

The first one, thinking about the reward he now had coming due, shook his head. "Baron wouldn't like if we broke him." They started down the ladder, the one with the feet leading the way. Midway, the man at the top stumbled. The other gasped in horror, but the silent clay guard reached its arms and caught Tesla before his head hit the ground.

It made a rude but oddly poignant Pietà, the clay figure cradling the unconscious man. For a long minute, no one moved. Then the soldiers scrambled down the ladder. The one who'd stumbled assumed a protective bluster. "Where do we put him?"

Rappaccini broke his stare and shrugged. It wasn't his concern. He assumed there were sufficient cabins on the yacht. "Find a place. Best be sure there's a door with a lock."

❧

"Those fools of di Bari's," Haussmann said, narrowing his eyes, apparently determining the level of Rappaccini's personal foolishness. "So busy searching for gold, they nearly discarded the diamond." He entered the cabin with a smile. Having never caught such a feline in the act, Rappaccini had often wondered about the description 'the cat that ate the canary' until he saw that smile. The Baron's rapture might be a boon. He hoped to exchange some whispers with the girl on the train to Rome. With the Baron distracted by his treasure, this might be easier to accomplish.

After too short a time, the Baron stormed out of the cabin, as vexed now as he recently had been pleased. "Pfffttt! They've ruined him!" the Baron muttered, glaring at the surrogate for his anger. "Awake, but I can get more sense out of Lady Giulia's parrot. Your fellow imbeciles have ruined Nikola Tesla!"

The Baron stomped off to his own quarters.

Micah felt a stone drop to the pit of his stomach. This was the famous Tesla, the genius the Baron thought essential to Augustus's plans? He ought to have made the connection at once and done something. Not that there was anything much he could have done. Most of the damage had occurred before he'd clapped eyes on Kola. That is, Tesla. In any case, once the man's condition had been understood, Madame Blavatsky had set her little nurse to help. Madame B was, in her way, a professional and had the professional's distaste for excess. Now the patient had passed from her influence to his and he must intervene in whatever way might present itself.

If Tesla's mind could be salvaged and managed, the scientist was a pearl beyond price. If it could not be, or if Haussmann and the Emperor owned it, Micah would have to be ruthless and destroy it utterly. It would require delicate balancing, to reap the benefits of that brain while controlling it to the proper end, all the more challenging because Haussmann would be playing the same game with the advantage of operating openly. The man known as Rappaccini found this challenge exhilarating; it was why, as he had known from the day he joined the Service, the life he'd chosen was the best life imaginable.

There was a deep quiet in the yacht. Everyone seemed to be catching a few hours sleep except Rappaccini and the amphoraka who were both on watch.

Did the clay creatures have such an experience as sleep? Micah was curious. He climbed enough rungs of the ladder to bring himself face to face. Peering into the blank mask made him inexplicably sad. "I mean to help," he was moved to whisper. The familiar bluish light glimmered behind the eye holes; there was no telling what that might represent. Would it stop him, if he tried to enter Tesla's cabin? There was only one way to find out.

The creature never moved. Micah left the cabin door open so that he would not be trapped or surprised. He walked softly to the bunk. Tesla must have extreme resistance to the sleeping draught, just as Verdi had claimed. His breath was that of a man fully alert and his eyes, although unfocused, were wide open. Micah touched him on the cheek, to see if he would respond. Tesla turned his head.

"Hello, Sunshine."

Tesla could swear he heard a whisper of English, in an English voice. Someone was standing over him. He blinked to focus his eyes on the wavering shapes.

"It's alright," the voice continued. "Don't try to speak. I'm a friend, but we must keep this a secret between us two."

The man, whose form Tesla could finally identify, was the lean, elegant tool of Rome he had seen in the old woman's parlour.

"There's no need to worry, Mr. Tesla," the man murmured. "Whatever happens, you must trust me." Nikola didn't want to move. "Do you understand me? Don't say a word. Blink twice if you do." Tesla blinked twice. "Good. The Baron said he found you incoherent, but I have hopes that together you and I can make some sense. You've been heavily drugged, most recently with opium. In my work, I have seen the effects of opium. The influence will pass. You may be unwell for a time, but your head will clear."

The man's voice was soothing and there was comfort in what he said. "Yes," Tesla breathed.

"Very good, Mr. Tesla," the man squeezed his shoulder, as a friend might. "I am called Rappaccini. For your own safety and for mine, that is the only name by which you may know me. I don't know how much time we have together but, when we part, I will ensure that we will meet again. This boat docks at Lucco in only a few more hours. From there, we go by train to Rome. By the Emperor's private railway. He believes we are bringing his grandson a bride. He is wrong. They all are."

Tesla had no idea what the man was talking about.

"It is not the Princess we bring, but the girl with whom you were taken."

"Claude!" This one fact had gotten through. Tesla tried to cry out, but his voice sounded like a mouse's squeak.

"Shhh! We don't want the Baron to know you're alert. Don't speak until I say so. But you and I know," the man smiled, "the girl is an agent of Pinkerton's."

"Pinker...?"

"Hush!"

There had been a sound outside. Rappaccini moved away from the bunk. He spoke in Italian to someone on the other side of the door, someone who entered the room. Tesla painfully raised his head, only to see the face of his worst nightmare.

"Such an unexpected pleasure," Baron Haussmann purred. "Di Bari's fools didn't know the treasure they'd retrieved. Rappaccini tells me you cried out and he came in to see what was wrong."

Tesla shot a look at the other man who gave a meaningful nod. "Yes," he confirmed, as loudly as he could.

"What was wrong then?"

Before Tesla could think of answer, Rappaccini interrupted with smooth flow of Italian. "I don't know, Eminenza. He had not fallen from the bed and there were no injuries I could see. I could not question him. I was about to call you. With your many languages..."

"You speak English, do you not Rappaccini?"

"Si, Eminenza. But I thought you would prefer that the prisoner be kept ignorant."

Haussmann performed the girlish smirk that was part of his repertoire of smiles. He was, as he liked to tell people, a happy man by nature, and smiled often. It was a prudent underling who learned the language of those smiles. "I applaud your discretion, Rappaccini," he said. "As I have long suspected, you are superior to di Bari's usual league of fools. You have thought well, for all that your conclusion is wrong."

Rappaccini accepted the gentle rebuke gracefully, with his own inward smile for having selected the correct move. He was now free to speak with Tesla in English without raising suspicions. As long as they kept outside the Baron's own hearing, they could communicate openly, with no one to understand what passed between them.

Tesla's eyes were closing again. The Baron indicated they should leave. He locked the cabin door behind him.

"Watch!" he said to the amphoraka. The creature shifted its bulk to take up a position midway between the two locked doors.

Gesturing for Rappaccini to follow, the Baron went to his own cabin and poured a pair of brandies. He handed one to Rappaccini and took a generous swallow of his own. "What can you tell me about what they gave him?"

"The squadra who brought him had some...difficulties." He did not want to give an impression of assigning blame; he sensed it would not be taken well. "He was given a combination of substances. When Madame understood his distress, she assigned a healer to him. I do not believe he was given any additional medications until the sleeping draught that was administered tonight."

The Baron considered this. "Whatever was given to him needs to be expelled from the body, like any poison."

"Give him a purge and sweat him, then a few days of clean food and water." Rappaccini said. It was time for a display of confidence.

"I can't keep him drugged if I'm going to get any useful work out of him," the Baron fretted. "And I don't only need his mind to be sharp, I need it to be mine. I need him to work willingly. Pfffttt!" He twirled his glass so that the cuts in the crystal threw splinters of rainbow on his hand. "I had him two years ago, you know."

Rappaccini had been in Napoli at that time, working to attract the notice of di Bari's regional secundus. "Did he escape?"

"No. I let him go." He took a considering sip.

"Forgive, Eminenza, but that puzzles me."

"Vanity," the Baron shrugged. "I had promised to do so. I thought to get the best fruits of his genius by allowing him to feel some freedom. Once he had fulfilled his part of the bargain, I felt the desire to respond in kind. I have regretted that moment of indulgence these two long years."

"Today your generosity was rewarded," Rappaccini suggested.

"So it was, so it was." Haussmann looked hard at the centurion. "We soon reach Lucco. The Lady Giulia is meeting us there, to greet the royal bride." He said this with an astonishing lack of sarcasm. "I have decided I will accompany the ladies to Roma and present the Principessa to Caesar. You will wait here for me with our Mr. Tesla. This will give you two days for the regimen you suggest. Two more as we sail to Venezia. You are billeted in Venezia, are you not?"

"Si, Eminenza."

"Excellent. I would sleep now, Rappaccini."

The Lady Giulia arrived via the Baron's beautifully engineered railway lines, on Caesar's luxurious private train, to escort the bride to the capital. She brought an elaborate gown, white in token of the girl's virgin state, with an embroidered velvet waistcoat of Augustus's favourite imperial purple. She found the girl unconscious and as cumbersome as a sodden bolster. It would have taken four women to dress her; Giulia had brought only one. They had to leave her in the same crumpled travel clothes she had been wearing since being taken in Prague.

The legionaries carried the sleeping princess from the yacht on an improvised stretcher made from the silk bed cover. Giulia followed in a majestic huff. She was not at all pleased. Her plan had been to dazzle the English girl with the magnificence of the Second Roman Empire. The carriage had been filled with orchids. A delicate feast of peacock and caviar had been laid out on the gilt table. Asleep, all the glory was wasted on her.

As ordered, Rappaccini stood on the deck with Tesla to watch them leave. The Baron felt it would increase his hold over the inventor.

"Our Mr. Tesla has three sisters, Rappaccini," Haussmann had said. "Did you know that?"

"No, Eminenza."

"Ah, well. He has not been your subject as he has been mine. He appears somewhat coarse, but he is sentimental about young women. I understand he was much concerned about the one with whom he was found, the one those fools confused with the Principessa." Having seen only one girl, Haussmann found the confusion ludicrous to imagine. "Of course, I did not see the other, but the Principessa Maud has quite a distinctive appearance, does she not?"

"Si, Eminenza."

"I dare say they had some general similarities of colour and shape," he had sniffed. "We will make use of this and allow Tesla to see the Principessa from a distance. Let him think the safety of his own young woman is in his hands." The neatness of the idea had pleased the Baron.

Now Rappaccini kept close to the still-groggy scientist. "You must not say a word," he cautioned. He told the lie he wished were the truth. "She is well. She is merely feigning, to keep them off their guard. She will be listening to everything they say, to use it later to her advantage."

"Why don't we rescue her!?" Tesla's lethargy was replaced with a wild glint in his eyes and he seemed ready to spring. It required a trained, muscular clamp on his arm to keep him in place. "There are two of them and two of us. The old man will not fight."

"No, but the Lady Giulia will. I have met with more than one lieutenant who claims to have the scars on his back to prove it. And you forget…" he nodded toward the amphoraka who stood temporarily on the dock. Nikola refused to look at it. Since regaining consciousness, he hadn't once acknowledged it, though it was often hovering nearby, if such a massive thing could be said to hover.

"Then why did you bring me here, if all I can do is say goodbye?"

"You must not say a word! We are here because the Baron wants you to think you stand surety for her safety."

"If I do not do as he asks, he will harm her?"

"Not a hair on her head, I assure you." This, at least, was pure truth. "Not as long as he thinks she is the English princess. Now hush!"

The Baron had appeared at the top of the ladder. Rappaccini approached the old man and offered a hand. Haussmann raised himself up on deck and smoothed his coat, "though why I bother, I don't know," he observed. "Eight hours on a train will spoil the lines completely. Rappaccini, I leave Mr. Tesla in your competent hands."

Rappaccini gave the proper salute, Tesla looked down at his shoes and the Baron disembarked.

The two men remained on deck, their eyes following the strange little procession. A few minutes after the Baron's back had disappeared, the amphoraka, which had been hoisted up top by a specialized steam crane, shifted its weight and set the yacht swaying. They were alone, just the three of them and a skeleton crew.

⚓

He was of two minds about the entire situation. That was an inadequate phrase if ever there were one: "of two minds." His lip curled as he thought it. For Rianero/Fairservis, now cloaked in Rappaccini, two minds was a comfortable minimum. What he could have used now was two bodies, the extra one to go to Rome with the girl while this one stayed on the boat with Nikola Tesla.

It would have been preferable for the Baron escort his own prize to whatever laboratory gaol he had waiting up north. Micah had hoped to be sent to Rome with the girl and then somehow wangle his way into good enough graces to stay close to her for as long as possible, at least until her mind had cleared and he might finally learn her intent. But one must make do with the hand one is dealt. The girl was gone. While he had the opportunity, he would need to maximize his efforts with Tesla and recoup what advantage he might.

He knew his time was short. He treated the man as he had tended his mother over her long final illness, solicitously pushing a steady flow of clean water and food into him, distracting him with light conversation and having him take frequent rests. The sedation passed out of his system but, Micah discovered, the inventor was still not quite right in the mind.

Perhaps whatever had occurred on the ride from Prague had unhinged him, or perhaps he had always been like this and recent events had merely dissolved the barriers that had kept it under control; whatever the cause, Tesla's current state was not drugged but lunatic. There was a humid pallor to his skin, and a slightly clammy odor rose like an echo from his body. When instructed to eat, to wash his teeth, to follow from place to place, he remained docile; 'defeated' might perhaps be the better word.

He spoke about the past as though it were the present, then if questioned, would look at Micah as if it were the question that was in error. Agreeing with him was equally apt to rebound. Once, for example, Tesla spoke anxiously about the possibility his mother might be worrying about him.

"Don't be distressed," Micah assured him; "I'll see that your mother gets word that you're safe."

Tesla looked at him with a crafty grin. "Do you think you can trick me?" he asked. "My mother has been dead these five years!"

The scientist could seem lucid enough for an hour or two, but his sentences were often disjointed and there was something frenetic about the way he delivered them. Except when delivering one of his short, impassioned speeches, he wore a faraway look in his eyes. Sometimes he would stop in the middle of a thought to walk across whatever space they were in and stare fixedly at some minor thing that had drawn him: a hinge fastened by unmatched nails, a bird on the horizon.

Micah kept his tone calm and tried to maintain a reassuring and soothing presence. It was critical that Tesla trust him and that they form some kind of bond but, towards the middle of the second day, he began to worry he might never accomplish this goal.

"The girl…" Micah needed not another syllable. In Tesla's mind, there was only one girl.

"I thought you said we were not to speak of her!"

He had. Until now, whenever Tesla had raised this subject, he had diverted the conversation, afraid of agitating the inventor beyond control; but he needed to make an emotional connection and this was the only avenue available. He would have to take that risk. "We can make an exception just this once. The crew is gone ashore and the Baron isn't

166

expected for some hours." He sat down on the banquette and poured them each a glass of the barley water he'd made with his own hands when the Italian cook refused to believe Tesla would not recuperate on wine. "How did you come to know her in Prague?"

"Not in Prague. In Chicago. I worked for a time with her father. Her father is Frank Monteith."

"Why do I know that name?" Micah was beginning to have the feeling he had missed something in his excitement at learning Tesla's identity. There was something else, but what?

"The inventor. The great inventor. There are very few men I admire…" Tesla plunked himself down opposite, stretching his long legs so that his boots were resting on Rappaccini's banquette. With the gears clicking in his head, Micah hardly noticed. "Oh, there are a lot of clever men who hit on some idea and make it sing. But he is the only person who could match my understanding of the concepts we used to build the radio-operated digging apparatus. And the scope of that man's thinking! Of course you know he invented Vitriflex, the translucent silicon they use for aership windows."

Fairservis hadn't. He was not as attentive to science as he perhaps should be; politics was more his forte. But that name sounded oddly familiar.

"And he knows more about Prometheum than anyone living. He pioneered industrial applications of the compound's propulsive properties. Then there's the Franklin emulsion process for photographic plates, the aether spectrometer, the Franklin hinge…Can you conceive of a mind that might encompass all of that?! Other than my own, that is." Tesla took a another greedy gulp. Micah noted that his hunch about fluid intake had been a sound one. He also perceived that whatever mental weaknesses Tesla might suffer, a low self-opinion wasn't one of them.

Micah was curious about one thing. "Why 'Franklin' if his family name is Monteith?" he asked.

"To honour his ancestor, the great inventor and philosopher Benjamin Franklin. His own proper name is Franklin."

Of course! The legendary Sir Alastair Franklin Menzies, the man at the head of the American branch of the British Special Service. "Monteith" must be some sort of cover name. Micah was even more impressed by his talents than Tesla. The more shocking revelation was that the female spy was apparently Sir Alastair's own daughter. If one had a trained agent who bore such a resemblance, it would have been the obvious decision to make, but if that agent were your own child…Despite his predisposition to be skeptical of outsized reputations, Micah had to acknowledge a grudging respect for the fabled Sir Alastair. A man who could be that cold in the pursuit of duty was someone he could learn to admire.

"Oh yes, of course," is what Micah said to Tesla. "He's a great man. We have mutual friends. In England."

"You do? Can you get word to him?"

"About you? I had expected…"

"No, about Claude! That the Emperor has her!" Tesla had that wild look again.

Micah assumed this to have been Sir Alastair's plan all along. Apparently the inventor didn't know of his hero's other life. "Yes, of course. I will do everything in my power. But remember," when Tesla's face turned like that, Micah knew he was about to lose him, "for both your sakes, we must play along with the Baron for a while."

"To see her carried out like that!" Tesla grabbed a handful of hair in anguish; Micah was learning that Serbians were even more dramatic than Italians. "So fragile and white. To have to stand and watch and not even be allowed to say goodbye. Not to be able to look into her eyes and reassure her that I am here for her. Her eyes are so beautiful, like quicksilver, don't you think?"

Micah startled. The girl on the boat, the girl now on her way to Rome and Caesar, had eyes the colour of amber. Could this be another slip in Tesla's mind? Micah knew that she was the girl who had attacked him with the bit of glass. She was the same one who had tried to escape that first night, wasn't she? He thought back to that meeting in the corridor. She had been like some wrathful goddess, her eyes blazing…cold. As lightning. His stomach plummeted. Grey. Why could he remember this now and not before? Sweet merciful God, the girl on her way to Rome really *was* Princess Maud!

&.

Haussmann returned that evening, literally humming with pleasure at the success of his journey to Rome. He had left the Principessa still asleep— could Rappaccini credit it?—but Caesar was most pleased all the same. Augustus had met the train himself and had personally seen to the Principessa's comfort, even pushing a lock of hair from her face with a truly paternal tenderness. The Baron's eyes grew moist at the telling; he dabbed at them with a pristine square of lawn.

Asleep though she be, she had been accorded every courtesy due to a royal bride. Her household had been established in the Villa Borghese, such a delightful little jewel box nestled in the most charming gardens! Lady Giulia had selected all of Maud's ladies as well as personal guards, and would herself keep rooms in the villa until the Principessa had adapted to her new station. As the Baron was taking his leave, the Lady's own seamstress had arrived to take the Principessa's measurements and begin her wardrobe.

Courtesy had been paid to the Baron as well. There had been a particularly fine banquet last night in his honour, no expense spared. As a nod to the absent Principessa, dessert had been tiny pastry crowns, gilded with gold leaf and containing a gold-flecked custard that had been frozen in Alpine snow. It was understood that the British were most fond of custard.

Best of all, Haussmann had been given a blank check to expedite completion of his pet project, the restoration of the Colosseum. The work had moved forward in fits and starts for years, hampered by the prodigious cost of such a monumental reconstruction and Caesar's alternately waxing and waning enthusiasm. With Augustus determined to celebrate the imperial wedding there, no cost or effort would now be too high.

"Well?" the Baron said, finally drawing a breath. He had the tiniest bit of threat in his twinkling eyes.

"See for yourself, Eminenza." Rappaccini pointed at the window in the door to the dining cabin. A calm and alert Nikola Tesla sat at the table, eating a roasted bird. There was no hint that his earlier paean to Claude's beautiful eyes had blossomed into a fit so prolonged as to exhaust him until he had slept like the dead for four hours. It was an enormous relief when he woke and demanded food. "He is a little bored, now, I think. He asked for a book, but there were none in any language he could read."

"Ridiculous that he has so little Italian," the Baron said with a little pfft of impatience. "He's a Serbian. They've been under the administration of the Empire longer than he's been alive."

"Perhaps he comes of a Nationalist family," Rappaccini suggested.

"He will have plenty of time to learn. I hope he doesn't pick up that bastard Venetian patois instead." The Baron stifled a yawn. "I will speak with Mr. Tesla tomorrow. It has been an eventful few days and a good night's rest will be welcome. I have given the captain my instructions. We will sail north as we sleep. I will dine alone in my cabin. Good evening, Rappaccini." The Baron nodded politely and started toward the stern.

"Very good, Eminenza." Rappaccini saluted, relieved to not have to manage a confrontation tonight. He would now be able to enjoy his own dinner. A carafe of good wine would be particularly welcome.

"Oh, and Rappaccini," the Baron gave the penetrating look that always seemed at odds with his somewhat foppish personality. Well done."

Now that he had everything he wanted, the Baron was pleased to take his time. He breakfasted in his cabin, giving Fairservis time to settle Tesla and prepare him for the eventual meeting.

"I don't know what he plans," Micah warned, "other than having you work on some project for Augustus. Do what he asks and know we will find a way out. And should I act cold or even cruel, know always that I am your friend."

"And hers," Tesla insisted.

Until such time as Micah was certain that Tesla made a trustworthy collaborator, it seemed prudent to allow him to continue to believe that the girl in Rome was his Claude. "And hers," he agreed.

11 - BABES IN THE WOODS

Taking the air on deck, the Baron was happy to discuss the future with the two younger men. "In a few hours we will arrive in Venezia, a city of great charm and of considerable interest to an engineer such as myself—to you as well, I should imagine. Indeed, were it not for the stench of the canals, it would be quite perfect. You are quartered there, are you not Rappaccini?"

"Si Eminenza. La Serenissima is a most beautiful city."

"Once I have completed work on the Colosseum, perhaps I will turn my attention to the canals. Have you been to Venezia, Signor Tesla?"

"No, Baron."

"A great pity." The Baron seemed genuinely sad, shaking his head like an old dog. A happy thought occurred to brighten his face. "I know! We will put in at San Marco and I will have the boat go on to meet us at the Fondamente Nuove. In that way, I can at least show you some of the beauties of the place before putting you to work."

Before Tesla could find the courage to ask what his work might be, the Baron had gone to speak to the captain and wasn't seen again until they had come within sight of land.

Watching the wonder bloom on Tesla's face as Venice shimmered into view, Micah recalled his own first sight of the Queen of the Adriatic. It had been one of his mother's favourite memories. His parents, in the first happy years of their all too brief marriage, had spent some enchanted weeks here. For their son, sight unseen, the city was a memory of a life that had never been. Returning to Italy for the first time since his childhood, he'd lived for nearly a year in Naples, establishing himself as Benvolio Rappaccini, a young man with a future. When Rappaccini had managed to get himself recruited by di Bari and was summoned to Venice, he had been more afraid of disappointment than of discovery; if the place had been banal, it would have cut deeper than a knife. He'd stood on the ship, as Tesla stood now, hardly breathing. It had rained that morning, and the sun shone with the soft diffusion of light passing through the pearly walls of a shell. He could still feel the sigh, his chest opening with piercing sweetness, at the first sight of the Salute, which had been rendered more magical than ever through the veil of that light. From a distance, it was the sheer impossibility of Venice that touched the heart. No child who, with head on the pillow and eyes heavy with the onset of sleep, had ever dreamed a city, could have dreamt a more fantastic place. Close up, some of the fairy tale aspect disappeared into crumbling walls, the stink of fish and sewage, and as much jostle and bustle as Smithfield market, but the vitality was as engaging as the distant fantasy had been. Not even the abundance of uniforms, nor the numerous Imperial decorations, could spoil it. Sometimes Micah felt a measure of guilt for the gratitude that his double life had opened the door to this city.

The Baron nimbly threaded his way to what was still, despite Augustus's fiercely monitored borders, the Drawing Room of Europe. While they sat over coffee at Florian's, the Baron pointed out the beauties of the Basilica and the Campanile and at last told Tesla his assignment. "You will be working with the amphoraeka. It will not be the first time you have worked on their arms." Haussmann tittered; "it's an amusing pun in English." Both of the younger men regarded him blankly. Controlling his mirth, the Baron explained that Tesla was to prepare the creatures for battle with weaponry that could be integrated with their bodies. "Much more practical than having them wield battle axes. To start, a blade should fit neatly and ought to be simple for someone of your gifts. After that, a greater challenge. Caesar observes that some type of Greek fire would be apt as well as effective."

It was clear that, had he been a fox, Tesla would have gnawed off his own paw to get out of this trap. Rappaccini fixed him with a steading gaze but it was ignored. Under cover of retrieving a dropped spoon, he bent passed the inventor's ear and hissed the one word, "Claude!" Tesla swallowed hard.

The Baron, prattling on about vehicles that could efficiently convey a platoon of the massive troops, had blessedly missed the incident. As they ambled down the winding alleys towards the Fondamente, he kept up a running commentary on the scenery, never acknowledging the mournful silence that shrouded Tesla. The brief flutter of excitement had died as soon as the Baron explained his undertaking. The scientist's feet dragged on the stones. Now and then, Rappaccini had to give him a little prod to keep him moving. He allowed himself to be led to the waiting yacht like a sleepwalker and was silent for the remainder of the journey.

Haussmann had reasoned that the Venetian lagoon would make an excellent natural prison and so, a year before, had established a laboratory on Murano, where it disappeared neatly among the glass furnaces that lined the small island. Before leaving Dubrovnik, he had wired di Bari to have his agents in Venezia ready the place for immediate occupancy. Without a boat at his disposal, Tesla would be securely marooned.

The yacht pulled up beside the innocuous dock. When the crew had made it fast, the Baron disembarked, followed by Tesla and Rappaccini. A loud and treacherous creaking alerted them to the amphoraka shifting heavily from deck to dock behind them. The Baron produced an old iron key and unlocked the door.

Empty thought it felt, the building seemed clean and well aired. There was not another person in sight though, as the Baron led them through the rooms, several amphoraeka could be spotted in the shadows, four or five in addition to the one from the boat who now stood beside the entrance. The men toured the well-furnished living quarters—bedroom, study, kitchen, even a water closet and bath—before reaching the workroom.

It was, as the Baron said, "original to the *fornace*, which is what they call a glass furnace here. You know, Mr. Tesla, we must start to teach you Italian." A high-ceilinged room, it was generous enough to have accommodated half a dozen master blowers and their teams. Now it was filled with obviously new equipment of various kinds, as well as whatever materials had been suggested by the engineers the Baron had consulted. "And lit with electrical lamps of your own design, you will be pleased to note." Tesla showed no reaction, but the Baron was nearly dancing with pleasure.

"The challenge, as you will recall Mr. Tesla, is that no metal can be incorporated into the fabric of the bodies of the amphoraeka and, for anything that might be attached to them, you are only to use metals that were known to the ancient Egyptians. For the vehicle, you may use anything you please. If you don't see it here, you need only ask and it is yours. But for the weaponry to be attached…gold, silver, copper, lead, bronze, iron…you understand. We tried once to encase a steel blade in an arm with an unpleasant result."

"Do they die?" Rappaccini asked, all innocence.

The Baron chuckled. "Not to worry. They're like stone walls; blows, even blades and gunshot, glance right off them. We had one, early on, wander onto a railroad track. That was before we'd learned how to…eh, train them…to ensure they would follow orders. This particular one stood directly in the path of an oncoming train and refused to budge. The front of the engine folded up like a concertina. All that happened to the amphoraka was an arm breaking off. As Mr. Tesla well knows, we can easily replace those."

"And the people?" Tesla asked, his eyes as wide as if he had witnessed the scene. They were the first words he'd spoken since they arrived.

"Very sad." The Baron dabbed his eye with his omnipresent snowy handkerchief. "Some died. The engineer, of course, and others. And many were injured. Such is the cost of progress. We learned much from that day." He brightened at a random recollection. "One little boy was found wandering a nearby field. He'd been thrown clear of the wreck. Sooty as a sweep, all scratched and bruised, but entirely intact. Quite miraculous. Playing with the wildflowers and singing to his little self in the sweetest voice. Caesar was most taken with him, still keeps him in his household. The sweetest voice. What was I saying?"

"No metal," Rappaccini said helpfully.

"Yes, yes. Anything at all for the vehicle, or even for something they might be made to handle. Not that they have hands as such," he briefly compressed his fingers so that his hand showed like an amphoraka's as a pad with but a single split, "but you get my point. No metal to be attached, other than the ones I've already mentioned. Those are all benign. Caesar's own special one, the prototype, as it were, for what you see," the Baron gestured expansively as if to encompass every amphoraka in Italy as well as the one whose eye sockets glowed blue in the corner of the present room, "the 'Golden One', as it is called, is literally painted with liquid gold and to no ill effect. It was that clue that helped us to an understanding, though it took several ugly experiments to reach our conclusions," he added with a moue of distaste.

"I can't," Tesla muttered. The ranks of bottles and tubes in their racks, shelves and shelves brimming with bins, tools in neat bright rows on the benches…The room began to oscillate. He would have toppled over, had Rappaccini not grabbed his elbow and steadied him just in time.

Haussmann, who had been admiring the rugged authenticity of the original furnace, heard the scuffle and turned. "Mr. Tesla!" he exclaimed, "you are unhappy!"

Tesla hunched his shoulders and looked at his shoes. For himself, he would have gladly struck the old man dead and exultantly faced his own inevitable death at the hand of the trecika, but what would happen to Claude? He dared say nothing.

"Now then, Mr. Tesla, you know I'm not a cruel man," the Baron said, sounding almost hurt. "I want you to feel safe and comfortable. Aren't these pleasant rooms? You even have a small garden." He opened a door in the blackened wall. The stream of sunlight made the room seem dim by comparison. A faint sweet breeze ruffled by.

"I'll be alone," Tesla mumbled.

"Alone? You have the best bodyguards in the world to protect you. They can't cook or clean for you, of course; you'll have to do that yourself."

"I'll have no one to talk to. And what if I need something? Something for my work," he said with cunning.

"Someone will come every few days to check. I'll have Rappaccini come on the food boat. You know him."

Tesla looked hopeful. Rappaccini displayed obvious annoyance.

"I will speak with the Conte di Bari myself." The Baron's tone brooked no dissent.

"Si Eminenza." The salute Rappaccini sketched was only minimally respectful. This pleased the Baron more than fawning submission would have. Men like Rappaccini, though Haussmann would not have been able to explain what he meant by that, must learn they were not in control.

The centurion retained his disgruntled aspect as they parted from the lost-looking Tesla and took the yacht to di Bari's headquarters in the Castello.

Having checked in with the tessarius, he parted from the Baron with another terse salute and made his way to the Cannaregio, where Rappaccini allegedly kept his mistress and Micah kept a distant cousin who was as invincibly loyal as she was (for form's sake) pretty and who, more importantly, rode like a demon.

❦

The Pinkertons were finishing dinner when Thompson brought the wire. Lord Pinkerton glanced at the paper. "From Tucker," he said aloud.

"Excellent!" Joan said brightly. "We'll leave you, then." She had no idea what the cables said, but she knew that Tucker meant Italy and any word from Italy was particularly important. She had also been told it was important for her to keep Nan Hudson occupied so that she wouldn't trouble herself over what her brother and niece might be doing in Prague. Tonight she would take Nan to the Lyceum to see the latest piece by Mr. Pinero. Mr. Archer, who Joan trusted as being a good Scottish critic, had written well of it. Allan had planned to accompany them. "I'll give

Thompson your ticket on the chance you'll be able to join us at the interval. Come, Nan."

Pinkerton nodded absently and began to read. Tucker reported that the Emperor's plan had moved too quickly for the Princess to be extracted. She was in Rome. Also, Pinkerton was to advise Sir Alastair that the inventor, Tesla, was being held in Venice. As for the other young women, Tucker had been told that they had last been seen alive and well in Dubrovnik, and were said to have been released by Blavatsky, but Horner had been unable to learn anything further of their fate.

Pinkerton wished he'd passed on the rich lobster bisque and limited himself to lemon sole and peas. The heiress to the British throne was in the hands of mad Augustus, as was the man who appeared to be the best hope at defeating him. If they were lucky, the innocent granddaughter of a wealthy—and, moreover, political—Liberal baronet was captive somewhere in Ragusa, together that other mysterious English girl. That all four captives had last been seen alive was cold comfort. Pinkerton's intestines were twisting into knots that would have done a sailor proud. He would ring for a chamomile tisane to settle his digestion and then compose a wire to Menzies. There was no need to speak with the Queen before morning. Perhaps Joan was right; he should speak with Dr. Gull about a sleeping draught.

Maud awoke screaming. Even before she opened her eyes she knew something was terribly wrong. The bedclothes were silk and the room smelled of gardenia, a flower she had always found suffocatingly sweet. Her thoughts were jumbled with traces of a nightmare that she somehow knew was not dream at all but shards of broken memory. She had been shopping with Gertrude. Then some men...a black beard, a sting in her arm, blood...Poor Captain Piper!

That last memory made her scream and, once she started, she couldn't stop. The images crashed like Devon surf against her mind. The woman with the pale stare. Tile floors in an intricate pattern that wouldn't stop moving. A room with a fountain that spun around and around, and birds...she felt a special giddiness when she thought of the birds, a sick sensation that had something do to with colours doing what colours oughtn't do. Her eyes turned grey in the mirror. Not a mirror, a girl...The scream stopped, choked in her throat, and she grabbed at her corset for a...what? For something sharp, a weapon...where was her corset? She screamed again, the sound roaring up from deep inside her, filling her ears and shaking the bedposts.

If her mind had been clear, she would have expected her screams to draw a crowd; and if she could have heard the clatter of running feet in the hallway, she wouldn't have been shocked when the door blew open, filling the room with people. There were a pair of frightened maids in an unfamiliar livery and a worried little man with the large bag and pocket watch of a physician, all hurrying up to the bed. A soldier entered with his sword drawn, pushing everyone else aside as he inspected the scene for intruders.

Finally, the blackest man Maud had ever seen filled the doorway. He made a deep obeisance in her direction, causing her to press herself against the headboard, the bedclothes clutched under her chin. He was not tall, but his muscles, bulging out of a bronze leather doublet and kilt, were terrifying. He bowed again, more deeply still, and stepped back to admit a small, pale woman.

As a character entering on stage in a play, the woman would have looked like a joke but, in this room, the power radiating from her tiny figure made her inspire fear rather than laughter. She strode on golden high-heeled sandals that glittered with emeralds. Her purple silk draperies were fastened at the shoulders, antique fashion, with emerald and diamond clips. More emeralds and diamonds dripped from her ears and long neck, and were roped through her hair. Beneath the yolk-yellow curls, her face appeared even more raddled than it was because of the cosmetics she employed in an attempt to look younger: her eyes were ringed with kohl, her thin lips smudged with carmine and there were doll-like dabs of rouge centered on her cheekbones.

She drew near to the bed.

Maud felt she would have to scream again, but instead she sneezed; the woman reeked of gardenia.

"Your Royal Highness," the woman said with regal nod. Her voice, thickly accenting the English words, had the chill musicality of ice tinkling in a crystal pitcher. It made Maud want to swallow, but her mouth was too dry.

"Where am I?" Maud tried to be imperious but it came out as a croak. How long had it been since she'd spoken? And where was Gertrude?

"Welcome to Roma, Your Royal Highness. *Benvenuti a Roma*." The woman sketched a curtsey. Behind her, the maids curtseyed nearly down to the floor and the men bowed. "I am the Lady Giulia," she continued in Italian. "You shall call me *Zia*, Aunt, as I shall be so once you have married Gusto."

"Married?" Maud tried to clear her throat. She wondered if she had misunderstood.

"Yes of course." The Lady Giulia had the smile of a boy pinning a living butterfly into his specimen case. "To Prince Napoleon Auguste," she cooed; "my beloved nephew and Caesar's heir."

Maud opened and closed her mouth like a landed fish. No sound came out. This was a nightmare, Grandmama's worst nightmare come true. She felt her chest rise and fall, but no air seemed to be reaching her lungs. She reached out a hand, flexing her fingers, grasping frantically at nothing.

The doctor scurried over and put his fingers on her wrist. Consulting his pocket watch, he made grave medical sounds and shook his head. Giulia looked down her nose at him. Meeting that gaze, he seemed to shrink until he was smaller than the Lady. Giulia pointed an elegant bony finger at the leather bag.

"As the Baron instructed," she said. He began to fumble at the catches. She fixed Maud with her pitiless black stare and smiled again. "We must not have you making yourself ill. You are unsettled from your journey, that is all. You will soon be calm. Your maids will bathe you and you will wear one of your beautiful new gowns. Then you and I will take the air together. We are going to become good friends." It sounded more like a threat than a comfort.

Maud felt a hand grab at her ankle from under the sheet. Before she could twitch it away, something stuck her between her toes. The pain was little more than an insect bite, but her heart ached and the tears rolled down her cheeks.

Giulia sketched another curtsey and withdrew as majestically as she'd arrived, trailed by her bodyguard and the soldier. The doctor made an apologetic bow and hurried away.

Alone, the maids eyed her cautiously. When it was clear that she would no longer scream and would not bite, they came close enough to help her from the bed and through a connecting door into a marble bath. "*Pace, Principessa*," one of them said, daring to pat her hair, "all will be well."

By the time she had been lowered into the tub, her heart flutterings had subsided. Her anxiety seeped from her pores into the warm, scented water. Perhaps all was well. It didn't seem to matter; nothing seemed to matter very much.

❦

Claude awakened to a sensory barrage. Her head felt like lead, her back ached and something was poking her in the ribs. She could swear she heard twigs snapping and she caught a whiff of some very fresh spoor. Though her eyes were open, she could see nothing at all. The blanket must have slipped over her head. She pulled it off and felt a button. Not a blanket; her coat. She moved it and tried to lift her head, gingerly, an inch or two from where it was pillowed on her other arm.

Slowly, the world came into focus. There were short grasses at eye level, and an unfamiliar weed. She tried to push herself up off the ground, but the arm she had been sleeping on was numb as a post. It took some doing to struggle into a sitting position. Whatever had been digging into her ribs now made an uncomfortable bump under her bottom. She reached with her working arm and dragged out a leather bag. The large brass buckle must have been poking her. She unfastened it and peered inside. There was food. The idea of food was disgusting. Just the smell made her gorge rise and she stumbled upright to vomit, leaning heavily on a nearby tree.

It was a large tree. Some kind of beech, her hand told her from stroking the bark. Steading herself, she started to survey her surroundings. She was standing in a small clearing ringed with more such trees. She tried to look beyond them and saw a foliage-thick darkness. A forest then. How had she wandered so far from the tent? Her mouth felt disgusting now and she was so thirsty! There must be a stream nearby or they wouldn't have stopped here. She would have to find it. And where were Father and Leski? She shook her head to clear it. She remembered something about a vision quest. Was that it? Had they smoked a pipe and sent her forth? Why couldn't she remember?

She heard a groan and turned toward the sound. It was strange, but until now she hadn't noticed the other mound in the clearing. It was a young woman, someone she knew. It was Gertrude Bell. What an idiot she was! This was no family camping trip. They must have escaped from the Blavatsky somehow. How had they done it? She couldn't remember at all. How far were they from the city?

She picked her way across the rolling ground to help.

"Your Royal Highness!" Gertrude cried, "are you alright?!"

"I'm not your princess," Claude replied. "I'm Claude Monteith." It seemed silly to say that aloud. "How do you do?" she added, sticking out her hand. That made it impossible not to laugh.

"How did we get away?" Gertrude asked, when she'd caught her breath. "Where are we?" Her limbs were causing her more trouble than Claude's, but her mind seemed less confused.

"I don't know. I can't remember anything between dinner and now. I'm not certain I can even remember dinner."

"Where is Princess Maud? We wouldn't have gone without her. I know I wouldn't have."

"Nor would I. I'm on the case."

"What case?" Gertrude looked at the satchel beside her on the grass. "You mean this? What is it?" She kicked it with her toe. It shifted and they could see some straps of leather peaking out from underneath.

"Food. We each seem to have one. That's not what I meant. I mean I'm on a mission. A job. My father's actually, but now mine. He's a spy. He had a message in Chicago, from the Queen…" Claude was having difficulty shaping her thoughts into sentences. She bent down and pulled the straps. Water skins, she saw with some relief. Handing one to Gertrude, she pulled the tip off the nipple of the other and took a mouthful. She sloshed it around her mouth and spat it out.

Gertrude took a large swallow.

"Best to only take what you need," Claude cautioned; "we don't know how long they'll have to last us."

Gertrude rubbed her eyes with her knuckles. "I wish whatever was in my head would go away already," she complained. "Nothing makes sense. I keep seeing and hearing the strangest things."

"Me, too," Claude confessed. "Talking birds and roots that reach up like hands and grab you by the ankle. And I can smell colours, I think."

"Roots?" Gertrude lifted her hands.

"Well, maybe you see different things. I think we're on vision quest. We see what speaks to us. Apparitions. We have to fight them to see the truth. It's difficult, but we can do it. The Sioux do. We have to try. We can't stay here in a forest. We need to find our way out and get help."

None of this made any sense to Gertrude except the last bit. "Where is Maud?" she repeated, insistently.

"She was the one they wanted." Claude concluded unhappily, "they must have her."

Surprising herself, Gertrude burst into tears. She was not a weepy young woman by nature.

Claude patted her shoulder. "She'll be alright. They want her alive." She regretted the baldness of the statement as soon as it was said, but Gertrude didn't seem to mind.

"I know," she said. "Captain Piper told us all about it. Poor Captain Piper." Her eyes filled again and she blinked furiously to contain the spill. "The Emperor wants her to marry his grandson."

"We have to assume the Emperor has them both, the Princess and Nikola. I know they want him alive, too."

"They want Kola?"

"His proper name is Nikola Tesla. He's an inventor, like my father. I could kill those villains for what they've done to his mind. I would do it, too, personally. I would kill them, without a speck of remorse." Claude plucked a hefty branch from the ground and, with an odd horizontal sweep, sent it whirling dangerously across the clearing at the height of a man's neck.

"You said your father was a spy." Gertrude's curiosity was greater than her surprise at the sudden bloodthirstiness of her companion.

"He's a lot of things. And you and I are going to make our way out of this place, wherever it is, and get to Prague to tell him everything, so that he can find them both and bring them back." Gertrude brightened at the conviction she heard in Claude's voice. "We should eat something first," Claude continued. She'd sat down on the ground and spread the contents of both satchels on her skirts. She gave them each a bit of cheese, then broke a loaf in half and split one half between them.

Gertrude sat beside her and looked. "There isn't much, is there?"

"Only enough for a couple of days. Just enough time for us to get good and lost, and die without soiling someone's conscience," Claude said grimly. She packed the remainder carefully away. "We can stretch it to three, maybe four if we're careful. After that, we hope I can find some good foraging."

"You mean berries and mushrooms?" That was the only type of foraging Gertrude knew.

Claude nodded. "Roots, as well. And herbs of course. Some wildflowers. If we can find a source of fresh water, I can keep us going for weeks."

"You know all this?"

"I've been raised to it. These aren't any woods I've ever seen, but I'm betting I can find our way through them. At least we're both wearing boots, though yours don't look particularly stout. I suppose we can be grateful we weren't wearing ball gowns and slippers when we were abducted. Not that that city clothes are much better." She looked down at her skirts in disfavour. To Gertrude's shock, she bundled them up and threw them over one shoulder, displaying her bustle. She started undoing the tapes.

"What are you doing?!"

"Making a walking skirt that I can walk in. I suggest you do the same. Ah! No need to hide this any more." Straightening her flattened skirts, Claude reached inside her waistband and pulled out a silver chatelaine. As Gertrude watched, fascinated, she unfolded tiny scissors from what looked like a metal wafer and made a small cut in her petticoat. Once she'd started the tear, she picked up the fabric in both hands and ripped all the way around the hem. She cut a piece from it and, braiding her hair in a club, used the bit of silk to tie it back. She wound the longer strip neatly and tucked it into her satchel. "Keep your eyes out for some smooth stones," she advised. "If we're stuck here long enough, we might have to do some hunting."

Gertrude had decided to take her new friend's advice and was jettisoning her own bustle. "Which way do we go?" she asked, ever practical. "No matter how much you know, we can't survive indefinitely."

Claude shrugged. "We were in a costal city. With some connection to the Italian Empire, wouldn't you assume?"

"Yes, but where are we now?"

"How far would they have taken us? I'm willing to wager we're still south of Prague. So we head north." She slung a satchel and a water bag from shoulder to hip and picked a fallen branch from the ground to use as a staff. "Coming?"

Gertrude did likewise, though she had to discard three or four branches in the course of the morning until she found one that suited.

It felt good to walk among the trees with the smell of ground cover crushing underfoot. They talked a lot, glad of the freedom to do so, even though much of what they said didn't quite make sense. Claude often stopped to converse with animals that Gertrude couldn't see. Gertrude would sometimes be moved to throw her arms around a tree that told her it wanted to dance.

They walked all day, with no sign of another human being, only birds and once or twice a rustling sound to indicate there might be animals nearby but out of sight. When they grew tired, they sat for a time and took a swig of water and a bite from their meagre supplies. For a few hours after such a break, the world seemed more confusing, but Claude was always able to confidently point them north. She hadn't seen her spirit animal, but whenever she sank too deep into the vision quest, she would listen for Leski and he would move her forward. He guided her in other was as well. Late in the afternoon, Leski showed her some patches of thistle. She filled both their pockets, instructing Gertrude to nibble the roots when she was hungry. This would stretch their provisions.

"Where do we sleep," Gertrude said suddenly, and Claude understood that the sun had begun to fade. A forest like this probably had wolves or possibly even bears. They had no weapons, only a handful of stones and their walking sticks. At the next small clearing, they used those sticks to scrape a circle of bare earth. Claude gathered moss and twigs. Tonight she'd use one of her precious matches to strike the spark. She built a tipi of dry branches above it and nursed the fire along until they had a steady blaze. It might be dangerous to sleep near a living fire, but it seemed more dangerous not to. They stayed awake as long as they could, but eventually they both fell asleep.

Sometime in the night, Claude woke. The fire was low. She sat for a while, calm and alert, listening to the sounds of the night. Creatures rustled through the trees and skittered on the ground, but nothing large that she could sense. Above her was a patch of black sky and a waxing gibbous moon. It was a moment ripe with portent, but nothing happened. She fed some more branches to the fire and went back to sleep. When she woke again, it was morning and Gertrude was pulling the satchels down from the tree limb where they'd hung them for safety.

The new day was much the same as the one before. They pressed on in the direction Claude assured Gertrude was north. They found more thistles and again gathered as many as they could carry.

"Why not the stalks?" Gertrude asked, munching on a root.

"You need to cook them. Even if we had water, we have no pot. Though I suppose we could wrap them in leaves and make mud. If we had water." Claude still hadn't found a hint of water. They were consuming less of the food that both girls had begun to suspect was drugged but which was sustaining them, and more of the greens they found. The duration and intensity of their visions was lessening, but they were getting lightheaded now in a different way, from dehydration. When they spotted an open patch filled with dandelions, even though it was a little west of north, Claude decided they should take half an hour to harvest them, to bite on the stems and use their teeth to strip out every bit of moisture.

As the light began to dim again, they knew they must begin to look for a clearing for the night. They kept pressing on, acre after acre, but nothing presented itself. Claude was wondering if they might have to find a climbable tree and take turns sleeping in the branches, when Gertrude stopped dead in her tracks.

"A fairy!" she breathed, in a tone of wonder.

"What?"

"A fairy. Just ahead of us. Hovering in the air. How lovely!" Gertrude began to ran.

Claude ran after her. "It's another vision, Gertrude," she said, trying to hold her back.

"No it's not," Gertrude insisted, straining forward. "Look!"

She pointed. A ball of blue light danced in a loop and sped away from them. Claude could see it too. They had never shared a vision and her own mind seemed unusually clear. It must be something real, some kind of energy. Gertrude was convinced it had some kind of intelligence. Anything seemed possible to them now.

"It wants us to follow!" She began to run. Claude ran after.

Whenever they got near enough to almost touch it, the light bounced, as if it were laughing at them, and sped off again. It wove through the trees, never dipping up or down but staying just at the level where they could see it. They had been tired to begin with, at the end of such a hard day. Now they were becoming exhausted and breathless. Claude stumbled once and it was hard to make herself get up from the ground. Only Gertrude's calling, "hurry! hurry!" kept her moving on.

Suddenly, the blue light winked out.

"Hello?!" Gertrude called. "Please where are you?" she pleaded; "Where did you go?" There was no answer and the light did not return.

Claude sank down to the ground to catch her breath and nearly hit her head on a pile of stones. The moonlight showed her what seemed to be bits of a chimney. She hauled herself up again and grabbed Gertrude's arm. "It's a house!" she said.

"I told you it was a fairy!" Gertrude said happily.

It wasn't really a house, but it had once been some sort of cottage. All that remained now were the ruined fireplace and part of an adjoining wall. With the hearth to protect it, Claude felt she could build a larger more robust fire that she expected would last most of the night. She tried to show Gertrude how to coax a spark from two sticks and some dry moss and start a flame. They sheltered by the wall and slept soundly.

The next morning, Claude explored the area. There must have been a vegetable garden once. She found a few allium growing wild and pulled them up. Near the ruined walls, she saw feathery purple and green clusters of wild sorrel. This was the more valuable treasure. She'd hoped in vain that the house might have a well. Their water skins had sunk dangerously low. The taste of uncooked sorrel would be strong, but she knew the leaves held precious moisture.

As they were preparing to move on, Gertrude was still jabbering about her 'fairy.' How clever it had been, to find them a safe place to sleep, and something they could eat.

Claude had been examining the path that had led them to the cottage. She looked closely at the trees and the shadows on the ground. "No!" she moaned.

"What is it? Should we not have eaten those leaves?"

"The leaves are fine. It's this!" Claude gestured around her in frustration. "Your fairy or will-o-the-wisp or whatever it was has taken us…Oh! We're turned all around. This path leads East! We're entirely off course. We may have undone all our efforts and we're running out of time."

Gertrude was silent. There was no answer to this. "We'll be alright," she said, because someone had to, even if at the moment neither believed it.

"Let's go," Claude said, shouldering her burdens and picking up her stick. She turned in a slow circle, scanning the scene like a sailor, but there was only one way out of the clearing. "This way," she said.

Though their hearts were low, they walked stoutly. Much of the time their legs seemed to move of their own volition, the heads above them swimming feverishly.

The sun seemed particularly hot today, as well as bright. The trees seemed blacker. The birds were louder and more raucous. The girls stopped to rest on a fallen log. Gertrude had a bit of cheese. Claude couldn't make herself eat, but sucked on some pebbles she picked from the ground, a trick to make herself less thirsty.

"Eat something," Nikola said. "There's still a piece of chestnut gateau." She moved her head from where it was resting on his shoulder and smiled at him. His curls were flopping into his eyes. He looked like a worried puppy. About her! He was in so much danger himself, but she was the one he was worrying about. She felt a warmth spread inside her chest. He must have opened the door and set the Prometheum with his own hands. She didn't know what to say. Maybe she didn't have to say anything. She smoothed the hair back from his brow. It wasn't black; it was brown.

"You must trust that I serve your best interests," he said, in a resonant baritone. His eyes were a startling dark blue with a thick fringe of the blackest lashes. Below his strong, high cheekbones, there were deep vertical crease in his cheeks as if someone had trailed her fingers through a pot of honey. He leaned his head closer to hers and her heart began to spin like a gyroscope.

There was a shrill scream overhead. Claude blinked. She was alone on the log. Above her, a falcon swooped elegantly across the sky, about to catch up some poor victim in its beak. Nature was so cruel and so beautiful. She was exhausted in so many ways that she almost wished falcon had snatched her.

"Claude?" Gertrude called. "Do you think these mushrooms are alright? They seem like the ones we find at home."

Expecting nothing, she trudged over to see. Actually, they were fine. She gave a weak but encouraging smile. Gertrude started to twist them handily at the base of the stem and Claude opened up her satchel to receive them. They were nice mushrooms and it looked like there were enough for them to live off for a day.

Claude knelt down to help and her hand touched the spongy moss. Mushrooms! Her nostrils flared and she pulled in a deep breath. The air at ground level had the faint smell of damp. Closing her eyes, she moved her head in an infinitely slow arc, sniffing the air. Finding the spot where the smell seemed strongest, she rose slowly and started in that direction. She walked as quietly as she could, her ears straining for any sound, even the slightest squoosh under her feet.

"Claude, what are you doing?" Gertrude called.

"Hush!" Claude said. "There should be water nearby." She kept moving, pushing at all her senses to expand and help. Gertrude, clutching a bundle of mushrooms in her skirt, hobbled after her.

"There!" Claude breathed. Gertrude was perplexed. It was merely a small bunch of what looked like green onions. "They won't grow unless there's damp," Claude said, her excitement rising.

They walked even more deliberately now. Gertrude looked hard, trying to see what Claude might be seeing. She noticed a small dark patch on the ground between two trees. "Claude, is that water?!"

Claude walked over and bent down to look. "No," she said, straightening her back. She stopped halfway, her hands on her knees. "But *that* is!"

The leaves were thick but she could just make out a small rivulet several hundred feet away. She broke into a staggering run, Gertrude right behind her. It didn't look like much, but it was moving. Claude followed it upstream aways, hoping it would widen some. It didn't, but she saw some birds alight and take a sip before flying off. She wanted to cry with relief. "It's sweet! Gertrude, it's sweet!" Squatting down, she cupped her hands and splashed it on her face. She could feel it being absorbed into her skin. It felt wonderful. Gertrude squatted too, her hem dragging in the blessed mud. They drank until they felt swollen with water. Their teeth ached from the cold. Pouring out whatever drops of probably-tainted water were left in the skins, they refilled them from the stream.

The stream did not run as true to north as Claude would have preferred, but they followed it for the rest of the day. People who lived in wooded areas usually built near water. Perhaps if they followed it long enough, they might find some houses or even a village. If not, at least they would have potable water to keep them alive a few days more.

When they found a likely clearing, Claude had them stop, though it was earlier than they usually made camp.

"Shall we eat the mushrooms?" Gertrude asked, proud to have made a contribution.

"Not yet. I have an idea. What do we have left of the food?"

Gertrude checked the satchels. "Half a loaf, a piece of cheese the size of two thumbs and a bit of dried meat."

"Let me have the meat. And two of your hairpins." Claude pulled out the long strip of silk from her bag and ripped it in two. She tied a piece to the end of each of their staffs. Gertrude handed her the hairpins and she carefully bent them before fastening them to the other ends of the strips.

"Fishing poles!" Gertrude exclaimed.

"If it doesn't work, you get my piece of cheese," Claude grinned. The water had changed everything. She was as full of high spirits now as if it had been one of her family adventures. She used her little scissors to cut two ribbons of dried meat and stuck them on the improvised hooks.

The fish must have been as hungry as the girls. In practically no time they'd caught enough for a good sized meal. Once gutted awkwardly with sharp sticks, an allium was tucked inside each to give them flavour. After the fish were wrapped in oak leaves, the packets were plastered thickly with mud and placed in the fire.

They burned their fingers a little, poking out the cracked mud cases with sticks, and they burned their tongues on the hot, oniony fish, but it was wonderful. Sated for the first time in days, they watched sparks fly out of the fire and spiral against the black night.

"In the morning, we can roast your mushrooms in the embers," Claude noted. "That'll be nice for breakfast."

"I could learn to enjoy this," Gertrude remarked contentedly. "To think, people lived like this for thousands of years."

"Some still do," Claude observed.

"When we get through this," Gertrude said, carefully emphasizing the 'when', "might I come and visit you in America sometime?"

Claude stuck out her hand the way men did back home. "Shake on it," she said.

12 - CAPTIVES

When Baron Haussmann returned from Venezia, he found a messenger camped out in his foyer. The boy was waiting to take him to the Villa Borghese, where Giulia was having the unusual experience of something not going according to her expectations. Just as Princess Maud was meant to have be impressed by the majesty of the Empire on the train, she should have been awed and grateful to be accepted into the bosom of the Imperial family. Giulia had planned a charming set of diversions for the girl she would treat as her own daughter.

How different Giulia's life might have been if she'd born Patre a son. She wondered more often how different the world might have become had she herself been born male. Would the circumstances of her birth have mattered then? The first Caesars hadn't let themselves be thwarted by such petty things as legitimacy or even incest. No, it was being born female that had been her one insurmountable flaw.

As it was, with Patre having every intention of staying in this world, she had dedicated her life to supporting him. She'd been his helpmate always, for all the years since leaving childhood behind. Should he, despite his determination, pass on, rather than ruling the Empire herself, as she justly deserved, Giulia would have to wield her power behind Gusto's throne. This young princess, married to Gusto and providing him with an heir of the body, would either be the instrument of Patre's remaining in this world or the surety that his line—their line—would continue to rule over Roma. Either way, Giulia would be there to support and guide the girl.

For Giulia to remain in control, the girl must come to trust her. Instead, she recoiled. Fully alert, the girl would scream like an eagle and become violent. She would kick and claw, and even try to bite her attendants. The doctor had been scalded with coffee from an upended breakfast tray. Giulia herself had been narrowly missed by a hairbrush hurled across the room. One day the girl had seemed calm, only to try and jump from through an open window the minute the maid had turned her head; the windows were now kept locked. In another context, Giulia might have admired her fighting spirit. Here and now, it was making any civilized dealings impossible. There was no option but to continue to keep the girl drugged and biddable.

"It's well for you that Blavatsky provided you with that case," Giulia snapped at the Baron.

Haussmann gave her the sweetly puzzled look he continued to think that, against all evidence, she found disarming. "It was only appropriate that I transfer it to you, Daughter of Light, along with the responsibility."

She slapped him across his smug face. The red mark would fade within the hour, but it temporarily relieved her frustration. She had spent an awkward half hour in the garden, trying to snare the silly girl's attention and coax her into eating a bit of veal. Whatever was in those vials certainly quieted the girl. She didn't have a word to say for herself. Giulia could have gotten more from a statue. Somewhat erect and appropriately groomed and garbed, she looked rather like a statue as well. Peculiarly tall though she was, the English princess was lovely. There had been plenty of opportunity for Giulia to admire her profile; all the girl wanted to do outdoors was gaze at the flowers. Still, it would be far worse to have her screaming or trying to run.

Perhaps it was for the best to keep the girl this way until she became accustomed to her new station, or at least until she'd been formally presented to Patre. Patre preferred women to be quiet. Giulia was, to her own knowledge, the sole exception to this. From what she had been able to gather over the years, even Mama had been expected to know her place. Giulia was different. There was no one Caesar trusted as he trusted her. She might be barred from succession, but he had no truer heir.

"You will need to return to Dubrovnik," she ordered the Baron. "The Blavatsky must supply you with more of this substance." She clapped her hands briskly together. A page hurried over with a pitcher of wine and two glasses. At her gesture, the Baron poured. The left side of his face was a pleasing match to the chianti. She lifted her glass and took a sip. "Blavatsky would do well to provide a modification that will allow her to be somewhat more sociable."

The Baron agreed. "The Principessa must come to accept her new life, not avoid it."

"It might ease the way if there were a person she would talk with. You have a way with the ladies, Baron, or so you have often said. And you speak English." Giulia said the last word as if it left a bad taste in her mouth. "That might…comfort her." She took a cleansing sip of wine.

"I am happy to serve, Daughter of Light."

A servant brought a tray of hothouse fruit to the table. The young man peeled a grape and placed it between Giulia's lips. She gestured for the Baron to help himself.

Taking up a small pearl-handled knife, Haussmann began to peel himself a peach. The skin fell to the plate in a single perfect coil that soothed him. He speared a slice and popped it neatly into his mouth. The sweet burst of juice was a delight. He would go to Blavatsky and return with a solution that would satisfy the Lady Giulia and Caesar.

Giulia had been watching him fuss.

"I will see the Principessa before I leave," he assured her.

"Mmmm." She seemed thoughtful. "And then you will be putting all your efforts into Patre's Colosseum. Do we not have anyone else at Court who speaks sufficient English? What about that attractive centurion who was sent ahead to Dubrovnik. The young Neapolitan who looks so stern?"

"Rappaccini, you mean?" So the young man had caught the Lady's eye. "Di Bari's man? Yes, he speaks English well enough. Indeed, that is why I have him minding Tesla for me in Venezia now."

"I would have him assigned to the Principessa for a time." She cocked her head and smiled, watching the Baron master his pique. "It would be a sacrifice for you, I know. But Caesar would be most grateful."

"But of course, Daughter of Light," Haussmann said, pushing away his plate. The peach had been quite spoilt for him. He'd hoped that with Rappaccini on duty it might not be necessary to medicate Tesla. Rappaccini. Pfffttt! how could one young man have become so indispensable? "An admirable idea for the short term. While naturally not as dear to his heart as the welfare of the Principessa, Mr. Tesla is also most important to Caesar's plans. Perhaps once the Principessa is comfortable, Rappaccini might be permitted to return to Murano."

Giulia nodded graciously. It was not a promise. Giulia did not make promises. It was a gesture of good will that cost her nothing. First let her see what this Rappaccini might be able to achieve.

᠊ঌ৯

The Conte di Bari was extremely anxious to make Baron Haussmann happy. If that meant sending his most reliable centurion to Murano three times each week, so be it.

Di Bari knew the assignment concerned an important prisoner being held on the island, but that was all he knew. The Baron had not volunteered more and not even Caesar's own spymaster might question the Baron. Whatever Rappaccini had been instructed to do when he got there, he wasn't pleased about it. Each time di Bari gave the order to go, the centurion didn't bother to disguise his repugnance. He would grunt out "Si, Eminenza" and shake his head like a wet dog, then almost stomp out the door. His attitude surprised di Bari, who had always found the young man as keen as he was industrious and competent. Certainly the Baron must have found him impressive, to have specified it must be he who performed this errand. It would be a shame if Rappaccini were to do anything to forfeit the Baron's patronage. Di Bari would have to invite the young man to dinner and counsel him.

Rappaccini stood at the dock, frowning and glowering ostentatiously at everyone he saw. He checked the supplies against his list as they were loaded onto the boat. In addition to some materials the Baron's agents hadn't thought of, such as beeswax and redacted sulphur, Tesla had ordered lengths of iron tubing and specific sizes of brass screws. It had taken an entire day to locate everything. On his last visit, Tesla had also begged him for some citronella. It was early in the season, but the inventor was already proving a magnet to the lagoon's mosquito population. The pastries, and a large pot of Cousin Elettra's lamb ragú, were Micah's own addition. Between depression and limited culinary skills, the inventor was looking thin and peaked. It was in everyone's best interest to keep him as robust as possible.

When they docked on the island, the trecika guarding the door marched over to inspect them. Rappaccini held up a bronze disc that the Baron had given him for that purpose. The creature promptly stepped back and allowed him to pass. There was a symbol on the disc that looked something like a scarab beetle, with the large panels of the carapace carved as three glyphs that made no sense to his eye. Micah had made several rubbings of this disc. One was hidden at all times in the leg of his boot, one was about to be smuggled to Tesla between the pages of a book. The last was in his flat, awaiting the opportunity of his or Elettra's slipping north into Corinthia. A safe courier was waiting there to carry it on to Prague, where Tucker's last message from Pinkerton indicated that Sir Alastair was carrying on the work that Tesla had begun. Anything that might be a key to controlling the amphoraeka had to be useful to their efforts.

Wearing the additional layer of arrogance that he had recently veneered onto his characterization, Rappaccini waved the disc and pointed to the men who were lugging iron tubes out of the boat. The trecika took up their bundle as if it were a handful of faggots. It headed for the fornace, just as two of its fellows appeared from the building and headed for the yacht. It was fascinating. They, too, lifted cargo from the deck. It was as if the first creature had somehow instructed the others as to what needed to be done. This was something else that needed to be relayed to Tesla and Sir Alastair.

"Two hours!" he snapped at the men who stood on deck with empty arms. They tugged their caps and scattered gratefully in the direction of the nearest *osteria*. Although there seemed to be more amphoraeka in Venezia of late, they remained a strange enough phenomenon that the average person preferred to avoid coming too close. It was an intelligent instinct, he thought. The things were as large as two men and smelt of newly-dug graves. His nostrils flared just thinking it. Pretending at an indifference he didn't feel, he swaggered up to the unlocked door, shouldered his way in and headed to the kitchen with the food.

Tesla knew how to boil water, but had to be shown what to do with the fettucine. He looked into the pot with interest. The aroma of the sauce wafted over from the other pot. He actually felt hungry. He hadn't been eating much. He did, however, like to spend time in this kitchen. The trecika couldn't follow him in, not even by ducking under the lintel—there wasn't enough room between the stove and the sink and the table—but they didn't seem to mind him lingering here. He had the sense that they respected his need to eat, that they felt sentimental about it. He knew it was mad to be attributing feelings to the creatures, but he couldn't help it.

"Maybe it's because I'm alone with them," he explained to Rappaccini. "It's so quiet here. I find myself talking with them, just to hear the sound of a voice. The way old women talk to their cats. I would swear that they understand me."

"The way old women feel about their cats?" the Italian Englishman smirked. "You're right, Tesla. You're too much alone. But there's nothing much to be done about that. I'm here almost too often as it is. Any more and we'd draw suspicion."

Tesla could hear this idea and understand. He had remembered this morning that Rappaccini was expected. It had kept him focused enough that he had been able to think. The days were so hard to bear, and his sleep was torn by nightmares featuring the Baron, but as long as he knew Rappaccini would keep coming, he could hold on to that thought and pull himself through the worst hours. So strange. When he was well, he could stay alone for weeks and not think anything of it; but when he was ill, he was terrified of a few hours of silence, lest he start to hear voices in his head. He stomped through these rooms, singing sometimes, to fill the space with sound. More often he talked aloud. It was better to talk to the monsters than to talk with ghosts. "I still think they understand," he confided, with a queer glitter in his eye. "There's one especially. I think he remembers me from Rome."

"He?"

Tesla nodded several times. "I can't think of them as 'it'. There's something in them. I can't explain, but I can feel it."

Skirting the issue, Micah told him about the rubbing he'd hidden in the novel, and what he had learned about Sir Alastair—Frank, as Tesla called him—working in Prague. The inventor brightened considerably for a bit and managed to consume a reasonable portion of pasta.

"What are you planning?" Micah asked, as their allotted time grew slimmer. "I fear that the Baron might turn up at any time, unannounced. You must have something to show him."

Tesla had thought of that himself. He was an intuitive thinker, but now he was masquerading as the type of engineer he had always mocked, the slow and steady tortoise who made endless drawings, multiply rendering the same few ideas. His workbenches were littered with crumpled sketches, each showing a small flaw that Haussmann might easily discern. He laughed slyly. When the Baron came to inspect his progress, as the Baron surely would, he would see this evidence of fruitless industry and draw the conclusion Tesla wanted him to draw—that, in subjugation, his thinking was constrained by fear of error and his progress was correspondingly slow. It had taken him only a day to generate enough sketches to indicate a fortnight's work and he could now focus on what he had decided would be his best goal: something that would look effective but in practice would not quite deliver.

The ultimate delaying factor, something that even the Baron would have to concede, was that those strange monks in Roma were the one ones allowed to mould and alter the amphoraeka. Whatever Tesla did by way of creating armaments would needfully be theoretical. Even if he had been the most willing of recruits, he would have been limited in this way. Therefore, if he made his attempts credible enough, the Baron would bring his sketches and models to Rome. It would take days or perhaps weeks there before the failures were discovered, and when they were, it would seem to have been a legitimate effort. Tesla believed he could buy a great deal of time in this way. "And every hour I can prolong this," he added, almost happily, "is an hour more for Frank to perfect my automatons."

"Tesla, you are every bit the genius people say you are," Micah told him, admiringly.

*

"Si, Eminenza!" Rappaccini gave his sharpest salute, together with an eager, avaricious grin. The Conte could see exactly what his centurion was thinking: another special request from the Baron, with assignment to the Lady Giulia's own household. Here was advancement! Everyone in the mess would envy him!

"You are to report at once."

"What about Tesla?"

"I will find someone to deliver his groceries," di Bari sighed. He was a Legate, a spymaster, not a tessarius.

"He speaks no Italian."

"We have no other English speakers to spare." Those di Bari had under his command were scattered across the globe in more obviously critical positions. It would take weeks to find a replacement and recall one. Too bad Soderini, the young tribunus he had hoped to claim from Roma earlier this year, had been abruptly reassigned by Caesar to no one knew where.

"He is Serbian, Eminenza. He also speaks good German and some French, surely enough to let his needs be known." The Count's face cleared. "A family man, if I may be so bold," Rappaccini suggested.

"Eh?"

"He is not well." The Centurion tapped his temple suggestively with his forefinger. "He can be erratic. Also melancholy. Someone accustomed to the changeable temperaments of children might best suit."

"Thank you, Rappaccini. You may go."

"Have I leave to visit Tesla to explain? He will otherwise be expecting me."

"Yes, yes," the Count was already reviewing his staff for potential nursemaids.

With another enthusiastic salute, the Centurion had gone.

On the boat, he made expansive small talk about his path to promotion. A few ribald jokes were aired at the expense of the Lady Giulia. When they reached Murano, he gave the pilot a generous handful of coins. "Have a round on me. In honour of my good fortune. A round or two," he amended, with a wink.

The men touched their caps and grinned before rushing away. With anticipations of bettering himself, the centurion was a much happier, friendlier man. *This* Rappaccini would be missed!

Humming cheerfully, Rappaccini strolled to the door and, ignoring the trecika standing eternally outside, unlocked it. Only when it was closed behind him did a cloud show on his face. What was an excellent prospect for Rappaccini was a mixed blessing to Micah. He would be in position to help, perhaps even rescue, the Princess, but he would be leaving a loaded weapon in the hands of the Baron.

Tesla was in the workroom, hunched over the drafting table. He seemed unaware of the amphoraka whose shadow merged with his.

"Good morning, Tesla," Rappaccini said in a conversational tone.

Tesla looked up. Micah could swear the trecika shifted slightly away. "Hello. Did you bring more pastries? The chocolate ones were the best."

Micah reached for a piece of foolscap and a pencil and started to write. "I'm making you a dictionary," he said. "A food dictionary. The names of things you like to eat, or might like. So you'll know what to ask for."

Tesla scowled. "I don't want one. I don't want to learn Italian."

"It would make your life more comfortable."

"I hate what it represents. It would mean I might live out my life here."

Micah thought for a moment. "I understand," he said. "But it's wise to understand the language of your enemy."

"Everyone is my enemy. Should I understand every language known to man? If a mad dog tries to bite me, do I learn to bark?" He let out a few yips and began scratching at his ear.

"I am not your enemy," Micah said carefully. Tesla was having a bad spell. Or perhaps this was how he usually was and the man he met on his previous visits had been the exception. Tesla had hinted that he drew strength from anticipating these meetings. This meeting hadn't been scheduled. If this was an indication that Tesla's mind went astray between visits, he might go quite mad with Rappaccini gone to Rome. "I am your ally. We are working together, to thwart the Emperor's plans."

"The Baron, you mean," Tesla said.

"The Baron does what the Emperor requires." Micah began to correct him and saw the trust fading from his eyes. "Yes, of course the Baron. Baron Haussmann who had you kidnapped and is holding you against your will. But if we work together, we can turn his designs back on him and bring him down."

"How do I know you're not a spy," Tesla said with cunning.

This was a tough one to counter, for of course Micah was a spy but Tesla was in no shape to process the explanation. "I'm a friend of Frank's," he ventured. "Remember? I'm working together with you and Frank...and Frank's lovely daughter..."

"Claude!" Tesla groaned, holding his head. "They took her away! They're going to hurt her if I don't help them," he whimpered.

"No they won't," Micah began to reassure him. It struck him that he could turn this fear to his advantage. "They won't because I will be there to stop them. The Baron has ordered me to Rome, and the young lady..."

"You must go to her!" Nikola jumped up and practically shook him. He was a stronger man than he appeared to be. "You must protect her. You must!"

To control him, Micah pulled him into an embrace. "There, there," he said, because it seemed the appropriate soothing thing to say. "I will see she comes to no harm. And while I'm in Rome, someone else will come here in my stead and bring you things. You'll be well taken care of until my return."

"You must never leave her side," Nikola said, in a fervent whisper more potent than a shout. "Never. You must promise me."

On the trip back to Castello, the men were completely occupied with trying to keep themselves and the boat steady. They didn't register the silence of their new favourite centurion as he stood watching Murano dwindle to a speck.

Tesla too would disappear; first into his own mind and later, when the Baron couldn't get what he wanted, from the face of the earth. Micah didn't have a place in his life for friendship and if he did Nikola Tesla wasn't a likely candidate but, despite his best attempts to cut off the part of himself that had softer feelings, he pitied the man. As he pitied Princess Maud, and the plucky Miss Bell and his beautiful lock-picker, though he tried not to wonder what had become of them. He wanted to save them all, to preserve the nation that had given him sanctuary but, most of all, to bring down Caesar Augustus. The last was first in his priorities, and by accomplishing it, he would serve a greater good. Revenge would be both sweet and cleansing. To make it come about, something would have to be sacrificed. Someone. For the moment, the Baron was calling the moves, but Fairservis would find a way to take control. When the opportunity arose to do so, he must be prepared to use it to his best advantage. He must not allow sentiment to guide his decisions. He must always be the player and not the piece on the game board.

Pinkerton had taught him to reinforce his bridges, not to burn them; one never knew when one might need to cross back. Rappaccini made an effort to be jolly in his farewells to the crew and leave a pleasant impression on their drunken memories. Crossing the piazza, he nearly collided with a barrel-chested uniform that was emerging from a bar. It was Izano, a higher-ranking centurion with the bluff good nature of a childhood bully who'd stumbled into a felicitous occupation. Rappaccini hadn't seen him in several months. He missed him. A spy could wish for no better drinking companion than Izano. In his cups, he confided much that he shouldn't and by the next morning would forget saying anything beyond one's name.

"Rappaccini!" Izano kissed him soundly on both cheeks. "Good to see you! How long has it been?"

"I was thinking the very same thing!"

"Come, have glass of wine." Izano draped an arm around his neck and steered him back into the bar.

"A quick one," Rappaccini agreed. "I have to catch an afternoon train to Roma. New assignment."

"Roma? Very nice. Sounds like a promotion."

"I don't know," Rappaccini said, with clearly false modesty. "I seem to have made a favourable impression on Baron Haussmann, that's all."

"Then we both have reason to celebrate!" Izano doffed his uniform hat and pointed to his forehead. Centered there, only two-fingers-width away from the bridge of his nose, there was a tattoo. It was a strange symbol, but looked so familiar.

"Where have I seen that before?" Rappaccini mused aloud. In the dimness of the bar, he noticed that the green ink gave the mark an eerie luminescence. "Is it shining?"

Izano shrugged. "Some kind of chemical. Like glow worms. It frightened my wife half to death first time she saw it. It's so that they'll see it in the dark. The trecika, that is. Though I can't say I ever thought they 'saw' the way we do."

That was why it seemed familiar. It was the same symbol as on the bronze disk. He hadn't used the disk today, he realized. He hadn't expected to be going out to Murano and had left it in his gun locker in the barracks. Yet the amphoraka on the dock had made no move to check him. It was as if the creature knew he was permitted on the island. Did the monsters think? Could Tesla be right about them?

"I've had tattoos before but this…" the fellow rambled on. "Hurt worse than the time I got into that knife fight with the Turk who used stinging nettle on his blade. Good trick, that one. Keeps your opponents off balance. I would have been a memory if it hadn't been for Padilla taking him from behind and slitting his throat." Izano lifted his glass to toast his absent comrade and took a healthy swig.

Rappaccini topped off the glass from the carafe. "But what's the purpose to it, Izano?"

"It's so they'll follow us, take commands."

"Us? Is there an entire cohort of men with peculiar green tattoos?" Rappaccini joked.

"No joking matter, Rappaccini." Indeed, Izano looked graver than was usual at the onset of inebriation. "There are ten of us in Venezia alone. We train on the mainland. It would put a strain on La Serenissima to support extensive forces. No doubt in Roma you'll see many more who wear these marks. I know there are others like us in Firenze, Milano, Napoli…This is only the beginning." He stood suddenly, pulled his shoulders back and, as his chest inflated to its full impressive expanse, lifted his glass to the room. "Caesar Augustus, his health!"

"Caesar!" came the hearty response of several of the other drinkers in the room.

"And to the Second Roman Empire!"

"The Empire!"

"The Empire," Rappaccini raised his glass along with the others.

Izano resumed his seat and mopped his face with a large handkerchief. "Great preparations are being made," he confided. "I wouldn't be surprised if whatever assignment you have from your friend the Baron is a part of it."

Rappaccini nodded his agreement. It was the assignment from which he was being removed, however, that was part of the same thing as Izano's activities. The plans for the amphoraeka involved the weapons and vehicles the Baron had tasked Tesla to design. Even without these designs, Augustus's plan, whatever it was, was already being deployed. Venice was the important place for him to be, not Rome; he knew that now. He would have to leave today—one could not refuse a direct order, especially not from that source—but he must find a way to return again as quickly as possible.

❧

It was a fair walk from the train station in Rome to the Castel. Micah welcomed the exercise. The Italian trains were elegant to look at, but the accommodations were hardly comfortable unless you booked first class, a luxury that a centurion of his rank would not consider. In a country where everything was monitored, a spy must be more than usually careful to conform to his cover.

He also wanted to enjoy the last hour that might belong to him for a long time. Once he checked in, he would constantly be on display. For the duration of this walk, he could relax and appreciate the beauties of the city. One had to acknowledge that Haussmann had done an exquisite job. Rome couldn't have been more splendid in the days of the first Augustus, and Haussmann's city was surely cleaner and better lit. Turning onto a broad marble avenue, Micah paused to admire the prospect. If one re-dressed the modern Romans in togas, it was easy to fancy one was strolling through the past. The ghosts must feel so comfortable since Haussmann had brought back their city. There was even something suitably antique in the customary surfeit of Caesar's beloved gold-leafed eagles and bullion-fringed purple banners. All that ruined the illusion were amphoraeka. All at once, there seemed to be so many of them. Micah frowned. Was this part of the growing cohort to which Izano had referred? People didn't seem to be paying them any mind; either they were used to seeing them or engaging with Tesla was causing him to see more of the creatures than there were. There were definitely two guarding the gate to the Castel. He had no symbol on him, but they let him pass without incident. Perhaps they were meant only to intimidate by their presence.

"Baron Haussmann asks that you report to his villa once you're settled," the Tessarius said with a pleasant enough nod. "I'll send a page with word that you've come."

"Thank you. I know how crowded facilities are in Roma. Would you suggest an appropriate rooming house?"

"We can easily accommodate you in the barracks." Closing the leather roster on Benvolio Rappaccini's signature, he opened a key cabinet. "I have rooms prepared." He ran his finger down the rows and unhooked a set. He scrawled a rough map on a slip of paper and passed it over with the keys.

"Thank you." Rappaccini didn't bother to hide his surprise. On other visits, Rome had been so packed with soldiers that, even with recommendations, it had taken hours to find a bed in a dormitory.

"There have been a number of reassignments of late," the Tessarius said blandly.

Rappaccini took the keys, saluted and went to find his billet. According to the sketch, his rooms were in that part of the Castel used as a kind of Old Soldier's Home. The only 'reassignments' from those rooms were to what Madame Blavatsky called 'the Other Side.' There was usually a long waiting list for vacancies. He had no superstitions about taking a dead man's place and the rooms were likely to be more comfortable that he could have hoped for, but he wasn't happy to be here.

On prior visits to Rome, he had sought out the Ospedale. Old soldiers had time to talk and long memories. A man might glean a lot from fulfilling the charitable impulse to visit the elderly. Unfortunately, his mother had died without telling him of his strong resemblance to his grandfather, or perhaps it was that she'd only known her father-in-law as a haggard fugitive and couldn't see his reflection in the fresh face of a small boy. To some of the ancients in this place, the connection was immediate and clear.

"You have the look of the family of Tuscany," they would say carefully, eyeing him top to toe. He would shake his head and shrug it off.

Zacuto, who had lost a leg to the Turk and whose back was hatched with the scars of flogging from a lifetime of speaking plain, said "You're the image of old Leopoldo, God rest his soul" and spat through his gnarled fingers to ward off the evil eye.

"I'm Neopolitan. I share a distant connection, many generations back." His smile had spoken of weary tolerance for a familiar question. "Nothing more. I hope Caesar sees no such resemblance; it would certainly do me no favour."

This had been sufficient deflection for an afternoon's chat with a lonely old man who was grateful for any company but, if such men had to be spoken with daily, there might be a real risk of slipping. He passed under the arch with some trepidation. The small courtyard was much as he recalled except that it was deserted. No Bath chairs had been wheeled onto the paving stones, positioned on to catch the sun. The benches near the small fountain were untenanted and the coating of wet leaves spoke of their being so for more than a few days. He heard nothing other than the gurgle of the fountain and a hint of birdsong.

Pushing open the door, he called out a cheerful "buongiorno!" His voice rang hollow in the foyer. He headed towards the solarium, where there were usually a few heated games of dominos and briscola in progress. A few husks, swaddled in blankets, nodded in their chairs while a diminutive nun read aloud from *La Divina Commedia*. She looked at him briefly, then continued her reading. It was obvious that she considered him an intruder. He bowed respectfully and withdrew.

Where was everyone? Had some influenza swept through and carried off the aged populace? If so, it would be sad but hardly secret; why had there been no mention? He shifted his bag, which had achieved maximum weight in the last quarter hour, and mounted the stairs in search of his door. It lead to a spacious, well-lit chamber furnished as a parlour. It boasted a sleeping alcove and its own water closet. The windows looked out on the courtyard. If he had wanted to be in Rome, this would have been a pleasure. As it was, it was troubling. Why was such a desirable room available to a low-mid-level centurion? There was no time to think about it now. The Baron would be awaiting his presence. He pulled out his kit and washed and shaved. He reluctantly buttoned up the shirt he'd travelled in. He'd have to see about getting someone to press his others before he had to meet the Lady Giulia. He'd been in her presence before, but he sensed that when he met her this time he would register an impression; he wanted to look impeccable. He put a small bit of pomade in his hair and combed it off his face. This would have to do.

It was no surprise that the Baron kept a fine table, Micah reflected, spooning up the last grains of a delicate asparagus risotto. He didn't flatter himself that the excellence of the meal had anything to do with him. The Baron made no special praise of it, other than to ask his opinion of the wine. "Do you know wine?" he asked, in that way of men who did.

Micah had learned that, when asked this question, it was wise to espouse abashed ignorance. Men were vain about their knowledge of wine and were warmed by his shortcoming. "No," he said, holding the fragile glass up to the light to admire the blonde liquid, "but it's very nice."

"From my own vineyards in Tuscany."

If his father's lands had not been confiscated before his birth, Micah would have had vineyards in Tuscany. In the darkest shadows of his heart, he wondered if these were one and the same. As it was, being raised without a father and subsequently in the household of a Scot, he knew nothing of wine but what he had been able to pick up here and there over the years. The madam of a Paris whorehouse, a woman who claimed to have been the mistress of Dumas père, had taught him a surprising amount about fine champagne. Now, based on the length of the Baron's digression, he would apparently have the opportunity to learn about the Tuscan whites. He paid careful attention.

The sole was accompanied by a straw-coloured wine with a more mineral taste. After explaining its finer points, the Baron relaxed into the topic of the Rappaccini's assignment.

"The Principessa has been put through a severe trial of nerves, and I fear that the compounds Madame Blavatsky was required to use reacted adversely with her constitution. Nobility, my son, is not robust. She didn't wake for some days after you saw her leave the yacht. When she did, she was fearful and, yes, enraged. But rather than allow her to exhaust these emotions naturally, the Lady Giulia required instant compliance. The Lady Giulia is not a patient woman. It is not in her nature and life has never required that she cultivate the art of seeming. She's kept the Principessa dosed ever since. The young lady sleeps much. When awake, she moves like a shadow. This does not please the Lady Giulia either." The Baron shook his head at the contrariness of the Lady.

Sad to tell, the Principessa did not have many good hours and her days were kept short. Rappaccini had arrived too late in the day to meet her. She dozed most of the morning. After luncheon, she would take her place in the gardens, staying there for several hours. Occasionally she could be led to the aviary, but she seemed to have some fear of birds. When the day cooled, she would return indoors where her only occupation was to sit at the piano and play simple tunes no one could recognize.

The Lady Giulia attempted daily to converse with her. Some of the younger ladies of the court had also been introduced, but with little success. Ginevre, older sister to the groom-to-be, had the most effect but the sensitive nature that had helped her to make contact also caused her to feel extreme distress when in the company of the melancholy English girl; she could not go too often nor stay too long.

"It sounds such a sad life," Rappaccini observed.

"It is hoped that your arrival might change that," the Baron countered. "Someone to speak with her in her own tongue. Currently, she seems to drift in a dream, even those few hours when she is awake. She has little appetite. There was great concern that she was growing too thin. It was necessary to find the times she is most amenable to food and plan her meals accordingly. Much attention is given to urging her to eat. We've brought the best pasticciere in Firenze to create delectable little cakes to tempt her." The Baron sounded wistful that the pastry chef was not catering for him.

"Must she take any such medication, if it has this effect?" This was extremely dismaying. At least he'd been able to establish a connection with Tesla and even reason with him at times. The Princess had been drugged to the point she probably had no idea where she even was.

"It is for her own protection, Rappaccini. She becomes quite violent when we withdraw it, even if only for an hour's delay. We fear she might harm herself. It is hoped that the new compound will avert this behaviour while providing more waking hours. I have already seen a change, though not enough to satisfy the need. To be blunt," he twitched his nose in distaste; the Baron disliked bluntness, "the Lady Giulia wants her broken like a saddle horse, to embrace the loss of freedom and befriend her captors."

They regarded the thought as if it had been set on a plate between them. Neither of them liked the taste.

"Ach!" the Baron tried to wave it away. "It will all come right, once she's well enough to meet young Gusto. Young women," his eyes grew moist. "When they think they are in love, all is right with the world." He changed the subject then, and began to grill the Centurion on Tesla's state.

"He was not pleased when I said I was leaving," Rappaccini couldn't resist saying.

The Baron brightened. "He's well enough to voice an objection; excellent! How is the work progressing?"

"I'm not an engineer like yourself. I saw many drawings, plans and the like, but I cannot say what might be made of them."

"I will have to go to Venezia for a few days and see for myself. This is excellent, Rappaccini! I see you are a young man to watch."

The lamb arrived, and with it a wine the colour of apricots. Taking a sip, Micah felt it bloom in his mouth like the same fruit. He let his surprise and approval show on his face. "This cannot be from your Tuscan vines!" he exclaimed.

The Baron laughed. "No, this is from my vines in Alsace, my ancestral home. You have a palate!" he declared. "It would be criminal to neglect it. While you are with us in Roma, you will dine with me regularly and we shall see about your education."

"'Scusi, Eminenza. Speaking of Mr. Tesla..." He was curious about something and they'd drunk enough wine that any excessive boldness could be dismissed as owing to it. "I'd heard the servants' gossip, but what exactly happened to the other young ladies, the ones that were taken along with the Principessa and Mr. Tesla?"

"The Baron dabbed his lips with his napkin and sighed. "Madame Blavatsky released them," he said, "as one releases a wild bird that has been healed of a broken wing. She had them taken far enough from Dubrovnik to confuse the trail and left them to find their way."

Appalled, Micah was careful to sound clinically impressed. "Abandoned on a roadside. Strange, but presumably effective." Now he was glad he'd let Tesla continue to think it was Claude who was in Rome. It was kinder.

"Not a roadside," Haussmann admitted. Perhaps the wine was having its effect on him and making him sentimental. "A wood, I believe she said. But she gave them food and water. What is meant to be will out. Madame Blavatsky is a great believer in Fate, you know." Haussmann steered the conversation back to the wine, and then to the grappa he had selected to accompany their cheese.

It was past curfew when he left the Baron's company, but Micah decided to walk back to the Castel by the longest route he could work out. Contemplation of the fates of the young women had cleared his head, but his reflexes were softened by alcohol. A walk would help return him to possession. He might not know much about wine, but in his time at Oxford he had learned how to mitigate its effects on his body. He was still drunk by the time he reached the Ospedale, but only he would have recognized his condition as such. He could feel it as an excess of sentiment, particularly when his thoughts wandered to the lovely Claude. Surely a woman of such spirit and resourcefulness could survive whatever challenges the Blavatsky's Fate might present. Yes, he was still drunk, though his body was under his control; blade to blade with a clear-headed professional he would not have acquitted himself well.

He walked as quietly as the tiles would allow. Even the swaddled men he had seen earlier, however far gone, would be capable of being disturbed by clatter. A slice of lamplight seemed to prove his point. He tiptoed past the open door and heard the great wheeze of lungs straining to draw sufficient air.

"Who's there?" It was so silent in the hallway that the graveled whisper just reached his ear. "Come in, please. I have no fear of you."

Curious, Micah slipped into the room. He immediately recognized the old man propped up by the pillows. Grey and sunken-cheeked as he was, it was the one-legged reprobate, Zacuto. As his visitor drew near enough for his features to be seen, a weak smile lit the worn face.

"Close the door," he instructed, "and sit here by me."

Micah did as he was told. When he was perched on the edge of the bed, Zacuto placed a hand over his and sighed as if releasing a great burden. "It is my friend young Tuscany," he said.

"Now, Zacuto," Micah remonstrated gently, "you know I am no such thing."

"I know what I know," he replied. "What brings you here at this hour?"

"I'm returning from dinner. I've been assigned to Roma for some time. They have me billeted here. Zacuto, what's happened? Where is everybody?"

"Reactivated." The old man framed the word in someone else's inflection and smirked. "So they call it. Translated is more like."

"But all of them? I was last here not three months ago. What was it took them and how did you survive?" Even as he said it, he wondered if Zacuto truly had. The man looked as if he had but few hours of life left to him.

Zacuto shook his head. "Not dead," he corrected. "They yet live, if you can call that life. Better to be dead and at peace. I ask only for peace."

Micah was puzzled. "Are you tired? Do you want me to leave?"

"No!" Zacuto grabbed at him. "Please Benvolio, or whatever your real name might be." Before Micah could protest, the old man cut him off. "There is no need to pretend with me. I see your blood in your face, in your walk." Zacuto struggled to sit forward. Micah adjusted the pillows behind him and waited for him to catch his breath. "You think I am the only one who saw? We made a vow…" he pushed out the words, his body convulsing with the effort. Alarmed, Micah rose to get help. The old man clamped down on his arm with a grasp like the bite of a mad dog. "No! No one must hear. Only you!" He leaned forward and gulped the air down as far as it would go. A little before he was able to, he resumed. "I was with Leopoldo, almost to the last. He knew there was no hope; he smelled it in the stars, he said. He ordered us to go far from him, to save ourselves. Only weeks later, not even a month, he was taken. Some of us were hunted down as well. Others…Some of us are meant to survive. As I have again, for the last time, and now I know why. To tell you…" He tried not to wheeze. "To tell you what they have done."

He seemed feverish, but Micah sensed that his mind was as clear as ever. "I won't leave until you have told me," he reassured the old man. "Take the time you need."

"I may only take what time I have," he answered, with a touch of his customary spark. "They came here one day to speak with us, two legates, representatives of Caesar's. We were told we were to receive a great honour, a reward for our years of service. Only the best, they said, though in truth they took all but those whose minds had already wandered from their bodies."

Recalling the state of the cocoons in the solarium, Micah nodded his understanding.

"They took us in groups of five—a hand they called it. We were brought to the ruins near the Porta Magica, at the third hour of the day.

Some kind of chapel, it looked to be, some ancient kind brought out of the ruins. I was in Alexandria, you know, and Cairo, with Napoleon. This had that flavour. They gave us something to drink, and washed us. There were men there in blue robes. Not as Caesar affects for his household. Foreign. Men the colour of tanned leather with no hair on them at all." He pointed weakly to his own eyebrows and grimaced. "None at all."

Micah tried to imagine a face without eyebrows. It would have an inhuman aspect. To even a hardened legionary, that would be more disturbing than the worst battle scars. He squeezed Zacuto's hand, urging him to continue.

The old man tried to smile. "It was like the opera, except the music was shit," he observed. "All flutes and drums and cymbals. And that eunuch of the Emperor's singing like a woman. There were women as well; young girls who danced. Virgins. At least one was. For the moment." He fixed Fairservis with his clouded eyes.

Understanding dawned. "You mean...right there?"

"Not even with a man." The memory brought a look of disgust to his face. "They held her down, the other girls, all of them in some kind of trance as we all were by then. They had a dog, a black mongrel...." he shuddered. "They required a sacrifice. Afterward, they killed the dog. Cut off its head. And we couldn't move to stop any of it. Whatever had been in that drink, it was as if our bodies were encased in mud. Which was the point of the exercise."

Micah waited patiently until he realized the old man was waiting for him to react. He wasn't at his best; he didn't know what was wanted. "The point of the exercise?" he finally asked.

"Our bodies encased in mud," Zacuto repeated, underscoring the significance of every word.

Micah didn't want to believe what he was comprehending, but it all made sense. What Izano had said about the swelling ranks of the trecika, the evidence of his own eyes of the disappearance of the old legionaries...What better source for 'recruitment' than men who had already given their lives to soldiering?

"Translated," he recalled the word Zacuto had chosen before. The old man squeezed his hand and relaxed back into his pillows.

"Translated. I could see it. The light went out in their eyes and they would fall and then, in one of those clay monsters...it was like a candle had been lit."

"But not you. You survived."

"They wouldn't accept me," he wheezed. "They couldn't. I'm a Jew, you know."

"They take Catholics, I assume, or there would be no one to take."

Zacuto smiled in wily remembrance. "You could feel when the moment came, when something began to tug at your soul and try to pull it away. I thought of Yakov wrestling with the Angel. 'I am too old to fight,' I thought. And I began to say the *Sh'ma*, the Jewish prayer, in preparation to depart this life. It saved me."

"Some of the Catholics would have done the same," Micah reasoned. "I would have done so myself, tried to say the last rites, even without a priest."

"The Jews need no priests," Zacuto said, simply. "The prayer is between ourselves and our God. But it's not about that. It's the language itself. We are the People of the Book, you know. Every Hebrew word, every letter has its ancient power. For all its age, Latin is young and less potent. Our faiths, those priests and mine, shared the same dawn; their Gods cannot steal from Yaweh. I spoke the words and the rope went slack. One of the priests saw what had happened and put a gag around my mouth but it was too late. They could not stop me from thinking the prayer. I prayed and I prayed until it was dawn and the magic dissolved. They could not break the Covenant. The ordeal burned up what strength I had and left me as you find me. I thought surely they would kill me, and knowing what had happened to my comrades, I welcomed death. But instead they brought me back to my bed, to allow me to die as my God would will. I shouldn't have lived more than a day. I did not know that I was waiting for you, my friend." Zacuto smiled with great sweetness, washing Micah in a flood of warmth. "That was eight nights ago. Tonight, I think gladly, will be my last."

They sat in comfortable silence together, Zacuto's hand resting lightly on the younger man's hand. It had been years since Micah had felt a tear on his cheek. He let it dry, unseen by eyes that remained open for some hours before the light finally fled them. When it had, he withdrew his hand and gently closed those eyes. He kissed the old man on the forehead and slipped like a shadow from the room. He was careful to leave the lamp and the door as they had been when he'd arrived. The nuns would find Zacuto in the morning and never know he had had any visitor other than Death.

13 - VERFARKAS

Claude and Gertrude stumbled on what looked to be the remains of a campsite. There was a sizable circle of grass that had been trampled flat. The mound of cinders at the center were cold, but Claude's nose told her they couldn't be more than a day old. Her instinctive reaction was joy. Somewhere, not so far away, were other people! Even if she and Gertrude couldn't speak their language, whoever it was could be made to understand that they needed to get out of this forest.

At first Gertrude was excited too, but her mood began to change as they continued their speculations. "I've read Mr. Stead in the *Pall Mall Gazette*," she said, her lips pulled into a tight line at the memory. Defenseless women weren't always saved. They might be sold into slavery, the worst kind of slavery, even by the very people they trusted to protect them. "We have to proceed with caution."

Back home, Claude had heard stories of girls being captured and forcibly adopted into tribes. As an almost official Lakhota already, Claude had always felt safe in the woods, but as Gertrude pointed out, these weren't the woods she knew; she was in Europe now, or thereabouts.

Still, the possibility of help was irresistible. Claude started looking actively for the trail these campers would have left. They decided they would follow it, but keep their own presence concealed until they had judged it to be safe.

"Of course," Gertrude noted, "there's no real way to know until it's too late."

On that philosophical note, they took up their new path.

They never saw another soul that day, but the signs of human presence grew clearer.

Claude had decided they should wait until it was fully dark to build their fire. She wanted to see if she could make out any other firelight glowing through the trees. She could not.

It had troubled her to realize that if they were to continue tracking these others, they would have to veer away from the stream they thought of as their lifeline. There was nothing left of Blavatsky's rations; their satchels were empty except for what they had picked up off the ground. The last few days they had lived mostly off fish. Most important, of course, was the water. They knew from experience that their skins held what was at best a three-day supply. Right now they were as strong as they would be, and the visions came only occasionally. Were they willing to bet that, if they left the one source of drinkable water they knew, they would find another in time? It was a difficult decision and one they discussed deep into the night. In the end, once again, there was no choice but to gamble. They couldn't live in these woods forever.

Feeling prematurely nostalgic, they breakfasted on fish. They cooked more than they could eat and stowed the rest, wrapped in dry leaves, for later. They drank themselves full to bursting and filled their skins. Finally, they turned their backs firmly on the stream and headed in the direction Claude had said was marked by the mysterious others.

As they were building their fire, they heard the sound of twigs snapping underfoot. They froze. Holding their breath, they scanned the trees around them. There was nothing, not so much as the flash of a tiny rodent. Claude glided silently around the perimeter of the clearing, as she was able to do. Nothing. They were disappointed. It had been their first hopeful sign all day that they might be coming close. They settled down to eat what they'd found along the way.

With nothing that the animals couldn't dig up with their own paws, there was no reason to hang the satchels in trees. Instead, they used them as pillows. Claude lay back, taking up her star-gazing pose. The moon was full tonight, no longer gibbous. How many days had they been wandering this forest? She tried to reckon it, but before she got past the second day, her eyes had closed and she was fast asleep.

Claude was jolted awake by something she never heard. A moment later, there came a howling sound that seemed to penetrate her very bones. It sounded almost like a coyote. Did they have coyotes here, or was it some kind of wolf?

She had feared something like this since their first night, but had gradually relaxed her guard. There hadn't been any large predators that she could tell. The forest was either peculiarly empty of them, or the ones that lived there didn't like the smell of humans.

She shook Gertrude awake and warned her. "We must build up the fire. Hopefully that will be enough to keep the animal, whatever it is, away. But if that fails, if it comes anyway, we'll need to climb a tree beyond its reach," she explained. "Get our things together. If we have to run, we don't want to lose what we have, especially not the water skins."

They sat as close as they dared to their augmented blaze, eyes and ears patrolling the trees for a sign of life. Claude thought that if the animal were the size of a coyote and she caught it off guard, she would be able to beat it back. She doubted Gertrude could do much, but she knew it would give her confidence to feel armed so they both gripped their walking sticks tightly.

"Do you still have those flat stones?" Claude asked, as conversationally as she could manage.

"Yes. Why, should we throw them if something comes?"

Claude reached in her own bag and pulled out the somewhat draggled pieces of petticoat. She should have thought to tear off another strip, she realized, but she wasn't about to do that now. Not when she might have to run at any moment. Fortunately, silk was strong. "How many do you have?"

"Five or six, I think," Gertrude started to look.

"I need only four."

Puzzled, Gertrude dug in her satchel and fished out the stones. Claude tied them to the ends of the strips of silk. She stood with a grunt of satisfaction. Taking one strip in each hand, she began to twirl them slowly. As she got the feel of the weight and balance, her speed increased. Claude bent and twisted, all the while keeping the stones flying through the air at the end of the ribbons. Finally she let them come to a rest and sank back down on the ground. "Now we have a weapon," she said panting.

"What do I do?" Gertrude whispered in awe. Was there anything the American girl couldn't do? She was beginning to feel that an Oxford education might be lacking in some regard.

"Run," Claude answered succinctly.

"Run? That seems...."

"If it gets to where I have to use this, I can't be worrying about whether or not I might hit you, too."

Put that way, it made a good deal of sense. Gertrude resolutely clutched her staff. If there were anything to do before running, she was determined to show she could do it.

They sat for long enough that their backs began to feel sore. Claude fed in some more branches. Perhaps it had been her imagination after all.

But no! She heard the intake of Gertrude's breath and looked up from the fire. On the other side of the clearing, just between the trees, she saw pairs of green eyes. Two, then three, then six or seven. They appeared so quickly. She gestured for Gertrude to remain still. Their bodies blended into the shadows, but as best as she could judge the height of their eyes, the animals were sitting. One or two had some silver in their fur that caught the moonlight. Definitely some kind of wolf and beautiful, in a wild dangerous way. The fire was holding them back. As long as the girls kept feeding the fire, they would come no closer. With any luck, the wolves would tire or get bored and go away.

One of the animals in the center of the row lifted back its head and bayed loud. It was a chilling sound but not, Claude thought, as terrible as the sound she had heard before. Perhaps it was because she was wide awake now. The howler must have been the leader, because all the others lifted their own muzzles and joined in.

"We're fine," Claude said, trying to calm herself by calming Gertrude.

"Of course we are," Gertrude said stoutly. "We have a fire, we have weapons...."

There was a crashing sound in the trees behind them. Claude jumped to her feet as a pair of enormous creatures hurtled through the brake. There was something canine about them, but they were longer and taller than any wolf. They were covered not with fur but with a leathery hide tufted with coarse-looking grey hairs. There was a gaunt, starved look about them, and their eyes were the red of fresh blood.

The creatures let out a wild howl. *That* had been the sound that had awakened her. "Run, Gertrude!" she yelled, shrugging her coat off her shoulders. Her arms free, she started to twirl her makeshift bolos. "Run NOW!"

Gertrude didn't wait to be told twice. She scrambled up and started across the clearing, pointing her staff like a spear.

"Not that way! That's where the wolves are! Run to wherever these things came from!"

"Run to wherever these things came from!"

Gertrude ran for all she was worth. It went against everything she thought she stood for to run away from a friend in danger, but she knew Claude was right. If she stayed, she would only be a liability.

She needed to find a climbing tree. She was glad she'd played with her little brothers and knew how to go about it. Compared to the things Claude knew it was nothing, but it was more than many young women of her acquaintance would know to do. She found an oak with a reasonable limb and dug her stick into the ground to help herself clamber up. She had already lost track of which way she'd come; she hoped she would be able to find the campsite when it was alright to come back. How would she know? Would Claude have to find her? That didn't seem right. She hoped her stick would still be there when she came down. It was a good stick. It suited her well. Why was she getting sentimental about a piece of wood when there was a girl out there fighting for her life?!

She listened but couldn't make out which sounds might be those horrible creatures. There was no way that Claude could survive this night, incredible brave girl though she was. Gertrude fought back the urge to cry. There was no time for that sort of thing. She had to think of herself as a soldier, like Billy Lacelles. She could mourn her comrade later. Right now she had to keep herself alive. As long as she lived, there was a chance of making it back to civilization and getting help for Maud. Gertrude climbed to the next sturdy branch, and the next one after. Far enough, she decided. She settled herself with her back against the trunk and tried hard to pretend she was home and playing hide and seek with Maurice.

It was unthinkable, but she must have dozed; she felt herself snap to, the way you do if you've drifted off. She almost hit her head on the tree trunk. The night seemed quiet. That is to say, it seemed only as noisy as she'd gotten used to, sleeping in the woods all these nights. Perhaps the battle was over. She would wait a little while longer and try to find her way back. Looking out into the trees, Gertrude spotted what might be the campfire. Well, it was some kind of warm-coloured light down below. What else could it be?

She tried to spin out another hour by reciting long passages of *Paradise Lost*. When she ran out of words, she decided it was time to leave her perch. Keeping her face turned in the direction of the campfire to mark her way, she slowly reversed her climb. She wondered why it was always so much more difficult going down. Perhaps it was because you couldn't see where you were heading. The final limb was the worst. She let herself down and pointed her toes, but still couldn't feel the ground below them. Had she jumped to get up? She might have; she'd been that frightened. Or perhaps she had turned herself around and was on a different side of the tree; maybe there was a hole there…A hole; that did not bear thinking of! She squeezed her eyes shut and let go. She fell with a soft skid, which wouldn't have happened if she'd remembered to bend her knees, and she landed on her bum. Hugo would be laughing at that one, she thought. Scrambling up, she dusted off her skirt and groped for her stick. There it was, right where she'd dropped it. She picked it up and started toward where she was certain she had seen the campfire.

Gertrude was rather proud of the way she was finding her way through the woods. Once, when she thought she heard something large scuffling in the bushes, she hauled herself into the nearest tree without a second's hesitation. It turned out to be nothing, but it gave her a chance to peer down from a height and check her bearings.

She soon reached a spot where she could see the yellow firelight glimmering through the trees. It didn't seem at all familiar. She was no child of the Western Frontier, but she was an Oxford scholar and she was English enough to fancy she knew the difference between one tree and another. She took a sniff as she'd seen Claude do, though to what end she didn't know. She decided to proceed with extreme caution.

Walking as she had been shown, in the way that least disturbed the twigs and other such that snapped beneath one on the ground, she moved closer to the brake. There was a smell of cooked meat! She swallowed hard. She hadn't had meat since Budapest. She took an involuntary step forward before catching herself—if there was meat on the fire, then it was definitely not her campsite, unless…she shuddered. No! She pulled herself back. That was too horrible to contemplate! She shook her head as if to banish the terrible thought. As she did so, she must have reached out her hand, or perhaps her staff, because a cowbell started clanking and a horse whinnied loudly; then she heard a cacophony of pots being clanged and people shouting and a shotgun going off, and she heard herself wailing "Stop! Stop!" in the shrillest possible voice, like a child's, and a tall, dark figure jumped out from behind a brake.

"*So keres?!*" The man yelled, jerking her arm. Her stick dropped and she was pulled into the clearing. It said something for her state of mind that she was relieved to hear it was a wholly human voice. Then she remembered— it was humans that had abandoned her and Claude in the forest in the first place. She began to struggle, but the man was larger and stronger than she and soon had pinned her arms behind her. Being immobilized didn't stop her from screaming. She screamed long and hard until her throat rasped and her breath was coming in gasps, when she finally understood that it didn't matter if she screamed because there was no one to hear except the stony faces facing her.

The old woman said something and the man pushed her forward. Perhaps the woman was not so old. Although the hair that showed beneath her kerchief was mostly white, her voice was strong and she moved, albeit leaning heavily on a stick, with great energy. She looked at Gertrude in curiosity and from every angle. She felt the fabric of her skirt and murmured something. The man who was holding Gertrude thrust her left hand out and toward the old woman, who took it and turned it over slowly. She examined the burns from Gertrude's struggles at making fires, and her torn, dirty nails. Her black eyes bore into Gertrude's with the same intensity as Madame Blavatsky's pale ones. Then she smiled, and Gertrude found it oddly comforting. She said something that might have been a greeting.

"Hello," Gertrude managed to stammer.

The woman tried again. Whatever she was speaking, it sounded like many languages stitched together: perhaps some Greek, and something that sounded almost like Roumanian. Gertrude had picked up a few phrases in Bucharest and tried them now.

"Hello," she repeated. "*Bună ziua.*"

The woman laughed and let loose a glad tirade, leading her to the campfire. Her capture followed close behind, still watchful.

"I'm sorry," Gertrude said apologetically. "*Imi pare rau. Vorbiti engleza?*"

Eventually, employing her excellent school German supplemented with a combination of energetic pantomime and an inspired pidgin of words borrowed from every tongue she could call on, Gertrude was able to explain about Claude and the horrible beasts. She knew she had gotten through to them when she saw the looks her listeners darted around the sheltering circle of trees.

"We must help her!" she concluded.

The large piratical man who had initially captured her, and whose name she had learned was Milosz, shook his head. He looked at the old woman to explain.

"There is no help," Dika said, holding Gertrude's hand between her own. "We must hope your friend is dead."

Gertrude wasn't sure she'd been understood. "Claude has the skill to fight," she insisted. "She may still be alive!"

"The *vérfarkas*," the old woman explained, "he is a man, cursed in his blood to change when the moon is full. Stronger than any beast and with those passions as well as the cunning of a man."

Finally, Gertrude understood. Vérfarkas. 'Vér', like 'were'. The creatures she'd seen were werewolves! Why hadn't she known at once. Like any child she had been deliciously scared by such tales, but had never suspected they might be real. "But surely they can be killed!"

"The only thing that can slay him is silver mixing with his blood…When we must come to these woods under the fullness of the moon, we cast bullets of silver." Milosz pointed to the rifle in the boy's hands. "We met the pack earlier. The two who attacked your camp escaped. We have only one bullet left."

"Then we can help…"

"You said you were attacked by two. We have only one bullet. And your friend has no weapon," he continued remorselessly. "If she lives, she will have been injured—a bite, a cut. Once her blood is poisoned by theirs, she will join their ranks."

"It is better to be dead," Dika reiterated with some authority. Gertrude wondered if someone near to her had been bitten by such a creature. "We will wait for morning."

Milosz nodded. "In the morning we will find her. And if she lives, we will use our last bullet to save her soul."

After than, she huddled miserably by the fire in silence. They offered her some kind of stew, but she had lost any ability to eat. Dika led her to the back of their wagon and bade her share the straw mattress covered with blankets. It seemed years since Gertrude had slept on anything other than bare ground, and she fell asleep the minute her head hit the pallet.

&

"Not that way! That's where the wolves are! Run to wherever these things came from!"

Gertrude would have to take care of herself, for now both the creatures had focused their attention on Claude. They circled her, confused by the spinning cords. There was a stink about them that made her eyes sting. One reared up on its hindquarters and tried to bat the moving shape with a foreleg, like a cat chasing a butterfly. The stone whizzed by and cracked its paw. The thing snarled, showing evil yellow teeth. The other, the smaller one, seemed to think her attention was diverted and skulked around behind her. It was about to pounce when she let fly one of her makeshift bolos. Her release was perfect. The weight of the stone, spinning through the air, wrapped the silk like a rope, binding together the creature's hind legs and causing it to fall face down on the dirt. Growling, it began to drag itself forward on its front legs. The larger creature was coming at her from her other side, its muzzle dripping, the claws of its forepads raised to strike. Whatever these monsters were, they were out to kill.

Her thoughts crackled like an electrical current. An injured animal is the most dangerous of all. When you have two enemies, you cannot disable both at once unless you can cause them to harm one another. She feinted to the side. The larger animal leaped toward her and she jumped out in the opposite direction, at the same time jerking her remaining bolo cord sharply down.

She had forgotten that she wasn't wearing trousers. In mid air, her skirt caught in her legs and she fell. But the jump had been enough to buy her time. The two rocks slammed up to meet each other, hitting the pouncing creature in its long muzzle. It fell hard, the full weight of its body landing on the head of its fellow on the ground.

Claude scrambled up. 'Use what you have!' Father said in her ear. Spotting her heavy walking stick, she kicked it up and grabbed it in both empty hands. She just made it. The unbound animal, enraged now, was back on its feet and starting to spring. It should have been unconscious. They both should have been. The bound one should have been crushed dead but its forelegs were starting to once again drag along the ground. How did you stop these things?

Wielding the stick as if it were a quarterstaff, she started circling backwards. If she could get to the creature on the ground, she should be able to stamp on its feet with the heel of her boot and cripple it. That would be one entirely down. The monster that was still standing faced her; it circled as she did, almost toying with her. She could swear it leered at her, as if the beast knew what she was doing and found it amusing.

Claude was just where she wanted to be. Her next move would need to be swift and certain. She jumped backward and over the belly-creeper. Pitching her weight forward again, she stomped hard on the animal's front paws. It yelped in pain and she went flying face down into the dirt. Again she'd miscalculated the skirt. Trying to move, she felt a searing pain in her ankle.

All the years Father and Leski spent training her and she would die today, not because she fought like a woman but because she was dressed like one. Well, she wouldn't die alone!

She flipped over. Her right hand brushed against her staff. She grabbed for it. The larger creature stopped circling, opened its jaws and charged. She thought of Father and Leski and forced herself into a seating position. As the beast lunged, she twisted the staff to just the correct angle and rammed it firmly between the yellow teeth and into its throat. "*Hokahey!*" she yelled with all her might, the woods ringing with the sound.

The monster gave a horrible scream. Its body convulsed, blood and bilious green foam spilled from its throat, but instead of dying, it rose up again on its hind legs. The staff was caught in its head. It swayed above its haunches, pawing at the stake with its forelegs; it seemed to be trying to shake it loose.

Claude tried desperately to get up, terrified that she would faint from the pain in her leg. "Why don't you die!" she screamed hysterically, beating the air with her fists. "What is this? Magic?!"

From nowhere, she remembered the folk tales Aunt Nan would tell when she was particularly nostalgic for the Auld Country. There was always something about silver...Or was it cold iron? No, that was for fairies. For monsters it was always silver or had better be; that was all she had.

The wounded beast had almost freed itself from the pole and was once again coming toward her. Fumbling with one hand, she managed to unhook her mechanical pencil from her chatelaine. It seemed so paltry a thing to wield against this beast, but it was her only hope.

The monster sprang at her, crushing her against the ground with its terrible weight. She felt its fetid breath in her face. She raised her arm, ignoring the fearful weight and, with the calm certainty that she was already dead, she plunged the silver stick into the creature's eye.

It collapsed heavily on top of her.

With a surge of strength she didn't think she had, Claude managed to roll over. She found herself on top of the monster. With a final grunt, she pushed herself up enough to roll off and onto the ground.

The thing didn't stop her. It reached once towards the three inches of silver protruding from its eye. The sound it made was almost human. The other eye rolled back in its head and it was still.

For several minutes, there was no sound other than Claude's labored breath. Then the wolves, who had never moved in all this time, threw back their muzzles and bayed once again. The green lights faded away as one by one they withdrew into the woods.

Claude heard an odd scratching sound and turned her head. The smaller creature, its head turned guiltily toward its partner, was pulling itself painfully away toward the fringe of trees, dragging its still bound hind legs along the ground.

Claude, too spent to do otherwise, watched it go. She let her head fall back. The tears streamed over her cheeks and dripped on the ground. She felt she might lie there forever.

Somewhere, she heard a branch snap in a tree, and a soft, careful footfall. "Gertrude?" she whispered.

"Martyia!" the voice was male and seemed to be pleading.

"Who are you?" she asked weakly.

The man muttered something in a language Claude didn't understand, then knelt beside her, lifted her into a seated position and said something in another. She shook her head. "*Sprechen sie Deutsch?*" he asked

"*Ein bissen,*" she said. A little. She was trembling and in pain.

"*Wasser,*" he said, holding a tin canteen to her lips. She took a sip and coughed. He patted her back and made her take another sip. "You killed the vérfarkas," he said.

"Vérfarkas?" she asked, dully.

"The monster that is the wolf. *Ruv.* I don't know the German," he said apologetically. "Vérfarkas is the Hungarian."

Were they in Hungary then? Her head was spinning. "Who are you?" she repeated. "Where is my friend, where is Gertrude?"

"I am Yoska. I don't know where is Gertrude. I saw only you. You and they." He pointed to where the dead beast lay not far from them. She looked and shuddered. "You have slain them," he said in awe. "I thought you were Martyia, come for my life, but you are Angel of Death only for *trushal odji,* the hungry soul of wolf."

"That's no wolf," she said.

"No," he agreed. "Is vérfarkas. Is creature of enchantment. No one can slay vérfarkas. I have never seen such a battle."

She looked at him sharply. "You saw me fight these things? Where were you?

He pointed up. "In tree."

"In a tree? You sat in a tree and watched? Why didn't you help me?!"

He shrugged unhappily. "No one can fight vérfarkas. You were to die, or even worse. I as well, if I did not stay in tree."

"What could be worse than dying?" she wondered, but she said it in English and he did not understand. Her hair was all over the place. She pulled it back and started to braid. As she lifted it from her shoulders, Yoska gave a wordless moan and recoiled, his eyes rolling back into his skull in fear. Was there another one?! She turned to look where she thought he was looking. There was nothing there except the animal she'd slain, and her coat, which was covered in gore. Her mouth went dry. She'd find some other way to stay warm at night; she couldn't bring herself to even touch that coat again. It would have to be burned.

She looked at him, to ask if he would put the coat on the fire. It wasn't a beast that he had been staring at in such fear, it was her!

"Blood!" he whispered, pointing. Her shoulders, once she'd lifted her hair, were stained with more of the creature's fluids. If she had been anywhere near the stream, she would have jumped into it and rubbed herself raw with hands full of gravel.

"It's not my blood," she said. "It didn't hurt me. I'm fine."

"Not yours?" he said warily. "You're sure?"

She touched each of her shoulders in turn, her face wrinkling in disgust. It was all on the surface. "Not mine," she repeated confidently.

It seemed to matter. Yoska came close enough again to see for himself, touching each shoulder and moving her blouse to see if it stuck. His relief was palpable. He bent his head and kissed her hand the way she'd seen Catholics kiss the hands of priests. "You have great and holy powers."

It was ridiculous. She tried to push him away, sending a twinge of pain through her leg. He saw her grimace. "You are hurt?"

"Not bleeding," she said quickly. "My leg. I think I broke it."

Yoska unlaced her boot and eased it off her foot. Delicately but firmly, his fingers probed her ankle. She gritted her teeth against the pain. He smiled, and she noticed his two front teeth were gold. "Is not break. Is only turn." He whipped the kerchief from his neck and bound up the leg. "We wait for the light. I will take you my camp. My people will help."

"What about Gertrude? I told her to run." Claude pointed towards the trees where she'd last seen her friend.

"My people will help find your Gertrude," he said simply. "You have slain…"

"I know, vérfarkas."

"Very good!" His face split into a delighted grin. When she didn't smile back, his faded. "You do not understand," he said soberly. "They are evil. Blackest kind of magic. They slay many of our people. You have done a service. We must do the same."

He gave her some more water and then handed her a small bottle of drink. She looked at it suspiciously. "*Feuerwasser*," he said.

"I was given drugs. Poison. Very bad. I have dreams…"

"I make myself," he said with a grin. "Is good." The smell reminded her of Aunt Nan's bad-tasting medicinal brandy. She hoped it would have the same fortifying effect and drank deep. Yoska smiled approvingly. "Now you rest," he said. "I will watch with fire." He found her satchel and tucked it under her head.

❧

When Claude opened her eyes, dawn was staining the clearing. She blinked sleepily at the dying embers of their camp fire. She'd had the most terrible dream.

"Gertrude," she tried to call her friend. Her throat was extraordinarily parched. She needed her water ration. When she tried to get up, she felt the pain shoot up her leg. Not a dream then. What had happened?

She tried to shake her thoughts into order but it seemed that the harder she tried to make them mind her, the more the swirled around in her head. The wolves baying, announcing those horrible creatures. She squeezed her eyes tightly but it wouldn't go away, those ghastly dripping muzzles and blazing eyes coming at her…what had Yoska called them…the vérfarkas.

Yoska. Why had he disappeared? If it hadn't been for the kerchief, she would be sure she'd imagined him. No, he had been there alright, but who was he? He had watched and done nothing to help. He said he was a man. Or did he say that? Maybe she just thought that because he looked like a man.

Claude dragged herself painfully upright. She was grateful for the pain. She could feel her mind trying to float away, but the pain kept bringing it back. Wouldn't this ever stop? Would Gertrude and she spend the rest of their lives at the mercy of whatever drugs the Blavatsky had stuffed into their bodies?

Where had she put her walking stick? She needed it now. And where was her other boot? Ah, there it was! She unlaced it all the way and tried to push her foot inside but it was no use. She could tell now that her ankle wasn't broken, but until the swelling went down she was stuck. What was she going to do? And where was Gertrude?! Please let her have gotten safely up some tree, like Yoska said he had. But shouldn't she have come back by now?

"Gertrude!!" she called, as loudly as she could. She turned in another direction. "Gertrude!!" She turned again and screamed.

There was a naked man on the ground, tall and thin as a lathe. You could count his ribs through his sallow skin. His hands and feet were horny with callous. Her walking stick lay beside him, stained with blood. Please let this be vision quest and let it go away now! She couldn't turn away.

Something silver seemed to be poking out of his eye. She retched. It was her pencil. She staggered back and fell. The pain blossomed in her head and her sight turned inward. She could see the pain, like drops of iodine spreading on a glass microscope slide. It was very large and she was very small. If she fell into it, she would be washed away. She raised her arms to dive.

"Urme!"

A voice called her back and she was staring again at the horrible corpse.

Yoska came running into the clearing holding a cap full of mushrooms. He followed the direction of Claude's eyes and grimaced. "I apologize, my Urme. You should not have to see this."

"I killed a man! I have never in my life…"

"This was not a man, Urme. Gyorgi died a year ago."

She covered her face with both hands and shook her head. "I killed him and never asked forgiveness. You even thank a bird or a rabbit for giving up its life so that you may live," she whispered.

"He would have killed you without a thought." Yoska's voice was sad but definite. "He had no mind to give it." Putting down the mushrooms, he strode resolutely over to the body. He made the sign of the cross, mumbled something she could not hear and, with one firm tug, pulled the pencil free.

Before her eyes, the body shriveled, dwindled to skin-covered bone and then to bone-shaped dust that crumbled to the ground. Yoska broke a branch from a nearby birch and used it to trace the dust with some pattern she could not make out. He then broke the birch into four pieces and pressed them into the clearing at the four points of the compass.

When he had done, there was a tear in his eye. He knelt before Claude to hand her the pencil. She snatched it back and recoiled from him.

"Did I see that?" she whispered. "What demon are you to do something like that?" She wouldn't look at him. Her hand shaking, she wiped the slender silver tube on the grass.

Yoska recalled what she had said the night before. She had brain poison. This was fate. She did not understand that she held his *kumpania* in her debt; here was a way to begin to repay it. They had come to the woods at full moon for two reasons—to redeem the soul of Gyorgi, and to gather an herb that was prized for clearing such poisons from the brain and blood. Before the pack had come upon them last night, they'd already harvested some of the *dramego*. When he got her to the camp, Dika could brew a *chao*. First he needed to get some food and water into her.

Weak though she felt, Claude would not hear of it. She needed to find Gertrude. The morning kept slipping out of view and the events of the previous night came rushing back like a sequence of images flickering through a praxinoscope. She could see her friend running frantically past her. Gertrude had done well, Claude thought with approval. She had obeyed orders. Had it been enough?

Claude couldn't stop the nagging feeling that if Gertrude were safe she would have found her way back at first light. Had there been more of those creatures in the woods? Had she lost her way? What if she were lying injured somewhere, or wandering around lost, the way they had done those first days. Claude became more and more overwrought. Her head started to throb. She could feel it growing bigger, like a bubble.

Yoska tried to reassure. His voice sounded far away and hollow. He said they would go to his camp, and his friends would help them search.

Claude didn't believe him. There was something so strange about this so-called man, this Yoska. She could see a kind of halo, not like an angel's golden haze, but a smudge the colour of a bruise that surrounded his entire face. And the way he moved had something of a slither about it. He didn't want to help her find Gertrude at all. He wanted something evil. He thought he was tricking her, but she would have to trick him instead.

She let him help her wedge her foot into her boot and tuck up the laces so that she wouldn't trip. He handed her the satchel and water skin. She took her staff, as well. It was stained with blood but it had helped to save her life. She felt about it now the way she would a trusty sword. And with her ankle throbbing at every step, she needed it more than ever.

While Yoska, or whatever his demon name might be, buried the embers and the burnt bits of her coat, she carefully scanned the section of trees towards which Gertrude had last been seen heading. She thought she could see where her friend had passed. Fortune was with her and Yoska chose to start toward that general vicinity. It was no great effort to lead him between the very trees she'd noted.

As they left the clearing, he tried to take her arm. "No," she said cagily; "it's better if I follow you. If I stumble we don't both fall." When he tried to object, she assured him she had her stick to lean on.

She also told the demon it was easier for her to walk without speaking. Let him get used to hearing nothing from her. It would be easier to disappear. She soon found a rhythm to walking with her bad leg, a way to push her staff into the ground and use her good leg to drag the bad one forward. It got easier in time. It still hurt but the pain became part of her and she could move through it.

They reached a large tree. The demon passed it by without a second look, his eyes on a sinister path she could not see. What Wakhangli Mani showed her were the broken branches and a deep hole, as if someone had driven a post into the ground. She put her head against the trunk. "Show me," she whispered into the bark.

Yoska moved ahead along some trail he seemed to know, not noticing that Claude had stayed behind at the large tree. She circled it slowly, spotting a few inches of mashed ground cover that looked like someone might have fallen heavily on it. Flattening herself with her nose to the ground, she slowly scanned the dirt and moss until she could make out the ghost of a footprint.

Without knowing it, Gertrude had left her a trail. Claude followed, as her mentors had taught her. She was careful to hide from the demons. The one who called himself Yoska had disappeared from sight, but there were others. Claude knew how to hide herself by shifting her skin to bark and her hair to leaves. She couldn't see the demons, as she had to keep her eyes closed in order to disappear, but she could smell the sulfur as they pressed by and feel the oily film that lingered behind them in the air. As a tree, she was sometimes able to speak with a passing bird. The birds were able to help her when she lost her way and they helped her fight the one demon that spotted her, an owl with a woman's head who swooped down so low that its claws nearly caught in Claude's hair. It had streaming grey curls and odd moonstone eyes, and it laughed and laughed and laughed. She fought it off with her fencing sword, and the birds pecked out its eyes and it burst into flame.

Claude smelled smoke and coffee. She noticed the crude alarm strung along the perimeter. There was Gertrude, sitting by the fire beside an old woman and a boy. A tree, standing still, she watched. When Gertrude left the side of the fire and moved to the shadow of the caravan, Claude threw herself on the ground, wriggling on her belly like a snake.

By daylight, Gertrude could easily see the black string that looped from tree to tree, at chest level, around the entire perimeter of the camp. There were four or five cowbells dangling from it. If you hit the string at any point, they would all start to clang, which is what must have happened to her. It was a clever alarm system against night-time intruders.

She cradled the chipped enamel mug in her hands and waited for the coffee to be cool enough to drink. It smelled strong. She wondered if it was strong enough to give her the nerve to look for Claude. If Claude were alive and had been bitten or scratched…she couldn't bear to think about it. How could she stand there and watch while Milosz put a bullet through her friend's heart. She was too much of a coward for that. No, she would have to stay right here by the caravan and wait.

She had never seen such a caravan close up, no less thought of sleeping inside. It was a rickety wagon, but the sides were painted in wonderful designs that reminded her of her step-mother's Dresden plates. They were gypsies. She knew that now, but had been so confused last night that she hadn't seen it. There were gypsies back home who camped by the moor every summer. Father always said to watch your pockets when you saw them in town, and her stepmother had never let any of the children go to the fair for fear they might be kidnapped. How horrified her parents would be to see her now, sitting in the middle of their camp! Oh, she'd been kidnapped alright, but by an Emperor, not by gypsies. The gypsies had only been kind to her. As for dirty, well, after living rough herself for all these days she saw things differently now.

"Hsst! Gertrude!" The whisper that broke into her thoughts was coming from the ground. She peered around. It was Claude! She was nearly invisible, lying flat on her belly between two nearby trees. Gertrude went running towards her. "No, get down!" she hissed. "If you walk, you'll set off the bells!"

"I know!" Gertrude said. She was so relived to see her friend alive and whole that she said it with some asperity. She squatted down, the better to hear, and noticed the stains on Claude's blouse. She blenched. "You're not bleeding are you?"

"No." Now it was Claude's turn to be brusque. "That's what the demon wanted to know, too. Why, I wonder? You're not a demon." She cocked her head and looked at Gertrude appraisingly. "No, you're Gertrude alright." She smiled. Then, just as instantly, she frowned, struggling to sit up. "I must get you away. I see the signs, you know, all around here." she pointed to the caravan. "Can't you read them? They're all demons here…"

"They're gypsies, that's all," Gertrude said, matter-of-factly. It had made such sense to her that Claude would be emotional, that she only now realized that her friend was having a recurrence of what they called the vision quest. "Don't you have gypsies in Chicago? Come and meet them." She held out her hand.

"The horse has a mane of fire! How can you not see?!" Claude pointed a trembling finger at the extremely large but stolid black-pointed bay. Her colour was heightened and the pupils of her eyes swam wildly.

Neither of them heard Milosz until he pulled the cocking handle of the rifle pointed down into Claude's face.

"No!" Gertrude cried, throwing herself across Claude's body.

"Step away, Miss," Milosz said grimly. "Your friend is cursed. See the blood?"

"It's not her blood. She told me…"

"Lies!" He spat over his shoulder. "Move away."

"Milosz, no!" Yoska crashed through the trees, breathless, accompanied by clanking bells.

"Yoska!" Dika cried joyfully as she and Beznik hurried to embrace him. "*Devlesa avilan!*"

"*Devlessa araklam tume,*" he said fervently, allowing himself to be hugged and kissed and pulled toward the fire. All the while, they spoke rapidly in their language. Milosz hauled Claude to feet and prodded her to follow. Gertrude noticed a limp and turned herself into a crutch.

Yoska spoke for some time, occasionally acting out what looked to be a horrible battle. A look of incredible sadness came over his face as he told the last part of his tale. He looked at Beznik beseechingly. The boy nodded once, turned and walked rigidly away to the far side of the caravan.

When Yoska had done, Milosz looked at Claude with great respect and kissed her hand. Dika was not so easily satisfied. She looked Claude up and down, frowning all the while, then said something to Yoska.

"She does not believe your friend could have fought as Yoska describes," Milosz told Gertrude. "She thinks he may have been enchanted and only thinks he saw this."

"I don't know what your friend said he saw…" She was frustrated. Yoska had spoken Romani and she still didn't know what happened.

"He saw a single *gadji*, a woman, fight off two vérfarkas with a dead branch and a rope with two stones," he said solemnly. "One, she destroyed with a small stick of silver. The slain one was one of our kumpania. Gyorgi, father to that one," he indicated Beznik, whose shadow was just visible.

"I'm so sorry," she whispered. That poor boy! No wonder he wanted to be alone.

"Gyorgi was infected last year when we came to harvest the drarnego. If your friend has put him at peace, we are all in her debt."

Dika stood, holding out a hand to Claude. "Come," she said.

"She wants to examine your friend, to be sure she wasn't cursed," Milosz explained.

"It's alright, Claude," Gertrude said encouragingly, in English. "Go with her."

"If you say it's okay," Claude said.

Gertrude watched them enter the caravan.

"She seems so mild," Milosz said, perplexed.

"Her mind is...she sees things that aren't here," Gertrude tried to explain. "We were given some kind of drug. We thought it would go away but it keeps returning."

Yoska went to dip some water from the large tin can into a pot and set it on the fire. Dika was going to make a pot of chao.

When Dika and Claude exited the caravan, Claude's bloodstained blouse had been replaced by a loose scarlet tunic that was belted over her skirt. She had refused the offer of Dika's velvet festival skirt, but her shoulders were wrapped in a shawl, the colour of egg yolk, with a silky black fringe and embroidered flowers. Dika wore an expansive smile.

Milosz and Yoska smiled in response. The sunlight glinted off of Yoska's gold front teeth. Gertrude didn't know why, but she found herself laughing aloud.

"*Chivani*," Yoska addressed Dika with a respectful bow, "will drarnego help the lady?"

She cuffed him playfully. "Have you become a healer now, Yoska? Shall I give you a skirt?" She turned serious once again. "I hope so. We don't know what they were given." She looked at Gertrude questioningly. Gertrude shook her head; they didn't know.

Every year, their kumpania made their way to the border of this *vesh* as it was known to be favourable to drarnego, an herb with the power to heal the illnesses of the mind. The herb had inestimable value and was traded to *vitsas* as far away as Greece and Ireland for other needful things. Drarnego had to be picked at a certain time of year and, to ensure its efficacy, only under the full moon. This forest was also known as the territory of the vérfarkas, which made gathering the herb a dangerous mission.

As chivani or chief wise woman of their kumpania, Dika had to come each year to perform the harvesting rituals. She would take only a small party with her, usually only Milosz and one other. This year, Beznik had been included as they had had hoped to find Gyorgi and destroy him; as oldest son, it was his obligation. Seeing the vulnerable boy, Gertrude rather thought it was a mercy that Claude had spared him the horrible task.

The copper box that Yoska fetched from the caravan held what was what was left of last year's harvest. The drarnego that had been gathered the night before would need to be slowly dried in the sun, something that would be done when they returned to the camp outside the forest where the rest of their kumpania was waiting. Dika opened the box carefully, so that the precious dried herb wouldn't blow away. It emitted a flowery scent that reminded Gertrude of violets, but with a resinous note. When the water was poured over it in the teapot, she also thought she caught a whiff of copper. She asked about this and received a look of approval from Dika. Drarnego should always be stored in copper, she was told; the metal mixed with the herb and increased its potency.

The chao must steep for seven minutes and be stirred ante-clockwise nine times with a copper spoon. It must be drunk hot and plain. Dika handed a cup to each of the girls. While Gertrude felt fine at the moment, she acknowledged that she had previously thought herself rid of the visions only to have them surface again later. Whatever the Blavatsky had dosed them with, it seemed to have a lingering repeat effect. If this tea would purge it from their systems, she would almost bless the werewolves for leading them to it.

Gertrude angled herself so that she was directly facing Claude. If Yoska's observations were accurate, Claude had been in a deep fugue almost since dawn. She might be more likely to drink if she saw Gertrude do it. "To your health," she said lightly, touching her cup to Claude's as if they were flutes of champagne. Mentally crossing her fingers, she took a sip. It didn't taste like any tisane she'd ever drunk; it had a perfume taste, like church incense, mixed with hay. She gestured for Claude to copy her and drained her cup. Claude followed her example, making a small face when the first taste hit her tongue but continuing.

Gertrude handed both cups back to Dika. "How long will it take?"

Dika shrugged. "I don't know if it will work. I'll see to her leg now." Claude winced but didn't protest when Dika pulled off her boot and unwound Yoska's bandanna. The wise woman called for a pot of arnica ointment and massaged it into the injured ankle, then bound the leg with a length of thin cotton. Gertrude watched carefully. It was a less bulky bandage, making it easier to slip the boot back on and lace it loosely.

"We harvest again tonight, *chavi*" Dika said. "Do you want to help?"

"Oh, yes!" Gertrude said. Now that Claude was sitting intact beside her, she could start to enjoy this part of her adventure.

14 - ROMAN RUINS

Brushed, polished and sporting a pristine uniform tunic, Rappaccini reported to a temporary shed beside the Colosseum that served as the field office for the reconstruction efforts. Baron Haussmann greeted his arrival with the merest sketch of acknowledgment. His attention was on weightier matters: what ought to have been the final consignment of travertine for the outer wall had arrived from Tivoli a fortnight late, and a good ten percent of it did not meet the Baron's exacting specifications as to colour.

The Baron was famous for cloaking his anger. Unlike other *capos*, he never raged but voiced his corrections moderately, with a steely charm that brooked no refusal. Right now, only someone familiar with him would understand that he was in a most unpleasant mood.

"Sacconi over there," he chewed his assistant's name like a sticky toffee, "suggests we make do with what we've been sent and decorate the upper tier of Colosseum like wedding cake."

The very young man was kneeling by a large sheet of drafting paper, shading a sketch to indicate an attractive placement of the darker stone. He knew they couldn't wait for replacements. With the Principessa secured, the wedding had been promoted from 'someday maybe' to a looming deadline. There was no choice but to work with what they had.

"This is my memorial!" A mournful sigh deflated the Baron's round little belly. "When I'm dead and gone, this is what I leave behind me—the restoration of Roma."

"A masterpiece." Micah meant it. By whatever questionable means it had been accomplished, the city was a formidable achievement.

Ignoring the compliment, the Baron turned a shrewd eye on his visitor. "I know there are those who sneer at my efforts and say I'm nothing but a copyist. They don't understand the challenge of respecting the purity of classical lines, of echoing it in every new building and road. And now, instead of a crowning glory, I'm dumping a heap of guano at the foot of the Palatine hill." Making his selection from a shelf of crystal decanters, he poured a fortifying grappa and knocked it back.

Unsure of the expected response, Rappaccini chose to keep silent and shrug in what he hoped was acceptable protestation. The gleaming amphitheatre, even had it been a purely modern construction, would be one of the most impressive buildings he had ever seen. For appearing to have been snatched whole out of its proper century without a scratch, it was miraculous.

"Have you inspected the mosaics in Caesar's box?" Sacconi paused in his sketching to wipe the charcoal off his hands onto the front of his smock, which bore previous marks of such treatment. "They'll be ready for grouting tomorrow, but not unless you approve them."

The Baron nodded, resigned. "Come," he said to Rappaccini, stepping over Sacconi's drawing. "You may as well see the disaster close to."

The silhouette of the building alone was enough to send a thrill through an Italian boy who had been nurtured on the stories of Ancient Rome. It was unsettling, however, to pass through the actual portal. As he followed the Baron's rapid progress between the inner and outer walls, Micah had the sensation of being sucked through a temporal field of polar proportions and magnetism. The atmosphere clung as heavily as wet wool.

"Most of the inner wall is original," the Baron called over his shoulder.

Perhaps that explained it. Micah ran a surreptitious hand along the stones, wondering if he were touching anything his ancestors had. Were their ghosts watching him now? It would be nice if his parents might be, from whatever Heaven he liked to think had welcomed them.

Mounting the stairway to the first level, Micah followed the Baron out onto what was being called the Promenade, the expensive seats. He blinked in the sunlight and tried to grasp what he saw: a bowl that could hold the population of a small city. Below him, carpenters were working on a vast wooden floor, laying it in sections across a catacomb of weathered grey stone. He leaned in to get a better look. Had the noble gladiators had waited, down there in those trenches? Was this where the menagerie had stalked, and where absurdly brave Christians prepared for the unspeakable trials they would have to endure before their exhausted souls would be allowed to shed their bodies and meet their Maker? He was peering into the setting of his boyhood's most turbulent imaginings. He had a fierce urge to shout, "bring on the lions!"

Predictably, he had never assumed that his own ancestors were among those who had either been fed to the beasts or pitted against one another. Many of his ancestors hadn't been anywhere near the great capital; they had presumably been in Gaul fighting the invading legions or, in Grandmother Violet's branch, doing the same thing daubed with British woad. But his Roman forbearers, if they had in fact been the Patricians that his mother had implied, must have sat right here; exactly where he was standing. The perception was electrifying. He scanned the arena, trying to absorb it. Row upon row of stone seats, like threads on a screw. He was looking at the playing ground precisely as the early Fabii or Rufii would have. They really would have sat here. Though from what he knew of his family in more recent centuries, if they'd bred true, his Roman ancestors were just as likely to have been stuck at home on game day, sitting in a warm tub and opening their veins in retribution for some untimely manifestation of Republican fervour.

Some things never changed. With all that had been restored to the capital, it was no accident that the Iulium Forum, the forum of Gaius Julius Caesar, had been left concealed to the degree at which it had been identified. It would be dangerous for the Baron to raise a memorial to Rome's Republican past, or to remind men of the only Emperor who had been assassinated by men of State rather than by either treacherous family members or his own Praetorian Guard. The current Caesar had certainly neutralized that last threat. Micah spotted the bulk of some of Augustus's Praetorian Guard at the exits. Mindlessly loyal, clockwork toys whose gears moved to a single pattern, they guarded as they had been commanded. The wisps of light that gleamed from their eye sockets threw cobalt sparks in the shadows. Micah thought of what Zacuto had said. Perhaps one of these had fought for his grandfather against Augustus, but would it, would he, remember that now? Did they know what they once had been?

This uncomfortable chain of thought was broken by a substantial crash, followed by an echoing and ominous silence. The trecika didn't move from their spots; it was obviously not within their capacity to react; but Micah sped towards the source. He nearly collided with a man in a leather apron who was running, even faster, for the exit.

The crash had come from one of the two grand boxes. Historically reserved for the Vestals, it was destined to be the showcase for the bridal pair. The Baron had designed it in deliberate contrast to the classic snowy Carrera marble of Caesar's box, winking at it from the other side of the arena. The confection of opalescent Venetian glass was rubble now. The ground was littered with bright shards of what appeared to have been a chandelier. On its way down, it must have collided with the bridal thrones, breaking off bits of glass flowers. The gilt chain used to hoist the chandelier hung lank in mid-air, the bottom link split open; this was the cause of the accident, a flawed chain. The running man had, no doubt, been the workman unlucky enough to have been pulling it when it broke. Perhaps not so unlucky. He had only lost his job. If something like this had happened during the reign of the first Augustus, he would have been stabbed by the *pugio* of the nearest centurion.

The Baron prowled the rubble with a feline combination of claw and velvet. A workman crawled beneath the thrones and retrieved a branch from the chandelier, the clusters of rosy grapes appearing miraculously intact. The man cradled it like an infant and looked as if he were about to cry.

"I will send Sacconi to deal with this," the Baron said quietly. "You will sift through this…this wreckage. You will retrieve whatever is possible and you will help him make an inventory of every piece that was destroyed. To the smallest leaf. Venezia will not be allowed to sleep until they have duplicated all of it. And every one of you will work double shifts for the next fortnight to make up for this loss. Unpaid. We have no time for carelessness, no time for mistakes. Caesar expects to hold the Royal wedding here in two months time. Do you want to be the one to tell Caesar this can't be?"

Micah didn't hear the grape man's abject reply; the pounding in his head was too loud. He had known time was short, but this was the first he'd heard of his deadline. He had merely two months to somehow prevent this wedding from going through. How? With Rappaccini stationed in Rome, Micah was isolated nearly as effectively as if he were the one being held behind the walls of a gated villa. He would have to learn the exact date of the anticipated ceremony and somehow get word to Pinkerton. And he would have to hope for some kind of help from the Princess.

"Enough of this," the Baron flicked his eyes away from the groveling workmen and strode towards the nearest exit. "Come," he said to Rappaccini for the second time that day. "We are expected at another restoration project."

❧

It was difficult for Micah to accept that the bleached shadow in the garden was the very wildcat who had gone for his throat with a jagged bit of glass. The distinctive chestnut hair, elegantly dressed, was dull and lifeless.

Her thinness exaggerated her height, but with the vitality gone from her frame her stature no longer impressed.

"Principessa," the Baron said in the wheedling tone the childless use to try and charm children. "I've brought a young friend to meet you. Someone who can speak with you in your own tongue. May I present Signor Rappaccini."

"Your Royal Highness," he said softly, bowing low in the direction of her hand, as though she'd extended it.

The Italian-accented English caused her to bring him into focus. She jumped from her chair and scooted around to put the wrought iron table between them. Her eyes, as flat as tarnished brass only seconds before, darted rapidly from side to side. Her hands fluttered in vain along her bodice. "They have taken my corset," she muttered. "They have taken everything."

She recognized him then, as a figure from her nightmare. It would be difficult to make the kind of connection the Baron wanted him to make. To gain her trust enough to reveal his true mission might be impossible.

"She fears me, Eminenza," he murmured. "She remembers that I was in Dubrovnik."

"Pfffttt!" This was not the Baron's day to cut his losses. "Caesar sent for you because we need success, not excuses. Look at this!" Raising his voice, he flicked his ringed hand as if Caesar himself were doing the pointing. Maud was trying to disappear behind the fan-backed chair. "Hiding, like that workman who broke the chandelier. Where is the majesty? Where is the *ton*?"

Micah winced. He knew the girl spoke Italian and was understanding almost every word. He saw a small lift to the corner of Haussmann's mouth; it seemed the Baron knew this, too. He was giving Rappaccini the opportunity to come to her rescue.

Micah thought rapidly. He must adjust his masquerade and allow his honest dismay to show. If he appeared to fall in with the Baron's plan, he might perhaps turn this to his own advantage as well.

"Oh, my lady!" he said, forcing his voice to break and pressing his fist to his chest in the vicinity of his heart. He hoped the Princess was as fond of romantic novels as other young women her age. "What have they done to you?" Taking a single unobtrusive step that he judged would not raise the sense of threat, he leaned as close to her as he dared. "I'm desperately sorry, Your Royal Highness," he murmured, in his best public school accent. "They have done everything to keep me from your side, but I am here at last to protect you."

He tightened himself to his most military bearing. "Eminenza!" he said, more sharply than Rappaccini would ordinarily dare address a superior. He glared ostentatiously at the Baron who, just as ostentatiously, drew back. "You must show respect to the Principessa!" He made it sound like a challenge.

The Princess warily began to unfold.

"I am your servant, Your Royal Highness," Micah bowed again in her general direction, careful not to pressure her with eye contact. "Your wish is my command. If you prefer me to leave, I will leave, though I would much prefer to stay."

Still gripping the back of the chair, Maud appeared to waver. Her glance flickered toward the Baron.

"I have no time for games," he sniffed. "You may stay if you choose, Rappaccini. I shall see myself out." He turned, in an elegant display of faux pique, and left.

Micah was alone in the garden with the Princess. Pretending to be embarrassed, he craned his neck to survey the garden. No servants. They were alone, except for the Golden One. Standing where the head of the path met the villa's terrace, the clumsy thing had the peculiar beauty of ruined abbeys and very old graveyards.

"If you try to hurt me, I will scream," Maud whispered. "She won't like that."

"She?" For the first time, he looked directly into her face.

She pulled her eyes from his to look over his shoulder, down the path. "Her. That horrible statue thing. My guard."

"You mean the Golden One?" He was relieved. He'd been afraid the Princess was so far gone that she was speaking of herself in the third person, but it appeared she had some awareness of her surroundings after all.

"Is that what they call her?" she asked, listlessly. "No one has said."

"Why do you think it's a 'she'?" It seemed a curious choice. Before his talk with Zacuto, he'd never assigned a gender to the amphoraeka. Since then, he'd thought of them as male; there was certainly nothing feminine in their aspect.

Maud shrugged. "I don't know. But she is."

They faced each other across the width of the table, neither certain of what to do. "Please, Your Royal Highness," he said humbly. "I cannot take a seat unless you do."

With ingrained good manners, Maud nodded and slid into the chair that had been her shield. Micah pulled another chair so that it was a good foot away from the opposite side of the table.

"Thank you," he said, with the shy smile he'd perfected when the Pinkertons had sent him away to school. As had the masters and parents, she automatically smiled back.

He waited a moment to let the silence become natural, then smiled again. "We are at liberty to speak freely."

"You tried to hurt me there, in that place."

He shook his head. "No, My Lady. You tried to hurt me. I only tried to stop you from calling out. I wanted to talk with you, as I do now."

She frowned. "You're trying to confuse me. Everyone wants to confuse me. It's so hard to think." She rubbed her temples fretfully. "Sometimes it begins to get clearer. Like now. But only for a little while. Then the pain starts and they give me my medicine and it all goes away."

"I was told they changed your medicine. That you should be feeling better."

She smiled wryly. It was like a sunbeam pushing through a break in the passing clouds. "Better enough that I know it's not right. That I'm not right."

For the tiniest moment, Micah felt as if she were truly present. He grabbed at it. "Princess, I don't know how long they'll leave us to speak alone, or how long you'll be able to listen to what I'm saying. Believe me when I say that I am your friend. But this must be our secret, or I won't be allowed to return." If only she hadn't been the heiress to the throne, he would have reached for her hand to reassure her. Instead, he held her eyes with his until she nodded. He believed that she understood. He hoped she would remember. "I will get word to your grandmother that we have spoken…"

"She'll be furious! I was foolish. We should never have left Bucharest. And Mama…" She looked like someone who would cry but had no tears left to shed. "Mama will think I'm dead."

"Your mother thinks you're safe in London. We will get you home before she need ever know otherwise."

"They'll never let me leave here. They say they are going to marry me to that boy, the one that Grandmama said I would never marry. It's all my doing. Gertrude didn't want…Oh my God, Gertrude! It's all because of me! What have I done?!"

She looked so frantic that this time he did take her hand. He held it firmly between both of his. "Miss Bell was set free," he said, relying on the technical truth to give his voice conviction. "Along with the other young lady."

"Free?" She wanted to believe him.

"Free," he confirmed. "You needn't worry. You must get back your strength. And we must work together, you and I."

"I'm a prisoner."

"You are a royal bride," he corrected.

She shuddered and squeezed her eyes as if to make the garden disappear.

"No, Princess, you must listen to me. For us to succeed, you must play a game. Understand this: Augustus and his people disregard how you were brought here; in their minds, you're a guest, the most honoured guest there could possibly be, a future member of the family. They expect you to be impressed and grateful. Your fear and your very righteous anger are an affront to the story they've fabricated. This is why they dose you with medicine that saps your mind. They want you to fall in with their plans. Now I need you to do the same."

She stood with such force that the iron table nudged forward. "What are you saying?"

"Please, Your Royal Highness! Sit down!" he hissed. "If your distress is noticed, I'll have to leave." His warning was too late. The golden amphoraka was already headed toward them. He spoke quickly. "You must pretend to cooperate with them. When they speak of a wedding, don't fight. Pretend you are too shy to say much. Act as if you've accepted your state. I will do the rest. You must trust me."

He had tried. He couldn't tell if she was hearing him through the panic. He could feel the amphoraka's shadow on his back. "*Altezza*, I'm afraid I've exhausted you," he said in loud Italian. "It has been an honour, one that I sincerely hope you will allow me to repeat."

She gave a weary nod and collapsed back into her chair. He bowed low and, with all the nonchalance he could muster, walked past the mountainous guard to the gate. He would try again tomorrow.

❧

There were whorehouses enough in Rome, but none with the peculiar service Micah required. Instead, using an old family code that he had resurrected for just such a prospect, he inscribed a note on the sticks of a perfumed fan. The Baron was sending a courier to Venice with the order for the glass. Rappaccini bribed the page to deliver a gift to his mistress.

Elettra would re-code the information and get it, along with his address in Rome, to Tucker.

Micah speculated as to what it must be like to be on the receiving end of his own messages. Surely by now the PM and some of the senior Secretaries had been briefed, if not all of Whitehall. What would happen when the Queen learned that a wedding date had been set? In relative terms, the abandonment of the other young ladies would mean nothing on the world stage, but what were Sir Alastair and Miss Bell's family thinking?

This was Pinkerton's concern, not his. Micah was still the only agent on the ground and likely to stay so. This mission had too many personal elements for his comfort. Spying was meant to be an extraordinary kind of hunting; one could not successfully hunt in a field riddled with house pets. He needed to review his assets and start playing with the possibilities.

❧

After several days of being shown to the garden, Micah was surprised to be conducted into the villa proper. Every inch of wall and ceiling of the diminutive palace was encrusted with decoration; against all odds, the effect was charming. It was difficult to see it all at once. Staring up at a ceiling fresco of Apollo's pursuit of Daphne, he nearly missed a miraculous marble depiction of the same subject.

"How beautiful!" he said, not intending to say it aloud.

The usher, a retainer of some years and dignity, stopped to allow him to admire the piece. "Bernini," he said. "Created for this palace. We have several such treasures here."

"Bernini," Micah repeated in wonder. "Do I know him?" He squatted a bit, to get a better look at the feet of the fleeing nymph, her toes stretching into roots as she began her transformation into a laurel.

"Pardon my saying, Signore, but if you were Roman you would. You are of Napoli, yes?" The man tapped his ear.

Micah nodded. He was frequently reminded of how recent the unification was, and how superficial.

"Before we had Baron Haussmann, Signore, Roma had Bernini."

It was a deadpan delivery that left it to Micah to decide what the old man had meant to imply. Before he could attempt to probe further, he was interrupted by Mozart. Someone was trying to play "Voi che sapete."

The usher led him into room with a mantel and floor of sea-coloured marble. The wall panels were picked out in a companionable hue, to compliment a ceiling painting of Venus rising from the foam and other aquatic works of art. Even the piano was a delicate blue-green, with painted garlands of pearls and seahorses. It was the Princess who was sitting there, following his instructions and doing well. Judging by the richness of her jewels, the youngish woman with her mouth open in mid-warble was the Augustus's granddaughter Ginevre.

"I'm sorry," the Princess had broken off playing as he entered and was apologizing to their audience of two. Her colour was improved. Perhaps the adjusted medication was making a difference. "My hands. They don't do what I want."

"Perhaps I might assist," Rappaccini offered, rising from his bow.

"*Molto galante*," the Lady Giulia said with approval. Her eyes raked him from boot to crown.

The Princess gave him a grateful smile as she vacated the bench for a chair by the window. Taking her place at the keyboard, he smiled encouragement at the furiously blushing Ginevre and touched the keys. The girl stood there frozen, like Bernini's maiden, her face turned to the ceiling as if petitioning the painted goddess for deliverance. "It is not necessary..." she stammered.

"But I have interrupted your concert!"

She shook her head and hurried to a seat near Maud's.

Rappaccini appeared crestfallen. "Then I shall have to make it up to you." Without glancing at the music, he began to play the aria the Princess had attempted.

"The Centurion has hidden talents." Giulia remarked to the faithful Apollinaris, standing behind her.

"You play beautifully, Signore," Maud said.

He shook his head and smiled. "Only this music," he said, continuing to play. "It would not be an exaggeration to say I learned it at my mother's knee. Her own mother had been a singer." With the reputation of performers in Italy, he had just placed his mother firmly on the wrong side of the blanket. It was the simple truth. It was also useful that Rappaccini be seen as hungry with ambition. "A small career, but Cherubino was her signature role."

"Is that not a castrato role?" Lady Giulia asked with a curl of the lip.

It is if one perpetuates the barbarity of castration, Micah thought, but he merely smiled politely and shrugged. "Men enjoy the tease of a pretty girl in *pantaloni*."

"My father's eunuch shall prepare to sing it at our next banquet," Giulia decided. "You shall attend and judge the performance for yourself. Do you sing, Centurion?"

"My only gift for music is to enjoy it."

"I'm sure you're too modest. Sing for us now, won't you." It was not a request.

"As you wish, My Lady," he assented, letting his fingers run over the keys, creating a moment in which to select a song. He had an irresistible urge. "As the principessas have begun this opera, you might indulge me to continue. I have not the richness of voice, but if you would excuse a poor performance…" Smiling pleasantly, he struck the opening chord to Figaro's subversive cavatina. *If you want to dance, my dear Count, I will be the one to play the tune.* He sang as blandly as he could, a bubble of amusement tickling his chest.

Fortunately, while he could still continue to pretend ignorance of the implications of the lyrics, a servant appeared to announce that tea was ready to be served.

"An English tradition we have adopted in honour of our new daughter." Giulia's slant-eyed simper was chilling. She rose and placed a hand on Apollinaris's muscular arm. "Do join us, Centurion."

Rappaccini bowed his gratitude. As he had insufficient status to offer his arm to either of the younger women, he followed behind them to the garden. When Ginevre turned on the walk, Maud lagged sufficiently to speak with him.

Her voice quavered "I've had no waking hours to myself today. I had so looked forward to your visit. Now it would be rude to converse in English."

"Inadvisable," he agreed. "I will ask the Baron intercede with the Lady Giulia, to reserve an hour a day. He'll make her understand that our talks are important to maintaining your peace of mind."

"Is there any word from my grandmother?" she whispered. Ginevre was not so very far away; though it was believed she understood only the usual Italian-related soupçon of French and Spanish, one could not be to sure.

"Yes," he lied. He didn't want to upset the apple cart. In any case, he might reasonably assume Tucker would have wired his message to Pinkerton today. "She is relieved to know you are safe. She is furious with the Emperor. Plans are being made."

He was correct as to both assumptions.

❧

"What does he think to accomplish by this?!" Brandishing the transcription of Agent Horner's decrypted wire, Queen Charlotte of Greater Britain stalked back and forth across the room in a towering rage. She had been clutching it for hours, ever since Pinkerton had handed her the page.

Lord Pinkerton, the Foreign Secretary and the elderly Prime Minister stood silently, careful not to exchange glances that might betray their own annoyance. It was very gracious of the Sovereign to have offered them seats in her presence, but there was no point in sitting if they had to pop up every time the Queen felt the need to pace. The pressure of the current situation was strain enough, without the added exhaustion of jumping up and down. In any case, her question was rhetorical. They were all fully briefed on the latest campaign in Augustus's secret war. They knew exactly what the mad Emperor thought he might accomplish.

"This is the 19th century, for Heaven's sake, not the 9th! You can't simply snatch a princess and think you can walk off with a kingdom in your pocket!"

"All the same, ma'am," said the Foreign Secretary, "he's thrown something of a spanner into the works." Lord Rosebery was a modern man. He had even married a Jewess—a lovely woman and the greatest heiress in England, but a Jewess nonetheless. He was a *very* modern man. He knew about such things as 'spanners' and 'works.'

"As long as this remains secret, there is no blemish on the Princess's character," the Prime Minister asserted.

"On the *Princess's* character?!" Now Her Majesty was furious with *him*. "The Princess did not ask to be abducted, Mr. Gladstone!"

He continued, his gravelly voice calmer than most in the House would have credited him with managing. "Even so, were her abduction were to become common knowledge, the eligible princes…"

"You don't think, Prime Minister, that Britain is a tempting enough prize to balance out any perceived flaw?" When the Queen looked like that, it was like being sized up by an angry lioness.

The Grand Old Man didn't quail. "As it is, we must acknowledge the difficulty of finding a suitable prince who is willing to accept the role of his wife's deputy. The late Prince Consort was an exceptional man. There are many princes, and their advisors, who would consider this…ah…situation to be sufficient grounds for eschewing the role of Consort and demanding to rule beside her."

Her eyes blazed. "Then we must waste no more time! We must bring her home now!"

"We can't send our armies into Rome, Ma'am," said the Prime Minister as evenly as if he had not said it before, "unless we are prepared to ignite a full European war. We would have to go through France…"

"The French have no stomach for another war," Rosebery opined. "The Republic is still tenuous."

"They will once it's too late," the Queen promised tartly. "If he had Britain, Augustus would scoop up France like a handful of seashells. The day I die, mark my words, he'll have his troops engaged. And don't suppose Augustus won't have me dead the minute he minute he has legal control over the heir to my throne."

"Surely Ma'am..."

"Please, Mr. Gladstone, there is no need to try and muffle your peerless honesty on my account. Never mistake your Sovereign for a womanly woman. Nor a stupid one. Should my granddaughter sign a marriage register in Rome, it's as good as her signing my death warrant. If he could penetrate Our defenses sufficiently to murder my family, why should I be sanguine about my own chance of survival?"

"Have faith in Agent Horner and Sir Alastair, Your Majesty," Pinkerton urged.

"I do, Lord Pinkerton. Though I would prefer to occasionally hear from Sir Alastair in his own voice." The warmth in the Queen's voice was replaced by a tinge of acid.

"We are agreed that is critical that he lead the efforts from Prague."

"I will not demand his presence, Lord Pinkerton, as I continue to have sufficient trust in your organization to respect your authority. However, you might inform Sir Alastair that I would very much want to see him before me...shall we say at the first reasonable opportunity?"

In the days of the Queen's ancestors, glares like that had been followed by a trip to the Tower. Pinkerton tried not to twitch as he bowed. "Aye, Ma'am." He wondered how he ought to phrase the non-command to Menzies.

"We must continue to plan for the worst." The Queen once more took a seat. Without seeming to know what she did, she rolled up the paper and began to tap on the arm of the chair. Just as the weary men were about to give in to the temptation to sit, she jumped up again. "I advise you Prime Minister, of a decision. We are resolved to modify the Act of Succession to exclude the Princess Charlotte Maud of Wales." There was a grim note of victory in her voice. "Publish that to the world! Let Our will be plain to allies and enemies alike. That will put a crimp in his plans! Let him see how easy it will be to claim a throne in the name of the publicly disinherited."

"The act will favour Princess Alberta of York," Lord Rosebery assumed. There were nervous frowns on all their faces. The older of the little Yorks was still too young to write her own name.

The Queen shook her head. "Woe to the land that has a child as a king. Especially with Augustus waiting. No. I've been thinking. The instrument that Emilie signed to marry Belgium removed herself and her male children from the Succession, but there are two Princesses as well."

"Both unmarried." Rosebery rapidly searched his memory. "Though the elder…"

"Is affianced to William of Württemberg, yes. The younger, Louisa, is not quite old enough to ascend, but only by a year. Little enough to risk and it would be a brief regency at worst. Emilie's abdication papers must be carefully reviewed. It must be determined whether, under the Second Act of Settlement, I might still select her girl."

It was unnerving to hear the Queen assume her own imminent demise. "I'm certain I speak for us all, Ma'am, when I say that, whatever instrument you sign, please God we won't be required to act on it."

"Thank you, Lord Pinkerton."

❧

The Baron, occupied with other matters, was unavailable. Micah's daily meetings with Maud continued to be marred by the hovering flock of royals. He never was able to more than whisper a few reassuring words to the girl before the Lady Giulia or Princess Ginevre was at her side.

One afternoon, Rappaccini and the Lady's ubiquitous equerry were made to stand at attention on the terrace, while Prince Gusto joined the women for tea. It was the first meeting of the presumptive bridal pair. Even from this distance, it was easy to see that it was not a resounding success. Giulia's mouth hardly stopped moving. The Prince kept turning to his sister for reassurance.

Maud was making a brave effort. Each time she said something, Gusto ducked his head twice and smiled too hard. One couldn't decide if the young man was smitten, terrified or some combination of the two. At one point, he upset his cup. In the ensuing fuss, the Princess threw a beseeching look across the garden.

After that, Micah decided he could wait no longer wait to speak with the Baron. If necessary, he would linger around the Colosseum all day to catch him. He was preparing to do so, when a message arrived instructing Rappaccini to present himself at the Villa Alsaziano.

"You won't be attending the Principessa today," Haussmann said, dispatching the last of his frittata and dabbing at his lips. Rappaccini had been shown to the courtyard, where he was enjoying his breakfast among the lemon trees.

"Have I done something to displease her?" Micah knew he hadn't, but he was concerned that the Lady Giulia might have decided to take offense at his Figaro after all.

"Not at all, dear boy," the Baron waved the napkin towards a chair and gestured for the servant to pour his visitor a cup of coffee. "If anything, you have been too successful; you and Madame B's new formula."

"Too successful?" Relaxing into his seat, Micah gratefully accepted a pastry as well. He had cut short his own breakfast to get here.

"As we'd hoped, between the change in her medication and the comfort of your little chats, the Principessa had, so to speak, come among us at last. Unfortunately, she enjoyed these extended periods of clarity so much that she attempted to prolong them even further. Or perhaps, as the Lady Giulia insists, it was the introduction to her future husband that inspired the act." The Baron gave what was meant to be an arch little laugh but turned into more of an uncomfortable throat clear. "A noble attempt, whatever the impetus, but unwise."

Micah noticed that the Baron's forehead was furrowed in what appeared to be concern. "Eminenza?"

"Yesterday evening," Haussmann explained, "she refused the injection. Her doctor tried to dissuade her, reminding her of the results of previous attempts. She observed that in the past she had been fighting the circumstances of her being in Roma. Now, she was not only feeling much stronger but, having greater peace of mind, was able to accept her situation. Her determination was admirable. One is reminded that she is indeed born to be a Queen."

Hearing his own words echoed, Micah felt a measure of guilt. "Will she be alright?" He had to know and even Rappaccini would ask.

"Fine, fine," the Baron replied with unconvincing ease. "Still, it was a bad night. The doctor prescribes bed rest and quiet. Perhaps tomorrow she will be allowed a brief visit. No doubt you would be a more soothing visitor than the Lady Giulia, though it may take some diplomacy to make that point." As if for luck, he began massaging the scarab on his finger.

"Eminenza, I am about to be very blunt, and apologize for seeming forward." It was Rappaccini at his most conniving. "Will the lady require such medication always? She will someday be our Empress. And this weakness in her, what might this mean to a future heir?"

"Your patriotic concerns are laudable," the Baron allowed. "I will say that they are shared at the highest level. There is a plan to wean her off the medication, but not until after the wedding. It must be done very gradually to insure there are no adverse effects. You, Rappaccini, play a critical role in this plan, as you will continue to attend on the lady and present a figure of trust to bolster her strength of mind. In time, if we are all patient, the lady will assume full command of herself. As for you, Rappaccini," the Baron held him with a foxy smile. "For you there may be a very bright future indeed."

Rappaccini pushed his features into the lines of smug satisfaction that the Baron would expect. Behind the mask, his mind clicked rapidly. When he had learned Tesla's identity, Micah felt instinctively that the inventor was his strongest piece to play in this game. Lately he had been diverted by his pity for the Princess, but any remotely plausible plan for freeing her depended on her active participation. As long as Maud remained in thrall to the drugs, her control was limited, as was the amount of time he would have to get her safely to a medical facility. It wasn't as if he could steal a ptery to smuggle her out; Caesar considered flight an abomination and had banned it, like so much else, from the Empire. Compassion was a luxury that Micah could ill afford. For the sake of Queen Charlotte's kingdom, he must abandon her heiress and find a way to back to Venice.

"You seem surprised, Rappaccini." The Baron's voice broke into his thoughts.

It didn't take much acting for Rappaccini to appear flustered. "I ask only to serve, Eminenza," he said quickly.

The Baron smiled benevolently. "You should know how very well you are doing here. So well, in fact, that you do not require my presence. I've decided to make a little visit to Murano. I can't make the work at the Colosseum go any faster. I will take the opportunity to make the glassblowers anxious and, while I'm there, cheer myself with our genius's progress. The word from di Bari is very encouraging. It is reported that Mr. Tesla works around the clock."

ॐ

"We understand that your efforts are critical." Pinkerton took a small sip from the glass that had been poured for him. His old friend had excellent taste in whiskey and kept his own private stock at the Diogenes club.

"Understand?! Not one of you would have any comprehension of what my efforts are. I only hope my work on the automatons won't be undermined by whatever Tesla is coerced into doing for the enemy." Frank pinched the sides of his nose between his thumb and forefinger and massaged the bridge unhappily. He was recalling the day Tesla came down to breakfast distraught, having dreamed his mother had died. It had taken hours to calm him; then the telegram had come from Serbia, saying it was true. "You don't know how fragile that man is. Augustus will have broken

244

him as casually one breaks a wee egg. It sounds brutal to say this…Understand that I'm not being heartless, but it would be better for the world if Tesla were to fall apart entirely than for him to bend his talents to Augustus's will."

"I do understand. And I'm not arguing with you about any of this Menzies. I only ask that you fly in occasionally and not wait for a royal command…beg pardon, invitation…" Pinkerton expected his mild jest to soften the atmosphere. He was disconcerted to see Menzies jerk his head violently in response.

"A command is the only thing that could bring me here now," he hissed. He seemed about to say something more, but the waiter had arrived with the trolley. The discretion within the paneled walls of the Diogenes Club might rival that of the Service itself, but he was not about to take chances. The two men sat silent, while the server deftly jointed and sliced a crisp-skinned capon that neither of them was likely to enjoy.

After the trolley had passed back through the swinging doors, Pinkerton tried again. "I won't insult you by pretending to understand how you feel, Menzies. If Joan and I had ever been blessed…I can't imagine what it would feel like, to lose a child." It hadn't been necessary to be Her Majesty's leading spy to have figured out the identity of the 'other girl.' He thought of the last intelligence Agent Horner had been able to share and his heart gave a sympathetic lurch.

"I assumed you would understand." He poured himself another couple of fingers of the peaty malt. "Dinnae fash. She's not lost, Pinkerton. Merely misplaced. You don't know my lass." His voice was firm with conviction and a good bit of pride. "She'll be fine. Aye, it tears me to pieces, not knowing where she is or what she might be going through. But I'm certain she's coming back to me."

Pinkerton took another sip from his own glass. It had been a long time since he had allowed himself to enjoy a wee dram. Joan might say otherwise, but he thought it might actually help his digestion. He was uncomfortable. With all he had seen and done, how could Menzies delude himself like this? He had the most rational mind of any man Allan Pinkerton had ever met.

Frank raised his eyebrows. "I know you're thinking I'm a bampot, but I assure you I'm sane as Sunday. Aye, it would be natural to think the worst. Those first days, I was frantic with it." He tapped his cravat, just below the knot. "A man can't live like that. Then, Firewalker had a vision of her, walking through some trees."

"A vision? I thought you didn't believe in magic!"

"I don't. What you call magic is nowt but something we don't yet have the science to understand. Someday, when I have the time, the mysteries of the human mind…What was I saying? Aye. Firewalker knows absolutely that she's not gone, and if he swears to it, so do I! Don't think I'm staying in Prague out of superstition. I've even bought a bloody Bohemian foundry!" The expression on the other man's face made him laugh; not a big laugh, but a true one. "Out of my own purse, Pinkerton! What I'm saying is that I have a job to do. We'd have lost months if we'd tried to pack it all up and relocate. Far more efficient to have Firewalker join me there."

"That's why you work in Prague, not why you stay there!" Pinkerton had decided to lose his patience. If Menzies would admit to being nearly mad with anxiety, he might have been absolved for hiding; but if he continued to insist he wasn't, he had no excuse.

Frank pinched the sides of his nose again and cleared his throat. "You've never seen my lass," he finally said.

Pinkerton thought back. He had seen her as a small child, before Menzies had moved across the sea. He had a vague memory of a pretty little thing with a cluster of red-gold curls, but nothing more.

Frank's mouth twisted in a rueful grin. He produced his leather wallet from an inside pocket and pulled out the graduation picture. It had gotten a bit rubbed looking in these last few weeks. With a sigh, he turned it face down and slid it across the table, as if the two friends were playing at some high-stakes card game.

Pinkerton rested a hand on the back of the small piece of pasteboard and lifted it carefully. Almost immediately, he put it back down and polished his thick spectacles. He needed to be certain of what he thought he saw. He held it closer, then a bit further off, attempting to assure himself that his weak eyes did not deceive him.

"Don't tell me you never guessed." Frank was amused.

Pinkerton raised an eyebrow. "I suspected; but it's not a question one can actually ask." Not even, he thought, of the man you consider your closest friend. "No wonder you've kept her in America all this time."

"I had other reasons." Frank picked up the photograph and spoke as if the girl in the picture could hear him. "I'd no idea about this. If I had, Firewalker would have known to keep her on the other side of the Atlantic. I had no blessed idea at all until that night at the Embassy, and then it was too late."

"There was nothing you could have done." Pinkerton said reasonably. "It *was* too late."

Frank tossed the remainder of his excellent whiskey down his throat and poured himself another glass. "And she demands to see me, does she? The last person in the world I want to see right now is her. That's why I've kept away, Pinkerton; I can't trust myself in her presence."

"The Queen doesn't know," Pinkerton said quietly. "When your wire said not to mention the other lass, I took you literally."

"Then when it comes out, it'll be best for your own sake to feign surprise." Frank considered the discussion at an end and prepared to address his food. A final though caught him and he paused for a moment with his knife in mid-air. "I'd appreciate it, Pinkerton, if you'd continue to keep my sister in the dark."

"Naturally," Pinkerton sighed. The silver club-monogrammed cutlery might as well have been the Sword of Damocles hanging over his head. He pushed the peas around on his plate, doubting he'd be able to swallow one of them.

Frank nodded his thanks and jabbed his fork into a slice of roasted bird.

❧

The rule was that one did not speak to the Queen until spoken to. Frank didn't have to wait. The minute the doors had closed, Charlotte jumped from her chair and practically attached him with her fists. "Where have you been?!"

Frank instinctively grabbed her wrists in his own strong hands and held them down. "You know where I've been. I've been in Prague, building machines of war and moving heaven and earth to get your lass back." He kept his voice conversational and mild, which had the effect of making her anger seem petulant.

"I see absolutely no reason why you couldn't do that from London," she fumed.

"Because Tesla's lab is in Prague." He released her hands and held up his own in supplication. "Charlotte, I'm not in the mood for an argument. You commanded me to come…"

"I very specifically did not command you!" Her eyes glittered in triumph.

He laughed. It was a mean laugh. "Oh, aye. The Jesuits lost a jewel when you were born female and Protestant."

"Greater men than you have said so."

They stood only inches apart, their bodies rigid with challenge. For a long minute there was no sound other than the faint tick of the smallest hand of the ormolu clock.

Frank held his tongue and waited for her next stroke. Whatever he said today, he would never be able to unsay. He no longer cared. Prague was perfectly civilized; if he had to, he could comfortably stay there forever. Or there were places he knew in North America that were not part of Greater Britain and would be happy to have him.

She broke the lock and swept grandly to her chair.

She spoke quietly, forcing him to follow her. "You came to London, after all these years, because I needed you at my side. I still need you. The only reason you're in Prague, Frank, is because you don't want to be here with me."

In ordinary confrontations, the seated position was the weaker. Not so when the other party had no option but to stand and when the sitter kept her eyes looking straight ahead. Frank had to lose the power of eye contact or bend his head to an awkward angle.

"I have to be in Prague because Nikola Tesla isn't. Perhaps Tesla wouldn't be in Italy now if you'd been honest with me."

That made her look up. "What has one thing got to do with another?" she said impatiently. "Augustus had his hands on your genius once before. You told me yourself, the poor young man was frightened to death they'd find him again."

"This time they picked him up by accident. Augustus had men hunting all across Europe for your granddaughter. It was Tesla's bad luck to be in the company of a lass who looked exactly like her."

"What are you talking about, Frank?" Charlotte didn't like the pieces that were starting to come together in her head.

"Perhaps," Frank said in the same measured tones he would use to talk a lecture hall through an experiment, "Tesla wouldn't be in Italy now if he hadn't been walking Claude home from the restaurant while I was sitting in the embassy, trying to control my shock at the first sight of your granddaughter. Imagine, Charlotte, how differently it might it have gone if someone had mentioned the resemblance in time for me to get my lass back across the Atlantic, or at the very least hide her. But only one person had ever seen both lasses, and that person never saw fit to tell me."

"But your daughter is Chicago!"

"What is it you've told Lowthian Bell about his lass's whereabouts? Well, Ma'am," Frank bowed smartly; "that's where my daughter is as well. When last seen, they were together."

Frank heard his words linger in the air. He felt depleted, but oddly relaxed. He had said it. What next? Did he want her to rail at him? Would he have been satisfied to see her crumple and weep? Frank honestly didn't know.

Once upon a time, a young man had fallen in love with a queen. He had never expected her to act like…What was it she always said? Like 'a womanly woman.' And he had never wanted her to. He adored her as she was. He felt grateful even to be hurt by her and, when he walked away, along with his scars he had carried the greatest gift of his life. All these years later, he found Charlotte no less desirable. Miraculously, she still desired him. He had been enchanted all over again. He knew the constraints imposed when a sovereign took a lover, and had acceded to them. It had not made him as happy as he'd hoped.

Working in companionable near-silence with Firewalker, Frank had been able to think much about his discontent. He had concluded that, even from a goddess, desire without respect was not worth the having. He wasn't a dazzled young man any more. He had tested himself in the world, he had the dignity of achievement. And he had learned a great deal about love; his daughter meant more to him than her mother ever had.

It had been the truth, what he'd told Pinkerton: that in his heart of hearts, he knew Claude would be well. He didn't want Charlotte's pity. What he needed was for her to acknowledge that what had put his daughter—their daughter—in jeopardy had been her lack of respect for him. There would be a leveling of the playing field or, though there could never be a permanent severance as long as either of them lived, she would be accepting his resignation on as permanent a basis as he had at his disposal. Either way, he would find his peace. He stood, relaxed and quiet, waiting.

She didn't move. At first, she didn't know what she wanted to do. Never since Charlotte's childhood had anyone had spoken to her like this, with such total disregard for her reaction, not even Albert. She was a little thrilled, but more angered and offended. He had crossed the line. That was not how a subject spoke to his Queen. She had an urge to slap him, but that seemed too weak and personal. She could order him out of the room, out of the country, and he would have to obey. She must rise above this; Sir Alastair Menzies was too useful to send away.

Sir Lowthian had been told that his granddaughter had elected to stay with Maud while she stayed in a secret location, being protected from an unspecified threat. Horner's true message, that he was unable to say what had happened to Miss Bell, had been reported to the Queen. Why had no one said that the girl, Claude, was with her? She would choose to excuse the effrontery now that she understood Frank's distress. She knew what it was to lose a child...children; Augustus had taken her sons, now her granddaughter.

Charlotte closed her eyes and imagined Maud as she had last seen her, paying her respects before heading off to Bucharest. The Princess had worn that look of embarrassed relief that she often had when excused from duty. She'd made a proper curtsey, then, disarmingly, flung her arms around her grandmother's neck and kissed her goodbye. As Charlotte conjured that charming, infuriating girl, the vision blended with a distant memory of a solemn toddler and the photograph Frank had left had left on her pillow. It was very nearly one face. She had known that. Why hadn't she told Frank from the first? Why had she denied what she'd felt, looking at that stranger and knowing in one breathtaking stab that the stranger was her daughter?

Charlotte didn't remember opening her eyes, but she could see Frank standing in front of her, his hands dangling comfortably at his side. The way that he held his body communicated ease. She had been turned around in so many ways that she couldn't begin to make sense of it all, yet his face was as untroubled as if he had simply told her the hour of the day. How could he bear it?

"No more secrets," she said.

Frank nodded. This, then, was what he'd wanted: a shared trust. "We will get them back," he said, so much more kindly than he had said anything that day. "Both of them. You must believe this, as I do."

It was her turn to nod. "How much does Pinkerton know?" she suddenly thought to ask.

"All of it," he said. "For all these years, too, the old devil." It was a reason to smile.

"I suppose you'll be returning to Prague at once." Her voice wavered slightly.

"I think that I must," he agreed.

"Would you sit here with me first, for just a little while?"

He brought a chair as close to hers as it would fit. They sat, sharing the silence, her hands sheltered between his, until the clock struck the hour and he had to go.

15 – LA FORNACE

Pushing himself up from the workbench, Nikola Tesla nearly spiked his hand on a vagrant sprocket. He'd been bent over the close work long enough that he felt as neckless as a turtle. He needed to step back for a bit and reset his vision to the greater picture. Picking his way across the room to check his sketches, he nearly tripped on the cairn of crumpled paper that rose against the leg of the drafting table.

"Idiot!" he scolded. "How often must I remind you, young Kola? Safety first!" He ripped off the old-fashioned glass magnifying goggles and began to massage the sockets of his burning eyes. His hair, badly in need of a barber, stuck out wildly from the constant raking of his fingers. His forehead was already streaked from swipes of a grubby hand. It had been some days since he'd last remembered to change his shirt; the one he was wearing was stiff with a millefiori of food stains and workshop grime.

None of this mattered because there was nobody there to see it. Bosco, di Bari's white bearded *attendante*, would arrive tomorrow with the groceries. His would be the first human face Tesla would see in the week since his prior visit and his rusty German, the reason he'd been selected for this rota, the first sound of human speech other than Tesla's own.

Tesla hardly registered this. Once the Italian Englishman had left for Rome to protect Claude, time lost its meaning. In a room lit by electricity, it lost its boundaries as well. Alone but for his impervious guards, he slept when he was too tired to forestall it, rummaged in the kitchen when he was hungry, and otherwise hunched over his workbench, working on the puzzle he had set for himself.

His mind never felt fully awake. Even so, it had been clear how to arm the amphoraeka. He could see them, a series of bronze gears and springs that would propel a bandolier, to be slung crosswise over the clay body.

Each loop would hold a hollow copper bolt, one chamber of which would be tightly packed with wadding that had been soaked in a mixture of oil and combustible salts, the other with iron filings and lead pellets. As the next bolt rose to the shoulder, the mechanism would automatically load it into a kind of crossbow bonded to the clay arm. The creature would merely have to raise the arm to be perpendicular to the ground, then snap it parallel. The bolt would fire, while a flint strike would ignite the wadding. In sum, the missile was a modern shrapnel shell, adapted to the ancient Egyptian parameters set down by the Baron. It was, of necessity, a crude weapon but, when wielded by the amphoraeka, it would cause as much destruction as more elegant and advanced engines of death. The primitive technology had been child's play to design, far beneath his innovative genius.

The challenge was building in the critical flaws. It wasn't helping that the creatures kept interrupting his concentration with their attentions. From the moment of his arrival on Murano, a trecika, which he was nearly certain was the very same one he'd originally seen at the Baron's villa years before, had stuck close by him at all times except when he retired to his bedroom upstairs. Most recently, Tesla hadn't bothered with his bed but had taken to catching a couple of hours on the low divan in the room beside the workshop. Whenever he awoke, the creature was invariably standing guard by his head. The other four, including the one who mostly guarded the dock, had become equally attentive. When he voiced his thoughts, he had the sense that they were listening and that they understood. More than that, he could swear at times they were trying to contribute to his work. Sometimes Number One stood so close behind him that Tesla would see two wavery blue spots reflecting on the drafting paper.

"The loading mechanism must catch," Tesla mumbled. "The Baron will surely test that at once. He's clever, you know. Clever and evil, for all his manners and smiles. What am I missing here?" He looked at Number One and watched the eye jets flicker. "You don't know either, do you? Maybe I need a break. Maybe it's time for food again."

Tesla shuffled out to the kitchen and loaded a plate with some cheese and sausage. "Bread's stale," he noted. "I must add it to the list. Though I suppose he will know to bring me bread without my having to say. Did I ask for beer last time? I wonder if he will bring it or if they are afraid for me to have it. And something sweet. Honey would be nice."

He walked past the hallway guardian and bobbed his head in greeting. "I do get so hungry sometimes," he said, conversationally. "You know how it is. Though you can't, can you? Well, that's how it is."

He was still chattering away when he returned back to the workroom. "When does he come, the guard? Why can't I say what day it is? I could keep a calendar. No, I wouldn't know where to start. Who can say? Soon, I hope. The cupboard is getting bare."

Number One loomed up behind him, its presence prodding him toward the garden. "I have work to do!" he objected. The creature nudged him inexorably toward the mullioned glass door. "You think I need the air, do you? What do you know? I have a golem nursery maid!" He fell onto the stone bench in laughter, the thought so hilarious that he nearly tipped his provender into the weeds.

He set the plate down. A tiny striped cat darted out from somewhere, snatched a piece of meat half as big as its head and tried to drag it behind a large terra cotta pot that it erroneously thought would make it invisible. Tesla thought it was the funniest thing he'd seen in a year. He couldn't stop laughing.

Number One's monumental shadow spilled over him. The creature was bent forward as much as it could without tipping over, a long branch tucked into the bifurcation of its hand. It seemed to be tracing a line in the patch of dirt around the bench. It did that sometimes. One morning had been cold enough to have a fire; in the afternoon he had found the creature by the hearth, or as close to the hearth as it could fit, moving a poker through the ashes. It was another thing that made him feel the creatures could think.

"Are you drawing me a picture?" he snickered. "Or maybe you're a tutor as well as a nursery maid. Maybe you're teaching me my letters."

The creature continued to laboriously scratch the dirt.

The kitten shook its prey in its teeth and made adorably fearsome noises. Tesla hastily downed the cheese before the ball of fur would get any additional ideas. He could smell flowers and a rotten whiff of lagoon. The sun was bright. Closing his eyes, he turned his face to greet it. It felt good.

When he finally opened his eyes, the trecika had stopped whatever it had been doing. Tesla stretched slowly, feeling every muscle unfold. "Thank you, Number One," he said. "This was a fine idea." He started to swing his legs over the bench, but the creature held out the branch and stopped his feet from hitting the dirt. "What...?"

Tesla looked down. The pattern scratched awkwardly into the bald patch were letters. "It's writing!" He looked at the creature in awe. Moving carefully so as not to smudge them, he shifted his legs so that he could try to read it.

H - I - L - F - E. "Hilfe!" He jumped in excitement, his feet throwing dust over the letters. "Help! There's some kind of mind inside there, I knew it!" He started dancing around the creature as if it were a maypole. He stopped short to look into its eye holes. He would swear the blue light was pulsing stronger. "You can think! But how can you tell me what you think? You can write, but you can't hold a pencil. Even with what you can hold, the control you'd need...Look how hard it was to scratch out five letters, and all these letters are straight lines. What to do, what to do?" Tesla stuck his fingers straight through his hair, sending it fluffing out like black dandelion seed. The loading mechanism forgotten, his eyes were alight with a new and enthralling puzzle.

He crouched on the ground, one hand on the bench to help him keep his balance. The excitement was making him dizzy. "*Hilfe*," he whispered. "Help." He tapped his fingers absently against the stone.

The trecika moved closer to the terra cotta pot and hit it with the branch, copying Tesla's rhythm.

Tesla looked up. The trecika repeated the sequence. Tesla realized he'd been tapping out "Hilfe" in Morse Code and the creature had copied him. Of course! It could communicate percussively. He could teach it...He was struck by a thought that terrified him by its implications.

"Do you understand what you just did?" he said, almost as quietly as the kitten who was now hiding behind the olive tree.

One short, three long; J. One short, one long; A. Ja. Yes. It understood.

Tesla's heart skipped a beat. He swallowed hard and willed it to start again. At once he was acutely aware of being in an open space. The trees might have ears. Even if they did not, the drumming might travel across the water and reach anyone. He stood very slowly. "Come inside," he said. "It seems we may have much to discuss."

An hour later, Nikola Tesla was on the floor of his workroom, curled like an unborn child, his arms clutching his knees to his chest. The clay giant stood within arm's reach of a stack of crates, a light wooden mallet in the cleft of its hand. If a statue could appear spent, it did. It seemed an eternity since that precious moment in the sunlight when Tesla couldn't stop laughing. Now he couldn't stop weeping.

The dots and dashes had revealed things that Tesla wouldn't have wanted flitting across his worst nightmares—and Tesla's nightmares could be like a Renaissance depiction of Hell. Part of him wanted to pry his arms from his own knees and throw them around any part of the trecika that he could reach. A second part wanted to run screaming to the dock and hurl himself into the lagoon. Still another part, the part that had to win, wanted to tear Caesar Augustus II into a million shreds with his own teeth.

Sandtmann. That…thing, that lump of clay was Dov Sandtmann. The flicker in the vessel, what the ancient Egyptians had called the ka, was not some generic life force but the actual double of the living man. Closing his eyes, he saw a pale, freckled young man, earnest, but vibrating with life. Sandtmann had loved to laugh, an unexpectedly round laugh from his wiry frame that had always made Tesla, not much given to high spirits, laugh too. There was nothing to laugh at now. He willed himself to open his eyes again and look at the creat…at Sandtmann.

"We will fix this," he said. He didn't need to fake the conviction in his voice.

"NO," Sandtmann tapped.

"Yes!" Tesla insisted, scrambling to his feet. Without hesitation, he put his hand tenderly on the massive forearm.

"NO FIX," Sandtmann tapped. "ONLY END."

Tesla craned his neck, forgetting there was no face to look up into. An inarticulate cry broke from him before he could stop it. He leaned his head against what had been his friend and inhaled the dark aroma of the earth. Within the carapace of each amphoraka burned an individual human soul. At base, it was no more mysterious than his own consciousness. But where he was free to fight the pains of this world and endure or quit it on his own terms, they were imprisoned at another's pleasure, with no recourse but an eternal, tortured present. That was a darkness even Nikola Tesla could not imagine.

ѦѦ

Once he had marshaled his emotions, Tesla gathered all his amphoraeka guards in front of the fornace. He felt like a mouse in a forest. He had to step back into the doorway, so as to be able to look up and address those flickering eyes. "As you know," he said, with more diffidence than another man would have in the same situation, "I've been speaking with Sandtmann here. We are old friends." It warmed him that he truly did know which of the mountains of clay was his old friend. He had sensed a difference even from the first, though he hadn't known why. "I understand now. I will help you. Together, we will find a way."

Until that moment, the extent of his focus had been minor sabotage. His fears for Claude had undermined his ambitions, weakening his motivation and blunting his creativity. He had limited his goal to buying time for Frank. Dov's revelation challenged him to push aside that fear.

Now he knew that it was not sufficient to neutralize the threat of Caesar's Roman army; he had to destroy the amphoraeka entirely.

They wanted him to. They told him so, through Sandtmann, via the shared band of soul wave they used to communicate. The prisoners yearned, nearly universally, for release. It was up to Tesla to free these tortured souls who wanted to, finally, die. There were hundreds already depending on him, and more to come if he did not succeed. He knew he had to try, even if he lost everything in the process.

The amphoraeka completely retained the memories of the men they had been. Augustus might have 'recruited' Sandtmann because of his connection to Rabbi Löwe and the Golem of Prague, but the lawyer had been a gifted amateur engineer. Not only had Tesla been heard when he'd spoken his thoughts aloud, but he'd been understood, and now there was a way for his listener to respond with intelligence. Though he had no fingers with which to hold or shape, he was of excellent use as a sounding board.

With Dov's help, Tesla worked around the clock, pushing himself to the limit. He ought to have made better progress, but as difficult as it had been to try and design a weapon that would reliably malfunction, it was proving impossible to devise one that could be wielded by the amphoraeka and utterly destroy them.

The problem was not in their will, but the magic that held them. In their chests, beneath the symbol the Italian Englishman had copied from the disc, was a scroll that bound them in servitude to Augustus, forcing them to obey his designated deputies who were known by their display of that symbol. This same symbol prohibited them from turning on one another and, possibly worst of all, made it impossible to willfully self-terminate. In addition to inoperative weaponry subtle enough to escape the Baron, Tesla needed a way to enable a self-destruct while evading the magic ordinance. His design would need to be employed with 'correct' intent, to not breach the spell, yet still have the desired effect.

He had determined that the head was the one vulnerable spot on the massive body. From what he could puzzle out, it functioned as a kind of *serdab*, the hidden chamber the Egyptians built into their tombs. In a tomb, the serdab was meant as a viewing chamber, as the ka of deceased was expected to want to observe the rituals that the living performed in his honour. Such cruel irony! No one honoured the souls imprisoned in the amphoraeka. Instead, the living compelled them to perform actions that might have shamed them in life.

The head was needfully hollowed out. The vanity of imposing a Napoleonic beehive shape made for thinner walls than a simple brick or globe shape might have. Tesla deduced that if the head were shattered, the soul would fly free. That the Emperor or his minions had thought of this was obvious from the bronze helmet with its long chin guards. It was more than a military decorative note; it was protection.

"Such a blasted pity they're bronze," Tesla said crossly. "If they were iron, we could rig some sort of electrified magnet from a dirigible. Imagine, an entire legion lifted into the air by your helmets and whisked off to some wasteland…"

Sandtmann gave the thigh slap that represented laughter.

"I know, I know. The aership would sink like a stone. Remember when we used to think the next war would be fought from the sky? That was what we were afraid of. We could never have imagined this sort of thing."

Tesla sat on the floor with his back against the tree-like clay legs and thought hard. Could he engineer some sort of ricochet that might allow the amphoraeka to take 'permissible' outward aim but cause the shot to rebound precisely into the eye holes and cause the head to explode? Closing his eyes, Tesla tried to visualize such a thing. "Ha!" he laughed aloud, a hard laugh that doubled him over and hurt the back of his throat. "Ridiculous! Even I couldn't do that! Don't you think, Dov?" He hadn't voiced this particular brainstorm, so the amphoraka stood silent as a monument. Nikola didn't notice. He was lost in a dark sky of thought, trying to connect his vagrant thoughts into constellations. The optimal solution would be projectiles fired at the amphoraeka from an opposing force. Even then, it must be the right ammunition and aimed precisely into the eye holes. Only a machine could reliably perform with that kind of precision. An automaton. Behind his eyes, Nikola Tesla envisioned ranks of automatons marching across a field of vibrant green grass. The sky above was the cerulean of a robin's egg and the sun glinted off their metal bodies. He saw their arms rise as one and take aim. A hundred singing bullets scored the air, arching over the field to land in what looked like a wall. Like compass needles snapping to true North, the bullets snapped to meet their marks, pairs of holes behind which a faint blue flickered hopefully. He could feel the explosion in his bones as a hundred clay heads erupted and collapsed to dust within the bronze shells. The wall of clay stood solid as a cloud of blue smoke lifted towards the sky and the air filled with celestial music. It was beautiful.

Tears came to his eyes and Tesla thought longingly of Prague. If only he could get back. Or if he could get word somehow to Frank, if he could provide the measurements and calculate the angle to hit into the holes…Frank would surely be working on his clockwork men. Frank could punch the code into the titanium ribbons, and the gears and sprockets would spin into obedient alignment.

That man, the Italian Englishman, knew Frank. If only he would come again, Tesla would give him this information. But the Centurion was in Rome protecting Claude. Was Tesla truly ready now to risk her safety by pressing for his return? He castigated himself for this weakness.

Claude had surprised him and slipped into his heart before he could push her away, but she was only one soul. He must think of the amphoraeka. The fragments of the transformation that Dov could remember and had attempted to spell out were too broken to build a picture that made any sense. Instead, though he knew full well that it hadn't happened that way, Tesla envisioned his friend's gentle curiosity changing to horror as a stream of clay poured over him and encased his body.

Then there was his last image of Claude, carried off the yacht by soldiers, one hand dangling helplessly from the litter. Her sleeping face had been so white that the scattering of freckles stood out like ink spattered from a bad nib. Crackles of fire had glinted in the loosened hair that had streamed almost to the ground. He had yearned to run to her but had held still, for the sake of her life.

The battle in Tesla's heart was tearing him apart. If he were to risk that life now, he must sell it dearly; he must do as much as he could to find a solution here, within these walls, before wasting what might be the only chance to reach out. He pushed his cramped legs off the floor and wobbled toward his workbench.

"SLEEP," Sandtmann admonished.

"I can't," Tesla mumbled. "We need to work."

"TWO DAYS." Sandtmann had a ready reply. He positioned himself between Nikola and the table. "FOOD. SLEEP."

"It's not two days," he protested, then he lost his footing on a piece of wire and careened into a shelf. Perhaps Sandtmann was right. They needed him to be strong. The amphoraeka did, Claude did. "Yes," he said. "You're right, Dov. Food first and then I will see if I can rest."

༄

On his last visit to the fornace, Bosco had been disgusted with the dirt and disarray. He was under strict orders not to disturb the inventor's work— but he could at least impose some cleanliness. Entering the workroom to remove the piles of soiled crockery, he noticed appreciably more activity than on his previous visit. The walls were covered with diagrams, and not always drawn on paper. The workspace was cluttered with gears and cables in unfamiliar configurations. Tesla, completely absorbed in his mysterious work, ignored Bosco's carefully rehearsed German conversational gambits. The younger man had an almost fevered look about him; his eyes were overly bright and his face well flushed.

Bending to retrieve a bread board and knife, the attendante spotted what he thought at first was a child's toy train half concealed by a wad of crumbled foolscap. He took the liberty of lifting it, thinking to put it on the nearest surface. Tesla, turning to reach for his magnifying goggles, caught him with the model in his hands.

"'Scusi, Signore," Bosco apologized, reddening; "this is not safe on the floor."

"It's garbage," Tesla said.

"My grandson would not say so." Bosco looked at the tiny vehicle. It wasn't a railroad car, but something that was meant to move along a road, like a cart but without a horse.

"Give it to him," Tesla replied with a dismissive wave. He slipped his goggles over his eyes, reached for a tray of delicate tools and bent back over his work.

That was their one and only exchange of the day. When Bosco and the servant left a few hours later, Tesla didn't even notice, no less thank them for the scrubbed kitchen, cleaned grates and fresh linens. Bosco reported it all to di Bari, except for the gift of the toy; that was for Massimo, not for the Conte.

Tesla was so absorbed in his calculations that he didn't hear Sandtmann urgently tapping the warning from the trecika on the dock. He was aware of nothing outside his own thoughts, until a hand brushed his shoulder. Even then, he didn't realize it was a human hand. "Stop it, Dov," he mumbled, shrugging it off. "I'm sure I ate something today."

"I'm glad to hear that, Mr. Tesla."

Whirling to face the sound, Tesla found himself nose to nose with Baron Haussmann. He dreamt so often of the Baron that he thought he was dreaming now and instinctively struck out with his fists to fight off the specter of his enemy.

Haussmann grabbed at his arms and pushed them down. The younger man had been driving himself relentlessly for days but, however weakened he might have been, he was fired by panic. He jerked away with such strength that the Baron's wrist was sorely wrenched. "Hold him!" the Baron ordered the amphoraka that stood by the garden door.

Sandtmann had no choice; Haussmann had the glyph carved into his jasper ring. He stepped away from the door and, bending forward, gently encircled Tesla with his unyielding arms.

"What are you doing, Dov? Let me go." Tesla twisted and struggled to get free. "Oh, for God's sake, this is crazy. Why can't I sleep without these dreams? I need to wake up!...Why won't you let me go? I thought you were my friend!" To Haussmann's astonishment, Tesla started pounding the clay forearms with his fists, as if he thought any human hand could make an impact on these creatures. "Oh, just let me go!" he moaned; "let me land one good punch...If I can make it explode, I'll wake up and it will be over..."

The Baron shook his head sadly. The poor man was clearly not in his right mind. Rappaccini had reported leaving him calm and as stable as one might reasonably expect. Di Bari's man had mentioned drive and determination, but no hint of madness. Perhaps it was not a good thing for a genius to be left for too long on his own, especially a genius the Baron could recall collapsing catatonic under circumstances less trying than these. If he didn't do something to stop it, Tesla would exhaust himself. Sane or not, it would be days before he would be worth anything with his fingers mashed to a bloody pulp.

Still massaging his wrist, Haussmann walked briskly out of the fornace and towards the dock. "My bags!" he trumpeted, "and come! I have a message to send." The sailor raised his hat in salute and disappeared from view. Haussmann passed the amphoraka who stood in dumb guard at the front door. "Bring my baggage from the dock," he commanded. He had planned to stay the week with his old friend the Contessa d'Este, a hostess whose attention to the niceties of life matched his own. He was so impatient to check on his prize that he had asked the captain bring him straight to Murano first. Now it looked as if he would have to remain on the island. He needed pen and paper.

Tesla had stopped struggling with the amphoraka and was standing nearly still in the clay embrace. His head was tilted back at an awkward angle and he seemed to be talking to the creature. "I don't understand," he said in low, puzzled tones. "Why won't you put your arms down? I promise I'll be careful. I won't hurt myself. I'm not tired, so it can't be lack of sleep, not this time. I must need food. Let me go to the kitchen and find a piece of cheese. I'll eat it in the garden. You like when I sit in the garden. Why won't you answer me, Dov?"

"Utterly deluded," the Baron murmured, as he wrote rapid but elegant excuses to the Contessa, beginning with apologies for the lack of appropriate stationery. He would scrawl a less elegant note of instruction to di Bari.

Tesla's head snapped down and swiveled to look at the table. He rubbed his eyes in disbelief. "I see him again!" he whimpered. "Oh my God, this isn't a dream. I'm going mad!"

"You are not mad, Mr. Tesla," the Baron said in reasonable tones that reflected the exact opposite of what he was thinking. "I have come to see what progress you have made."

Tesla spat at him, with less force than accuracy.

From the Baron's perspective, the trajectory was mercifully truncated; the gob of spittle glanced off his boot. It was a small blemish, but distasteful nonetheless. He would have much preferred to exchange the sullied footwear for another pair and leave these for di Bari's man to polish, but it was imperative that Tesla be brought to what there were of his senses and that must begin with the acceptance that the Baron was indeed physically before him. Haussmann whipped out his pristine white handkerchief and, with as much deliberation as a tenor with a piece of stage business to convey, daubed at the spot. "You see, Mr. Tesla? I am as corporeal as you." He thought to try and lighten the tone. "As real as your clay friend here that you seem so fond of."

Tesla's body shook as he yelled out a stream of incomprehensible Serbian that the Baron assumed were the wildest invectives. He resumed his pounding on the amphoraka, writhing in fruitless attempt to get out or even to position his leg for what would have been, had there been bones, a bone-breaking kick.

The baggage had arrived not a moment too soon. Haussmann unlocked his small trunk and hastily extracted a small Moroccan leather case, congratulating himself on having had the forethought to obtain it. He had hoped, even so, that he would never need to use it, but in this state Tesla was a danger to himself as well as to the Baron. He unfastened the thongs, unrolled it and, with a deep sigh, filled a syringe.

Now that it was necessary, Haussmann could only hope that what he had would be efficacious. He recalled the story he'd been told of the passage to Dubrovnik; Tesla had fought and the agents had needed to apply an entire pharmaecopia to keep him docile. The Baron had no exotic mixtures from the Blavatsky, but merely honest laudanum and morphine, and a knob of hashish, such as any man of the world might have in his kit.

He tried to be gentle, but a glimpse of the syringe caused Tesla to buck in the arms of the amphoraka and roll his eyes like a mad horse. The Baron couldn't even roll up his sleeve, but was obliged to plunge the needle through the layer of soiled cotton. The opiate acted with gratifying and rather surprising effect. Perhaps the previous occurrence had altered his resistance, or else his current neglect of food and rest had weakened him. In a matter of minutes, Tesla fell limp; the amphoraka had to catch him before he fell to the ground and cradle him like a sleepy child.

Free to get his bearings at last, the Baron cast a fastidious eye over the scene. Di Bari's man had done well to have the rest of the house cleaned, but when he returned with the servant, something would need to be done about the workroom. The man, however, couldn't wait. Haussmann frowned. Tesla needed a bath and an immediate change of linen. The limp body smelt as pungent as week-old soup. He would have to bathe the man himself, then let him sleep off the opium. Let it never be said that Georges-Eugène Haussmann couldn't roll up his sleeves when circumstances demanded. What he could not do, however, was carry the Serbian. He regretting not having the forethought to install a ramp or a hydraulic lift in the *fornace*. The amphoraeka couldn't mount stairs; it occurred to him that might be a worthy future project for his pet genius. As distasteful as it was, he might have to wash the man in the kitchen.

"Eminenza?" The sailor stood on the tiles in the entryway, looking more uncomfortable than the lack of land legs could explain. He gulped visibly. "Your message?"

"Ah yes. Excellent." The Baron snapped his fingers, then pointed a thumb in Tesla's directions. "I will need your assistance first. Carry him."

Once he had Tesla settled, he would attempt to salvage something edible from the kitchen and then see if he could make any sense of the intriguing collection of drafts and assemblies he had seen heaped around the room. With the unconscious inventor safely tucked into the only bed, the Baron would have to make do with the rough divan; but glory never came without a price. Tomorrow, clean and rested, the genius should be in a more cooperative mood and the Baron wanted to be ready to make the most of it.

The Baron slept soundly in his rough nest. Just as he was allowing the sun's fingers on his brow to coax him awake, he was jolted to his feet by the blood-curdling scream of some uncivilized jungle hunter.

Tesla thundered into the laboratory. He was a fearsome sight, eyes and hair wilder than ever. With the sailor's help, Haussmann had managed to clean him off but he hadn't wanted to risk a shave. It had even proven too difficult to shrug the leaden limbs into a nightshirt; the Baron had deemed it sufficient to tuck him between the previously untouched sheets of his bed.

Now the man appeared framed in the doorway like a Caravaggio, mother-naked save for one of those sheets caught over one shoulder and trailing behind him. Oblivious to his state, even to the screws and rivets crushing into his bare feet, he flew from table to shelf, sweeping aside a crash of gears and cables, snatching up papers and crumpling them to his chest. He seemed possessed by some fire that burned through his gaunt face in hectic spots of colour.

Turning away from the maelstrom to collect himself, Haussmann watched the sheets dragging through the tawny dust that seemed to collect in any space that held the amphoraeka. For the first time, it occurred to the Baron how many of his servants' efforts must be spent cleaning up after his own complement. There was a price to be paid for impervious, incorruptible security.

"Hold him," Haussmann said wearily; "gently, please." As his instructions were guaranteed to be carried out, he was free to leave the room. "I will return in half an hour's time, Mr. Tesla. I hope by then to find you amenable to conversation."

The Baron went to perform his morning ablutions and dress, keeping an ear peeled for further violence. All he could hear was the occasional banging. Later he would send for someone to check the pipes; if this noise went on continually, it might drive him as mad as Tesla.

By the time he returned to the workroom, the Serbian had either come to his senses or tired himself out with struggling. He more or less stood where the Baron had left him, the clay barricade supporting him. When the Baron instructed the amphoraka to let him go, Tesla slid to the floor, landing heavily atop his scattered papers.

"Get dressed, Mr. Tesla," the Baron said mildly. "I will attempt to prepare some potable coffee."

From what the Baron could tell, considerable progress had been made. He would have preferred to know better. Most of what he learned was by examining papers and constructions with his own eyes. He needed to know more, but he was unable to get any word out of Tesla. For two days he tried every proven conversational gambit known to humankind, but all failed to elicit a response. Delicious wit, provocative observations, insults that ought to have led a man to raise a fist, everything hung in the air only to dissolve as if unheard.

Even when Haussmann directed the attendante's servant to sweep through the laboratory, Tesla stayed as silent as any amphoraka. Perhaps he was afraid the Baron would tranquillize him again. The efficacy of that syringe, welcome at the time, continued to puzzle the Baron; he had been told opiates passed through the man like water.

Haussmann tried a more pedestrian tongue-loosener but, unlike any man in his acquaintance, Tesla didn't even become garrulous when drunk. The inventor wept into his glass, but after a substantial amount of grappa had been absorbed, all that met the Baron's ear were the lyrics of a German student drinking song and, just before Tesla passed out with his head on the table, a piteous sighing "Claude."

Not one to give up easily, Haussmann decided to try the remaining option in his kit. The next evening, before sitting down to the calamari the Contessa's chef had sent to sustain him, he grated hashish over Tesla's portion. He was rewarded by a prolonged stream of dreamy babble that implied an obsession with the Egyptian monks who built the amphoraeka and ended, before the exhausted Tesla stopped as abruptly as he had begun, with something about calculating bulls-eye trajectories and needing "an algorithm for the automatons." It was all nonsense, but the Baron was encouraged to hear words at all and decided to continue with this course.

After a good night's sleep and a hashish-sprinkled breakfast omelette, Tesla was prodded to discuss the sketches that the Baron had been examining on his own. The inventor became animated, occasionally laughing inappropriately, as they looked at his model for the crossbow loading mechanism. Haussmann was pleased with this. Caesar might have hoped for something more exciting, but would it actually have been practical to insert tubes in the amphoraeka's arms and have them spewing Greek fire? How would the compound have been fed into such tubes? No, Tesla's crossbows and spears were much more sensible. Haussmann was amazed at how sensible, considering he could hardly get a comprehensible sentence out of their creator.

The Baron established a productive routine. A hashish-laced breakfast resulted in a prolonged ramble. When Tesla stalled, like an engine that had run out of steam, Haussmann left his drained genius in the charge of the amphoraeka and used the boat to spend the afternoon in the more salubrious atmosphere of the Contessa's palazzo. Upon his return to Murano, he fed Tesla a carefully spiced evening meal, resulting in another prolonged warble before bed. The Baron was pleased. This wasn't perfect, but it was most satisfactory.

Tesla's mind was too fogged for him to appreciate how much information he was giving away to the Baron. He felt his body switch gears from dozing to expansive, then jolt to a stop. It happened over and over again, but it was all feeling, not thought. In his dreams, he was an automaton. In his waking hours, only his aching muscles told him he was not still dreaming.

Tesla came to his senses in freezing, stinking water. "Help!" he sputtered. Something burned below his armpits. There was a jerk and he was hoisted by ropes, out of the water and onto the dock, by a trio of amphoraeka. As soon as it was certain that he was alert, Sandtmann tapped out the signal for 'distress' and lumbered back to the fornace.

The shock of the lagoon had been the only option. Sandtmann had observed these days carefully. The Baron wouldn't stay away long; there wasn't much time. Sandtmann had practiced what to say and rattled it out as rapidly as he could: Kola was saying too much; the Baron did not yet know more than was safe, but at this rate he soon would.

Tesla understood. "Whatever he's giving me…It makes my words come out. I can't stop them." His head was too thick for useful thought. All he could do was weep.

One of the amphoraeka on the dock signaled. Sandtmann had time to beat out a single word. "ILL."

"Yes, Dov. I feel terrible."

"ILL" he pounded, frantically, again. Then he froze at the workroom door, in the statuary pose the Baron would expect to find.

Haussmann breezed in, an orchid in his buttonhole, a box of pastries in his arms.

"Ill," Nikola repeated.

"I don't doubt it," the Baron said testily. "That banging again! I must have these pipes checked out."

The Baron was particularly taken with the designs for a vehicle that would enable the transportation of an entire cohort of amphoraeka along the network of fine roads he had been personally responsible for building across Italy. It was engine driven, using Prometheum for propulsion, with paired wheels that were cleverly designed to push along a slatted belt. It would move like a railway car, laying down its own tracks in an endless loop. He instinctively grasped the wisdom of this: greater stability for the heavy load, and even some ability to move where the roads had not yet penetrated. This vehicle would well serve Caesar's greater imperial purposes, but what truly engaged the Baron was the thought of more peaceable employment. How much simpler the work on the Colosseum might have been, for example, if such a vehicle had existed to ferry the stone from Tivoli.

The difficulty would be the Prometheum. Augustus would not permit the use of this substance, even if anyone would sell him enough to power such an engine. There must be some alternative. He longed to discuss this with Tesla, but was in a bind.

Since that afternoon, Tesla had repeated the word "ill" over and over again. Haussmann couldn't determine what he meant. He was pale and weak, but no more than might be anticipated from a routine of drugged work and drugged sleep. Could it be one of his crippling headaches coming on, like the one he'd had in Roma? Haussmann had feared for the young man's life then, as well as his sanity, but the headache had inspired a breakthrough. If Tesla felt a headache coming on now, was it better for the Baron to try and avert it, to preserve what access he had to the man's brilliance, or was the possibility of a major stroke of genius worth the risk of shattering that mind?

Haussmann needed time for thoughts of his own. He decided to forgo the evening's sprinkle of hashish in lieu of a soothing dose of laudanum. This would give the Baron an extended night to spend in the workroom alone, poring over the sketches and models, weighing his options.

Tesla been so hungry of late but tonight, plagued by his conversation with Dov, his stomach felt wobbly and he lost his appetite. He pushed his food around on his plate; any forkful that came near his lips made him feel nauseous. The wine that the Baron insisted he drink looked like blood. The first mouthful gagged him. Quickly bending his head, he somehow managed to spit it into a breadroll. After several such spits, he covered the roll with meat. Noticing the reduced level in his glass, Haussmann topped it off and, with a pleased smile, urged him to drink some more. While the Baron was deliberating over the pastries, Tesla managed to pour most of it into a nearby vase.

Now he stared restlessly at the shadows on the bedroom ceiling. Thoughts were chasing one another across his brain. How much had he given away to Haussmann? How much more would he be unable to keep from saying? And what had Dov meant by "ill"? He was achey and his digestion was uneasy, but that was no doubt due to whatever the Baron had been feeding him to loosen his tongue. The low-level throbbing he felt in his temples was only an ordinary headache. There was bad luck for you. For once, he would have been grateful to surrender to one of his headaches. He had been told they made him catatonic for days. Two or three days of silence, with the Baron learning nothing beyond what he could puzzle out from the sketches and models that Tesla had designed to mislead...Was that Dov's plan, that he should feign a headache and buy some time to marshal his thoughts and make plans? Was that even possible? He knew what his headaches felt like, and he had been told what they looked like. The doctor at Carnegie's sanatorium had taught him about self-hypnosis. He might be able to create the illusion, but not for more than half a day, not remotely long enough.

What was he supposed to do?

Tesla twisted in his sheets. It was so hot in the room! He slipped quietly across to the washstand. He soaked his sponge in the ewer and squeezed it gently over his shoulders, drenching his nightshirt. He opened the window and stood in front of the bars with his arms spread wide, until he caught enough of a breeze to feel cool again. He stretched out on top of the bedclothes, exhausted.

Tesla didn't respond to the delicious breakfast aromas wafting up toward his room. He didn't respond when his name was called rather loudly from the foot of the stairs. Haussmann wondered if he had overdone the laudanum.

Throwing open the door to the room, he could see Tesla was still abed. "Mr. Tesla!" he called, in his most jovial voice, but the younger man did not seem to hear.

"Pffftt!" The Baron strode resolutely to the bed. Tesla's eyes were open and twitching rapidly, like a dog having a bad dream. There was sweat beaded on his forehead, but his teeth were chattering. His breathing was labored.

The Baron sighed from the depths of his round little belly. All his concerns had been rendered pointless by malarial ague. He wasn't going to get anything useful out of Tesla for a week at the very least and he had no one to blame but himself. The fever was well known in the lagoon, but the security of an island prison had been so appealing that Haussmann had blithely disregarded the possibility.

He heaped the shivering man with blankets and went to prepare a hot water bottle. Waiting for the kettle to boil, he wrote a message for one of the amphoraeka to deliver to the waiting boat. Di Bari would have to procure some Warburg's Tincture for him right away. And he'd need a nurse, one he could trust completely. Di Bari, he remembered, had a telegraph. Blavatsky could be asked to send him that healer who had been so protective of Tesla.

Haussmann couldn't stay in Venezia indefinitely. Time was precious; there was the Colosseum to finish, and other contrivances for the wedding. Once he was assured that Tesla was on the mend, he would head back to

Roma with the plans and models. Perhaps the monks would be able to accomplish enough to mount some kind of display of the crossbow devices. Caesar would be thrilled. There would be plenty of time to outfit an army later.

16 - KUMPANIA

Gertrude Bell had never spent a more enthralling two days: the tea; the caravan, which she had learned to call the *vardo*; Yoska's teeth and Milosz's ruby earring; the deference shown to Dika by both men as well as by the boy Beznik. And the ritual of gathering the drarnego by moonlight: oh, she could hardly wait to repeat that tonight!

She wished she could write it all down. She *would* write on her white (or what used to be white) petticoat, but all there was to write with was Claude's pencil, which she couldn't think of without a shudder for where it had been. In any case, she didn't want to risk offending the gypsies by taking notes. The *Rom*, she corrected herself. She would have to rely on what all her teachers had always called "that fine memory of yours."

When they got to Prague, maybe she would write a monograph, to make up for the term she was missing. She had no idea what day it was, but she had only planned to be in Bucharest for three weeks and it was well beyond that now. What a happy thought! Not the part about missing Trinity Term, but her awareness of doing so. It was excellent confirmation that the drarnego had indeed worked.

What an amazing herb! She wondered if it grew anywhere in England. Maybe if she dug some up by the root, she could somehow keep it alive and get it home. She was quite a good gardener. The Rom seemed to feel that the forest and the ritual were integral to the virtues of the herb, and though her recent experiences had made her more willing to accept the possibility of such influences, a cultivated version might still perhaps retain enough efficacy to be of value. She fervently hoped that the vérfarkas would stay away so that they could complete the harvest. She wouldn't have thought that the injured one would chance another encounter with Claude, but Dika thought otherwise.

"It will want revenge," she'd said darkly. "Between us, we have destroyed its pack. It will be searching the vesh for another to join, and track us as soon as it can. We must hope it cannot in this moon. What happens in the next is of no consequence. When we finish the harvest, we will be gone for another year. That will be time enough to plan."

Gertrude squinted up at the sky. The sun was straight overhead. It was time, she thought, to wake Claude, who had fallen asleep on a clump of grass directly after breakfast.

Dika stopped her. "Let her sleep."

"She's sleeping so much." Gertrude was concerned. Since partaking of the drarnego, Claude seemed withdrawn. Not that Gertrude could honestly judge if this was unusual. It was curious to consider, but she didn't know what Claude was really like. They had met only a couple of weeks ago, and for much of their acquaintance their minds had hardly been their own. Still, she had entrusted her life to this girl multiple times already, and wouldn't hesitate to do so again.

"She used all her strength in her fight with the vérfarkas," the Chivani reminded her. "Powerful men have fought that battle and lost. She must have great powers. Yoska is not convinced she is not urme." Dika looked as if she was not quite convinced either.

"She's no more magical than I am," Gertrude asserted. "Her father trained her to fight. He's...It seems that he's a most unusual man. Claude is skilled in many things. They left us in the forest with nothing, only the least amount of food and water and even that was drugged by the Emperor's bitch." She coloured a little. She had really wanted to say 'jackal' but it had never occurred to her to learn the German word. She only knew 'bitch' because of being set to translate that story from the Grimm brothers, the one with the dogs. She assumed she'd made her point as Dika's expression changed from curiosity to pure hatred. "Claude kept us alive, even with her mind...with both our minds disturbed."

"Emperor?" Dika asked, loudly and significantly enough that Milosz and Yoska stopped whatever work they were doing to join the women.

"Augustus," Gertrude said promptly. "The Italian emperor. Caesar, he calls himself. We were kidnapped..."

Dika gestured for Gertrude to wait. When they were all settled by the fire, she said, "now tell us what you know of the Emperor."

"Not very much," Gertrude admitted. Then she did her best to tell all that she did know.

Milosz spat in the fire. "He is our enemy as well. Not only of our vitsa, of all the Rom."

"It's a famous story to our people," the garrulous Yoska began. "Years ago, Augustus Buonaparte, the man you call 'Emperor', had a sister who loved one of our men."

Dika interrupted to explain. "Our people went often to Roma then. Napoleon was greatly interested in Egypt and in the ancient learnings that have been lost."

"Like Augustus!" Gertrude exclaimed.

Milosz disagreed. "The father is not like the son."

"The son began like the father, " Dika observed. "But chose a different path. Napoleon craved knowledge, as some crave opium or drink. His son wanted only the power that comes from knowledge. Even as a youth, Augustus was dangerous. Today he is a *drabarno* of the blackest kind."

"You cannot imagine what curses he has heaped upon his soul!" Yoska exclaimed. Milosz spat again, this time through forked fingers.

"Napoleon believed," Dika continued, "as many do, that the Rom came once out of Egypt. That is why the *gadje* use the word 'gypsy', you see." Gertrude nodded vigorously, her eyes shining. She adored learning things like this. "He treated our people with respect. He would invite our people to Roma and meet for hours with the chivanis and the *vaidas*, the chiefs. Emilian was the son of a vaida, likely to someday succeed him. A very handsome boy. He could sing so beautifully, they said he could charm the hare into the pot and the vérfarkas deep into the forest. He came with his father to visit Roma. In the palace, he met Napoleon's daughter Paulette. She also was very beautiful, some say the greatest beauty of her time, and was known to have a most loving heart. They were very young." Dika turned up her hands as if to say that was all one needed to know to understand.

"It's like a fairytale," Gertrude breathed. "The princess and the gypsy. In a story, he would be a prince in disguise."

"He was a prince!" Milosz said sharply.

Gertrude startled guiltily. "Oh, I know he was," she stammered. "That's not what I meant…"

Dika smiled sadly. "You are a gadji, chavi. You see it as they do. Anyone but the lovers would have seen the same. You cannot have a match from two different worlds."

271

"But why can't..." Gertrude didn't know what she wanted to say. She had never been in love, but she wanted to think that love could conquer anything.

"Some things are greater than love," Dika said, understanding her thoughts. "Blood is greater. Blood has a more powerful call and will not let go. If Emilian and Paulette had been given time, they would have understood this. There would have been sorrow, but they would have known it was right to part. They weren't given that time. Paulette's young brother Augustus couldn't abide the thought of his sister loving a boy of the Rom. The two were invited to a banquet. Augustus drugged their food with something that turned their limbs to ice. Once they could no longer move, he made his sister watch as he took a knife and began to butcher her lover like meat for the table." Gertrude made an exclamation of horror, but Dika pressed on with the nightmarish tale. "First he cut off his ears and nose, to kill his beauty. He cut off Emilian's *kar*, his manhood, and stuck it in his mouth. And only then, while Emilian would still be alive to know, he carved the beating heart from his breast."

There was a long silence around the campfire. Gertrude could feel her own beating heart trying to break through her ribs.

"They threw his body in the river," Milosz said dully. "They had not even the respect to return him to his people."

"What did Napoleon do?" Gertrude asked when she could find her voice.

"He never knew," Dika said. "They say Paulette lost her reason for a time. Who would believe if she told? The only other witnesses were Augustus's personal guards and a poor boy who served at table. The boy somehow escaped and made his way to the camp. The kumpania vowed to take revenge. The women were to leave Roma at first light, the men remaining to see that justice would be done. Augustus was too quick for them. That night, his guards came with torches and set the camp ablaze. Few survived—only enough to keep the story alive. None of our people have ever returned to Roma. Those kumpanias who travel near to his borders remain well hidden from authorities and do what they can to work against the Emperor's power. He is our sworn enemy." Her smile was without humor. "It seems that by helping you, we also help our cause."

"The rule of hospitality has many rewards," Yoska observed.

"When we are finished in the vesh," Milosz said, "we will bring you to where our people are camped. There must be a meeting of the Elders, but then we will take you to as near to Budapest as our people go. You can get help there?"

"Yes," Gertrude said promptly. "We'll go to the British Embassy. They'll help us get to Prague, to Claude's father."

They moved camp to another spot for the night, close to another patch of the herb. The Rom seemed to be able to find their way around the forest as easily as Gertrude could get from Lady Margaret Hall to the Ashmolean.

Claude, somewhat revived, had asked to walk beside the wagon. She wanted to scout for signs that the beasts might have passed by. Dika had vetoed the request. The swelling had gone down, but her ankle was not up to bearing weight. Instead, she sat beside Milosz on the driver's box, craning her neck and comparing notes with him on the flora.

Gertrude, meanwhile, tried to convince Dika to let her dig up a few specimens. Dika was skeptical of the plan. She had seen her share of gadje gardens. They were a form of captivity, the plants in their rows, pressed to grow at another's will. The Chivani didn't believe that cultivated herbs could ever have the power of those that grew wild and free. However, if the crop tonight was abundant, she was willing to humor Gertrude; she even gave her a basket to use. She cautioned that if the plant survived and took root in Gertrude's distant home, it must always be cut under the full moon, and only once a year and according to the ritual. Gertrude swore solemnly that she would always honour Dika's mandate. The older woman patted her benevolently on the head. The girl meant well, but in the end it would not suffice. You cannot transplant the old ways.

They were wary again that night. Once the moon was up, they moved as silently as possible to where the drarnego grew thickest. Milosz patrolled the area, his one silver bullet in the rifle's chamber. Claude had Beznik help her into a tree where she could watch and listen. From time to time, she allowed herself a peep at Dika, swaying and bending gracefully in the moonlight, her hands weaving the spell like articulate moths. She felt peaceful. These people weren't like the Lakhota but they made her think of them. They knew who they were.

The harvest was completed without incident and was abundant enough that Dika allowed Gertrude her sample. Gertrude said a few solemn words, apologizing to the plants for taking them from their home. When Dika realized what she was doing, she stood with her hand fondly on the girl's shoulder, whispering some words in Romani for her to repeat. Gertrude used a sharp stick and her fingers to dig out around the roots. In case the soil itself had some special properties, she scooped a generous amount into the basket, made a hollow and gently set the tiny world and its precious denizens into that nest.

Dika heaped her harvest over the fruits of the previous nights. When they returned to the main camp, she explained, the sprigs would be scattered between layers of gauze and set on drying racks. After the herb had fully dried, it would be time for their kumpania to move on to the next stage of their annual migration.

As they had the night before, everyone slept in the vardo. They rotated their watch in teams of two, one holding the gun and one sitting on the box behind the horse, who remained harnessed. They were ready to run at any time. They didn't have to.

Dawn arrived without incident. Claude, who had sat the last watch, looked at the blush of sky peeping between the trees and smiled. It was hard to feel happy knowing that Nikola and Princess Maud were prisoners, but she couldn't help her lifted spirits. What was it Aunt Nan always said? Beware of what you wish for, for fear you might get it. Claude had spent so much time complaining that no one treated her like an adult. Lately she had been adult more than enough. All she wanted now was to let Father lift the burden from her shoulders. She could almost feel his strong arms hugging her the way he did, so tightly that her corsets would creak. Tomorrow at this time, their little party would leave the forest, and she and Gertrude would begin their journey home.

❧

It was the longest day. Everyone seemed anxious to push through it faster, and then get through the night. They drove to what would be their final campsite, built a fire, and rubbed and watered the horse. They ate their meal as the sun was setting, then packed up the vardo, to be ready to go.

By the time they finished the night's harvest, everyone was so on edge that Milosz suggested they not wait for first light to leave the forest. The moon was so bright tonight, he could easily find their way. They were discussing this when they heard the unmistakable howling in the distance.

Yoska started throwing dirt over the fire. Fortunately, Milosz had harnessed the horse immediately after returning to camp. He leaped onto the driver's box with the gun. It took his considerable strength to hold the massive bay until the women piled into the vardo. The horse was already trotting when Beznik jumped on the box in back and held tight to the bar. Yoska had to race to catch up with the moving caravan and clamber up beside Milosz. He grabbed the gun.

The howling was getting louder. It was a full pack and they were getting closer. Milosz snapped the reins again, giving the horse his head.

Suddenly, Beznik gave a shout. Yoska wheeled around on the seat and jumped down into the caravan with the rifle. He ran the few feet to the back, the women scattering out of his way as best they could in the swaying wagon.

Yoska looked through the tiny window. The vérfarkas were close enough that he could see the muzzles of the leaders, their teeth shining under the moon. He unlatched the window and pulled it back on its hinge as far as it could go. By placing the rifle sideways, he was able to slide it out to Beznik.

Still holding the bar with one hand, Beznik cocked the rifle and fired the last silver bullet. The report shook the wagon. There was a scream and it seemed as if one of the monsters fell. So did Beznik. The kickback had lost him his footing; he slid off the box. Yoska let out a yell, but there was nothing he could do. The window was so small, not even a child could have gotten out.

Yoska stumbled towards the front. "Turn around!" he yelled up to Milosz.

Gertrude looked out the window. "Stop!" she screamed as loudly as she could. "The werewolves have Beznik."

The vérfarkas had reached where Beznik lay sprawled on the ground.

"There's no helping him," Milosz shouted back. "The rest of us still have a chance."

There was a blood-curdling scream of human anguish. The largest of the pack threw his muzzle into the air and with a yelp that sounded like triumph, ripped out the boy's throat. The others of the pack fell upon his body and started to gorge themselves.

Inside the vardo, Dika sat ramrod straight on a trunk, her face a mask. "At least he will not survive to become vérfarkas," she said flatly. Gertrude started to weep. Yoska had to pull her away from the window and push her back into her seat.

Milosz pushed the horse as fast as the terrified beast could run. The caravan bounced on the roots of trees, jarring them to the bone and rattling their teeth. Otherwise they did not move. It was too horrible.

Claude jumped up and made her unsteady way to the front. "Milosz," she yelled over the rattle and clatter, "stop! You have to let me out!"

He shook his head fiercely and called back "No!"

"You have to!" She leaned forward as far as she could and spoke into his ear. "They don't want all of you. Once they're not hungry any more," she shuddered, "they'll only follow us now if they want me, if they want revenge."

"What can you do except die? I know what Yoska said he saw you do, but this is a pack. You can't fight them all at once and we have no more silver bullets."

"You don't even have a gun. Beznik fell holding the rifle."

He shook his head again. "You may be a great warrior, but you've been injured."

"I have a plan. I need a clearing with some good climbing trees. Start looking for one. I'll be right back." She drew back into the vardo. "Trust me, Milosz," she called back.

She snatched her water skin from the shelf and, after shaking it to be sure there was something in it, slung it across her shoulder. "I need something to use as a weight," she said, pulling out the napkin she'd kept tucked inside her pocket for weeks.

Dika nodded and handed her a small lump of lead used for rivets. "Anything more?"

Claude nodded, tying the lead up in her napkin. "A knife. And a handkerchief or another napkin. Sorry, Gertrude," she said, dumping the dirt from the basket into the cloth Dika gave her. "If we get out of this alive, you can get more." She tied the corners into a bundle and hooked it to her belt. She was already on her way back to Milosz when he called out.

"Urme!" They'd all been calling her that. Gertrude said it meant some kind of fairy or angel, she wasn't sure.

He had spotted a clearing and started to slow the horse. She gritted her teeth and clambered painfully up onto the box. Midway through the clearing, she tossed out the weighted napkin. It sent up a small puff of dirt where it landed. 'Step one, check' she thought. Her heart was racing. Her plan was on!

She stood, one hand on Milosz's shoulder to steady herself. "Drive as near as you can to that tree," she said; "the one with the low branch."

He did as she asked. Ducking his head to avoid hitting it, he missed seeing Claude grab the branch with both hands and swing herself up. She kicked her good leg over to straddle it and paused to catch her breath. Step two would be complete once she'd backed her way to the crotch and braced herself.

When Milosz noticed she was gone, he let out a cry. "She's gone!"

Gertrude looked out the back of the vardo and saw her friend sitting on the tree limb, slowly edging toward the trunk.

"Let me out, Milosz!" she demanded. "Slow down and let me out. She's injured; whatever she's trying to do, she can't be out there alone!"

"If all of us die, her sacrifice and Beznik's are pointless!"

"She's not going to be a sacrifice!" Gertrude said. She had always wondered, watching her brothers and cousins, what it must feel like to be a boy and jump off the hay loft in the barn. She was going to find out, only there wouldn't be hay. She saw a cluster of bushes coming up on the right. Before she could think too much, she jumped into them.

For the merest second, it was like flying, but then the branches were brushing her face. Remembering how Billy would call out to the younger boys "tuck and roll!" she tried to curl into a ball and protect her face. She slammed into the bush. It was hard, but not as hard as the ground would have been and a big improvement over hitting a tree. She was thrown onto her side; she did roll, though she was completely out of control. Every part of her body seemed to strike something and all the air rushed out of her lungs. She lay there panting until a voice in the back of her head started to scold her; if she didn't get up, she would surely end up feeding the werewolves. That got her up and staggering back to where she last saw Claude. 'If we live through this,' she thought, 'I'm going to be covered in bruises until Christmas.'

She used a low branch of the same tree to climb up to a spot just above and behind her friend. "It's only me," she whispered

Claude was glad to see her, but also annoyed at having a hostage to fortune. She didn't know what to say, so she said nothing but continued ripping the hem of her skirt where the last Prometheum capsule still nestled.

"What are you planning to do?" Gertrude asked.

"Make a Prometheum bomb," Claude said matter-of-factly.

"A bomb?"

"An explosive device."

"I know what a bomb is." Gertrude was a little offended. "But how...I thought Prometheum was a type of fuel."

"It generates combustion. Housed and set correctly, it can safely propel machines, including vehicles. But Prometheum can also be used as weaponry. Or it will be," she answered grimly. "They think I don't know, but that's what Father and Leski have been working on for years. They call it the 'Joshua bomb'; the walls will come tumbling down, you see? Combustion is explosion. Father and Nikola used Prometheum to blast holes for mines in Pittsburgh. It's cleaner than dynamite charges and proportionately more powerful, Father says. Although there's still a lot we don't know about it." All the time she'd been talking, Claude had been working fast. She set Dika's napkin in her lap and slowly dribbled water, mixing the dirt to a stiff paste. She squirted a little water onto her hand to clean it. Using the bone-handled knife, she carefully slit the lead capsule almost completely around its equator. "Open my needle case," she instructed; as long as Gertrude was here, she might as well be useful. Claude bent back the two halves of the capsule and tucked the little 'w' between the thumb and forefinger of her left hand, like two tiny cups. Her right hand scooped up some of the mud. "Now stick the needles into the shells."

"Point up or down?"

"Doesn't matter. Just put half in each."

Fumbling a little from nerves, Gertrude managed to stand a few of the silver needles into each half shell.

"Good," Claude said, satisfied. "Now run, Gertrude! Use the limb you climbed up and cross to the next tree. Keep off the ground 'til you get to the far side of that other tree, then run as fast as you can and catch up with the vardo. Milosz will be watching for you, I know he will..."

"I'm not going. I ran last time..."

"And both our lives were saved. With any luck, they will be again. We can't take a chance. We need to be sure someone gets back to Prague to tell Father. I told you the name of the hotel..." She cleared her throat. "Run damn it!"

Gertrude hugged her quickly and went as instructed.

The wolves came, howling, having followed their scent and the sound of the caravan.

Claude mounded the mud over the needle-studded capsule. Holding her breath, she turned it gingerly until it was upside down in her right hand. It held stable. She would be relieved, except now she had to worry about whether it would explode when she needed it to. There was no time for worrying. She took the rest of the mud and heaped it over the bottom of the capsule halves. It didn't take much to make it more or less round.

She froze.

They were coming! Their muzzles and forepaws were red with Beznik's blood; she could smell it from the tree.

As they passed into the clearing, they hesitated for a second to sniff he air. They were confused. They couldn't see her in the tree, but they could smell that she was up there somewhere. There was also a strong scent of her on the ground. They were drawn to the handkerchief like filings to a magnet. She set her mouth in a grim smile and raised her throwing arm.

"Hokahey!" she whispered with fierce pride. She hurled the ball of mud with all her might. It landed, with pinpoint accuracy, right in the midst of the pack. As it hit the ground, the impact set off the Prometheum. The mud exploded outward and the needles flew into the monsters. Such small splinters of silver, but as they hit their marks, the brutes screamed and fell as if they'd been hit by cannon fire. It couldn't have been a minute since she threw her makeshift bomb, and it was all over. The woods were as still as death.

Claude gripped the tree limb beneath her with shaking arms. It was over. She'd done it. The entire pack lay on the ground, their ugly bodies sprawled like a heap of poisoned weasels.

She hoped Milosz would come back for her. She tried to call out but, the way it sometimes happens in nightmares, her voice stuck in her throat. She put the thumb and fourth finger of her right hand into her mouth and blew a two-note piercing whistle. Would they know that was her? Well, at least they would know it wasn't a werewolf. She leaned back and waited.

There was a rustle in the tree behind her.

"I told you to run," she said, tired.

"I did," Gertrude sounded offended. "You were absolutely right, and I did. I heard the bomb go off. I knew right away you hit them. It got so quiet. I was afraid maybe the explosion had killed you, too. Then I heard your whistle." Her voice lifted. "Do you think you could teach me to do that? You know all the most useful things!"

"Thank you," Claude said.

"If I could help you down, I would, but I think we should wait for the Rom. They'll come back for us; they will."

"I know they will."

The horse was jittery and wouldn't come near, so they had to leave the vardo on the path a little away. They stared in awe at the pile of dead monsters. Yoska climbed into the tree and carried Claude down on his back.

The men took a spade and walked back to give a proper burial to what was left of Beznik. They returned with the rifle, and with the buckle of his belt, which they would give to Lenka, the boy's mother. By that time, the women had a small but comforting fire going, as far from the beasts as possible, and Dika was boiling water to make a restorative chao that smelled remarkably like rum toddy. No one felt like sleeping. They sat close together around the fire, telling stories, until traces of light bled across the sky.

When the sun had risen, Milosz and Yoska walked to the other side of the clearing to perform a grim salvage, turning the naked corpses over and over again until they found the needles embedded in their skin. Each time they pulled one clear, the dead vérfarkas would shrivel and turn to dust. When all the bodies had disintegrated, Dika, drew the ritual pattern with a birch stick and completed the ceremony to free the cursed souls.

Yoska brought the handful of bent needles to Claude.

"You keep them," she said, gently pushing him away. "They're no good to me any more. Melt them for bullets."

The caravan made its way through the trees, the rutted path growing wider with the miles until it eventually became a road. Emerging from the shadows of the forest, Gertrude and Claude blinked in wonder. The open fields seemed like a lush green sea, rolling towards islands that were farms and clusters of cottages.

The horse perked up its ears and walked with a new lightness. They reached a small village, neither prosperous nor shabby. No one paid them any mind as they made their way along the main road, past the pump and the green, to the far side of town to where the vitsa was camped.

The girls saw a loose ring of vardos and one or two open wagons, a little over a dozen in all. As their own caravan entered the camp, a shrill shout rang out and a barefoot tot came running into view. With a glad laugh, she hurled herself at Milosz. "Dada!" she cried.

He scooped her up and sat her on his shoulders. She took the cap off his head and put in on her own.

Everyone laughed and the rest of the vitsa poured out to greet them. There were cheers and hugs and slapping of backs. Then Milosz set his daughter down and approached the eager woman who'd hurried from the blue vardo still holding the sock she had been darning. It was hard to see her broad, hopeful smile shrink and crumple as she missed the one face she had been waiting for. Milosz bowed low in front of her. She tried to pull away as he pressed the belt buckle between her resisting hands. He wrapped an arm around her shoulders and drew her in. No one could see her face, but the wail that wasn't muffled against his chest broke the heart of everyone who heard. He led her back to her vardo, whispering in her ear. Dika followed with a draught she had prepared on the road.

Yoska gathered the rest of the vitsa around the fire that held the center of the camp. Slowly and with great passion, he told the story of their harvest journey. He spoke Romani. Gertrude and Claude could only pick out a few words here and there, but Yoska's art was so persuasive that they could tell where he was in the story. When he came to Claude's battle with the two vérfarkas, one or two of his listeners looked at her out of the corner of their eyes and sketched the sign of the cross. There was a deep sigh and a few approving nods when he revealed the end of Gyorgi. The reaction was more heartfelt when he described Beznik's sacrifice. Every eye turned respectfully toward's Lenka's vardo; even the men's were wet with tears. Yoska's version of what he understood of Claude's final stand against the pack brought an awe that was tangible. Men whipped off their caps and those nearest her shrank back, leaving a respectful foot or two of clear ground between them.

There was a rapid and somewhat histrionic consultation, ending with firm graspings of forearms that seemed to signal agreement. People started to drift away to whatever had been interrupted by the caravan's arrival. Yoska turned to the girls, spent but well pleased.

"It is decided to adopt you both into the vitsa," he announced, flashing his gold teeth. "This is great honour. Not even the oldest here can recall it in their lifetime."

The girls nodded. Though they weren't certain what the distinction might mean, they could accept the magnitude of honour.

"We will have a festival tomorrow. When the herb has dried, we will move north as planned. Milosz and Dika must stay with the kumpania, but I and some others, we will take you to where you want to be, to Praha."

After the evening meal, all the women in the camp gathered outside Dika's vardo with lanterns. Part of the adoption, the Chivani explained to the girls, was that they would carry the mark of the kumpania on their bodies. She lifted her skirt to show her bare leg. On her left thigh there was a circle and star above a pair of parallel lines. Within the circle were some squiggles.

"The road and star," she explained, pointing to the lines, "are carried by all the vitsa. The moon is the mark of our own kumpania, we who seek the drarnego. You can never forget what is here in your skin."

Gertrude, squinting under the yellow lamplight, saw the pattern come together. "Nine and seven!" she crowed.

Dika beamed at her. "You need only remember the copper," she said. She pointed to the ground where, in deference to their gadji softness, a layer of blankets had been spread.

Claude went first. Slipping off her drawers, she reclined on her right side. Dika rubbed a spot on her thigh with spider venom to numb the surface. "Even so it will hurt," she said, considering, "but I dare not give you anything to stop it. Your bodies are too recently clean."

"I'll take some of what Yoska keeps in his flask," Claude grinned. "And maybe a stick of wood to bite down on. Don't look so alarmed Gertrude," she added, as the women nearest Dika lifted their lanterns. "Maybe you should start your drinking now!"

It was a good idea. By the time Dika had finished and Claude's eyes were wet with blinked-back tears, Gertrude was what sailors call "three sheets to the wind" and singing a Romani song the others had been teaching her—apparently a very bawdy Romani song, based on the women's raucous laughter. She took her own tattoo with a combination of shrieks and giggles, and the occasional Romani curse that she had picked up from Yoska on the road and which set the women laughing again. Her final long swig from the tin cup of liquor was greeted with cheers.

The women helped Gertrude to her wobbly feet and pulled both girls into a dance that snaked toward and around the big campfire. One of the men had been playing melancholy tunes on a fiddle. As the women reached him, he switched to a sparkling dance and the women matched their steps to the music. A few pulled tiny cymbals from their sashes. Yoska produced a tambourine and soon everyone was joining in the wild dance under the stars.

When they had to part ways on the road, it felt like a family parting. Gertrude in particular, with her earnest fascination for every aspect of Romani life and quick ear for language, had insinuated herself into the kumpania. Claude remained wrapped in a fabric of myth and was more revered than loved. Before the girls were allowed to climb into the borrowed vardo, there were several rounds of kisses and tears. They were embraced by every pair of arms and most firmly by one-armed Ion, the former master thief.

Dika handed Claude a napkin containing a few dried sprigs of the herb. "You seem to lead an adventurous life."

Claude accepted the bit of linen as if it were diamonds. "I will put this in copper as soon as I reach the city," she assured her.

Dika nodded, pleased, and kissed the girls on both cheeks before turning her back and walking away. Gertrude watched the retreating back with a twist of her heart. She stood with one hesitant foot on the box, her basket of drarnego plantings cradled under one arm. Somehow she felt that she now belonged to this world, too, and was loathe to leave it. Claude understood, but she had been through this before and knew that whatever affinity they felt and even received in return, they were nothing more than privileged visitors here. "We have to go," she whispered, giving her friend a gentle push to climb.

It was harder still when they had to leave Yoska and his cousins at the edge of Prague. "Our kumpania does not come into the city," he had explained earlier. "If ever you have need, you can send word at the White Beet on the King's Road, where we have friends."

"*Latcho drom!* Travel safely!" they called to the travelers before looking away, as Yoska had wisely suggested, and starting down the road.

"Latcho drom!" they heard them call back.

Claude had seen the tiniest bit of the city and Gertrude had taken only the one ill-fated walk. Knowing the direction from which they'd come, they continued in the direction Claude said was Northwest. After about an hour they began to pass people in the streets.

"What we look like," Gertrude murmured. She hadn't thought about her appearance while were with the Rom but, now that they were surrounded by Europeans, she could feel herself shrinking under the scornful stares.

"We've survived kidnapping, drugging and being set upon by werewolves. I think we can tolerate a few nasty looks." Claude glared at a couple who were frankly gawking. The girl clutched her escort's arm with a whimper and he hastened her away from the draggled pair.

"I want to go straight to the Embassy," Gertrude fussed. "I'm going to take a two-hour bath, wash my hair until my scalp stings and burn this suit. I hope the Hutchinsons still have my bag."

"We're not going to the Embassy. It's afternoon. Father will be at the workshop. I have to go straight to him."

"If it were my father, he'd be at the Embassy," Gertrude objected. "Or riding herd on whatever authorities are out there trying to find us. Yours is a spy. He's probably on the road right now, looking."

"You don't know my father," Claude said. "Others can search. He'll be in the workshop. He's the only one who can finish Nikola's work, and now that's more important than ever." Claude felt a guilty pang. She hadn't thought about Nikola in several days. "I wonder if he's alright," she said, a lump rising in her throat. "Nikola, I mean. They didn't send him out with us. Do you think...?" She couldn't finish the sentence.

"I doubt Madame Blavatsky would have been so angry at those men if she meant to kill him," Gertrude asserted. "Remember? How she lit into them for giving him that powder?"

"A powder, is that what it was? I thought there was something about an injection. The Italian was so fast and I hadn't yet gotten used to hearing it."

"There was an injection. Quite a strong one. And when that didn't work, they forced him to swallow this powder that...that Madame said could cause a man to believe himself a walking corpse. But I'm sure he's fine now," she hastened to add. "She had that nurse taking such good care of him. That was kind, don't you think?"

Claude looked at her oddly. "From the woman who was all too glad to scramble our brains until we thought we could hear colours and smell sound, and then left us to die in the woods? Oh, kindness itself."

Gertrude shrugged. "I've been thinking about this. It gave us a chance. We survived. The Emperor might have killed us outright."

"And the Blavatsky woman could have told him that she had done, and then sent us somewhere safe. I don't know what her motives were, Gertrude, but kindness had nothing to do with it."

They walked in silence for a time, each haunted by the memory of a pair of strange, pale eyes and wondering what lay behind them.

Some of the buildings looked familiar. Claude's pace grew quicker and more sure. "I think know where we are now!" There was joy in her voice; she'd spotted the spiky black towers of the Tyn Church. "See! There's the Old Town Square. You can see the clock tomorrow." Ignoring the glares of the passersby, she lead Gertrude swiftly along the quickest of the routes Nikola had taught her and was soon winding down streets that felt beloved. Grabbing Gertrude by the elbow, she dragged her into the alley that led to the warehouse.

"There's no one in there," Gertrude objected. "See how it's boarded up? It's deserted."

"No it's not. The windows face the courtyard out back." Claude knocked at the door and waited impatiently. There wasn't a sound. Claude stamped her foot in exasperation, then turned sheepishly to Gertrude. "What an idiot! I guess that drarnego leaves a few holes." Instead of turning away, as Gertrude expected, she knocked again: an elaborate series of knocks and pauses. This time she waited patiently.

Gertrude heard nothing, but Claude must have as she spoke, in a quiet, conversational tone, to the door. "Father, it's me." The door flew open and her friend was crushed against the chest of a grey-haired man not much taller than she but with, apparently, enormous strength in his wiry frame. He pulled her inside.

Gertrude, feeling invisible, followed and closed the door. The building felt old and the musty smell of an unused space lingered in the air. Despite what Claude had said, she could see no windows. The space seemed shallow, too, only a few body lengths from the door to the wall. It occurred to her this might be a false front of some kind. Whatever the famous Nikola had been working on, it had been something secret.

Most of what Gertrude could see in the dimness were shelves, piled with metal clutter of the kind she supposed an inventor would need to have around. The fittings were makeshift and rickety, but everything was scrupulously clean. Everything except herself, she thought with chagrin.

She wasn't the only one waiting. A tall man stepped out of the shadows from where he'd been watching the reunion and turned the full power of his black eyes on Gertrude. There was something of the Rom about him, a contained wildness, except that he was more contained and, beneath that she could sense, wilder still. He reminded her of nothing so much as the Tower ravens, with their glossy black plumage and cruelly clipped wings. She realized with a thrill that this must be the man Claude had spoken of so often when her mind had been disturbed. She hadn't expected him to be so beautiful.

"How do you do," he said, his American-scented English somewhat different from Claude's.

At the sound, Claude broke away from her father and saw him for the first time. "Oh, Leski!" she cried joyfully, flinging her arms around the unbending figure. "How wonderful! You saved our lives in that forest!"

"Mit'anksi," he said in a tranquil tone. He patted her head with affection. "I saw you were well. I told Wohitika Capa. But who is your companion?"

Claude blushed. "Where are my manners! And after all we've shared! Miss Gertrude Bell, Mr. Lemuel Firewalker. And this is my father, Mr. Franklin Monteith."

"Miss Bell," Firewalker bowed gravely. "I am pleased to make your acquaintance."

Gertrude bobbed politely. "I am so pleased to meet you, Mr. Firewalker." Now that she had a better look at the older man, she realized she knew him. "Sir Alastair?"

"Miss Bell." Frank gave a delighted smile. "It is even more of a pleasure to meet you again. You are a braw lass indeed." He took her hand and bowed over it.

"When could you have met Gertrude, Father?"

"When she arrived from Budapest with the Princess. I met them both that night at the Embassy." His face darkened. "While someone was dragging you off to Dubrovnik. I would never have forgiven myself if...I would never have forgiven her..." His voice trailed off until it was a whisper.

"Is that where we were, Dubrovnik? How do you know?" It was Gertrude's turn to blush. "Of course, how silly of me. You're a spy."

Frank shot his daughter a look. She looked back, exasperated. "We were in the direst of circumstances and she was the only person I dared trust. And we were drugged. Who can control what they say when they're drugged?"

"You seem well enough now," Frank said dryly.

"Thanks to the drarnego," Gertrude piped up. "The Rom were so generous..."

"It's clear this is going to take some telling." Frank looked them up and down. "I think we need to get you both comfortable and fed. I've taken a wee house nearby," he told Claude. "I'd like Miss Bell to join as there, if she has no objection. I'd rather know where both of you are at all times." Gertrude nodded, a little relieved to not be separated from Claude. It still felt as if they needed to be together to be safe. "Lem will go to the embassy and fetch your bags. And he'll bring back some food. We've established a relationship with a fine cafe..."

"And I will wire Lord Pinkerton." Firewalker said, pulling on his coat and hat and heading for the door.

"Wait, sir! My family!" Gertrude couldn't believe that, in the excitement, she'd nearly forgotten them. "They must be worried to death! Please wire them too. Tell them that I'm safe."

"Dinnae fash," Frank assured her. "Your family is under the impression that you're keeping the Princess company while she's in hiding for her protection."

"They believed that?" Gertrude was incredulous. "I disappeared without a word to anyone. My parents might believe such a story, if it came from someone important enough, but certainly my grandfather has been kicking up a fuss."

"I understand he was, uh, a wee bit forceful in his questions. As well we can both imagine." He chuckled.

"You know my grandfather?" She hadn't expected that.

"Miss Bell, your grandfather *is* aluminium. Both of us being in metal, so to speak, it's only natural that we've met now and again. Rest easy. Even Sir Lowthian Bell had to believe that story once he'd heard it from the

Queen herself. But aye, a letter or two would add credibility to the narrative. Write. We'll ask Hutchinson to send them in the diplomatic pouch."

"What about Aunt Nan?" Claude asked.

"Oh, I left her with the Pinkertons," he said, checking his pockets for the keys. They were in his own coat, which he had forgotten was hanging on a nail. Claude handed it to him. He smiled fondly at his daughter. "She thinks you've been here all this time, you and Tesla, working with me. Can you imagine the sooch if I'd told her you were missing?" He hugged her again, his eyes a little bright, and whispered, "I knew you'd come home alright, lass."

It would have been wonderful to soak for an hour, but there was only one bathtub in the little house and now that the possibility of being clean was so very near, neither girl could bear to wait for long. While Gertrude took the first bath, Claude went to the room Frank said would be hers. All the things she had left in the hotel were there, carefully put away as if she had been living there these last weeks. Her brush and hair-catcher were on the dresser, her gowns in the wardrobe with her French-heeled boots neatly placed on the floor below them. She had to blink back tears at this show of faith. She quickly pulled out her wrapper and slippers for Gertrude and left them on a chair outside the bathroom. Back in her room, she removed Dika's shawl from the stained leather satchel that had never left her. She lifted the fabric to her nose and took a deep breath. It smelled of fire and drarnego. She folded it carefully in tissue and placed it with her things. The red blouse would need to be washed. She doubted what was left of her walking skirt could be salvaged and she knew her poor brave petticoat was a rag. It used to embarrass her a little, that she preferred silk to cotton. Now that the tensile strength had saved her life she would never wear anything but.

She unlaced her boots and eased off her dusty boots. Her toes wiggled gratefully in her reeking stockings. She supposed she could boil the hose clean, and all her underwear, too, but she might as well burn the lot and be done with it. She could hardly wait for Gertrude to be done. The idea of the smell and feel of clean fabric against her skin seemed like heaven.

She really was being an idiot today! There was no need to wait for Gertrude. Father hated baths. Wherever he planned to stay for any time, he would find a way to rig a shower bath, even if it were little more than a few lengths of copper piping hanging from a meat hook. Heaven only knew how much she longed to wallow in a tub of hot water, but she needed cleanliness even more. And she was starving. She wondered what Leski would be bringing from this cafe of theirs. Whatever it was, she hoped he'd be bringing a lot of it.

By the time Gertrude had finished her bath—she had to fill the tub three times before she felt clean—there was a small fire crackling in the room she had been assigned. She sat on the slipper chair by the hearth, helping her hair to dry and wondering why she felt so cramped. It was a nice enough room, plain as one might expect from a rented house, but pleasant and tidy. The bed looked so soft she wanted to climb in right now and yield to it. Yet she couldn't stop thinking of the smell of earth and bark, and of a lush indigo vault with the moon shining out from it like a silver coin. She'd been lost, uncomfortable and afraid for her life, but would she ever again feel so strong and free?

She might have sat sighing for hours if there hadn't been a knock at the door. It was a girl, come from the Embassy with the bags. Mr. Firewalker had sent her in the Embassy carriage, she said, round eyed at the privilege. Now that it was no longer a bachelor establishment, Mrs. Hutchinson insisted on sending someone to keep house. Alice was not a ladies' maid, she admitted, but if Miss Bell required any assistance, she would be most pleased to help. Gertrude smiled. She was a student, she explained to the girl, and most accustomed to tending to her own hair and garments.

She proceeded to get off the chair and do so.

Gertrude followed her ears down the stairs. The sounds were coming from the kitchen. Everyone was there. The girl, Alice, was busy at the sink. Mr. Firewalker, who seemed accustomed to such tasks, was setting out the food on the scrubbed deal table.

Claude and her father leaned across from one another, elbows on the table, as they talked intently. No wonder Claude had gotten down so quickly. Her hair looked as if she'd only rubbed it a couple of times with a towel and maybe pulled a comb through. Seeing the damp chestnut tresses streaming down her back, Gertrude was irresistibly reminded of her schoolroom days with Maud.

"It's amazing how much you look like her!" she marveled. She hadn't meant to say it aloud.

"Bosh!" Claude couldn't have been more dismissive. "The Princess is a beauty!"

"Have you never looked in a mirror?" Gertrude rolled her eyes. She felt Frank's full attention turned on her.

"Miss Bell? I've wanted to hear an opinion other than my own. I did only see the Princess the one time. More than a superficial resemblance?"

This man was a scientist as well as a spy. Gertrude felt she needed to weigh her answer. She tried to view Claude as a stranger might. She rifled her memory for pictures of Maud: in the schoolroom; at balls and at court; more recently, giddy with mischief at having imperiously requested the use of a ptery and been granted it.

"Remarkably so," she said finally. "The princess is a tiny bit taller. And Claude is older, but with her hair down…" She opened her hands in surrender. "You're not at all alike as people," she spoke directly to Claude now. "But if someone didn't know you, or if you were dressed alike…It's really the eyes that make the difference." She looked back at Frank, smiling in recognition. "Claude's eyes are exactly like yours, sir. But the rest of her…I suppose she must resemble her mother's family."

"I've always supposed as much," Claude agreed. "But I thought my mother was French. The royal family are mostly German, aren't they? Or Habsburg?"

"There's some distant connection." Frank said hastily. "Unofficial, mind you."

"Through the Fitzrichards?" Gertrude found this intriguing. The Queen's uncle and predecessor had been famous for his illegitimate progeny.

Frank tapped the side of his nose. "And the Stuarts and the Menzies hail from the same clan lines, if you go back far enough."

"I'm sorry." Now Gertrude was puzzled. "I seem to have things muddled. Is the family name Menzies or Monteith?"

"Monteith," Claude said.

"Monteith isn't the name I was born with," Frank told his daughter. "In my line of work, it isn't always wise to travel under your true name. Our family name is Menzies. I changed it when you were very small and we moved to America."

It was like that day when the agents had come and she had started learning the truth about her father. "Is there anything else I should know, *Sir Alastair*?" Claude said icily, standing to glower across the table.

"You're wearing trousers!" Gertrude exclaimed. Claude was wearing a pair of what seemed like men's woolen pants, but they fit her as if they'd been made for her.

"Yes of course," Claude retorted. "And if I'd been wearing them when I faced those blasted vérfarkas, I would never have sprained my ankle."

"Your ankle?" Firewalker, paused in filling the glasses and knelt beside her to look.

"It's fine now. The Rom took care of it." She shooed him away and sat back down.

"What are vérfarkas?" Frank asked.

"Hasn't she told you?"

"I was waiting for you."

"We're all here now," Frank observed, picking up his knife and fork. "Start at the beginning."

As concisely as they could, Claude and Gertrude told what they could remember of their abductions and tried to put together a coherent picture of their days in Dubrovnik, when they had so rarely drifted back to reality.

"I tried to insist I was the one she wanted," Claude recalled. "I thought it would be what you'd have wanted me to do. But the Blavatsky woman…She had the most peculiar eyes. And the way she said it. 'You are not the princess we seek.' My mind could barely focus, but I remember this one thing so clearly; it seemed so strange," Claude mused. "I was devastated that I'd failed. I wanted to make you proud."

Frank reached across the table for her hand. "I'm always proud of you," he said. "If you don't know that, I'm the one at fault."

Claude smiled and squeezed back. "I know," she said. "I thought of you often." She turned to Firewalker. "Both of you. It made all the difference, having you with me." A shadow passed over her and she sighed. "If only I'd been able to help poor Nikola. You know, I thought at first that I was taken because I was with him, but really it was the other way round. Those men treated him horribly. His poor mind! It was worse even than when his mother died. Do you think Madame Blavatsky is still taking care of him?"

Frank cleared his throat and started to massage the sides of his nose. Claude regarded him with suspicion. "Father? What do you know?"

There was no point in beating around the bush. "I'm sorry, lass. Augustus has him."

"No!" she slammed her fist on the table and setting the dishes to rattling. "How? How did they find out who he was? I'd swear they didn't know. I never called him by name, and he always referred to himself as Kola."

"I don't know how they found out. I only know that they did, and they have him somewhere in Venice. He's alive and safe."

"Safe? Oh, Father, it's what he dreaded! You know he'll fall to pieces if he hasn't already." She fell back into her chair with a sob of despair.

Frank reached for her hands again. "Pinkerton has a man there, one of his best, keeping an eye on him."

"If he's so great, this spy of yours, then why doesn't he get him out?"

"He's working on it, lass. We all are. We'll get them both back, Tesla and the Princess."

She shook her head. "His body maybe," she said with a small sniff. "Not his mind."

"We have the drarnego," Gertrude, practical, reminded her.

"That will only counter the effects of whatever drugs might be in his system. I don't think it can heal his mind. But I suppose we can try." Claude tried to sound firm. A moment's weakness was an allowable indulgence; more than that was out of the question. "Remind me, when we do our shopping, I need to get a small copper box for the dried leaves. And a spoon."

"And more silver needles," Gertrude reminded her.

"Silver needles?" Frank was perplexed.

Gertrude looked to her reluctant friend. "You have to tell this part," she said. "I can't. I don't know it all."

Claude nodded and took a deep breath. She told her Father and Firewalker of what she had thought was a vision quest: of the things she'd seen and heard; and how all the skills they'd ever taught her had kept Gertrude and herself alive. The story spilled out of her. She hadn't thought she'd remembered so much until she'd started the telling. The hardest part of the story was her battle with the two monsters.

Her voice was the only sound in the room. The men didn't say a word. Gertrude was equally riveted. The only version she had heard was Yoska's, which had been overly imaginative and told in rough German. Claude's more laconic description was twice as chilling.

For all that it was summer, the atmosphere in the room was as clammy as a London fog. Frank left the room and returned with a bottle of brandy. He poured a small, therapeutic glass for each of them. They drank in silence until the girls were able to continue and tell the story of poor Beznik. When Claude finished describing her Prometheum bomb, Frank hugged her so hard that Gertrude thought she heard ribs cracking.

"What do you think of that, Lem?" he chortled. "A true Franklin! My lass is worth more than all the sons in the world!"

Gertrude hadn't known a girl could blush so red.

Firewalker, in his sober way, was also beaming. "It was all well done, mit'anksi."

"You're not yet done with inventions, my lass," Frank told Claude. "Wait until you see the improvements we've made to the automatons."

"Gertrude, didn't I tell you? I knew you'd be working on them!"

"We'll make better progress now that there are three of us."

"Can we see them now?"

"Tomorrow," Frank said firmly. "If we go to the workshop now, you know what will happen. We'd still be there at midnight. I think you and Miss Bell should have one proper night's rest."

It sounded too heavenly to refuse.

17 - CAPRICIOUS FORTUNE

The Princess's futile attempt to release herself from the medication had been more debilitating than initially divulged. Dottore Catoni prohibited visitors for several days.

Effectively off duty, and with the Baron out of town, Micah had more time to expand on the Roman version of the network of resources that he had built in Venice and that his Italian cousins had in play in Naples and Florence. Dressed in workman's clothes, a soft cap pulled low on his forehead, he lingered in dingy *birrerias* and *caffès*, cementing alliances with men of political passion. He took extensive walks through the city, mapping it with his feet as well as his head, paying particular attention to areas of egress and to those twisted warrens of abiding poverty where a person might easily disappear.

For more immediate purposes, the centurion Rappaccini continued to be seen loitering hopefully near the Villa Borghese for an hour or two each day, charming maidservants and cultivating the fellowship of footmen, guards and grooms.

Micah also made careful reconnaissance of the presumptive site of the (prayerfully, never-to-be) wedding. This was pleasure as well as business. The Colosseum was an endless source of fascination to him.

Sacconi, busy as he was, was always willing to make time for the Baron's favourite Centurion and point out things of interest. Micah was especially enthralled by the efforts being made below ground, in the stone maze that Sacconi taught him to call the 'hypogeum.' Before his current assignment, he had once spent several months exploring a similar region at D'Oyly Carte's new Savoy Theatre. Disguised as a member of the chorus, he successfully uncovered an Italian spy who had concealed himself in the orchestra as a second trombone. Along the way, Micah saw a great deal of the hidden world of wings and traps and flies that surrounds a stage; but even the ultra-modern, all-electric Savoy was nothing compared to what Sacconi revealed to him beneath the legendary Roman arena. The tunnels and niches of the hypogeum held a small city of dressing rooms, storage rooms and rooms whose original purpose had been mercifully obliterated by time, as well as a wood shop, a working forge, an armory, what looked for all the world like a dry dock, and two machine shops to support the intricate system of winches and pulleys and fans that sustained the entire complex. He watched some workmen testing out a set of hydraulic lifts that he was astounded to learn were carefully restored originals.

"The ancestors used to flood the arena to stage naval battles," Sacconi explained. "These were used to hoist scenery above the water line. At least, that's what we can figure from descriptions of the time."

"Does Caesar plan to flood the arena?" Rappaccini asked, in some awe.

"Someday?" Sacconi shrugged. "Why not? If they could do it then, why shouldn't we be able to do it now? That and more." He scanned his list. "You must excuse me. I am off to the Istituto to inspect the progress on the seat cushions. The Baron will not accept them if they aren't perfect."

"The Baron is a demanding master," Rappaccini observed.

Sacconi allowed his usual mask of good humor to drop. "Were it not for the Baron, I'd be building sheds in Pisa with my father and brothers. That is, if there'd been enough work for one more man. Otherwise, I'd have been conscripted for farm labour. He sent me to school in Switzerland, had me trained in math and engineering...You're a soldier. The Empire always has schools for soldiers." This was said without resentment, as a matter of fact. "But for men like me...I couldn't dare to dream of this. Whatever he asks me to do, I must think it a privilege to serve him."

It was well that he'd made such good use of that time. When Rappaccini was finally allowed back to the Villa Borghese, he saw that the work of several weeks had washed away like a sandcastle meeting the tide.

The Princess had regressed to the same state of lassitude that he'd found on his very first visit. Although functionally alert for longer periods of time, she'd been demoralized by her inability to fight off her dependency. Her body craved the drug and she was too weak to resist that craving.

Moreover, without the Baron to intercede, a mere centurion was unable to budge the Emperor's family from their constant attendance. Micah had only a few minutes safe speech with her at any time. She was gracious and sweet to her visitor—had he spent any time with her before her abduction, he would have been surprised at just how gracious and sweet—but the spark that he thought he'd kindled was gone. The Princess was a sleepwalker. It only confirmed his earliest impressions. Somehow Rappaccini needed to get himself reassigned to Venice.

❧

Madam Blavatsky was as efficient as the Baron had anticipated. Warburg's Tincture hadn't even begun to take effect on Tesla before the little healer arrived from Dubrovnik. She was an exotic figure in her Eastern draperies and sandals, a filigree of red tracings on her delicate hands and, the Baron couldn't help but notice, nearly naked feet.

Her chest of supplies was nearly as large as she. The Baron sent an amphoraka to take it from the boat and was pleased to see her recoil. It was not in his nature to find pleasure in the fear of others, but this fear would be her security and his peace of mind.

Haussmann greeted the young woman with the respect due to her mistress. He would have exerted himself to set her at ease except that she insisted, with trembling dignity, on being brought directly to her patient. With the nurse here, Haussmann felt free to decamp to the Contessa's palazzo that very afternoon. Why shouldn't he enjoy the delights La Serenissima had to offer? Tesla was doing nothing but sleep.

After a satisfactorily epicurean breakfast the next morning, the Baron returned to the fornace and spent several hours in the workshop. Drawings were sorted; some were placed in a leather portfolio. Selected models were crated up. Today he would take the boat back to the Dorsoduro. Once he was assured that the young man was out of danger, then he would depart for Roma.

Sandtmann and the other amphoraeka watched what they could of what the Baron took, and worked to remember what they saw.

Tashi had been taught many things by Madame Blavatsky and, before that, by the aunts who had taken her infant self to their care. Other things she knew by instinct or perhaps, Ama said, from a former life. It was her path to be a healer. Her karma had led her to Ama, and had crossed with the karma of this poor broken man. She knew it was wrong to feel anger, but she had been angry when Ama had separated them in the carriage. She'd sensed a wrongness in the shape of the world, a wrongness that hadn't abated even after she returned from the woods and Ama called her to the solar to meditate. With each step she took, Tashi felt she put out a foot to walk on ground that wasn't there. Her relief at the Baron's call had been as great as her concern for Kola. The fabric of the world was whole again. She had hurried to assemble all she might need to take with her, but Ama, in communication with the Masters, had already done so.

Ama, as benevolent as the sun, as nurturing as rain, gave Tashi all that she might need and more, including much wise advice and her special blessing. They would not meet again in this lifetime, Ama informed her, but they were bound forever.

Tashi had no plans for forever, but she knew exactly what she had to do now. Warburg's Tincture was immediately replaced by Madame's own cinchona brew. Bandages, to be kept constantly moist with an aromatic oil, were wrapped as a neckcloth and around the patient's wrists. In a fleeting moment of clarity, Tesla was terrified to feel himself bound and let out a yell. He was so weak that the sound disappeared in his chest, but Tashi saw his shoulders jerk forward with the effort. Standing where he could see her, she touched a hand to either side of his face, assuring him that she was real. The little nurse slept on a pallet on the floor beside Tesla's bed. She tended him as he shuttled between burning and freezing, fed him by hand, and massage his throbbing temples with a soothing balm. She sang the same lilting chant that had comforted him in the house in Dubrovnik.

At the beginning and end of each visit to the fornace, the Baron mounted the stairs to check on the patient's progress. Tashi let him enter the sickroom, but stood fiercely beside the bed until he left. It was her inner voice that told her to do so; Ama had given her no instructions about the old man who was not quite Italian, only about the younger one.

Rappaccini played the piano, while the two royal maidens worked on a bit of tapestry. More accurately stated, Ginevre bent over the frame and carefully drew her needle through the linen. Maud toyed with skeins of coloured silk, taking them from her sewing basket and sorting them into heaps that were related in ways only she might understand. With his own mind free to wander, Micah tried to conceive of ways he might smuggle Nikola Tesla off Murano. Should he leave a decoy in place, or would that not be worth the risk to Tucker? They could stage Tesla's suicide, but how might this be done without the Baron blaming Rappaccini?

"A melancholy tune, Centurion. Not what I would choose to delight the ears of a bride."

He had been so engrossed in his schemes that he hadn't noticed Caesar's entrance. He jumped from the bench and gave his deepest bow.

"Altezza, if I have offended the ladies or your illustrious self, I offer my most humble and sincere remorse. Please. I had not thought…"

Augustus pushed away the apology with the back of his hand. Micah noticed the large cabochon emerald, carved with the same symbol as both the Baron's ring and the bronze disk used on Murano; it was the scarab glyph that controlled the amphoraeka. "The young often confuse melancholy with sentiment. Resume your seat, Centurion. We will educate you. Rafello?"

The curly-haired eunuch stepped out from the cluster of attendants that had followed the Emperor. He cradled his ever-present lute and began to sing a French folksong of cloying sweetness. Augustus sat between the two young women, holding the nearest hand of each. He stroked their fingers in time with the tune, his eyes half-closed in bliss. Micah couldn't stand to watch; he turned back to the keyboard and began to delicately follow the castrato's lead.

"A valuable thing, education," Augustus crooned, as the song drew to a close. "Perhaps someday it will make you a courtier, Centurion; but not so quickly. You are a new man, with much to learn. You interest me, Centurion. I hear your praises from a number of corners and, if my granddaughter's taste can be trusted, you are considered pleasing to look upon."

Micah chivalrously averted his eyes from Ginevre's vivid flush.

"An ambitious young man, I would say. Ambition is a character with two edges, like a sword. I notice you have been most assiduous in your attendance on my daughter. Has he amused you, my pearl?"

Augustus lifted Maud's chin with his finger and examined her face.

Micah held his breath in fear. From whence had sprung this unusual enmity? He had been acutely circumspect in his dealings with any member of the Imperial family and their household. To his considerable relief, he had rarely met Caesar. Did Augustus suspect something? Or had Rappaccini's swagger been so successful that Augustus thought he was trying to seduce the Princess?

Nearly anything Maud would say might damn him now.

She said nothing. She didn't even blink. It was as if she weren't present.

Her lack of reaction satisfied Augustus. Releasing her, he pursed his lips in a parody of mirth. "Perhaps, Centurion, you overestimate your charms. Young women can be fickle, can they not? No matter. I am planning a charming diversion for my pearl of great price. An excursion to a delightful little island."

At a loss for how to respond, Micah decided Rappaccini would smile eagerly.

"A *family* excursion," Caesar continued, pointedly. "It is time for my pearl to learn to love her bridegroom. Your attendance will not be required."

🙚

It was a subdued Tesla who was eventually led down the stairs. His eyes were deeply shadowed and his body seemed to hang on his bones like a worn-out suit of clothes. He had an air of having come from far away.

Haussmann was delighted to see the scientist on his feet. "We must get you back to strength! Take a fortnight or two as a holiday and do nothing. Nothing at all! I would send you to the mountains but frankly Tesla, even in your weakened condition, I can't trust you." The Baron gave a rueful chuckle. "You must rest yourself here. Whatever your good nurse here requires, whatever might please you to have brought, you need only ask. I return to Roma tomorrow. The monks should find plenty enough to do with what you've already drafted. When this other business is concluded, I'll return and we will continue on together, you and I."

Tesla nodded; that was all he had the energy to do.

Tesla woke in the middle of the night. Weak as he was, his body was tired of sleeping; he had slept so much during this illness. He was hungry. He swung his legs carefully over the side of the bed, so as not to disturb Tashi. He had forgotten that, now that his fever had passed, the little nurse had finally agreed to sleep on the divan in the workroom. His feet grazed the floor and he tried to stand. It was surprisingly complicated to make his body obey. The bedpost helped.

Tashi had insisted that, after a prolonged diet of broth and barley water, his stomach needed to be gradually re-accustomed to food. She had fed him like a baby today: toast fingers dipped in boiled egg, weak tea with honey, a bit of fish with no sauce. It wasn't remotely enough for a grown man; no wonder he felt so weak. There must be something else in the kitchen. Also, he would like to have a few minutes alone with Dov; it would be good to reassure him that all was well.

Moving slowly and keeping both hands on the bannister, Tesla slipped down the stairs as softly as he could. Almost as if he had known to wait, Dov was standing outside the kitchen. Tesla grabbed the huge clay arm for support and pushed himself up on the balls of his feet, to be as close to his friend's face as possible. "You were right, Dov," he whispered. "I *was* ill. Malaria they say. But I'm fine now." He couldn't hold himself up any longer, so he patted Dov on the chest. "Just a little hungry. Don't worry. I'll be fine."

His eyes were accustomed to the dark, but things had been shifted around. Nothing was where he remembered it being. He wanted a wedge of cheese, but couldn't find any. He settled for another slice of bread, which he slathered with some kind of jam. Peach or apricot, he wasn't sure; his tongue still wore the fever coat that made everything taste dull. The bread helped to fill the hole in his stomach, but it wasn't enough. He started opening cupboards and found a hard cured Italian sausage that seemed promising. He bit off a piece. It was salty and not all that easy to chew, but it was meaty and presently seemed like the most desirable food in the world. He kept biting and chewing, occasionally taking a swig from the pitcher of barley water Tashi had left in the ice closet, until he'd polished it off.

It was lucky that he was standing by the sink. There wasn't even time to burp before his stomach rejected the whole salty, fatty, jammy mess. It came spewing out with such violence that he could hardly hold onto the ledge. Even when there was nothing left inside, his body kept heaving until he thought his stomach itself would come flopping out like a slimy, deflated red balloon. Tashi had been right. The strain was too much for a body only recently racked with malarial shakes. He heard the blood thundering behind his ears, and the fireworks began to explode.

"Nooo!" he moaned, falling to his knees.

Outside the kitchen, Sandtmann began to swing his arm against the wall. The pounding broke into Tashi's dream, which changed briefly to a dream about drums before waking her. She flew towards the noise to find her patient collapsed nearly unconscious on the kitchen floor.

She couldn't raise his body but, with more strength than might have been supposed, managed to drag him through the doorway by his legs. She made up a bed of cushions on the workroom floor and rolled Tesla onto it. His eyes reacted strongly to the lamp. A quick examination satisfied her that it wasn't the ague. She covered him with the blanket she had for the divan and put a damp cloth over his forehead and eyes.

The amphoraka took up a position in the corner, watching. Though Tashi had gotten over her initial fear of the creatures, they made her uncomfortable. Her skin prickled in their presence. She looked up at this one now and felt inexplicably sad. She nodded and left him standing sentry while she went to scrub out the kitchen.

It was a fleeting headache, almost a reflex. If he hadn't been weakened by the malaria, it might not have happened at all. Tesla was awakened at dawn by the first light of day and a stupendous idea.

In the thrall of a vision, Tesla lost all judgment. He knew only that he had seen perfection and was compelled to bring it into being. Rushing past his sleeping nurse to his work table, he began to sketch. If this worked in life as he'd envisioned it, the amphoraeka would be like gods. No man would be able to stand before their might. He sketched madly, without a single false stroke, then stumbled upstairs to his bed and fell into a sound sleep.

Sandtmann moved slowly to the table. He remembered Kola's visions. The notes on these pages were likely to be pure genius but, whatever they might be, until his friend was alert enough to grasp what he had conceived, it was essential that the Emperor's Baron not see them.

Dov hoisted a massive clay arm and dragged his hand so that the papers were pushed to the floor. The room held few hiding spaces, and none that an oversized statue might reach. It would be simpler to destroy the sketches; he need only tear them to bits underfoot. He couldn't bring himself to do it. The only acceptable option was to place them where they might be overlooked.

He thought he could push them under the divan, where Tashi slept the sleep of the just. It was a delicate procedure. He slid his foot forward. His body weight was too great; the papers began to crumple like a concertina, exactly what he'd wanted to avoid. If only this detested carapace could bend! That something so simple should be unworkable. All he wanted to do was sweep some paper under a piece of furniture. Of course! Why must he overcomplicate things? Kola had always laughed at him for it. There were no brooms, but there were plenty of long sticks of copper tubing propped against the shelves. The longest came easily to reach. He held it between his hands and pushed at the now-crinkled pages, inching them out of plain sight.

Haussmann arrived with a complement of soldiers to load his crates and folios onto the boat. The precious archive would travel with him in his private railway car to Roma.

Tashi was in the kitchen, making a list of supplies. The room, the Baron noted with admiration, was sparkling. There was nothing like a woman's touch.

"He sleeps," she told the Baron, before he could ask. "He was restless last night. Now he sleeps."

"Are you certain you can handle him?" the Baron asked. "I will have di Bari send you someone…"

She shook her head. "Now all will be well. Now he will listen."

The Baron nodded. She was probably correct. Nothing like a little illness to keep a man in line. "Signor Bosco will come every day. You need only ask for something and he will bring it."

She pressed her hands together, as Madame's people did, and bowed from the waist.

"Yes, well then. Should you need to contact me…"

Once again, Baron Haussmann returned from Venezia to find a messenger camped out in his foyer. He had begun to detest the sight of the unnaturally deferential urchins in their ill-fitting livery. Spotting one at his door was like opening an umbrella in the house; something unfortunate was certain to rain down on him. Today, it was an invitation to join the Imperial family holiday. Rather than spending the next ten days in the Colosseum, where his attentions were sorely needed, the Baron would be spending them in Capri. Moreover, his pet centurion had been explicitly uninvited.

"I don't know what I might have done to offend Caesar, Eminenza," Rappaccini very nearly whined. He thought it wise to be preemptive and had bribed one of the Villa Alsaziano's servants to alert him to the Baron's arrival.

"Nothing to concern yourself about," the Baron sighed. He wouldn't have minded being in the Centurion's shoes right now. It was inconvenient to be in the bosom of the Imperial family when one had responsibilities elsewhere. "You are a fine looking young fellow, Rappaccini, and the Principessa is at ease in your company. Caesar quite wisely wishes to ensure there is nothing—perhaps I should say no one—to distract her from admiring the qualities of her future husband."

"I understand, Eminenza." He bowed his head and attempted to look nobly resigned. "Then will you be terminating my assignment and returning me to my commandante?"

Haussmann shook his head. "I prefer that you be available, should the Principessa require, when we return from Capri. There will be much to do between now and the wedding. After that, I expect to have more challenging work for you, in Murano."

"I understand, Eminenza."

The Baron looked at him thoughtfully. "I believe you do. You've done an excellent job for me Rappaccini. There's no reason why you shouldn't have a holiday as well. Your woman must be longing for your presence."

"How did you...?" Rappaccini's mistress was, deliberately, an open secret, but he had never discussed her with the Baron. Had the Baron been doing his own spying?"

"Aha!" the Baron twinkled. "I was certain that a man of your virtues would have a beautiful young woman tucked away somewhere."

"In Venezia." Rappaccini shrugged with obvious false modesty.

"Perhaps she deserves a holiday as well. Lake Como is lovely at this time of year. You might take her to Vienna, if she's fond of music."

"There wouldn't be time, Eminenza."

"Nonsense. We won't be returning to Roma for nine or ten days. Take all of them. Enjoy yourself. You've earned it."

"Thank you, Eminenza. That is most generous." Rappaccini bowed.

"And Rappaccini..." the Baron stopped him. "I have everything nicely in hand in Venezia, and I consider you off duty, but as long as you're passing through, if you wouldn't mind taking a quick look in on Tesla..."

&

On the chance that the sight of the Imperial yacht might distress the Princess, Rappaccini had been asked to be among those escorting the royals to the port. The physician, who was included in the party to Capri, stood at her elbow.

They need not have worried. Maud had no recollection of her voyage from Dubrovnik; she'd been reliably unconscious the entire time. Today she stepped from her coach onto the pier with the slow grace that had become hers, and with not a bit of hesitation.

Rappaccini bowed deeply and moved away. His heart could not afford pity.

A few hours later, a centurion lounged in the smoking car of the Venice-bound train, stretching his legs to better admire the deep polish of his boots, and commandeering refreshments with military insolence. It was expected.

Micah sorted his plan while the countryside shuttled past the windows. The Baron's sympathetic lechery had provided most of it. He would install Tucker on Murano, and instruct him to let his beard grow and skulk in the shadows. Neither of them were assassins, and it was distasteful to contemplate the act, but they would have to deal with Blavatsky's little minion; there was no choice. Then, with Elettra's help, he would disguise Tesla as his mistress and they would travel openly together to Prague. It was bold, but with a heavy enough veil it should work. He would wire Pinkerton from the Embassy. They could get some good British security in place to protect Tesla's workshop. At the end of his holiday, Rappaccini would return to Rome. As long as someone remained in the fornace making a mess and eating the food, di Bari's attendante would be none the wiser and, with the Baron remaining in Rome until the wedding, neither would anyone else. It wasn't as though the amphoraeka could talk! Tucker would be perfectly safe.

Yes, it was a plan that would work. A pity he couldn't rescue the Princess as well, but he was merely a British spy, not a mythical Greek hero. He thought he was doing well with the hand he had been dealt. He hoped Pinkerton and the Queen agreed.

The gardens at the Nido D'Aquila had always been a delight to the senses. They had been a pet project of Caesar's mother, Ginevre of Lorraine, a gracious gentle lady with a love of gardening and an unfashionable preference for the local flora of Capri over transplanted curiosities. When the young Georges-Eugène Haussmann was assigned to organize the terraces and the drainage, he had found it as much a pleasure as a great honour.

The Baron raised his flask in silent salute to her memory. It saddened him that she hadn't lived to see more than the first seasons of growth. She had made something truly lovely. If he couldn't be doing what he needed to at the Colosseum, there was some solace in this beautiful place that he shared with the ghost of his younger self.

That ghost was a dangerous companion, a reminder of a time when Haussmann had been his own man, when dreams had been untainted by what might have to be traded to see them brought to life. Not that Haussmann had ever been an innocent, not even as a youth. His practical Alsatian father taught him that to court the affection of the great was to rise in the world. As a young engineer, helping to raise Alexandria from the rubble, he'd grasped that his own ambition was to build cities. The favour of the ruler would be necessary to his future. While the Great Napoleon lingered through his final years, voiceless and half paralyzed from the apoplexy, Haussmann played a careful game of courtship with Augustus, the heir. Wielding flattery and discretion, he turned himself into his own pawn. He learned when not to speak, when not to act and which ideas to forfeit. He allowed himself to think that the bargains he made were trivial. In particular, he taught himself not to judge Augustus's actions. In order to do great things, one had to be ruthless. Just as it was necessary to clear the slums that had grown over the bones of ancient Roma, it was necessary for Augustus to protect his empire by consolidating his power; slum dwellers were displaced and rebels died. If taxes were so high as to be punitive, it must be thought of as the price of building a strong empire. If freedoms were curtailed, if education was limited, this was the price of peace until the unity of Italy had been established for a sufficient number of generations to ensure it would remain so.

For some time Haussmann thought himself succeeding in a clever masquerade, that he was manipulating Augustus into supporting his schemes. Burying himself in his work, he pretended not to see beyond his boulevards and shining buildings. By the time he realized that he had become Augustus's man in all but the most hidden corner of his soul, it was too late. He could remember that day: the day some thirty years ago when he was introduced to the Golden One. At first he thought the rude statue to be another of Augustus's humorless jokes. It was Giulia's behaviour that convinced him of the truth. Giulia kept one hand resting lightly on her rounding belly, the other clutching desperately at Augustus. Her eyes were overly bright and she had the hectic manner of the deranged. Until that day, Haussmann had kept his eyes firmly shut against the nature of the relationship between Augustus and the niece he called "daughter." That day, the veil lifted from this and other incontestable truths. The man with one arm around the young woman and the other caressing a gilded block of clay was not merely eccentric and uncompromising; he was mad.

Even as Haussmann silently acknowledged Caesar's total madness, he understood the degree of his own entrapment. It would have been impossible to escape with his life. Georges-Eugene Haussmann was not prepared to die, so he trained himself to forget what he had previously ignored. Did any deity exist to judge him, and his scientific nature was not convinced there did, then he was already damned for his complicity. For the rest of his life, he abjured no deed that would further the one creation he knew would exist beyond his lifetime: Roma. Whenever ghosts threatened, or when the sentimentality of old age caused a temporary weakness of the heart, as it had once with regard to Tesla, the Baron need only walk the boulevards or contemplate his elegantly crafted scale model to remind himself of the vastness of his achievement. There was little point regretting the means to such a glorious result.

The Baron was only melancholy because he was away from his masterpiece. He breathed as deeply as his aging lungs would allow, \the mingled fragrance of lemon and rosemary bringing him, as always, tranquility. His own trees had begun as cuttings from this grove. It would please him no end to linger here alone with the lemons and his better memories. Alas, he was expected soon at a picnic on a cliff.

&.

The tent pavilion shimmered white against the deep blue sky and, in the distance, the deeper blue waters. Dining couches, draped with silken covers, had been carried up the path so that the Imperial family might lounge in traditional Roman style. The men wore tunics and togas, the women, stolae; all were garlanded with greenery and flowers. Chitoned servers circulated with heaping trays of summer fruits and *frutti di mare*. Rafello perched with his lute on a dramatic slab of ash-coloured rock, the clear notes dancing on the air. Every detail was precisely as Augustus had specified. He ought to have been blissful. Instead, he glared across the tent, his famous brow furrowed in umbrage.

Adjusting his scratchy wreath, the Baron followed the glare to a double-couch. Prince Gusto had his mother's gentle brown eyes and a sweep of dark hair that softened the Buonoparte brow. When he did manage to smile, his smile was very sweet. He was tall enough for most, nearly of a height with his bride, but he rarely held himself to his full height. The Principessa, crowned with sweet freesia, the soft white folds of her gown spilling over the sides of the couch, looked more like sculpture than ever. Reposing side by side, like figures on a tomb, the young pair barely acknowledged one another. "They make a handsome couple," Haussmann assured Caesar.

"Pah!" Augustus wiped his mouth and reached for another fig. "Where is the heat in that boy?"

"The Principe is a little shy of her, I think. She is very beautiful. And, excepting his honoured aunts and sisters, she is the grandest principessa he's ever met."

"At that age, I would have been chomping at the bit to tumble her. If I had been told she was my bride, I'd have hauled her out to the wildest part of the gardens to steal a kiss or two at least, maybe grab a quick feel."

"He is beautifully mannered, as befits a prince. Very chivalrous."

"He's weak!" The Emperor's left arm was troubling him again. He signaled for Khristos, who he'd taken to having follow him throughout the day. The muscular Greek was almost instantly kneeling beside him, kneading the offending limb. "If only I could be certain that the cock would function as well as the mind, I wouldn't wait another hour to perform the Ceremony. But I dare not risk it, not until I have absolutely guaranteed another heir of the blood. I cannot mate them soon enough for my needs. I only hope the boy is up to the task."

"On the day, he will be as up to it as any bridegroom," the Baron assured him, understanding none of this except the last expressed hope. "And once the benediction is pronounced, she will have no choice but to welcome him with open arms."

"Open legs is all that matters," Augustus grumbled. "I have half a mind to do the job myself, in this old body. But not before they are duly married, with pomp and ceremony enough that none in the world can contest it. There mustn't be the slightest shadow of illegitimacy over her child." Any trace of lechery had been replaced by purest calculation. "Only in the name of a legitimate heir to England's throne may the Third Augustus," his raised eyebrows in Gusto's direction were as good as quotation marks, "rightfully reclaim Britannia for Our Empire."

The Baron waited in well-considered silence. It was not politic to acknowledge receipt of such confidences.

"It will be a long year." The Emperor spoke again at last. "And my doctors would do well to see that I last it out. Tell me Baron, how prospers your other efforts on my account?"

The Baron risked a mild pleasantry. "You mean what news from the Rialto?"

Augustus looked at him blankly. "From Venezia, Baron. What news from Venezia?"

❧

Rappaccini went straight to the barracks, to say hello and buy a round of grappa for some of his fellows. He told some mildly salacious stories of life in Roma and bragged about his current leave.

"I can't do without you, Young Rappaccini; that's what the Baron said."

"He never did!"

Rappaccini nodded. "Embraced me with tears in his eyes, like a father. Told me to take my woman on holiday and, eh, get my strength up."

There were envious snickers. That was the point. He wanted to be sure word got around that Rappaccini was taking his mistress on a romantic holiday with the Baron's sanction.

He signaled the barkeeper for another round and set down a generous tip. "And now you will excuse me, gentlemen, but I must share the glad tidings with the lady in question."

First he went to pay his respects to his commandante. Di Bari was out, but Rappaccini had a brief gossip with the Praefectus and let him know he'd be visiting Murano on the Baron's behalf.

The Praefectus confided that Bosco would be pleased to be able to miss a day. It was clear that the usually complacent attendante was not enjoying his assignment. In fact, he had been heard to say that he would rather handle feedings at the zoological gardens than tend to the Baron's guest.

Micah was so frustrated that he could have ripped the hair from his own scalp. His plan depended on a cooperative Nikola Tesla. The inventor might be slightly mad, but until now he'd shown eagerness to thwart his nemesis, the Baron. It was that residual spark, as well as the treasure in his brain, that had always made him the stronger candidate for escape, but the Tesla that he found in the garden of the fornace was as much a shadow as Princess Maud.

"You look well." Micah tried a falsely jovial clap of the shoulders. "If I hadn't been told, I would never have guessed you'd been so ill."

"I am well cared for," Tesla said listlessly.

"The Baron seemed extremely pleased with your work," Micah said, perching casually on the other end of the bench.

"Then he hasn't spotted the flaws. That's good." He plucked a blade of grass and cupped his hands over it, trying to make it whistle.

"Excellent," Micah agreed. "What progress have you made on the other front?" Tesla looked at him blankly. "Weren't you trying to learn more about what might be used to destroy the trecika? Some information I could try and get to your Frank?"

"I had some thoughts. But not anything useful."

"Talk me through them. I'm not an engineer but trying to explain them might help."

"They're all dead ends."

"I'd still like to see them."

"Nothing to see. I didn't commit it to paper." Tesla gave a wan smile. "A good thing as it turned out. The Baron had hours here on his own to comb through everything. Then he packed it all up and took it with him."

Micah was confused. "How does he expect you to work if he took everything?"

"I'm on holiday." Tesla gestured grandly at the stunted garden. "With Tashi here, I don't even have to worry about feeding myself. I can spend all my hours sitting in the sun and having meaningless conversations with imaginary friends."

"You know I'm not imaginary, Tesla. Could your imagination do this?" Micah pinched the inventor on the wrist.

Tesla barely flinched. "Probably."

"Wait until tomorrow when you have a mark to show for it."

Tesla laughed. "Are you a Catholic, Italian Englishman? Haven't you heard of people displaying the stigmata? The mind." He tapped his temple. "All powerful."

"We need to get you back to Prague." Micah stood decisively, as if he were about to haul the other man onto a train right there and then.

"Why? There's nothing I can do. It's missing." Tesla rubbed his head despondently. "Everything is missing. Let Frank do it. He can, better than I. He'll take care of everything."

"Without you?"

Tesla shrugged. The amphoraka was more communicative.

Micah had to wake the man. Tesla still thought the prisoner was Sir Alastair's daughter. "You haven't even asked about your young woman."

He didn't expected an explosion. Tesla jumped up to face him, his face flooded scarlet. Before he could raise a hand to block it, Tesla had jabbed a finger into the base of his throat. It was a singularly effective thrust. Micah doubled up, trying to catch his breath.

"You said *you* would protect her!" Tesla hissed. "If she's been harmed...I *would* kill you, you know. You see now how easily I can do it." He bared his teeth and leaned too close. Micah could smell his breath, sour from illness.

"She's well," he croaked. He compelled himself to stand upright and look calmly into the crazed eyes. "She's very well. And completely safe. I meant to reassure you."

"I shouldn't have done that." It was reflection, not apology. "I'm glad she's well. That's fine then. Now I need to sleep. This is too hard. I can't do this any more." He spun around, and stumbled through the workroom door.

Still gasping painfully, Micah followed. He would have followed Tesla up the stairs except that Tashi, who had heard the clatter from the kitchen, stopped him and led him back to the workroom.

"What was that about?" He couldn't speak without coughing.

Tashi shrugged. "He was sick."

"I know. Malarial ague."

"No. The night before the old man left. He was sick. He wants to be empty."

This made no more sense to him than Tesla's behaviour. "You're a nurse. Would you have something...? My throat."

"Some tea," she nodded. She seemed about to head back to the kitchen when she gave an odd shudder and turned back. She pointed to the low divan with her little sandaled foot. "There. I think he," she jerked her head in the direction of the ever-present amphoraka, "wants you to have this."

"This?" There was nothing to see except a heap of neatly folded bedclothes.

In a single fluid motion, Tashi squatted and pulled out a mess of papers. They were schematics and notes in a familiar scrawl.

"Tesla kept these for me? He said the Baron had everything."

"Not Kola. This one here." She flicked her hand briefly at the amphoraka, simultaneously acknowledging and ignoring it. "I hear them together."

"Talking?" This couldn't be possible. Micah had spent enough time with the creatures. If they could make a sound, he'd know it.

She shook her head. "Not with words. With sounds like this." She brought her little fist down once on the table. "They think they're quiet, but I can hear. I don't understand them."

"Why do you think these are for me?"

"They were hidden from the old man. When I found them, I went to put them on the table. Then I could feel him watching me." Her shoulder's twitched again. "I knew he did not want them to be found, so I left them where they were. So they are not for Kola to have either."

"But why me?"

"He stares to keep me here, and does not stop me," she said simply. "And Ama told me to expect you. She says that your karma, like mine, is linked to Kola's. You are the one who acts. What you decide, I am to follow."

"Thank you." Micah was abashed that he had even thought about eliminating this woman. She was turning out to be his greatest ally. "You speak English well," he observed.

"We have the English in my country." She pressed her palms together and bowed. "I will put a kettle for you. Then I will see to my patient."

Micah spread the papers out so that he could see them. He could make neither head nor tails of the drawings, but assumed they must be important.

"So, Signore," he addressed the amphoraeka. "Can you explain these to me?"

The amphoraeka didn't move an inch.

"If you can speak, this would be an excellent time to do so." The effort made him cough again. Coughing hurt worse than speaking. Micah pulled the chair out from behind the table, so that he could gaze comfortably up at the clay face. "I have some knowledge of your kind," he said conversationally. "A man I knew, a man I respected, told me something I will now tell you, as a show of good faith."

When he had told Zacuto's story, bringing a surprised tear to his own eye, the creature still had not moved. Micah sighed. "Well then, if you have no objections and I cannot read them, I will see if I can find someone else who can. With any luck, in Prague." He carefully stacked the pages on the table, to roll them into a cylinder.

A tapping sound made him look up. The amphoraeka was hitting his leg with a piece of copper tubing. The rhythmic beat reminded Micah of something.

"Your pardon," he said, trying to concentrate. "Would you please begin again, more slowly?"

This time, Micah understood. It was Morse Code. He had to transcribe it to understand the rueful sentence. "I DID NOT THINK TO PRAY."

❧

Rappaccini had booked a sleeper car, as was mandatory for a rising young centurion taking his mistress on holiday, but he could not sleep. There were too many thoughts chasing around Micah's head, things he had discussed with the amphoraka who he must learn to think of as Dov Sandtmann. He dared not write them down, not in a train full of Romans with a series of border crossings yet to come. He needed to rehearse the facts until he was safely in Prague. With any luck, the Ambassador would be able to tell him the whereabouts of Sir Alastair Menzies. If not, at least he would have a secure wire at his disposal.

Leaving the loyal Elettra curled demurely on her couch, he wandered down to the smoking car to indulge in brandy and cigars until the first streaks of dawn painted the sky.

❧

As the day began to cool, the light that suffused the room shifted to a flattering lavender grey. The Lady Giulia stretched across her couch, a voluptuous stretch that rippled from her throat all the way down through the arched and bony foot that she used to kick away the *pescatore* who had so satisfactorily completed his commission. The young man rolled to the floor and, clutching his garments to cover his private parts, scurried from the room without another word. She admired his celerity almost as much as his lean, tanned flanks.

Apollinaris had chosen well; but then who should know her taste better than he, who lived only to please her? She liked them broad-shouldered, with a slim waist and hips, and long legs; tall men, who amused her by looking down, as if they could ever make Giulia Buonaparte feel small. It had been vexing of Patre to bar the Baron's pet centurion from their island excursion. He was just the type she favoured. His face was handsome as well, those piercing eyes and the mobile and somehow mocking mouth. He intrigued her. She could smell a hunger in him, the kind of hunger that made men ripe for the picking but also made them think they could be dangerous. It was diverting to flirt with men who thought themselves dangerous. When they became tiresome, it was simple enough to get rid of them. She had left her fancy alone all these weeks, saving the centurion for a time like this when she might savour the indulgence. Were it not for the delightful array of available alternatives, Patre's fiat would have quite spoiled her holiday.

She stepped onto her balcony, past the fluttering gauze curtains, and looked out towards the Golfo di Napoli. The sea breeze was a delicious caress along her bare skin. Ah, well. Perhaps it was better this way. Sapphire waters and mythic stones were all well and good, but the most wonderful thing about Capri was the simplicity of life. So many luscious toys to play with and their lack of ambition made for such a refreshing change from Roma. No wonder so many of the first Caesars had been drawn to this island.

Tonight they would be dining by torchlight in the grotto. Patre found the gloom titillating; he hoped it might midwife a spark between her pathetic nephew and his insensible bride. They had no more life between them than the pieces in a mantel grouping. The boy was clearly besotted, turning moist orbits around the girl like a dog with an ailing master, but it was making no impression and, if you asked Giulia, it never would. The girl was a cypress with a distant smile; really, you could get more response from an amphoraka! Ah, well. Patre's illusions aside, there was much to be said for dull compliance. It was certainly preferable to her raving like a caged animal. The pair would be wedded and bedded before the summer ended, whether the girl remarked it or not. In this state, when the

Ceremony was eventually performed she might never even notice the change. As long as the Principessa persisted in this half life, she might preserve her life indefinitely. It would certainly make things simpler on Monday.

Thinking ahead to Patre's little garden party made Giulia smile. Like those of the former Medici palazzo in Firenze and the park around the Villa Borghese, these gardens were always open to the public. Upon assuming the leadership of a united Italy, her grandfather had found this tradition already established and had embraced it. With so many Imperial properties available, Patre had been able to continue this sop to the people without having to follow his father's example of actually mingling with them. Monday, however, would be different. Caesar would graciously interrupt his domestic repose in Capri to meet the visiting public. In exactly the kind of bold stroke Giulia most admired from Patre, even before the family had left Roma, news of this had been carefully leaked to the Empire's allies and receptive ears in the emphatically unaffiliated states. There was certain to be a large turnout of well-placed locals, avid for favours and gossip. The gossip would not disappoint.

&.

At the mouth of the grotto, water as dark and rich as the finest Alizarine ink bled into the velvet sky. Centuries after the hands that had chiseled it were dust, wind and tide had weathered the once raw span of shelf to match the mottled shadows of the stone walls. Only the soft lapping sound told of where one blackness met the other. The air was cool; in comparison to the pervasive sun warmth of day, almost chilly. Maud's evening dress was of silk tissue, too thin for such a night, and the curious style they affected here provided endless accommodation for an opportunistic breeze. She shivered and reached for her glass. The wine was warming and, no matter how often she drank or how deep, the level never seemed to change. Caesar's servants hovered ceaselessly. Terror resulted in a measure of attentiveness second only to that of love. Maud had learned much about terror, when she could remember it.

There was warmth also to be found radiating from the body beside her, from the shy boy they said was her bridegroom. She could regard him calmly enough; he was no one to fear. She had met young men like him before, in another life. In that life, she had also met young men who were worldlier, some who were bolder or more handsome, and others who were pleased at their own cleverness. She had never met a bridegroom; that had been yet to come. She remembered the night of her ball; Father, so handsome in his uniform and ribbons, teasing her mercilessly about the three candidates he and Grandmama had invited to attend.

Maud was surprised to feel the softness of a handkerchief being pressed into her hand. She hadn't noticed her own tears. The young man leaned closer, his eyes wide with concern. "Please don't cry," he whispered. "Patre won't be pleased. Are you feeling unwell?"

"I'm cold," she said, because she was.

"I could hold you." His voice was tentative. Under the flickering torches, she only imagined him blushing.

"I don't like to be held," she said, because she didn't, not any more.

"It would only be to keep you warm," he said humbly.

"I don't need to be warm." Casting her glance around the grotto, this was something she had suddenly realized.

Where the cave opened up like a the proscenium of an opera house, a representation of an enormous sea monster appeared to thrash in the torchlight. Another flame tickled the chin of a stone Bacchus twice the size of living men. Other torches, few but with their flames doubled by their twins at the water's surface, threw menacing shadows and illuminated the shapes of the other diners in fleeting bursts that shifted with the wind. In one flash, the leering face of Caesar glowed like molten brass and cast a yellow light on the nearby ear of his confidante, the simpering Baron. Another brought a glimpse of the Lady Giulia, mercilessly teasing her faithful Apollinaris, unaware of the mockery the cruel torchlight made of her own face and withered limbs. The few members of the Court who had been invited to this family dinner were obscured by the shadows but sensed as the hissing of gossip and the occasional caw of drunken laughter. Always barely visible by the spectral pallor of their gowns, Gusto's sisters huddled with the aunt who had raised them, as if all three were awaiting sacrifice.

Maud shivered again. Gusto put a tentative arm around her shoulders. She had no energy to resist, only enough to raise her glass to her lips and take another sip of wine. "I don't need to be warm," she repeated. "I am dead already, and this is Hell."

A shifting breeze caused a torch or two to flare. Spotting the young couple, Augustus sighed with satisfaction. He couldn't see their faces for the shadows, but they had drawn close to one another and Gusto's arm was wrapped protectively around his bride. "More wine!" he called. "Ha! Did I not tell you, Baron?"

"Yes, indeed! Well done!" Despite his hearty concurrence, the Baron could not have said why his master was so pleased; he hadn't been listening. Wine flowed too freely this night and the Baron was pensive in his cups. The grotto was not a place that pleased him. He enjoyed nature that had been tamed by men, like the gardens. Here, all traces of man smacked of impermanence, as if they might be erased by an impetuous wave. It made him feel like a flea on the pelt of the universe, a passing annoyance.

The pretty young server who refilled their glasses was relieved to not have gnarled old men's hands sliding over her body, squeezing and probing where the priests said hands should not go. She was also concerned. It was odd that neither man was paying her any unwanted attentions. Had she done something to offend? She looked nervously from one to the other. Each seemed lost in his own thoughts. Would she be punished? Should she stay or go?

"More wine!" an imperious voice called from behind her. A voice she would do well to obey. The Lady Giulia. She picked her way carefully over to where the Lady was draped over the compliant body of Apollinaris like a rug, her face resting against his chest. Because it was a family dinner, he was privileged to dine with her instead of standing guard behind her chair.

Apollinaris's eyes gleamed in his dark face. At her approach he reached up with both hands, a glass in each. After the girl had filled one, he carefully brought his arm down to where Giulia could see. She propped herself up on her forearm to accept it, her elbow digging into his ribs. Apollinaris never so much as twitched; nor was there a change to the stolid set of his features when his mistress, having taken a long swallow of wine, balanced her glass on the flat of his abdomen and moved her freed hand along his beautifully moulded leg.

They silently pitied Apollinaris below stairs, in the same way they pitied the blind or legless beggars in the Forum. His adoration of his cruel mistress was incomprehensible, but they could pity his crippled heart. The girl watched him with a sympathy that he refused to acknowledge. He held her gaze as steadily as he held the second glass. She filled it and, at the dismissive jerk of his head, drew back into the shadows to await the next call.

Maud could still hear the hisses and murmurs and laughs. She could still see the leering faces. She could still feel the warm arm trying to create a shelter where none would ever be found. "More wine!" she called.

❧

Ginevre of Lorraine had spent many of the happiest of her final hours resting in the spot where the garden began, the pergola protecting her from the sun whose sparkle always, to the very end, gladdened her eye. Today a small dais had been set on the floor of sea-blue tiles to exhibit her son to the eager eyes of his guests. Caesar Augustus sat on a low-backed seat of ivory brocade that perched on the shoulders of a quartet of gilded sphinxes. A half-wreath of gold laurel leaves encircled his formidable brow. As was his wont, he was draped in a toga of Egyptian cotton, the purple folds obscuring the elegant tailoring of what was, in a nod to the ostensibly casual nature of the event, a suit of creamy linen. The Lady Giulia stood by his favoured left shoulder, a similar stola bisecting the gown that matched her signature emeralds.

They made a brilliant picture. Yet each person who came to bow or kiss hands found his eyes drawn to the high-backed chairs in the shadows behind them.

Ordinarily Prince Napoleon Auguste had the perpetually cowed air of a dog that had been routinely abused by its master, and the equivalent constant yearning to be loved. Today he wore his impeccable summer suit with a waistcoat and cravat of soft rose. The unusual flush of colour, a straighter spine and a bit of a sparkle lent him, if never majesty, then at least presence. His unremarkable features were enhanced by visible pleasure as he, like everyone who neared the pavilion, gazed at the young woman beside him.

Inches and worlds away, Maud stared placidly at nothing. She was adorned in a cloud of maidenly white silk gauze. The gown, like the jewels, had been expressly selected by Giulia, ensuring they were both bridal and Imperial. The bright chestnut hair, tumbled into Classical curls, had been wound with pearls. A large pearl pendant, famous from a popular portrait of Ginevre of Lorraine, hung from her neck. Silent Maud was the magnet that drew the attention of every guest. Her height and distinctive colouring were as good as a calling card, and the older guests recognized a familiar echo in her face.

No official mention was made of either of the young people. It wasn't necessary. Maud's position, behind Caesar and beside his heir, spoke volumes.

It spoke to the Spanish Ambassador to Rome. He kept a villa on Capri and had hastened there at first whisper, taking with him the Ambassador from Mexico, with whom he was attempting to repair relations. He was glad he had invited Mexico to be his guest on Capri. If Rome were about to have a toehold in the Americas, it was more critical than ever for Madrid to repair relations with Tenochtitlán.

It spoke to the Russian Ambassador, who lost no time in reporting back to St. Petersburg. Relations between the major powers was always a delicate balancing act. A British alliance with Rome would upset the turnip cart. He also jotted a brief note to his counterpart in Stockholm. The King there had voiced some thoughts of a marital alliance with Britain through his younger son. The Tsar had similar interest in Axel of Sweden.

And it murmured, in carefully modulated tones, to the Swiss Resident, who congratulated himself on his prudence in having ventured from his villa on the Via Aurora on the basis of a dropped hint. Sipping chastely at the excellent prosecco, he watched closely and committed it all to memory. As soon as he returned home, he would pen a circumspect letter to the embassy in London.

18 - SPECIAL SERVICE

The warehouse, as Gertrude discovered, was a very different place once you got past the entry way. Except for a small bit of loft at one end, it was all one room. The walls, rising unbroken from the brick floor to the roof, were very tall. Though not a large building, it might have almost felt cavernous, were it not filled with so many fascinating things. The granddaughter of Sir Lowthian Bell was not unfamiliar with such places, but this one was stocked with things she had never seen before. A web of tubes and wires was suspended overhead, some leading to a smelly, dangerous-looking machine that she was told generated electricity. A live fire burned inside of something that looked like a marriage between a forge and a kiln; presumably used for casting small metal objects, it was ringed with what could only be described as a moat and was cautiously located, she was relieved to note, only yards from the courtyard door. The shelves and the zinc-topped tables were crammed with tools to which she couldn't put a name and covered with confounding assemblages. It was almost disappointing when a particular contrivance of flasks and tubes turned out to be for nothing more exciting than brewing coffee, a beverage that Sir Alastair and Mr. Firewalker consumed in even greater quantity than the Rom.

Work areas were carved out by overhead light, unusually bright and originating from buzzing globes that were far removed from the electric lights she had seen in England. Where pools of light met the soft grey diffusion from the dirty windows, dust motes spiraled in profusion. Behind that shimmering curtain was one of the most astonishing sights Gertrude had ever seen in her life: a troupe of metal mannikins lined the wall, like a dream of metal soldiers by someone who had never seen a real one. A patchwork of silvery and golden and bruise-blue metals, they were larger by a head than the tallest men; and what an odd head that was, with a coil of wire stretched between the bolts that sat in the position of ears, and a clownish face that was three metal tags and a squiggle of solder. Arms and legs were articulated, with gears and cables at the shoulders, elbows, wrists and knees.

Sir Alastair made one of these 'automatons' move. He did it with a mysterious box, which was covered with buttons, levers and a couple of protruding spikes. Gertrude would have thought they would be wound up with a very large key, but Claude explained that whatever it was that made them move had something to do with the wire curls, and with bits and pieces behind the little doors in those barrel-shaped bodies that made Gertrude think of small stoves.

The metal man stepped forward, away from its fellows, and walked around the room in a proscribed circle. Sir Alastair then, somehow, instructed it move through a series of motions that could have only been pattered on a cricket bowler.

"Look, Gertrude! It can throw! Oh, well done!" Claude clapped her hands and laughed in glee, before popping open the mannikin's chest and poking her fingers around.

Gertrude was awed but completely at sea. Nothing here had been part of her education. The conversation of the other three was an incomprehensible stew of "propulsion," "mass" and "trajectory." Except for that odd tombstone rubbing, even the pictures on the wall were diagrams of machines. She perched herself on a stool, to wait quietly. Now that she was back in civilization, she supposed she should be thinking of going home. It felt somehow disloyal to Maud to go on with life, but what else was Gertrude to do? She was useless here. Perhaps Sir Alastair or Lord Pinkerton might write a letter to her tutor; Miss Rubin would be furious with her for all the reading she'd missed. Or would she be allowed to return to Oxford now? According to Sir Alastair, the story was that she was somewhere with Maud. She might have to stay in hiding indefinitely. She must have a talk with him later.

For now, she would try to keep busy. She picked up a notebook from a stack on the table. The stampings on the back cover and flyleaves were unfamiliar; it wasn't a British notebook. It must be Mr. Tesla's. If it was, he had atrocious handwriting. Even if it were in a language she knew, the content was unlikely to make any sense to her. Perhaps she could go to the Embassy and borrow some books. Surely that would be allowed; the Hutchinsons knew she was here. She might prevail upon Mrs. Hutchinson to take her shopping. Whatever she had thrown in her handbag for that madcap excursion to Budapest was insufficient for her present needs.

She leafed through the book, looking for a blank sheet that she could tear out to make a list. Gertrude loved to make lists; there was something so settling about it. As she flipped pages, a sketch caught her eye. It wasn't an engineering diagram. The lines were tentative, as if Tesla hadn't been sure of what he wanted to draw. Perhaps he had been drawing from memory. She held the page to the light to get a clearer look. It appeared to be an Egyptian hieroglyphic. How curious! And oddly familiar. She raised her head to think where she might have seen it before, and her eyes went to the rubbing on the wall. With a flicker of excitement, she walked over to compare the two. There was a semblance, yes, but they were not the same. The elements they shared nagged at her. Where had she seen a similar design? She wondered if Mr. Tesla had drawn any more hieroglyphics that might help her remember. She went through the notebook slowly, making sure to turn only one page at a time and examine both sides. This was the only picture of its type. Intrigued, she thumbed through a couple of other notebooks. There was nothing like the little sketch, only the kinds of jottings she assumed a scientist would make. She returned to the first book, this time trying to read the paragraphs around the sketch. The handwriting wasn't impenetrable, only unfamiliar and agitated, as if it had been written on a train. It was a memoir, she realized, not a work journal at all. They seemed to be notes about his time in Rome. As a student of modern history, she really had an obligation to read them. Putting aside the unresolvable question of the drawings, she settled in happily.

"Gertrude? I said, aren't you starved?" Claude leaned over her shoulder, casting a shadow that made it difficult to see the page. "You're miles away! Whatever are you reading?"

"Huh?" She had been so engrossed that she had forgotten where she was. They were all standing nearby, as if they'd been waiting for her. Gertrude was flustered. "Oh, it's something your Mr. Tesla wrote. Fascinating. He says a lot about those creatures."

"What are your thoughts, Miss Bell?"

"Oh, I'm not a scientist."

"You're an Oxford scholar. I'd be interested in hearing your perspective." Sir Alastair's keen appraisal made her feel as if she were sitting her entrance examination all over again.

"There was this one thing. He says a lot about the priests, the ones who make the amphoraeka. Egyptians, he implies. I noticed this hieroglyph." She flipped to the drawing and held it up. "It's not clear why he drew it, but it might also have something to do with amphoraeka. Do you see? This part is a little like the symbol for eternal life. That rubbing you have, Sir Alastair, it has something like that as well."

"You're familiar with hieroglyphics, Miss Bell?"

"Only what I could learn from the exhibit cards at the museum. Oxford has few courses of study open to female scholars. I don't know if there's an Egyptology syllabus at the University. We're not even permitted to matriculate in Latin and Greek."

"Gertrude has a gift for languages, Father. We were with the Rom for what, a fortnight? She was already speaking Romani."

On the heels of his initial relief at seeing her alive, Frank had marked Miss Bell as an unnecessary complication. They couldn't risk her being seen by anyone who might mention to her family that she was not, after all, hiding somewhere with Princess Maud. Carnegie would have her, if he asked, but the Carnegies' social circles might overlap with that of the Bells. There were secure places in Switzerland that might do, but that would be a dull and lonely exile for a young woman. The one option he hadn't considered was keeping her here in Prague. Listening to her explain what she had gleaned from Tesla's diary, he had second thoughts. Miss Bell knew more about the current situation than almost any member of Her Majesty's Special Service. She demonstrated an acute intellect that was already engaged on the work at hand. It seemed wasteful to toss away such a gift. Moreover, he understood the bond she had forged with his lass. Frank believed in using what you had. Unofficial though it was, what he had were the first two female agents of Her Majesty's Special Service.

"Miss Bell," he said, once she finished her train of thought. "Would you consider staying on and working with us? It would do us well to have you."

"Of course she'll stay, Father. We wouldn't have it any other way, would we?"

Gertrude turned a bright pink, which added depth to the colour of her eyes and momentarily endowed her with an unusual gloss of beauty.

Firewalker flashed one of his rare smiles, causing Gertrude to blush brighter still. "I agree that we would be most fortunate to keep her. However, mit'anksi, you must allow Miss Bell the same privilege of decision that you would want."

"Oh, of course I'll stay," Gertrude.

❧

Frank read the note quickly, his face alive with curiosity, and stuffed it into the fire. "I'm off to the Embassy to retrieve an intriguing package," he said, pulling off his leather apron and reaching for his coat. "It seems we are about to meet Pinkerton's protégé, the impressive Mr. Horner."

"Has the Ambassador met this Horner before, Wohitika Capa?" Firewalker asked blandly.

"I have my doubts. According to Hutchinson, the gentleman in question has presented the correct credentials. Notice, however, that the Ambassador sent a note and not the man."

"Then you doubt the gentleman is Agent Horner, Sir Alastair?"

"We shall have to see. Horner is dug in deep in the bowels of Rome. I should hardly expect him to appear in Prague."

Claude pushed her magnifying goggles up to her forehead in order to fix her father with an anxious stare. "You don't think this is a trap?"

Frank pushed them back down over her eyes and gave the top of her head a kiss. "It's a guarded Embassy, not the docks of Shanghai. At worst, the lad is an impostor, which would of course raise a few wee questions. We'll know soon enough."

Not much could be accomplished with Claude jumping to her feet every time she heard a mouse skitter.

Firewalker set a fresh cup of coffee in front of her. "Patience, mit'anksi. It's only been a short while"

"It doesn't take long for something horrible to happen," she noted, grimly.

Firewalker placed a steadying hand on her shoulder. "If something had happened, I would know."

"Would you, Mr. Firewalker?" Gertrude's face was lively with interest. "When we arrived, you told Claude you'd known we…she, that is, was safe. Is this something your people know how to do?"

The corner of his mouth twitched. "When souls with whom you share a bond depart this world, you feel it. But what I refer to now is more about machinery." He reached into his pocket and produced a round item the size of an old-fashioned snuff box. It had no obvious markings, nor any buttons or knobs that Gertrude could see.

Claude grabbed it from him. She pulled down her goggles to look more closely and turned it under a light, her clever fingers probing the edges until it sprang open like a clam shell. A tiny oval filament popped straight up from the center of what appeared, except for ring of clockwork surrounding a minute cluster of crystals, to be a compass. The bezel was marked in degrees. "What is it? That loop looks almost like a radio wave receiver…"

"It's of limited use. The two units must be within twenty miles of one another."

"Two units?"

"They're built in pairs. The mate to this one is in your father's pocket. Should he be in danger, he would send a signal. This one would shake. We would use it to track his position."

"Fascinating!" Gertrude breathed.

"Why haven't I seen this?" Claude demanded.

"It was developed for the Service. Your father is often discreet about such inventions. This is one time he had reason to regret this habit." His expression was shadowed so briefly, it might have been a trick of the light. "He blamed himself when you were abducted. He thought you might have been able to signal him, if he'd given you a transmitter."

Claude blinked in astonishment. "How ridiculous. Why would he have thought I might require something like that? Even if he had, I was dead to the world until I was on a boat halfway to Dubrovnik."

"You can't blame chance. Instead he blamed any number of people."

"Poor Father. Not knowing can be the worst thing." She weighed the little gadget thoughtfully in the palm of her hand. "This might be a useful thing to have. Do you think it could be made smaller; perhaps a little lighter?"

Frank was back in time for dinner, practically whistling with excitement. "It really was Horner. Interesting lad. He's still in position in Rome, but he managed to find a way to come to Prague quite openly. With some important papers from Tesla on him, no less. I invited him to join us tonight, but he has his fiction to maintain. He's staying at a hotel in the Nove Mesto, in the guise of a Roman soldier enjoying…" It dawned on him that his audience included young women; he broke out in a cough.

"An assignation?" Gertrude provided helpfully. It sounded like something from one of those books she never read.

"Aye. Remarkably able young man," he hurried on. "We'll have him with us tomorrow."

❦

Frank gave Claude a quick hug before rushing out the door. He had arranged to rendezvous with Agent Horner at the cemetery after breakfast and bring him to the warehouse. As he reminded them all, some discretion was called for. "I should be there in half an hour with another clever lad for you to confound. And I promise to never tell your Aunt Nan that you met him in britches."

Spies had a noiseless way about them. Gertrude never seemed to hear Sir Alastair enter a room. Absorbed as she was, in her reading, it wasn't surprising that she hadn't noticed his arrival until Claude screamed.

It was a blood-curdling scream, more like a primitive war cry than shock or fear. Gertrude's head jerked back and she dropped the Univerzita Karlo-Fernandiva's copy of *Pictorial Language of the Ancient Egyptians* with a dusty thud.

Framed by the inner doorway, a most peculiar tableau was presented to her eye. Sir Alastair had made his way into the room by a few feet. Claude, her eyes blazing, had run past him towards the other man. Her mouth was curled in what could only be called a snarl, her entire body shaking with rage. She gave every indication of wanting to pounce, but she was unable to; the unflappable Mr. Firewalker stood behind her, holding her hands away from the face of the new comer.

It was, Gertrude realized with dawning shock, a face that she knew from a nightmare. Even without the black uniform tunic, he was unmistakably the sinister Italian from Dubrovnik.

"No!" Gertrude gasped.

Sir Alastair raised an eyebrow. "Do I take it then that you ladies are familiar with Agent Horner?"

"Agent? Agent my foot! He's one of the Emperor's men. Repetto..."

"Rappaccini," the man corrected, in what sounded like a perfectly authentic Eton drawl.

It was like throwing oil on a bonfire. With a shriek, Claude tore herself from Firewalker's restraining grip and flew at the visitor. "You locked me up!"

"For your own safety." He stepped neatly aside and she fell forward.

The fall didn't stop her; she curled into a tight ball and rolled her weight at his legs, knocking him off balance.

"Ha!" With a quick twist, she had him face down on the ground and was kneeling on his back. "You stood there and watched that woman poison us! You let her leave us in the woods to die!" she started striking him with her fists.

"I didn't know…." Instead of fighting her off, he was groping the air behind him.

"Claude, stop!" Gertrude was just as angry as her friend, but this was no way for a lady to redress her wrongs. Not only was it inappropriate, it was dangerous: he was a man; he was stronger; he might hurt her. "Oh, Sir Alastair, make them stop!"

Gertrude had no name for the expression on Sir Alastair's face. "She needs the practice, Miss Bell," he said blandly. "We haven't trained in months. I expect Agent Horner can take care of himself."

At that moment, the agent found what he was after—a tight grasp of Claude's ankle. He gave it a yank and she fell backward. He used the opportunity to flip himself over and crawl toward her. She started to scramble to her feet.

"I am working under cover for Her Majesty" he grunted. "I thought you were, too!"

"You thought I was a spy?!"

It gave Claude pause, just for a moment but long enough for him to use the opportunity to bring her down again.

"I thought you were meant to switch places with the Princess." If she were a man, he'd have thrown a solid jab at her nose instead and ended this ridiculous wrestling match. "I tried to find you alone and speak with you, but you…she…She tried to stab me with a piece of glass!"

"Well done, the Princess!" Claude chortled breathlessly.

"Maud tried to stab you?!" Gertrude found this as equally astonishing as the struggle on the ground. "Where did she get a piece of glass?"

"We swapped. I…oof!" The arm Claude had been using to push herself upright was jerked out from under her. "I made her take my corset!" she yelled.

"Good lass!" Her father approved from the sidelines. "In Dubrovnik? And you had a bit of glass?"

"Broken glass. I forgot about it," she grunted into the floor. "I've probably forgotten other things as well." She rolled over and glared at her adversary "I. Was. Drugged!" she gave a mighty push that sent the agent rolling away from her.

"And I," he gasped, when he could. "I was walking a bloody tightrope with a blindfold on and both hands tied behind my back!" Their eyes locked across the two yards that separated them. Both of them were finding it difficult to catch their breath. "I thought you were there to work with me. Until Tesla told me who you were, and by then it was too late…!"

A fresh flash of anger lit her face. "You hurt Nikola!" she sprang from a crouch and dove, collapsing across him and sending her knee into a spot of legendary tenderness.

The spy's mouth opened in a soundless scream.

Firewalker sighed and strode over to the human bundle. "Enough, mit'anksi. I think you've had your say." He pried her off of her victim and pulled her gently back to where Gertrude stood frozen in amazement.

"I'm afraid my lass has got the better of you, Horner." Frank helped the agent stagger to his feet. "No hard feelings, I hope."

"If she were a man…" the younger man muttered, his eyes crushed in pain.

"Och, aye. Unfair advantage," Frank's eyes sparkled will ill-suppressed glee. "If you have cause to fight with a woman again, you must remember not to fight like a gentleman." He uncapped the flask that Firewalker handed him and pressed it to the agent's lips.

Micah swallowed gratefully. "Who thinks to fight a woman?"

"True of my generation. Yours as well, I see. And yet, you assumed she was an agent like yourself. Interesting. Perhaps the time has come for women in the Service."

"My mother worked for the Service."

"Did she? I didn't think Pinkerton warm to the idea."

"In Italy. She was in a position to gather intelligence and send it to Britain. I don't know how she found her way to Lord Pinkerton, but I know he was grateful for her efforts."

"Then you *are* Italian," Claude accused him with some relish.

"My allegiance is to Greater Britain. But by birth, yes." His blue gaze was steady and his voice was calm. "There's no shame in that. The states of Italy have given much to the world. Don't condemn a people for the villainies of one man."

"Well said, Agent Horner." Frank tried to signal his daughter to restrain herself. He thought the agent had sufficiently proven his self-control for one day.

"You sound so English!" Gertrude couldn't help but exclaim.

"Children adapt, Miss Bell, if they're wise and there is much incentive. I was sent away to a public school when I was young. If you know boys, you know how rigorously they enforce the status quo."

"I have brothers."

"Then you know. A strange boy could have no greater incentive to adapt than the hope of being accepted, or at least ignored, by his classmates."

"So you were raised to be British," Claude said dismissively. "And a talented actor. That still doesn't explain why you didn't try to help us. The Blavatsky woman planned for us to die in those woods."

"I didn't know. Haussmann had me on the yacht that night. A girl...a young woman was brought on board, asleep. Drugged. I had no way to tell you apart. I knew there was a difference in your eyes but I couldn't sort it out." He threw up his hands in an unusual show of exasperation. "I thought it was *you* on that yacht, the agent who was meant to double for the Princess. And I thought the Princess and Miss Bell were safe. I was shocked when Haussmann told me what had happened. I'd been so certain that Madame Blavatsky would never knowingly take a life. You have no idea how relieved I was last night, to learn that you had survived. I'm glad I never told Mr. Tesla otherwise."

Before Claude could lash out again, Micah held up a hand to forestall her. "Haussmann is holding Mr. Tesla is in Venezia," he said, quickly. "Venice. I assure you that I've done everything I could to make him comfortable. He's as well as can be expected. I saw him two days ago. When I return, I promise I'll pass him any message you want to send. As I told Sir Alastair, I wanted to bring him to Prague. I had a plan. And it would have worked if the man hadn't given up!"

Even Claude could see the authenticity of his frustration. "He isn't well," she whispered, bunching the knee of her trousers in a fist.

"He's had better days," Micah agreed. "I would have thought he'd move mountains to outwit Haussmann. I don't understand why he's chosen to give up now."

"Fortunately," Frank hinted, "he's sent us his work."

"More accurately Sandtmann did," Micah remarked. Still moving a little stiffly, he walked to the false entrance to retrieve a large, shabby portfolio tied with cheap string. Taken at a glance with his scuffed boots and paint-stained canvas jacket, it created the unremarkable impression of an affably struggling artist.

"You've recruited one of Haussmann's men? Horner, I am impressed."

"Why does that name sound familiar? Father, didn't Nikola once have a friend called Sandtmann?"

"He still does" Micah lifted the portfolio onto one of the tall zinc-topped tables. "A very good friend." As he removed the papers, he told them about his talks with Sandtmann and Zacuto. Firewalker took rapid notes.

Several times, Frank stopped him to walk to him back through some part of the story. Claude and Gertrude listened in silence, feeling only the human drama of the trapped souls.

"Sandtmann saved these," he concluded. There was a note of strain in his voice, as if some piece of this had touched him more than he wanted to acknowledge. "I don't know how he managed it, but he hid them from Haussmann and even from Tesla himself."

Frank turned his attention from the agent to the papers, beckoning for Firewalker to join him.

"Why?" Claude wanted to know. "Why hide them from Nikola?"

Micah shrugged. "Sandtmann had a feeling. He watched Tesla write these pages almost automatically, after being unwell, and he sensed that there might be something different here than in the other work. Something 'honest' is what Sandtmann said, and that's what worried him."

"Nikola said his headaches helped him solve things that had seemed impossible," Claude recalled. "Maybe whatever he saw would have done exactly what the Baron was hoping and make the amphoraeka even stronger."

"Why take the risk of bringing them here, Agent Horner?" Gertrude asked. "Wouldn't it have made more sense to burn them?"

"You study the strengths of an enemy in order to learn his weakness. If Sandtmann is correct, then studying Tesla's ideas might give Sir Alastair the key to destroying the amphoraeka."

"I'd have rather Nikola come to tell them to Father himself."

"I did try to bring him, Miss Menzies. He said he couldn't do anything more, but that Sir Alastair could."

"Monteith. Miss Monteith," she corrected absently. "I still don't understand. Perhaps he didn't trust you enough to come with you."

"Claude!"

"Never mind, Miss Bell. I understand. He does trust me, Miss Men…Monteith." Micah was the last person to argue about someone's choice of name. "He trusted me enough to let me know what you mean to him." Pretending not to notice the flush in her cheeks, Micah fixed his eyes on the opposite wall. "Ah, good! I see my courier made it through."

Gertrude looked to where he was pointing. "You sent that? Then you know what it says?"

"Well, no. But does that matter? We know what it does."

"What is it then?" Claude demanded.

Micah had put the coded message on a scrap of paper separate from the rubbing itself so that, if intercepted, the courier might swallow it. Obviously the courier had gotten through. He was puzzled by their confusion. "It's the command symbol that controls the amphoraeka."

"Oh!"

"Miss Bell, is everything alright?" Firewalker had seemed to be deep in consultation with Frank, but at the sound of her voice, he was at her side.

"Oh, yes, Mr. Firewalker." She gave him a shy but radiant smile. "Mr. Horner says he knows how this hieroglyph is used."

Firewalker nodded. "The amphoraeka must follow the commands of those who carry it. Yes, so he wrote to us."

"Why didn't you tell us?" Claude was reproachful.

"We thought we might learn more from Miss Bell's studies if she could pursue them without bias."

Gertrude nodded. "It's true. I would might have started to focus on symbols for 'obey' or 'rule.' I would have missed much of what I've learned."

"There's a similar symbol on the bodies of the amphoraeka themselves," Micah noted.

"Similar? Not the same?" Gertrude asked.

"I think not."

She went to the shelf for Nikola's journal and opened it to the small sketch. "More like this?"

He looked at it carefully, then looked at the rubbing again. The small sketch seemed incomplete. He couldn't be certain.

Gertrude retrieved *Pictorial Language of the Ancient Egyptians* from where she had dropped it and started thumbing through it. "You see, they both have the *ankh*, the key of life. And I believe this bit here is meant to be the *ieb*, the heart. The ancient Egyptians believed that the heart was the seat of the soul, you see. When a man died, it was said that his heart had departed his body." She looked up, beaming with scholarly enthusiasm. "They thought their gods would weigh the heart against a feather, to see if the person was worthy of the afterlife. The feather was truth, you see. Or perhaps 'justice' would be more accurate. If the heart was too heavy with sin, then the person could not pass on."

"Is the feather part of the symbol?" Claude asked.

"No." Gertrude seemed disappointed. "I thought it might be."

"Perhaps," Firewalker suggested, "it's because these souls are not allowed to pass on. You must continue your studies, Miss Bell. Learn what else these symbols might tell us."

Frank had left off his study of the papers. "I concur. Perhaps there is something in this that we can use to our advantage."

"What do Nikola's notes tell you, Father?"

Frank rubbed the bridge of his nose. "Time will tell. There seems to be more attention to the creature itself than to the weapons it might carry. Schematics for a kind of armor: wheeled plates for the feet, and a shell to protect the head."

"The amphoraeka already wear a kind of helmet." Micah indicated the shape.

"Then it would seem the head is the Achilles heel, so to speak."

"Tesla said something once." Micah tried to remember. "Something about aiming for the eyes."

"Ah, this explains the visor! Limited mobility must likewise be an issue."

"Speed?" Micah thought aloud. "But they move quickly for their size."

"Unidirectionally," Frank observed.

"How do you…?"

Frank slapped a sheet of paper over the rubbing. "Notice how the wheels are mounted on this plate? Designed to change direction on a whim. I might adapt this for the automatons." He grinned. "Only fitting, don't you think?"

"Tesla's spoken of his automatons. I didn't quite believe him."

Frank jumped up with the energy of a man half his age. "Lem! We must give Agent Horner a demonstration! Horner, prepare for a treat!"

It was the first opportunity to share the potential of the invention with someone new. Frank and Firewalker were proud to display every gear and gesture. Despite his obvious and gratifying wonder, it was clear that the agent's comprehension of the achievement was insufficient to communicate back to Tesla as Frank would have hoped.

"It doesn't matter if I understand," Micah kept repeating. It was true, even if it was becoming increasingly embarrassing to admit this within Claude's hearing. "Tesla's washed his hands of the business. He said it was now up to you."

"But see here, Horner," Frank persisted, jabbing his finger into a metal arm from which the skin had been peeled back to reveal a series of pistons and tubing. "If we increase the thrust and adjust the aperture here, then if we calculate based on…how tall do you say these creatures are…?"

Micah stood tall and ran the flat of his hand from his head to the automaton. It touched the top of the shoulder cap. "Very nearly the same. I would say the amphoraeka are three…no, four inches taller."

Frank referred back to the sketches Sandtmann had saved and made some rapid calculations in the corner of the page. He nodded happily and beckoned Claude to read them. "That lad and his intuition! See how perfect that angle is? Your Aunt Nan would say he had the Sight, eh lass?"

"Probably. Not that he needed it this time, Father. Remember, this wasn't a random design. He always meant them to match against the amphoraeka."

"Aye, but he didn't know about the head then. No, he must have sensed it from the start, able lad."

"What does it all mean?" Gertrude wondered aloud.

Firewalker, standing nearest, heard her. "If we make the adjustments Wohitika Capa describes, assuming the relative height is correct, we will be able to create aiming sequences for several optimal distances."

"Remember my bomb, Gertrude? If Father's correct about the implications of that visor thing that Nikola drew, shooting something like that…well, not needles of course, but something with that kind of force directly into the eye holes will blow their heads wide open."

"And that would kill them?" Gertrude knew she sounded stupid, but she didn't see how something that wasn't alive could be killed.

"If it would set their souls free, then yes!" Now that he understood what Sir Alastair was talking about, Micah could vigorously support it. "How many rounds can your machine men carry? And how quickly can they be made to aim and fire, do you think?"

"Twenty rounds apiece," Frank said promptly. "Ten in each arm. Speed depends on whether we alternate or exhaust one before firing the other."

"If you don't alternate, you'll set the balance off," Claude observed, recalling the delicacy of the gyroscopic mounting of the main engine.

Micah made a quick scan of the room. "Augustus's army is growing every day. Who knows how many there will be by the time he decides to move. You've only got a few dozen of these machines. It's not nearly enough to blow them all up."

"Aye. But now that we know what to do, I've a proper foundry here in Prague that we can re-tool. We'll have a true manufactory to get the job done. Firewalker will fly back to America to fetch the Prometheum we'll need." He chortled with satisfaction.

The thought of Prometheum detonations had sent Claude back to that night in the forest. She envisioned herself hurling round after round of explosives. She could feel the concussions and smell the smoke. There was the sound of shattering clay. She couldn't see them, but somewhere in the distance, souls were dying. She was horrified.

"Oh, why do men think killing one another is the only answer?!" she cried. The others stared at her.

"Lass, we're talking about an army led by a maniac."

"But isn't there another way? There are people in there, we know that now. Why do we have to blow their heads off?"

Micah was affronted. He had risked everything to bring the information that might help to destroy these creatures. "For one thing, they're a menace as long as anyone can command them. For another, I've spoken with them or at least with one of them. They *want* to die."

"It's the same point," she retorted. "They want to die *because* they can be commanded, because they're slaves."

"You say most of them were soldiers, Mr. Horner. Of course they want to die," Gertrude reflected. "It's terrible, what was done to them. They want their honour back. I imagine they'd prefer to take at least some of their tormentors down with them."

"They can't," he said flatly. "They can't kill anyone who has the glyph, they can't kill one another, they can't suicide."

"What about sabotage?" Frank wondered. "We know they can work on their own. Tesla's friend Sandtmann did as much by getting these plans to you. They can't disobey a direct order, but what if there were no orders? At night, while the commanders sleep, I dare say they could destroy a fair bit of property."

"One time, yes. But as soon as someone woke the first commander, they'd be assigning command in pairs with a new protocol for twenty-four hour watch." Micah knew the Roman army.

"Miss Bell makes a good point about honour," Firewalker observed. "If nothing else, they would regain some of their honour by trying."

"You're all missing the obvious solution," Claude sighed testily. "You have to free them, remove the obligation to obey. Don't destroy them; destroy that symbol!"

"Oh, easy as pie," Micah snorted. "Hunt out and steal every cartouche in Italy, burn the tattoos off the heads of the field commanders…"

"Not the commanders, idiot! Off the amphoraeka."

"How?" Gertrude asked, hoping her friend had an answer. The thought of all those souls would be haunting her forever. "You mean, if we could figure out what the symbol meant, we might be able to draw a new one? Perhaps something with the feather..."

"Claude, lass, don't be foolish. We'd need an automaton for every amphoraka. The logistics..."

"Oh, I don't know," she said petulantly. "Spray them down with a fire hose and melt it away."

There was a stunned silence as they digested this. Then their minds started racing.

"But they're resistant to water," Gertrude said slowly. "It said so in Mr. Tesla's journal."

"Aye, Miss Bell. We couldn't wash it away in any case. Agent Horner says the symbol is etched somehow."

"It appears so, sir."

"I wonder if we might devise some compound that could fill in the lines. Erase the image that way. If there were such a substance, something that would stick, then aye, we might build an appliance that could spray it." Frank swept his arm as if training a hose across a wall. His eyes had the vacant stare of vision. "Something like that could cover eight, maybe ten at a stroke. What do you think, Lem?"

"If there were a compound that would stick fast to the clay, it might work. Of course, we'd still need to brand them with some kind of counter-sign, as Miss Bell suggests."

"Eventually. For a start, it would do to disable what they have. Pity it has to remain theoretical." Frank let go of his vision and sighed with regret. "Aye. If only we had an amphoraka to experiment with."

Micah laughed so hard that he coughed. Claude looked daggers at him.

"With any luck, we soon will. Sandtmann had the same idea."

"Sandtmann is coming here? Nikola's Sandtmann?!" The daggers dropped.

"I wanted him to. He's from Prague for one thing, which would have made it easier for him to make his way here, but he insisted that Tesla needs him. Instead he's sending a volunteer who was stationed near the northern border. They require no rest, but once out of the empire, he has to stay concealed. It may take some days."

Firewalker nodded his understanding. "Avoid settled areas as much as possible; otherwise travel at night. Will this being know this?"

"He'll be one of the old Legionaries; he'll know better than you or I."

"Maybe better than you," Claude noted.

"How were you able to get one of them to fall in with this?" Frank wondered.

"I was holding the glyph, you see. I keep a copy in my boot." Micah pointed to the rubbing. "So I was able to 'command' Sandtmann to find a likely volunteer and to transmit my 'command' for him to head off. They had no choice but to obey."

"Well done, Horner!" Frank was impressed.

"It was Sandtmann who figured it out," Micah admitted. "He was a lawyer once, you see."

Agent Horner parted from them at the door to the workshop that evening. He had, he reminded them, a cover to maintain. He and Elettra would be dining in their hotel before attending a performance at a concert hall known to be frequented by visiting Italians. They had also planned an outing for the following day.

"We'll have you with us again before you return to Venice, I hope."

"Oh, yes," Micah assured him. "Tomorrow night we will have a very public lovers' quarrel. Then I'll be on my own for two days, and Elettra will shop and pretend to pout."

Frank was the only one who appeared pleased to hear this. The girls found it difficult to separate the Pinkerton from the sinister Italian centurion, and Firewalker was looking forward to restored tranquility. They could all, however, agree that it had been a productive day and looked forward to a relaxing evening in the little house. Their mood was only slightly dampened when Alice handed Frank the note that the Embassy driver had left for him. He read it quickly. "Pinkerton," he said before placing it on the fire, as if that should be explanation enough.

Frank waited until after they'd eaten to say that he would be flying to London in the morning. The girls ran off to pull together some things they wanted him to carry. Firewalker wasn't so easily distracted, but there was nothing else Frank had to tell. Pinkerton hadn't said what it was about. That made them both uncomfortable.

❧

Pinkerton was in the automobile that came to fetch him from Shooter's Hill. He looked ten years older than on Frank's last visit, but wouldn't speak in front of the driver.

"She's waiting for you," was all he'd say.

"I was hoping to have a wee visit with my sister before…" The expression on his old friend's face stopped him. "Aye. But if I can't, I have a package for her, from her niece. And some more letters for you to pass along to a certain industrial baronet."

Pinkerton brightened slightly. "Aye, I nearly forgot to say how happy I am for you. That wire was the only bright thing in weeks."

"A good sign," Frank said, "for those as believe in signs."

Pinkerton didn't look like someone who did. An hour later, Frank understood why.

It wasn't only the Queen who waited, in full sail, at Windsor, but the elite few that Frank thought of as the first ring of the Privy Council. Before he could even properly kiss hands, a letter was shoved under his nose.

"They've all read it," she said impatiently. "The question is, now that word is out, how are We to counter?"

Frank scanned it rapidly. He felt himself grow rapidly cold, then warm with anger. "Why are we to believe…?"

"The Swiss Ambassador!" She flung the title like a challenge. "From the Swiss Resident in Rome. Impeccable, damn them both!

"Ma'am!" Archbishop Benson was honestly shocked.

"I think we might excuse Her Majesty's language under the circumstances," Rosebery murmured.

"No, Lord Rosebery, the Archbishop is quite right. My apologies to you. And to the Swiss gentlemen; I owe them a debt of gratitude, not a curse. It's the damned Emperor of Italy who deserves my curses, and may they be the least of what rains down on his head. Augustus Buonoparte should rot in Hell for all eternity, and I do not apologize for saying so!"

"Amen," muttered the Queen's ancient cousin, the Duke of Nova Scotia. The Archbishop, wisely, didn't say a word.

"And where was your precious Agent Horner in all this, Lord Pinkerton?"

Frank stepped forward to face her. "Begging your pardon, Ma'am, but I was with Agent Horner yesterday in Prague. I swear he knows nothing about this."

"In Prague? I thought he was in Rome, trying to extract my granddaughter from the clutches of this madman!"

"He is. Augustus himself ordered the lad away. He said it was to be a family holiday."

"Family," she said bitterly. "He's stolen a member of my family and put her on display like a hostage! I want the world to know…"

"Do you Ma'am?" Lord Rosebery asked, his voice carefully level. "Thanks to our Swiss friends, we have a list of the dignitaries who were present. It's small enough, and mostly those whose word would be questioned by our allies. Switzerland says her name was never spoken; those who were present drew their own conclusions. We can say they were mistaken, control the damage."

"And let him get away with this?"

"We have discussed this before, Ma'am," the Prime Minister reminded more sternly than might be quite appropriate. "You cannot accuse the Emperor of kidnapping unless you are prepared to go to war."

"And that, Ma'am," said the War Secretary with a bit of a tremble and his eyes fixed straight ahead past her shoulder; "that, we agree, we are not."

"But Augustus did it," the Queen fumed.

"His agents did," the Foreign Secretary respectfully corrected. "He could easily claim to have rescued her from misguided renegades."

"No one would believe that for a minute!"

"Nonetheless," Lord Rosebery continued smoothly, "we know that an accusation would be excuse enough for a war that might embroil all of Europe."

"Austria would jump at any reason to try and reclaim the lands lost to Napoleon," the Secretary for War could speak strongly about that. "And with Italy distracted on two fronts, the Turks would block up the Aegean and attempt to regain Greece."

Pinkerton nodded his agreement. "Russia would join in a trice. Alexander is panting for an opportunity to expand his influence. Isn't that so, Menzies?"

"Aye, in theory. But all of you are forgetting the unnatural army Augustus has been building for himself."

"And where is the result of the study I commissioned on the Act of Settlement? Gentlemen, all I hear from you are excuses, not solutions!"

"With all due respect Your Majesty, these are facts. We can't gauge the power he controls, and we don't want to first be learning this on the battlefields. We're making great strides in Prague, but until we're ready to fight him and win, we can't risk crying havoc and letting loose the dogs of war."

"We must continue as we have done, Ma'am." In the heavy silence that followed Frank's pronouncement, the Prime Minister sounded even more doleful than usual.

"But what about this?" the Queen snatched the letter out of Frank's hands and brandished it like a flag. "This is the final straw!"

"It could not have been Princess Maud!" Rosebery gave a credible imitation of astonishment. "The Princess has been with her mother in Roumania all these months."

"And why has no one seen her there for so long a while?" catechized the Archbishop.

"She's…ah…fallen ill!"

"Isn't the Queen of Roumania always visiting lepers?"

"Oh, do be quiet, James!" the Queen said crossly.

"The Duke has a thought, Ma'am," Rosebery smiled with some satisfaction. "Perhaps not lepers, but Queen Elisabeth is known for her charity: hospitals, poor houses. In theory, anyone in her party might be exposed to every illness under the sun."

"What you are all saying is that we have no choice but to play a waiting game."

"He wants us to make the same mistake that he made in invading France," added the Prime Minister, who was old enough to remember.

Pinkerton nodded in agreement with the Grand Old Man. He had spent so much of these last few years studying Augustus Buonoparte that he felt sometimes he could see into that wicked brain. "He's taunting you, Ma'am. He wants us to move before we're ready."

"When will we be ready, Frank?" the Queen asked, when only themselves and Pinkerton remained. She sank listlessly into a chair. Frank started for the drinks cabinet, but she raised a hand to stop him. "Please, just tell me the truth."

He shrugged. "We're that close now to having a way to fight those creatures. Your Agent Horner, Pinkerton, he's got one of them on its way to Prague. Impressive lad, Horner."

"You're not serious!" What little colour was left in the Queen's face drained away. "One of those monsters?!"

"They're soldiers. And now we have some working for our side. But even with that, it might still take some months for us to have everything in place. The Council is right. We have to wait until we do."

"I can wait for revenge. I can. And I will find some legal basis to sign the succession over to Emilie's Louisa. What I cannot do is sit quietly by while Maud is wed to that boy! I do not understand this, Lord Pinkerton. Why can't your agents get my granddaughter out of Rome? Why can't you, Frank?"

Frank knelt down beside her and, pretending Pinkerton was miles away, took one of her cold hands and held it between his. He reminded himself that, in a history of saying difficult things to Charlotte, this would simply be one more. Taking a deep breath, he told her everything young Horner had told him about the Princess's condition. When he had done, it was Pinkerton who was dabbing at his eyes with a handkerchief. The Queen sat like a monument.

"Please leave," she said, when she finally spoke. "Both of you, gentlemen."

"I had to tell you."

"Yes. You did. Thank you, Frank. But please; I cannot bear to have anyone near me. Not now."

"Aye. I'd expected to return to Prague, but I could stay…"

"No, thank you. When I'm ready, I'll…"

"Send for me. Aye."

The men were moving quietly to the door when she stopped them. "Frank?" she said softly.

"Aye?"

"Your…Claude. Lord Pinkerton told me. She's returned to you. She's well?"

"Aye. She is."

"That's something then." She closed her eyes and they left her.

§

Pinkerton dragged Frank back to his house. "You can deliver that package yourself," he commanded. "We'll have the aership take you back as soon as the sun comes up. It would do us both some good to make someone happy today."

Frank had to assume his sister was happy to see him, though with Nan it was never so simple as that.

"Look what the cat dragged in!" she greeted him. "The Prodigal Son took less time to return than you did."

"Nan, you know better than most why I have to stay there."

"Aye, but nae so much as a visit in all this time? Dinnae tell me you've never been in London. Aye, you can tell me; but you know I'll nae believe you."

"Aye, I've come once or twice; but only to see the Queen. Then back to Prague the same day without time for so much as a wee dram. Those aerships are a real miracle," he added slyly.

She gave him a little push, the way she had when they were children, and looked at him with fond exasperation.

"I brought you a gift," he said, handing her the heavy bundle. "From Claude. She said it was something you wanted."

"So she remembers she has an auld Aunt? I was starting to wonder. Nae so much as a postcard from the lass." Her eyes narrowed suspiciously and she glared at her brother. "You're nae trying to soften me up? Dinnae tell me Claude's engaged to that Serbian!"

Frank honestly hadn't seen that coming. He automatically started to laugh, then recalled where Tesla was now and felt it catch in his chest. He doubled up. It was a painful wheeze, all the worse for having to pretend it was amusement.

Nan looked concerned. He rasped out a chuckle and waved her away. "Dinnae fash yourself, Nan. There's no time for courtship. Nor postcards for that matter. We've too much work to do. Now open your package. She'll want me to tell her what you said."

She painstakingly untied the knots, then wound the string into a tight ball. After removing the brown paper and folding it into a neat square, she opened the cardboard box and peeled back a layer of paper tissue. She reached in and carefully removed the piece of cut crystal. Speechless for a moment, she held it to the light.

"She said it was a rose bowl," he said helpfully.

"I ken what it is," she said, her voice unusually soft. "It was thoughtful of Claude. I'll write and tell her thank you." She set the bowl down on Joan Pinkerton's walnut side table and tilted her head from side to side, admiring the effect. "Though I wonder if maybe I liked the other one a wee bit more." She sighed and cleared her throat. "Unco thoughtful. Has she been brushing her hair every night? You look as though you've been eating well," she regarded him critically. "I hate the thought of the two of you living in a hotel like a pair of salesmen."

"Dinna fash yerself, Nan. I took a wee house for us. We have Firewalker, and Mrs Hutchinson sent a good lass from the embassy; you'd like her."

"I could have come back to keep house for you."

"You'd be bored to tears in Prague, Nan. We're in the workshop all day. Long days. And at night it's all we can do to eat before we fall into bed. I'm much happier thinking you're enjoying London with Joan and her friends.

Nan frowned. "I dinnae ken why, but I ken you dinnae want me there. There's certain to be a reason, there always is with you; but you notice I haven't asked it."

"You never do."

She gave the dry little laugh that meant she was honestly amused. "I ken how it pains you to have to tell a falsehood. You may be a bold liar in the Queen's Service, Frankie—I'd say you must be, or nae doubt you'd have been dead long before now—but even when we were just a pair of wee bairns, it ate you up inside if you had to tell me ought but the truth."

"It was just as hard to tell you the truth. I still remember telling you it wasn't a fairy circle behind the cottage, but me and Angus Carmichael learning how to smoke."

They both laughed then, heartily. Pinkerton, coming to show Frank to the guest room to freshen up, brightened at the sound. Even a small moment of respite was a victory these days.

19 – AN AUDACIOUS VENTURE

Micah snuck out of the hotel at dawn. From what he could tell, other than the usual array of itinerant musicians and painters, the only Roman presence in Prague was a score or so of soldiers on holiday, none of whom would be likely to rise much before noon. Still, Verde, or had it been Rosso, had some contacts here; it was only good sense to be as discreet as possible and make his way while the streets were empty. As he passed the old Jewish Cemetery, he heard an unmistakable tapping. He found Sandtmann's volunteer concealed among the confusion of lurching stones. Keeping to the shadows, he led the amphoraka to the warehouse. They waited in the narrow alley, to one side of the door, until someone would come and open up.

"Good morning Agent Horner," Firewalker said quietly, turning the key in the padlock. "And good morning to you as well, sir. I presume you are Mr. Sandtmann's associate?"

Micah nearly jumped out of his skin. He was certain they were standing deep enough into the alley to avoid detection. He inched forward. Firewalker wasn't even looking in his direction. The man had opened the door and was holding it wide.

"There's no one behind me. I suggest you enter quickly."

Micah gestured for the amphoraka to come forward, catching his breath as it filled the doorway. It was a close fit. The crest of the bronze helmet nearly grazed the lintel.

"How did you know we were there?" he demanded, once they were both safely inside.

"I saw your footprints. Both of you. You were trailing dew. You must have been in the cemetery. And there was a scent of damp clay unusual to this place." Firewalker calmly appraised the creature before him. "Fascinating. I hope you don't mind my staring, sir. I don't mean to be rude. It's an honest curiosity; you are unique in my experience."

The blue jets in the amphoraka's eye holes flared briefly.

"Please make yourselves comfortable. Have you breakfasted, Agent Horner? We'll see about getting you some food."

"Thank you, sir. If it won't disturb you, I'd like to see what our, uh, friend can tell us about himself and his journey here."

Firewalker waved him away and set to work preparing the coffee apparatus for the day. Micah led the amphoraka to the other end of the large room. As they passed the ranks of automatons, he felt sure he saw the creature hesitate for just a step.

"*Niente di cui preoccuparsi*," he said, keeping his voice as friendly as he could. He had been assuming the amphoraka was Italian but was he? Sandtmann wasn't. For that matter, he couldn't remember what language he'd used when speaking to Tesla's friend. "Nothing to worry about," he repeated, just in case. Perhaps all languages were the same to the dead.

When the women arrived, they were still talking. They were using a pair of copper tubes that Micah had picked up from one of the tables.

Claude was tempted to clap her hands over her ears at the racket. Instead she strode over to the creature with her right hand outstretched. "Hello," she said kindly, touching her hand to the clay wedge that was his. "Welcome to Prague. Thank you so much for coming all this way to help us. I'm Claude. And you are…"

Micah couldn't take his eyes off her. Her sang froid was astonishing.

Gertrude saw his face and made a disparaging click with her tongue. "For heaven's sake, she faced a pack of werewolves with a sewing kit," she whispered. "This is at least a friendly monster."

The amphoraka took his length of copper tubing and beat out a rapid pattern

"We must teach you Morse code, Miss Monteith," Micah said blandly, turning back from Miss Bell.

Claude shot him a foul look. Picking up a convenient hammer by the business end, she flipped it in midair to grasp the handle and briskly rapped out I-D-I-O-T on the workbench. "Brrr! We can't be doing that all day long. We'll all be deaf before lunch." She tossed the hammer aside, coming within a hair's breadth of Micah's arm, and regarded the amphoraka thoughtfully. "There must be some less, uh, cacophonous way that we can communicate. Mr. Garibaldi, can you bring your hands together like this, to clap?"

He couldn't. She requested a series of arm movements, watching carefully to see how he might carry them out. Sometimes, she had him repeat one.

Her instructions were peculiar enough to be intriguing, but something interested Micah even more. "Why is he doing as you say?" he finally asked.

The amphoraka, Garibaldi, raised an arm and pointed to the wall. Claude was standing in front of the rubbing of the command glyph.

For some reason, this struck Gertrude as hilarious. She laughed so long that it became contagious. Garibaldi struck his thigh several times with his hand, which they assumed was his way of laughing, a thought that set them off afresh.

"Oh! That was almost as much fun as listening to Yoska at the campfire, the night we got our marks!"

"That's it! I'll be back before you know it!" Claude gave her a quick hug and ran out the door.

"Bring back some food for Agent Horner, mit'anksi!" Firewalker called after her.

Claude was still running when she returned to the warehouse. She was in such a hurry that she nearly collided with her father at the door.

"You're back!" she said, bestowing a breathless peck on his cheek. "Did Aunt like her rose bowl? Wait until you see what arrived during the night!"

She flew into the room, dropping a napkin-wrapped egg sandwich in front of a bemused Micah, and headed to the shelves on the back wall. "Now I'm sure there were some leather thongs in here..." She rummaged through some baskets and gave a cry of delight.

Frank sipped his coffee and stared wordlessly as his daughter fluttered around the clay giant with fists full of strings. The amphoraka didn't move. It was like watching the Lilliputians restraining Gulliver.

Gertrude finally had to ask. "Claude, whatever are you doing?"

"Finger cymbals!" she exclaimed, with a radiant smile. "When Mr. Garibaldi strikes his leg with his hand...you see, right here? It's the only spot where he can touch. If I tie one cymbal here and the other like so..."

She'd finished the final knot and stood back admiring her work. "Mr. Garibaldi, I'd like you to meet my father."

The amphoraka raised his arm a few inches and carefully brought it down. There was a small, pleasant chime.

She sighed with satisfaction. "Oh that is so much better, don't you think?"

YES, he answered.

"Fascinating," Firewalker murmured.

"Aye." Frank moved closer to the creature and tilted his head. He liked to be able to look a man in the eye. "Mr. Garibaldi, is that right? I'm very pleased to meet you. You can call me Frank."

They all gathered around the amphoraka, asking him questions, listening to his answers ring out in his charming new voice. Frank and Lem touched and prodded his carapace, tossing observations back and forth and making copious notes. Gertrude had pressed a sheet of paper against the symbol on his chest and was rubbing with a bit of charcoal.

It was all a pleasant buzz in Micah's head. He sat on his stool, his half-eaten sandwich in one hand, his eyes focused Claude, in her men's trousers, a smudge of dirt on her cheek, her glorious hair scooped back as though it were a nuisance. He thought that he had never seen anyone look so beautiful or seem so alive. Suddenly Micah couldn't catch his breath. He compared the vivid woman before him with the memory of the poor sad Princess trailing up the ramp to the Imperial yacht. However could he have confused the two? *This* was his lock picker, the woman who had so inconveniently stirred his blood under Blavatsky's roof. He felt as though something were collapsing inside him.

The Russian woman's caution sprang to mind: "You have walls within you. I would fear the repercussions if they were to be breached." It was like being doused with a bucket of freezing water. She was correct, of course, the cagey old bitch. What was he thinking? Those walls were what kept him safe. He couldn't survive a day in his world without them. He gave himself a mental slap across the face. He was tired and hungry, there was too much on his mind. It was a momentary weakness. Yes, she was an attractive woman. He had met plenty of attractive women before. He would push this aside, just as he'd done in Dubrovnik. Fortunately, she hated the sight of him. That would make it easier for him to harden himself against her. Once he left Prague, he would never have to see her again.

Until now, Frank and Firewalker had been plodding along in Tesla's footsteps, progressing steadily, but with no spark to push them beyond the obvious. Now everything was different, not merely because they had a genuine amphoraka to work with, but specifically because they had met Garibaldi. For hour after hour, he tapped out his life story while Gertrude and Micah took turns writing it down. The person inside the clay was not an ordinary centurion, but had been a commander under Napoleon. He had spent his entire life fighting for the future of his people. When the Great Unifier was stricken by apoplexy and Augustus assumed the consulship, Garibaldi stood with the Carbonari to defend the freedom of the Italian people. Escaping to France, he fought against Augustus in the Gallic War. In the years that followed, he and others like him had fueled an underground war to liberate Italy from oppression. Many died in the attempt. Some were caught and publicly executed in horrible ways, to set an example. Garibaldi was singled out for what he said was the cruelest punishment of all, becoming one of the first souls to be transmigrated into clay and compelled for thirty years to obey the orders of the tyrant he had fought so hard to bring down. No wonder that he volunteered when Sandtmann sent out the call.

Gertrude's hand was so swollen from writing that she sat at the dinner table soaking it in a basin of whatever it was that did for Epsom salts in Bohemia. She couldn't have cared less. Giving release to thirty years of angry silence! Never in her life had she felt so useful. It was a good thing that Claude's cymbal idea had worked out or they all would have gone mad, as well as deaf, from the pounding.

Sir Alastair wanted to begin at once on a machine for artificial speech, but Mr. Firewalker had reigned him in and reminded him of their priorities. Apparently part of Mr. Firewalker's job was to restrain his employer's wilder flights of inventive fancy. He did so with remarkable tact. She shot a covert glance across the table to where he, Sir Alastair and Claude were discussing the adhesive properties of various resins. His severe features were lit with passion, but his tremendous dignity never faltered. Gertrude felt Agent Horner's clever eyes watching her; her cheeks reddened.

"I found Mr. Garibaldi's revelations fascinating, didn't you Mr. Horner? And so poignant?" Gertrude's grandfather had taught her that the best defense was to seize control of the situation.

"Poignant?"

"It was kind of you to offer to sleep in the workshop tonight and keep him company."

"Kindness is not a useful trait in the Service, Miss Bell. My offer was simply expedient. I am, you will recall, supposed to be at odds with my paramour and must not show myself at my hotel until tomorrow evening."

"You could have stayed here, with us. Sir Alastair offered to make up a bed in the parlour."

He shrugged. "I'm on duty, Miss Bell. Mr. Tesla's former accommodations are sufficient and appropriate."

"Still, you can't deny being moved by what Mr. Garibaldi told us. 'If I am free and I can speak, there is life.' The bravery of his spirit!"

Mr. Firewalker, who seemed to be able to listen to a different conversation with each of his ears, broke in. "It changes everything, Miss Bell. I agree."

"Agree with what, Leski?" Claude asked, following his voice.

"Because of our own decency, what we've learned from Mr. Garibaldi must change how we proceed. You were quite right, mit'anksi, in urging us not to destroy the amphoraeka. Once they have voices, even so small as a pair of brass disks, some of them might choose life. We must do what we can to allow them that choice."

"Aye!" Sir Alastair punched his left fist emphatically into his cupped right hand. It made a satisfying smack. "Our programme for the automatons should focus on two sets of actions: one, to obliterate that hieroglyph that obliges the amphoraeka to obey; and the other, to shoot at anything human that tries to stop them! When Britain faces Rome, these puir souls will be free to choose life or death as they will." He knocked three times on the edge of the table and grinned. "Aye, it's good to know where we're headed at last!"

Gertrude started to applaud with the others, but was stopped by a terrible thought. "We've forgotten something!" she said, jumping to her feet in a kind of panic. "What about Maud? If we don't rescue her, she'll be married to the Emperor's grandson before any of this can happen."

Sir Alastair got up from his seat and put a fatherly hand on her shoulder. "Aye, Miss Bell. It may well be turn out so. We'll see her free, dinnae fash. But before that, I know it isn't fair, but she may well have some very hard times. She'll be needing a brave friend, puir lass, when we bring her home. It's good you'll be there for her, Miss Bell."

He let her cry into his shirtfront until she was steady enough to flee from the kitchen and up to her room.

§🐚

Claude was restless from Gertrude's outburst. She felt obscurely guilty being safely in her father's house, in control of her own mind and body, free to do whatever she wanted tomorrow. Yes, she and Gertrude might have easily died in the woods; but they hadn't. Her more sensible self knew that they had fought hard to come through, but another piece of herself felt only lucky. She was uncomfortable to think that Fate could so easily have dealt her the opposite hand. If Madame Blavatsky had thought that she was "the princess we seek," she would be the one who was locked away in Rome.

It must be horrible to feel so totally abandoned. Nikola had given up in despair. Claude still didn't quite trust Agent Horner's motives, but she believed his report. She knew Nikola's weaknesses as well as his strengths. He was the kind of person who could easily die from deciding there was no more point in living. If he left Italy alive, it might take years in a sanatorium to bring the light back to those beautiful sad eyes. Hot tears streamed from her own eyes, soaking the pillow. Those few wonderful days they'd had here together seemed hardly more real than the castles she'd built in the air when she was fifteen, writing "Claude Tesla" in her diary. She had bought back her life, but what about the life she could now never have?

She wanted to kill someone. Not some *thing* like a werewolf, which was only a kind of beast after all and killed for its own survival. No, she wanted to kill the people who had deliberately poisoned their lives: hers and Nikola's and poor Princess Maud's. She wanted to take a knife and plunge in into Caesar's heart, to split that Baron's head open like a coconut. As for Madame, if Claude had the chance, she would kneel on that fat body until the last breath of air was pressed out of the lungs, then pluck out those spooky eyes with her bare fingers!

Claude sat up, grabbing her knees to her chest. Her heart was racing so fast it didn't seem her body could contain it. She was frightening herself. She had never felt this kind of rage before. Wakhangli Mani had always said anger was poison; she was beginning to understand what he meant. She made herself lie flat on her back and pretended she was a rag doll, each limb growing soft and floppy. Her heartbeat slowed and her breathing mimicked the rhythm of sleep. Her mind, however, refused to relax. Her anger was spent; so was her grief, but the thoughts wouldn't leave.

If only the Princess had been strong enough for Agent Horner to smuggle her out. How awful for her that her efforts to stop the drug had only made things worse. She must despise herself. If she had to keep living this way, if she had to go through with that marriage and wait however many months until the automatons were armed and there were enough of them for Britain to crush Augustus, all the drarnego in the forest wouldn't be enough to bring her back.

Nikola and the Princess, both lost. Claude felt so helpless. She yawned. A bit of memory slipped in, looking in the basin of a fountain and seeing herself reflected in duplicate. To the remembered sound of tinkling waters, she finally drifted off to sleep.

۹

Groggy from her restless night, Claude headed over to the warehouse after everyone else had gone. As she entered the open workspace, a blast of water whooshed by her face, missing her by inches. She screamed, dropping the basket of bread and fruit.

"Blast, Father! What in the name of…!"

"I didn't hear you coming, lass; your foot is that soft." Frank was unapologetic.

"You might have put my eyes out!"

"Do you think?" He regarded her thoughtfully. "Don't move from where you are."

She stood there while he took a folding measure from his leather apron and held it to Garibaldi's chest. He then brought the same measure over to her. His thumb came to her forehead. He gave a grunt of satisfaction. "Aye, not too bad for a first test. What do you think, lass?" He pointed to her attacker. It was an automaton, standing with one arm extended. A hose, strapped to that arm, led from a bucket hanging from a rude harness on its back. "Just a wee change to the algorithm and I'll have it exactly where we want to be, and you can begin punching the tapes."

Frank had been running calculations since sun-up. He was, as he liked to put it, firing on all cylinders. Agent Horner had been set sweating over a bubbling vat of some viscous substance that he and Firewalker had concocted. To Gertrude had been delegated the more delicate task of transcribing a message for Tesla onto rice paper, using the juice of crushed berries for ink, "in case yon Horner has to choke it down before he can deliver it." Now that the shops were open, Firewalker was on his way to purchase a specific type of gramophone that Frank thought he might be able to motorize to play through the night and keep Garibaldi company.

Her father seemed so happy. Claude hated that she was about to ruin it for him, but she felt she had no choice. With purpose in her stride, she walked over to where Agent Horner was stirring his presumably sticky mess. The reek nearly stopped her before she arrived. It smelt like an uncomfortable marriage of pine trees, blood and tomcat spray.

"You get used to after the first five minutes or so."

She wrinkled her nose in distaste but resisted the desire to pinch it closed. It was important to appear strong. "I don't see why you have to. It would seem simple enough to mechanize that."

"Presumably, once your father has a final formula. For now, I'm to keep stirring. He comes by every now and again to check the consistency." He rotated his right shoulder with a grimace. "Playing the Baron's errand boy is making me soft."

"Your fighting skills could use some practice."

"So could your small talk."

This was not the time to antagonize him. She cleared her throat. "When you met me that first night in Dubrovnik, when I tried to escape, you really thought I was Princess Maud."

He nodded. "She was still a girl when I'd last seen her and the resemblance…" You overwhelmed me, Micah wanted to say; and I lost my better senses. Instead he twisted his lips into a mocking smile. "You were certain imperious enough for royalty. When I saw the two of you side by side the next day, I assumed you must be working for Pinkerton, that he had planted you in Europe as a decoy and it was only bad luck that they'd found the Princess as well. I was more than a little annoyed with Pinkerton for not having warned me."

"It would have been a good plan." She tried to act nonchalant. "Only think what would have happened after the wedding, when Augustus made his grand announcement and it turned out he'd married his heir to a nobody."

"It would have made him a figure of ridicule throughout all of Europe and far easier to topple. Now he'll only appear vicious."

"Only? Isn't vicious is bad enough?"

"He's an Emperor. If he gets what he wants, how he got it won't discredit him much in the world's eyes. That, Miss Monteith, is your lesson in politics for today."

"Then we have to be sure he's discredited." She ignored the sarcasm and ploughed ahead. "I need you to sneak me into Rome. I want to exchange places with the Princess."

He started to laugh. Her stare drilled into his head and he froze.

"You're serious."

"Agent Horner," Frank called to him. "Keep stirring!"

"Deadly serious."

"I'm sorry, sir!" He put his hands back on the stick. "Don't be ridiculous," he muttered.

"It's not ridiculous. It was your idea."

"It was not!"

"Yes it was."

"If the two of you are planning a rematch, you'll have to wait until Agent Horner is finished with that batch of resin." Frank came up behind Claude and put a restraining hand on her shoulder. She whirled around to face him. "What's up with you, lass? You look exactly like your...like your Aunt Nan about to tell me a hard truth."

"I want Agent Horner to exchange me for the Princess."

"I've already told her it's ridiculous, Sir Alastair," he cut in.

She rode right over him. "There must be a way to get me into Rome. Then Agent Horner would be able to sneak her out with no problem, because everyone's attention would be on me. You know, like sleight of hand. Don't you see?"

"It's not ridiculous," Frank said slowly. "But it's too dangerous."

She took a deep breath and drew her self up to her full height, her eyes level with his. "It isn't dangerous at all. You've all said so: it's too important for Augustus to keep the Princess alive. All I need to do is pretend to be Maud, marry the Prince and wait patiently as long as necessary. "

"It might be months, lass." Frank shook his head.

"I know how to wait, Father. When I have to, I can even be patient. I can bear it far better than she can. Most important, the marriage would be meaningless."

"You couldn't possibly!" Gertrude could no longer pretend not to hear them.

Claude turned a steely eye on her. "You should know better than anyone that I absolutely can."

"Can isn't should," Gertrude answered stoutly. "It's a mad thing to do."

"I thought you were her friend."

"I am. But now I'm your friend as well. What purpose does it serve to lose you both?"

"Don't think like a friend, Gertrude. Think like a scholar. Agent Hunter has shown what purpose it would serve. This is a great game of power. Surely it's worth the risk of a pawn to put the Emperor in check?"

"In theory," Gertrude unhappily had to admit.

Claude smiled. "In practice. And it's not much risk. Unlike the Princess, I'll absolutely know that you'll all get me out in the end. In the meanwhile, I'll have Centurion Ravioli here to protect me." She turned to address her father, her voice strong and steady. "If someone were holding a Prince of Wales captive, and the Service had an agent of sufficient resemblance to pull it off, wouldn't Lord Pinkerton be obligated to try?"

Frank blinked. "God help me, lass, but he would."

"Well, then." She pecked him on the cheek and smiled happily, as if it were all settled. "Ever since I graduated Vassar, I've been itching for something useful to do."

What had Frank expected? This was what happened when you raised up a child in your own image. For years, Nan had been honking about like Cassandra and he had refused to listen. The thought of his sister made his eyes roll skyward. "Thank Heaven that I saw your Aunt the other day," he grumbled, trying to contain his fear and his pride. "I won't be able to look her in the face again until we get you back home."

Claude looked at Firewalker expectantly. He had listened quietly to the rough outlines of the plan. His face betrayed nothing, but that was hardly unusual. He chewed thoughtfully on a breadroll, then washed it down with a generous sip of coffee.

"Well Leski?" she asked, unable to bear the silence a moment longer. "What do you think?

He took another sip. "Agent Horner," he tendered. "You've told us the Princess is dependent on drugs, that the difficulties presented by this dependency are what led you to divert your attentions to Mr. Tesla."

"Yes." The shadows shifted on Micah's face. "I see your point, Mr. Firewalker. The Princess might not survive the escape."

"And in her place, Miss Monteith would presumably be similarly dosed," he continued.

"Of course she would. Oh, Claude, not again!"

"You're forgetting something, Gertrude. How much of the drarnego do we have?"

"Enough for one dose. Possibly two."

"Perfect. Half for the Princess. And the other half for me, when the time is ripe."

"Would you be able to remember...?" Gertrude began doubtfully.

Claude cut her off breezily. "We can show Agent Horner how it's done."

Micah slashed a firm negative with both his hands. "No. Mr. Firewalker is correct, this is out of the question."

"It's something the Rom gave us," Claude explained. "It clears the drugs from the system."

"I wouldn't dare doubt you," he assured her darkly. "But you don't understand. The Princess's body has been acclimated to the drugs. The dosage level they're administering now would be dangerous to a clean body."

She opened her mouth to speak, but he cut her short.

"A single dose might kill you," he said bluntly, "before we had a chance to try your Romani herb."

"Could Maud try again to give them up?" Regardless of where her heart was, and right now it was flopping like a pancake, Gertrude always tried to consider all sides of a problem.

"There isn't enough time to do it safely. In any case, they won't allow her to try. The Baron was clear about that. Not until well after the wedding."

"How are the drugs provided?" Frank asked abruptly.

"There's a Court physician who has charge of them. Catoni. He comes to the villa to inject her."

"Would it be possible to swap the vials? Replace them with water...?"

Micah was disappointed in Sir Alastair for the weakness of the proposal. "It might work once, but every day?"

"Would he be susceptible to a bribe?"

"Wakhangli Mani!" Claude was shocked; not at the idea, but at the source.

Firewalker shrugged. "Men are known to be, mit'anksi. Particularly the wasichu."

"This one would be too much in fear of his life," Micah asserted.

"If only they'd given her pills or powder," Frank mused. "It would be simple for Claude to pretend to take them."

"Too bad Maud doesn't give herself the injection," Claude joked bitterly. Her father sat up sharply, as if he'd touched a live electrical wire. "What? You have an idea!"

Frank leaned so close to Gertrude that she jumped. "You know her best, Miss Bell. Would she do it?"

Gertrude was confounded. "Voluntarily give herself...? Why?"

Like her father's, Claude's mind raced under pressure. "Because she knows she needs the medication, but it's embarrassing that people see it administered in this way. It would be, wouldn't it? Embarrassing?"

"In truth, mit'anksi, I believe it would be the opposite. As long as someone else is administering the dose, the Princess can tell herself that it's happening against her will. If she were to do the deed herself, she'd become her own jailer. That's a great deal to ask of someone, even in their own best interest."

"If she were told it was the first step to rescue? I think she might safely be told that much." They'd already determined that it would be to risky to tell Maud about the plan in advance. "What do you think, Miss Bell?"

Gertrude was troubled by Firewalker's observation. "I don't know. And I'm not certain I understand. Do you mean that she would be injecting herself with water."

"We've seen what happens when the drug is withdrawn from her body," Micah objected.

"Then you *are* going to give Maud the drarnego!"

"Any treatment should wait until we have the Princess in hospital."

Gertrude was about to contradict Sir Alastair when Firewalker spoke again. He was grave and respectful. "It would be best to consult your kumpania, Miss Bell. Safer for the Princess. They are the experts with this herb. They would know best what quantities might be needed, or if it would be efficacious at all in this regard."

"Point well taken," Micah agreed. "The Princess's condition is precarious. We ought not upset the balance."

"My object," Frank broke in; "was to remove the *physician* as a complication, not the drugs. If the Princess were in the habit of administering her own injection…"

Micah grimaced. "You don't understand. Every member of that household is a spy. The maids would notice. After we made the exchange, Miss Monteith would need to inject herself with whatever was in those vials."

"Or pretend to do so," Frank grinned, his eyes twinkling. "Years ago, Pinkerton had me undercover in China. I masqueraded as an opium addict for six months. Learned a clever trick with a needle." Father and daughter bent their heads together and started to talk excitedly. It was the same each time he allowed Claude to work with him on one of his cases. Once he made the decision, he'd push aside his reservations about the danger and the two would lose themselves in the excitement of a *Boy's Own* adventure.

Micah was not pleased. "This allows a critical piece of planning to rest on a supposition. As Mr. Firewalker observed, it seems a great deal to ask of the Princess."

Gertrude felt that her old friend's character was being ravaged by this discussion. "Maud is a fighter! Even when she doesn't need to be."

"I've seen that, Miss Bell. I admire the effort she made to work with me. But she's not herself any longer. I saw it in her eyes. Like Mr. Tesla, she's given up."

"She mustn't give up now! Surely when she hears that Claude and I are safe…"

"She's always thought you safe. What else was I to say when she asked?"

"Then you must say that you've spoken with me and that I'm asking her…" Gertrude thought back to their shared schoolroom and clapped her hands. "No! Say that I am *challenging* her to do it. Maud can be very competitive, particularly where I'm concerned."

"I would gladly, if I thought she would believe me."

"We must make her believe you. I could write to her."

"What if someone else read it?" he countered. "I don't think anyone around her reads English, but I'd hate for her life to depend on that."

"Something else then. Some item of significance that she'd know came from me. The Tudors and Elizabethans always seemed to have a ring to send." Gertrude made a moue of dissatisfaction. The modern monarchy had a distressing lack of significant jewelry.

"Would a photograph do?" Mr. Firewalker asked. "I brought my kit from Chicago."

ॐ

Time was short. After Rappaccini returned to his paramour tonight, Agent Horner might only safely steal a few hours more in the warehouse before his return to Venice. They worked rapidly on the details of the plan. What hours were left were used in a furious debrief, teasing out as much information as possible on the world in which Claude would find herself.

She sat side by side with the Italian Englishman, listening intently and blessing her well-trained memory. The benefit in impersonating someone who was living on the fringe of consciousness was that a few mistakes would not be fatal. Maud might reasonably be expected to forget where she was or who she was talking with. Still, it was important for Claude to know as much as she could about the major players and how the Princess reacted to their presence, as well as to have a general sense of how she spent her days.

The agent was a thorough and patient instructor. How odd that he wore the same skin as Rappaccini; they couldn't have seemed more dissimilar if they had truly been two men. This man, though self-possessed, bore himself modestly. He was respectful of her Father and Leski, and spoke kindly to Gertrude. As for their own differences, she had to admit they were as much her fault as his. She dimpled to recall the outcome of their skirmish. Some men wouldn't have been able to set that aside and work with her, one professional with another, as Agent Horner was doing.

Preparing to sketch out a rough floor plan of the ground floor of the Villa Borghese, he stood to stretch his legs and fetch a piece of drafting paper. She found herself staring. He had borrowed some of Nikola's work clothes from a nail in the loft: a pair of worn corduroy pants and a loose shirt. Out of his black Imperial tunic, his slim, muscular body was just as feline, but lacked the threat beneath the surface; he wasn't coiled to pounce. Father made a joke and he laughed, a natural full-throated laugh, throwing his head back and displaying a mouth full of white teeth. Claude found herself fascinated by his neck. It rose from the collarless shirt, a strong, beautiful column of muscle. She imagined her hand touching it, tracing the ropy vein to his clavicle. It brought a fiery blush to her face, a blush that didn't subsided when he caught her stare with his dark blue eyes. She felt a clench somewhere below her belly, as if she'd caught a butterfly there and it was fluttering its wings. She felt hot and embarrassed, and at the same time she wanted to giggle.

Why did he make her feel these things, this calculating untrustworthy man? She had dreamed about Nikola Tesla for years. Nikola was the first man she had ever loved and, before all this had happened, she thought that he finally loved her too. The life she imagined for them would have been one of shared work and content. What she had felt just now was nothing like content. It was startling and turbulent, and she wanted to feel it again. What was wrong with her?

"Your eyes!" he exclaimed, staring back.

She wouldn't have thought her face could feel any hotter. "What about my eyes?!"

"It won't work!" He sounded genuinely crestfallen. "We've forgotten all about them. Sir Alastair, this can't possibly work. When I first saw the two of them, I didn't know which was which, but I could see it was the obvious way to tell them apart."

"It's true," Gertrude's voice was soft with regret. "Even when my mind was utterly confused, I could always tell."

"And the Imperial household has been closeted with the Princess for months now. They'd notice in an instant."

Claude jumped to her feet, sending the stool beneath her clattering to the floor. "Damn it!" She didn't care who heard her say it.

Frank seemed oddly unperturbed. "Maybe it's not a problem."

"Of course it is, Father. I can't wear dark glasses all the time."

"Dark glasses? No, of course you can't, lass." There was an enameled iron cabinet tucked below the bit of loft. He brought out a Mason jar and set it carefully on her table. While he washed his hands, Firewalker spread a clean sheet of white paper next to the jar. The others watched curiously.

Claude bent for a better look. The jar seemed to be full of water, except for a few coloured flecks at the bottom. "What is it?"

"A wee thing I started working on during the Mexican wars. For the Service. Something told me to have Lem pack it up." He plunged his hand into the jar and fished out one of the tiny things.

"It can't be a weapon; it's far too small." Leaning over Frank's shoulder, all Claude could see was a coloured dot.

"In as much as deception is weapon, this would be an aid to that end."

Claude unhooked the small magnifier from her chatelaine. She had recently added this useful item having realized, in the forest, the danger in having to rely on a few paltry matches. "I don't understand. It looks like a bit of glass."

"Not Vitriflex? Look closely."

"No," she said promptly. "Too thin. You've never been able to press Vitriflex so thin. This is nearly as thin as a fish scale."

"Clever lass," he said approvingly, reaching around to give her cheek a pat. "You place them against the eye. Like this." He dampened his forefinger with the tip of his tongue, then touched it against the disk. The disk stuck and he lifted it ever so carefully. Holding his eye open wide with the fingers of his other hand, he gently touched the disk against it. "The curve fits to the curve of the eye, and the wetness causes a wee bit of suction." He removed his finger. The brown circle stuck there.

"Oh! You have a brown eye! Does it hurt?"

He smiled broadly. "Seems strange at first, a bit of pressure like a new boot. But once you becomes accustomed to it…"

"But why invent such a thing, Sir Alastair?"

"Well might you ask, Agent Horner, as one who might have need of it someday. Our agents can grow their beards or shave them, change the colour of their hair, brown their skin with walnut juice…The one thing you cannot do is disguise your eyes. Imagine if we had been able to have a dozen men safely in Rome years ago. We might not be in this position now."

"Agent Horner has blue eyes, not brown." Claude noted automatically.

"So he does, but Agent Horner has the advantage of being genuinely Italian. And his eyes aren't a British blue."

"No. They're quite dark. Like deep water."

Gertrude shot her a keen look.

Claude didn't even notice; she was too fascinated by her father's piebald eyes. "So this is a kind of mask."

"Aye, for now. Someday, once I've perfected the technique, maybe there might be other possible applications. Imagine if I could shape the curve of the lens in such a way that it might have a corrective effect on the vision."

"Would that be possible?" Gertrude was amazed. "It's so small!"

"In theory, Miss Bell, aye it would. Descartes proposed it over two hundred years ago. And it seems inevitable I give it a try. My honoured ancestor did, after all, invent bifocals."

☙

Gertrude brought Mrs. Hutchinson a small pot of seedlings, entreating her to tend them for a month until she would return to Prague to retrieve them. The Ambassador's wife was diplomatically sanguine about cooperating with plans that couldn't be explained. She also graciously allowed Gertrude to borrow the Embassy carriage.

It was a good thing she had. With such a long list of errands, Gertrude would have never otherwise been able to accomplish everything. She made a mental note to send the good lady some very British luxuries as soon as she got to London.

It seemed that she needed something from every corner of the city. Clothes were easy to find; copper spoons and boxes a little less so. Sir Alastair's own list was left with a pharmacist in the morning, with the bundle to be retrieved some hours later. Finger cymbals, which Claude had insisted on obtaining for Sandtmann, had been a bit of a challenge until someone at a music store provided the address of a woman who supplied costumes for the ballet and opera.

It was late afternoon before Gertrude was able to send the carriage back to the house at the Josefov with the fruits of her labors.

She had left the most important errand for last, the message that so much would depend on. Turning her back on the castle, she strolled the upper end of the King's Road, hoping it would not be difficult to find the house she sought. She needn't have worried. It was exactly as Yoska had described it, a pistachio green building in the old style, with a large white beet hanging from a wrought iron arm above the archway. Opening the door, she found herself in a small courtyard.

An old man was spilling over the sides of a weathered bentwood chair, a skinny yellow dog at his feet. Both were apparently deep in slumber until she walked by. Then he opened one bloodshot eye and growled. So did the dog.

She stopped in front of him. "I'm sorry, I don't speak Czech," she said in German.

"Nobody home," he said in that same language. "Go away."

"I have a message for a friend," she persisted. "I was told to leave it here."

"No friends," he grunted. "Go."

"No," she said firmly, folding her arms. "I shan't." Switching to halting Romani, she said "I have a message for my vitsa and I won't go until you agree to take it."

He stopped pretending to be asleep, but looked no less disgruntled. He was a most disreputable looking man, unshaven rather than bearded, wearing mismatched clothing so riddled with holes that it must have been the dirt that held them together. Pushing his greasy cap back from his greasier hair, he regarded her skeptically.

"Your vitsa!" He spat three times onto the cobbles.

"Yes," she said, wondering if it would be effective for her to spit, too.

He and the dog held their ground. It was a stand off. She understood she had no other choice.

"Oh very well then…" She bend down and quickly pulled up her skirts and petticoats to display two inches of bare thigh.

He leaned forward with narrowed eyes that went from the patch of skin to her face and back again. He nodded sharply and she let her skirts fall back with a sigh.

Then, in a preposterously contrary exhibition of manners, he sprang to his feet and kissed her heartily on both cheeks. "*Droboy tume Romale!* Come, we have drink!" He grabbed her by the hand and led her through the courtyard to another door. The dog, in a delirium of tail wagging, followed.

20 - INFILTRATION

Pacing restlessly past the uniformed doorkeeper, the black-clad centurion frequently checked his timepiece. "*Basta!*" he fumed. "We're going to miss the train." Inside the hotel, his woman fussed endlessly with the angle of her cunning little bonnet. Micah spotted the cab turning down the street.

"Call me a cab!" He pushed past the uniformed doorkeeper and yanked the woman away from the pier glass so hard that she nearly tripped over her yards of emerald taffeta.

The cab stopped. With an imperious toss of coin to the doorkeeper, and another to the boy who scurried to help with the bags, Rappaccini handed the dark beauty into the cab. It wasn't empty.

The shadows of the back seat neatly hid the woman in blue. She attempted to appear blasé, but her cheeks, behind the dotted blue veil of a ridiculous hat, were flushed with nervous excitement.

He briefly raised his eyebrows before climbing in.

The railway station was filled with travelers. The woman in green melted quickly into the milling crowd.

"This way, *cara mia*," Rappaccini drawled to the woman in blue. It was fascinating that four small words could be made to sound so arrogant.

"Si, *mi amor*." The woman tilted her head in an attitude of adoration.

It was amusing, but it would be dangerous to take the game too lightly. Taking Miss Bell by the elbow, Micah gave her arm a little pinch. Swaggering as if he owned the station, he strode towards the platform at a pace slow enough to accommodate the glide required by the torrent of blue and purple ribbon flounces that was, according to Elettra, the latest word in fashion for the kept women of Italy.

Only Italian trains ran across the borders of Augustus's Empire. The string of dark red carriages, picked out with arabesques of gold paint, gleamed as if they had been enameled yesterday and the brasses shone like burnished gold. Even if it seemed a bit old fashioned when compared to trains on other platforms, the effect was rather splendid.

The brutish man at the gate wore a great deal of gold braid on his sleeves and had a bayonet slung over his shoulder. He inspected their papers as if he were authenticating the Ten Commandments. Impatiently tapping his foot, Rappaccini held out his hand. The official glared at him and slapped the documents down hard.

The Centurion didn't flinch, but coolly folded the papers and slipped them into his tunic. He deliberately did not look at the woman on his arm as he propelled her to their compartment, but he thought he felt a small shiver. He understood; the minute she boarded this train, she would effectively be entering Italy. He paused to fleck imaginary dust from his cuff, enabling her to gather up her skirts and her courage, then helped her mount the two steps to cross the Rubicon.

§♠

After disappearing in the crowds at the station, Elettra Rianero made her way to the ladies' cloakroom. She tucked her feathered bonnet into her carpetbag and mussed her dark hair. The elaborate green overskirt was whisked off, revealing a simple black one. Drawing a thin shawl over her bodice, she crossed the ends behind her waist. She rubbed her eyes hard, to redden them.

She felt a twinge of apprehension. She had run errands for the family from the time she was old enough to keep secrets; however, this was a foreign land, where they spoke languages she didn't know. Moreover, her cousin was using her papers to slip Signorina Bell into Rome. Without her papers, Elettra was a non-person. If she made a mistake before making contact, there would be nowhere for her to turn.

She picked up the bag, assumed a posture of great weariness and trudged out of the station. Anyone who noticed her at all would assume her to be a servant or perhaps a midwife returning home after a long delivery, someone not worth looking at twice. With no other option but to trust to her cousin's instructions, she made her way to the Josefov and a small cafe on a quiet street.

❧

Despite the early hour, Rappaccini had ordered champagne to be brought to their compartment. He over-tipped the steward, who took one look at the woman's ensemble and gave a knowing wink. She made a pretense of ignoring him in a very grand manner.

Turning the key in the lock, Micah loosed his tunic. "That will ensure no one disturbs us for several hours. I'm afraid we'll have to make an appearance in the first class dining carriage for dinner tonight, but other than that, you should be able to relax until we arrive in Venice."

"I wish that were possible." Miss Bell unpinned the frantically embellished hat. He noticed that, in order to set it on the seat beside her, she had to lean forward before swiveling to the left. Elettra was slightly longer in the waist than she. Miss Bell looked supremely uncomfortable.

"Change into your own things. I'll pop out to the smoking car for a cigar."

She seemed like the kind of girl who would bravely protest. He ducked out before she could do so.

When he returned, she was wearing something much less turbulent and reading a book. Reaching up to the luggage rack, he pulled down a hamper of dainties provided by the hotel in Prague.

"I daresay you'll be more than ready for this now. See what there is. I'll open the champagne." He could see the surprise on her face and smiled. "As long as we have it, we might as well enjoy it. Certainly you've earned it. To your release from my cousin's wicked torture device," he said, handing her a flute.

"To success," she corrected. "For all of us."

"Quite right you are." He took a sip. As he should have expected, it was prosecco, not champagne. Pleasant enough, but he couldn't help thinking that Dumas père's purported mistress would have disapproved. "Ah, I see you're reading Boccaccio," he remarked, to cover an amusement he would not have been able to explain.

"The Italian shelves at the Univerzita's bookstore didn't run to novels. It was either this or *La Commedia*. I thought *Il Decameron* more appropriate to my, um, role."

"I admire your commitment to detail." He did.

They tucked gladly into the picnic, talking all the while about Boccaccio and Chaucer, punting on the Isis and similar University tea party topics. Until now, he had thought of Miss Bell more as an adjunct—to the Princess or to that hellion, Miss Monteith—than as a person in her own right. In her own right, he learned, Miss Bell was a gentlewoman and a scholar. Armed for this mission with nothing beyond her loyalty and a stout heart, she reminded him of the men who were the backbone of the Service, the quieter sorts who buckled down and got the job done.

"How kind you are being to me!" she said impulsively.

He broke off, puzzled, in the middle of an anecdote about a venerable Classics tutor and the Elgin marbles. "Pardon?"

"We hated you in Dubrovnik. We thought you were cold and heartless." Gertrude's manner was never other than frank. She regarded him with unsentimental compassion. "But I think you must be a very kind person. It must be painfully difficult, to do what you do; though you do it exceedingly well."

He knew that Miss Bell wanted nothing more than to extend the hand of friendship, but men in his position did not form friendships. The unforeseen danger of his trip to Prague was that he had enjoyed those collegial hours and let his guard down. He might be in a closed compartment now, still speaking English with a decidedly English girl, but Rappaccini would be back in Venice by morning. Whatever had been open and easy in his manner shifted subtly. He shook his head. "I'm afraid you're mistaken. Kindness is not a quality I've ever had the urge to cultivate. It wouldn't be useful in my line of work."

She was openly puzzled by his response. "I only meant that I'm grateful for your courtesies. You've taken such pains to make me comfortable."

"Your well-being is critical to the success of this mission," he drawled, leaning back into his seat. He tilted his head so that he seemed to be looking down his elegant nose. "Don't mistake my intentions for anything more." It was cruel, but it was certain to discourage her.

Miss Bell flushed with equal measures of anger and embarrassment. "I can only say the same!" she said sharply, whipping open the Boccaccio.

He hoped she was not the sort to hold a grudge. Dinner tonight would be a public affair and they would have to play at being lovebirds. With a touch of sadness, Micah pulled out a volume of Jules Verne that he'd bought for Tesla in Prague.

Provided they both have reading material, two people can share a railway carriage in total silence for a surprising long period of time.

They arrived in Venice late in the morning, confederates if not friends. Gertrude's temper had cooled before dinner; as ever, her own good sense had seen to that. All that was left was a measure of disappointment that she'd been let down by her usual knack for taking the measure of people.

Sir Lowthian always said that if she had been born male, she'd have been a natural for the diplomatic service. Agent Horner had dented her confidence. Well, whatever else he was or wasn't, the man was a professional and she would do her best to live up to his standards.

Today that meant waiting patiently in his rooms, the legendary city of Venice tantalizingly within reach but entirely prohibited, while Agent Horner went to check on Mr. Tesla.

Tonight, they would both take the southbound train that curved past Florence on the way to Rome. Rappaccini's commission papers allowed him unrestricted passage in the officer's smoking car. He had secured a second class berth for Gertrude in what was euphemistically called the "ladies' carriage," where she would be as inconspicuous as possible until she disembarked. Inconspicuous and alone.

Frank tried to be matter-of-fact with his goodbyes, but was no more successful than when he'd sent Claude back to college after her holidays. He hugged her a little too tightly and mumbled something incomprehensible into her hair.

His anxiety made her even more determined to be strong. "Dinnae fash, Father," she said brightly.

He usually laughed when she tried to speak Scots, but not now. He loosened his grip on her and managed a smile. "You make me proud, lass," he said finally, and gave her forehead the kind of kiss that parents give as blessing.

She was glad there was so much work to do with the automatons and Garibaldi. He would be too busy to worry much, he and Leski both.

The courier who took the diplomatic pouch was told only that his two mysterious passengers would leave him in Bern. The young men were dressed for the country in rough britches and boots, each carrying a large rucksack. Their faces were obscured by soft caps. They didn't speak at all during the flight. After the first quarter hour, the courier didn't either. When they landed, the pair slipped away from the airfield. It was a few-mile tramp to the bicycle shed, where telegraphed instructions to a Swiss-based Pinkerton had ensured that a pair of machines would be waiting for them.

For several days, Claude and Elettra pedaled through the beautiful but strenuously rolling landscape, stopping only for the occasional meal. The sunlight soaked into Claude's face and arms. Her mind drifted. When it drifted to thoughts of Nikola, she pushed them away and worked at improving her Italian by imagining arguments with the insufferable Agent Horner. Her body became one with the machine that she rode: her legs pumping, her lungs rhythmically accepting and expelling the sparkling air. The first night, they found a tavern with a room to let. The next night, they had to negotiate for hay in a barn. Both nights, she fell almost instantly into a deep and dreamless sleep. It was easy to forget what awaited her at the other end of this journey.

❧

In Prague, the plan had seemed bold but plausible. With each hour that passed, Micah wondered increasingly why he'd ever agreed to it.

His visit to Murano served only to confirm Tesla's abdication. Sir Alastair's letter spurred a fleeting interest, but the fat wad of rice paper was almost immediately set aside. Trying to salvage something from the afternoon, he taught the little nurse how to communicate with Sandtmann.

A few hours later, with some qualms, Micah settled Miss Bell into her compartment and launched her on her solo way to Firenze. Miss Bell was the most dependable piece on the board, but there was too much around her that could not be predicted.

He had no way of knowing if Tucker had received their message. The timing was ridiculous. The scheme had too many variables and involved too many amateurs. Micah tried not to think of all the ways things might go wrong. He couldn't think of anything else.

He arrived at the Castel just after dawn, groggy from lack of sleep. The tessarius on duty handed him a note from the Baron, left the evening before. Micah had thought he would have at least a day on his own before the Imperial family returned from Capri. He had to mentally rearrange a few moves. Already.

A cup of coffee and a quick shower later, a smartly-groomed Rappaccini presented himself at the doors to the Villa Alsaziano. Gallante refused entrance, stating that the Baron would be found at the Colosseum. Not for the first time, Micah wondered why a man as relentlessly charming as Haussmann would hire such a sour major domo. He felt Gallante's glare follow him as he retreated down the street.

Unlike his man, the Baron was delighted to see him. It might have been more accurate to say that the Baron was delighted, period.

"How well you look, Eminenza!" Rappaccini greeted him.

"It's good to be home," the Baron twinkled. "I feel as if I'd been away for a year! Sacconi was just about to show me what we've accomplished while I was away."

The old man was wreathed in smiles. Everything seemed to make him happy. He admired the parti-coloured stone of the nearly-finished upper tier as much as if he had never envisioned it any way else. Reviewing the restored bridal box, he complimented the exhausted workmen so heartily that several blushed red around the ears. Stopping by a rail to catch his breath, he gazed upon the completely-laid arena floor, his eyes limpid with what could only be described as love.

"Molto bene," he sighed with deep satisfaction.

Micah noticed that Sacconi sighed as well, only his was a sigh of pure relief. The assistant mumbled something about having to meet a shipment of Grecian silver and hurried away.

Haussmann ushered Rappaccini back to the field office. He opened a box of marrons glacés, offering it to his guest. Micah suppressed an inward shudder; it was far too early in the day for that much sugar. Rappaccini plucked a confection from the box with a gracious smile.

"So, Rappaccini," the Baron asked, having downed his first chestnut in two bites; "did your lady enjoy her holiday?"

"It was most satisfactory, thank you, Eminenza. One little spat, but it was quickly put to rights." He flicked a finger at his wrist, indicating a bracelet.

The Baron laughed. "The magic of gold, to instantly restore a lady's good humor! Or was it silver?"

The slim bangle had been the least that Elettra deserved. "Fortunately for my pocket, there is a jeweler in Prague who is, ah, pleased to show respect for the Imperial uniform." Rappaccini smirked. He was glad for the opportunity to drop the name of the city. It had been one of his earliest lessons: if you were transparent when you could be, people rarely suspected you of concealment.

"Excellent. And now you are refreshed and ready to return to duty."

Rappaccini allowed himself a slight air of injury. "With due respect, Eminenza, I have never forgotten my responsibilities. I made certain to stop by Murano, in both directions."

"Of course you did, Rappaccini," the Baron nodded briskly. "This is why I have come to rely on you as I have. And how did you find our Mr. Tesla?"

Rappaccini shrugged. "Sitting under a tree, dozing in the sun. He said you had given him a holiday."

"More like a period of convalescence. Malarial ague is quite debilitating, you know. I prefer to have him husband his strength for now. He has done quite well by me. The monks are making good headway with the weapon he designed. I plan to include an exhibition as part of the wedding festivities. It should be most impressive. Perhaps Mr. Tesla should be there to witness the fruits of his labor." He enjoyed the thought. "Yes! And after, you will return to Venezia with him for a while. The Principessa will certainly not be needing you on her honeymoon."

"Does the Principessa have need of me now?" Rappaccini looked at his feet, trying to appear self-deprecating.

"She will be very happy to see you," the Baron said, without hesitation.

"But will the Emperor?" he asked delicately.

"Our little family outing was quite the success. The bridal pair were adorable. The Emperor was more joyful that I have seen him in a decade. In this mood, he would give the girl anything she'd want, within reason. As it makes her happy to speak English with you, he has magnanimously ordered that you be assigned to her detail. Permanently. I will send word for her to expect you tomorrow, at your usual time."

Micah wouldn't have used the word "happy." The Princess no longer seemed capable of so definite an emotion. Everything about her spoke of resignation.

He was pleasantly surprised that, except for the Golden One lurking on the terrace, they were, to all appearance, alone in the garden. "It has been a long time since we were allowed such privacy," he observed candidly, after kissing her hand. "Should I be honoured, Your Royal Highness? Or insulted that your guardians think me so slight?"

"It is I who is of such little threat. They are sure of me now." She was as wan and thin as the first time he had seen her in Rome. She was also, he would swear, a little drunk.

He took the seat across the table, as she indicated. "Perhaps they shouldn't be."

"What do you mean?"

Leaning slightly closer, he fixed her with a steady eye and kept his voice low and even. "Help is coming, Your Royal Highness."

He couldn't tell if the flicker he saw was hope or fear, but it was immediately surrendered. "You're just saying that." It was a listless whisper. "I know there's nothing anyone can do."

He shook his head. "You're wrong. There are those who are working on your behalf. But you will need to do something very difficult, in order to help them."

He reached casually into his tunic and pullout out a small piece of pasteboard. "I thought you might enjoy seeing a photograph of my recent holiday in Prague," he said loudly, just in case there were ears among the shrubberies.

She took the card. Her hand trembled. "Gertrude!" For a brief moment, he thought she might faint; then two spots of colour bloomed in her cheek.

Firewalker had posed Miss Bell in the Old Town Square, and framed his picture so that the famous clock was visible beyond her. She had a broad smile plastered across her face and seemed to be waving.

The Princess let the photograph fall to the table. "But we never saw the clock. Oh, this is cruel of you!"

He picked it up and put it back in her hand. "I told you; Madame Blavatsky let her go. She has been staying in Prague. She told me to tell you to look closely at what she's holding."

"You spoke with her?" She was as alert now as she was capable of being.

"Yesterday. Now look."

Maud peered obediently at the photograph. "It looks like a hat."

"Yes. I expect it has some significance. She also said to tell you, and I am quoting her exactly, 'this time you must do as I ask.' Although what that has to do with a hat…"

She looked again. This time, her eyes widened in wonder. "I nearly bought that hat. The day we were…That day. Gertrude hadn't wanted us to leave the Embassy. But I insisted. If only I'd listened to her…" her voice faltered and the tears welled up in her eyes.

"Then you must listen to her now," he said matter-of-factly. If she hadn't been a princess, he would have touched her reassuringly on the arm. Instead, he could only place his hand casually on the table between them. "Even if you won't want to do it, you must do as she says."

She nodded, as if hypnotized. "Yes, I must."

"Miss Bell…Gertrude asks that you manage things so that you administer your medication yourself."

"No." It was a reflex, more a breath than a word.

"I know it's unpleasant…" He breezed along, as if he were asking her to conjugate a page of irregular verbs or eat a bitter vegetable. "But then a doctor wouldn't have to follow you wherever you go. You would have some autonomy."

She furrowed her brow and repeated herself. "But why?"

"Ah, you mean why would Miss Bell ask it? I'm afraid I cannot explain why, but it's necessary."

The shake of her head was infinitesimal, as was her shudder, but Micah saw them both. "I couldn't…" she faltered; "how could you think…?"

"Not I," he corrected. "I said you would never agree, but Miss Bell seemed to think otherwise. She said you would follow her advice. This time." He'd deliberately paused before adding the last two words.

She didn't so much as blink.

He took back the photograph with a small grimace of regret. "I'm sorry, Your Royal Highness. We cannot risk having someone find this in your rooms." He made a show of looking at it, almost as if he were speaking with Miss Bell. "She will be disappointed when I tell you said no."

"You're going to see her again?"

"Eventually. I had hoped you would, too. But first you would need to take control of your medication. Ah, well." He slipped it into his tunic and changed the subject. "How did Your Royal Highness find Capri?"

Micah walked the longest route he could devise back to the Ospedale, giving himself some time to review the audience. He hadn't expected the Princess to clap her hands and tell him it was a marvelous idea. On the contrary; she might easily have had him thrown out. But she hadn't, and as soon as she had balked, he had moved on.

As limited as the time was, he must move cautiously. Princess Maud was hanging on to herself by the merest thread. If it weren't possible to separate her from the court and execute this improbable plan, if the wedding went ahead, Micah wasn't confident that her sanity would last far beyond it.

The photograph had been a clever idea. When he next saw Miss Bell, and he devoutly hoped that day would be very soon, he would thank her. He wished it hadn't been necessary to take it back. If the Princess could have kept it, he would feel more certain of victory.

It had gone well enough, considering. He would try again tomorrow and push a little harder.

꧁

On Agent Horner's map, Claude thought Lake Lugano looked like a monkey climbing a post. The curl of the monkey's tail touched on the boundary line, and its arm reached directly into Italy. "Why don't we row across at night?" she'd asked him. "Isn't that how smugglers do it?"

"Not at Augustus's borders," he corrected her. "The waters are too well lit. There are raft-mounted oil lamps with large reflectors, and the centurions who patrol the area are ordered to shoot first and ask questions later." There wasn't sufficient time to have them slip through the unguarded mountains, and a well-patrolled twelve-foot fence snaked through the more passable bits of frontier. The plan was for them to rendezvous with Tucker at a sleepy border town that he had cultivated for his own transit.

By the time she and Elettra crossed the causeway at Bissone, Claude was no longer astonished by dramatically-shadowed mountains. She had become inured, as well, to charming clusters of plastered red-roofed houses with neat shutters and window-boxes. They followed the monkey's leg to its southernmost tip, then made a beeline south through village after Swiss village. The way seemed so inevitable that Claude was paying little attention to Elettra. She was caught off guard when the other girl disappeared from the main thoroughfare.

The place looked no different from other towns they had pedaled through. Claude skidded to a halt and dismounted. She wheeled her bicycle back to where Elettra had turned off. The street was so narrow that two cows wouldn't have been able to pass down it side by side. Close-packed houses made cool shadows that were initially pleasant after the hot sun; they seemed less so the further she came from the main road. There wasn't another soul in sight. Her hand went absently to her sternum to feel the locket Father had given her, a comforting bump beneath her shirt. The houses, like many she'd noticed on their ride, only had windows at the second story level. Seen from the high perch of a bicycle seat, this had seemed interesting, a logical architectural adaptation to deep snows. Experienced on foot, the blind-faced walls loomed like cliffs of weather-stained plaster. After days with the rush of sun-washed air in her face, they were oppressive.

There was something uncanny here. Against the stones, the clop of her boots was uncomfortably loud. She kept peering over her shoulder to see if someone was following her. Her toe caught between two cobbles and she tripped forward, her front wheel scraping against a door. She shuddered, more than the bump warranted. As if someone were walking over her grave, Aunt Nan would say. The street intersected with a wall of dressed stone. Steeling herself for what might come, she jerked the machine to the right and strode toward the patch of light with manly determination.

The return to sunlight made her squint. A pair of old women brushed by, their arms full of flowers for the church. There were laughing screams from a game of tag. In a dirt alley nearby, a group of men were playing some kind of boules. It was a town, just a town. How ridiculous she'd been, scaring herself over nothing, and quoting Aunt Nan to boot! Perhaps she was more anxious about this mission than she had allowed.

A sharp whistle drew her eyes to the center of the rough plaza. Elettra was standing by the well, beckoning impatiently

Wheeling their bicycles across the cobbles, they parked them at the side of the tavern. Inside, Claude sought out a dim corner. Elettra fetched a couple of steins of beer from the bar and settled across from her. "Relax," she advised. "We have lots of time." A young barmaid, who had to be the daughter of the house, skipped over to their table. She fluttered her eyes shamelessly as she set down a wooden board with a round brown loaf and a chunk of cheese. The studied indifference with which Elettra tossed her a coin was so clearly modeled on Centurion Rappaccini that Claude was hard-pressed to not laugh; she had to pretend to blow her nose on her sleeve. Elettra hid her own smile in her beer.

"You'd better be careful or you'll be engaged before we leave here."

Elettra tore off a bit of bread and threw it at Claude. She was a very convincing young man.

They made their way to the churchyard at nightfall. Sitting on the lumpy ground cover for hours, concealed by a thickly ancient tree, Claude felt as though she were waiting to go on in a play, a feeling that was reinforced by the sounds of choir practice floating through the darkness from out of the church.

Eventually, a figure stumbled down the road and lurched through the gate. He paused to lean against the wall and light a clay pipe. The flicker of the match briefly illuminated his face.

"Tómas!" Elettra jumped up stiffly and hobbled to meet him.

Their Swiss respite was over. Fighting a rising reluctance, Claude pulled herself to her feet.

Though the messenger from his Swiss counterpart had come as near to Mercurial as discretion and the lack of Italian technology would allow, there hadn't been time for elaborate planning. Agent Tucker opted to rely on a simple, direct approach. He had put two years of considerable effort into building the feckless character of the Rappaccini family servant. The regular border guards at this post had long since stopped any pretense of formality; they had shared too many a bottle and done well from his ineptitude at games of chance. On a few occasions when his younger brother Vito had accompanied him, they waved the lad through. Tonight, the 'brothers' would be accompanied by their cousin Claudio, who had gone a bit wild and could scarcely be said to be conscious.

"Can you act drunk?" It was the first thing Tucker said to her after Elettra introduced them.

"Of course." The very strangeness of the question was confirmation that the mission had truly begun.

"I don't mean tipsy," he pressed her. "I mean like you can't see a hole in a ladder."

"Just tell me what you need. I can mimic anything from a sip of brandy on an empty stomach to a breathing corpse." Familiarity with the drinking habits of men was one of the inadvertent consequences of her unconventional upbringing; though, to her mind, the miners and machinists of her childhood had been innocents compared to Archibald Spafford and his Yale cronies.

What Tucker wanted was for her to be so apparently drunk that any guard earnest enough to question them would decide to wave them on. He rubbed dirt on all their faces and splattered their clothes with beer. Claude's canvas jacket was rubbed with the contents of a small jar, a noisome paste of whey and gruel. Keeping to the darkest shadows, they left the churchyard and made their way to the bend that led to the crossing point.

After a few experiments, including a nauseating one that had Claude balanced face down with her stomach pressing on a bicycle seat, they decided to leave her seated, her legs dangling and scuffing along the ground. She leaned forward, much of her body supported by the handle bars. One arm was draped around Tucker who walked beside, guiding the bicycle. She was instructed to keep her eyes closed and make no sound other than the occasional groan.

Weaving and stumbling, Elettra followed behind with the other machine. She whistled broken bits of a rude song. When they were within sight of the guards, she let the bicycle fall and had to scramble to pick up the bags and strap them back on. Tucker castigated her in loud, thick-tongued Italian.

"Halt!"

❧

Maud was too exhausted to fight any longer, and too exhausted to feel guilty about it. It was easier to yield, to drink too much wine and set herself afloat on a sea of nothing. In this new limbo, she hadn't cared whether Rappaccini would ever visit her again. Then he returned to prick the bubble and let in the outside world in two words: Gertrude Bell.

Gertrude, her friend and the epitome of everything Grandmama wanted her to be. Gertrude was asking the unreasonable, just as the Queen always did. It was so unfair of them! Maud was tired. All she wanted to do was sleep and forget. A part of her wanted to ask to have this man banned from her presence. In a day or two, he wouldn't even be a memory. But he had said that she hadn't been forsaken.

Her heart, which she had silently mourned and put to rest, was breaking all over again. To be strong enough to do what Gertrude asked of her, or what he claimed Gertrude asked (because another voice in her head whispered it might well be a lie, though to what end she couldn't fathom), she would have to believe there was a reason for it. Why would anyone be so cruel as to ask her to take up that needle in her own hands and willingly inject the substance she so shamefully required? The man would not say, or could not say, but there must be a reason. That 'must be,' that was hope. A tiny spark, almost buried inside her, heard this and rallied. It hurt. As much as she craved it, she no longer trusted in hope; and yet, she couldn't make herself deny it.

ॐ

Tucker's blurred voice turned obsequious. The young guard would have none of it; he had been thirsting for some excitement; he demanded their papers.

Claude's pulse raced. She fought hard against the panic; she had to be sure her body stayed soft.

Tucker's rambling excuse, heavily larded with honourifics, was to no avail. She felt the other man draw closer to the bicycle. Elettra loudly drew in her breath, a noise she covered by pretending to hawk up a gob of phlegm and spit. The sound made Claude's gorge rise.

It was a fortunate reaction. At that same moment, the avid young guard chose to put his hand under her chin and lift her head in his direction. Eyes still closed, she opened her mouth and repeated the retching sound just as he got a whiff of rotten milk from her jacket. Shouting an unfamiliar word that sounded very ugly, he dropped her head and jumped back to avoid what must have seemed like imminent splatter.

An older voice, blunt with bored authority, joined them. She could hear the change in Tucker: this was someone who knew the wayward

Tómas. A joking tone coloured the pleading as he repeated his story, with disparaging mention of "my brother, who you know" and "young Claudio."

The older man laughed and thumped Elettra on the back. "Ow, Signore! My head will fall off!" she moaned.

The older man laughed again. Claude could feel him looming over her. "Young idiots," he sighed. "You too, Fontana. Why are you stopping men who are coming back home? You should be watching the traffic going the other way."

Claude heard the gates swing open and felt the bicycle lurch forward.

"Grazie, Dottore," Tucker repeated fervently. "Mille grazie."

"Mille grazie," Elettra mumbled, staggering behind.

Tucker wouldn't stop until they were a solid mile away from the checkpoint and hidden by a clump of trees. His own bicycle was waiting for him there. He led them along unmarked dirt roads, lit only by a slice of moon. A little before dawn, they arrived at a nearly invisible farmhouse. Tucker knocked quietly at the back door. It flew open immediately. The old Republican farmer greeted his comrade Tómas with an almost military salute. The girls were ushered to a room where a battered tin tub waited in front of a small fire. By the time they emerged, cleaned and changed into their next costumes, coffee and hot food were waiting on the table.

Tucker had a gig and a sturdy horse waiting for them in the barn. He had also planned their route, and provided safe houses where they would stop along the way. Claude would add a thick veil to her dowdy black gown. She would travel as a widow, accompanied by her nephew (Elettra, still in male clothing). They would leave immediately after breakfast and make their way to the city she must remember to think of as Firenze, where Gertrude would be waiting for them.

Maud had a customary chair in the garden. She wouldn't have called it her 'favourite,' as that would imply that she liked it beyond all other chairs. There was nothing in Rome that Maud liked beyond anything else, only those things that, while she had still had the strength to care, she hated less. She closed her eyes and tilted her head so that the sun would bake crimson dots through her eyelids. A soothing hum of insects nestled within the silence. When she sat like this, it was easy to imagine herself dissolving into the air.

She was roused by a cleared throat and a rattle of cups. She had ordered the tea herself, earlier that day. It was to be brought at the hour appointed for the Centurion's daily call. By the sound, they were arriving together.

The Centurion gave one of his elegant bows. She hadn't extended her hand, or he would have kissed it. At her nod, he took the seat opposite with the barely-suppressed excitement of a well-trained hound before the chase, his clever, spying eyes searching her face while she poured out for both of them.

Fussing with the cream and sugar, she had not yet spoken when he rose hastily and bowed again. "It is gracious of you to join us, Principessa," he said loudly, in Italian.

Maud turned her head to see Ginevre, nearly at her elbow. Upon their return from Capri, Augustus's granddaughter had been moved into the villa, to live with her until the wedding.

"I didn't know…" Ginevre stammered, turning her usual deep pink. "I don't like for Maud to be lonely." When an Italian said the Princess's name, it sounded like it rhymed with 'loud.'

There would be no confidences today. "My sister is most attentive." Maud poured a cup for her uninvited guest.

Ginevre ducked her face to stir her tea. "If I had known the Signore would be here, I would have gone to see to your gloves."

"The Principessa is very kind."

She blushed again. It was preposterous that she was nearly thirty. Her timidity stripped the years from her and kept her girlish. "Moud can't be seen in an ordinary store."

"It would not be appropriate," Rappaccini agreed.

"In London, they would sometimes close the store for us." Maud remembered, as if it had happened to a girl in a book, walking through Mr. Liberty's faux-Tudor galleries with her detail following behind. She could almost smell the cologne that the usher daubed on his handkerchiefs. Floris lime, such an English scent. Would she really see England again? Maybe if she did as Gertrude asked? She thought she'd trapped the moan in her chest until she saw them staring. "I have been permitted to see nothing of Rome," she said, dully.

Ginevre shifted unhappily in her seat. She seemed so artless. Perhaps she honestly didn't understand that Maud was a hostage.

"A fitting capital for Caesar's empire," Rappaccini oozed. "I've seen nothing to compare with Roma. Although, to be fair, I've seen little of the world."

"Where did you spend your holiday, Signore?" Ginevre was emboldened to ask.

"How kind you are to ask, Principessa. I visited Prague. A fine city, but not a patch on Roma."

"I was in Prague once. With my friend Gertrude." This time, what came into Maud's mind was a photograph of a girl in front of a clock, a girl wearing a broad smile and carrying a slightly silly hat. She didn't so much make a decision as feel it tumble out: "Gertrude was a good friend to me. I would do anything to see her again."

There was an awkward silence. Then the Centurion held out his cup for a refill. "I apologize for my presumption, Altezza."

She lifted the pot and poured. "There's no presumption, Signore. It's my pleasure to grant your request." He lifted an eyebrow. She nodded, then covered it by quickly indicating the silver dessert stand. "You should have another cake as well."

"Yes, of course. Excellent." He turned his attention to the plate as if it were filled with gems.

"We have a fine pasticciere," Ginevre murmured bravely. "The best there is, Patre says. He had him brought here from Firenze."

Rappaccini pounced enthusiastically. "A lovely city! Are you fond of Firenze, Principessa?"

"I haven't been since I was small," she admitted. "I remember the gardens were wonderful to play in."

"Ah, yes!" he gushed. "Not the majesty of Roma, of course. But so much beauty. And the shops! Now that is a city for gloves!" He smiled charmingly, encouraging Ginevre to appreciate his little jest. She giggled.

Maud wished they would leave her alone, that she might sit quietly and dissolve again. Wasn't it enough that she'd communicated her decision?

Rappaccini stabbed a finger at the sky, to show inspiration. "I wonder if perhaps away from Roma, in Firenze let's say, it might be possible for the two of you to shop together as sisters do."

The limits of Ginevre's life were transparent. Her face lit up, then just as quickly dimmed. "Patre would never allow it."

"Ah." The Centurion returned his attention to the cake plate. "Would any of these have almonds?" he asked. "I'm very fond of almonds."

❧

When Signora Gori's little maid let her into the *penzione*, she was whispering, as usual. Gertrude didn't pay her any mind. She had been enjoying her stolen holiday in Florence; her mind was on her visit to the Duomo.

"Ayyyeee!!!"

The wail made Gertrude jump. She turned automatically to the other human in the foyer. The maid rolled her eyes like a horse about to bolt and flattened herself against the ugly wallpaper. She stammered something under her breath. The only word Gertrude could pick out was *sorella*.

Sister! Her foot catching on the hall runner, Gertrude skidded into the stuffy parlour. Swaying on the settee was a pile of black laundry, the source of the painful noise. Signora Gori looked about to rise from her seat opposite, but was preempted by a lanky young man, half-swallowed by his rumpled linen sack jacket and a badly-knotted neckerchief. He awkwardly patted the bundle, mumbling *"pace, pace"* over and over. His eyes slewed around the room as if he would rather be anywhere else in the world.

"Claud...ia?" Gertrude panted.

"Zia Elettra! *Meno male!*" The young man threw his arms around her, whispered something about seeing her tomorrow and disappeared out the door. He was gone before Gertrude realized 'he' was Agent Horner's cousin Elettra.

Gertrude put her own arms around the shuddering, moaning Claude. "My apologies, Signora. My poor sister...Thank you for taking such good care of her in my absence."

"It was no trouble at all, Signorina Rianero. If there is anything I can do to help, anything at all..." Signora Gori's face was alight with unusual interest.

Gertrude smiled politely and shook her head. "I think it would be best for her to have a little rest in our room."

As soon as the door clicked closed, Claude fumbled off the veiling. "That felt like forever!" Her face was as moist and puffy as a steamed pudding, small tendrils of hair clinging damply to her forehead. "I thought I was going to smother in there."

"What was that about?!" Gertrude jammed the side chair under the doorknob. Signora Gori didn't hold with locks.

"When I told her I was your sister, the one who was expected, she insisted I have a glass of lemonade in the parlour. Then she sat down to give her sympathies about my poor blessed husband. I think it was 'blessed.' Not that it matters. She wanted to know everything. The woman was relentless!"

Gertrude was perplexed. "She hardly asks me anything at all. I had two pages of village details all memorized, but she couldn't have cared less. As far as she's concerned, if isn't in Tuscany, it's not worth knowing about. Mostly I listen and smile, while she goes on and on about the glories of Firenze. I keep expecting her to trace her pedigree back to the Medici."

"I think she's one of those old women who loves misery. She wanted all the particulars of my poor husband's last days."

"Oh, dear! What did you say?"

Claude flicked the air with her hand. "Aunt Nan had a friend whose husband died of a cancer. She used to talk about it in excruciating detail. All I had to do was translate it into Italian. When there was a word I didn't know, I fumbled until Elettra joined in. I wasn't in trouble until the old biddy started on the funeral. How would I know what goes on at an Italian funeral? I fell apart."

A momentary panic showed on Gertrude's face.

"Deliberately," Claude laughed, in good spirits now that they were safely reunited. "I deliberately fell apart. It's an excellent way to not have to talk. I started wailing and grabbing at Elettra. I thought about faking a faint, but I was certain that if I did she'd insist on pulling off the wretched veil. You came just in the nick of time."

"Since you mention it, that does seem a bit extreme. I know Italy is old-fashioned, but…"

"The veil is the whole reason Tucker made me a widow. We don't dare let her see my face. I ought to have been wearing my wig as well, but it was so hot today…"

"We'll be gone before she ever sees Maud. Even if she did, she'd never guess it wasn't you." Gertrude dipped her handkerchief in the pitcher on the washstand.

Claude took it gratefully. "You're looking at the wrong problem." She sat on the edge of one of the beds and started daubing her face and neck. "In a few weeks, the local papers are going to be full of pictures of the royal wedding. No one can think they saw the bride walking around the streets of Florence with you."

It was a sobering reminder for Gertrude. Once she'd made it safely out of that dreadful ladies' carriage, away from all the nuns and crying babies, these last few days had been something of a lark. All at once, the gravity of their mission was oppressively real again. She sank down across from Claude, the sad creak of the bedsprings underscoring her mood. "Where did Elettra go? I have her papers."

"Pisa. To make your arrangements. Let the Signora think there's some kind of manly carousing involved. She'll stop by tomorrow to say goodbye and fetch them. What are you and I meant to do now? Where are we on the schedule?"

"There's a stall we're to check each day for a message. On the Ponte Vecchio. It's quite near the palace and always full of shoppers. When they arrive, we go to the park the next day to watch."

"What if they don't arrive?" Claude twisted the damp handkerchief around her fingers, then jerked it so that it made a soft thwack. "Do you think he'll be able to convince her?"

"I don't think he'll stop trying until he does."

Claude sucked thoughtfully at her lower lip. "So the only question is whether they'll be allowed to come."

❧

This plot of theirs was like nothing so much as a trapeze routine where the artists take unreasonable risks to fly at each other at great heights, because they hold the conviction that they will be caught. Each of their small band had to achieve their separate goals, while trusting in the others to do the same. Micah wasn't easy about putting his trust in others. At least his own next move was one in which he had the utter confidence: he would use Haussmann as a cat's paw to get them to Firenze.

The surest way to get the Baron's support would be to persuade him that the idea was his own. Ginevre had provided the perfect lead. He had only to describe the pathos of that tea party conversation. Micah hurried straight from the royal tea table to the Villa Alsaziano, tingling with the dangerous electricity of contest.

"I never thought I would pity a princess, but I admit must admit that I did. Both of them, Eminenza." Rappaccini shrugged. "It seems sad that they can't do as all women do."

"A holiday with your own lady has given you new eyes." The Baron's own eyes grew sentimentally damp at the image of thwarted girlish delights. "Every bride," he declared, "has the right to experience something...ah, something bridal!"

Rappaccini assumed an air of false approbation. "Caesar shows his love, as well as his wisdom, in wanting to protect her. Ah, mio," he sighed thoughtfully. "If only *Roma* were not so full of prying eyes."

"Rappaccini, once again you surpass my expectations!" The Baron clapped his protégé on the back and rang for Gallante to bring wine.

"Eminenza? I don't understand."

"It is Roma that is the obstacle! Exactly! If they were elsewhere...Perhaps go to Firenze, make the Lady Ginevre's dreams come true. Yes, a sisterly pre-nuptial excursion before the Principessa's face appears in every newspaper. It would be perfectly safe."

"It would be a gift to the Lady Giulia as well," Rappaccini said slyly. It was no secret that Haussmann's relationship with that lady was delicately adversarial, particularly when it came to matters of taste. Surely it rankled that, having monopolized all Maud-related decisions since fetching her from the yacht, Giulia had annexed the aesthetic decisions around the wedding, choosing everything—the gown, the jewelry, all the bridal decorations for the Colosseum—without so much as asking his opinion. "She is too great a Lady to ever say, but with so much to do for an event of this magnitude, I would think it too much, for even of a woman of the Lady Giulia's unquestionable abilities, to continue her tender care of the Principessa."

The Baron's face was lit with his most roguish twinkle. "You make an excellent point." He couldn't countermand Lady's orders, but there were other ways of crossing her. Giulia would be furious to have the girl out from her under her thumb for even a few days. "It would be a true blessing to remove that burden. And I believe the Emperor will agree." Micah did not expect the readiness with which the Emperor agreed, but the Baron knew Augustus better.

The Emperor listened graciously to Haussmann's ideas. He always did, except when the man was wasting his valuable time. Decades before, he'd learned that the Baron was more easily managed if he thought his opinions were being taken into consideration. Not that Caesar Augustus II had to manage anyone. It was more efficient to command, and the results didn't significantly differ. But Haussmann had been part of his life for longer than anyone and, in his limited way, was the closest thing Augustus had to a friend.

Today Haussmann was suggesting that the English Princess might enjoy a trip to Firenze with his pathetic granddaughter. It was an interesting proposal.

"Surely it would be to everyone's advantage for her to appear to have settled into her state. What could be more normal and natural than for a bride to shop?"

Augustus bridled a bit at that 'appear.' "Our holiday in Capri was even more of success than I had hoped. You know that, Haussmann, you were there. The girl has embraced us entirely. Have I mentioned that she's asked Dottore Catoni to allow her to assume responsibility for her own medications?"

Haussmann was impressed. He had thought the Principessa's demeanor had seemed more disheartened than embracing. "Well then! I would think that deserves some recognition."

Indeed. And for her to be accompanied by her future sister was matched perfectly with the illusion of young love and happy family that Caesar was anxious to promote. He was surprised that Giulia, who stuck so close to the girl, hadn't suggested it. Perhaps he shouldn't be. The English girl was his daughter's natural rival. She would be Empress someday, and mother of his line. It was to Giulia's advantage to try and keep the girl beaten down. She would be furious to think that the girl might gain the confidence to challenge her. His barking laugh confounded the Baron, who had no idea what might have caused it.

Of late Augustus found himself compelled to delegate responsibilities to others. His Sybil had located "aud in B_est" not a minute too soon. This body was failing fast. More and more, he found it necessary to conserve his strength. There was no one he trusted more than his Giulia, and it had certainly been appropriate that the adoption of the English Princess be led by the ranking female of his family; but, just as the Baron's relationship with the Lady was adversarial in matters of taste, the Emperor himself often felt compelled to reign in his daughter's thirst for power.

"A happy bride, yes. Let them go to Firenze, Haussmann. Goldsmiths, leather workers, and a nice secure palace to keep them safe. I'll give the order myself. Send your Rappaccini to escort them. Giulia is so busy with all the arrangements, she'll never notice they're gone. And if she does," Augustus smirked. "She can answer to me." Yes, the English Princess would someday be Empress. Someday soon. It was time for his daughter to adjust her aspect to the sun.

21 – THE BOBOLI EXCHANGE

Claude fingered a bauble casually, so that she could angle her head and get a better peak through the side of her veil. Yes, it was unmistakable; a basket of plums from Agent Horner.

"You have exquisite taste, Signora."

"It's very beautiful. Such skill!" She held the cameo to catch the sun, then put it down.

"Not another like it in the world."

"I'm sure. My, are those plums?" It would be more conspicuous to ignore them. The man was a purveyor of gold, not produce. "What an unusual idea."

The jeweler lifted the painted basket from the shelf. "A gift from a satisfied customer." His fawning smile did not reach his eyes, which skimmed over everything on the bridge but her. "Please, Signora, honour me by taking one."

"How kind," she said. She plucked one cautiously, as if it might explode.

"Not at all. They should be eaten while the moment is ripe."

She agreed hastily, with a slight correction: "yes, while they're ripe."

"Ah, yes." He fussed ostentatiously with an arrangement of watch chains.

Catching up with Gertrude at the next stall, they continued their daily stroll across the bridge.

"What would you like to do today, Sister?" Gertrude asked, linking arms.

"We should enjoy the last day of our holiday. Is there something else that you want to see? We must be sure to see it today."

Gertrude looked at her blankly.

"Before we depart from this beautiful city," Claude said, emphasizing the '*partiamo.*'

The penny dropped. "The message…"

Claude put the plum in her hand and continued coolly. "I think perhaps tomorrow we should visit the Boboli gardens."

❦

Rappaccini tactfully steered the royal ladies in the direction of the shady cypress alley, where the statue of *Patience* marked the turn-off to a hidden lover's knot garden that was so perfect for his purposes. At the slow glide they favoured, it might take half an hour to reach it.

Ginevre was enchanted, touching every other leaf and cooing over every statue and fountain. The mouse's eyes actually sparkled, and she had revealed an unexpected ability to prattle. It had been the same yesterday, on the Ponte Vecchio. She exclaimed over even the most ordinary trinkets with a joyful air of discovery. After this walk, he was taking them to a nearby street of small shops, where fans and shawls and other such elegant fripperies were said to be on offer. He expected her to be transported by ecstasy.

He wished it were more obvious to him what Maud was feeling. So much depended on her reaction tomorrow afternoon. Her face was a placid mask, but she leaned on the handle of her parasol as if she were otherwise in danger of toppling over.

Micah felt a little off-balance himself. He was still surprised that Augustus had agreed to the excursion and set them off so quickly. Not only that but, according to the Baron, it had been Caesar's own recommendation that Rappaccini escort the girls. He couldn't stop wondering why. Augustus had shown a clear dislike of him. Was this a test? Certainly no one could suspect what they were planning.

"Oh! I didn't remember how beautiful it was!" Ginevre paused in the middle of the path, her hands clasped together as if to hold the garden to her heart.

He had to smile. The day of the tea party, he'd instinctively understood that including the bashful princess in his plan would vastly increase their chances of success. Her enjoyment gave an air of authenticity to their excursion. Any added complications from her presence were far outweighed by the advantages: she made a perfect blind.

❧

The public gate to the gardens was guarded by an amphoraka. The paths closest to the Imperial Palace were conspicuously patrolled by a few uniformed guards. Claude and Gertrude made an effort to appear as nonchalant as the other visitors, so that neither would take notice of them.

They were glad they had given themselves plenty of time to search for the path that Agent Horner had described. The grounds were vast. They wound their way past trim formal gardens and pocket rambles that had been carefully tended to look wild. An avenue might lead to a grand fountain, set in an ornamental pond. There were a great many statues. It helped to know that *Patience* was a female figure; they didn't have to stop to read the inscriptions on all the creatures and men. Sometimes they would find a pretty spot with a bench and sit quietly for a while, until Gertrude felt compelled to check her watch again. She checked her watch too often; she couldn't help it. The penalty for being early is that waiting becomes interminable.

Claude tapped her hand to get her attention. "Are you alright?"

"A little nervous. Aren't you?" Marooned in Italy, Claude would be in far greater danger than she.

"Remember in the woods, when I told you to run? I'm referring to the time you actually listened to me." They shared a weak laugh. She took Gertrude's hand and squeezed it. "It's like that. I can't waste my energies borrowing trouble. As things happen, I'll do what I have to do. When everything is over, then I can afford to be nervous."

A quarter hour sooner than they should have, they paid their respects to *Patience*. As the Tuscan Underground had assured Agent Horner, the entrance was recessed and somewhat overgrown. Ignorant eyes would skip over the secluded garden, never recognizing it for what it was. The concealed spot they found had a good view, but wasn't made for comfort. By the time the walkers breached the garden, Gertrude's left foot had fallen asleep and Claude had woven a small antimacassar of leaves and grass.

An unfamiliar female voice alerted them to peep through the greenery.

"Oh, Signore! I'd forgotten all about this place! I used to hide from my brother here!" The young woman, whoever she was, was addressing Agent Horner. Whoever she was, she seemed eager that he share her excitement.

"Gusto wouldn't hurt a fly. He cares too much."

The second speaker was Maud, but a Maud so changed by these two months that Gertrude felt herself gasp. Agent Horner had warned them, but it still came as a shock to see her exuberant friend replaced by a wax doll. Even Maud's voice sounded lifeless.

Gertrude turned to Claude for her reaction, but Claude was glued to her peep hole. Of course, she would have to be. This would be her only opportunity to observe at first-hand the changes that Horner had described and which she would be expected to impersonate. This was the main reason they were in the garden today. This, and also to give him a sign that all was well.

It was up to Claude to signal. Gertrude hated to break her concentration, but there was no choice. She couldn't make the complicated American birdcall. How long would it be before Agent Horner assumed his message hadn't been received? Would he think perhaps that Claude hadn't made it to Florence?

Gertrude looked back at the trio in the garden. Rappaccini appeared as easy and confident as he had at every railway check point. That didn't mean a thing. She had learned not to make assumptions about the man. Maud seemed deeply fatigued. Would she soon ask to leave?

Gertrude leaned closer to Claude, hoping the sensation of her shadow would be enough to get her friend's attention. When startled, Claude was prone to reacting automatically. The subtle approach didn't work. She gingerly Claude's arm and pulled back. The arm flew out. If Gertrude hadn't thought to move, she would be doubled over, trying to catch her breath.

Claude whirled to face her target and stared reproachfully. Using the finger alphabet she had taught them in Dubrovnik, she spelled out "W-H-Y."

Unable to recall the letters quickly enough, Gertrude pantomimed flapping wings.

Claude bit her lip in chagrin. She took a deep breath and, cupping her hands to her mouth, flooded the air with a series of avian trills.

"Even the birds here sound happier than the ones in Roma!" exclaimed the stranger. "I'm so glad we came to Firenze, aren't you, Moud? When you and Gusto are married, perhaps Patre would let us live here."

Maud nodded graciously. "It's peaceful here."

Rappaccini flashed his white teeth in the direction of the birdcall.

The stranger spun around, coming closer to the hedges. She was less of a girl than her mannerisms had suggested. "Shall we walk to the grotto before we go to the shops? Moud will love to see the grotto." She started back in the direction of the cypresses without looking to see if the others were following.

"To the grotto, then, as it pleases Ginevre," Maud smiled sadly. "It's good that someone is happy."

Rappaccini bowed. "Yes, Your Royal Highness," he agreed, changing to English and speaking a little too loudly. "I think this place has the capacity to create happiness. We shall return here tomorrow and see."

※

Signora Gori had been told that beautiful Firenze had, alas, not proved comforting to the widow and that the sisters were leaving to attempt a sea-side cure. The Signora was disappointed, but found solace in that the fee for an additional week's stay, paid in advance, was forfeit. After checking their bags at the railway station, Gertrude made arrangements with the browbeaten driver to meet them outside the Boboli Gardens at two-thirty sharp.

At one-fifteen, they strolled through the gates carrying a small picnic basket between them. Without speaking, they made their way steadily towards *Patience*. Neither could think of anything to say.

They crossed the small garden and passed through the gap in the hedges. Once they were in position, Claude removed the veil and hooked it carefully on a twig. Gertrude took the pocket mirror from the basket and held it open for her as she popped open the back of her locket and, dampening her forefinger with the tip of her tongue, placed a small amber disk in each eye. Claude winced. It felt as if she had grit in her eyes. It hadn't hurt when she'd practiced wearing them in Prague.

"Are you alright?" Gertrude whispered.

"My eyes are dry. We slept so little last night. I'll be fine." She would have to be, she thought grimly. She lowered her lids slowly and tried to make her tear ducts well.

Gertrude hugged her. The impulse surprised them both. "Good luck!" she whispered. "You'll be wonderful. You always are."

"So are you. But what brought that on?"

"They'll be here soon. There probably won't be time to say goodbye, and then…" The significance of what she was saying hit them both.

"Good luck. And let me say that there's no one with whom I would rather wander drugged through a Hungarian forest." Claude tried to make it a joke, but it didn't come out funny. Her eyes really did tear up. She forced herself to smile.

It wasn't long before they heard a familiar Eton drawl on the other side of the hedge. "You must trust me, Your Royal Highness. You will be glad you allowed me to escort you here again today."

Gertrude peered through a convenient hole in the leaves. "It's only the two of them," she whispered to Claude.

"We should wait a little. The other girl might have fallen behind."

As if he'd heard her, he added "I went to a great deal of trouble to ensure we had this hour to ourselves."

Claude wasted no more time. Her trills rose over the song of the local birds.

Agent Horner approached the hedge. Maud, her hand still resting on his arm, followed without knowing why. About a foot away from the gap, he turned to look into her eyes. "My Princess," he said gently. "I have a happy surprise for you. But you must promise to be calm. You mustn't raise your voice, or we risk being discovered. In fact," he had a flash of inspiration; "it might be wise if you were to put your hand over your mouth, on the chance you might be tempted to call out."

She frowned in confusion, but lifted her white lace mitt hesitantly to her lips.

He smiled encouragingly. "Someone is here to see you. A friend. Miss Bell…"

It was difficult to see which penetrated Maud's consciousness first, the sound of that name or Gertrude's appearance in the gap. The Princess gasped. She would probably have screamed had it not been for Agent Horner's forethought. Instead, she clamped her hand over her mouth to stifle it. Gertrude ran to embrace her. Maud began to tremble.

"It isn't really you. I'm dreaming." She barely whispered it. Burying her face in Gertrude's shoulder, she wept soundlessly.

Agent Horner stepped away, to keep watch at the entrance.

Gertrude held her close. "I'm here, Maud. Everything is going to be fine." She had to say it several times before the Princess would lift her head. When she thought Maud could absorb what she had to say, Gertrude repeated Agent Horner's caution. "Now Maud, you must stay very calm and quiet. I am here to take you home. Do you understand?"

Maud started to shake again. "Home?"

Gertrude put a protective arm around her shoulder. "You must be strong. And you must follow everything I say, without question. Yes?"

Maud nodded.

"Excellent." Gertrude took a deep breath and blew it out. That had been the easy part. "Well, then. Augustus must continue to believe that he holds you here and there's only one way to do that. Maud, I haven't come here alone."

This was it! On the other side of the hedge, her heard fluttering wildly, Claude prepared to strip off her widow's weeds.

Gertrude led the Princess through the leaves.

"Hello, Maud," Claude said quietly. "Remember when we swapped our corsets? We're going to do it again."

Maud looked as if she might faint. They had anticipated this; Gertrude had a vial of sal volatile ready to snap under her nose if she did.

"Maud?" Gertrude said, a little sharply.

"You're not real!" Maud's fear was palpable. "I dreamed you. It was the drugs, the one that woman gave me!"

"I'm as real as you are, Maud. Touch me." Claude took her hand firmly. Maud tried to jerk it away, but Claude held tight until the other girl's palm was touching her cheek. "You see. We look alike, that's all. Remember? How we confused everyone? You and Gertrude and I. Nobody knew which of us was you."

"Ye-es." Maud pulled back and turned to Gertrude for confirmation.

"Oh for goodness sake, Maud," Gertrude said testily, as she often had when they'd shared lessons. "We were in a room with three beds. Of course there were three of us there."

This was sufficiently concrete to be reassuring. "Yes. It was like looking in a mirror, except the eyes in the mirror were…" She looked back at Claude. The beginnings of a smile turned instantly to a look of horror. If Gertrude hadn't been holding onto her, she would have bolted.

Claude, by now undressed down to her petticoat, was getting impatient. "There's no time!" she hissed.

"She wasn't prepared for this, Claude. She needs a few minutes." They glared at each other. Suddenly Gertrude understood. "Your eyes!"

Claude felt like a fool. Of course the Princess would think she was hallucinating. She gingerly removed the lens from one eye. "Princess?" she coaxed. "Maud, look at me. I'm wearing a kind of mask."

Gertrude had to forcibly turn Maud to face her.

"You see?" Claude held out the finger with the coloured dot. "It's a disguise, to make me look exactly like you."

Maud looked warily from the finger to the one grey eye. As she watched, Gertrude fished out the mirror again and Claude pressed the lens back into position. Maud's face cleared.

Claude smiled with relief. "Good. Now you must take off everything you're wearing. We need to swap, every stitch down to the skin."

"Down to the skin?"

"Yes. I'm assuming your maids help you dress and undress. I can't be seen in my own undergarments."

"Your hair isn't dressed like mine." Maud said doubtfully.

Gertrude paused in the act of slipping the muslin polonaise from the Princess's shoulders. It was encouraging that Maud was alert enough to take an active interest. Furthermore, she was correct. Beneath her little chip bonnet, her hair was dressed in an elaborate pile of curls. Claude's hair was pinned up into a serviceable but hardly fashionable knot. Even if they had an hour to do it, they didn't have the skill of the Princess's maid.

"Take it down," Gertrude advised. "You can say...hmm..."

"Oh, something about passing a tree and getting caught by a branch. I've done that, you know."

"You could say that you had *un emicrania*." Maud sighed. "I often do."

"Emicrania?"

"Sick headache. Your head was hurting; you had to take it down." She started to pull the pins from her own hair, wrapping them in the handkerchief she had tucked in her sleeve.

Claude tried to stop her. "You don't need to take yours down as well. We have a wig for you."

"These are gold. Everything here is gold."

Claude was beginning to realize how much she didn't know. They had only few minutes left. She needed to know other things that Agent Horner would not be able to tell her. "What is your maid called?"

"Leonora is the one who came here, the one who does my hair. She's the kind one. In Roma, there is also Silvana." Maud sighed again and rubbed her temples fretfully. "I don't like her. She reports everything to Giulia. They all have to, but Silvana wants to."

"You must tell me what you call the members of the Imperial family. And your rooms. How do I get to your rooms in Rome? What do you do all day, when Agent...Signor Rappaccini isn't with you?"

Maud's face crumpled and she covered her face with her hand.

"You're pushing her!" Gertrude was angry and protective all at once, the way she often felt when she had to mind her small half-siblings. With Maud this fragile, she had a sinking feeling the rest of her adventure was going to be as trying as it was hazardous.

"Blast!" Claude muttered. "I need her to tell me!"

Gertrude petted and coaxed until Maud calmed down. She helped her to disrobe, slipping in questions so casually that Maud answered without thinking.

Even with Gertrude playing ladies' maid, it took a good twenty minutes to complete the exchange. This wasn't nearly enough time for Claude to learn everything she needed to know concerning Maud's life in captivity but, thanks to Gertrude's deft handling of the Princess, they did at least extract the most critical bits.

"Have you done?" Agent Horner had returned to the hedge and was speaking through the leaves.

"Just about," Gertrude told him. She looked from one young woman to the other, and back again. They appeared to be the exact same two young women she'd started with. Everything was in place. A thought struck her. "Claude, where's your locket?" Her own was safe around her neck.

Claude patted her bodice. As well as the glass compartment with two additional sets of lenses, it held a transmitter that was dormant now but would someday signal to tell her that the mission was at an end. It was like having Father nearby. "No one will notice."

"And what about your chatelaine?"

"Oh, I can pass it that off as something we bought here in Florence."

"No you can't," Horner stated bluntly. "That thing is a tool box, not an ornament. Let Miss Bell have it."

"No!" She understood that he was right, but she had become superstitious about that chatelaine. She wanted it near her.

"Giulia will paw through all your things when we get back. She'd have it in the trash in a minute."

Claude gritted her teeth. This man would be her only ally and she couldn't stand him. She especially hated that smug way he had of imparting information, as if it made him superior to know something someone else didn't. She did, however, trust him. "Then you can keep it for me." She examined the items dangling from the various chains. It would be hard to be without any of them, especially her new clasp knife, but one object was a necessity. After Gertrude's incident at the House at the White Beet reminded them of an additional risk to her masquerade, Leski had prepared a paste of tinted wax and tree gum, another legacy of Father's mysterious tenure in the mysterious East. She unhooked the silver clamshell that contained the precious lump and threaded it on the locket's chain, reluctantly handing the rest of the chatelaine to Agent Horner. "Pass it back to me after the wedding. They won't be watching me as closely after that. It can get mixed in with the gifts."

388

"The wedding?" Maud sounded surprised.

"Yes, of course," Claude said calmly. "Everything has to happen just as it would if you were here."

"It's time." Gertrude had checked her watch again. They had to be out front to meet the carriage.

"Then Miss Monteith… 'Scusi. Altezza. If you would join me, please."

Claude crossed quickly into the garden, before anyone could think to hug or cry.

Agent Horner inspected her from head to toe and smiled. "Perfect. Now Miss Bell, it's our turn."

Gertrude took a small leather bag from the picnic basket and set it on top. It contained a hypodermic needle and a handful of blue glass vials.

Agent Horner removed a case from his tunic and unrolled it. Still hiding behind Gertrude, Maud gave a strangled cry.

"Please, Your Royal Highness, don't be distressed." There was surprising compassion in his voice. "Now you understand why it was necessary for you to perform the injections. You will need to keep stable until you reach home and proper medical attention."

Having carefully switched the contents of the two cases, the Agent bowed deeply, and with more sincerity than Rappaccini was ordinarily seen to do. "Ladies."

Claude barely had time to say a final "good luck" before he was steering her across the little garden and out towards *Patience*.

"Your hair is down," he said in a low voice.

"I have a migraine, Signor Rappaccini," she said grandly. "*Un emicrania.* The pins were making it worse. When I return to my rooms, I will lie down and rest."

He grinned appreciatively. "I'll familiarize you with our apartments before you do. We should be able to make some other time to speak alone before leaving the city, to see how well you learned what I gave you in Prague."

"Where is Ginevre?"

"In town, with one of the other guards and her maid. I told her I'd assumed she would want to buy a surprise bridal present for the Princess, and made an appointment for her at a purveyor of embroidered leathers."

"Embroidered leathers?"

"She seems to be enamored of gloves."

Before they left the secluded garden, Gertrude tugged the veil down over the Princess's face. She didn't expect her to remain compliant until they reached British soil, but she hoped it would last at least until they were safely out of Italy. She pressed Maud's fingers around one handle of the basket, grabbed the other handle for herself and set a deliberate strolling pace. They were two women who had enjoyed a picnic and, having sufficiently admired the grounds, were on their way home for the mid-day *riposo*. It was critical that Maud not hesitate and draw the attention of either the amphoraka or any of his human counterparts.

In a few minutes that felt like an hour, they breached the gate. The graveled footpath dipped dangerously toward the road. Picking her way carefully in her unfamiliar hobnailed boots, Gertrude used the basket to steer her charge. She wondered what was going on behind the black silk. She and Claude had shared so much that they knew the language of one another's gestures and posture. Maud, through her own trials, had become a closed book.

The apron of the cobbled piazza seemed improbably wide. Gertrude craned her neck to see across it. There were several carriages in a row, all equally black and respectably plain. Gertrude moved briskly along their ranks, looking for the forlorn driver with the drooping mustachios. He was nowhere to be found. According to her watch, it was nearly ten past two. She had learned that the attitude to time was different in Italy than it was back home, but she had been so specific with that man!

She stood by the box of the end carriage, trying to establish whether one could simply claim a vehicle at the curb, as one might back home. A fat man blustered up and brushed her away with a handkerchief as red as his face. Before Gertrude could protest, he climbed in and the driver pulled away. Meanwhile, the other carriages had all driven off. There wasn't a horse or a wheel in sight.

She stared helplessly up and down the road. The wicker connecting her with Maud was vibrating with tension. Gertrude felt a degree of exasperation that, were she not so committed to being sensible, would have verged on hysteria. All she wanted to do was convey her royal cargo to a railway station and endure the fewest possible uncertain hours before arriving in Pisa. How could she have thought that this benighted Empire was at all charming, with its miserly rail travel and irresponsible people?

There was no choice but to walk. The station was only a couple of miles from here. She could easily cover it in the time they had, but she wasn't sanguine about Maud. The Princess had never been much for long walks. Would she be able to do it now, in her current state of frailty? More worrisome, what if she panicked along the way and did something foolish?

It was now gone a quarter past. 'No time to hesitate, Bell,' Gertrude prompted herself. She squared her shoulders and nodded encouragement to the Princess. "Let's go," she said brightly.

"You said there would be a carriage."

"It didn't show. Don't worry. The station isn't far. And it's a shame, really, that you've seen so little of the city. We'll walk along the river for a bit, to avoid the crowds, and take the next crossing. It'll be a lovely walk, you'll see."

She headed west along one of the quieter streets, distracting Maud with cheerful small talk. The few people they passed nodded in an automatically friendly manner but otherwise ignored them.

Somewhere behind them, a man's voice shouted *"Arrestatevi!"*

Maud dropped her end of the basket and started to wring her hands.

"Pick it up!" Gertrude urged. It couldn't be a soldier; there hadn't been remotely enough time for anyone to notice the deception. "We need to act normal. There's nothing to worry about. Probably just someone after a pickpocket. There are even more of them here than at home."

Maud didn't seem convinced. There was a sound of boots slapping hard against the pavement.

It took all the self-control Gertrude could muster to stop from breaking into a run. She spotted an open door on the street, the kind that usually led to a courtyard. "Now! Pick the basket up!"

This time Maud obeyed. Gertrude angled towards the door, forcing herself to move no faster than she had before.

The sound of running came closer. "Arrestatevi! Signora!"

She refused to look behind her. Reaching the door just in time, she twisted to push Maud and the basket through first. Before she could lift her foot over the raised threshold, a strong hand gripped her elbow.

"Signora!" The man sounded more relieved than martial.

Gertrude whirled around to face him. The furrow in the man's brow matched the droop of his outsized mustachios. It was the driver from the livery service.

"Where were you?!" She dug her fists into her hips and stamped her foot. She was certain Claude would have slapped his foolish face.

"As you said, Signora," He sounded injured. "I came to the piazza. I looked, but you weren't there. Then I saw your companion. I remembered her, a widow woman, so like my Zia, God rest her soul. I left my horse with a boy and followed. When I could see for certain that it was you, I called out. But you wouldn't wait." He reproached her as if it had been she who'd been late.

"I did wait. I waited a full quarter hour! I assumed you weren't coming."

"Why?" He shrugged and scratched his head.

"Oh, never mind," she said crossly. It was still preferable not to have to walk those miles with Maud.

He bowed, scooped up the picnic basket and headed back in the direction from which they had come. Holding out her hand to Maud, Gertrude followed. She was exhausted already and the journey had hardly begun.

§

Closing the door, Claude allowed herself a brief sigh of relief. She must once again be grateful for the insufferable man's professionalism. Agent Horner had sent the Princess's maid on a shopping expedition, making certain to include a few items that would be difficult to find. She had a few precious unobserved hours. Father had warned her that Royalty led public lives; there would be no locks in Italy.

She made a quick survey of the enormous, over-decorated room, opening every drawer and cabinet to familiarize herself with the contents. Claude found almost as many items of apparel for a flying visit as she had in her entire wardrobe back home. Royalty must change their clothing four or five times a day! Presumably Lina…no, the maid was Leonora. Leonora would be responsible for popping her into the correct costume for each hour and occasion.

She froze. She'd seen something move, out of the corner of her eye. It took a slow scan of the room to understand that it had only been her reflection in the mirror. This reminded her to toss the handful of gold hairpins on the vanity.

Claude realized she was tiptoeing through the room, acting like exactly what she was: an intruder. She frowned at herself in the mirror. This wasn't good. She was the Princess. She must begin acting like the Princess.

Her first step would be staging an epic headache. The room had a glorious view of the gardens, the afternoon sun infusing the leaves with a jewel-like splendor. Whispering a valedictory blessing on Gertrude and Maud, though surely they were long gone by now, she resolutely pulled the heavy draperies closed. In the cool grey cave that resulted, she discarded her unfamiliar garments, letting the beautifully embroidered muslin puddle to the floor. The pile was too neat. She carefully added sufficient disarray to give the impression that she had undressed in haste.

The thin silk dressing gown was the least fussy garment she found in the armoire; even so, it was foaming with lace and stuck with ribbons, more like attire for a doll than for a woman. She had gathered that the Lady Giulia selected everything, down to the trimmings on the Princess's chemise. She dreaded meeting that woman, possibly more than she dreaded meeting mad Caesar himself.

Claude moistened Maud's handkerchief with water from the pitcher. After soaking up the heat all day, the bed would be stifling; she fell gratefully onto the pale blue brocade fainting couch instead. Folding the handkerchief over her eyes, she blocked out the last of the light. The damp linen felt cool against her skin. Her hand grazed the edge of a light shawl that was draped over the back of the couch. She pulled it down to use as a coverlet. With the excitement draining from her body, she was surprised to realize that she was tired. It would be nice to sleep.

A shaft of muted light penetrated Claude's closed lids and awakened her gradually, as light will do. She blinked drowsily and turned on her side. A piece of cloth slipped down over her face. She brushed it away.

"Altezza?"

The soft female voice was unfamiliar. Claude struggled to push herself up to a sitting position, but her elbow got caught by a froth of lace. She was about to swear, when she remembered where she was and turned it into a yawn.

There was more light, of the cool, blue, summer evening variety. Someone, the maid, she realized, was opening the draperies to let it in. She had slept for hours.

"How are you feeling, Altezza? It's time…"

"Un emicrania," she said, aiming for fretful. "I was walking in the gardens, with Signor Rappaccini…" She lifted her hand to her head in an eloquent gesture of pain that she remembered from having seen Ellen Terry play Ophelia in New York.

The maid, Leonora, looked concerned. "You should not go down to dinner. The cook can send up a cup of consommé. Come, let us get you to bed."

As appealing as that was, Claude decided it was better strategy to resist the urge to hide. She had to meet Ginevre some time. Right now, the residue from her alleged headache would be a good mask for any mistakes she might make. Latching onto her impersonation with zeal, she began to shake her head, then winced and, keeping hand on her forehead, waved the other in the negative. "I've slept so much, I'll need to tire myself again before I go to bed. It will do me good to join them."

Leonora didn't look happy, but she nodded. "I'd prepared the *pisello* organza."

Pisello was Italian for pea. Claude didn't remember seeing anything of such a definite colour during her peep at the Princess's wardrobe. Maud's gowns were of an almost aggressive maidenly pallor. She gestured her acceptance and fell back against the tufted curve of the couch.

Leonora cleared her throat. "Altezza? It's seven o'clock now. Don't you want to…?" She clamped her mouth shut on whatever words were in her mind and stood still, her hands folded over her stomach.

It took an uncomfortable second or two for the penny to drop. Seven o'clock! Claude's first thought was astonishment that she had slept for more than three hours. Then she remembered the single most important piece of information Maud had shared in the garden, the routine for her medication. There were two injections a day. After each, she needed to lie down for a while; even after the morning dose that followed a night's sleep. Because of this, the doctor had habituated her to having the evening dose administered at seven o'clock so that she would be able to keep her eyes open at dinner.

"Yes, of course," Claude said vaguely. "Thank you, Leonora. I hadn't realized the time."

She got up from the couch, walked stiffly to the bed and sat on the edge. She opened the drawer to the bedside table. Carefully ignoring the maid's presence, she removed the case, which Agent Horner…No, *Signor Rappaccini*. She must start to think of him so. It would be disastrous were she to slip and call him by the other name where someone might hear it. *Rappaccini* had given her the case, to restore it to its proper place. At the time, she had thought it wise to hide her locket behind it. She surreptitiously touched the chain now, for luck.

Claude took the syringe from the roll, fitted in a needle, and smoothly drew up the saline solution from one of the vials. She raised the knee of one leg so that the heel was resting on the coverlet, and poised the tip of the needle at a place between her big toe and the one beside it. She wouldn't be using Father's little trick, not yet. For as long as the saline supply lasted, she was to perform a genuine injection; if the doctor were to examine her when they returned to Rome, she needed to ensure there were some marks between her toes. She dipped her head so that her hair would obscure her face. If Leonora were watching, it was critical that she not give herself away by reacting to the prick. With a grateful thought for the practice that

394

Father had put her through, she pressed the plunger, counted to fifteen in her head, then very slowly pulled herself up. She put the kit away. Maud had said the maid would collect the vial; she dropped it casually on the bedcovers.

"The *pisello* organza, Leonora?" she murmured, falling back on the pillow.

"Si, Altezza." Leonora covered her with the shawl from the fainting couch.

"That will be nice." She closed her eyes. She opened them again when she heard the door close. The tube of blue glass was gone.

Claude wanted to run around the room and whoop. She had passed her first exam!

Maud leaned her head against Gertrude's shoulder, pretending to sleep while her friend, typically, read a book. There was something indisputably authentic in that act of reading. It enabled Maud to pretend that there was nothing extraordinary about sitting in a second-class railway carriage in Italy, swallowing her terror each time someone shifted or cleared their throat.

When they finally reached Pisa, they carried their handbags to a quiet corner to wait until the passengers who disembarked with them would leave the terminus. Once the coast was clear, Gertrude hustled her into the vacant Ladies' Cloakroom and made her change. The clothes in her bag were for a boy: breeches and a canvas jerkin. Maud had never worn breeches. They made her feel so exposed. Gertrude also insisted that she remove her corset, to change the way she moved. Once upon a time, she would have resented Gertrude sounding like such a know-it-all. Now she found it reassuring to be bossed by her.

They tucked one another's hair into flat caps. Gertrude gave a final tweak to her red neckerchief and patted the battered leather satchel she had slung across her chest. Maud knew that it held their most precious possessions: a few important papers, some money and the case with her despised but necessary medicine.

"All present and accounted for." Gertrude cuffed Maud cheerily on the shoulder, the way the boys always seemed to do. "*Andiamo!*" she said, picking up one of the bags. She strode forward with a bold, almost cocky air. Maud wanted to stay inside and hide, but she had no choice. She took up the other bag and followed silently, half a step behind.

She had no idea where they were headed. She assumed it must be too far to walk, as Gertrude headed confidently across the road and organized a donkey cart. The cart was as slow as it was bumpy; it took forever to get to the water.

The father and son who owned the *Faustina* were waiting impatiently by the chubby-hulled sailboat, checking the sun as if it were a clock. They ignored the two awkward youths until Gertrude showed them a token, some kind of medal on a red, white and green ribbon.

The son immediately grabbed their bags in his large, calloused hands and plunked them into the *gozzo*. The father, Enrico, explained that they must leave very soon if they were to blend in with the others who fished the evening tide. There was scarcely enough time to avail themselves of the noisome waterfront privy before they were scrambling into the boat and the men were pushing off. Young 'Rico, who was nearly as sea-weathered as his father, skillfully twitched the lines to swing the boom.

The men, a laconic pair, worked together almost silently. The sail caught the wind and the gozzo glided swiftly out into the sunset waters.

Gertrude sat still, all of her energy suddenly spent. Maud leaned her head against her friend as she had in the train, dreamily watching the shifting colours and the occasional sea bird. She had no idea how much time had passed until she felt the traitorous aching in her back and a flush of heat. Now that she was safe, with Gertrude, everything that had happened since that morning in Prague was nothing but a bad dream. She would deny this intrusion that would force it all to have been real. She only hurt because she wasn't used to going without a corset, and she was hot because she was overdressed for a summer night. She shifted her body to ease it. Closing her eyes, she tried to focus on the sound of water lapping softly against the side of the boat.

As long as there was any light, they stayed within sight of the other fishing boats. Once there was dark enough to conceal their absence, Enrico, who had been holding steady on the rudder, pushed it away from him. The boat made a sharp turn north. They would be hugging the coast of the Ligurian Sea, he explained. To avoid being observed by local fishing fleets, they would travel by night and put in to shore before dawn. There were havens all along the coast where they could shelter during the day.

Gertrude thought this seemed a very sensible plan. "How long, will it take, do you think, until we get to Nice?"

Enrico lifted his face, as if the breeze on his cheek might help him to think. "If we have more nights like this one," he ruminated; "good nights for sailing, it would be three days maybe. If we lose the wind, or if we have rain, it might be as long as six."

He suggested his passengers get some sleep. If they were hungry, he advised, there was food and wine in the tin locker.

Maud, who had been admirably calm, began to whimper.

"We're fine," Gertrude assured her.

"No." Maud gripped Gertrude's arm so hard that it hurt. Her hand was clammy. "My...my medicine."

"Why didn't you say?!" Gertrude flipped the satchel open and handed her the leather case. "Goodness, how would I know unless..."

Her eyes white with frenzy, Maud practically tore it open. She pulled off one of her boots and the stocking from the same foot. "I can't see," she muttered frantically. "There's no light. No light!"

Enrico took a match from his pocket and lit a small lantern that hung from a hook beside his seat. He passed it to Maud without a word.

Gertrude wondered how much these men had been told. She assumed that they were Republican or some other kind of anti-Imperial partisan, or Elettra wouldn't have chosen them; but until now, with Maud's leg gleaming in the yellow light, she had no a clue whether Enrico had known his passengers were women. It didn't seem to faze him a bit. Neither did the sight of Maud plunging a needle between her toes. It was a sight that made Gertrude shudder.

Maud shuddered, too, but hers was one of release. Gertrude could see the tension ebb from her body, one muscle at a time. Her eyelids fluttered closed. She didn't even notice when the syringe was slipped from her fingers.

"Is it helping?"

"It will," Maud breathed. "It'll take a few minutes, but it helps to know that it's on the way."

"Is this how it always happens? You feel pain like that, so suddenly? How horrible!" Gertrude was as curious as she was concerned.

"I should have taken it hours ago."

"Why didn't you?!" It was so like the Princess, to expect one to read her mind. Gertrude had vowed to stay sympathetic, but she was exasperated and reverted to the tone she usually used with Maud. "How would I know when you were supposed to take it? You only had to say."

"I didn't want you to see. To make it real. I wanted it to go away..." Her voice faded to almost nothing. The soft lantern light picked up the tears that were trickling through her lashes.

Gertrude was abashed. It was as Mr. Firewalker had said. She must curb her habit of lecturing Maud and remember that the Princess was not well. "It *will* go away," she said with more conviction than she currently felt. "When we get you home and you have a doctor to help you."

"What if I can't get home? He just said it might take six days to get to Nice alone. Six! They only gave me enough for the trip to Firenze. One or two more in case of breakage. It won't be nearly enough. I need...I can't go on without it. Oh, Gertrude! I'm so ashamed!" The tears were streaming now. She covered her face with her hands and rolled over on her side.

"It's not your fault," Gertrude leaned over and whispered in Maud's ear. Her heart was breaking at the ruin beside her. She couldn't imagine what the Queen would do when she saw. "Don't worry. It'll all be well."

She passed the lantern to Enrico. He doused the light.

They sped across the dark waters. Gertrude kept making soothing sounds until she was certain that Maud slept. Then she opened the case and touched the vials, counting them. Twice a day; she had known that much of the routine, only not at what time. There was exactly enough here for five more days. She thought unhappily of some of the other bottles in her satchel. Sir Alastair had prepared her for this eventuality.

22 – ROYAL PROGRESS

The first quiet morning was almost idyllic. Just before sunrise, they docked in a cove off Porto Venere that Enrico implied, with a wink, his not-too-distant ancestors might have used for smuggling in the days when Italy was still a scattering of contentious duchies and principalities. After breakfast, the men unrolled their blankets on the sand and fell fast asleep in an instant. Gertrude and Maud, who had rested during the night, began the arduous task of reconciling the Princess's body to a half-strength dose of her accustomed medication. There was no alternative. Even if Enrico's more optimistic projection proved true, there was not enough of the drug to see them through the journey home.

Some hours after the morning injection, Maud's body noticed that it had been short-changed. The reaction began, exactly as Sir Alastair had warned: her skin grew warm to the touch, but she shivered as if cold; her eyes rolled in her head; she jabbered anxiously about nothing. Gertrude had been given some medicine that was supposed to trick the body into thinking it had been given more of the drug than it actually had; she dutifully ground the tablets into powder and forced the Princess to swallow it. When Maud burned with fever, she stripped her to her underclothes and drenched her with sea water. When she shook with chills, Gertrude ransacked their bags, stuck two pair of stockings on the Princess's feet for warmth and rolled all their skirts and petticoats around her like a cocoon.

On the second day, Maud's bowels cramped and her muscles began to ache. Gertrude brewed pots of an herbal tea that Mr. Firewalker had given her to combat the cramps and dehydration, then dripped the tea into Maud's mouth, one spoonful at a time. She did the same with the broth that Enrico concocted from fish bones when it became clear that Maud could not swallow bread and cheese.

For two days, they were stuck on a shingle of rock south of Sori. The Imperial Navy was running night maneuvers off the coast at Genoa and fishermen in more than a dozen coastal villages had been warned to stay clear of the waters. To Gertrude's other burdens was added the pressure of lost time. Every day the *Faustina* remained in Italian waters, they risked being caught; and each delay ate away at the limited supply of the drug.

It was difficult enough to care for her patient on shore; night at sea, when a spasm could set the gozzo tilting into the waves, was misery for everyone. One night, they pressed on through hours of driving rain. Whenever Maud began to retch, Gertrude would prop her over the side of the gozzo, holding their sodden bit of canvas overhead like a tent.

Gertrude had always prided herself on rising to the occasion. She was beginning to think that this was the arrogance of the untested. When Agent Horner explained about the Princess's dependency on the drug, she'd been confident of her ability to handle the situation. Only Sir Alastair understood what it really meant. She, and probably Claude, had assumed Maud was suffering through something similar to their own experience of confusion and distress that could be fought against by a strong enough will. She knew differently now.

She ran herself ragged trying to keep up with Maud's needs. She caught her rest in fits and starts, waking whenever the other girl made a move or a sound. She forgot to eat, unless one of the Enricos put the food in her hand. How had Elettra found such wonderful people to watch over them? "Grazie," she said, hoping her face and voice could make the words mean what was in her heart. "Tante grazie, mille grazie."

Because Maud was too incapacitated to do it herself, twice each day, Gertrude drove the needle home (another reason to be grateful for Sir Alastair's foresight). Each injection provided a brief respite, but once Maud's body understood it had again been deceived, the cramping escalated and the hallucinations resumed. The men continued not to say much, but she noticed that Enrico senior sometimes watched them with pity in his eyes.

If this was how Maud's body reacted to a half-dosage, Gertrude didn't want to imagine how much worse it would be if there was nothing left to give her at all. She prayed that Dika had received her message.

❧

Caesar Augustus II lay on his boat-shaped bed, his head elevated by a purple silk bolster, his hands gripping the carved acanthus leaves on the rails. A film of perspiration beaded his face and neck. Behind him, a terrified page stood wafting a large palm-leaf fan.

During luncheon, the Emperor had complained of a tightness in his chest. He called for his masseur. Khristos put a bracing hand on his master's clavicle and immediately pulled back, his face awash with alarm. "Dottore Catoni must be called, Altezza," he stuttered, ducking his head frantically in Giulia's direction. Augustus rasped that this was ridiculous, that he only needed the man to attend to his cramp. Giulia chose to trust the more objective Greek.

Hours later, the crisis had not passed. A divan was carried into Caesar's chamber, so that the Lady Giulia might hold her vigil in comfort. Apollinaris stood watch over her, his bulging arms crossed over his breastplate. Rafello perched on a gilded stool at the head of the Emperor's bed, playing softly. The masseur remained nearby, should his skills be required; so did the two Egyptian priests.

Prince Napoleon Auguste sat awkwardly in a chair that had been placed for him at the foot of the bed. He had been standing by the door, until the usher tasked with the Lady's sustenance was struck by the impropriety of the heir to the throne being situated like a servant. The Lady Giulia glared, but permitted the chair to remain. Gusto, though uncomfortable sitting there, felt he had no option. He still didn't understand why it was necessary for him to wait there. There was nothing he could do. He couldn't even give comfort; his grandfather was never anything but scornful of his kind heart.

Everyone's full attention fixed on the craven little physician as he released another careful drop of fluid into the Emperor's open mouth.

The extract of foxglove had begun as an ancient receipt, one of many unearthed during an excavation on the Palatine Hill. There was some evidence that the villa had been the house of the *Mater Patriae*, the Empress Livia. The scrolls in the alabaster jar, discovered in a room that would have been well hidden even when the structure was new, were more than usually interesting to Augustus II. After determining the precise results of each formula, he had spent years experimenting with subtle variations.

Catoni quaked with each dose, praying that the Emperor would survive it. It was by Caesar's own calibration that the preparation being administered to him now would control his heart and not utterly cease its function. If he had miscalculated, however, he would not be the only one to pay the ultimate price.

The suggestive presence of the Lady's equerry didn't help Catoni's nerves any. Watching the Emperor's breath, he held his own. He experienced a moment of sheer dread when the hands loosened their grip on the bed rails, but the barrel chest continued to rise and fall with an increasingly even rhythm. He bent low over the Emperor's face. The lips were losing their bluish tinge. Perhaps this dose had done the trick, at least for the time being. Caesar's eyes flew open and drilled into his. The physician sprang back in alarm, causing the Lady Giulia to startle and gasp loudly.

Caesar licked his lips. His mouth was dry. In an instant, the masseur was at his side with a pitcher. Catoni soaked a cloth and gingerly wrung it to moisten his patient's mouth without trickling water down his throat. Caesar struggled to raise his head. The masseur positioned himself at the edge of the bed, sliding behind his master to support him.

When his thirst was slaked, Augustus turned his head away from the physician. He beckoned for Giulia to come closer. She lifted his hand and kissed it, then knelt by his side, so that her ear was near his lips.

"Tell the boy to go," he whispered.

"Are you certain, Patre? I have the feather and the scarab stone." She patted the waist of her gown where a tiny reticule of gold mesh hung from a chain. "I will keep it with me always now. You need never fear to be caught unprepared."

He smiled weakly. "You are my treasure, Giulia. The only one I can depend on. But all is well."

She shot Catoni a challenging glance.

The physician rolled his eyes heavenward and checked his patient's pulse. "It would seem the crisis has passed," he said, miserably. "But I will stay here tonight."

"We all of us will," the Lady declared. Apollinaris and the Greek hurried to lift her divan and place it beside the Emperor's bed. "But you," she clapped her hands twice for attention, then waved the backs of her fingers in Gusto's direction as if to shoo him away. "You may take your leave."

The confused Prince bowed and scuttled away before anyone might change their minds.

❧

The *Faustina* floated silently off the coast until the sun began to tip the waves with quicksilver; then slipped, at long last, into an abandoned jetty at the eastern end of the port of Nice.

Gertrude tidied herself as best she could, resuming the boots and jerkin that she'd abandoned some days back. Her hair was too rigid with salt and sand to do anything other than fold the long plait as it was and stuff it into her soft cap. Maud was currently unconscious. By this time, Gertrude had no scruples about asking Enrico's help to dress the insensible girl. He did it with solemn care, as if he were decking the statue of a saint for parade. Whatever compensation Elettra had arranged, it couldn't possibly be enough for what Enrico and his son had done for them. Somehow, someday, she would have to find a proper way to thank them.

So little of what she had brought to Florence was worth salvaging that it fit easily into a single bag. 'Rico hoisted it over the edge of the boat, then lifted Maud and stepped off onto the dock. Gertrude stumbled after him. She wanted to fall to the French boards and kiss them.

Enrico, fussed nervously with the mooring cleat. "I don't like to leave you here. The other girl, she can't walk."

'Rico held Maud solicitously, waiting to be told where to set her down. Gertrude started scanning the dock, looking for a convenient crate or a pile of ropes. "Don't worry. We have friends coming to meet us."

The old fisherman wasn't convinced. "But how? We didn't know until last night that we would be here today. And how would they know to look here?" He gestured to the deserted buildings by the dock. "This is a secret place."

"They are the kinds of friends who know secrets. And they will have arrived days ago." Gertrude gave him her most confident smile. She wasn't entirely certain herself, but she wasn't going to let Enrico know. He'd risked too much already to get them out of Augustus's realm. "They would have been checking the docks every morning. We have only to wait a few hours."

"Signorina!" 'Rico called.

Gertrude spun around to see what had disturbed the usually stoic fisherman. A man had materialized at the other end of the dock, tall and broad-shouldered, with something piratical in his appearance. His boots rang on the boards. As he drew nearer, they could make out a dark head, shaved nearly to stubble, and glowering black eyes. Gertrude caught the wink of a large ruby from one ear. To the shock of both the Enricos, she ran towards this devil, arms outstretched.

"Milosz! *Devlesa arakam tume!*"

Milosz would not be convinced that the barely conscious girl, drooping in his arms like a wilted tulip, was not his friend Claude. He humored her with a nod, but Gertrude could see he didn't believe her.

He led Gertrude behind the abandoned sheds. It was a token of how distracted she was by the first two legs of the mission that she expected to see a vardo camped there. Fortunately, Milosz had been more practical. The waiting vehicle was a shiny blue steam-driven automobile with yellow wheels.

A skinny young man grabbed her bag and hauled it over the side of the back seat. Milosz paused from covering Maud with a rug to help Gertrude up. She didn't conceal her astonishment well. Milosz caught sight of her face and laughed. "It's Pascal's. The boy is car crazy!"

Though he hadn't yet filled out, the boy was as tall as Milosz and had the same look about him. He hopped into the front seat, put his hands on the wheel, and turned to wink at her, over his shoulder. "*Vive les machines!*"

Milosz ran around back to prime the boiler. The engine caught; the automobile began sputtering and clacketing. He jumped into the front beside his nephew, who lowered his goggles and turned the valve.

The racket and bouncing roused Maud, who came to with a jolt and a scream. Gertrude clamped a hand over the Princess's mouth to muffle it. She was bitten for her troubles but swallowed her own scream, concerned that they not call any additional attention to themselves. It was essential that Maud slip into London as invisibly as she had slipped out of Italy. Gertrude felt conspicuous enough being in this very modern steam car, but perhaps her self-consciousness was merely the effect of a fortnight in Italy; thus far, the few people who passed evinced only mild curiosity and the occasional wave.

Gertrude's attempt at explanation was drowned out by the chugging engine. As she tried leaning closer to Maud's ear, the vehicle hit a stick or a bit of rock. Her head snapped back so abruptly that she bit her tongue. It was too much. "Pull yourself together, girl!" she yelled through her pain. "Your grandmother would be mortified to see you like this!"

Maud went rigid. Milosz, craning his neck to see what the noise was about, looked into the golden eyes. He tempered his usual fierce smile into one of pity. "Apologies, Gertrude. But she does look very much like Urme."

She nodded. She hoped Augustus and his people were equally mistaken in what they saw. With a guilty start she realized that was the first thought she'd spared in Claude's direction in days.

"She has a sickness?"

Gertrude massaged her injured hand. There was nothing to be done about her tongue. "It's almost time for her medicine. It would be better to wait until Dika can see her." She lisped the words with difficulty, glad that Maud did not understand Romani. "Is the camp nearby?"

"No camp. We go back to Grenoble for Dika." Milosz was enjoying the speed of this vehicle. He hung over the back of his seat with a wild grin. "We were outside Linz when your messenger found us. Too far even with our fastest horse. We took the railroad."

"The railroad?" It seemed an unlikely form of transport for the Rom.

Milosz winked. "Boxcars are a fine way to travel. But this time, to respect our Chivani, I bought tickets. Sitting for hours, packed shoulder to shoulder with so many gadge…" He made a face. "I breathe better in a boxcar."

"Why is Dika in Grenoble?"

"She stays with the mother of this one," he jerked his head in his nephew's direction. "They live there. In a house. Her husband is gadge. We get Dika and tomorrow we go on to Rouen."

"Tomorrow to Vichy!" Pascal corrected. "Next to Blois. Milosz said to stay clear of Paris, Mademoiselle. And *then* to Dieppe and Rouen."

"Three days? How long until we get to Grenoble?"

"If the boiler behaves, I can take us to almost 50 kilometers an hour!" Pascal caroled proudly.

Gertrude threw up her hands. She hadn't thought to memorize the map of France.

"Before moonrise," Milosz clarified.

There was no way that she was pulling out a needle in a speeding steam car. "We'll need to stop then," Gertrude called back. "As soon as you can spot a quiet place."

❦

A private rail spur led to Caesar's palazzo in Rome, where a closed carriage waited to take the princesses on to the Villa Borghese. Rappaccini was not permitted to accompany them; the Lady Giulia had given the driver explicit instructions. Agent Horner had warned Claude that the Lady might blame him for her temporary loss of control over the royal prisoner. The standing order for his daily visits to the Princess were Caesar's, but the Lady had ways of erecting impediments. It might be some days before she saw him again.

Under cover of helping her into the carriage, he gave her hand a reassuring squeeze. He bowed and shut the door. She didn't need to be an actress to follow him with sorrowful eyes. The pang in her chest was genuine. There had been few chances for private conversation, but she'd felt secure having him near. Sitting beside Ginevre in the dim carriage, she was totally alone.

Ginevre had been a boon in Florence. Claude had dreaded putting a foot wrong but, that first night at dinner, she had only to ask "did you see many pretty things?" for the Italian princess to launch into a stream of happy babble about the shops she'd visited and the ornaments she'd bought. For their remaining time in the city, it was the same. Ginevre brought the exuberance of a small child to everything they did. Claude didn't have to do a thing beyond keeping a slightly melancholy smile on her face and giving the occasional nod.

Now, the mere sight of Rome had subdued Ginevre, reducing her to the faded presence Claude had been primed to expect. They made the brief drive to the villa in silence.

The carriage doors opened. Blinking in the sudden spill of yellow light, Ginevre smiled nervously. The bewigged footman, his chartreuse satin livery dripping with gold lace, looked as if he had just exited from an opera. The haze from his glass lantern only added to the air of unreality. Claude allowed her eyes to empty as she was escorted to the Villa's entrance. Staring ahead into nothing, she felt her slippers crunch on the gravel, then tap against the smooth stone of one of the twin stairways. They passed under the portico. Though it was only just twilight, the darkness there was nearly complete.

The sparsely gaslit entry hall dazzled by comparison. Before Claude could get her bearings, a frightened girl came running from an inner room to hurled herself into Ginevre's arms.

"Oh, Ginevre! At last!"

"What's wrong, Irene? Why aren't you at home with Poppet?"

"She brought me here to wait for you. You must come," she insisted, pulling Ginevre by the arm. "Patre has been ill! Zia Giulia is with him. Gusto as well. They would never call for Gusto unless it were serious!"

Ginevre blanched. Sparing a single guilty look over her shoulder at the Princess, she allowed her sister to drag her towards the door.

"Patre." That was what they all called the Emperor. So Augustus was not well and his heir had been called to his side. That *did* sound serious. What would happen if he died? Claude wished she could speak with her father right now. Even Agent Horner would do. She wondered if Lady Giulia had given her instructions before or after the Emperor had fallen ill.

This mission might turn out to be a very short one. Surely they would cancel the wedding if Augustus were to die. Once he was gone, they would have to realize how mad the abduction had been. Perhaps they would send her home. They should be relieved to see the back of such an inconvenient hostage. Or would they seek a more permanent solution to this predicament, would they want to make sure that the addled Princess never had a chance to try to tell her tale? Claude felt a touch of ice down her spine. She resolutely pushed it out of her mind. Hadn't she warned Gertrude about borrowing trouble? Worrying about something that might not happen would only dilute her focus from the situation at hand.

The facts were that Augustus was ill and the family was gathering. What should she do now? As Claude, she would grab the opportunity to try to run. Or maybe she wouldn't. How far would she get before some guard would stop her? In any case, it was improbable that Maud would try to escape and Claude's priority was to preserve her impersonation. What would Maud have done? The Princess she'd seen in Florence was beyond action, unless someone were there to lead her. Would Maud react at all to the knowledge that her enemy was gravely ill? Most likely she would hide in her rooms and hope to be forgotten.

A servant hurried by with a tray, pausing briefly to bow. Hesitation was a bad idea.

She should look as if she knew where she was going. It was no small trick to reconcile the mirrored gallery, with its kaleidoscopic marble floor and ranks of statuary, with the floor plan Agent Horner had given her to memorize. She started slowly in the direction opposite from the one Ginevre had taken. The music room led to an unlit room of less obvious purpose. All the rooms on this level flowed into one another; it made navigation tricky, but after a false start she found the first actual door that she had seen since entering the villa.

She just missed being spotted again; a faint clatter of footsteps receded from the landing. Holding firmly to the polished rail, she advanced upward. Now she must depend on the instructions Maud had whispered in the garden. Hoping she could rely equally on the Princess's accuracy and her own memory, she turned down a corridor and counted doors. She paused, her hand hovering over the knob.

The door opened by itself. Fortunately, it opened inward or it would have hit her. As it was, Claude flinched. From the other side, a pinch-faced woman glared at her. She must be the disagreeable maid, Giulia's informer, Silvana.

"Altezza," she croaked, bobbing a meagre curtsey. "You will want to refresh yourself after your journey."

Claude followed her wordlessly, through the storm of lace and blush satin that was the bedchamber, to an antechamber that held the bath. The water was steaming and redolent with gardenia. It made her sneeze. The crow woman smirked at the sound. There wasn't time to think whether this reaction was good or bad for her impersonation. The woman began to undo the bodice of her creamy linen travel ensemble. In Florence, under Leonora's kinder ministrations, Claude had become accustomed to this process. It wasn't until the woman began to undo her corset strings that she remembered: assuming that even the drug kit might be subject to scrutiny by those who packed and unpacked the Princess's bags, she'd tucked her locket down the front of her chemise this morning. Her hand flew up to stop it falling when the corset was released. With luck, she might be able to use some sleight of hand to whisk it out of sight and tuck under a towel or something until she had a solitary minute to find a more permanent hiding place. That, however, wasn't her biggest problem.

It occurred to her that the maid was intending to bathe her. She hadn't bathed in Florence. She had only been without underthings when Leonora put her into her nightdress, and then the room had been nearly dark. This bathroom was gaslit. As soon as her drawers came off, the mark of the kumpania would be glaringly obvious on her thigh. She needed a few minutes alone with the precious contents of her silver clamshell. How could she get rid of this woman? Claude thought quickly. By trial and error with Leonora, she'd learned that there was one time she might have a reasonable expectation of privacy. With a little gasp, she made herself go rigid, then bounced on the balls of her feet.

Silvana ignored the hint. She prodded Claude's hand, where it clutched her chemise. "Come now, Altezza. The water will get cold."

Claude pretended it was the most natural thing in the world to have her intimate functions known by strangers. "I would relieve myself first, Silvana," she said, allowing an injured note to creep into her voice.

Silvana said nothing but managed to convey the opinion that an unscheduled call of nature presumed on the proper order of things. She snapped herself upright and stalked back to the larger chamber. Claude followed trailed behind her. A door was cunningly concealed in one of the papered walls; the maid flung it open and lit the candle inside.

Acting as if Silvana weren't there, Claude stepped into the tiny closet. The door closed, and she leaned against it. She hadn't realized she was holding her breath until she let it out. The etched mirror sconce magnified the single flame, but the light revealed only a cushioned seat, over the usual chute, and a matching footstool. She pulled down her drawers and quickly pressed some of the wax paste over her Romani tattoo. She hoped that

Father was correct, that it would stay in place when wet. She left the locket on the floor; the concealing shadows would do as a temporary hiding place, until they left her alone tonight to sleep. She pulled the tasseled rope, sending a loud sluice of water down the chute. Father had been correct about the Italian plumbing; it was, confoundingly, almost modern.

The delay hadn't improved Silvana's disposition any. She must be a very good spy. There was no other excuse for someone this unpleasant to be assigned to the Princess. Claude would need to be extraordinarily careful around her.

The undergarments were pulled from her body and she was plunked into the marble tub. Silvana scrubbed so roughly that Claude expected she'd be red for hours. She feared for her bit of camouflage. As the sponge broached the knee of that particular leg, she fixed the maid with a doleful look. "Why don't you like me, Silvana?" It seemed the kind of thing a subjugated Maud might say. From Silvana's reaction, she was correct; this appeal seemed to have been tried before. The maid threw the sponge aside and opened the large towel to cover her as she rose from the bath.

"It is not necessary for you to dress, Altezza," she said brusquely, reaching for a dressing gown. "The Lady is with Caesar tonight. Everyone is to dine in their own rooms."

Moist and most thoroughly clean, Claude drifted out of the bathing room. She wondered what to do with herself. If her bags had only arrived, she could read. She allowed herself to collapse gracefully into a convenient slipper chair.

Silvana cleared her throat for attention. There was a troubled look on her face. "Your medication, Altezza. Dottore Catoni is with Caesar…"

She blinked once, a tick of Maud's that she had noted in the garden. "I administer my own medication now. Did you forget, Silvana? I have sufficient for tonight. Where is my case?" Presumably a fresh supply of drugs would be forthcoming, but the physician had fortunately provided a couple of extra for the journey, in case of breakage. It was even more fortunate for Gertrude and Maud, she reflected, to have that additional day.

The small handbag had obviously been delivered. Flushing as if she had been reproved, the maid retrieved the case from a console table and carried it over. Claude fitted together a syringe and serenely drew up the fluid from one of the last measures of saline. She was relieved to not have to attempt Father's trick for the first time under those eagle eyes.

She performed the injection and withdrew the needle with a blatant sigh. Relaxing back into the tufted brocade, Claude stretched out the hand that held the empty vial. She waited until Silvana bent to accept it, then looked into her face. "Someday I will be Empress," she murmured, apropos of nothing. She doubted that Maud had ever said that to Lady Giulia's spy; or, for that matter, to anyone.

Through her lowered lashes, Claude could see the revelation hit. Caesar was unwell. This girl would indeed be Empress someday, perhaps someday soon. It might be well for Silvana to start buttering her bread on both sides.

The woman was no fool. "I will ring for your dinner now, Altezza," Silvana mumbled. "If that is your wish."

❦

Rappaccini betook himself to the Villa Alsaziano the next morning, to sulk over his disbarment.

The Baron was having his own issues with the Lady's high-handedness. Caesar had been incapacitated for hours before he'd learned a thing about it, and that little had come not by way of Giulia but through one of his own spies in the Palazzo.

The force of Caesar's personality was such that Haussmann often forgot his sovereign was his senior by three years. For the first time ever, the Baron considered the possibility that his Emperor might predecease him. It was not a pleasant prospect. The Lady Giulia would have her claws out before Augustus was even in the ground, or however it was that Caesar preferred to dispose of his remains. If the Baron were to be allowed to live out his life in comfort, he would need to ensure that he was indispensable to the heir.

The key to this, he thought, was Tesla. He must impress upon Prince Gusto that Tesla's genius, not Giulia's conniving, would be the power behind his throne. As well as being dazzled by the demonstration of cross-bolt weaponry, Gusto must register the man who had devised it, and that it was only thanks to the Baron that Roma held the services of that man. Yes, Tesla must definitely appear at the wedding.

Haussmann brushed away Rappaccini's sulks. "Caesar was unwell. She will forget all about it once he's back to strength."

This was the first Rappaccini had heard about the Emperor's illness. He looked abashed.

"Nothing to concern yourself about," the Baron continued. "But as long as you are prevented from fulfilling your duties with the Princess, I think I will take advantage and steal you for a while. Before I send you to Venezia, I have another errand that requires your particular knowledge and discretion."

The Centurion displayed his customary air of smug competence and bowed deeply. "Si, Eminenza. But what about the Principessa? She will be expecting me…"

"With her wedding only days away, Rappaccini, the Princess is unlikely to require diversion. However, if you are unable to take your leave, I will call upon her myself and explain your absence"

❧

Gertrude stumbled drowsily along the dark path to the house. Lala, a delicate woman with Milosz's sparkling black eyes, smiled shyly at her guest. "*Bienvenu chez moi*," she said. "My husband gives his apologies, but he is already asleep. He must be up before the sun, for his work."

"*Devlesa arakam tume.*" Gertrude surprised her with the traditional Romani response. We found you with God's help.

Dika patted Gertrude fondly. "You remember your lessons." She briefly probed her face and seemed satisfied with what she saw there.

Lala had put her bridal bedlinens on the settee in the front room, and made up a pair of pallets on the floor for the other women. She apologized for the modest accommodations. "My husband and I would have gladly given you our bed, but the *Chivani* insisted on this."

Dika nodded emphatically. "Your husband needs his sleep. This will serve us well. And if I have need of the kitchen, you won't be disturbed."

"Thank you," Gertrude said. "It is very good of you to help us. You have no idea how wonderful clean sheets look to me right now," she added, with a smile. Milosz carried the sleeping Maud from the automobile and deposited her gently on the settee. Dika laid a hand on the Princess's forehead and checked her colour.

"She had her medicine a couple of hours ago," Gertrude felt compelled to explain. "She should rest easy." With Lala's help, she undressed the Princess and covered her with the light cotton blanket.

"You rest now, too, chavi," Dika said. "We talk in the morning."

Gertrude yawned. "I've been sleeping all day," she protested.

"Then you have a chao with me, and tell me about your friend." The older woman put her arm around the younger and led her to the kitchen.

It was a large room, the heart of the little house. The iron kettle was no doubt perpetually on the boil. Lala set a brightly-painted teapot before the older woman, with the utmost respect. Dika produced a packet of dried leaves from the folds of her sash. When the water hit the herb, it released a scent that both soothed and stimulated.

Breathing it in, Gertrude was filled with a sense of well being. To her own surprise, she started to sob. Like a summer thunder storm, it didn't last long but it was necessary to clear the air. When she raised her head again, Dika pushed a cup into her hands. She drank thirstily. Dika waited patiently until she was able to speak.

She told the Chivani everything she knew about Maud's condition, both what she had been told by Agent Horner and the Princess, and what she had observed for herself. With increasing authority, she spoke about their efforts to reduce the dosage. When her pidgin Romani failed, Lala helped by translating her French.

Dika listened with characteristic total absorption, asking the occasional pointed question, refilling their cups until the pot and Gertrude had both been drained.

"Sir Alastair thought we should wait until she has a doctor," Gertrude concluded reluctantly. "But we can't. The drarnego *has* to work. This is all that's left." She took out the final vials that held any fluid and set them down on the table. "At the current dosage, that's only enough for tomorrow."

Almost ceremoniously, the Chivani picked up one of the blue glass tubes and removed the stopper. She brought it up to her nose. Finally, she touched the cork with the tip of her tongue. She shook her head. "When I gave you drarnego, you and Urme," she used the nickname with a hint of fond respect, "the substance you had been given was simple, something to upset the balance of your mind. This is nothing simple." She sighed deeply and folded her hands on the well-scrubbed table. "There are herbs here that I know, but others I do not. There is some poppy, but not so much as should cause the body such craving. Drarnego will undo much of this, but not all."

"But you can help her!" Gertrude looked at Dika beseechingly.

"Each person is so different. It is a great mystery, that what is meat for one can be poison for another. I can purge the substance from her body. But there is something else...in the body, the mind, the soul...I do not know. Something binds her to this drug. That I cannot change. After the poison is gone, her road will be long, and never easy."

Maud woke the house with her screaming. She had awakened to find herself in a strange bed, her thoughts a scramble of gardens and boats and a bone-rattling road. Dika was the first to reach her side, which made her scream all the more.

The noise brought Lala's husband clomping down the stairs in his nightshirt, rifle in hand, nearly colliding with Pascal and Milosz who were flying from the attic.

Muzzy with sleep, Gertrude stumbled over to the settee to quiet the Princess. Maud's eyes were white with terror. She chokingly whispered that a witch was trying to kill her. Gertrude held her close and rocked until she relaxed.

Dika sent the men back to bed, Gertrude's embarrassed apologies floating after them.

Maud and Dika fell quickly back to sleep. Gertrude was unable to. She lay on her pallet, trying to pretend she was in her rooms at Oxford. She ached for that oasis of calm. Adventures, she decided, were not entirely to her taste. It wasn't the physical hardship she minded, so much as the turmoil. As fascinating as it was to explore the world, she was beginning to think she was better suited to feeding her curiosity with books.

§

Part of the Princess's routine was her daily visit to the garden. Passing through the French windows, Claude's eye was caught by a large flash of gold. Horner had explained that the Golden One currently resided, if that were the proper word, at the villa and would be standing guard on the terrace. Claude had thought she could envision it, but the reality was staggering. It was only a head taller than she, smaller than Garibaldi but of proportionate bulk, the entire mass coated in unbroken gleam as though someone had up-ended a vat of molten metal.

Seeing it in the sunlight, she couldn't tear her eyes away.

The blue jets shimmered. Claude was embarrassed to have been caught staring. "*Sei così bella*," she apologized; you are so beautiful.

As soon as she said it, she realized her mistake; no one spoke to amphoraeka, except to give commands. It was lucky that no one had witnessed this. She hurried from the terrace, pausing by the nearest rosebush to bury her face in the sweet blossoms and regain her composure.

Her task had been far simpler in Florence, with only Ginevre and Leonora to deceive. Both of them seemed to like or pity Maud. As long as she was docile, they were happy enough to accept her. She had made a little joke once—a very little joke; Agent Horner had immediately caught her eye and indicated this was not something the Princess would do. "Don't get cocky," he'd whispered later. She hated when he was right; nevertheless, this entire charade weighed on him having been so.

The Princess's customary table was, of course, exactly where he had said to find it. The afternoon was warm, heavy with the buzz of insects and the dusty sweetness of summer flora. In her heart of hearts, Claude had felt some disdain for what she considered to be the Princess's weakness in resisting captivity. It was humbling in the extreme to discover how easy it would be, even without the assistance of opiates, to sleep this life away. She dug a fingernail into the soft spot at the base of her wrist, to arouse herself.

She had spoken directly to an amphoraka. What other mistakes might she have made today? Along with her morning tray, Leonora had brought the happy news that Caesar had turned the corner; the Princess had looked at her blankly, as if she weren't quite certain what that might mean, then applied herself to her morning injection. Father's trick had gone off without a hitch, the liquid trickling harmlessly into the chair cushions. The kind maid's observation that the Lady Giulia would remain with Patre today had been met with something approximating a smile. Neither of these reactions had been taken amiss.

Later, she had been stuffed into this dotted-Swiss confection and prodded towards the music room, which had been, mercifully, empty. Unless Maud had previously expressed a dislike for *Greensleeves*, her hour there was unlikely to have caused any comment.

The other girl, Ginevre's sister hadn't joined them for lunch. Presumably, with the Emperor on the mend, she had returned to wherever it was that she lived. Ginevre was as much downcast as if someone were standing over her with a whip. As the Princess rarely spoke unless spoken to, it was a mostly silent meal. Claude carefully continued to toy with her food and eat lightly. With her appetite blunted from inactivity, this was likely to become the easiest part of her charade to maintain.

She wondered what other mannerisms would soon become habitual. Since swapping clothes with Maud, she manipulated her body as if it were a puppet, inwardly holding her breath after each move. Every interaction was fraught with potential for exposure.

"Moud! Look who's come to see us!" Ginevre's slippered feet scampered towards the table. She sounded happy again.

Expecting to see Rappaccini, Claude opened her eyes and turned with a glad smile.

She should not have been so glad. The gawky young man in the overly elaborate tunic had to be the Prince.

"I've asked for lemonade. You like your tea, I know." The very thrust of Ginevre's chin was apologetic. "But the day is so hot."

Claude wafted a hand in what she hoped betokened accedence. Gusto took the opportunity to seize it and kiss it.

She had no idea how Maud would react to this! Would she smile? Would she recoil? She remembered what Agent Horner had advised: when unsure how to react, don't. Claude was chagrined that she felt so lost without that insufferable man. Maud regarded Gusto as benign; she remembered overhearing the Princess say something to that effect in the Boboli. She decided to leave her hand limp and allow the kiss to pass unremarked. It must have been like kissing a leaf. He let go, quickly enough, to slide into the seat beside hers.

Revived by her brother's presence, Ginevre launched into a chronicle of her adventures in Firenze. Claude sipped quietly at her lemonade. Whenever Ginevre turned to her for corroboration, it sufficed that she nodded vaguely. Each time, she felt the Prince staring at her with a mixture of longing and fear.

To put him at ease, she gave him a tremulous smile. The poor boy— it was impossible to think of him as a man—was so happy he probably wouldn't have twitched if she'd picked up a welding torch for an impromptu reshaping of the iron railings.

She hadn't expected the Imperial family to be so pitiable.

Though she cringed under Dika's penetrating gaze, Maud had no remembrance of her night terrors. When Gertrude explained that they were going to withhold the drug, she paled but did not protest. She obediently drank the drarnego chao.

Together, they waited to see what would happen. Conversation was a good distraction. Now that they were safely in France, they could speak freely. Gertrude was especially eager to hear all that Maud could bring herself to tell about her captivity. She didn't acknowledge it even to herself, but on some level she was afraid that Maud's mind would not recover from this ordeal, and it was important to learn what she could while the memories were still there.

When the tremors began, Maud lashed out hysterically. "It's happening again, just like before! You said this would cure me!" She began clawing at Gertrude's arms, her nails leaving red gouges.

Gertrude slapped her across the face. "Listen to me!" Maud was shocked enough to do so. Gertrude was shocked at herself. "I said it would *help*. It will make it easier to get that poison out of your system. Eas*ier*, Maud. It can't be easy. I'm sorry."

Dika fed Maud a steady stream of drarnego chao, supplemented by Mr. Firewalker's herbal brew. Gertrude had shown Dika her other supplies on that first day. The Chivani rejected Sir Alastair's tablets with a knowing smile. "These can only try to fool the body," she explained. "They are not meant for healing." However, she was most respectful of the content of Mr. Firewalker's packets. Gertrude had quickly come to consider Mr. Firewalker a most superior person. She felt a glow of pride that Dika, who she held in highest esteem, would pay him this complement.

The drarnego did make the withdrawal easier, though it was only because she had a basis for comparison that Gertrude was able to make this claim. The physical discomfort was considerably reduced. Most strikingly, Maud remained coherent. Once the Princess realized for herself that her harshest disturbances were caused by her own panic, the spells of hysteria abated. Her most severe symptoms were a persistent low fever and the trembling, which never entirely subsided. It was not much worse than a mild influenza.

They stayed in Lala's little house for four days. When the patient was cleared for travel, the two young women bid a grateful goodbye to their rescuers. Maud stopped Pascal from helping her into the automobile. Composed but pale and insubstantial, she was still a shadow of the Princess who'd set out to find some fun. She looked at the assembled faces intently, learning them by heart, and then she bowed. "I don't know how to thank you," she said finally said. "My family owes you a great debt."

Dika returned the bow. "There is no debt between us. We share friends." The Chivani smiled fondly at Gertrude. She gestured to include the mixed company of French and Romani and added, "we share an enemy, as well."

"I feel as if we're always saying goodbye," Gertrude said plaintively, after recovering some of the air Milosz had hugged out of her lungs. He and Dika would be traveling east at their own pace, returning to the kumpania. The journey to Rouen would be simple enough that Pascal could take them on alone.

Dika kissed her on the forehead and handed her the drarnego. Maud was to continue taking it for another fortnight. "*Ashen Devlesa,*" she said God go with you. "Latcho drom."

If Pascal hadn't already lost enough days getting them to Rouen, he would probably have begged to come with them, but the position in the manufactory in Le Mans was an opportunity of a lifetime and the young mechanist dared not delay any further. It was just as well. Gertrude wasn't sure she would have had the heart to refuse.

He stroked the side of the ptery, his eyes moist with longing. "You can fly this, Gertrude?"

"Yes." She remembered Sir Alastair's happy surprise at learning that, like his daughter, she had something of this skill. She had hidden her reservations well. Her confidence was stronger now that the two-seater he'd organized turned out to be the same military model as the one they had 'borrowed' in Bucharest. It was one thing to puzzle out a new set of controls; it was another thing entirely to do it while flying across the English Channel.

She rolled up the sleeves on the padded jacket Sir Alastair's factotum had thoughtfully provided, hoping they wouldn't roll down in the wind and get in the way of her fingers. The garment was tailored for a man, of course, and unlike Maud, she hadn't the height to wear it without some adjustment.

Pascal stowed their bag and assisted the Princess, whose body was still not reliable, into the back seat.

Gertrude shook the canteens a second time, making sure they were sound. "The one with the ribbon is the drarnego," she said, handing two of them up to Maud. You'll want it as soon as we land."

Pascal gave a final tweak to the buckles of Maud's harness and, with obvious reluctance, clambered down from the aercraft.

Gertrude gave him a boyish cuff on the back before realizing what she'd done. She grinned, embarrassed. Since she'd begun walking around in breeches, she had picked up some inconvenient habits. She hoped they wouldn't prove difficult to break. "*Bon courage*, Pascal." She stuck out her hand to shake his. Might as well be hung for a sheep as for a lamb. "Monsieur Bollée will be lucky to have you!"

He shook it gravely. "Bon courage, Gertrude. Mademoiselle." He waved up at Maud, who blew a kiss back. He beamed with embarrassed delight.

Gertrude swung up into the pilot's seat. She pulled on the soft leather helmet and flight goggles that she had lugged all the way from Prague. Before she covered her face, she looked over her shoulder at Maud. The Princess looked happy enough to laugh. Gertrude's spirits were equally high.

Gertrude reached inside the neck of her jacket to fish out the chain that held her locket. She prised it open with her fingernail and pressed the button inside. Unlike Claude's, the mate to this one wasn't with Sir Alastair but had been sent by courier to England. When they landed, it would alert Lord Pinkerton's man to come and fetch them. She tucked the chain safely away. It made a tiny vibration against her chest.

She slipped on her gauntlets and gave a final wave to Pascal. "Au revoir!" she yelled. She put her hand on the throttle. Before he could reply, the ptery came to life, the roar drowning out everything except the exultant laughter in her own head.

❧

Gertrude spied the black automobile heading towards them, even as the wheels were still coasting to a halt on Beachy Head. As soon as she could, she stood upright, sucking down the sea air—the *English* sea air—as if it were her first infant breath. Nothing had ever been so delicious.

She turned to Maud with a radiant smile. "We did it!"

Maud's smile was guarded and never reached her eyes. She made no attempt to move.

Gertrude leaned into her compartment and released the buckles of her harness. "Time for the drarnego," she ordered, briskly. "It's nothing but wheel ruts, as far as I can see. You don't want to try drinking from a flask while we're bouncing over them."

A jumpy gentleman, who introduced himself as Mr. Chandler, handed them down from the ptery and into the closed back of the car. His silent companion hopped into the pilot's seat that Gertrude had just vacated and reactivated the engine.

"Our bag!" Gertrude called. It was too late. The ptery was already coasting toward the edge of the cliff, the wheels clearing the chalk.

"Nothing to worry about, Miss." Mr. Chandler got in with them, taking the reverse-facing seat. He tapped a small Vitriflex window to get the driver's attention. They began to move. "We'll see that the bag finds you in London."

No doubt it would, eventually. Gertrude was glad she had kept hold of her battered leather satchel, with Dika's gift inside.

It was an uncomfortable drive. Once or twice, Mr. Chandler asked them how they were, then looked away as if he thought he ought not have asked. He jumped when she attempted to make polite conversation. Gertrude didn't assume that all Pinkertons were like Sir Alastair or Agent Horner, but this one's evident nervousness surprised her. Maud, who had seemed happy until they landed, had withdrawn into herself and would say nothing. In the end, Gertrude relaxed against the seat, turned her eyes to the windows, and watched England rolling by.

23 – DAMAGE CONTROL

For whatever reason, it had been decided that the Princess shouldn't see herself in her own wedding gown. Claude didn't know whether she would have been horrified or collapsed into hysterical laughter; either way, she was just as glad to not have a mirror. It was difficult enough to stand submissively on the small platform, trying to ignore Ginevre's awed admiration and the incidental reverent murmur from Leonora, with nothing to do except shuffle a few degrees when so instructed by Lady Giulia's tame modiste.

A pair of assistants crawled around her, re-pinning the deep flounce of curlicued Milan lace on the underskirt. The Signora had already expressed her displeasure at the carelessness of these minions. The flounce was decidedly dragging. When calibrated a few weeks ago, it was to have been placed so as to just skim the ground. Claude knew the difference was to do with Maud's slight advantage in height. Fortunately, it was minor enough that the modiste would dismiss it as error.

Claude thought that when this interminable fitting was over, she might claim fatigue; perhaps *un emicrania* if necessary. It would be blissful to be alone, even if only for an hour. She congratulated herself on having asked Rappaccini to add a bookstore to their shopping itinerary in Florence. At the rate at which she read Italian, the handful of volumes she had selected should last her at least through the honeymoon.

The honeymoon. It was odd how detached she felt from the inevitable sequel to this wedding, as if the experience (and being thoroughly educated she understood, intellectually, exactly what that was) would appertain to someone else. She could certainly bear it better than Maud would have; that was all that was important.

Really, a honeymoon was the least of it. Managing Gusto would be a piece of cake. What she didn't like to contemplate was everything else that could happen. If the Augustus began to trumpet his victory immediately after the wedding, Britain would likely have to attack at once; with nothing to counter the amphoraeka, it would be an ugly war. The best move for her side would be for the Emperor to wait until he thought he had cemented his claim to Britain, until his newly-minted granddaughter became pregnant. Claude shuddered. The clinical detachment with which she could consider the marriage bed didn't extend to carrying a child. She had heard whispers that there were things one could do to prevent this; she wished she'd been a little more curious, but it had never occurred to her that she might need this knowledge. She would have to hope, devoutly, that Father and Leski would have the automatons ready to invade before she found herself with an additional hostage to fortune.

Claude was so distracted by this line of thought that, when she heard the loud report, her instinct was to duck.

It was the door to her apartments, being flung open by a heavy hand. The hand belonged to a muscular black man, clad mostly in bronze leather. Stepping inside, he struck a martial pose, one hand on the hilt of a large sword that was presumably as sharp as it was decorative. Ginevre, Leonora and the modiste snapped to a stiffness that was very nearly a salute, then dipped from the knee into formal curtseys. The two minions, having scrambled to their feet, crouched back into the most obsequious of bows.

The woman who strode in on absurdly high gilt heels, had to be the Lady Giulia. She was painted like a cheap doll and hung with more jewels than even the most nouveau of riche would have worn to a ball back home. The antique style of her gown left her skinny arms bare and revealed an angry collarbone. The mustard silk clashed with the unnatural colour of her curls and, taken together with her emeralds, gave her skin a greenish cast that emphasized the lines and shadows of age. She was an appalling sight.

Once again, Claude had to stifle a desire to giggle. According to Agent Horner, she could show fear to this woman, if fear were warranted, but was otherwise to maintain her sleepwalker's trance. She fixed her gaze on the door to the water closet, keeping it there as Giulia approached the platform and circled her, raking her from head to hem with cruel eyes. The tiny woman's powerful confidence made Claude feel oddly large and ungainly.

"You seem fatigued, Principessa." Her voice was too rich to be shrill. She wielded it like a whip. "I hope your little excursion to Firenze was not too much for you."

Claude craned her neck down, as if looking from far away. "It was Patre's idea that we should go," she said, with as little tone as possible.

Behind her careful mask, Claude could see Giulia absorb this remark, wonder if the dozy Princess could have intended it as a taunt, and ultimately dismiss the idea as preposterous. It was a satisfactory reaction. Even when it wasn't hand-to-hand, a battle was a battle; there were feints one might make to feel out the boundaries of one's opponent. Claude was beginning to see the sense in those sedentary games of strategy that she had always found boring. Perhaps, before she had become hampered by the drugs, Maud ought to have been able to change the dynamics of her situation. Claude chided herself for this uncharitable thought.

"Did you enjoy your little treat, Ginevre?" As bullies will, the Lady had turned away from the non-responsive Princess to a more gratifying target. "I hope you comported yourself with more than your usual dignity. You were, after all, representing the Imperial Household."

"Yes, Zia," Ginevre stammered. "I bought you a gift. One for Patre, as well."

Claude was impressed by the Princess's forethought.

"Such a loving heart," Giulia purred. "I would have expected you to have asked after your grandfather's health by now. Were you not concerned to learn that he was ill?"

"Oh, yes, Zia! I didn't sleep a wink last night. But this morning, we had word that all was well. And Gusto came to visit…"

"Gusto would hardly be an authority in this matter. But yes, the crisis has passed. Enough that Patre requested I leave his side specifically to come here and see how his 'pearl' had fared on her journey." She shot another gimlet look at Claude. "Have you nothing to say?"

Claude adjusted her expression to one of mild puzzlement. "May I step down?"

"The ingratitude!" Giulia fumed. "If you were not who you are, he would never stand for such disrespect for a minute! Well, do not expect to be excused forever, Principessa. Things will change soon enough, once it is secured."

Claude wondered if she were supposed to understand this reference.

Stalking to the door, Giulia snapped her fingers at the modiste. "Finish. And do something about those sleeves. They're a horror." Before she exited, she turned to face Claude again. "Patre is hopeful that he will be well enough to dine in company tomorrow." Her smile was as sharp as a fang. "Expect to join him."

Before the door closed, Claude caught a flash of gold in the shadows.

❧

Allan Pinkerton brought the news to Windsor, that her granddaughter and Miss Bell were at that very moment flying across the Channel. He seemed ten years younger than he had the previous afternoon. If it were anyone less dependable, Charlotte wouldn't have believed the report.

It was Frank's doing, he explained. He had few details to share, other than that somehow, with Agent Horner's assistance, Frank had connived for Miss Bell to smuggle the Princess out of Italy. Their plan had begun weeks ago, but they hadn't wanted to tell her until they were certain they had succeeded. Somehow, after that horrible day when he had told her the truth about Maud's condition, Frank had made it happen.

Sensing the girl would do best in her own bed, Charlotte pushed aside her aversion to Kensington Palace to be at her granddaughter's side. She refrained from swooping down the moment they arrived, first allowing Dr. Jenner's nurses to make Maud comfortable. Before entering the room, she knocked softly.

In her white nightdress, propped up by her pillows, Maud looked like a suffering child. Her eyes were smudged and enormous in her wan face. The only remnant of the vivid young woman who had left London in April was the bright hair, streaming down her shoulders. Ignoring the fussing and bowing of the nurses, the Queen sat on the edge of the bed. She put her arms around her granddaughter and held her, stroking her hair and whispering how grateful she was to God for bringing her home. She could feel the girl's body slowly relax.

"You're not angry with me?" Maud whispered.

Charlotte kissed her on the forehead. "There's nothing to be angry about. A terrible thing was done to you and you were very brave. I'm proud of you."

A single tear ran down Maud's cheek. Charlotte hugged her again before releasing her.

"Now you must rest and get well."

Maud nodded. "Is Mama here? It must be awful for her."

"She's with your Aunt Elisabeth. We've let her think that you've been traveling with Miss Bell. We thought it for the best."

Maud nodded again. Her eyes began to droop with exhaustion. The Queen stood slowly, so as not to shift the mattress and disturb her. The nurses bowed again. This time, she acknowledged them with a gracious smile.

"Where is Gertrude, Grandmama?" Maud spoke just loud enough that Charlotte could still hear her. "I don't want her to leave."

"She'll stay as long as you want. Now rest."

Maud sighed and melted into the pillows.

Charlotte watched tenderly until her eyes were closed. The Queen had much to learn and digest, but the grandmother was at peace. She must wire Frank. She wanted him here so that she could see his eyes when she spoke with him. Now that this was over, she hoped he wouldn't run back across the Atlantic. She would not order him; she would ask.

❧

The Queen's own physician had been waiting on the gravel drive with two nurses and a cane-bottom wheelchair. Maud was trundled up to her rooms, to be bathed and popped into bed. Gertrude was prevented from accompanying her. Instead, she was conducted to a small sitting room and subjected to an examination as stringent as any Oxford tripos.

Unlike Dika, who allowed her to tell the story in her own way, Dr. Jenner had a series of specific questions to pose. When she volunteered information outside his line of questioning, she could see him reject the information. He was particularly dismissive of the drarnego.

Gertrude refused to be put off. She was determined to ensure that Maud completed the full course of Dika's treatment. "The drarnego tea will reinforce the progress she's made but, as you can see, she's still quite fragile. With rest, simple food, her body…"

He held up a hand to stop her. "Young lady, I believe I will be the best judge of what the Princess needs. I have asked for your account only because I understand my patient may be unable to provide one of her own."

Dr. Sir William Jenner was one of the most admired doctors in Britain. He was also a self-satisfied old man who looked like an angry fish. Sitting across from him on a low chair, still in her grubby male trappings, Gertrude felt at a distinct disadvantage. "I have the utmost respect for your expertise, Sir William. I must also respect someone whose knowledge in this particular area surpasses that of either of us."

"Your Gypsy woman."

"In their tradition, the Rom have preserved knowledge that we have not."

"Miss Bell." He didn't actually shake his head, but she could feel him thinking to do so. "Thank you for being so forthcoming. I commend you for your splendid care of the Princess. Now I really must attend to my patient." He actually pulled out his pocket watch.

Gertrude Lowthian Bell was not accustomed to being patronized. She jumped to her feet and put herself between Jenner and the door. "I have seen the efficacy of this herb, Sir William. It is truly remarkable. The drarnego healed my own mind, and I have seen how much it helped the Princess. Certainly there would be no harm in her continuing to take it."

The hand came up again. "My dear Miss Bell. As you admit, you yourself have undergone a considerable ordeal. I will accept that you believe that this herbal tea enabled you to recover. It is far more likely to be the result of your own robust nature than of a magic potion brewed up by an old Gypsy woman."

"I might remind you," she said acerbically, "that an old Russian woman created the drugs in the first place." She stalked out.

Gertrude regretted her show of temper almost immediately. As long as the Princess remained under Jenner's care, access to her would be under his control. She would probably have to apologize. She consoled herself with the thought that Jenner was a highly-respected physician. His treatment wouldn't cause Maud any damage. He might even have some clever, modern ideas to speed her recovery. And if he insisted on remaining close-minded, if he wouldn't continue the drarnego as Dika had advised, Gertrude would find a way to do it herself. She wondered how she might get a message to Sir Alastair.

"Is there anything I can get you, Miss?" The maid met her with a small but respectful dip.

"Has my bag arrived?" If the leather handbag had indeed found its way here from the ptery, she would at least have a night gown to sleep in. Tomorrow, she would arrange to borrow a suit and go straight to the shops.

"Oh yes, Miss. We've unpacked all your things." The girl opened the wardrobe.

It was full; moreover, it was full of familiar garments. The room was the same one in which she had occasionally stayed during her brief tenure as Maud's schoolmate. For a split second, Gertrude wondered if she might have left some things behind three years ago. Then she realized she was being ridiculous; she'd only had the bluebell pongee made up in time to bring to Bucharest. Scanning the other items, she understood: not only had Sir Alastair sent whatever she had left in Prague, but he had seen to it that all of her things were retrieved from her Aunt. She was touched that he had thought of this.

"Would you like for me to draw you a bath? There's plenty of time. Dinner won't be for another hour. Her Majesty said there's no need to dress. It will be only herself and you."

It was unusual but, all things being equal, dining tete-a-tete with the Queen would hardly be Gertrude's oddest experience in recent months.

&

Queen Charlotte had fresh reason to look with favour upon Sir Lowthian's intelligent granddaughter. Miss Bell was admirably composed for a young woman who had passed the better part of a fortnight in an Italian fishing boat and traveling through France with a family of gypsies. It made for diverting dinner conversation.

"There's one thing I don't understand, Miss Bell. How is it possible that we haven't heard a word from Agent Horner? Surely the Emperor must be furious at the Princess's disappearance."

Miss Bell appeared perplexed. "I know that you've never met her, Ma'am, but I can assure you that Miss Monteith looks enough like Princess Maud to be her twin. You would have to know them both very well to suspect there'd been an exchange."

"Miss Monteith?" Charlotte felt a wintry draft of insight.

Miss Bell thought she understood her sovereign's confusion. "Sir Alastair's daughter is called Monteith."

"Yes, of course. I had forgotten." Charlotte forced herself to smile. Her granddaughter was safe, but now her daughter was in Augustus's hands. Surely this hadn't been Frank's idea! How could this have been allowed to happen?! "Tell me, Miss Bell. How exactly was the, ah…The substitution. How exactly was it effected? I know the general lines, naturally, but I am interested in hearing the story from your unique perspective."

&

The dining room of the Imperial Palazzo was designed for State banquets with dozens of guests. Tonight there were only three and the armed guards standing behind. The Lady Giulia's guard was the formidable African, as impassive as an amphoraka, who seemed to accompany her everywhere.

They waited together in silence, at the end of a pristine acre of white linen. At the midpoint of the nearly-empty table stood a liveried page. He pulled at the tasseled end of a cord that wound through a series of pulleys to a large mat of woven straw that hung overhead. For a while, the only

426

sound in the room was the slight creak of the panel swinging back and forth.

The long wait went from uncomfortable to menacing. The summer air wafting down the table was warm, but anticipation blew a chill draft on Claude's bare shoulders. She nearly jumped at the peal of trumpets.

Through the portal of yellow Sienna marble came a pair of armed centurions, bearing the Emperor on a purple silk litter. They set him on a bench across from Gusto and herself.

Claude had looked upon the face of evil twice before. Gwendolyn Fortescue, who'd destroyed men for her own gain, had been beautiful and mostly charming; only those that she'd forgone to charm had seen the frigid calculation in her eyes. The landlord, who had rented rooms to shop girls for the delight of killing them, had been bland and innocuous; according to witnesses, he had remained so even on his walk to the scaffold.

This man, the most evil of all, was a weary old man with a big head. A muscular servant had to prop him up on some cushions, to enable him to recline on his side and face the table. Even so, he radiated power. Giulia, whose own power belied her petit frame, was diminished in his presence. Tired or not, his black eyes glittered with intelligence. They were the first eyes she had encountered in Rome that looked for more than they expected to see. Claude steeled herself to not react as they probed her face; his was the only examination that counted.

"Did my pearl enjoy her holiday in Firenze?" he crooned. His voice, like the Lady Giulia's, had a certain musicality.

"There was much to see." Claude kept her voice free of animation, but allowed the Princess to offer an observation. "The Duomo was beautiful. Ginevre and I saw many fine shops."

"You see, Giulia? Three whole sentences! Surely the holiday was a success." He smiled with satisfaction. In repose, the combination of his oversized brow, hooked nose and thin lips might be forbidding but, she noted, it was the kind of face that would be as amiable as the expression it showed. Giulia's expression, for all that it was technically a smile, was not nearly so pleasant.

Emboldened, the Prince asked where they would be going for their wedding tour. Giulia nearly snapped his head off. "As Patre's heir, you have responsibilities here in Roma, Gusto. Your wedding tour will have to wait."

The deflated Gusto sagged in his seat and turned his attention to the salad of tomatoes on his plate. It was challenging for Claude to maintain her façade. She itched to lash out at the stupid woman. There was no call to treat the Prince like a fool, just because he was kind.

"What have you to say, my pearl?" Augustus asked. "Would it disappoint you, to remain here after the wedding?" He looked intently at Claude for her reaction.

She displayed none. "As it please you," she said, listlessly. She blinked once and added, "Patre."

The answer contented him. Augustus beckoned to his servant to assist him with his meal.

Giulia was not so easily appeased. She looked sharply at Claude. Claude was careful that there was nothing to see.

For the rest of the night, Claude felt the Lady's eyes weighing her every gesture. She found herself taking refuge in her glass. In Florence, Claude had immediately learned that the Princess was expected to consume a great deal of wine. She had developed a few tricks for maintaining that illusion without actually dulling her senses. She thought that if she appeared deep enough in her cups tonight, Giulia might leave her alone.

Giulia, who imbibed a great deal and must have a hollow leg, was relentlessly vigilant. Claude was seriously considering whether it might be wise to pretend to pass out, when Augustus claimed fatigue and bid them goodnight. The Lady Giulia immediately reassigned her attention to the Emperor and followed him to his apartments.

Gusto saw Claude safely back to the Villa Borghese. Giulia's rebuke had silenced him for most of the night. He slouched, dejected, against the tufted cushions. The clopping of the horses hooves added to the ineffable air of melancholy in the carriage.

"They shouldn't treat you like that. You'll be Emperor someday, and you'll be a better one than your grandfather." Her own words surprised her; Claude must have drunk more than she'd thought.

A wonderful change came over Gusto's face. "Do you think so, Moud?"

In for a penny, in for a pound. "Yes. Because you'll care about your people."

He put an arm around her shoulder. When she didn't pull away, he kissed her cheek with shy confidence.

It seemed prudent to pretend that the movement of the carriage had lulled her to sleep. A guard carried her up to her room, where Silvana undressed her and put her to bed.

❧

Madame Blavatsky's major domo greeted the Centurion at the door and ushered him inside. He gestured to the dark, carved chairs. "If you would kindly wait here, sir, I will bring the package. I will not be a minute." He bowed and disappeared into the shadows.

Micah waited until the spice-coloured robes had whisked entirely out of sight. Someone unfamiliar with the place might not have noticed, but he sensed it immediately: the building was uninhabited. The numerous wall hangings, with their intricate painted stories, had been replaced by anonymous swatches of tapestry. He heard no wind chimes. Even the smell was off; a scent of incense lingered in the air, but it lacked the accompanying body of smoke. Walking lightly, so that his footsteps wouldn't echo, he entered the large room where Madame held court with her acolytes. It looked for all the world like an ordinary ballroom. There was not a cushion to be seen.

Gephel seem unsurprised to find him there.

"Where is Madame?"

"Gone. Caesar's men will not find her."

One had to admire the Blavatsky's craftiness. If Augustus had expected to leave her holding the bag for the kidnapping, he had been severely out-maneuvered. "You will follow?"

"Not until she sends for me. I was to remain until someone came to replenish the Princess's supply of the compound. I will leave today, to await her summons elsewhere."

Trying to unravel the meaning of this development, Micah hefted the small tapestry holdall. "And what will happen next month, when the Princess requires more?"

Gephel looked at him with a curious admixture of admiration and wariness. "Ama left a message for you."

"For me? You're certain of this?"

"Oh yes. The centurion who walks in shadows. She hoped that you would be the one the Baron sent."

"What if he'd sent someone else, or perhaps even come for it himself?"

Gephel shrugged. "I was to give the bag to whoever came. Anyone else would have been told that Ama was in private meditation and could not be disturbed. No one would know. Not for another month."

"Another month?! And what of the Princess then? She is dependent on these drugs." Though Micah knew full well that Princess Maud would require nothing more from this source, he thought of two young woman abandoned in the woods and his outrage came naturally. "For a woman of great conscience, your Ama is curiously heartless when it comes to disposing of young women."

"This is your message, sir." He closed his eyes, as if he would read the printed words from the inside of his eyelids. "What is contained here is sufficient for the needs of your Princess."

"What is that supposed to mean? I have no patience for Madame's puzzles."

Gephel shrugged again. He was simply the messenger.

"But she hoped that I would hear this. Hoped, but didn't know?"

"Ama has always said, not everything is revealed. Not even to the Seven Rays."

"Something must have been, ah, 'revealed' to made her decamp." He delivered this in Rappaccini's most sardonic, patronizing manner.

The steward was unruffled. "Ama said only that the time had come. Something unexpected had occurred, some decision the Masters had not foreseen. I am not privileged to know what. They were not pleased."

"You should be careful in what you say, Gephel. You make your Masters sound all too human."

"No, sir. Ama says this is meant as a lesson in humility. The soul cannot achieve perfection. Even those that ascend may only ever strive for it." Gephel drew the familiar circular obeisance with his arms.

There was nothing more to learn here. Tucking the bag under his arm, Micah followed Gephel from the room. He looked back over his shoulder at the emptied house, wishing he understood the implications. "Now that I've seen this, aren't you concerned that I'll tell the Baron?"

"Ama was not concerned," the steward said, serenely. "It will be known when it is known. Namaste."

"And you will be long gone." Whatever had inspired her, one had to admire the Blavatsky's craftiness.

Before continuing on to fetch Tesla, there was something else Micah needed to do. He slipped down a narrow street, where a set of stone steps led to a patch of shore out of sight of the quay. He had discovered it while exploring potential avenues for escape, the first time he'd arrived in this city. In the light of day, his black tunic made a sharp contrast to the sand. He crouched low against the rocks, still uncomfortably exposed to anyone who might casually look in this direction.

He set the holdall on the flattest bit of ground within reach, and unbuckled the straps. It would have been preferable to do this in Venice, in the privacy of his own rooms, but there was a slim possibility that one of the Emperor's men might have been instructed to take possession of the package as soon as he stepped back on board. Once it left his hands, the opportunity would be lost for good.

The blue glass vials had been rolled in wadded silk for protection. There were so many of them, a month's worth for a Princess who required two injections each day. Balancing on the balls of his feet on the uneven ground, he unwound the first roll. Working as quickly as he could with the fragile glass, he began pouring the contents out into the sand, then rinsing each vial and refilling it with sea water.

Micah felt the pressure of time. The boat might not be in view, but he was exposed to the sight of the casual Ragusan eye. A precipitous breeze caused a few drops of the compound to splash his face. It was odd that he could smell only the iodine tang of the sea. Micah had a keen nose, and it was practically in the fluid. He had no idea what might be in this compound, but he would have expected to catch some kind of scent. Bringing the empty tube close to his nostrils, he took a deep sniff. Nothing. Curious now, he picked another one from the roll. He carefully removed the tin cap, eased out the cork and inhaled. Still nothing. Sticking his little finger into the opening, he tilted the tube. He gingerly withdrew the damp fingertip and touched it to his tongue. Water! It was nothing but water!

He plunged his hands into the bag and pulled out a roll from the bottom layer. Two of the vials there, selected at random, also held water.

He tried to remember the exact words of Gephel's message. *What is contained here is sufficient for the needs of your Princess.* Of *your* Princess.

Micah rocked back on his heels, trying not to fall over. He reflected, not for the first time, that of all the curiosities he had encountered on his mission in Rome, Helena Blavatsky was the greatest mystery.

❦

Sir Alastair and Mr. Firewalker spent nearly all their waking hours at either the workshop or the foundry. Alice had been too well trained to lead a visitor to them, even if he had arrived in the Embassy carriage. She left Lord Pinkerton in the parlour with a pot of tea and ran to fetch Sir Alastair to the house.

Pinkerton was too upset for tea. Last night, he had been summoned to Kensington and roundly castigated by the Queen for not telling her something he hadn't known himself. Frank had played it close to his chest and, because it was Frank, Pinkerton had allowed him to do it. He had disclosed only that he and young Fairservis had hatched a plan by which the Princess might be smuggled out of Italy while he continued to work on Tesla's secret weapon.

Pinkerton had been trusted with nothing but the information needed to carry out the retrieval portion of this plan. Miss Bell's story had been as much a revelation to him as to the Queen. Even without Her Majesty's command, he would have flown to Prague at first light to confront his old friend. His anger simmered with the waiting. When he heard the door to the house slam open, he stomped out of the tiny parlour. "So help me God, Menzies, whatever were you thinking?!"

Frank met him with a thump on the back and an infuriating grin. "Miss Bell made it through, aye? Auld Lowthian has got himself an able, braw lassie."

Pinkerton pushed him away. "Aye. But what of your own bairn? How could you do this?!"

Frank turned solemn. "It was Claude's idea. I won't pretend I was happy, but I couldn't argue it. Have you seen the Princess, Pinkerton?"

Pinkerton shook his head. No one had, except for the Queen and her doctor.

"From what your lad Horner told us, the lass wouldn't have lasted much longer. By getting her out of Rome, we bought ourselves the time to finish what Tesla began. Did you happen to come by aership?"

"It being only myself, no. Ptery. You can fly us back. Her Majesty is expecting us both for dinner."

Frank rubbed the sides of his nose. "Then she's bound to be disappointed when I don't show. It won't be the first time I'll make her angry and it won't be the last."

"Menzies, you cannot play this game with her..."

"This time it isn't about us, Pinkerton. Right now, I cannot afford to lose so much as an hour. We are...Come. You'll see. Then you can go home and tell her about it. And send me back an aership, while you're at it."

❧

Having finally met Augustus, Claude understood that it was Giulia who was the biggest threat to her continued masquerade. For once, she didn't have to pretend to Maud's lethargy; a night of the Lady's scrutiny had exhausted her. She spent the morning resolutely in bed. After a light luncheon, brought on a tray, she allowed Leonora to dress her for her daily respite in the garden. She appreciated Maud's attraction to the place. It was peaceful, especially with something to read and a pitcher of lemonade.

She thought that the Golden One, watching from the terrace, must find it peaceful, too. The creature seemed to prefer being out here.

Claude was dozing over her book when the tapping jolted her awake. It was a walking stick, moving towards her on the path. She turned to face the sound. Though she had never seen him before, she knew at once that this was the Baron of Nikola's nightmares. How was it that these decrepit old men held the power to destroy lives? She stared at him, thinking that she would enjoy nothing more than grabbing up that stick and pressing it hard against his windpipe until his eyes bulged out of his head.

The Baron misinterpreted the faint smile that teased the corners of her mouth. "Altezza." He bowed with much flourish and kissed her hand. "Your Royal Highness," he continued.

She tilted her head inquiringly. Why was he speaking English?

Through a tangle of fulsome courtesies, he eventually made his way to the point: Rappaccini had been sent away on business. "*Your* business, I assure Your Highness."

How upset was she allowed to be? Tears were always acceptable, but at this distance would be difficult to fake. She settled for a trembling lip, then dipped her face behind her book.

She took some pleasure in remembering that unless she offered him a seat, which she was not about to do, the elderly gallant must remain standing in her presence. There wasn't much he could do, except hover nearby and attempt to placate her with promises that the Centurion would absolutely be present at her wedding and would no doubt be restored to her service immediately after.

She refused to respond. When this stream eventually ran dry, he cleared his throat several times. "Altezza?" he finally submitted. "Have I your leave to go?"

With a tiny sniff, Claude lowered the book. She waited just long enough to increase his discomfort, then nodded curtly. "Please do. I will see you out." Now that he had disturbed her equilibrium, she preferred to spend the remainder of the afternoon in her room. It would cause no comment; she had been in the garden long enough.

She allowed him to take her elbow and lead her to the terrace. He kissed her hand in what he certainly thought was a charming manner and toddled off through the garden gate.

Still staring blankly after him, she relieved herself by muttering one of the rude Romani phrases Yoska had taught her. She wasn't certain what they meant, not exactly, but there was something satisfying about the sounds they made.

A shadow fell over her. Whirling around, she found herself level with the chest of the Golden One. The creature hadn't come so close to her before. It seemed to want to make contact.

"I was wishing the Baron goodbye."

It bumped against her.

"You don't believe me?" she joked. "Don't tell me you understand Romani?"

It bumped against her again, twice in rapid succession.

"Who are you, I wonder?" she said, thinking aloud in English. "You have no glyph." She gingerly placed a hand in the general area where Garibaldi's mark had been. It wasn't smooth—no portion of an amphoraka's surface could be said to be smooth—but it was unbroken. There was no mark there now, nor had there ever been. Did that mean no one could command the actions of this particular prisoner? If not, why did the Golden One stay here? Why did it not destroy itself?

With Horner lost to her indefinitely, Claude needed an ally in this place. She hoped it would be worth the risk she was about to take.

"If there were somewhere we could go, a place where no one might hear us, I could teach you a way to talk."

Escorted by the Golden One, the Principessa was allowed to pass without question. The amphoraka, seemingly well acquainted with the park that surrounded the Villa, effortlessly led her about half a mile away. They stopped at an ugly little clump of trees, just uphill of a small clearing where a crew of workmen were busy with pipes and stones.

With two spoons, hastily filched from the lemonade tray, and the ribbons from her bonnet, Claude was able to rig up a reasonable substitute for finger cymbals. It was almost as if the Golden One knew what to expect. Claude tried to remember what Agent Horner had said about the way the amphoraeka communicated with one another. She had scarcely tied the final knot before the chimes started spilling out.

"I AM PAULETTE," they spelled.

"Paulette Buonaparte." Claude touched the carved golden curls in wonder. "Of course you are."

"YOU ARE NOT SHE."

"I am a friend," Claude replied. "A sister." She didn't know whether the amphoraeka saw through those flickers of blue or some more ambiguous agency, but she took a long step back to ensure her body would be in view. She lifted the hems of her skirts. "You know this mark, don't you? The road and the star? The moon…" she touched her finger to the circle, remembering the night it was made. "The moon is the mark of my own kumpania. Your story is remembered."

"IT IS NOT ALWAYS GOOD TO BE A SISTER."

Claude understood. "Your brother did this to you."

"AND MANY THINGS. I TRIED TO DIE. HE WOULD NOT ALLOW. HE MADE ME THIS. FOREVER."

"Not forever." Claude looked into that gilded mask, trying to fathom the misery of the soul inside. This was not a counsel easily given. "You must have learned since then," she began as delicately as she could. "From the others. You have no mark. There's nothing prohibiting you from any action you want to take. You might choose to die, at any time." The spoons didn't move. Did Paulette think this an insult? Another thought struck her. "Or you could leave here. Go to the Rom. The would accept you as family."

Finally, an answer came. "SHE WOULD NOT COME. I THOUGHT I COULD LEAVE HER BUT I CANNOT. SHE NEEDS ME."

"Giulia, you mean?" Claude doubted the Rom would accept Augustus's child. They were ruthless in their stand against evil. Not that it mattered. "No, I don't imagine she would leave Caesar. She seems devoted to her father."

"NOT HER FATHER." Paulette responded. "EMILIAN."

At the beginning of the year, Queen Charlotte had determined that, prior to any formal confirmation of status in the succession, the Princess should make a tour of Greater Britain, to see something of the empire she would rule if she became Queen. It was to be an independent tour, with Maud herself as the principal player. The ambitious itinerary, weaving through the British Isles and stretching across the Atlantic to Her Majesty's American Territories, had been meant to begin in July.

As long as Maud was thought to be in Bucharest, it hadn't been difficult to conceal her disappearance from the British public. However, once July drew near, it became more complicated. Engagements were postponed indefinitely while the Princess was said to be recovering from a mysterious illness that she had contracted abroad. Gossip mounted steadily as more and more engagements were canceled. Some Britons actually read foreign newspapers, the less reputable of which made sly hints that were difficult to ignore.

Notwithstanding Maud's fracturable state and Dr. Jenner's admonishments, the Privy Council insisted that the security of the Nation required her to immediately set the rumours to rest.

With Gertrude Bell, the only person who she appeared to trust at this juncture, holding the reins, Maud was sent that very first day to run the gauntlet of Rotten Row in an open chaise. It easy for people to believe in the Princess's illness after that. Pale and sometimes seen to tremble, she pressed herself deep into the extra cushions. The cadets with whom she had flirted in the past were pained when she greeted them by name but was unable to so much as smile. Cadets are notorious gossips; they did more good for the Queen's cause than the society women whose attention and mouths she had hoped to enlist.

Pinkerton returned to the Palace straight from Shooter's Hill too late to prevent this outing, but he protested vociferously against further appearances. If Augustus got word that Maud had been seen in London, the entire Roman operation would be at risk.

The Council was insistent on staging one more appearance. The following night, the Princess was seen waving languidly from the Royal box at the Opera House. Those in surrounding boxes reported hearing her companions voicing concerns. One particularly powerful gossip heard a familiar male voice say "With all due respect, Your Highness should have done as I advised. I wish you had not been so insistent on returning to public life before you'd quite recovered. I fear the fever has returned." The entire party disappeared after the second interval.

The next morning, the aer-yacht Boudicca was seen to depart from Shooter's Hill. The unusually indiscreet Palace chauffeur let it slip to the aerodrome crew that it was headed for a favoured cure spot of the rich and powerful.

8.

Rappaccini's orders hadn't included Tashi, but it was only prudent to bring her along. To his surprise, she suggested that Dov should come as well. With a shared language, the two had become firm allies. As Tashi needed a few hours to pack whatever she thought might be needed, Micah had enough time left for a quick stop by the flat in the Cannaregio. He hadn't seen his cousin since she'd disappeared into the crowd at the Prague terminus. The last thing he expected was to find her deep in discussion with Tucker.

"What are you doing here?" The two men shouted almost in unison.

"Trying to figure out the fastest way to get you this." Tucker thrust a tightly rolled piece of onionskin into Micah's hands.

"I was going to come down to Roma to look for you," Elettra said. "I was trying to decide whether it would be more convincing to accuse you of cheating or pretend I was pregnant."

Micah's code book was hidden under a floorboard. Once Tucker realized what he was about, he stopped him. "I decrypted it already. It's from our friend in Prague. Instructions for you. You only have to decide what you need Elettra and myself to do."

❧

The final fitting of the bridal gown was the most public private event Claude had ever experienced. All the senior ladies of the court had come to observe, some trailing their maids. The Lady Giulia's party included the omnipresent Apollinaris, who carried a large casket of some sweet wood. It must have been heavy, but he would not set it down.

The Golden One stood by the open door, the lintel being too low to allow her to pass through. Claude was relieved that no one seemed to think twice about her presence. Paulette had taken to spending time in Claude's company, even indoors. It was too dangerous to tap out a conversation in the Villa; but if no one else were within earshot, Claude could talk to her. Paulette was hungry for stories of the outside world, especially anything to do with the Rom.

Today was as much a rehearsal as a fitting. She sat in her dressing gown while Leonora, trembling slightly under the scrutiny of all those eyes, proceeded to dress her hair according to a style of the Lady's devising. There were minor snags and adjustments as Giulia editorialized the practical application of her design. Claude was surprised by the ripple of girlish curls, bound with an intricate network of braids. Wasn't the point of this marriage for the bride to appear regal? Then she remembered: dressing her hair high would diminish the Prince at her side. She could only imagine the heels on poor Gusto's boots.

The last pin was set in place. Giulia rose to inspect the finished work at closer proximity. She circled slowly, viewing Claude's head from every conceivable angle. The woman's heavy perfume was extremely irritating. Claude couldn't stop a violent sneeze. "'Scusi," she said. Leonora darted in with a handkerchief and dabbed at her nose. The maid had a startled look.

Before Claude could register anything more, everyone's attention turned to Apollinaris, who stepped solemnly forward and knelt on one leg by the vanity table. Steadying the casket on his knee, he opened the lid. Nested in folds of dark velvet was an exquisite diadem: tiny diamonds, perhaps hundreds of them, set in rays around a trio of pale green stones of a kind that Claude had never seen before.

"This was made for my grandmother, Ginevre of Lorraine," Giulia said. "It was given to your bridegroom's grandmother, the Empress Philippine, on her wedding day and you will wear it on yours."

Claude leaned in to get a better look, when a whiff of gardenia caused her to sneeze again. It caused a suppressed titter among the younger spectators. Leonora, the handkerchief poised for application, seemed more shaken than amused.

Claude heard a rapid set of thumps from the doorway. E-Y-E. She swiveled to face the mirror. One of her eyes was grey. The amber lens must have popped out when she sneezed. No wonder Leonora was shaken. What would she have thought she'd seen?

"'Scusi," she said again, jumping from her seat and snatching the handkerchief from the maid's hand. Covering her face in evident embarrassment, she sped towards the water closet.

She fumbled for the hole she had made in the underside of the footstool and dug out the locket. Thank goodness it was here! If she'd put it in the drawer, as she had originally thought to do, even Maskelyne himself couldn't have mustered sufficient sleight of hand to get it now. Forcing herself to slow down, she undid the precious compartment, delicately extracted another lens and pressed it against her cornea. With no reflective surfaces here, there was no way to confirm that it had settled correctly. She wished she'd had the foresight to hide a small mirror. Cupping her hand to catch it lest it fall, she winked slowly. It shifted. She thought it felt right. She hoped so; she couldn't stay here all day.

She pulled the rope and counted to ten before exiting.

Only the Lady Giulia had not politely averted her eyes from the door. Less curious about the princess's distress than piqued by the interruption to her moment of grand theatre, she radiated impatience and distain. Claude turned away from that smirk, pretending to be cowed. After she resumed her seat, Giulia recalled the attention of her audience with a little cough, then lifted the diadem from the box and bestowed it like a sentence of hanging.

The purpose of the coiffure became evident; Leonora anchored the sparkling crescent with a row of matching hairpins that bit firmly into the braids. At least she wasn't expected to keep it in place with posture and will power alone. The ornament only appeared dainty; Claude felt she was carrying Garibaldi's helmet on her head. It was a strain to remain impassive when Giulia handed Leonora the matching earbobs.

The maid bent close to fasten them. "Are you well, Altezza?" she asked in a low voice.

"Quite well, thank you." Testing the balance, Claude pivoted her head slowly until she was squarely facing Leonora. Once the other woman had registered her pair of amber eyes, she murmured confidingly, "did you ever have such a sneeze, Leonora, that you thought you might have to…?" She made her voice trail off and looked shyly downward. Under cover of adjusting a curl, Leonora gave her shoulder a discreet pat.

Claude stifled a sigh of relief.

She allowed the modiste's assistants to dress her, raising and lowering her arms when instructed, remaining mute when pins stuck her or one of her longer curls was caught by a dress hook. Plain and lace-flounced underskirts settled into place, this time hanging precisely as intended. They had to tightened her laces painfully for the pointed bodice, with its deep décolletage and the merest whisper of a sleeve. The split overskirt rose, puffed, to each hip, where it was caught with large jeweled rosettes. More embroidery than cloth, the exquisite fabric flowed back to follow her like a stream. It would be an effort to walk at anything other than a snail's pace.

Her hands were slipped into mitts of white glacé kid that her dressers rolled, like a second skin, up to her elbow. When all was in place, Giulia fasted a diamond collar around her neck and a number of bracelets on each wrist.

The ladies cooed their admiration, while the dressmaker's girls made final puttering adjustments to invisible flaws until the Lady Giulia pronounced it done.

The worst part of this mission, Claude thought, was how constantly helpless she felt. Standing frozen and dumb on the platform, she could only imagine herself facing the vérfarkas in this getup. She surely would have died. Unless she could have gathered the train up and netted it. Or perhaps tucked the earbobs into one of the mitts and use it as a cosh? For some reason, this line of thinking calmed her. This, and knowing that Paulette had interceded for her; Agent Horner might be beyond reach, but she was not without a friend.

&.

The Spanish Ambassador to the Second Roman Empire rummaged happily through the diplomatic pouch: a gossipy letter from his sister; a new novel by Valdés; and a collection of newspapers, including recent copies of *The Times* of London and *Le Figaro*, as well as the usual ones from home. He settled in for a pleasant afternoon of reading.

Rumour in Roma was that the russet-tressed noble lady, whose name was carefully never mentioned, would make an important appearance at tomorrow's gala opening of the new Colosseum. He had been watching the

British press with the avidity of a pickpocket at a bazaar but, thus far, there hadn't been a peep. He unfolded *The Times*. Within minutes, he was calling for his valet and his volante. Within an hour, he was in audience with the Lady Giulia.

The page who brought the message to the Villa Alsaziano was more than usually jittery. He refused Gallante's silver salver; Caesar had insisted the message be placed in the Baron's own hand.

Baron Haussmann attempted to conceal his impatience. He understood it was not the boy's choice. He made a point of smiling charitably before opening the note, a smile that turned almost instantly to alarm. The Emperor commanded his presence at once, his and that of the centurion Rappaccini. Armed guards were waiting outside to escort them. Armed guards!

Haussmann's nimble mind flew over the events of recent days, trying in vain to uncover any that might have caused such a reaction. He sent Gallante for Rappaccini who, in light of his extreme competence, was currently residing in the guest wing. Tesla was proving to be a tiresome houseguest. Without the little nurse and that one amphoraka for whom he'd formed a deluded attachment, the Serbian would have been completely unmanageable.

Rappaccini appeared with admirable haste, smartening his tunic as he loped down the ramp. Handing him the note, Haussmann was gratified to see momentary discomfort ruffle the usually smooth face.

For the brief duration of the ride to the Palazzo, they exchanged neither word nor glance, but sat between the guards and feigned composure.

Claude's eyes slewed to observe the silent guards to either side of her. After verifying the Princess's return from Florence, the Emperor had let her alone. Claude had assumed he was convalescing, husbanding his energies for the big event. Why had he sent for her now? And in such a way? Something was very wrong.

Augustus reclined on his couch, a young page fanning his brow. Giulia, the ubiquitous Apollinaris behind her, was seated near enough to reach his hand. As the Baron and Rappaccini entered the garden, the pretty eunuch ceased his playing and melted away. The atmosphere tasted of iron.

The two men bowed with elegant subservience. Rappaccini prepared to give his arm to the Baron if necessary, to help him up. Augustus did not signal them to rise. While they were still on one knee, he snapped his fingers. The page grabbed a newspaper from the Emperor and gave it to the Baron.

"Tell me, Baron, what does this mean?" Augustus spoke in a cool, low voice that was more dreadful than any bellow. "The picture speaks many volumes, but I do not know if I should trust the Ambassador's translation." Rappaccini noticed the Spanish Ambassador among the cluster of courtiers.

The Baron read the English sentences as rapidly as he could, then passed the paper to Rappaccini without comment. The article was two days old, little more than a paragraph of thanksgiving for Princess Maud's recovery from what was described as a lingering fever. It was accompanied by a small photograph of two young women waving from a carriage in a park. Micah felt it as a punch to his belly. He pretended to have some difficulty in reading, hoping to buy time for thought. When he couldn't stretch the time any longer, he handed the paper back to the boy and employed Rappaccini's unconcerned shrug. He tried not to feel the boring stare of four black gimlet eyes.

Haussmann cleared his throat. "Surely these are the young women the Sybil left in the forest. The two British spies. Are they not, Rappaccini?"

Rappaccini nodded. "The Baron is most assuredly correct, Divina…Altezza." He bowed his head to touch his extended knee. "The decoy, and the female companion of the Principessa."

"Ah yes, the decoy. The British Queen thought to confuse my forces."

"She underestimated your powers, Divina."

"The British speak proudly of the freedom of their press. Do they lie or is this decoy so convincing?"

"I saw the impostor in Ragusa, Divina. There is some resemblance. From such distance and from a moving vehicle, enough to easily fool a casual observer."

"Why were they allowed to leave Ragusa alive, Baron?" Giulia spat the last word.

The always urbane Haussmann nearly stammered. "The Sybil would not violate the laws of her spirits, Daughter of Light. To do so might deprive her forever of her powers." The blasted woman had not said this exactly, but the words sounded compelling in the Baron's mind as he formed them. "She abandoned them in a forest, with only a drop of water and food between them, and not in their proper minds. 'It will out as it is meant to be,' she said. I never thought they would survive. I told her it would be kinder to kill them outright."

"Has the Principessa's medication been retrieved from Ragusa?" Giuila's eyes narrowed to calculating slits.

"Yes, Daughter of Light," Rappaccini assured her. "I received the package myself at her door. I was told it would be enough for the next month."

"That will be sufficient for our needs. See that it is brought to me at once. As for Madame, Patre," Giulia added with relish. "Your Sybil may have finally outlived her use."

Augustus dismissed his daughter's intimation. He was more concerned with addressing immediate danger than issuing punishment for the failing that had caused it. "And yet the young women did survive. And they have made their way to England, to speak of everything they saw."

"Their minds were upset by the same compounds as the Principessa's," Haussmann stressed. "Nothing they might remember would be believed. The newspaper shows not a hint..."

"Be that as it may, Queen Charlotte can have no doubts that we hold her heiress."

"Surely this report proves that you have Britain in your power, Divina." Lunging on one knee was not most effective posture for persuasion. Rappaccini bowed his head again and tried his utmost. "Their Queen is afraid. Look how she struggles to conceal the absence of the Principessa from her people. A fever? For so many months? Ridiculous! And now this pathetic effort to create the illusion of her presence. How the world will jeer at Britain, Divina, when the marriage has been performed and the truth is revealed."

He had set out his saucer of cream, but could not judge whether Augustus was lapping it up.

Claude crossed the patio with as much dignity as she could muster, and as little concern as she could counterfeit. The guards stayed close behind, their nearness pressing her forward more quickly than she would have preferred. She felt like Mary Stuart. The comparison was not consoling, but it kept her head held high.

The Emperor certainly didn't lack energy now; some barely-contained passion made him seem twice his previous size. Giulia smoldered more than ever. Before them on the stones, in view of a wary circle of watchers, the old Baron and Agent Horner were down on their knees.

Claude swept a formal curtsey, nearly to the ground and bowed her neck in obeisance. "Patre."

"News from home, my pearl," Augustus said. His voice was not remotely charming. It was the voice of a man who had hacked his sister's lover to pieces while forcing her to watch.

A trembling messenger handed Claude a copy of *The Times*. All she grasped was the photograph. Her heart gave a happy leap; Gertrude had managed to get the Princess home. Her mission had been accomplished. Success was a brighter strength than desperation. "Gertrude!" she exclaimed, hoping Agent Horner would understand the joy in her voice.

"You know this young woman, my pearl; my pearl of very great price?"

She responded to the question at face value, allowing herself to become slowly agitated. "Yes, of course. She is my friend, Patre. We were together when...She was there. I thought she had been killed. He..." She pointed a trembling finger at the kneeling Centurion, then turned to address a few words directly to him, wishing there were some possibility of communication. "You said she was alive. I didn't believe you." She swept the Emperor another deep bow. "How could I have doubted your kindness, Patre? I am ashamed."

"Who is this other woman? The one with your friend."

The ice in Augustus's voice penetrated through to her very bones. He was not to be put off by an abject pose. She knew she must answer more carefully than she had answered any question in her life.

"I don't know," she said, lowering her voice to the merest breath. "I thought..." She remembered when Maud had seen her in the Boboli garden and hoped the memory would colour her body's behaviour. "Another girl who looked like me. I had never seen anyone...I thought I imagined her. And that horrible old woman...I imagined so many things. I still do, sometimes. Perhaps I am imagining this," she added craftily. She looked at the newspaper in horror and dropped it. "Someone is trying to trick me, to make me mad!"

She wondered if it would be taking things too far to tear at her hair and settled for covering her face with her hands.

The page snatched up the paper and returned it to the Emperor.

"You test our patience," Giulia snapped. "You are no more imagining this than I."

Claude assumed Maud's most beaten aspect and refused to blink until a tear trickled down her cheek. She hoped it wouldn't dislodge an amber lens.

Augustus held up his hand to top his daughter. "Basta, Giulia. It must be as the Centurion so cleverly surmised. A desperate ploy by the British Queen. We are indebted to the Ambassador for revealing this weakness to us." The rage had subsided, but suspicion continued to pervade his manner. He beckoned for the Princess to draw nearer.

Claude walked up to the couch and curtseyed again. While her head was low, Augustus placed a finger under her chin. She was trapped in a crouch, her face lifted close to his.

He touched the tip of a finger to her tear, then licked it. "I can see my pearl knows nothing of this business," he said, leaning forward until she could feel the heat of his breath. She closed her eyes and willed herself to not react. "She must not be distressed on the day before her wedding." His face was so near that, as he spoke, his lips brushed hers.

She didn't move until she felt the shadow leave her face, then she opened her eyes and cautiously rose. He was still looking at her. She felt herself blush.

Augustus snapped his fingers at the guards. "You will accompany the Principessa home. Rest well, my pearl. Tomorrow will be a great day."

Claude's heart ricocheted from rib to rib. She performed a final obedient curtsey and glided towards the archway. She dared not look back.

Augustus glared peevishly at the Baron and the Centurion. "Why are you still here? No doubt you have much to do before morning. And I...I have been much provoked and require some peace." He waved a hand at Rafello, who scooted forward and began to play. The Emperor's eyes began to close.

Giulia stroked his hand. "Ambassador," she called in her hard, clear voice. "Your service will be remembered with gratitude."

The Spanish Ambassador bowed gravely and withdrew, followed by all but the Emperor's immediate servants. A boy brought the Lady a bowl of scented water, to bathe the Emperor's brow.

Unwatched, Rappaccini rose stiffly to his feet and bowed. He held out his arms to the Baron, allowing the old man as much dignity as possible in the struggle to shift himself erect. The Baron leaned heavily. Micah could feel the old man's pain and a residue of fear as they inched their way across the patio. He had quelled his own disquiet; Miss Monteith—that astonishing young woman—had acquitted herself admirably.

The men inched their way across the patio.

"Apollinaris!" Giulia's voice rang out.

It had seemed certain that no one would hinder their exit. Micah's body tensed to fight, if necessary, to survive the day.

"Go with the Centurion and fetch me the package from Ragusa. We would not want the Principessa's medicine to go astray."

Micah had hoped to deliver the package himself and steal a few quick words with Miss Monteith. Waiting to feel the approach of the equerry's heavy tread, he was once again visited by the ominous sensation of being caught in a blind trapeze act.

24 – JUST CAUSE

Still groggy from the sleeping potion they had slipped her night before, Claude was lowered into a warm tub and bathed in scented water. They patted her dry, slipped on the new silk undergarments and arranged her on the fainting couch. She didn't think twice about such things now. A paste of white clay was applied to her face, to brighten her complexion. Cool slices of cucumber were placed on her eyelids to reduce the puffiness of sleep. She dozed behind them, while Silvana buffed her nails to a rosy sheen with a bit of soft chamois and Leonora brushed her hair with one hundred firm strokes.

Is this what a girl's wedding day is supposed to be like? Claude knew this made her odd, but she'd never thought about it. Even in her most deplorably girlish imaginings, she had envisioned herself and Nikola as already married, working side by side in a shared laboratory. Odd that Caesar Augustus had made that nearly true for a few precious days.

A ripple of anger dispelled her languor. She had been so absorbed in her mission as royal proxy that she'd lost sight of her personal stake in the matter. Augustus had been equally responsible for ripping her dream apart! If she hadn't felt it necessary to take Maud's place, she would be working day and night on the automatons to ensure that he was utterly destroyed. The swipe of a cold, wet sponge, Leonora removing the masque, sealed her renewed commitment. There was nothing special about today. This sham wedding was simply another hurdle to be cleared.

While Leonora painstakingly recreated the approved structure of braids and curls, Claude was free to sip Maud's beloved milky tea (to which she would never become reconciled) and nibble dry toast.

446

The door was flung open with familiar lack of ceremony. Giulia stalked in, with her usual human accessories close behind.

"Altezza!" Leonora fumbled; the comb caught painfully at the nape of Claude's neck. "I haven't finished…"

Giulia dismissed her whimpers. "Don't be a fool, Leonora. It's far too early. I am here to wish the Principessa…*my niece*…all happiness on this day." The Lady brought her cheek to Claude's and, looking at her in the mirror, bestowed a frigid peck. "You are very pale," she admonished, as if this were a choice rather than a fact of birth. "The arena is large. Patre would be most displeased if your features could not be seen. Fortunately, this can be corrected. I have brought some cosmetic preparations." Giulia stepped away and flicked her hand in the direction of her women.

A maid scurried forward and curtseyed apprehensively. She dipped a stylus into what looked like a pot of coal dust. Claude didn't move a muscle. As the girl traced the line of her eyelashes with this powder, all she could do was pray that her lenses wouldn't pop out.

Behind her, Giulia was giving Silvana orders: "count out enough for a fortnight and bring the remainder to Dottore Catoni."

Claude didn't have to see them to understand she was talking about a fresh delivery of drugs. Blast! They had been so busy that her morning injection had been entirely forgotten. It was pointless to hope that Silvana wouldn't cause a flap. Sure enough, she heard a string of slavish apologies. The face-painter was asked to pause and the Principessa's little case was set on the vanity table.

"It's hardly past the usual time." Claude turned a reproachful eye on Silvana. "You woke me so very early today."

Silvana handed her a vial. "We are fortunate not to have to lose more time waiting for the Dottore," she said sharply. "You must have used the final dose last night. You should have said. Had the Lady Giulia not brought this…"

"We are very fortunate. Thank you, Zia. You take such very good care of me."

Claude casually drew the fluid into the needle. Giulia regarded her skeptically. She flashed a guileless smile. "You must forgive me for being so distracted. Today is my wedding day." She tried to pull her knee up to her chest, but the little seat made the position awkward. She would have to move to her usual chair.

Frowning, Giulia stopped her. "You will undo Leonora's efforts." She held out her hand. "Give it to me."

Claude had no recourse but to hand over the syringe, the contents of which would be poison to her.

The room fell away. Giulia knelt before her with the grandeur of a king washing the feet of a beggar. Claude, trembling, raised her dressing gown above her ankle. Once her body absorbed the fluid, what would happen to her? Would she die quickly? That would be the most merciful end. If she were very lucky and her body survived, would her mind? She stared into the mirror and tried to imagine her own grey eyes looking back. "Hokahey" she whispered, inside her head.

Giulia was well-practiced; the needle smoothly penetrated the webbing between her toes. Apollinaris helped his mistress to her feet.

"Thank you...Zia," Claude murmured. She wondered how long it would be until her body registered the shock. Her heart was already beating too fast. She must fight the impulse to panic. It would be nice to have someone to say goodbye to; she looked at the doorway, but there was no flash of gold.

The world continued to turn slowly around her. The girl finished outlining her eyes. Giulia approved the result and swept out to begin her own toilette. With Giulia gone, Leonora's mood lifted. She hummed a little song as she braided and pinned. Silvana went to heat the curling irons.

Still Claude waited. They'll know now, she thought; they'll know that the newspaper was correct, that Maud is back in London. Augustus would be enraged. He would send the full force of the amphoraeka against Britain. War. Would her sacrifice have meant anything? Maud would live, but how many would die before Father and Leski can send the automatons to defeat him?

She had never imagined waiting for death to come. She had always assumed she would meet it head on, but there was nothing here for her to fight. At least she could give herself the comfort of drawing her last breath with Father beside her heart.

Claiming she needed to answer a call of nature, she tried not to wobble on the way to the water closet. The weight of the locket in her hand felt like love. She kissed the case and looped the chain around her neck. Regretfully, she removed it. It would be noticed too quickly there; someone might take it away. Instead, she fastened the chain together with the string that closed her drawers and tucked the locket inside the waist band.

She kept a hand in her lap all the while that Leonora worked on her hair. When it was done, the two maids helped her to the fainting couch. A rolled towel was placed behind her neck, to support her head.

"We must see to your gown, Altezza," Leonora said. "You will want to rest now."

They left. Claude held onto the kindness in that voice. She lay still, afraid to move. It had been almost an hour since the injection. She would rather feel pain than this terrible anticipation. The drug was coursing through her veins but her skin was cool and dry, and she could sense all of her digits. Could the drarnego have made her resistant to whatever was in these vials? She wasn't even lightheaded, only a little sleepy. With one hand resting on the comforting lump of her locket, she yawned.

§•

To her considerable astonishment, Claude awoke to another cup of milky tea and a flock of harried attendants. It was so lovely to be alive that none of this bothered her. The primping, the weight of the jewelry, nothing mattered. She floated down the stairs as if it really were her wedding day.

After the event, the bridal pair would be driven away from the Colosseum in an open chariot, with Apollinaris at the reins, Caesar's unique Praetorian Guard marching behind. It would be a superb bit of spectacle.

However for conveyance to the arena, the Princess was stuffed into a closed carriage. Augustus was biding his time; he wouldn't reveal his new granddaughter to the people of Rome until the marriage had been performed and duly witnessed. None of the invited guests had been told the true reason for the event. The day had been presented as the official opening of the wondrous arena, complete with music and a military demonstration. Only when the Prince and the Cardinal took their places on the stage, would the truth begin to unfold.

§•

The Emperor's box had the stern beauty of a temple, a guise that was enhanced by the glory of the Golden One, positioned at the Emperor's side. On this day of days, Caesar Augustus was equally radiant, as radiant as the god he proclaimed himself to be.

There could be no more perfect setting. This building was indeed the jewel in the crown of his empire. Even under the Flavians, it could not have been more sublime. From his marble throne, he surveyed its magnificence and the throng of unsuspecting guests with equal satisfaction.

He cupped his hands to his mouth and leaned towards the passage from which the Baron was dispatching his minions on whatever sundry tasks remained to perfect the day. "Admirably done, Baron," he called.

Haussmann was disarmed by the unequivocal compliment. "I have been honoured to serve, Divina," he called back. He bowed low, his bald pate gleaming like the Colosseum itself.

Caesar turned an affectionate countenance to his beloved daughter. "You as well, Giulia. You have surpassed yourself in this charge."

A wide cloth-of-gold runner stretched to the center of the floor and a dais there, thickly banked with white blossoms. Without fanfare, a cardinal made his way along that aisle. There were curious murmurs from some of the more observant guests. Augustus smiled. Until Giroleme escorted young Gusto to his place, they would assume only that he was benevolently allowing the Church a token role in the festivities. They would never begin to guess at the truth until it was full upon them.

"The prize is ours, Giulia," he said, squeezing her hand. For once, her smile was as dazzling as her emeralds. "I am well content."

A silver peal of trumpets sounded. The moment of Caesar's greatest triumph was about to begin.

❧

Claude heard a silver peal of trumpets.

"Gusto's cue," Ginevre breathed. She made a few possessive tweaks of Claude's gown. "You look so beautiful," she said. Her admiration was honest. Ginevre's heart was big enough to revel in another girl's special day. "There's no reason to be nervous. Gusto adores you."

Claude wasn't nervous. She continued to be enveloped in a blessed haze. She was about to marry a stranger, and there was no telling what might happen once Augustus felt he legitimately owned the Princess, but all of this seemed trivial compared to the simple fact of her life.

Leonora pretended to re-pin an errant curl. Claude's hair had been so thoroughly coated with pomade that it was unthinkable that any tress could have slipped its moorings.

"Thank you," Claude murmured. "Thank you all for being so kind."

Silvana handed the bouquet, in its gilt holder, to Ginevra, who handed it on to her. Ginevre and Irene took their own bouquets and moved into position in front of her.

There was a second peal of trumpets. The Italian princesses began to walk. Claude could feel Silvana behind her, fussing with the drape of her train. Leonora pulled the veil over her face and stepped away.

"Bless you, Principessa." She whispered.

Claude began the long march to the entrance. She either felt terribly brave or like a complete idiot, she couldn't decide which.

§

During his final inspection of the Colosseum, Caesar had shown displeasure at the 'plainness' of the arena. With a heavy heart, Haussmann had given the order for eight gilded flagpoles, each with an eagle crouched upon its knob, to be studded around the top of his most beloved edifice. From each of these depended an inevitably gaudy bullion-fringed imperial banner. It was like trailing mud across a fine linen tablecloth. Though Micah's initial reaction had been one of pity for the Baron, he had reason now to be grateful for the enormous flapping sheets of purple silk that helped to cover his crawling progress along the building's rim and, even more so, for the flagpoles themselves, one of which would provide an excellent emergency mooring.

Tucker had reached him with Sir Alastair's message just in the nick of time. He still was hard pressed to believe it. Menzies had estimated it would take months before Tesla's metal soldiers could be equipped to neutralize the amphoraeka. How could he possibly be doing this today?

§

Just beyond the archway, Claude paused in the sunlight. Some spectators spotted her and cheered. "Don't look up!" she instructed herself grimly. She hadn't seen the Colosseum; Augustus had not wanted to risk a rehearsal; but, back in Prague, Agent Horner had described the marvelous arena to them in enthusiastic detail. She knew there were many thousands of faces looking on. She didn't dare look up now, for fear of losing her composure. When the ceremony was over and she and Gusto were seated safely in their box, she would have plenty of opportunity to admire it.

The impersonation of Maud's elegant glide had become second nature to her. She made a graceful figure, promenading down the cloth-of-gold aisle. Ginevre and Irene waited to rearrange her train after she mounted the platform. Gusto, as pale as his inane white and gold uniform, stood beside the Emperor's grey-bearded younger brother. Amongst this profusion of virginal splendor, the red robes of the cleric stood out like a pool of blood.

As she reached the Prince's side, the trumpets sounded again. The sound seemed to come from everywhere at once. There must be a ring of heralds, she mused, standing at the top of the building. The cleric, who Claude assumed must be a very senior kind of priest, gestured towards Gusto. He was staring too fixedly at his bride to notice.

The elderly Prince Giroleme nudged him. Red with embarrassment, Gusto reached for the hem of her veil. "'Scusi," he whispered, as if he were taking a liberty, and he lifted it off her face.

The entire Colosseum seemed to draw a collective appreciate gasp. Above this, a single strangled cry rang out: "Claude!!!"

The word was immediately overlaid by a fresh peal of trumpets, but not soon enough for Claude. She knew that voice. It was Nikola! Her heart twisted. It took every bit of discipline she could muster to not turn around.

Gusto reached for her hand. His own hand was shaking.

Suddenly, Claude felt a very different kind of shaking. Her locket was vibrating against her thigh. There was only one thing that could mean— the mate to the transmitter had to be within twenty miles of her; Father must be nearby! However improbable, what else could it be? She wanted to shout for joy. She wanted to scream to Nikola not to worry. She wanted to know where Agent Horner was.

The programme had promised musical performers and a thrilling show of Caesar's military might. The assembled guests were amazed, then titillated, to realize they were about to witness a royal wedding. They were settled in to enjoy the spectacle when the vast shadow spilled over the Colosseum.

Every face lifted as one. A single gasp cut through the crowd at the sight of the majestic silver aership. Those who had never seen such a thing shivered in awe. Even the more worldly guests braced themselves in anticipation.

The belly of the gondola skimmed the top of the arena. Micah Fairservis held onto a flagpole with one hand. A coil of rope plummeted toward him, the weight of the grappling hook sending it just beyond reach of his fingers. It sank past, grazing a few ears, setting off yelps of outrage, and hitting an aisle railing with a clang.

With no time to think, Micah let himself drop from the ledge. One foot somehow landed on the highest row of seats. The other stepped briefly on a fat man, who was too shocked to react. Ignoring the people in them, Micah clambered over the seats to reach the aisle.

The nearest centurion watched, agog, as the hook rasped across the stone, dragged by the drift of the aership. Micah dove into the aisle to pin it down. One of the barbs sliced the side of his hand; he was lucky it hadn't gone through his wrist.

"Your assistance is required!" Rappaccini barked. The rank indicated by his uniform commanded obedience. The very young centurion sprang forward. "Hold this!"

"Why wasn't I warned about this? Someone could have been hurt!" The youngster put his foot on the indicated bit of rope. He sounded more excited than troubled.

Rappaccini pulled out his handkerchief and bound his hand tightly, to stop the bleeding. "It worked well enough in rehearsal," he muttered loudly, leaving no doubt in the other's mind that the aership was part of the planned exercise.

The two men maneuvered the grapple to the rail, winding the rope twice to secure the hitch. Drawing the short ceremonial sword that was part of his dress uniform, Micah maneuvered the flat to reflect a flash of sunlight.

The aership pushed towards the south side of the arena. The rope stretched taught. Enjoying the irony, Micah ordered his unintended assistant to clear a path through the stands.

A figure appeared in the doorway of the gondola. Those in the upper tiers of the audience could see that it was an amphoraka. Greeted by a collective cry of astonishment, it slid down the rope.

It landed heavily, but upright. Micah rushed to unbuckle the harness. His eyes met a patch of black where a glyph had previously been visible. A small bronze nameplate had been pressed above an etched motif of ankh and feather.

Micah saluted solemnly. "General Garibaldi, welcome to the Colosseum."

Garibaldi chimed an acknowledgement. The cymbals, Micah noticed, were now more permanently attached with welded bronze bands.

"General?" the young centurion was watching the proceedings apprehensively. "I thought they were…They follow orders, they can't give them."

"Things are about to change in the Roman army," the senior centurion replied.

Except for those nearest to Garibaldi, every eye in the arena swiveled back to the aership. A penumbra of sunlight spilled over the elliptic shadow of the aership balloon. More figures had appeared, men in armor, jumping from the ship. Depending from handkerchiefs of shimmering silk, the bodies floated down as lightly as dandelion fluff. The audience held its breath in wonder.

From her position on the dais, Claude saw the sun glint on a patchwork of silvery and golden and bluish metal.

The utter silence was shattered by a triumphal male voice somewhere in the stands: "*Sic semper evello mortem Tyrannis!*"

Quivering as much with pride as with excitement, Claude searched the crowd for Nikola. Before she could find him, another voice rang out—the voice of Caesar Augustus.

"*Fuoco!*" the Emperor bellowed.

The display of Roman might was to have concluded today's festivities, so only some of the armed cohort of amphoraeka were already waiting in stairwells and niches around the arena. From wherever they stood, at the Emperor's command, fiery bolts arched through the air towards the aership.

Undermined by Tesla's hidden flaw, the arrows fell short. Many landed in the stands, among the invited guests. The Colosseum erupted in screams. Hair and clothing flared. Velvet cushions smoldered. Much of this occurred in the Promenade, sparking a frenzied evacuation of dignitaries.

The invaders were reaching the ground. A second round of fire came nearer the mark. A few of the descending parachutes were grazed, the silken fabric instantly devoured by bright fire.

There was the clamour of running feet and shouting commands. Rifle shots rang out: the cream of the Roman army attempting to restore order. Then the ponderous thunder of clay feet as the amphoraeka were called to form ranks.

A charred parachute dropped one automaton onto the sloping canopy of the bridal box. The metal soldier rattled down and sailed out over the floor of the arena. It fell only a few yards from the dais, its lower limbs crumpled from the impact.

Claude poised to run to the damaged machine, to see if it might be salvaged. Gusto pulled her back. The proximity of danger to his beloved was making him unusually resolute.

"You'll be hurt! Eminenza, Zio, we must get the women to safety!"

The two old men didn't wait to be told twice. They rushed the two princesses towards the nearest exit.

Claude attempted to wrench free of the ardent Prince. He grabbed both her wrists. Hampered by miles of silk and lace, she was unable to do anything other than dig in her heels. Pulling all her weight down and backward, she fell, dragging the bewildered Gusto with her. It was a bad fall. The weight of the diadem jerked her head painfully against the boards. Gusto landed across her. One of her arms was free. She used it to pinch his nose until the struggle to breathe caused him to roll over. The veil had blown back over her face. She ripped it off, unmooring some of the hairpins. The headpiece was even more excruciating now that it was unstable. She scrambled to her feet, pulling haphazardly at her hair.

Claude stared in horror. One of the burning parachutes had floated up and grazed the balloon of the aership. The balloon was quickly collapsing, the skin shriveling off a flame-licked skeleton of blacked struts. The gondola veered, sinking to the ground. One end hovered over a bank of still-occupied seats. People wailed in panic, pushing one another down the aisles into a flood of human lava.

Undeterred by either fire or the bullets bouncing off their bodies, the mechanical men that had landed safely began to form a curved rank at one end of the arena. Arms and legs pumping in splendid unison, the reflected flames adding grandeur to their silly faces, they advanced. The sight ought to have made Claude's heart swell with joy, but it was too busy breaking.

"FATHER!!!!" The howl came from a place so deep that her legs shook with it. She hurled the diadem to the ground. Tears streamed down her face. Fumbling at the hooks of her cumbersome garments, Claude staggered off the dais towards the wreck.

Again, a pair of strong arms pulled her back. She had managed to undo the overskirt. One firm jerk and she'd discarded it, together with its endless train. Encumbered only by underskirts, petticoats and bustle, she kicked at her would-be protector.

"Let me go!" she shrieked. "My father is in there!"

"No he's not." The familiar voice was oddly matter-of-fact, as if recording a measurement. "He can't be. He's sending the radio commands."

Claude spun around and threw herself against Nikola's chest, sobbing with relief. "Are you sure?" She rested her head against his clavicle, searching for the familiar smell of coffee and machine oil, but everything was obliterated by the reek of smoke.

"It's the only way." He sounded certain, if detached. His emotion seemed to be reserved for the automatons. "Truly splendid. The weaponry looks different from what I designed. I can't make it out. I wish we could get close enough to see. I suppose I'll have to wait until this is over."

As if to punctuate his words, what was left of the aership slid to the floor of the arena, trailing the last of its flaming halo over the seats behind.

The Colosseum was a seething cauldron, the sour smell of fear mingled with blood, singed hair and acrid black smoke. The air was filled with the sounds of death and human misery. A stampeding crowd, uncontrollable, choked every stairwell and aisle. The army had to take up arms against them to clear the access points needed to let in the amphoraeka that had been stationed outside.

On the floor of the arena, a wall of clay goliaths faced off against a row of shining metal soldiers.

As a single beautiful machine, the automatons raised their right arms at a precise 53-degree angle to their barrel chests. Each forearm had been replaced with a long brass nozzle, which discharged a vigorous spurt of tarry goo directly at the engraved glyphs.

From somewhere above, an amplified voice called out in Scots-scented Italian *"Siete uomini liberi ora. Siete liberi di vivere o di morire come si sceglie."* You are free men now; free to live or die as you choose.

Augustus was frothing with rage. Who dared to snatch the moment of glory from his hand?! It was that bitch, the British Queen; it had to be! How had she learned of this? Well, her ill-gotten knowledge would do her no good. The woman would learn what happened to those who crossed Caesar Augustus! It was insufficient recompense to see her evil machine blazing to ash. His amphoraeka would smite her soldiers, and the girl would be wedded and bedded before the sun went down on this day. And this would be only the beginning! The Baron's pet genius would build great machines to carry his amphoraeka. They would smash whatever would not yield. Gaul would return to Roma, and then they would cross the waters and take Britannia in the name of his new daughter. The Empire would be whole again, and all roads would lead to Caesar Augustus!

He stood by his marble throne, his hands gripping the sides to keep him upright, and roared his commands to his forces. Where was the girl?! He leaned forward to peer at the dais. She was trying to run, but the boy, amazingly, had her pinned. Perhaps the boy had some blood in him after all.

"Hah!" he roared. "Hold her!"

He felt as though one of the blazing crossbolts had pierced his chest. His legs were jelly. His hands clutched at air that he could not breathe.

Giulia saw him collapse. "Patre!" She leaned over him, removing the heavy gold collar from his chest.

"Now," he whispered through gritted teeth, the angry tears glinting in his eyes. "Now."

Patre was unconscious. Without hesitation, Giulia pulled the ring from his finger and placed it on her own. "Take him!" she commanded one of the amphoraeka that had been stationed in the imperial box. "And you," she signaled the other; "fetch Principe Gusto to the Temple!"

There was no time to lose. Even today, even here, she had worn the reticule with the feather and the lapis scarab. Sending Augustus's bearer on its way, she hurried down the private stairs. Apollinaris, Khristos and the two priests followed close at her heels. The nearest vehicle to the hidden doorway was the flower-decked landau meant for the newlyweds. Apollinaris threw her in and vaulted up to the box, seizing the reigns from the stupefied driver. The others piled into the back with the Lady.

No one noticed Rafello running behind, waving his lute over his head to attract their attention. They drove off. He bent over his knees for a moment to catch his breath. It took no great cleverness to guess where they were headed. He had seen the pain on Caesar's face, and the flailing clutch at his chest. He would follow them on foot and meet them there. He would be with his master. He had no other home.

Rafello heard an elderly grunting behind him. The castrato turned to see Baron Haussmann, his wedding finery mussed with panic. "Young man!" the Baron wheezed. "What is happening? Where is Caesar?"

Rafello didn't need to speak. He pointed in the direction in which the carriage had disappeared. There were tears rolling down his pretty cheek.

The Baron nodded his comprehension. Rafello bowed his curls with surprising dignity, and went on his way.

Haussmann looked up at the Colosseum looming magnificently above him. The epitome of his life's work. He felt his own tears raining down. Within those walls, terrible machines, wonderful modern machines were destroying the power of the Emperor's immortal army. Augustus himself was ill, powerless, perhaps even dying.

The Baron was too old to fight. He had only wanted to die quietly, in his own bed. He walked closer to the doorway and put his lips to the stone, kissing his favourite child goodbye. He straightened himself as best he could. Leaning on his knobbed stick, he headed in the direction of the Villa Alsaziano. Before he turned off the Via dei Fori Imperiali, he took one last look back at the shining white glory of the arena. No one could say it hadn't been well done, he assured himself. He had built to last. Rome would stand for another millennium. His heart lightened with peaceful pride. It was well done. He was an old man. He had earned his rest.

🙚

Gusto was white-lipped with fear. He wished he had fled with the others, but he couldn't have left the Principessa. Now there was no way out, not that he could see. The stands were chaotic and the floor of the arena a battle zone. Furthermore, a rough-looking stranger had muscled his way to Maud's side and was restraining her.

Though it was not in Gusto's nature to fight, his grandfather had ensured that he was properly trained in the arts of war. His chased steel sword was as sharp as it was decorative. He jumped from the platform and drew it, calling out a challenging "Ha!"

The stranger whirled around.

"Release her now!"

The stranger didn't seem to understand the words, but he took in the sight of the raised sword. His eyes glittered wildly.

It was the Principessa who spoke. "Oh, for goodness sake, Gusto, put that away."

"My beloved..."

"No, Gusto. I'll explain later. Please, put the sword down."

"What is he talking about?" Nikola asked.

"He thinks he has to protect me from you," she explained hastily. "He thinks I'm Princess Maud."

"You're not, are you? Wait, what's wrong with your eyes?" In an instant, Nikola's aspect changed from that strange, clinical detachment to one of extreme anxiety. "Why does everyone try to confuse me? The Baron and the other one, your father's friend. But he's not your father, not if you're not you..."

Claude certainly didn't need Nikola losing his grip just now. She popped the lenses out of her eyes. Grabbing him by the shoulders, she brought his face towards hers. "I'm me, Nikola. Look at me! I'm Claude."

Nikola relaxed but Claude's other 'protector' let out a scream.

"Moud!! Your eyes!!"

Claude dropped her hold on Tesla to take hold of the Prince's hands. "Gusto," she said earnestly, "I'm not the Principessa, I'm sorry. But I am a friend. I promise, I'm here to help you. You can trust me. You must stay calm."

458

A shadow fell over them and she screamed.

An amphoraka was towering over Gusto. It lifted the Prince in its herculean arms. Claude screamed again. There was no knowing why the creature had come for the Prince, but it could not be for any reason that was good. She had to stop it. Her eyes flew over the scene. Anything that looked like an ally was engaged in the melee on the floor, and Agent Horner, blast him, was nowhere in sight.

She threw up her hands in frustration and brushed against the heavy earbobs. Of course! She almost laughed. Her fancies hadn't been so fanciful after all. Though a cosh wasn't realistic. It had to be a projectile that would fly free, right into the eye socket. What she needed was a slingshot, but there was nothing on hand that looked like a frame. She jerked Nikola's arms towards her, pushing the elbows into a 'v.'

"Nikola, don't move!" She stripped off one of the elbow-length mitts and wrapped it around his hands. "Hey, you!" She yelled. "Yes, you; amphoraka! Whoever you once were! Look at me!"

The creature was so startled at being addressed that it stopped in its tracks for just long enough. She fitted one of the earrings, aimed and sent it soaring. The jewel smashed into the helmet's nose plate and rebounded, narrowly missing Gusto's head. The Prince, rigid with shock, didn't even notice.

"NO!" She fumbled for the other earring and shot again. This time, she aimed true. The sparkling missile sailed through the eye hole.

Claude's heart stopped.

Nothing happened.

"How?!" Claude was dumbfounded. "How can this be?" she raged.

"It wasn't combustible," Nikola said, in the detached voice he'd used earlier. "The head has to implode to release the soul."

The amphoraka was heading through the outer ranks of his fellows, which parted to allow him to pass.

"HORNER!!!" She had no idea where the agent was, but it felt better to scream for him than to do nothing. Where was Father, or Leski? She hated feeling so powerless. She wanted a weapon. She itched for a grain of Prometheum, to make another bomb. She was desperate to get off this stupid platform. She was desperate to do something, anything at all other than stand on the sidelines.

"What are you doing?" Nikola looked at her as if she were a strange machine.

"I don't even know." There was one thing she could do. She might be stuck with a thin pair of beaded slippers, but she had vowed in that forest never to get trapped by skirts again.

"I would never have believed it! You're superb!"

Claude's extensively visible complexion stained with a violent blush. Silk pantalettes felt brazen in a way that good stout trousers never had. She bent to grab up a fallen petticoat, when she realized that Nikola hadn't been looking at her. He had been looking *behind* her.

The lambent halo of the Golden One was serenely beautiful, even in the current chaos.

"Paulette!"

It was surprising that she was standing here and not with Giulia. Paulette had no glyph; as far as Claude knew, nothing commanded her except what remained of her broken heart. Claude wished there was a way to know what the Golden One was thinking, but no amount of thumping would ever be heard above this din.

Paulette didn't need Morse code to get her message across. She extended an arm. Looped above her hand, a rifle depended from its strap. The other hand pointed at the path that was closing in the wake of Gusto's abductor. It was confirmation of Claude's suspicions that Augustus meant him harm. Paulette was staking her own claim to freedom today.

Claude grinned and grabbed the rifle. "Take care of my friend Nikola!"

There wasn't time for Tesla to react. The moving wall of clay shifted. Whatever gap Claude disappeared into had instantly closed. He leaned against the platform, bemused. Where had she gone? After dreaming about her all these weeks, she had leaked through his fingers like water. Had he imagined her? He no longer trusted his own senses, and the gilded statue in front of him held no clues.

Waves of clay broke at the periphery of the platform where he stood, distracting him from anything else. The Army commanders must have aroused every amphoraeka in Rome: the unarmed now outnumbered those who had been fitted with Tesla's crossbolt mechanism. They flowed toward that end of the floor where his glorious automatons stood, shooting round after round of some viscous compound at their foes. Not at their heads, but at their chests. Nikola grasped this and was fascinated. He wished he knew more about the weapon Frank had designed.

After being hit, the amphoraeka would fall back and make way for the next rank. Nikola watched a pair of the stricken giants stagger off to one side, face each other, and blast their crossbolts into one another's eyes, a kind of suicide pact. A visible tremor shook the ranks as the shared soul-wave perceived their departure. This was only the beginning. More pairs followed them. Others who bore an obliterating splat of black where their command glyphs had been, moved through their unarmed fellows, appearing to consult before firing a bolt. A few uniformed men, the tattoos on their foreheads vibrant through the dust and smoke, were crushed trying to intercede. Bronze helmets rolled underfoot. Headless clay torsos studded the arena like standing stones.

Nikola was riveted to the scene, but didn't know if he believed it. It was too much like one of his own fantasies.

A woman's cry of horror cut through his reverie. Dov, carrying Tashi, had reached his side. The little nurse slid to the ground and threw her arms around Tesla.

"Kola! They are dying!"

"Only if they want to die, I think," he said, patting her absently. "Frank has given them the freedom to choose." He looked up at his friend. "Don't leave me, Dov. Please don't leave me."

❧

Claude ran zigzags through the mass of amphoraeka, dodging legs, ducking swinging arms, sometimes slipping in her thin-soled shoes. Darting past Gusto's startled face, she chose a spot to stand her ground.

"Oi! Trecika!" She yelled, as loud as she could. She hoped that was considered an insult. Whether or not it was, the creature paused. She shouldered the gun and yelled again. "Gusto, bend your knees and try to roll!"

The blue flames flickered. Claude sighted and pulled the trigger. Once again, her missile found its mark. This time, she was playing with fire. The head imploded, dust spilling from the helmet; the blue flames went out. Simultaneously, the empty bronze helmet toppled to the ground, the arms relaxed and Gusto dropped to the ground.

He fell hard, his feet slipped and he bumped onto his gluteus maximus. Claude tucked her own head down and slammed herself against him, shoulders first, to push him out of the way of the headless carcass. She could have spared herself the pain. Rather than capsizing, as she expected, it stood where it had halted, an empty clay urn. Gusto rolled onto his side, babbling every prayer he had learned at his late mother's knee. Claude dusted herself off. She tried to pull the Prince to his feet before he might inadvertently be crushed by the milling herd of amphoraeka.

"What do you think you're doing?"

Claude spun around. A pair of sapphire eyes shot sparks right through her. She couldn't tell whether the insufferable man was furious or amused.

"Someone had to save the Prince." The eyes raked her from top to toe, reminding her she was standing there in nothing but a bodice and pantalettes.

"You're not a soldier. You could have been hurt."

"Well who else was going to do it?" she said, slinging the rifle across her back. It felt good to be armed. "I didn't see you anywhere about."

"I was assisting General Garibaldi."

"It *was* Garibaldi! By the time I could see, there was only a shadow. It might as easily have been Leski."

"Garibaldi is invaluable." Horner seemed to be thinking aloud, his expression almost visionary. "The amphoraeka—the ones who choose to live—will look to him, naturally. More than that, he's uniquely able to rally the rebels. Italy has awaited this moment for longer than you and I have been alive. Outside these walls, the nation is rising! Io mi prenderò la rivincita!"

"But how? I expect everyone saw the aership, but why would they think…?"

"We put the word out, as soon as we had your father's message. Not only to the men I know here. We've got Tucker spreading the word in Milan, Elettra in Venezia, our cousins in Napoli…it's all part of the plan."

"There's a plan," she said coldly. "Really. Was anyone ever going to tell me?"

The rapt expression was replaced by his more customary condescension. "Oh, don't be ridiculous. I haven't been allowed near you since we got back from Firenze. I couldn't even tell you about replacing the drugs with seawater."

"WATER?!" Her enraged slap had to sting, but he didn't give her the satisfaction of flinching. "I thought I was going to die this morning and you tell me it was all for nothing?!"

He had no idea what she was talking about. "What was I supposed to do, throw a note over the wall?"

"Give it to one of those maids you said you 'cultivated!' You might have tried!"

"Maybe I trusted that you had everything under control. Where's Tesla?"

It was flattering, considering the source. Still, it rankled to have been kept in the dark. "On the platform. Safe. With Paulette."

"Paulette?"

She was pleased to know something he didn't. "Paulette Buonaparte, Augustus's sister. The Golden One. We've become good friends."

He inclined his head in respect, as if to say 'touché.'

"What does the plan say we're to do now?"

"I was supposed to tell you to get Tesla and the Prince back to the aership," he drawled.

She couldn't help it; she sniggered. So did he. The two of them stood in the midst of chaos, laughing helplessly.

"The hypogeum!" he blurted, when he could.

"What?" It was a funny word; she continued to giggle.

He put his hand on her nearly-bare shoulder and she stopped. Blue eyes pierced grey.

"I see you removed the lenses," he said, offhandedly. "I prefer you this way. The hypogeum," he continued smoothly, as if he hadn't just been extremely complimentary in the most offensive way. "The Colosseum's underground. It'll be safe to wait there until all of this is over. I'll find you then."

Claude angrily disavowed her blush. "Don't trouble yourself. My father will find me. Where is my father, by the way? Do you know?"

"I saw a ptery. It came in behind the aership. I don't know where it landed."

That made sense. "So, how do we get there, to the hypo-whosis?"

"The hypogeum. Use the East door. You'll have to get to the other side of the automatons. Then through the arch and down the ramp." He turned his attention to the whimpering Prince. "Come along, Altezza. We need to get you to safety."

Gusto allowed himself to be helped up. He must have found some reassurance in the centurion's uniform. He suffered the other man to put an arm around his shoulder and lead him through the disarray, back toward the platform.

୨◆

"Switch coats with me," Agent Horner demanded, unbuttoning his black tunic.

"Why?" Tesla was only being curious. He had already begun to comply.

"The rebels will be gathering in front of the Pantheon. Someone has to translate for Garibaldi. I can't be seen in an Imperial Uniform."

"I could go," Claude offered.

"No!" The three men shouted. They seemed startled by their unique concurrence. Both Gusto and Nikola reached out as if to prevent her from stepping forward. She pushed them aside.

Before she could protest, Horner lifted a hand to stop her. "*You* could, but the English Princess can't. As it is, I can't imagine how Her Majesty's Government plans to explain all of this. Catch!"

He pulled something from his tunic before handing the garment to Tesla. Her hand came up automatically and caught the flying object.

"The world must see without a doubt that the uprising is indigenous and just." The passion in his voice told her that his commitment to this went far beyond his assignment; it was personal, the first personal thing she knew about this exemplary spy. "Augustus will be deposed in favour of the Prince and a new order established. I'm already known to many of the leaders. And you need to get Tesla and the Prince to the hypogeum, before the Army realizes they're still here." He saluted. "I leave the two most important men in Rome in your very capable hands."

The lithe figure dashed toward the opposite side of the Colosseum. Claude stared after him. The chatelaine, clutched in her hand, was warm from his breast pocket. Her cheeks were warm as well. "It would have been nice to have had this sooner," she said tartly, but he was too far away to hear. It was hard to dispel the absurd glow of pleasure. The insufferable man had treated her like an agent and an equal. She would do her job well.

"Why is he leaving us?" The Prince was not sanguine about the loss of the only recognizable figure of authority.

"For your sake, Altezza. To keep the peace in your name. He's shown me how to get us all to safety. I'll explain when we get there."

"But Moud, the Army…"

"The Army is otherwise engaged. We must keep close to one another. We are heading for that archway," she pointed.

"Where they're shooting?" Gusto was horrified. "I will not expose women to such danger!"

Nikola agreed. "We're safe where we are. We should remain here. You and Tashi might be trampled underfoot."

Claude sighed. There was no time for this. "Gentlemen, this is not your decision to make. Paulette, please take Gusto. If you have to carry him, then do. Mr. Sandtmann, you take…" She looked around. "Where is Mr. Sandtmann?"

Tashi let out a voiceless wail and pointed into the endless stream of amphoraeka. Dov was heading into the thick of it. A deep pink scarf from Tashi's silk costume had caught on the chin-guard of his helmet and fluttered behind him.

"Dov, don't leave me!" Nikola yelled. It was the most emotion Claude had seen from him today. "Stop!!"

It was Claude who understood that Sandtmann could not. The human commanders had called for all amphoraeka within hail; his glyph did not allow him to refuse. He moved inexorably towards the automatons and the goo that would free him. That much was fine, but in the short term, regardless of whether Sandtmann ultimately chose to live or die, she needed him alive for Nikola's sake.

She spotted the broken automaton, not six yards away from the platform. It had been knocked about enough that it looked more like scrap metal than a clockwork man. It seemed safe enough to approach; if the Prometheum boiler were going to explode, it would have done so already. She bounded over to examine the wreckage. Father and Leski had incorporated the nozzle into the structure of the arm; it couldn't be removed without a workshop full of tools. The canister of resin, however, was detachable, strapped to the mannikin's back. The buckle had been squashed in the fall and wouldn't budge. Feeling whole again, she pulled the little clasp knife from her restored chatelaine and slashed the straps. The canister was too heavy to carry.

She ran back to the platform and, ignoring Gusto's pleas and Nikola's howls, retrieved her discarded train. It was long enough that she could remain upright and drag the container behind her on the ground. Keeping a grateful eye on Tashi's scarf, she dragged the container ahead of Sandtmann's current position to the feet of a decapitated amphoraka. Dumping out the canister, she slung the train across the giant torso. With a huge knot tied at the hip, it made as good a perch as she was going to get. Wrapping her remaining mitt around her hand, to protect against the heat, she dug out a handful of goo. Her foot digging into the knot, she used her free hand to hoist herself up to amphoraka height. Dov came within range. She wound her wrist and threw as hard as she could. The resin hit low on the moving target. She jumped down for another scoop and hurled again.

This one missed entirely, dripping uselessly off the shoulder of the figure next to his. She was running out of time. He was moving away.

"Mr. Sandtmann!" she yelled. "Dov! Wait! You can move more slowly and still obey!"

Aristotle it wasn't, but the logic was sufficiently effective to enable him to pause. She jumped down from the sling again, filled her hand and put herself directly in front of him. Raising her arm overhead, goo trickling down to her neck, she bent her knees and sprang up, slamming her hand into his chest. Somehow, enough of the resin stuck to cover the glyph. She panted with relief and smiled, placing her cleaner hand on one of his. "Claude Monteith. I've heard so much about you. Let's go get Nikola."

In the end, it was Claude who rode East in Sandtmann's arms. After her success in freeing him, it seemed a pity to waste the rest of the resin. With a faint tinge of regret for the fate of the lovely fabric, she again used the train as a sling, this time enabling Dov to carry the canister. Each time they neared an amphoraka, she scooped up a handful of goo and tried to mash it against the glyph. Away from the heat of the Prometheum boiler, the resin gradually lost its viscosity; she was able to help only half a dozen before it had cooled too much to stick. Reaching the head of the ramp, she dismounted and unloaded the spent canister. The others trailed slightly behind.

Nikola, clutching tightly to Tashi's hand, lingered by the firing line. Gears revolved and cables tensed. Brass nozzles swung into position. Hot tarry resin gushed with the force of a steam engine. Over and over, the automatons cycled through the pattern. Nikola stood as near as Tashi would allow, staring with the baffled pride of a new father. His ear sought out the underlying whirrs and clicks. The foolish smile on his face mirrored the ones he had welded onto his progeny.

She understood Nikola's fascination, but this was not the time for it. "Better go get him Mr. Sandtmann, or he'll stand there all day."

The patch of ground between the automatons and the ramp was empty of everything, save herself and some detritus that had blown down from the stands. It was peaceful enough that Claude began to feel self-conscious about standing around in her underwear. She slipped the remnant of fabric across her body like a tartan and patted it affectionately. It had turned out well for her that no expense had been spared on the Princess's wedding costume. For material that had seemed so frivolous, it had proven surprisingly strong. She had no idea what she might do with the scraps, but it would be a pity not to salvage some of it when this was over.

"Let him go!" Nikola's shout rang out in the gap between fusillades.

Two soldiers had rushed Paulette and, astoundingly, were trying to pry Gusto from her arms.

Claude reached for her rifle, but her trigger finger was covered in the tarry leather wrapping. With a great deal of satisfaction, she sought her magnifying glass and wiggled it hard until a hard beam of light bounced off it into the eyes of the would-be abductors.

The soldiers screamed and released their grip. Paulette, still clutching her great-nephew, moved toward Claude. One of the soldiers recovered enough to follow.

The soldier wore a forehead tattoo. He must have been so accustomed to amphoraeka obeying him that he didn't think to try and avoid Dov Sandtmann. He smacked into the wall of clay and fell to the ground. Sandtmann continued walking, his shuffling gait slamming his feet repeatedly into the man's ribs and belly.

Claude chose to turn away. They were both doing what had to be done.

Scanning for other uniforms, she herded her charges into the safe zone. "Run!" she insisted; it was safest to stay a moving target. Tashi tugged at Nikola, forcing him forward. Holding her burden close, Paulette moved at the fastest speed that her hulking clay legs could achieve. Claude stayed behind the automatons until she saw the others disappear down the ramp. Only then did she run after, swift as a deer.

෴

Where was the boy? Giulia was frantic. Patre's lips were blue with the effort of staying alive. Catoni, hastily called to the temple, concurred: there was not a moment left to waste.

Giulia knelt down to where the Greek crouched with Patre in his arms. There was no other option. "You must take me, Patre," she whispered with her lips against his ear, the certainty flooding her veins even as she said it. She had foreseen this eventuality and prepared for it. "I am an heir of the blood. Use me as your vessel until the line is secure, and then we will claim the boy."

It was a struggle for to whisper his reply. "Yes," he said, the pain washing over his face. "It is right that this should be. You are the only one…always…" He could no longer speak. She moved so that his lips could graze her forehead in blessing, then shifted so that she might kiss him on the lips.

She was filled with exultation. It is easy to have people who are willing to kill for you. True power is having someone willing to die for you. Her sacrifice was confirmation of Patre's greatness as well as the greatness of her own love.

Giulia surveyed the scene around her. The priests in their blue robes, their young acolytes, the musicians: everyone had been summoned and was ready.

She beckoned to Apollinaris. She pressed the reticule into his hand. The feather and the scarab were in his care. As Patre trusted her, he was the only one she could trust to do what must be done. Raising herself on tiptoe, she wrapped her arms around his neck. Even now she would not kiss him. Her last kiss had been for Patre.

He stepped away, his eyes shining with unshed tears.

The music hummed. She signaled to the maiden she had trained herself. The girl bowed and began to dance.

A scared boy held out the situla. Giulia pressed her hands firmly over his shaking ones and drank deeply.

Her hair flowed over her body like a bridal veil. With a beatific smile, she raised her arms in invocation. "Henu Nun and Naunet, of the Waters that flowed Before Time..."

⁊⃰

Claude waited for Sandtmann, hoping no soldiers would follow. For five long minutes, she crouched in the dimness at the foot of the ramp, anxiously monitoring the muffled din above. The trick with the magnifying glass wouldn't work down here. She would have to use her gun, and she would have to do it cack-handed. The resin had hardened over. It was impossible to unwind the bandaging. Her eyes trained warily on the top of the ramp, she inserted the tip of her clasp knife at the spot where the wrappings covered her wrist. An experimental push made it immediately evident that, even with her full attention, this approach would break the knife, slice her ulnar artery or both. Father had trained her to fight ambidextrously. That she couldn't shoot as well with both hands was an omission that she emphatically vowed to redress as soon as she got back home.

She felt the vibration of Sandtmann's feet before she saw his long shadow. He was thoroughly alone.

The hypogeum was a warren. Claude had no idea which way the others had gone. She didn't like the idea of calling out; there was no telling who or what else might have chosen to hide down here. Eliminating those corridors too narrow for an amphoraka to pass through still left a number of options.

She rejected the more forbidding doors, the ones sealed with crossbar latches or sheeted in metal. What looked like animal pens were easy to see into and dismiss as empty. One door led to a metal shop. She had Sandtmann wait while she scouted for a pair of cutters. Once they found the others, Nikola could cut the casing off her hand. That is, the Nikola she knew would be able to. She wasn't so sanguine about the Nikola here today. Though he seemed rational enough, he was incomplete. It was like visiting a house when the family had been away for the summer; everything was where you expected it to be, but the rooms were missing the intangible something that made them feel occupied.

She fitted the cutters into the cleft of one of Sandtmann's hands, keeping her own good hand free to open the next door.

Someone inside screamed. Without pausing, Claude shouldered the rifle and barged in. A troupe of girls huddled on a bench against the opposite wall. They looked to be between nine and twelve years old. She couldn't imagine anything more incongruous. In their gauzy tunics and floral wreaths, they trembled like butterflies. She had forgotten this had started off as a wedding day. There would have been an entire program of festivities. These must be dancers. The poor things were innocently waiting to be called. They clearly had no idea what was going on above their heads. What looked like a crazy beggar woman had burst into their dressing room, waving a gun. No wonder they were terrified.

"It's alright," she said, hoping her smile was more reassuring than her shredded costume. "I'm sorry if I startled you. There's been...um...a change of plans. There was a demonstration by Caesar's Praetorian Guard and things got a little out of control. But there's nothing to worry about."

They didn't look convinced. One started crying in wet shaking gulps. There was nothing Claude could do about it. It was a group of adolescent girls; one of them was bound to be a maternal type.

"You should stay right here until someone comes to bring you home. Someone will, I promise. You just stay put until then. Agreed?"

A tiny brunette with old eyes gave a begrudging nod and put her arms around the weeper.

"I'm going to close the door behind me." Claude addressed the evident leader. "It might be another couple of hours, but you don't have to be afraid."

"We're not afraid," the child said stoutly, glaring over her friend's heaving shoulders.

"Good girl."

Claude tied a bit of rag to the door handle, marking it for whoever might be sent. She and Sandtmann continued to open doors until they found the rest of their party hunkered down in a large empty room, Paulette standing guard within the door.

Nikola acknowledged them with a relieved sigh. "You're safe."

"The soldiers haven't followed. I think Mr. Sandtmann took care of them."

"I wish we had your cymbals with us, Dov."

Dov slapped his hand against the wall.

"Better not, Mr. Sandtmann," Claude warned. "We don't want anyone to hear us. I'm sorry. I can't imagine how frustrating it must be." She patted him kindly on the chest.

"I've been thinking about a communication device." Nikola remarked, almost cheerily.

"You and Father both."

"Good. We can work together again."

"First I have a much smaller project for you." She handed him the cutters. "Someone needs to be able to shoot this rifle. I have more experience than you. Gusto can probably shoot, but he's useless for now. Who could blame him?" She nodded to where Tashi was rubbing the wrists of the dazed prince.

"You are a very unusual young woman."

There it was again, that sense that strange detachment. They sat side by side on the floor, as they had in the workshop. It should have been familiar and joyful, but it was as if he didn't know her. She wasn't sure she knew him any more, either; another reason for her to hate Caesar Augustus.

Claude watched sadly as Nikola positioned her arm to rest against his thigh, to steady it. He touched a curious finger to the hardened bandages. She shivered, as if he had touched the hand beneath.

"What's in it?" It was the scientist asking.

She stayed just as matter-of-fact. "The resin? Another thing you and Father can discuss. He and Leski had only just started working on it when I left Prague."

Nikola slowly cut away at the casing. She winced. Under the thin kid, her palm and fingers were blistered. Claude had been so intent on her task that she hadn't felt the initial measure of hot goo seep through the rough bandage. Now the inner layer of leather stuck. Nikola pulled it off and the damaged skin came with it. She cried out. It was good to have an excuse.

The sound drew the little nurse from Gusto's side. She made professionally unhappy tsking sounds. "We have nothing I can use on this. Not even water."

"I just need to cover it for now." Claude frowned at the raw weeping flesh. It hurt like blazes, but there was nothing to be done.

Tashi nodded. "You have a knife."

"And a scissors." Claude handed over her chatelaine.

Tashi went to the far corner of the room and turned her back to the others. An amount of discreet wriggling was followed by a ripping sound.

Whatever kind of undergarment might be worn with her unusual filmy garments, the fine cotton lawn was probably the cleanest bit of cloth in the Colosseum. Tashi wound the strip over Claude's hand, keeping her trigger finger free.

A sudden jolt made Tashi lost her balance. She fell into Claude, sending them both to the floor.

"Ow! What the…" The floor began to rumble. Claude used her good hand to push herself up on her knees and look around. Nikola, standing against the wall with his hands on a pair of levers, refused to meet her eye. "Nikola, what did you do?!"

"Nothing!" If he were trying not to look guilty, he was failing miserably. "I was only looking at them."

The roof split open, sending a rain of debris sifting down on them. Nikola tilted his face towards the shaft of sunlight.

"Duck!" Claude yelled, covering her head with her arms. Paulette had hold of Gusto. Tashi rushed to huddle between Dov's legs.

A bronze helmet plummeted through the gap to where Tashi had been sitting a moment before. The little nurse gasped. Claude rolled across to Nikola. "You'll get yourself killed, you idiot!" She threw her weight behind his knees, forcing him down.

The room seemed to be rising. More rubble tumbled into the ever-widening gap: chunks of clay, bits of spent crossbolt, a rifle.

"*Fucile!*" Gusto shouted.

Dov stuck out an arm to catch it by the strap before it could hit the ground and go off.

"How did it understand?" Pale though he still was, Gusto had recovered sufficiently to think.

"They always could, Altezza. Only now that he is free, he can act on it." Claude smiled gravely. "There is much to explain. Once this is over."

"You seem to know a great many things that I do not."

The ceiling was entirely open now. Only light gravel and dust continued to sift down from the edges. The room-sized lift had risen high enough that the top of the shaft rose only a foot or so above Sandtmann's head.

Gusto tapped Paulette's hands. "Please, you must let me go. I have a rifle."

"Are you sure?" Claude asked. "I mean no disrespect, Altezza, but…"

By way of answer, Gusto headed determinedly towards Dov. He was only slightly unsteady. "I don't know what is happening or who these people are, but you have protected me. It is my duty to help." He unlooped the strap from Dov's arm.

As his head cleared the shaft, he raised the rifle and prepared to aim. He gasped.

Claude tore her eyes from this unexpected champion to follow his line of sight. Her eyes swept over the aftermath of what had certainly been the strangest battle in modern history.

The Colosseum was littered with shattered clay figures and human bodies. Survivors of both kinds strayed distractedly along the periphery. Most of the mechanical men remained intact. Yards from the East door, they stood as still in their curved rank as ever they had in the workshop. Smoke still rose from the stands. There were bodies there, too; some shot, others trampled in the crush to evacuate. The only sounds were the Imperial flags, flapping in the afternoon breeze, and Tashi's muted sobs.

Nikola headed towards his automatons. There seemed no reason to stop him.

Gusto lowered his rifle. "What do we do now?" His shoulders sagged.

Claude patted his arm. "I don't know. Someone will come soon to tell us. Why don't we sit down?"

As the amphoraeka had been unable to mount the stairs, the dais remained standing. They could sit on the edge and wait. Claude was hoisting herself up when a fierce glitter caused her to squint. It was Ginevre of Lorraine's diadem.

Claude was glad to see that the lovely, weighty crown was merely dusty, not dented and was missing only a few small stones. She placed it in Gusto's hands, closing his fingers around it.

He stared into the pale green jewels. "You are not Moud." It was a statement, not a question.

"I am not," she agreed. "I look very much like her."

"All this time…"

"Not all this time. I took her place in Firenze."

A few bedraggled white blossoms still clung to the sides, a poignant reminder of how this day had begun. Setting the diadem aside, Gusto plucked a rose and stroked the velvet petals. "I felt that something was different. I love her, you see." It was a rueful smile.

"I'm sorry." Claude didn't know what else to say. She unclipped the necklace and the one bracelet that remained on her arm, and slipped them into his pocket. He didn't seem to notice.

An alien birdcall broke through the eerie quiet. Claude pulled the pink scarf from her hair and waved it joyfully overhead. She was suddenly too tired to jump up. Anyway, the soles of her slippers were worn to holes and it would hurt to run across the littered ground. It was enough to beam at the two beloved shapes, loping across the arena to claim her.

25 - RESIDUUM

Tucker and Elettra had done their part in spreading the word: patriots across the length and breadth of Italy knew that this was the day the tyrant Augustus would fall.

Rome was abuzz with rumour. Much of the city had seen the aership; more had seen or smelled the smoke. They gathered at the Pantheon to call for Caesar to abdicate in favour of his grandson Napoleon Augusto. The ancient temple was full to bursting, the doors flung open wide; on the other side of them, the crowd overflowed the piazza, spilling into the streets. Men in rough jackets and soft caps jostled shoulder-to-shoulder with black-coated businessmen, aesthetes in bright cravats and robed clerics, all calling for the Emperor to be overthrown.

When Michael Leopoldo Rianero, scion of the martyred Tuscany, stepped out on the portico and presented General Garibaldi, grown men cried. The centurions who were lingering warily in the area, raised a cheer. A local cafe owner offered up every spoon in his inventory for makeshift cymbals and Baron Haussmann's young telegraph operator volunteered to teach the code to any who wanted to learn.

It was that same page who first told Micah about the Baron: how he had returned from the Colosseum and walked the villa, lightly touching his favourite possessions; how he'd bathed and shaved and changed into his favourite coat; how he'd called for his easy chair to be brought to the foyer, and a bottle of wine from his homeland; and how Gallante had found him, not an hour later, his head lolling back, his legs awkwardly sprawled, the wine glass fallen from his hand to the terrazzo floor. A small ruby glass vial was found in his waistcoat pocket; it was empty. There was a peaceful smile on Baron Haussmann's face. Before his eyes had closed, the last thing they'd looked on was his perfect gleaming model of Rome.

The death of the Baron saddened Frank, who had hoped to meet him. He wanted to understand why an engineer of his skill had forgone the future to restore the past. Frank spent as many hours as he could in the Baron's office at the Villa Alsaziano, where the British party set up temporary residence. Gallante was no more pleased than Tesla at this turn of events but, until the Baron's will was found, he could not refuse Prince Gusto's request.

Prince Gusto was now the First Consul of Rome.

Claude only learned of all of this after the fact. Following Father's instructions, she'd flown the ptery to Switzerland. Father's contact in Bern whisked her away, dirty rags and all, to his office, where she sent the telegraph to Pinkerton herself. Exhausted, she asked if Mr. Jackson would conduct her to the nearest hotel. Instead he suggested driving her to a discreet and quite charming inn where, until her travel arrangements were made, she could enjoy a restful mountain setting. To her embarrassment, she fell asleep on the road. She didn't remember much of her arrival, except that the unflappable Swiss staff welcomed her without so much as batting an eyelash at her dubious apparel.

She woke with the birds. Every bone in her body had that soft, fragile feeling, as if a long fever had finally taken the turn. The maid who brought her breakfast opened the shuttered windows; the air lured her with a delicious smell of pine and flowers. Claude slipped on a borrowed grey poplin gown that reminded her of a nursemaid's uniform. She would see where she could use Mr. Jackson's purse of Swiss money to buy a pair of walking boots and some clothes.

There was a knock at her door.

"Come!" she called.

"Hello! I fear I'm being rather presumptuous." Despite her words, the clipped voice on the other side was cheerful and confident. "They told me another Englishwoman had arrived last night and I thought you might require a guide…"

Claude flung open the door with astonished laughter. "Gertrude!"

Gertrude nearly fainted.

Interlaken was famous for its restorative properties. Tucked among the many local spas and hotels of were a few very exclusive sanatoriums, including the one in which Princess Maud was currently residing. No wonder Mr. Jackson had thought this a 'discreet' place for Claude to bide her time.

Gertrude's visits to the Princess were limited to an hour each day. The rest of the time, she and Claude were free to amuse themselves with long walks and rowing on the lake. All the while, they talked long and hard. Each found ineffable pleasure in the companionship of someone with whom she could be completely honest.

One afternoon, they returned from a walk to be told that a gentleman was waiting to see Claude.

"It must be Mr. Jackson, about my travel arrangements," she said regretfully. It seemed far too soon. "I could ask to stay another week."

Gertrude brightened. "Would you?"

"I'll explain that I met an old friend here. Father won't mind. I dare say I'll still get home before Aunt Nan does."

The man waiting in the private parlour was not Mr. Jackson. He was older than Father, his thinning hair and whiskers more grey than brown. His face alight with interest, he rose stiffly from his chair to greet them.

"Miss Menzies!" he said delightedly, extending a hand. "Such a pleasure! I haven't seen you since you were so high. I am Lord Pinkerton."

"Miss Monteith," she said, automatically, extending her own. So this was her father's oldest friend and chief of the Queen's Special Service. Really, the only spy she'd met who looked at all like one ought to was the insufferable Agent Horner.

"Yes of course. Miss Monteith. My apologies. And this must be Miss Bell, Sir Lowthian's granddaughter."

Gertrude bowed politely. "Lord Pinkerton."

"I expect you're wondering why I'm here." He beamed jovially. "I've come from a brief visit to Rome. I have heard so much about you, Miss Men...Monteith, that I wanted to see you with my own eyes. I told your father that I would transport you to London personally."

Claude was dubious. "I'm meant to be going home, to Chicago."

"There has been a change of plans. I'll explain once we're underway. I'll wait here while you get your things."

"Now? I was planning to ask Mr. Jackson if I might stay another week." She exchanged looks with Gertrude. "And anything you have to say to me can be said in front of Miss Bell. She has a right to know everything I know."

Pinkerton looked sharply from one young woman to the other. Despite the thickness of his spectacles, his glance was penetrating. Claude and Gertrude met the scrutiny calmly.

"I don't see why not," he decided. "The Princess will be returning home in a fortnight. You can travel with her. Assuming, that is, that she is not uncomfortable in your presence?"

Claude turned to Gertrude. "I haven't seen the Princess since Florence."

"I believe the Princess can be made quite comfortable, Lord Pinkerton, if you would secure permission for Miss Monteith to accompany me to the sanatorium for a visit."

Pinkerton nodded appreciatively at Gertrude's sensible suggestion. "Excellent. As to your other point, Miss Monteith, I am in complete agreement. Anything I have to share with you may certainly be shared with Miss Bell. In fact, I consider that in the course of this, ah, exercise, you have both been seconded to the Service. I need only administer the oath. But first, I think we ought to make ourselves comfortable and ring for tea."

Bubbling with more excitement than seemed appropriate for any old man, no less a government official, Lord Pinkerton told them everything that Frank had told him, beginning with an account of the hours that followed the events at the Colosseum:

Though less than robust, old Prince Giroleme had managed to get Ginevre and Irene safely back to their villa. They waited there for hours, knowing nothing and fearing the worst. When Frank arrived with Gusto and Paulette, the girls and their aunt Marie-Pauline, the one they called 'Poppet,' were hysterical with relief.

Upon being informed that the Golden One was his lost sister Paulette, a dreadful suspicion Giroleme had spent decades refusing to contemplate, the elderly Prince was felled by a seizure. A servant was sent to fetch Dottore Catoni. The terrified physician was found hurriedly packing a trunk, preparing to flee from Rome. He was fearful of the recriminations that might fall on him for having followed the Lady's orders with regard to the English Princess.

Dragged to the villa, Catoni told the family of a mysterious ceremony in Augustus's temple, at the end of which the Lady Giulia had thrown herself across the Emperor's cold body, screaming like nothing ever heard on this earth. Not even her man, Apollinaris, could calm her. The doctor had wondered if he dared administer a sedative, when she had abruptly pulled herself together. She kissed the Emperor's lips, covered his face with a cloth and removed a curious emerald ring from his finger. And then she fled, in a matter of minutes, together with her people. Catoni had urged the remaining servants to disappear, lest any try to blame them for colluding in the Emperor's death. When men were sent to the temple the next day to retrieve the body, they found only the Greek standing guard; whoever they had been in life, Khristos said, it wasn't right that the dead should be left alone.

News of the gathering at the Pantheon made its way to the villa. The Buonaparte family waited, paralyzed with uncertainty, to learn their fate. "Not to beat around the bush," Pinkerton observed, "the young man was inheriting a throne in the midst of a revolution." That Frank had assured them of a home in exile diminished, but did not remove, the dread.

They heard the shouts well before the rebel leaders, with Garibaldi at the fore, converged on the steps of the villa. Frank had been impressed with the dignity with which Gusto walked out to meet them. The Prince calmly informed the crowd that Caesar was dead.

Whatever their differences, the various rebel factions had already agreed that Napoleon's hard-won Italian unity was too precious to lose. The consensus was that his politically-innocent great-grandson would make an ideal figurehead for the new order. This decision also made it easier for members of the Army, regardless of their leanings, to support the new regime.

The cheering had been so loud, Gusto was certain his own death would be next. Instead, Garibaldi approached and, with Rianero still translating, tapped out their hopes that the Prince would assume the mantle of Head of State and, in concert with a revived Senate and a chamber of advisors, rule wisely. It was the inconspicuous Poppet who made the suggestion that Gusto take the title of First Consul, the title under which the Great Napoleon had led Italy.

Lord Pinkerton was of the opinion that, once the dust had settled, Italy might have a bright future. With only two telegraph lines in the country, the greatest initial challenge was in spreading the word. It had been necessary to send the Roman-based soldiery into the country to declare the new rule and to assist with controlling that minority who challenged it. In their absence, the surviving amphoraeka volunteered to keep the peace in the city. Riots, due mostly to an excess of high spirits, had been few.

Amphoraeka from across Italy were still streaming towards the Colosseum, where Frank and Firewalker were working out of the workshops in the hypogeum. Frank estimated that it would be a matter of a few more weeks before every glyph had been neutralized.

As word of the great change leaked out, men from across the globe were readying themselves to converge on Rome: exiled intellectuals, political enemies and members of the Italian nobility; young engineers and scientists seeking challenge; men of business, sniffing an opportunity. Pinkerton's aership from London had ferried several such forward-thinking men "including your grandfather Sir Lowthian, Miss Bell, and Sir Alastair's great friend Mr. Carnegie."

"You've said nothing of Nik...Mr. Tesla," Claude finally interrupted.

Pinkerton nodded. "Mr. Tesla has been invited to remain in Italy. Your father says that the First Consul's advisors made an impassioned plea for his help, but he expressed discomfort at the idea."

"You're being polite, aren't you?"

Pinkerton laughed. "You know both your father and Mr. Tesla too well."

Claude didn't add her own laugh to his. "Will he return to Prague, do you think? Or ought he be someplace like this, at least for a little while?" Nikola had been astonishingly clear-headed at the Colosseum, but his strange air of detachment continued to trouble her.

"I've never met the young man, but your father seems to share your concerns. Mr. Carnegie was requested to bring his doctor with him to Rome."

"Lord Pinkerton, who is this Rianero?" Several unfamiliar names had cropped up repeatedly in Lord Pinkerton's account. It was Rianero's apparent connection with Garibaldi that sparked Gertrude's curiosity.

"Ah, yes. That's the name young Fairservis was born with. You did know that he was Italian. Grandson of a Grand Duke, no less."

"Fairservis?"

Pinkerton laughed again. "He would have introduced himself as Agent Horner."

"Oh!" Claude flounced in her seat. "That insufferable man has more names than Lucifer!"

⚜

Less than a month later, their select band of conspirators were dining together at the Bell family town house. Claude had been in London for ten days, but had hardly seen any of it. Her wig had been jettisoned with the rest of the widow's garb. With insufficient time to get a new one made up, despite an obscuring hat and a misleading pair of smoked-glass spectacles, her movements were strictly constrained. Even a pleasant afternoon with

Aunt Nan had to be relocated from Fortum's tea room to the Pinkertons' drawing room, lest rumours start. It may have been mean-spirited, but Claude was fed up with having her life dominated by her freakish resemblance to Princess Maud of Greater Britain.

It was a relief, therefore, as well as a joy, to be seated now between her father and Nikola, with Gertrude, Leski and that insufferable man (who gave no sign of being anything other than a charming young British civil servant) across the table. Tomorrow would be the formal audience with the Queen, when they would receive her thanks for their part in saving Maud and neutralizing the threat of Caesar's immortal army. Tonight, they could enjoy a unique companionship. This should have been the happiest of evenings but, as it wore on, Claude's contentment gradually diminished to the point where she felt quite low.

Agent Horner, or whatever his name was, would be returning to Rome almost immediately. His talents, and his now openly-acknowledged connection to the family of Tuscany, made him a valuable player on the new scene. The Princeps Comitium, Gusto's advisory council, had offered him a position but he had chosen for now to serve his adopted country, as well as the land of his birth, by playing a more neutral role. Speaking about it, his eyes kindled with some of that same ardor he had shown just before leaving her on the floor of the Colosseum.

He had a new mission. So, it seemed, did everyone else.

With the last amphoraka duly liberated, and cymbals and nameplates welded onto every one that chose to live, Frank and Lem were free to leave Italy. Frank's services, however, were still required on this side of the Atlantic. He was looking at houses in London. From here, he would be better able to keep an eye on the new international free-for-all in Italy. London would also provide easier access to his foundry in Prague; the government was eager to explore the future of the automatons. For all that he made the decision seem so logical, Claude was shocked; Father had been so adamant about never returning to London. The very foundations of her world were shaken. Home wasn't merely the house in Chicago, it was the house with Father and Leski and Aunt Nan; it was knowing that, wherever Father travelled, this was also the place that *he* called home. She had naturally expected to someday leave that home, but marriage or other reasons for doing this had more the quality of dreams than plans. She had certainly never imagined her home might be leaving her.

It was small consolation that Frank was only distancing himself from his American life and not dismantling it. Lem would return to Chicago in a few days, to take control of the businesses there. Frank also announced, with one of his broadest smiles, that Lem would be assuming some of his more obscure responsibilities in North America. After so many years, the Lakhota's position with the Special Service had finally been formalized. Lem wore an uncharacteristic glow of pleasure. Beside him, Gertrude clapped her hands. She looked as if she wished she dared to hug or even kiss him. Claude jumped up and did, wondering guilty, for the first time in her life, about the other slights he must have silently suffered.

Gertrude had her foot firmly on the next step in her own path. She spent much of each day deep in study, so as not to find herself fallen too far behind when she returned to Oxford for Michaelmas term.

Even Maud, the phantom guest at this dinner, was moving on. The Swiss doctors and Dr. Jenner had all certified that she was well enough to fulfill her planned grand tour of Greater Britain. None of them would admit it, but Gertrude knew that it was Dika's drarnego treatment that had restored her body to health. Despite this physical recovery, an aura of fragility surrounded her. It saddened Gertrude to see the Princess subdued to this extent. As vexing as Maud had often been, as much as she had needed tempering and maturity, there had been something brilliant about her irrepressible personality. "I'm not sure that I like a biddable Maud," Gertrude confided to this very select company. "But everyone is so pleased about the tour, and Maud seems happy enough to be able to please them."

Claude felt the conversation wash over her like chill November rain, her discomfort growing as the evening wore on. It was hard to remember that it was only this winter that she had been moping around the house, frustrated at her inability to make an important difference in the world. What did Aunt Nan always say? "Beware of what you wish for, for fear you might get it." That the Franklin clan had a tiresome habit of speaking in aphorisms didn't make the burden of their messages less valid. Claude had gotten more than her wildest imagination could have conjured. These five months had been equal parts exhilarating and exhausting. As proud as she was that she had successfully seen it through, she was grateful that it was all over. However, there was a void where all the excitement had been. Everyone else had something new to engage them. What was she supposed to do now?

Once it became clear that the ladies would not leave the gentlemen at table, the Bell's butler offered brandy and demitasse in the drawing room. Claude chose to sit on the small settee, in the hope that Nikola would join her. With only a slight show of hesitation, he did. The others kept a compassionate distance at the other end of the room.

He sat with his knees apart, his hands dangling between them. She sipped nervously at her coffee. It felt strange to be together. This was their first opportunity to talk alone since the night they were abducted; Claude didn't count their brief reunion at the Colosseum. She could focus on him properly now. Uncle Andrew's doctor had pronounced him well, cryptically noting that Tesla seemed a bit too sane for what he had experienced. Nikola seemed strong to her; clear-eyed, although the shadows under them must have permanently darkened. Pale and pensive, he looked more like a Romantic poet than ever. She longed to brush the errant wave from his forehead; and yet, she did not.

She had been assuming that Nikola would return to Prague to work with Frank. He told her that, while he had given Frank permission to carry on with development of the automatons, he had declined the government's commission to personally continue. The mechanical men had been a vision of his long before he had thought of them as a way to counter the amphoraeka. Now his precious invention was tainted by bad memories. So was the workshop in Prague. So was...

"Me?" she asked. The intimacy that she had felt in the workshop in Prague was missing; that magical feeling that her life and his were bound together, was gone.

He ducked his head, embarrassed. "You are...You don't know how precious you are. In my heart, whether or not you want it, I will always be your friend." He cleared his throat. "You must understand that this is all I can ever be. To anyone. I can't risk that again, to feel that I hold someone's life in my hands. It's too great a burden. If I can't work, I can't live. And I can't work unless I can remain at peace."

Her smile was weak but sincere. "I do understand." She did. She remembered how she had felt in Dubrovnik, watching him fall apart. The burden had been too great for her as well. She held out her hand to him, at an unmistakable angle.

Taking it gently, he gazed into her eyes. An electric charge flooded her body. For just a moment, her heart swelled with joy.

"Thank you," he said, humbly. "You will always...I will always value...I would be honoured if you and Frank would visit me someday in Sweden."

"Sweden?"

The international speculators flocking to Rome had been drawn to Nikola like metal filings to a magnet. Everyone had tried to woo him. Most intriguing were a small delegation from the famous scientific community in Visby, with their talk of intellectual freedom. They had shown great respect to Dov Sandtmann, treating him as a man and not as a creature. The remoteness of the location, and the fact that Nikola knew not a soul in all of Sweden, only added to the appeal.

Nikola visibly relaxed, growing more and more confident in the telling of his plans. Making encouraging noises, Claude kept her face bright. Did the hollow ache mean that her heart had been broken, or was it merely badly bruised? Either way, it hurt so much. Her one attempt to be like other girls had been a dismal failure. She felt like such a fool. Eventually they joined the others. It was important to keep moving. Conversation passed without her notice. She laughed, without hearing the jokes. Someone was playing the piano; Claude didn't notice who, though she registered the music as comforting.

"Do I take it Mr. Tesla has shared his plans?" The insufferable man was at her elbow. The music had stopped. It must have been he, playing the piano.

"You already knew?" Her face flushed crimson. She felt an even greater fool.

"He told us on the flight over. I think he was hoping that your father or I would tell you."

He seemed not to be mocking her. If anything, he was being kind.

"Sweden sounds quite wonderful," she said brightly. "A scientific paradise."

"So they say. It may be exactly what Mr. Tesla needs to put all of this behind him. Not everyone is strong enough to move forward." He regarded her speculatively. She wished his eyes weren't such a penetrating shade of blue.

"We all have our strengths," she replied tartly. "It is well to know one's own."

He grinned. "Indeed. My apologies, Miss Monteith, for cutting this delightful evening short, but I am expected at the Pinkerton's for an early breakfast." He tapped his forehead in salute.

Claude returned his bow and watched him pay his respects to Gertrude. She couldn't wait for the other men to follow him so that she could retire to her bedroom and decide whether or not she wanted to cry.

ε

Lord Pinkerton sent a closed automobile to bring them to Kensington Palace. Claude was surprised at her own disappointment. She had secretly cherished the hope that the ceremony would be at Windsor Castle. As grand as they were, the Italian palazzos were overgrown versions of the millionaire mansions of America's various Gold Coasts. It would have been exciting to see a truly old castle, with turrets and such. Before she left, she would have to see the Tower of London, even if she had to dress as one of Gertrude's brothers to do it.

A liveried servant showed them into an antechamber. Claude couldn't tell if the Royal servants were trained to be imperturbable, or if they'd been explicitly warned to expect the Princess's doppelgänger. An attendant straightened their gowns.

Claude smiled appreciatively at her friend. Gertrude looked lovely, for all that she'd been in such a fuss over her dress. With the audience such a close secret, she had been unable to inquire at the usual channels as to what might be appropriate. The discreet dressmaker, sent by the Queen to see to Claude's ensemble, had advised her to wear the gown in which she had been presented at Court. Claude thought that the white duchesse satin showed Gertrude to her best advantage.

Claude's own creamy gown was well-suited to her complexion and the russet glow of her hair. The woman had taken her preferences into account, so the styling suited her as well; the simple lines of the silk charmeuse flowed like water. She knew she looked well. She felt good, too. Gertrude had laughed at them, but Duckworth's scalloped kid boots were as dainty as any dancing slippers; after running blisters at the Colosseum, Claude was determined to never again be caught out in thin-soled shoes. According to the same reasoning, and despite the dressmaker's gentle protests, she wore her chatelaine clipped to a thin diamante girdle.

She had spared the dressmaker the sight of her final non-traditional embellishment by not producing it until they arrived at the palace. She looped the shawl through her elbows now and squared her shoulders defiantly, daring Gertrude to stop her.

Gertrude's smile was rueful, but understanding. She bent to adjust the drape in back. Her nose gave a slight twitch. A faint smell of wood smoke and resinous violets still lingered in the gaudy yellow silk.

"It does make a statement," she said, squeezing Claude's hand.

If the brick façade of Kensington Palace had been a disappointment, the Presence Chamber was not. Though modestly proportioned for a royal audience chamber, one wall had been paved with mirror, in imitation of the Palace of Versailles. Echoing the opulence of that celebrated hall, Richard IV had hung the other walls with golden silk. Rainbow prisms dripped from the crystal chandeliers.

Claude and Gertrude were the last of their company to be ushered into this arresting chamber. The men were, as might have been expected, deep in conversation with Lord Pinkerton. Aunt Nan brought Lady Pinkerton to say hello. Aunt's opinion of Dika's shawl was writ clear across her face, but the occasion prevented her from speaking her mind.

Claude had not expected so many spectators at a 'secret' audience. Except for one who wore a full-sleeved clerical gown, they were a cluster of prosperous looking men in formal dress, a sea of black relieved only by various ribands and medals and stars. Aunt Nan explained that Father's surprising green riband was the sign of the Order of the Thistle. The other men, she whispered, were the Queen's Privy Councillors, the cleric being the Archbishop of Canterbury himself.

A white-whiskered man of unbridled energy broke from the huddle to embrace Gertrude, who cried out in surprised delight. She had been resigned to having none of her family in attendance. It hadn't occurred to her, though perhaps it ought to have, that the redoubtable Sir Lowthian might be made an exception.

Someone rapped thrice outside one of the chamber doors. A silence fell over the room as the Queen entered, followed by Princess Maud. Claude had been told countless times of the Princess's resemblance to her grandmother, but it was very different to see it with her own eyes.

Once you saw Queen Charlotte off a stamp or a coin, the likeness was astonishing. She and her granddaughter shared one face. Had recent experience not dimmed the Princess's light, only years would have distinguished between them. If anything, the Queen's vitality and inherent majesty more than outweighed her advancing years. Claude thought she had never seen a more beautiful woman, though a small nagging in the back of her mind said that perhaps she had.

Turning to whisper something to Gertrude, Claude caught sight of yet another member of the Royal family. She must have entered from the far door. It was astonishing how that face repeated from woman to woman. Claude was fascinated, until she noticed the yellow shawl hanging from the arms of the third woman. She was looking into the mirrored wall. Claude shuddered. She had always found it especially disturbing to not recognize herself in a reflective surface. Steeling her nerves, she looked again and stared hard. Despite all experience, she had never fully accepted the magnitude of the resemblance. Seeing them reflected together in the wall of mirrors, even she was stunned: if it weren't for the colour of their eyes, it would be nearly impossible to tell herself apart from Maud.

Claude turned in Father's direction, hoping to catch his eye, but his face was turned away. In the mirror, she could see that he was looking elsewhere. He was looking at the Queen. What was more, the Queen was looking back! She swore she saw them exchange a private smile. She wanted to squirm, as she had when one of her college chums confessed to having a 'pash' for Father. One simply did not think of one's parent in that way. Claude found herself harboring a sudden affinity for Hamlet.

It was so peculiar. She had never seen Father look at any woman that way. And the Queen…

Claude's body froze. All at once, she couldn't breathe. The blood was rushing behind her eardrums like a waterfall. Time fell away, leaving flashes of memory. The smell of sugar. A room full of children and candle-lit trees. It must have been Christmas. She was so tiny that all she could see of Father was his trouser leg, but she could feel his hand holding tightly to hers. Her new dress was stiff and tickled, but she felt very proud in it. A beautiful lady knelt down and hugged her, the most beautiful woman she had ever seen. Baby stars; the diamonds on her hair had looked like baby stars. "Are you an angel?" she'd asked. "My Mama is an angel." The woman…the Queen…the Queen had looked as if someone had struck her.

Claude felt as if she had been struck, by lightning. She knew, as surely as she knew that the sun rose in the East every morning. It was as tangible as the mark of the kumpania on her thigh. She'd thought that she had come to the end of her father's secrets. He had his reasons; she forgave him. This was different. This was about her life. She had been taught that her mother had died bringing her into the world; she had grown up with a measure of guilt for causing that sacrifice. Instead, the woman who'd born her had discarded her like an outmoded gown. She couldn't decide which was the greater hurt.

Father would no doubt say that he had tried to protect her with his lie. Had he expected he could hide forever? Maud was embarking on a grand tour. Her professional debut would be well-covered by the press. Eventually she would come to America. Even if Claude hadn't decided to smuggle Nikola's Prometheum to Prague, if she had never crossed the Atlantic and been mistaken for the Princess, someone would have been bound to notice the resemblance eventually. Would Father have dismissed it with the same explanation he'd given Gertrude in Prague, that flimsy hint of a connection with the Queen's cousins and a shared clan line? Had he ever planned to tell her the truth?

A tug on her arm brought Claude back to the present.

"Your curtsey!" Gertrude hissed, pulling her down.

Claude sank down into her deepest curtsey, the very one she'd practiced to deceive Caesar Augustus. Her head bent low, she caught a comforting tang of wood smoke from Dika's shawl. Her fingers twined the black silk fringe. She drew strength from that. It didn't matter whose blood ran in her veins; there were those who had chosen her. She had been adopted into the Rom, and she was little sister to Leski.

One after another, her companions stepped forward to receive an expression of Royal gratitude: Sir Micah Fairservis; Sir Lemuel Firewalker; Dame Gertrude Bell; even, despite his foreign nationality, Sir Nikola Tesla; though, being unable to explain the reason for their honours, it was doubtful that anyone would use these new titles any time soon. Father was now Lord Menzies.

Claude was the last to be called forward. She curtseyed again. Still bowing, she inclined her head to receive the sky blue riband that the Queen slipped over her left shoulder. A ceremonial sword touched her lightly; a rich contralto voice proclaimed her Lady Claude Monteith and told her to rise.

Monteith, not Menzies; her own proper name, the one that had been invented for her. She would be her own invention. Claude Monteith: tinker, warrior and spy. There was pride enough in this for any woman. She rose fluidly from her curtsey to faced the Queen with a cold and steady eye.

"You risked your own life to save my granddaughter's," Queen Charlotte said. "There are no words sufficient to express our gratitude."

"It is an honour to serve my country," Claude replied smoothly. "Your Majesty."

Maud stepped forward, as she had when Gertrude had made her obeisance, and embraced her. "Thank you," she murmured. They were only two words, but they came from her heart.

Claude warmly hugged her back. She could feel the Queen's eyes on them. "Good luck, Princess," she whispered.

Queen Charlotte and Princess Maud left almost immediately. The Privy Council were not far behind. Their own small party, plus Sir Lowthian, were driving to the Pinkertons' home for a celebratory luncheon.

"Lady Claude," Gertrude jostled her at the doorway.

"Dame Gertrude. Explain to me why I'm a Lady when you're a Dame."

"She made you a Lady Companion of the Garter!" Gertrude said, touching a finger to the riband with wonder and a smidgeon of exasperation. "It's an unprecedented honour."

Claude shrugged. "I'm sure there have been one or two before now."

Gertrude shook her head. "I don't know. I'll have to do some reading."

"You'll have to write me when you find out."

Gertrude seemed disappointed. "You're not staying in London?"

"No." She had made her decision when she made her curtsey. If they didn't want to tell her, she would pretend she didn't know. She would return to Chicago, where that was possible, and help Lem. She had seen enough of the world to last her for a long while. It was time for her to go home and find out where she belonged.

FOOTNOTE

Archbishop Benson lingered behind the other members of the Privy Council. "Lord Menzies, if I might beg a minute of your time?"

It took Frank a moment to respond; it would take a while for the new address to feel familiar. He smiled sheepishly. "My Lord, Archbishop."

Benson cleared his throat. "You must excuse my presumption, sir." He brushed a non-existent bit of lint from the white sleeve of his rochet. It was a delaying tactic.

Frank regarded him curiously. "Not at all, My Lord."

Benson cleared his throat again. "My predecessor, before he died, confided in me the details of a ceremony he performed at Balmoral some twenty-two years past."

Frank paled, his mouth drawn to a tight line. "Your purpose, sir, in raising this subject?"

"The young woman, Lord Menzies. Am I correct that she is the issue of that union?"

ABOUT THE AUTHOR

Merle Darling has been living in the imaginary 19th century since the age of seven, when she first read *Little Women* and *The Secret Garden*. This illusionary state of being was reinforced by a four-year stint at a 19th century college (complete with ivied walls and afternoon tea in the dormitory parlours) where she studied under fine 19th century scholars in the History and Theatre departments, practiced her knitting and learned to bake bread.

Her home is in an iconic 20th century city. She writes on the train, as she has never successfully kept a diary and therefore has nothing sensational to read.

ABOUT THE UPSILON KNOT

The story you've just read is set in 1887, in a world whose history is somewhat different from the one that ushered in the era in which you're living.

The world of *The Upsilon Knot* branches off from the world we know some 200 years before this story, when Anne Sophia, a daughter of Queen Anne of England, survived smallpox and lived to inherit the English throne.

Among the ripples from this point of deviation: there's no American Revolution; the French Revolution takes a while longer to come to a boil; the ambitions of a brilliant and charismatic young Corsican named Buonaparte focus on uniting Italy (taking a bite out of Austria-Hungary along the way) and gathering up some of the Mediterranean territories of the ancient Roman Empire.

Cultures, events and locales in this book are either the product of the author's imagination or are used in a fictitious manner. Although some of the characters in this book may have familiar names, they are *not* the people you read about in history books.

To learn more about this alternative world, visit www.theupsilonknot.com.

ACKNOWLEDGEMENTS

The Upsilon Knot began as a project for National Novel Writing Month. For over a decade, NaNoWriMo has inspired people around the world to stop dreaming and start writing. If you write, want to write, or want to support writing, please visit http://nanowrimo.org/

I was lucky to have a great support team during that inaugural month, many of whom continued to be amazing cheerleaders throughout the life of this project. There are too many of you to list you all by name, but I thank every one of you! For a wide range of knowledge and tolerance of my brazen reconfiguration of the historic record, I must single out Mike McDonald, Marc Lummis and Julia Rubin. And, for pep talks without number, Claire Nowacoski, Josh Thomas, Alan Salant and Honey Seltzer. For daily lollypops and *never ever* letting up, very special thanks are due to Yelena Brand.

I must also thank Keith Blount, who doesn't know me at all. Keith is the creator of Scrivener, the software that enables me to write (and rewrite) in bits and pieces that mirror the way I think, and somehow pull it all together to make sense. To learn more about this wonderful tool, visit http://www.literatureandlatte.com/.

Finally: my interest in alternative history has deep roots in my fascination with genuine history. It seems only right to thank my two favourite history teachers, who were as enormously generous with their support and encouragement as they were with their experience and wealth of knowledge.

For being the first person who taught me a History that went way beyond the memorization of critical dates, for sharing her genuine love of the subject, and for allowing me to argue, I can never give enough thanks to my 10th grade teacher at Forest Hills High School, Ronnie Hirschhorn.

For knowing the 19th century like a native, for teaching me how to do research, for appreciating my linguistic games while forcing me to learn how to organize my thoughts, and for standing in support of a double major in History and Theatre, I will always be indebted to my Vassar faculty advisor, Professor Anthony S. Wohl.

Ronnie and Tony, if you ever read this book, I can only hope you'll laugh!

www.ingramcontent.com/pod-product-compliance
Lightning Source LLC
Chambersburg PA
CBHW071630260626
47170CB00001B/39